CHILLER

CHILLER

STERLING BLAKE

BANTAM BOOKS
NEW YORK TORONTO LONDON SYDNEY AUCKLAND

CHILLER

A Bantam Book / August 1993

All rights reserved.
Copyright © 1993 by Sterling Blake

BOOK DESIGN BY GRETCHEN ACHILLES

Library of Congress Cataloging-in-Publication Data

Blake, Sterling.
Chiller / Sterling Blake.
p.   cm.
ISBN 0-553-09376-2
I. Title.
PS3552.E542C47 1993
813'.54—dc20   92-37845
                                                     CIP

S. F.

Published simultaneously in the United States and Canada

Bantam Books are published by Bantam Books, a division of
Bantam Doubleday Dell Publishing Group, Inc. Its trademark,
consisting of the words "Bantam Books" and the portrayal of
a rooster, is Registered in U.S. Patent and Trademark Office
and in other countries. Marca Registrada. Bantam Books,
1540 Broadway, New York, New York 10036.

PRINTED IN THE UNITED STATES OF AMERICA
RRH   0 9 8 7 6 5 4 3 2 1

To Dean and Gerda
For laughter, wisdom, and warm companionship.

CHILLER

PROLOGUE

The bomb exploded three yards away.

Alex's father had often quoted an obscure philosopher's saying, "God is in the details." Alex had gathered that meant some abstruse point. Maybe that if you looked hard enough, God's fingerprints showed up somehow.

The bomb taught him another meaning.

He was standing just around a corner of a steel kiosk, one of those little booths that sell chintzy last-minute gifts and cheap candy and utterly unmemorable memorabilia. Only this was Tokyo's Narita airport and nothing was inexpensive. He had been annoyed to find that he had to cash his last travelers' check to pay the airport tax, a stiff two-thousand-yen good-bye kiss from the Land of the Rising Sun. It was the last of his summer money. He decided that he might as well spend the leftover bills on a miniature samurai sword that he supposed would work either as a letter opener or as an assault weapon for midgets.

He had handed the tired-looking Japanese woman the bills. She had been busy arranging some plum blossoms for sale and turned to him, distracted, crow's-feet carved deeply in her face. She held a blossom in one hand.

Later, trying to recall the moment, he seemed to see his hand moving with languid, slow-motion grace toward the woman's worn, outstretched palm. In memory, something had alerted his subconscious, lending the events a sliding grace. The woman touched the bills, her hooded eyes dulled by fatigue, and then a wall of pressure struck her. Her face seemed to smear and dissolve an instant before he had the sensation of somebody hitting him in the head with a baseball bat wrapped in goose down. No sound, just massive impact. Then he was weightless, buoyant, the world beyond a blur of soundless velocities.

No smack of landing. No sudden jar. But then he was lying in utter silence on a granite floor as cool as an angel's kiss, staring up at the high, ribbed ceiling far, far away.

He had turned his head. Legs flicked across the milky foreground of this curiously flat, dimensionless scene. The disembodied legs seemed in a tremendous hurry for no apparent cause. Certainly he felt no great urgency himself. He turned his head again, finding it a great effort, the vertebrae going *rak-rak-rak* like a rusty crank-driven machine.

How had he gotten tired so fast? Steel sheeting lay curled next to him, its jagged edges glinting in the enamel-gray fluorescent light. The woman's kiosk, still helpfully if redundantly sporting a large yellow KIOSK sign, was now a shredded box lying on its side.

The Japanese built to last, and the rolled steel kiosk walls had lasted just long enough to blunt the explosion. He sat up, little chilly slivers running through his legs, ice in August. Bodies lay like rag dolls all around him.

It was odd, he thought, how wounded people look like heaps of clothing, as if calamity were a confused fashion statement. They were tousled lumps—slick raincoat, wool suit, a polished brown shoe turned at the wrong angle—but somehow no longer people anymore, just collections of their wrappings that had failed to protect them from the shrapnel weather here.

Pain started to seep into his elbows. His shirt was torn and bloody. Abstractly he noted the cuts and bruises where steel had peppered him. Metal was cold, so the icy threads he felt up and down his legs were steel. Logical.

The ethereal fog around him began to retreat, letting in movement, damp air, faces wide-eyed, pale, their O mouths beginning to shape screams. Daytime television with the sound off, he thought numbly. Everything happened beyond the glass wall of silence.

He got to his knees. A gliding, soundless world.

He stood up shakily. Rubbery legs. The woman was there with him in the silence. He found her a few feet closer to the shattered kiosk. She had been cut nearly in two by the blast. Blue-black guts trailed from her like fat sausages. Gray bones poked through her skin where the shock wave had crushed her ribs.

Yet her face was blank when he rolled her head up, her eyes open and still dull and tired and wanting to go home. In her hand she clutched a single plum blossom. Her body was already a cooling island in a spreading red-brown lake. He noted that her seeping blood smelled like freshly sheared brass, startling, pungent.

He had stepped back, his shoes sticky with congealing blood, when he saw dumbly that he could do nothing for her. Her body was limp and relaxed but her pale, knotted fingers would not release the fragile, perfectly formed plum blossom.

Don't let go of that blossom.

There is a moment that comes to everyone and changes them forever. No one ever forgets it.

Usually the moment comes in the quickening years of adolescence. For him it had been that frozen instant in Japan when he retreated from the spreading stain. The darkening rust-red pool seemed to grow a brown crust, hardening before his eyes into the soil that would soon yawn moistly open to accept her body, to enclose the corpse in a grip that would never end. The earth would suck her down into it, make her a part of it, dissolve her with its licking tongues.

The hungry earth. Mold, rot, rust. Gray deep ponds reeking of rotten eggs. Decomposition. Dust.

Among all the people in the milling airport he had been alone with a terrible fact he had now discovered—that the earth devours everything. That it swallows all life, finally, just as before his eyes a sticky emissary of the dank soil now oozed out of the torn woman and licked across the granite slab floor, searching for him, for anyone, for the fodder that could feed this organic mud-hunger but never satisfy it.

Yet the woman's rigid hand with its yellowing nails held vainly to the blossom. Somehow in his confusion he thought that if she held it, there might be some hope of hauling her back, even though the spreading brown pool had already claimed her.

Hold on, he had thought. *Hold on.*

Her body had taken some of the blast that would have ripped into him, shredded him, taken everything from him in one compressive instant. The kiosk and the tired woman had absorbed the worst of it. The fact that he was using up his last yen and that he stood at just a certain angle—that was a meaningless detail.

God is in the details.

An odd saying for his practical father, a white-haired man who didn't believe in God. But the details of their momentary geometry had made him live, to stride the green fields, happy above the underlying slag layers steeped millennia-deep in bones and rot, while the small, worn woman died.

She had given him time to heed the sign, the warning.

His hearing took a day to come back. He read about the terrorist attack in *The International Herald Tribune,* propped up in a Tokyo hospital. By that time the frozen, eerie moments had already begun to seem unreal.

As he lay on starched sheets for days afterward, he had plenty of time to think. He knew little Japanese so his mood was unbroken by casual chat. He had spent the summer as an American Field Service guest with a Japanese family, and they came to visit him, of course. That did not lessen his solitude. When they left after visiting hours there were still the long nights to get through. He had spent them staring at the white-tiled ceiling, thinking of the ribbed steel heights of the Narita vaulting, of the moment when he had seen what he now thought of as the Black One spreading out from the woman, searching for him.

It was coming to get him. To get the clever and the stupid, the glossy rich and the starving poor. Everyone knew it. That simple truth lay behind every event of every day, yet no one mentioned it. The Black One was the best-kept nonsecret of all time.

ONE

REBIRTHDAY

To Jacques Dubourg.

Your observations on the causes of death, and the experiments which you propose for recalling to life those who appear to be killed by lightning, demonstrate equally your sagacity and your humanity. It appears that the doctrine of life and death in general is yet but little understood. . . .

I wish it were possible . . . to invent a method of embalming drowned persons, in such a manner that they might be recalled to life at any period, however distant; for having a very ardent desire to see and observe the state of America a hundred years hence, I should prefer to an ordinary death, being immersed with a few friends in a cask of Madeira, until that time, then to be recalled to life by the solar warmth of my dear country! But . . . in all probability, we live in a century too little advanced, and too near the infancy of science, to see such an art brought in our time to its perfection. . . .

I am, etc.,

B. Franklin.

1
ALEX

Hold on, he thought. *That's all we can do, for now.*

Alex Cowell took a deep breath, sucking in the dry chaparral scent of the arroyo around him. A red squirrel scolded him from atop a gum tree. A palm farther up the slope clashed its fronds in the warm, shifting breeze.

He had gone for a walk to clear his head. Usually it worked, sharpened him anew. But today he had slid into the past and snagged on that moment in Tokyo. It had haunted him for years. He saw now that he would never be rid of it. That slicing, brutal instant had led inevitably across more than a decade, to this quiet, yet exciting moment.

He shook his head and turned back toward the boxy white two-story building. A warm wind came gusting down from the ridge, curling his black hair and plucking at his shirt sleeves with dry caresses, as though hurrying him along.

He had come back here among the gangly pepper and eucalyptus trees hundreds of times before, taking a break from work, tossing worn tennis balls for Sparkle. The big, gangly Irish setter had fetched with glee, bounding into the mesquite and manzanita, ignoring the barbs that caught her coat and lashed her muzzle. She had never lost her enthusiasm for the bouncing yellow prey, had seemed convinced since she was a puppy that they were a rare, delicious game animal. Her look of quiet pride and accomplishment as she bounded back to him, tennis ball compressed in powerful jaws, had always struck him as both noble and comic. Out here, racing through the underbrush, her simple joy had picked up his lagging spirits many times, jollied him out of passing depressions. He had missed that simple rite this last month.

He went back inside the building, threading his way through the chugging pumps near the rear door. He washed up carefully and pulled on his Angels baseball cap; maybe not medically orthodox but a comfortable way to keep his hair out of the surgical zone. Quietly he slipped into the operating room. Susan Hagerty nodded abstractly, busy adjusting the complex liquid crystal displays on the artificial kidney machine. The moment Alex stepped into the room he shed the memories of Tokyo, of Sparkle as a pup, and saw her as she was now.

An old dog lying on her side. A tad comfortably overweight. But her russet coat was still sleek, her long muzzle giving a comic look of professorial intelligence. Her abdomen and chest had been shaved for her operation, and that area was swathed in white bandages. Her lungs labored under the artificial stimulus of a respirator.

You'll fetch those tennis balls again, Sparkle. Just hold on. Then he slipped into his professional persona.

He automatically checked the kidney procedure the old-fashioned way, by judging the color of the cylinder that carried out the heart of the job: exchanging Sparkle's blood with the dialyzing fluid. The thick tube was a deep, rich red—good. Still, he set to work running a careful check on a humming ultracentrifuge.

A Dixieland number came on their six-disc CD player, rattling drum riffs through the austere operating room. Jelly Roll Morton from 1927, the spotty old plastic recordings digitized and precision-tuned so that the full-bodied bass and piercing trumpet sliced through the decades, sounding more pounding, alive, and vibrant than ever, the past recaptured. The bouncy beat put a touch of zest into their labors. Susan would have preferred a Mozart symphony and Alex favored sixties classic rock, maybe Jefferson Airplane's *Surrealistic Pillow,* so they had compromised on a hefty stack of Bix Beiderbecke, King Oliver, Preservation Hall, the sassy Barrelhouse Boogie Band, and Louis Armstrong.

Dr. Susan Hagerty hovered over Sparkle. She was a solidly built woman, good-looking in a homespun way, with a level-headed, calm expression that Alex found particularly reassuring now. She was the first woman he had ever had a true, professional relationship with, the joys of involving labor without any sexual nuances. That aspect was particularly welcome; he was still recovering from his divorce and needed to see women in a different light.

Susan ran on the beach regularly and had a quiet physical energy about her, the focused gaze of a woman who had made her way in life through concentration. As he watched she changed one of the IV bottles that trickled fluids into Sparkle and said crisply, "No sign of pulmonary edema."

"Great. Let's hope . . ." His voice trailed away. The unexpected plaintive note in it embarrassed him.

Hope seemed of little use here. His old friend seemed to be a small, fragile splash of color encircled by banks of shiny medical equipment.

Hope was a soft, vague thing compared with the hard metallic grays and greens of the OR.

Pulmonary edema was, as usual for medical terminology, a long term for a simple problem. Sparkle's lungs could accumulate fluids as Susan gradually brought her body temperature higher. Too much, and she would drown.

"I had some danger signals in the latest blood chem readings, though," Susan said in a flat, almost matter-of-fact voice.

Alex looked at the digital readouts on the bank of screens and knobs opposite Susan. The welter of information was confusing, and he was still trying to unravel the numbers when Susan said, "Traces of damage in the pancreas. Blood glucose was jumping around. Electrolytes were acting funny, too."

"So you—"

"Straightened out the electrolytes right away. Glucose is coming back, too. The pancreas has me worried." Susan worked steadily as she talked, calm and steady after many hours here. It had been a long, tough operation, and it wasn't over. They had started the day before, bringing Sparkle's stiff body in from the freezer where she had lain for days.

It had begun weeks earlier, when Sparkle began dragging her hind legs. The cause turned up when Susan, who worked on research at Immortality Incorporated, had done a routine angiogram, injecting contrast dyes and taking X-rays. Sparkle had a blood vessel tumor pressing on her spinal cord. It was a mass of small vessels buried deep, a fibrous tracery that pinched nerves and brought lancing pains. Not cancerous but growing, it had spread all through her before Alex had noticed that she wasn't eating very much, didn't go outside anymore, even to play ball, and slept more and more.

Susan had shaken her head in despair when she looked over the X-rays. She had worked with dogs as experimental animals and knew the dimensions of their problems. An operation to remove all the fine filaments would have been too much of a strain on the animal. A veterinarian whom they called in to consult had shaken his head and offered with a sad, kindly smile to put Sparkle down immediately.

It had hit Alex hard. No more would his big friend come bounding up to him after a tough day at work, slathering him with tongue-kisses, woofing greetings and complaints, eagerly snatching up a ragged ball for fetching, yelping out her transparent joy. No more.

So Alex had decided to try a long shot. As general manager and technician at Immortality Incorporated, he had access to methods and equipment denied to most people. And he knew Susan Hagerty, whose research in low-temperature preservation at I² was slowly bearing fruit.

He had to spare Sparkle the slow agony of the tumor. She was more than a pet, somehow. She had gotten him through his strident divorce, through his mother's dying, through innumerable evenings of wine-deepened depression, sitting alone and dateless in his apartment. But he could not accept her "merciful" murder.

They had cooled Sparkle down to twenty degrees below freezing, carefully adjusting her internal chemistry, injecting noncellular blood substitutes that acted like antifreeze. Her firm old head had trembled at first as Alex held her and murmured softly, almost like singing a lullabye, stroking her belly the way she always liked, avoiding the shaved and swathed patch where the cannulas connected into her. She had peered up at him with luminous deep amber eyes that held an eternity of loving patience, utterly trusting that this spreading chill in her was going to be all right somehow. With her last remaining energies she had licked his hand. She had gone without a whimper.

Auto mechanics can fix cars easily because they don't have to work on them while the engine is still running. The delicacy of surgery comes from the fact that patients have to remain alive while hands and instruments thrust deep into them. Surgery is itself a major, life-threatening trauma.

Matters are far simpler if the patient has already died.

Sparkle had gone on a voyage no other being had ever attempted. Held in stiff, chilled stasis, she suffered none of the slow erosion that living beings endure. Susan and Alex had used new drugs Susan was developing, "transglycerols" that allowed a body to avoid freezing even though it was colder than the freezing point of water. This gave Susan time to study the results of Sparkle's surgery. She had used the days to carefully trace the path of the tumor threads, dark strings like coiled snakes that had wriggled deep within her. It had been long labor, consulting the inner maps of X-rays, of PET and CAT scans, and of tissue samples. Susan had rooted out every fibrous remnant, taking biopsy specimens, cutting away with a laser scalpel, stitching up the widespread damage. She was an adequate surgeon and had worked on dogs and cats. The luxury of time at low temperatures, free of the need to keep the patient's body functioning, let her take meticulous care.

Ironically, it was only through killing Sparkle that she had any scrap of hope. She was now free of the insidious growths that had riddled her. Heart stilled, brain waves stopped, her purple eyelids lying so flattened it seemed that she had lost her corneas, Sparkle had glided through days of changeless time, dead by all the standards of medical science.

They had prepared her rewarming by injecting membrane stabilizers, to hold cell structure together. Then they had brought her up from the icy domain that claimed her by using carefully controlled radio frequency rewarming. The glycerols that gave antifreeze protection to her cells were hard to coax back out. Susan had developed new, simpler procedures and taught them to Alex. He knew biochemistry, but better, he knew how to listen, which usually is more valuable than bookish lore. Hand-eye coordination proved to be especially important in the bleached-light intricacies of the operating theater.

"Dura mater seems fine," Susan said. "No big surprise, though. It's just the sort of tissue the cryoprotectants should work best on."

Alex nodded, adjusting the ventilator settings. The dura mater was the tough membrane covering Sparkle's brain. Before Susan had developed her new methods, they had seen previous frozen animals develop fatal damage there as they cooled down. Ice expanded between cells, caving them in. This was a more insidious problem than "freezer burn," which was simply the loss of water from tissue in ordinary refrigerators. The major enemy of cooling as a method of saving patients came with rewarming, when cell walls could not reexpand naturally because they had been damaged. Susan's research had perhaps offset that. Perhaps.

Alex found himself petting Sparkle, stroking her fine pelt, hands seeking some sign of life from her familiar body. The coat was tangled and matted, and her shanks were chilly beneath her gray warming blanket. The respirator kept forcing the worn old body to go through its mechanical motions, but Alex wanted to feel some tremor of that mysterious other, the essence that changed a laboring mechanism to a living spirit, a mind capable of knowing joy.

Susan leaned over, fatigue lining her oval face. She had given more this day than he had, yet her hands remained steady, her voice calm and free of the skittering tension he felt, as she said, "She's in there somewhere, Alex."

"I hope."

"The memories that made her all that you loved—they're preserved."

Down in the cells of Sparkle's brain, hard-wired by chemical processes science was only beginning to fathom, she was waiting for him. The ravages of warmth and pressing time had not gotten to her yet. Or so their theories went.

He sighed. "Yeah. I know."

"And it's looking good." Susan tapped the liquid crystal display of Sparkle's internal temperature: 27.7 centigrade.

Alex worked in centigrade constantly, but somehow for matters close to the throb of living things, his mind reverted to the scale he had learned as a boy, just as he dutifully swallowed drugs for a cold but took his true, deep solace in chicken soup. "Let's see—that's eighty-two degrees Fahrenheit. She's almost there!"

"Try her brain waves."

He checked the electrodes attached to Sparkle's head, then scanned the screen. Soft hash, green lines jittering against a black field. No clear result, but the complexity of the traces alone tightened his throat. The last time he had looked there had been nothing, an ominous flat line.

This is all a research project, remember. An experiment. Chances are slim. Susan laid out the odds. I knew that going in.

He caught his breath. The green hash, which showed activity levels in portions of Sparkle's brain, now showed complex waves. They spiked up out of the spaghetti jumble, vanished, then returned.

"Hey. Alpha rhythm, good and strong." Waves snaked steadily across the 'scope face.

While I was outside, day-dreaming, he thought, *the old girl was fighting her way up from the cold. Coming back to me.*

He massaged Sparkle vigorously, as if life could ooze like a fluid from him into her. *C'mon, girl. Up from the dark depths. . . .* Her flesh was torpid and sluggish. Beneath his kneading fingers his old pet felt like chilly meat in a supermarket. But he knew that in medicine appearances can lie. That was especially true here, in a surgical procedure never tried before.

C'mon . . . just give us a flutter of life, anything, the most feeble stirring. We'll hold a party for you, throw a barrel full of fresh bright yellow tennis balls, take you rabbit hunting up the arroyo. A rebirthday party, Sparkle. His hands began to ache from the massaging. Did Sparkle's muscles seem a fraction more supple?

Susan said compassionately, "Don't expect a lot. This is the first time, Alex."

"I know, I know, but—"

"Totally new technology, and I'm doing it all by the seat of my pants. Don't expect—"

"She moved." He said it in a flat, factual voice, as though excitement might scare the tremor away.

Susan smiled sympathetically. "You're sure? The respirator sometimes induces an autonomic response in the rest of the body, and—"

"There! There it is again." He bit his lip. Eagerly he massaged Sparkle's legs with fingers that were beginning to ache. Her legs had twitched the way she did when she dreamed, chasing tasty rabbits over green summer fields.

Susan's eyes darted over the complicated displays that crowded around the operating table. They stood for long moments watching the shifting liquid-crystal numbers and graphs. Sparkle's brain waves showed fresh ripples, growing complexity.

"Blood chemistry is coming around. Her pH looks better," Susan said. "The perfusate is completely exchanged out."

"She's trembling."

"You're sure?"

"Look." Alex let go of Sparkle's legs. They began to jerk visibly.

"My lord," Susan whispered.

"See? She's—"

"That could be a simple discharging of—" Susan stopped, gazing at rippling digital indicators. Her look of rigorous scientific skepticism fell away like a mask slipping from a warmer, more vulnerable face. Susan was a handsome woman with chestnut hair and a square face that gave the impression of solidity. Even now this came through, despite the red bags under her eyes and a network of fine lines that webbed out from the corners of her mouth. Lipstick and powder and eye shadow might have hidden much of this, but not the leaden notes in her voice. Yet these, too, were banished in the next moment. "Heartbeat. Look."

A monitor now showed a steady pulse.

Alex glanced at the brain-wave spectrum. It was alive with shifting structure.

"Let's get her breathing on her own," Susan said.

Alex's eyes widened. "You're sure?"

"Come on. I'll show you."

It took a while to attach a plastic bag in place of the heart-lung machine. Alex rhythmically forced air in and out of Sparkle, following Susan's directions in concert with her own quick, expert work. He stopped regularly to see if Sparkle would start breathing on her own.

"Think it's safe?" Alex felt a lump in his throat. The dangers of taking her off the machine suddenly loomed before him. But then, he reminded himself, he wasn't the surgeon. Here his lofty Ph.D. in biochemistry qualified him to be a simple medical assistant, little more than a handyman with the equipment. The doctorate had been fun to earn, but even before he finished it, he knew he didn't want to do research in conventional areas. This was his calling. He liked working with his callused hands, fixing balky machines, doing the grunt labor around Immortality Incorporated, where something needed patching up all the time. He enjoyed understanding circuits, putting up drywall, framing in wooden supports for the suspension vessels, anything that transformed lines on paper into something solid that worked. And at this moment he was heartily glad that he did not have to make the decisions here.

Susan watched the displays closely, then nodded. "So far."

"Whoosh, this is hard work."

"You're tensing up, that's all." Above her surgical mask she gave him a wink. "Don't force it."

"Right. Right." Alex eased off, watching Susan for guidance at every step of the procedure. She carefully adjusted a dozen other settings. The body had to be restarted smoothly, letting the heart and lungs strike up their own rhythms. For long minutes he watched the regular rise and fall of Sparkle's chest, driven by his hands, and it was only when Susan touched his arm softly, much later, that he realized that his hands were no longer breathing for Sparkle. He let them drop to his side, aching. The gentle rush of air through her now seemed subtly different, almost like a repeated sighing, effortless, a natural flowing.

"She's back." Alex felt stunned, dumb.

"Back from the other side," Susan smiled, and Alex saw how pale and wan she was. He glanced at the clock and automatically made an entry in their operation log. Every detail of the procedure had to be exact, recorded.

Susan puffed out her cheeks, popped her eyes, and let out a great "Whoosh!" Then she sagged, leaning against the operating table. He realized that she had been on her feet, taking no more than five minutes away to gulp down some tacos, for ten hours.

"She'll need rest, therapy, constant monitoring." Susan had relaxed physically but was still plainly holding her emotions encased in a professional reserve.

"Sure, sure. . . ." He stared down in wonder at Sparkle. Her chest rose and fell smoothly, and he knew in the silent, sliding moment that he was watching a quiet, profound miracle.

"Back from freezing," Susan said. "A whole, intact, higher mammal. Never been done before. Never."

Alex swallowed hard. "Never. Goddamn."

"All the dreams, the stunts, the half-baked ideas . . ."

"And here it is."

"Got anything to drink?" Susan grinned, and as if on a signal, the tension broke. They embraced each other, whirling away from the operating table in a lurching dance, whooping and laughing and crying. The rebirthday party had begun.

2

GEORGE

An illegal panhandled him on the corner of Bristol and McFadden and he shot back, "Go with God, brother."

But his tone might as well have said, "Go to hell." He wanted to say, "You got more than me, Mexo," because that was the plain truth.

The illegal didn't speak enough English to understand him so he shoved the guy and spat on the sidewalk and walked on, knowing that it was dumb to draw even that much attention to himself.

Cops might see a chance to roust the illegal and check him out, too. Word could be out on him, even this far from Arizona. He doubted it. Hitchhiking didn't leave leads. Still, he couldn't get into police files until he got set up in a secure place again, with all his gear and interfacing software.

He walked down the broad street that was empty and asphalt-anonymous beneath the ceaseless, piercing morning sunlight, the way only California streets were, bland and strangely, quietly beautiful, and promising to become a slum the next time you looked.

His fingers curled back to touch his palms as he strode heavily along, arms swinging easily like beams carved out of hardwood by a sculptor who thought big and liked muscles. The veins in his neck bulged as he ground his teeth, thinking for the thousandth time about the mistakes he'd made, the ones that had put him here on the street, watching his back to see if a squad car was pulling alongside the curb nice and easy, just to take a look at him.

He was the kind of man who got that sort of attention. It was useful sometimes, kept people from getting in your way. It was a God-given gift, and he just had to suffer the side effects. The Lord gave no boon without some trial coming along with it, his saintly mother had said.

The early morning traffic growled and muttered beside him on McFadden. Except for keeping an eye out for cops, he gave it no notice. The men on their way to work noticed him, though. His suit was a light gray wool showing the wrinkles and wear of two days on the run. It held off the morning chill but hadn't been enough last night. His black hair was cropped close, neat and under control. His two days of beard bothered him, made him feel like trash, a grimy yellow newspaper in the gutter, but he would have to deal with it when he had toilet articles again. He wore the fifties-style white nylon shirts that you could launder and hang up in the shower of your hotel room. He liked them because they had a clean, functional feel. The white of them did nothing to lighten his face, which was like chipped concrete. His gray eyes absorbed the slanting spring sunlight and gave nothing back.

He knew what the men in the passing cars thought. They were mostly Chicano, a lot of them driving pickups and wearing baseball caps. To them he was an Anglo without a car, obviously a bum. Maybe he had stolen the suit somewhere, along with the black shoes that needed a polish but looked expensive. Any Anglo walking here had no money. They would remember the time when they had nothing, took buses to work, were still dodging *la migra,* angling for a green card or straight papers, and holding down two sweatshop jobs at a time—in places where the first thing you learned was the exits.

It had been okay for them to walk, back then, but they had been on their way up and knew it. This Anglo was on the way down. Had to be.

George watched their quick glances and read in their expressions all of that. With the women it was different. He crossed with the light at McFadden and Main, and a mousy woman waiting at the crosswalk in a Honda watched him stride solidly along, her eyes veiled by false eyelashes that made her look ridiculous. About one woman in twenty would take notice of him, and he knew just from their looks what they were wanting. They usually watched his hands, which were big and veined. His power often came through his hands and women knew that, sensed it, felt a stirring. He had used those hands on women before, to caress them and sometimes to slap them when they wanted too much.

He ignored the mousy woman, even though she turned to watch him march past. He had learned to pass them by when he had important tasks, and always when he was about God's work.

Today had to be devoted to himself. God helped those who helped themselves. He had spent the night sleeping under the Santa Ana River passover at Edinger and needed something to pick himself up, take the bitter chill from his bones. A good breakfast, like the ones on the farm when he was a boy, thick pancakes and plenty of molasses and big warm biscuits, maybe. But that would take money.

He found the Bank of America on Flower Street, just where the telephone book had said. He walked up to the twenty-four-hour teller and pulled out his first-line credit card holder. This was one of the old tellers, its keys worn, because this was a poor neighborhood. The banks never kept up the maintenance on these, even though from his reading he knew they made a big profit off the accounts serviced in places like this.

He took out his top-of-the-line set of cards, a full constellation for all major banks, in the name of Gary Pinkerton. He had been in a playful mood when he'd set them up, and now he ruefully saw that maybe that little joke, using the name of the first detective agency, had tripped him up. Some beady-eyed security hacker might have caught on.

He slipped the card into the slot, and the slit-mouth ate it eagerly. ENTER USER CODE, the video display commanded. He punched in his call letters and drummed his fingers on the spotted metal counter. PLEASE WAIT.

The words held there while he counted to ten. He figured maybe the phone lines were full, this was an old machine, and plenty of people all over Southern California were stopping off on the way to work, hitting the machines for shopping or lunch money. That would slow down the whole system.

But then he reached twenty, and finally at thirty he knew it was sour. He was turning away when the video screen flickered to blank. The slot did not spit his card back out.

He walked away fast. The banks were getting sharper all the time. Even this crummy old teller might be able to call the police. In a neighborhood like this they could be pretty hardnosed with customers and get away with it.

He went five short blocks down Chestnut and around a beat-up high school, turning regularly to see if any cop cars showed up behind him. He passed by a Denny's and felt in his pockets for change. Three quarters. He went inside and sat at the counter.

A woman at the end in a pink uniform one size too small noticed him and came over, even though he was sitting in another waitress's area. Swaying, lots of hip action. He ordered coffee and noticed a pack of Marlboros in her skirt pocket. He bummed one from her, making himself smile.

She smiled back, showing irregular, stained teeth, and lit the Marlboro for him with a Bic. She had to lean over the counter a little to do it, making sure he noticed her breasts, which were average size but pushed up by one of those special wired bras. He could see the boning through her uniform.

"You look like you've had a tough night," she said.

"Got the job done," he said because he couldn't think of anything else.

"What kind of job?"

"Uh, you know." He shrugged, hoping she would go away.

"Ummm." A broad smile, not showing any teeth. "Sounds like the kind of work I might like."

He grunted and she left. While she went for the coffee he twisted off the filter and dropped it on the floor. He hated those things. With relish he drew in a big chestfull, not caring about getting the tobacco fibers in his mouth. The waitress gave him another too-broad smile when she brought the coffee. She had dirty-brown hair and a lot of lines around the eyes, lines that makeup just crinkled around without concealing. Plenty of glossy purple lipstick, with chipped fingernail polish to match. Late thirties, he guessed. Showing the wear. Or maybe for a woman like her, the right term was *use*. Any woman who was interested in him now, the ragged way he looked, had to be desperate.

She licked her purple lips. "You new around here?"

George tried to think of a way to get rid of her while he watched the street. "Just passing through, sort of."

"You'll find there's a lot to do at night"—a significant look—"if you know the right places."

"Maybe I'll work nights."

"Yeah." The stained smile again. "You said."

He had made the cigarette last through the bitter cup of coffee. Just as he took the last drag, he saw two black-and-whites going down Chestnut headed toward the Bank of America. They were moving pretty fast but with no blinkers or sirens on.

The counter waitress started talking to him about the weather or the Angels or something as he watched the patrol cars turn toward the bank. He guessed they wouldn't figure he was on foot. But somebody could have seen him, and on top of that there weren't many places a guy on foot could go this time of morning. A prickly pressure built up in him, pulsing in his ears, thumping loud and strong so that he couldn't make sense of what the waitress was saying. His chest started to heave, tight and fast.

He threw the three quarters onto the counter, jerked to his feet, and started out. The waitress stopped talking, her mouth half-open to frame the next word of mindless patter, surprise turning to irritation. "Hey." She glared. "Hey."

He went out the back exit and trotted down an alley behind a Vons Market. It felt good to move. Muscles working, eyes dancing. He went half a block in the clean morning air and slipped into a doorway to think.

He knew this was probably not the smartest thing to do. He could have sat out the next hour in the Denny's listening to the waitress tell her life story, could have cadged some free coffee while she steered the discussion around to what movies he'd seen lately, using her eyes to suggest a whole lot more, and then she would have started hinting about doing something together tonight. But he liked to move when his body told him to. His instincts had kept him out of a lot of bad stuff and this time they told him to get some distance, fast. He never questioned his instincts—they were the work of God, and the Lord knew what was best for him. Maybe cops used the Denny's for a hangout, and after they answered the stop-and-question call at B of A they'd go there, notice him. His subconscious had a reason, his instincts, God's plan—it didn't matter what he called it, he had to follow it.

Down the alley a kid was unloading a truck onto the Vons dock. Boxes, dumpsters, trash. The kid looked like he was nearly through. George sized up the timing. He kicked at some packing material in impatience, slamming some two-by-fours against the wall. The alley danced in the pale blades of morning sunlight, colors popping in the air.

"Hey, you cleared out pretty fast, bud," the waitress said at his elbow.

He was startled, alarmed. She had approached on rubber soles while he was trying to plan, all caught up in his head, not on guard. He blinked and his mouth moved, but nothing came out.

"Guy like you, a girl notices, you know?" A sluttish smile, weakening at the corners with wobbling uncertainty. "Best thing I seen in a long time. Don't want to let a guy like you get away."

He looked at her nervous twitching lips, and his breath came in gasps. *A girl notices.* Would remember him if anybody asked.

"Well, you duck out like that, I take it kind of personal."

The trash-lined alley whirled around him, planes and angles sheeting up to the gray sky.

"And I liked you right off. Thought we might get together later?"

Bloodred patches flashed in the air around the woman's uncertain smile.

"Hey, look, I guessed you were keepin' outa the way of the cops."

Tight. His chest tight. "How?" He had trouble getting the word out.

"You got the look, y'know?" She seemed encouraged by his finally saying something. "Needing a place to maybe hole up?"

Colors arced like veins, burnt orange coronal streamers bursting out of her and dissolving into crimson stars. He opened his mouth, closed it. Watching the colors.

"You could come over to my place, rest up. Man like you needs his rest." The slanting morning sunlight showed the crinkled cosmetics in the lines of her face. Her bright red lips slid into a hesitant leer. "Not that you have to rest all the time. Y'know, you can have what you like."

Gaudy light, colors sluicing down from an oyster-gray sky and running in rivulets around her mock-coy, painted face. *Don't want a guy like you to get away.*

He sucked in a deep, fulfilling breath. Everything was clear now. The Lord had drawn His coat of many colors around her, and that made things simple.

"So hope you don't mind me comin' on to you like this, but long time back I learned the hard way that you see somethin', you go—"

He bent over and kissed her. It felt good to let the tightness steam out. Woman like this, that's what she wants. A shot of the hot 'n' heavy, they'd called it in high school.

She blinked with surprise and then returned his pressure. Her tongue slithered into his mouth, muscular and slick and wriggling. All the spit and goop with it.

Warm and quick and alive.

A moist, thick snake.

Then she was limp in his arms, and he was staring down at her loose face. Something had happened to her and he did not know what, or how, but as he shook her the neck and spine wobbled, no resistance. Face empty, pale. Arms dangling. No sound.

Long ago there had been the girl in the field, the one he met at night out there on one of his walks, and she had taken him into the hot 'n' heavy, too, and the next thing he had known then was her shrieks ripping open the thick night air. She had raked him with her fiery fingernails and staggered away in the Arizona dark, and he had not known then what had happened before between them. Just like now. Only this woman with the crows'-feet spreading away from her eyes, the brown eyes staring up at him, this woman did not scream.

Enough of this. He looked up and down the alley.

Nobody there. The kid working the Vons dock was out of sight.

No sirens in the distance. Just trash blowing in the breeze.

Big industrial-size dumpster beside the cinderblock wall.

Puffing, he crouched and picked her up. Surprising weight to her, but he rocked her up easily into a hug. He carried her to the dumpster. Had to move fast now. Yeah, heavier than she looked. Hoisting the body up onto his shoulder and then standing up was work. Grunting, he pulled the sheet-metal lid up. Setting his feet, getting the angle. He threw her in with one movement. Backward over the top, her head snapping back as if to look at him as she went over. Hair frayed with the momentum, face open, then gone.

Flattened cardboard boxes under his feet. He scooped up two; threw them in to cover her. The lid banged down as he sprinted away.

His thinking had been interrupted there, but now his head was clear. The strands and snaking threads of color were fading, crisping and fizzing in the slanting sunlight. He had trouble walking for a moment, his jimmy-john stiff against his leg, but he was proud of getting away, free.

He thought of a broad valley strewn with bones baked white beneath the rich sun. Faces flickered before him, faces forever stilled in expressions of surprise, fear, confusion. And colors sizzling around the wrecked heads, fiery plumes frying the faces, crisp, hot, vibrant.

The Vons Market was getting ready for the day. He slowed to a walk as he passed the piles of cardboard boxes and pine loading flats and more dumpsters. The kid had finished unloading. He was backing the Mack delivery truck out from the loading dock, grinding its gears. It had a steel tailgate, and George grabbed for that as the kid gunned his motor and started up. George pulled himself up easily and stood on the rear chrome bumper, holding on to the tailgate. The back doors were locked. The truck accelerated, the driver shifting through the gears as if this were a sports car.

He rode the truck for a fast few miles. The kid was hot to get somewhere and the smell of carrots filled George's nose as he hung on, the truck jouncing lightly on the turns.

He thought about the woman a little and knew he had been right. She had said she was going to try to hang on to him—*Don't want a guy like you to get away*—and she had guessed the cops were after him.

Well, she couldn't hang on to him. He had proved that. In mathematics, once a proof is done, you drop it and go on to the next problem. That was the way he wanted to run his life, and lately he had been getting better and better at that. George firmly put the woman from his mind and concentrated on the ride, on his plans, on this day. This day he had to dedicate to himself. And through him, to the Lord.

George jumped off at a traffic light because he saw a Security Pacific building down the block. He had a principle that God had given him when he was a boy, when he had learned to fight back against the bullies at school: The one sure way to get danger on your tail was to turn your back on it. People against you, you had to go right back at them, show them some spirit. If you got thrown, then right away you got back on the horse. He was going to ride Security Pacific.

He sat at a plastic table outside a Dunkin' Donuts, holding a Styrofoam cup he had fished out of the trash, so he would look as though he belonged there. Not long to wait for Security Pacific to open. That gave him time to strip all the Gary Pinkerton cards from his plastic accordion carrier. He said a fond good-bye to all twenty-three cards as he sliced them in half with a pocket knife and dumped them in the trash. Leave intact cards, and somebody would for sure try to pass them. He took out his backup, a small folder that had cost him several thousand dollars to set up and that had lain fallow for over a year.

The Security Pacific card of one Bruce Prior was virgin, just like the other dozen in the folder. He slipped them into his first-line plastic windows, enjoying the crisp feel of them. George felt the familiar tingling in his hands as he tuned himself up. Bruce Prior now had to take on an identity.

He rearranged his face so that the anger and irritation went out of it. When he was pretty sure he looked worried, he went into the men's room of Dunkin' Donuts and checked. Not bad, but he started to scowl as soon as he thought of anything else.

He kept working on his expressions while he did the job he had to get through first. Down with the pants, out with the jimmy-john. He wasn't sure what he had done with the woman back there in the alley, there were gaps in his memory of it. But it never hurt to get clean right after, that was for sure. He remembered the minister telling him that, many years ago, when he got caught in the church rec room, doing the hand-love with his jimmy-john after the Andrews girl felt him there and ran away. How good it had felt to clean it after, in the church men's room, all the foul smells gone. Same as now. He caught the musky reek coiling up from himself and figured that was from the woman exciting him down there. They carried filthy diseases, too. He used eight paper hand towels to be sure and felt better right away.

Back to business, all fresh. Time for repairs.

He washed his face and hands without soap because there wasn't any, just cold water and a wall-mounted blow dryer that was so low he couldn't stoop enough to get his face under it. He wet his hair and combed it with his fingers until it looked pretty good, like a guy who had just been in a hurry this morning. His black tie was still in his coat pocket but he had managed to mess it up by sleeping on that side. He wetted it a little and stretched it and put it on. The wrinkles still showed.

People always thought better of you if you dressed conservatively, plenty of serious blacks and grays. He stuck the tip of his tie under his belt and fiddled with his zipper until the tie got caught there, holding it tight so the wrinkles went out. With his jacket buttoned you couldn't see that or the dirty smudges on his shirt. He wet his fingers and stroked his pants legs until most of the creases came out. Lucky he hadn't been wearing one of his pleated outfits when he had gone out to a church dinner three days ago. They'd look like hell by now.

He had nearly walked straight into the cop screen around his apartment. A neighbor was having a loud party across the boulevard from his stucco apartment building, and there had been no street parking left at all. He'd seen that a block away and so had parked under an oak tree and started walking home, frowning at the loud rap music booming out of the party. Rap music!—gutter talk, no kind of music at all, and years out of date. It had irritated him to hear that trash cutting through the dry, cool Tucson evening. Especially after the sweet, flowing hymns he had been singing, songs that meant something and lifted you up on choruses of beauty.

But the party had saved him, because he saw the plainclothes guy walking away from it, maybe having just asked them to quiet things down a little. Mr. Plainclothes had cop all over him, plenty of stiff swagger and a third-rate suit.

George had slipped down an alley, fading into the shrubbery, and doubled around. There were two unmarked cars at the rear of his building and guys sitting in them, with one more standing in the shadows of the back stairs. They looked like serious trouble. Not local law, who were so dumb they'd park in front, probably under a streetlight so they could read the newspaper.

He had gone away and stayed overnight with a fellow parishioner family, good folks, giving them a story about a sudden need to fumigate the whole apartment house. They'd been kind of edgy about things, the way most people were around him, but they let him sleep over. The next morning he'd approached his place from three different directions. He did it on foot, in case they had an all-points out on the plates of his car.

Sure enough, from each direction there was a guy trying to look casual within a half block of the apartment. He had tried again that night, and they were still there.

Which meant the Feds, for sure. They could field special teams, take their time. Probably the interstate banking morons with their big computers. Which meant he was finished there.

But not finished for good, he thought, as he studied himself now in the men's room mirror and worked on his expression some more. Two days of hitching from Tucson had given him reddening sunburn and a mean squint. He got his mouth and eyes set so that he looked like a guy who had done plenty of manual labor and had the muscles to show but was basically just your average Joe. Worried, maybe a little confused.

He went into the Security Pacific with the opening door crowd. There were five desks to his left, two marked off with a little wood and brass fence, which meant the president and VP worked there. He looked over the three account managers at their desks. The best would probably be a young guy at the end, but he was already talking to a weathered Chicana woman in a sweater who was having trouble with her English.

George picked the next youngest account manager, a woman who looked to be midtwenties. The older they were, the more sharp and suspicious they'd gotten. As he sat down she gave him the neutral business smile they taught everybody these days and said, "How may I help you?" like a recording.

"Well, it's kinda funny," George said sheepishly. "I got one of your cards, but I don't have a local account yet."

"Oh, that's no problem."

"Kind of backward, I guess."

"Well, we probably sent you the card as an invitation, Mr.—"

"Prior. Bruce." He handed over the card, fishing it from his vest pocket so she could not see the plastic windows full of other cards.

She gave the card three seconds and said, "Let me just enter you and see."

He sat for five minutes while she clumsily went through her memorized routine, typing his card number in and looking for specs on the account, going through their national net. He casually moved his chair around so that he could see some of her screen. She had an obsolete monitor and made two mistakes with access codes.

He'd done nothing but charge a hundred bucks or so every month to keep Bruce Prior active and had paid off right away. It was a long five minutes, though, because there was a chance the cops at his apartment had somehow traced this identity. They'd had time to alert the networks. He had paid off the Prior with checks on Gary Pinkerton accounts, part of his perpetual cycling of money that kept him going. But unless the Feds did a thorough retrieval on every account he had, there would be no alert on Prior.

Unless they were on to him for more than that. There was always the chance that some stuff he'd covered up years back wasn't really buried. He put that thought out of his mind and watched the woman, ready to get out of there fast.

She smiled approvingly. "You've moved, Mr. Prior?"

"Right. New to the neighborhood."

"I see your previous address was in Tucson. A post office box."

"Got a better job out here."

"Congratulations. Well, then, perhaps you would like a checking account with us?"

"Sure. But I need some cash right away."

"I'm sure we can arrange that, too." She started taking out forms from her files.

"Don't have a steady address yet."

She frowned, then brightened. "You can use your employer's address."

That was what he got for departing from his standard story. He held his face steady, still working on the worried look, and added a little nervous touch of guilt. "They don't like us doing that."

"I quite understand. I'll bet Security Pacific wouldn't like it if I got all my bills here—there are so *many*!" Her merry little laugh had a mechanical edge to it, as if she had used it too much.

"How about I just come back in, say in a couple days, and give you my home address, once I've got one?"

"Well—"

He could see the cogs going around: Customer's left his card billing address, a P.O. box, no way to find him. Maybe something funny going on with the employer. Could be he didn't have a job at all now.

She said, "The assistant manager will probably . . ."

Now was the time to show the plastic. An embarrassed bobbing of his head while he held out his plastic accordion card holder, letting them unfold: Optima, Neiman Marcus, American Express, Broadway, Master-Card, Sears, Fuji, Visa, Nordstrom.

"Look, if these'd be any help . . ." He didn't have a dime in any of them, of course.

"Well, my, you *do* have a lot."

"Yeah, I travel plenty in my business."

She pushed back her chair, started to get up. "I'll just ask—"

"Do you know if there's a CitiBank around here?"

"Why, yes, there's—"

"If it's going to be a hassle, I'll just try them. I've got my main account with them."

She licked her lips and he watched her think. The assistant manager would see the customer walk out, figure maybe she had irked him. And how could a customer with that much plastic be a risk?

She licked her lips again and looked him in the eye. She saw something there, something that George knew he could use when he had to, because the Lord had put it there. It was his, a certain way of giving a window into his soul, so that people saw his inner truth, so that they trusted him.

She sat down, and he knew he was going to get the max on the card with no trouble. Ten minutes later he walked out with a thousand in his pocket.

He went three blocks from Security Pacific before he found a men's store that had light wool jackets in the window. He got two, one that fit right off the rack and another that could be tailored in a day. He got Oxford broadcloth shirts, gray slacks, charcoal socks with extra padding in the soles, two pair each of business shoes in black and brown, some Reeboks on sale, jeans, cotton T-shirts, Jockey shorts.

The store manager called in on the AmEx card. George stood casually chatting with the sales clerk, not seeming to watch the manager at all. The clerk went on about the weather, which George in his light-headed mood found funny, since they didn't have anything in California that counted for weather in his book. But he kept his face open and sincere while some talk went back and forth on the phone for long, stretching minutes. He got ready to walk out fast.

Then the manager hung up and came back all smiles. George had paid off the AmEx three weeks before with a Walter Humphries check on Nippon, so his bill today came in under the five-thousand-dollar limit. Humphries was a paper identity that he used to funnel cash, using a mail service in Nebraska that emptied the post office box once a month. That conduit was dead now too, he figured.

He walked down a sun-washed street, feeling good. A black-haired mutt lying under a weeping willow barked at him, then trotted over and allowed him to scratch behind its ears. Dogs had always liked George, a fact he had used several times. This one licked his hand and followed him until he had to kick it.

Two blocks away he got shaving gear, a toilet kit, and a Halliburton suitcase set, the burnished-finish kind he liked because they carried computers well. First-class stuff. The help was shorthanded in the shop that day and took his MasterCard without checking it at all.

While he packed the clothes in the Halliburtons, he saw a service station with a Budget sign across the street. Pretty soon Bruce Prior had rented a Chevy sedan, black, on a transfer from his Fuji card. All his purchases went into the trunk.

Within an hour more, Bruce Prior was eating corned beef hash with two poached eggs in a pseudo-fifties diner on Acacia. There were James Dean photographs blown up to make wallpaper in the men's room. Next to his red vinyl-covered booth with chrome piping there was a poster for the big new teen hit, "Rock Around the Clock." But the music was halfway decent, a lot of shoo-bop stuff, plenty better than rap-crap.

As he shoveled in the good salty hash, he smoked with relish the first Camel from a carton he had bought in a 'Bacco Barn. He put A.1. Sauce on the hash, and it got even better. The hash browns were greasy but he ate them anyway, lighting a second Camel and holding it between the fingers of his left hand while he forked in hash with his right. He liked easing the smoke out through his nostrils while he chewed. It licked the soft membranes there with a scorching tongue.

When he signaled for a second plastic pitcher of coffee the waitress came over to tell him that this was a nonsmoking section. He stared at her without saying anything until she blinked and looked away. He took two more forkfuls of hash browns and put out the Camel in the yolk of the last poached egg. Without leaving any money he got up and walked out without a word. Nobody followed him.

He was feeling good and knew that his fortune was no accident. He had planned for this, always had a backup line of cards and credit ready. The Feds could have cut it off if they'd had the right nose for pursuit. But they worked without the help of the Lord.

George decided to devote the next day to God's work, just to show he understood. There were tasks to do out here, many more than there had been in Tucson.

Holy ways were openly laughed at in California. There were evil practices here, lustful ones, family-destroying laws, the cesspool of Hollywood, corrupt judges, unspeakable pornography, and violations of natural order.

As he stood in the buttery sunshine and put the key into the brand-new night-black car that the Lord had given him today, George knew that this had all been ordained. The events of these days had moral heft, a solemn weight.

The Feds outside his apartment. The truck that had taken him away from the Bank of America. The Security Pacific woman who had changed her mind.

They had all been interventions. He saw that now.

The waitress, too, had been an intervention by the Devil forces that also walked this earth. And he had vanquished her. He could not remember that moment in the alley, only that she had tempted him and his jimmy-john and he had taken care of that somehow.

That, too, was part of his Calling.

He had received the Call to come here before, from a great minister, yet he had ignored it. The Reverend Montana himself had summoned him on the telephone.

George had a deafness, though, for yes, he, too, was a creature steeped in carnal sin, born to it, stupefied by the mesmerizing ornaments of this bestial world. In His silent, holy answer to George's lack of heed, the Lord had placed His hand upon the world. He had shaped events and brought George here. In the confusion of these last few days he had known that it was his fate to go to the Reverend. A Call had to be answered.

He got down on the broken asphalt right there in the parking lot of the diner, feeling it bite into his knees as the stones of antiquity had cut the flesh of martyrs, and thanked the Lord for taking a strong hand in his life.

He apologized for his fear, for his jittery anxiety, for his base and defiled nature, which struggled to climb up from the slime of the body and which could only redeem itself with pristine deeds. All along he should have put his trust in the infinite. His eyes squeezed tight and sudden tears of ripe joy oozed out onto his cheeks.

Then he got into his new car and drove away happily, whistling "Abide in Me," knowing with a granite inner strength that he had come at last to the place where he could fulfill his destiny and perform great works.

3
SUSAN

The emergency room was busy. Two Chicanos were brought in with pelvic fractures from a motorcycle crash. Both were getting prepped to go into surgery. A fifty-eight-year-old man had walked slowly in, complaining of pains shooting down his left arm. A young black woman with corn-row hair had vague cramps in her abdomen and was coughing up blood.

These occupied the interns at the University of California at Irvine Hospital, while the usual number of quick cases—bruises, fractures, sprains, contusions, foreign bodies inhaled or swallowed, dislocated shoulders, aches of back or head or stomach or ear—passed through like an unremarked, perpetual tide from the Sea of Statistics.

Business was brisk in the acute psychiatric ward, too. On her way into her office Dr. Susan Hagerty passed through the deceptively calm atmosphere there. Out of professional curiosity and a certain nosiness she allowed herself as a minor vice, she talked to the interns and looked into the three interview rooms.

An eighteen-year-old black girl stared intently at the glowing end of her cigarette, explaining in a dull, fast monotone how she had tried twice to kill her daughter, first by sleeping pills, then by suffocating her with a pillow. She did it to stop her child from crying. "I mean, I came in here to get some advice, you know? Some help. It's not natural. Not natural, a kid keeps crying that way alla time."

Susan was too experienced to be profoundly shocked by this. She was bothered, though, by the policy of allowing patients to smoke in the interviewing offices.

The next room held a man who had patiently tried to slash his wrists, using an ordinary paring knife, and seemed to wonder why it had not worked. Maybe there was something about how a knife functioned that he didn't understand.

In the end room a woman office worker was explaining why she could not walk. She kept floating up toward the ceiling, so her feet could not reach the floor to get a good grip on the Formica tiles. "That's why I can't make my feet work. It's real simple, you guys prob'ly see it every day. Do you think I can get workmen's comp?"

Outside there were patients already admitted and waiting to be seen. One older woman with frosted hair was crying softly into a pillow she held tightly. A teenage boy had a pillow also, but he was punching it hard, rhythmically, while his eyes stared out the window, expressionless but intent. Sitting farther away from them was a man in his twenties who kept himself aloof, ramrod straight and smiling at everyone, turned out in a torn, stained white tuxedo. He looked as though he was aching to tell the story, but he would have to be coaxed some first.

Susan liked these glancing brushes with the underside of the human psyche. She was well aware that she had burrowed into her work since her husband's death, and she missed a certain level of human contact. She kept up her connections—friends, membership on the board of the Chamber Music Society, old med school buddies—but the cartilage of sociability was not quite enough. At forty-four she felt awkward on dates, and she truly liked her own company.

Susan stood watching the man in the tuxedo, ruminating on this, and then headed down the hall. The usual chaos, all under control. Yet it helped somehow to see the range of human weirdness, the splintered pathways of pathology. Still, she could not suppress a sudden shiver. The abyss of the human mind was a murky, brooding riddle. In softly lit therapy rooms like this she sensed huge, shadowy monstrosities lurking unseen, swollen ugliness that rode behind the reeling eyeballs and lurched into the light only in twitches and oddities. Until, in some cases, the grotesque pressures ruptured forth, bile-sour and reeking, spewing into a surprised world.

She shook herself free of such thoughts, donned again her air of crisp efficiency. *Get real, girl.*

Emergency room staff were always fidgety about backup. A well-run hospital like UCI could handle a fresh ER patient every ten minutes. The problem was that they never entered at even intervals. Bleeding bodies and groaning, disoriented cases came at you in bunches, spun off Orange County's eternal armature. About one in four of those who turned up in the ER needed admission to the hospital. The rest went away with their cuts patched, bones splinted, traumas bandaged. Every time the patients needing admission bunched up, the senior physician immediately called in the ER backup.

Susan Hagerty was on call today. She had come into her office at UCI Gen in midmorning, poked a nose into the ER mostly to get a cup of the rich, rocket-fuel Colombian coffee they ran on there, and had hardly hung up her coat and started reading the night reports on her patients before her portable phone rang. It popped and went into annunciator mode so that she could not ignore it.

A disaster call always pumped up her adrenals. The programmed bleat for help circulated down from the chiefs of departments by an automatic phone tree—one of the few cases, in Susan's opinion, where computerization truly freed hands to do work.

Trauma center spat out a short report and ETA.

There had been a multiple car crash accordion-style on Interstate 5 in Irvine, near the border with El Toro. Trucks overturned. Traffic backed up for miles already. Helicopters aloft from police, CalTrans, rescue. This was *big*. CalTrans had already elected to send heavy lift choppers to pull cars out of the lanes as soon as the rescue teams could shuck the patients free.

No point in choppers from UCI; the accident was close. Ambulances would be here within three minutes, coming toward the hospital from the Sand Canyon offramp.

So it was back to the ER, on the double. As she walked rapidly through the bleached light of the corridor, interns, residents, and other specialists such as Susan began converging on the ER. Some wore wrinkled scrub suits, stained from tasks they had finished off in a hurry. Others were like Susan, in long white coats still starched stiff.

Nurses and staff were hustling ordinary patients out of the way, clearing the corridors and filling carts with fresh supplies. Her portable phone rasped again. There was a conference on the UCI campus that had called away most of the senior people. Bad timing. The chief of operations had put in a quick call to campus. Susan could imagine how it had gone. The secretary he had reached was unsure whether she should interrupt the seminar, until the chief barked into the telephone. UCI was nearby in miles, but not in mindset. It would probably be at least fifteen minutes before help arrived. Until then there was no more backup.

Distant sirens sounded like odd, strident bird calls. As Susan entered the ER she passed by the small black detector that alerted Trauma Central that she was on board. She picked up a headset and slipped it on, her portable phone going dead simultaneously, to avoid interference. She got an update on the spectrum of cases speeding toward them and frowned. Lots of damage. Five deaths already.

Trauma Central asked for help getting teams with the right skill balance for each case. Susan assigned at least one resident to each of the injured—wondering how long they could afford that luxury, as more cases came in—and then took a particularly bad case herself.

She studied the prelim, a computerized list on the ER data screen that dominated one wall. Her case was a woman, neck broken, multiple lesser injuries. And a police warning note strobed in red beside it.

The first bodies from the smashup arrived. Susan caught up to her self-assigned team at the entry ramp and helped the ambulance crew wheel her case in. The woman on the gurney seemed sturdy, her face tanned, probably had looked the picture of health only minutes ago. Now she was slack-jawed and pale beneath her layers of makeup.

Neck at an odd angle. Pupils dilated. She was already intubated, and a nurse was bagging her—driving air in and out of the lungs by pulsing a plastic bag.

Into the ER, working on her as they went.

"What's the police alert on this patient for?" she asked an ambulance attendant.

"She was in a dumpster truck that overturned in the accident."

"Driving a truck? What's—"

"No, she was in the garbage. Cops figure somebody chucked her, thinking she was dead. Truck empties the dumpster, doesn't notice her."

She thought of the acute psychiatric ward. So here it was—grotesque pressures finally spewing, foul and reeking, into a surprised world. A body—a *person*—thrown away, then spilled onto a freeway with the rest of the trash.

Then she swallowed her revulsion and said, "Ah. Then this neck injury could be hours old."

"I guess. She got awful banged up on the roadway, too."

That was clear. The rescue team had attached a physiological monitor to her, a book-size black hard-plastic slab with EEG and EKG leads. They had put into her an arterial stick carrying microelectrodes. These sampled blood chemistry, pressure, and flow. Susan punched its SPEAK button, and the monitor squirted its data to Trauma Central. Within two seconds Trauma Cen stretched the digital sandwich and translated the facts into a calm, flat voice speaking through her headset.

"Nonspecific slowing of EEG, consistent with concussion and metabolic injury. No sign of focal ischemia to brain."

Probable broken neck, Susan thought as they moved her to their work station, but no sign of cerebral bleeding.

Deep cuts in legs and arms. Angry red abrasions. The ambulance crew had done a good job with those; she checked the fresh white bandages quickly. Then, with the suddenness that to Susan was always like stepping off a step into free-fall nothingness, the intricate diagnostics dissolved before the stick alarm: the woman's heart had stopped.

A red light flashed on the jet-black telltale monitor. The Expert Systems Diagnostics Logic Package began muttering about cardiac arrest in her headset. The computer-generated voice was infuriatingly calm, she thought, cool and serene and remorselessly logical.

"Damn," Susan said. "Patient's gone into V-fib."

She and the nurse cut off the woman's pink waitress uniform, slicing it away at the arms. The nurse was a young man, and his strength came in handy, shucking away the bunched cloth. He chucked the remnants into a yellow plastic box for police evidence, stooped to pick up a wallet that had fallen to the floor, and finished the cut-away.

"Let's go. Shock her," Susan said.

Six minutes had elapsed since she started massage. The nurse handed her the defibrillator paddles. She checked the EKG display nearby and saw that she was getting irregular beats from the woman's heart, but nothing that settled into regularity. She fired the paddles. *Chud.* The body jerked, but the 'scope showed flat line.

Automatically she ran her hands down the woman's sternum to the landmark called the angle of Louis. She probed. "Let's ACD."

The nurse was there already with the molded gray cylinder, the hydraulic, power-assisted Active Compression and Decompression device. She positioned it, put her hand atop the mechanical diaphragm, and with a grunt started closed cardiac massage.

The heart is packed tightly between the backbone and the breastbone. She had felt it, a lump of inert tissue that had somehow decided not to go on. She had to persuade that muscular knot to start pulsing anew, tug it back into the thumping arena of life. The woman didn't seem to have lost a lot of blood, after all. Usually replacement of fluids and stimulation brought the heart back up. Usually. But behind the bland statistics lurked myriad special cases, patients with oddities of health or habit that all too often one only discovered too late.

She practiced an old mental exercise, thinking *down* into the woman's chest, *through* her hand, into the mass of unwilling muscle. Working through the ACD, a piston that amplified her effect, her hands pressed on the big breastbone. Susan thought of her working fingers, saw them sending into the woman's flesh bright yellow arrows of stimulant, rays of hope, crisp vibrant lightning.

She kept correct posture and concentrated on technique. All the mental focusing did no good if you goofed the essentials. Heel of the left hand coming down through the chuffing ACD, a third of the way up the breastbone. *Take it easy on this old cartilage. Oh, and while you're at it, don't collapse her ribs.*

Without blood circulation, the patient would begin to suffer damage from lack of oxygen. Her brain cells would begin their little deaths, starved for air, long before the more durable heart muscle began to deteriorate.

"Her name's Patricia Olin," the nurse said, jerking a thumb back over his shoulder. "See? Cops are waiting on this one."

Susan didn't bother to look. "Epinephrine," she ordered between strokes.

Hands came into her field of view, inserting intravenous lines in both arms, attaching catheters, taking a blood sample, all under the hope that she would restart the heart. With IVs, a brachial patch for fresh blood, a breathing tube down her throat, and a ventilator working, Ms. Olin was being buried in technology.

Susan felt her focus of attention narrow, the familiar falling away of all noise, sights, and smells that did not bear directly on the patient before her. The reeks and clangs and shouts faded. Every team leader wore a headset, which in theory was to help information flow faster, more quietly. She suspected they also doubled as earplugs.

Her own headset belatedly recited Patricia Olin's data, including an age of thirty-eight. Normally they came in already IDed. In a big crunch, niceties were set aside. A nurse had found Olin's insurance card and taken it to a nearby optical reader, which would track down her records and risk factors. But that would probably be too late for Ms. Olin, she guessed.

She puffed regularly, knowing that she had to keep her own oxygen level high or else lose a slight edge in her performance. Around her the ER was filling up. More bloody cases came in on swiftly rolling gurneys. It was a big smashup at high speeds. A resident shot questions at an injured woman at the next work station, only feet away, shouting over the noise.

Susan gave herself over to a well-practiced rhythm: shock, massage, listen. Five times, ten. The monitor whispered that pH was dropping. "Sodium bicarb."

The nurse gave the injections into the heart's right ventricle as Susan resumed massaging. Two more tries with the defibrillator paddles. Seconds ticked on.

She ordered a dose of epinephrine given IV. Another try. She blinked back stinging sweat. Some premature contractions that faded as she caught them on the 'scope.

Minutes stretched amid the babble and shouts and clatter swirling around her. Heart muscles moved on finer and finer scales, the overall movements ceasing. Dying. She stood in the eye of the hurricane, totally transfixed, concentrated, sending lances of waning hope down through her tiring fingers.

Wake up.

With some jolts from the paddles, Olin's arms flopped up and across her chest. It was as though for an instant the woman tried to seize control of herself and then her will wilted, helpless.

Fifteen tries.

Don't go.

She looked into Olin's face as she worked, though she knew you could tell little or nothing about a patient that way. The eyes might be the windows of the soul, but they were of no help in reviving the body.

Patricia Olin's eyes fluttered for a moment, as delicately as the wavering of butterfly wings, as though she were struggling up from some shadowy quicksand that sucked her down into a black pit, away from the sweet sun and open air. The movement brought momentary life to her face. Despite what her hands told her, Susan felt a flicker of joy. If only—

But a glance at the 'scope showed no true, steady response in Olin's chest. It was so easy to misread a passing tremor as a positive sign. She peered at the waxy skin with its sheen of perspiration and tried, as she worked, to see within the slack-jawed face the fragile, multisided person that was still somewhere in this phlegmatic body, these slabs of muscle and bone that resisted her probing fingers.

Abruptly she thought of another body, of a muscular, big-boned, strong man. Her Roger. Always eagerly athletic, especially in bed, Roger had been massive, muscular, almost daunting to her at times, and he had fallen away from her just as suddenly as this, a coronary while jogging, of all the ridiculous—

Seventeen. *No! Come back! Don't!*

Eighteen tries.

Nineteen.

"Blood pressure?" she prompted the diagnostics package. It reassured her that the pressure was not dropping much. So Ms. Olin had suffered few ruptured blood vessels from hydrostatic shock.

"So why isn't she responding?" Susan spat back.

"There are no significant indicators at this time," the bland, flat headset voice said.

The voice was undoubtedly right and just as undoubtedly irritating. Sometimes patients simply did not fit the standard profile. Usually you never knew why until after the autopsy. If then.

Last chance time. "Okay, let's open her up."

Things moved in a blur then, as if she were under water.

Closed-chest massage was moderately effective. She had considered using one of the "thumper" gadgets that sat on the patient's chest and delivered an optimal pressure pulse. But something in her liked hands-on medicine, even through an ACD. And anyway, her research side reminded her, the latest data didn't show them to be all that great.

So Susan "zipped her open," cutting swiftly through the left side of the chest with the big cutters. Patricia Olin's heart was a sullen red lump. She narrowed her field of view to it and seized the slippery knot with one hand. For a silent, dreamlike time she labored at the inert ball of muscle. All her will bore down through her hands—and it all came to nothing.

There came at last a moment when she wiped sweat away from her brow, panting, and glanced up. The attendants around her were looking at each other. Bottles of intravenous fluids clustered atop their poles, like ugly fruit on stripped trees.

Slowly, unwillingly, Susan looked at the impersonal hands of the big white clock. It had been fifty-two minutes.

Defeat flooded into her like a dark weight.

"I . . . I guess that's . . . all."

Her fingers numb, she automatically checked the other patients, each the focus of a buzzing cluster. Other faculty had arrived from the university and were handling matters well. A nineteen-car pileup, someone told her, caused by a jackknifed truck.

When are they going to start regulating those damned trucks? Susan thought sharply. *They do so much damage, so much—*

A wave of sudden, inexplicable grief burst over her. She made herself walk stonily out through the ER, checking to see if there was anything she could do, and at the same time trying to hold back the tide of emotion.

She got herself out into the enameled light of the hallway, pushing the door open and leaning against it. The air out here seemed fresher. She longed to get outside, go for a quiet walk, feel the sting of the sun, gaze up into the pale, crystalline sky. She blew her nose, bringing swarming into her sinuses the astringent cleanser smell a hospital never lost. That seemed to clear her mind, to pull her up from the funnel of concentration, and the first thing she registered was a police officer asking her if Patricia Olin had said anything on the table.

Despite herself, she laughed. The thin cackle came out with unnerving force. Susan gulped and made herself say slowly, soberly, "She never regained consciousness. The heart stopped on her way in."

"I see, ma'am," the patrol officer said, making a note. "We'll be getting in touch with you about this after—"

"Wait a minute. What happened to that woman?"

The officer blinked, his respect for physicians battling visibly in his face with reflexive caution. "It's an active case, and I can't—"

"No, damn it, why was she in a dumpster?"

The officer's lips pursed, and he relented. "We don't know. Just got a feedback, sayin' she worked in a Denny's up in the middle of the county. Walked out the back early this mornin'."

"And right into some bad luck," Susan said.

"Guess so, doctor. That's all I know."

She thanked him and pressed her back flat against the cool wall again. Aches seeped out of her. Slowly she noticed a hospital administrator nearby speaking in low, soft, sympathetic words.

But not to her. The target of this professional solace was a stocky woman in a honey blouse and brown skirt one size too small for her. The administrator was a thin, soft-spoken man gently trying to steer the woman into one of the small waiting rooms. The woman would have none of this.

"I want to see my daughter immediately!" she cried, snatching her arm away from the man's grasp. She turned abruptly to Susan. "Where is she?"

"Who?" Susan asked automatically. She felt for a door handle, preparing to retreat into the ER. She did not feel like dealing with relatives just now.

"Olin. Patricia Olin," the woman said adamantly. "I got a call from you people, I'm Donna Olin, I live just down the road, got here as soon as—"

"Please, just step in here," the administrator beseeched.

"No, I have a right to know, I've been waiting and I want—"

The woman stopped, mouth open, eyes widening, her irises like brown islands floating in lakes of white. Susan realized that the woman could see through the doorway behind her, to where the team had already drawn a sheet over the patient's face.

Or had they? Susan turned and saw that the team was still tending to the body, its face uncovered.

When she looked back, the woman seemed to wilt, swaying like a willow in a savage, silent wind. She babbled, crying between bursts of incoherent words. Susan put a hand out to comfort her and was brushed aside. The administrator was speaking slowly in low, calm tones, but the woman heard nothing, her eyes rolling in their sockets, lungs laboring, pale lips pulled back in a crooked grimace. Suddenly she snapped to attention, turned, and struck the wall with open hands. Furiously she beat the hard plaster in a sudden tornado of emotion, as if trying to drive the ER itself away. She shouted, cursed, kicked at the wall—and then collapsed, knees splaying outward, arms limp, making no attempt to cushion her fall.

Susan stood frozen, her mind whirling in an empty, frictionless void. The Olin woman struggled to get back up, her face closed in upon her own misery.

"No, no, I won't have that." Her mouth sagged as she argued emphatically with the air, focusing on nobody. "You can't *say* that."

"Say what, Mrs. Olin?" the administrator asked calmly.

"That she's—that she's just—" She gulped, blinked. With visible effort she pulled herself up, took a deep breath, her mouth firming. "Gone."

"If you'll kindly step this way . . . a little privacy . . ." Smoothly the thin man led her into a small waiting room.

No matter what you did, Susan thought, there was always some detail. No matter how efficient and sanitized and crisply run, in a hospital each death had some cruel, nasty detail. It might be minor, trivial, but it snagged in the mind and left a scar on the memory. And sometimes it was something sudden and awful, like this, as vivid as spurting crimson blood. This mother would carry this scene to her own grave. Such things happened. They had to. They arose from the noise and hurry and crowding of a place where daily, hourly, people died among strangers.

Susan made herself go back into the ER. She would be no good at comforting Mrs. Olin. That was what the buffer of assistants around so many doctors was for, though no one ever said so explicitly.

She stood silently and felt the hubbub ebbing in the ER, tension trickling away into rivulets of talk and cleanup jobs. To her relief, she was no longer needed. She told the operations chief that she was leaving, ignoring his puzzled glance. Her face must be giving away a lot.

A clerk stopped her as she left, guiding her to a small cubicle. She punched in on her phone, and her mind went on automatic, making the case report. The story tumbled out, data and treatment and impersonal slabs of facts. Robo-Doc. Strangely, it helped.

She climbed the external stairs slowly back to her office. The Saddleback Valley stretched like a jumbled-up board game, buildings jutting up through a white haze. The Indians had called this the Valley of Smokes, she recalled, because of the dry dust stirred incessantly by winds from the deserts to the east. Smog tinted this a ruddy brown and brought a prickling to her nose. Three stories below, palm trees lined the sweeping emergency driveway. A gust set their fronds to clattering, a sound both natural and strangely alien, like the clicking, impatient language of giant insects.

Only when Susan closed the door to her office did she notice that she still wore her bloody rubber gloves. She pulled them off and collapsed into her chair, a Norwegian leather tilt-back with a footrest that popped out. She needed the comfort. Her back muscles tensed up while standing at the operating table, storing her knotted frustrations, and then they protested hours later with stabbing spikes of pain.

Things had been going a bit too fast for her. The revival of Sparkle, the emergency in ER, the terrible way she had slipped up and let Mrs. Olin get the news. . . . She knew she would relive those awful moments in dreams for weeks.

She needed a break. No company just now, thanks, no quick coffee in the cafeteria. Something to take her out of herself.

The pleasure of working at a teaching hospital lay in the students and the research. An ordinary, workaday hospital dealt with the steady, awesome responsibilities of medicine. A university hospital did, too— but it also had in its bones the brimming promise of the unknown. Future ERs would see the same tragedies, pain, and grief, unless medical research found better ways of dealing with trauma.

With a beep her printer started sliding forth the typescript of her case report on Patricia Olin. Machine-translated from her voice code groups, it would probably be ninety-eight percent accurate, requiring only a quick scan. At the moment she did not feel like facing even that.

Time for a little fun. With a distinct tingle of anticipation, Susan plucked her working notebook from its slot in the bookshelf. She used a notebook-style computer that allowed her to write on the screen with a stylus. In an age of marvels, she still liked methods that echoed the jottings she had made as a schoolgirl.

She "refreshed" her notebook's memory from the big desktop computer where she kept her permanent records. Disks hummed to each other in their insect drone. Just as the transfer ended, something caught her eye. The systems log-in table, which kept track of her additions and editings, had an entry from two hours ago.

She had been with patients then, as scheduled.

Which meant that somehow, somebody had gotten into her files. When they knew she would be doing her rounds with the interns, not running any programs herself.

She tapped in commands, but there was no trace of what the intruder had done. No files missing. None even edited.

She sighed in relief. No damage, then. An accident, maybe? Her general directory was open to official additions, as per policy. Some misdirected inquiry from the hospital's main computer?

Or maybe not.

A chilly shiver ran through her. Sour, nauseated anger licked in her belly, a blood-deep, visceral revulsion at the violation of her private records. She gritted her teeth, whispered swear words. With leaden certainty she knew what had happened here. Some cunning snoop had broken in, looked around, and left.

Who? Why? Not a malicious vandal, or else her data would be scrambled, notes deleted, texts chopped and confused.

But her files could have been copied, of course. If the intruder wanted to steal her research. Or simply to know what it was.

Susan felt a gray, sinking dread. Yes—*to know what it was.*

She had heard the distant whispers of scuttlebutt about her work. Most of it came because she worked by herself, a woman alone, and didn't talk shop. There was no one here in her field, after all. But that didn't stop nasty rumors.

All the snooper had left was this single footprint in her log-in table. Which meant he was pretty good. Not expert, but good. Any competent technician or physician could have done it. In and out—for reasons she would never know.

But the chilly, bone-deep anger still churned in her belly. Scientific research was often abstract, aloof—but this was a digital rape, and she felt age-old, burning rage. For long moments she sat shock-still, mouth a grim line, fists clenched, nails biting into her palms.

Then decades of training took over. Resolutely, she unknotted her hands, stood, walked around, worked the stiffness out of her spine, yawned to stretch the rigidity from her face. *Fight it, girl.*

With a great, cleansing exhale she got rid of it all—the speculations, anger, worry, and anxious dread. Only a thin, ominous cloud hung at the back of her mind.

Physicians learned to drop segments of their lives into compartments, bang the doors shut, and come back later—if ever. She used that now. After getting control of her breathing and staring for a long moment into space, she was okay. She sat down, opened computer files, picked up her stylus, and began reviewing her work. *Dive on in. Don't let anything steal this from you, swindle away the simple pleasure of worthy labor.*

On the University of California campus at Irvine, she was the only faculty member working on cryopreservation—the techniques of freezing and storing tissues for later use. She was hot on a major advance now—Sparkle's groggy but solid revival had proved that. She had done successful trials with lab mice, sure—but a dog was far harder. Alex had talked her into suspending Sparkle, using the classic argument—*look, she's going to die anyway*—and practical, hard-nosed Susan had secretly expected to fail.

The crucial factor was a new class of specially developed chemicals she had developed—transglycerols. They had enabled Sparkle's cells to let their water escape as they were cooled, over a month ago. That had kept them from rupturing as Sparkle's water froze, because the ice then formed outside the cells.

In the cells lay the body's true structure. Function and memory were intricately housed in the little building blocks of all living beings. "Freezer burn" was nothing more than the microscopic ripping apart of cells as water expanded, turning to ice, slicing across membranes. It was like blowing up a balloon inside a room, pushing through the walls of ordered cell, fracturing the order that sheltered the family within.

Defeating that damage was the key. And she had done it.

As she worked over the notes from Sparkle's revival she felt a quickening, the old sensation that came seldom but was never forgotten: the moment when you discover something about the way the world is made, see it true and square. And you glimpse it before anyone else, like a high, distant valley unknown to humanity, its riches uncharted.

She sat back, her stylus working quickly on her notebook screen, filling in details from Sparkle's revival before they fled from memory. The most minor change in procedure could be crucial. She sometimes felt like Sherlock Holmes, obsessively noting what sometimes seemed like pointless trivia. Holmes had routinely counted the number of steps into a building, noted railroad timetables down to the exact minute, cataloged the colors and smells of countless muds and tobaccos, had been able to trace them from a few grains left by a villain.

She counted drops of solutions, noted the settings on instruments, knew the subtle tints of tissues under stress. Well, maybe it wasn't so odd. Arthur Conan Doyle, the creator of Holmes, had started out as a physician.

"Ah," she said aloud, "if only I had a Watson."

For some reason this made her mind veer into a familiar swamp of emotion. Roger.

They had been married nearly twenty years, had gone from early zesty passion to settled, comfortable intimacy. And then death's sharp scythe had cut him down with a heart attack. A quick death, the kind people called "merciful," as if being jerked into oblivion were something to be wished for. He had been her Watson, in a way, an amusing, dear sidekick—as well as an ardent lover. Her special hero.

There was a knock at her door. She was still half-immersed in her thoughts when she opened it to find Sidney Blevin, a colleague. *Not a candidate for Watson, no,* she thought.

She had never gotten through Blevin's cool, professional veneer to see what kind of human lurked beneath. He had a narrow face, hawkish nose, and sallow cheeks. Like many physicians, he kept rather poor care of himself. He sported a paunch ill-disguised by the baggy maroon sweater he wore beneath a lab coat, and his stringy arms spoke of little exercise. His hooded eyes studied her for an instant as though she were a specimen under a CT scan. As an oncologist, he read those three-dimensional hieroglyphics with ease.

"Susan," he said abruptly, "I've got the scoop here on your patient Lowenthal."

"Oh, good." She waved him to a chair.

She had called in Blevin to consult on the detailed CT scan of a woman Susan had admitted yesterday. Marie Lowenthal was a mother of three, married, forty-three—only a year younger than Susan. She had a persistent fever and vague abdominal symptoms. Marie had ignored her illness until it became obvious to her husband that she wasn't just having a bout with the flu.

"Here's the goods," Blevin said, advancing to her work table and calling up pictures from the hospital's top-of-the-line diagnostics. On her large, high-resolution wall screen the details were razor sharp.

"As you can see—" Blevin started to take her through the details, but she silently held up a hand.

The moment of first seeing fresh data was precious to her. Raw numbers spoke a subtle, supple language all their own. Graphs, charts, lab indices, a whirling blizzard of detail—she always sensed these as voices, some shouting, others whispering softly. It was easy to simply listen to the shouts.

Usually, the loud, obvious answer was also the right one. But not always. So Susan cherished this moment when she could turn her ear to the data by herself, listen for the quiet, telling murmurs.

The most common known cause of fever was infection, and the most common unknown cause of fever was infection. Many infections were hard to find. But fever could also arise from a hyperactive thyroid, from drug use, from a brain hemorrhage, from deep malignancy. An infection could hide in some cranny of the body for a long time, then reach the bloodstream, sending a shower of bacteria raging through the patient, shooting her temperature up. Then the body's defenses responded, white cells devouring the offending infection. By the time the patient came in, the bacteria that had caused the fever were gone, making diagnosis difficult.

So Susan had asked for an intricate inspection of Marie Lowenthal, bringing to bear the full resources of UCI's technology. And it had found what she most feared. This time the data shouted at her, and today, especially, it was not a truth she wished to hear.

"Big one," Blevin said casually. "Sitting right in the tail of the pancreas, tight and snug."

"Yes," Susan said, her face stony.

"Want to see it in 3D?"

She sighed. "No."

"Some interesting features," he prodded.

"Not necessary."

"She complain about any pain?"

"No . . . no."

"Funny. This far along, this big, they usually hurt."

Susan bit her lip. "She's a busy mother. Three children—she had to bring them with her on her office visit. A husband who works long hours. She probably suppressed it."

"Ummm." Blevin's hawk nose nearly touched the slick CT sheets as his finger traced the hints left by the malignancy.

It is like Sherlock Holmes, in a way, she thought. *We're hunting down the murderer. Not that swollen tumor. That's merely the weapon that will pull down a bustling, loving mother and wife. The true crime is committed by nature itself.*

"Pretty far along, I'd say." Blevin blinked owlishly. "Look at the detail these new computer programs give us! Aren't they great?"

"Yes. Great."

"Sure you don't want to see the 3D?"

Susan looked at Blevin's pale, oily nose as if it were a sickly fish from a deep, dark sea. Patients often complained that doctors weren't interested in them, only in their diseases. For a hovering, slow moment she felt for Blevin a sour metallic dislike, pooling in her mouth like the taste of aluminum foil caught in her teeth.

"I said no."

"Surprised it took this long to give her a fever."

"I imagine she's been ignoring the symptoms for some time," Susan said stiffly.

"Well, she's a goner."

Susan bit her lip, said nothing.

"You looked at the stats on this type?"

"Yes."

"Two months I'd give her, tops."

"Chemo?"

"This type, no percentage in it. Just make her throw up every five minutes for the rest of her life—which will be short. You going to be straight with her about that?"

"Probably."

"Dead meat, I'd say."

Susan's lips compressed into a thin, bloodless line. "Get out."

Blevin looked up from his sheets, eyes startled. "What?"

"I said get out. Now."

"Hey, there's no call for you to—"

"I don't refer to my patients that way. Ever."

He sneered. "You get too involved with them, I'd say."

"I care, of course." She struggled with conflicting emotions. The desire to be professional and distant. Her memory of Patricia Olin. Of Marie Lowenthal's children and their naked, hollow-eyed fear.

"Remember to keep your professional distance, doctor. Taking everything personally, it impairs your judgment."

"Go. Just go."

Blevin gave her an odd look, slipped his pages into a folder, and left. Numbly she watched him go, knowing that she had committed a stupid, rude, unprofessional mistake. But her mouth refused to open and apologize, to say anything at all. She was already thinking of what she would have to say to Marie Lowenthal, and somehow it was simply too much to bear.

Life was like a long march, an endless column of forlorn souls moving forward through surrounding dark. Nobody knows where you're going, but there is plenty of talk and the fools pretend to understand more than they're saying. There is merry laughter, too, and somebody is always passing a bottle around. But now and then somebody stumbles, doesn't catch himself right, and falls back a ways. Or just lurches aside and is gone, left behind. The dead. For them the march stops at that moment. Maybe they have a while longer, lying back there on the hard ground, already wreathed in fog—time to watch the parade dwindle away, carrying its lights and music and raucous jokes.

For us the dropouts are back there somewhere, she thought, *fixed in a murky landscape we're already forgetting.*

They fell farther behind every day. She could recall others who had stayed behind, years ago. With a little sigh or a grunt of agony or just a flickering of fevered eyelids, they left the march. And now they didn't know the latest jokes, or the savor of a fresh bottle of wine, or even what the hottest rumors were about. The march saddens as you go on. You remember them back there, wish you could tell them what's up nowadays, share a laugh or a lie.

And you knew that someday you will catch an ankle and go down and the murk will swallow you, too. Maybe it would be better if you didn't have that puzzled, startled moment of staring at the retreating heads, the faces already turning away from you. Maybe it was best if you couldn't hear that last parting round of hollow laughter from a joke you would never know, the golden lantern light already shining on them and not on you.

And it will happen to everyone you have known or ever will, Susan thought. Somehow she never got used to that.

And now she had to go up to see Marie Lowenthal.

4

KATHRYN

Immortality Incorporated was a two-story modular industrial prefab, like thousands of others in Orange County. Kathryn recognized the standard off-white paneling bolstered by a gray cinderblock facade, all enclosing the usual boring industrial square footage on a concrete slab. Behind these rectangular certainties, native scrub and spindly eucalyptus seemed to swarm down from a high ridge line like a fluid, following channels carved by runoff. At the base of the hill the thick vegetation parted, as though to keep a respectful distance from the building. She caught the crisp odor of citronella. A gust brought a thin flavoring of distant orchards. This Southern California semidesert had an ageless, eternal quality, the dry feel of centuries sliding by unnoticed.

Appropriate, Kathryn thought. Immortality took a long time.

The building stood alone at the flaring mouth of what she would have called a gully or dry wash but out here had to be termed an arroyo. Behind it she could see a backup electrical generator and chemical storage racks, all enclosed behind heavy chain fencing.

The only interesting touch was a band of mirror glass across the front at ground level. As she crossed the narrow parking lot she saw herself, hips swaying a bit more than she liked. Sexy Sadie—not the best image for her first day on the job, no. Remember to watch that.

She had long ago admitted that her relationship to mirrors was like that of politicians to opinion polls, so she allowed herself the luxury of a full, long look. Overall, a solid B, maybe B plus. The yellowish sunlight set off her auburn hair nicely, and her Navaho bracelet picked up the turquoise splashes in her patterned blouse. The off-white wrap skirt did not call attention to her B minus legs, which she had not yet had time to tan to the Southern California norm. She lifted her arms and did a turn, checking how the blouse tucked in the back. A minus, maybe. The ensemble struck a sleek contrast with the rugged hills and Santiago Canyon Road, which wriggled like a black snake into the distance. The overall effect reminded her of the stark black-and-white ads in *Vogue*— vaguely hostile women displaying themselves, with bare-chested guys in mirrorshades lounging around looking tough. She stopped before the silvered wall and combed her glinting hair with long fingers, twisted her mouth to see if her cherry-pink lipstick was right—great, a clear A—and then realized that anyone behind this one-way glass could be laughing at her. Feeling suddenly self-conscious, she pressed the doorbell.

After a long wait a tall, muscular man opened the door and peered out with a distracted look.

"Mr. Cowell? I've come to visit the facility? And I—"

"Oh, yes," Alex Cowell said vaguely. He had a square nose and lean good looks. His hair was fluffed up in the back, a cowlick barely suppressed, and his moustache was just long enough to suggest a man who cared little for his appearance and did his laundry when he ran out of socks.

"Oh, yes, right." Distracted, he glanced toward the rear of the building, from which came the faint cycle of pumps.

A bit nerdy, she thought. Rimless plastic lenses perched on his broad nose, giving him a curiously professorial look despite his cutoff jeans, torn blue T-shirt, and old air-heeled Nikes worn without socks.

As he stood aside she stepped by, getting a pleasant smell of musky maleness from him. She stood in the cool, still air of an unremarkable anteroom crowded by a Midway desk and gray steel chairs, but the walls caught her attention. Photographs filled one entire wall, mostly middle-aged men and women beaming at the camera, some in military uniforms, others caught fishing or playing sports.

Somehow, until these photographs, the reality of it had not hit her. *And they're all here, in a way,* she thought. *Or at least some hope still rests here.*

When she had applied for this job, straight from the classifieds, and first realized what Immortality Incorporated did, part of her had lurched back in horror. *They really do freeze people. It's not a joke.* But times were tough, and to save money to continue her college, she needed another part-time job to stack alongside her twenty hours a week at Fashion Circus. That was the hassle—nobody hired full-time these days if they could help it, to avoid paying all the benefits.

She had always believed her high school teachers—you could find out just about anything using the library. After reading up on the company and some cryonics history, and checking out their financial structure, her initial reaction—*what a bunch of creeps!*—had ebbed away.

She glanced back at Cowell. Kathryn believed in instinctive attractions, and this man definitely had the right stuff. Sure, this was a job, but life was short; she decided to have some fun with him. Cowell's name had come up in her library search on I^2 and cryonics. He was legendary among cryonicists, Cowell the controversial, known for his remorseless dedication. *Well, girl,* she thought, *let's keep the legend off balance.*

She broke this line of thought and turned to him. "Nice shirt."

She almost laughed at his disconcerted reaction. "Huh?"

"Ah, one of those men who never notices what he wears."

A guarded look. "I wouldn't say that."

"Much less what a woman wears."

"Like that dress?" he counterattacked.

"Ha! This isn't a dress, it's a skirt and blouse."

"Well . . ." He was a man who lived by technical distinctions, she could see that, and he was looking for a way out of this one. "Who cares?"

Ah, the so-what argument. "Who *cares*? You're trying to impress the public, sell them an idea that sounds like an outtake from *Night of the Living Dead,* and you say *who cares*?"

"We want people who don't go by appearances," he said stiffly.

"But *every*body goes by appearances." She smiled and sat on the corner of the green steel desk, feeling herself get into the swing. "You've got a look, whether you know it or not."

"So what's my 'look' say?"

She pretended to study him, starting at the face and moving down. *Nice strong thighs, actually,* she thought, allowing herself a little fun by extending her assessing gaze just a fraction too long. Sure enough, he reddened. "That outfit? Bleached-out jean cutoffs, tough-guy shirt, jogging shoes, scruffy moustache, shady eyes? You're saying, 'Yo, I'm a drug dealer.' "

A wry smile. "If only I made a drug dealer's income."

"You want to appear rich but unassuming, go for the army surplus look."

"I thought the rich wore designer sweat suits."

"Never. Psychologists and professional vegetarians, yes."

"You think you can dope out who people are by what they wear?"

The obvious truth of this was a central axiom of her life, of course, but she could see that admitting it would be a tactical error. The nap of fabrics, the heft of shoulder pads, choice of hemline, a subtle gathering at a bodice—all these carried such complex import, freighting every gesture with added meanings, that she was sometimes surprised that people could talk and look at each other at the same time. But she confined herself to saying, "I can read the obvious."

"Okay." He leaned against the wall, arms crossed in a standard judgmental-protective signal. "Read me."

"Ummm." Again she let her eyes run over his face, clothes, posture. "I'd say you were reasonably well educated, probably college degree, work with your hands a lot, have a sense for detail, thirty years old, unmarried but fool around."

He blinked. *Bull's-eye!* she thought. "What's that mean, fool around?"

"It means you're not dead." She gestured at the pictures on the wall. "Unlike your clients."

"Patients. Suspension patients." He corrected her automatically, still thinking over her assessment. "You know, you weren't far wrong."

About fooling around? she thought. *Let's hope so, unladylike though that might be.* Actually, she could deduce much more about women from their clothes. Men's wear was so predictable, off-the-shelf, boring. Men looked at cars as glamorous, and clothes as something that got them around. Women looked at cars as something that got them around—preferably to clothes, which were glamorous. Kathryn could glance at a woman wearing a dress on the street and instantly make a good guess at where she'd bought it, and why, what her house looked like, income level, what books she read (if any), and even a fair stab at how often she had sex.

Kathryn said in a lousy gypsy accent, "I have the all-seeing eye."

"Ummm. Couldn't be that you knew most of it already?" he asked slyly.

Well, the jig was up. Might as well wring a little more coquettishness out of it, though. "How could I?"

"Just now, at the door, I figured you were a call-in, somebody who saw that TV program on us last week and wanted to look us over."

"Why did you think that?"

He grinned. "The way you're dressed."

"Pattern turquoise blouse, white sheath skirt, red pumps, no stockings? Everyday wear."

"In Hollywood, maybe. Not here."

She smiled. "Okay, I'll 'fess up. I'm Kathryn Sheffield."

The effect was less than ego-boosting. Alex Cowell looked blank, then rolled his eyes skyward, recalling data from long-term storage. "Oh yes. Zeeman told me you'd come by."

"Right. I just moved here. I answered your ad for a part-time job. Mr. Zeeman hired me, twenty hours a week."

"Oh yeah. You were the only one who applied."

"More food for the ego."

"Your file's somewhere around here." He gestured vaguely. "Med tech trainee, right?"

"Sort of. General gofer might be closer."

"You know much about us?"

"You're in the newspapers a lot, mostly about lawsuits." The State of California was resisting allowing cryonics as a permissible means of "body disposal," as the *L.A. Times* put it.

His jaw stiffened. "We'll get through it."

Cryonics was a beleaguered idea, and only the utterly convinced had held to it through the years, building a few companies devoted to its ideas. She admired his resolute understatement, but on the other hand, this was the time to draw the line. "I, uh, should tell you that I'm not really a . . ."

"Believer?" Alex grinned. "Not necessary. Just do your job."

"I'm not hostile, don't get that idea. I mean, it's interesting. I need the work, to be honest. This recession is pretty bad. But the ideas, they're . . . interesting."

"Just so you're not opposed to it." Alex shrugged with good humor. She saw that beneath the nerdy veneer he was in fact quite a handsome man, with a strong, wedge jaw and dark, intense eyes. Many men poured themselves into interesting jobs and became couch potatoes who looked as though they ate exclusively at McDonald's, but Alex had a lean, compact grace. Vegetarian, she guessed.

"Glad to have you here." He stuck out a hand, glancing back toward the interior.

His grasp was warm and strong, and he gave her a quick, flashing

smile that seemed to imply some acceptance, some unspoken understanding. "It's Dr. Cowell, isn't it?"

He waved this away. "Biochemistry—marginally useful here, at best.
I did my thesis in longevity studies, lab rats galore. After a postdoc at
Stanford I got tired of routine stuff, wanted to follow my instincts."

"You do research here?"

"Sure. Nothing the National Institutes of Health will fund, though."
Again the broken grin.

Something told her that he had come to Immortality Incorporated
along a hard path. There was a coiled energy in him, the kind of gnarled
tension that can lead to great deeds or, turned inward, can simply fray
into neurosis, nervous tics, and obsession. Alex didn't have those signatures. He was casual in his cutoffs, not bottled up inside a lab coat or a
three-piece suit, like some Ph.D.'s she knew. After all, Einstein didn't
wear socks.

So she drew him out, getting the story about how a bomb blast had
drawn him into saving lives, leading eventually to cryonics. "Frankly,"
she said, "a name like Immortality Incorporated isn't great public relations—sounds like wackos."

"Yeah, I agree. But the company was founded in the first big spurt of
enthusiasm for cryonics, the 1960s. The old-timers like Zinnes make us
newer types keep the name as a sort of in-your-face raspberry to the
state medical board."

They spent a half hour filling out paperwork to the strains of Def
Leppard. Boyd Zeeman, the president of I^2, had hired her in the office
of his Huntington Beach pharmacy, after checking her references. Their
fragile finances dictated their style, limping along with a few poorly paid
on-site people, while volunteers stood ready to assist when a suspension
occurred. Their membership was climbing exponentially. "Last year, in
'ninety-four, we reached five hundred members and did eight suspensions. Most of the time it's pretty dead around here, though, so you'll
work with just me and a few others."

Pretty dead around here? But unconscious humor wasn't on for today;
Alex was focused, quick. By the time he was finished with the details,
Kathryn had forgiven him for forgetting about her arrival. He was still
distracted and immediately said, "Look, maybe you should start on
some simple job first, but I need help right now."

"With what?" Games were over.

"Got a dog back there, need to do some fluid cycling."

"I don't know much—"

"I'll show you what to do."

He led her back through a maze of medical equipment. I-Squared
was the flagship organization of the admittedly rather skimpy cryonics

fleet. He pointed out that they had much more equipment than their Northern California competitor, CrossTime Corporation—endless tall steel-gray cabinets of backup gear, gleaming gadgets, ample stocks of supplies. "Beefed up our capability all through the eighties. Started research then, too—until then it was a freeze-and-hope project, I'm afraid. I got into it to explore the basic ideas."

"But you could've done more, uh—mainstream research."

"You nearly said 'legitimate,' right?"

"No, 'respectable.' "

"I wanted to be part of a real revolution in how we think about death. See, the thing I learned back in that Tokyo airport was that I think like a cryonicist. I'm not afraid of death—I *hate* it."

His sudden ferocity startled her. "What's the difference?"

"Plenty. Fear paralyzes you. Hate you can do something about."

They passed through a long, high bay with a sheet metal roof. At first she did not recognize the tall, imposing cylinders there for what they were. Then she saw the heavily Styrofoam-insulated pipes and red-handled gate valves and felt the slight chill. Here they were—the suspension patients. They had given themselves over to Immortality Incorporated after being declared clinically dead, and now they coasted through their dreamless hours in liquid nitrogen. They dwelled in conditions colder than any place in the entire solar system, save the frigid outer planets. Only in such chill would time's erosions cease.

Kathryn had already wrestled with the whole spookarama of cryonics, the emotional baggage—associations with empty-eyed zombies and musty graves, creepy spiderweb necrophilia, horrid smells, squishy stuff underfoot, and things that go bump in the night. So she was surprised when she felt a sudden, strong reaction to the cool actuality of this place.

The blackness clutched at her for an instant then, the old dread feelings. Her eyes squeezed shut.

When she was six years old, her aunt Henny had come back from a trip to Europe with a used bobby's cape. Just the stylish thing, Aunt Henny had said, and without warning had thrown the heavy woollen weight over Kathryn's head. Sudden darkness, the thick swarming odor of damp wool, the vanishing of the sunny living room—and the jagged terror had welled up in her, the months of numb politeness stripped away. She had fought against the bobby's cape, tripped on a chair, fell. But the weight and dark stayed with her, seemed to wriggle up her nostrils with a moist, cloying insistence. She had screamed, *My mommy's dying!*—and thrashed and shrieked and grunted against the dark weight, and finally, when they got the cape off her, sobbed. In the still-bright living room the adult faces were white, stiff, big-eyed.

They had gathered to visit the cancer patient in an atmosphere of bland ordinariness topped off with forced laughter, and now little Kathryn had stripped that gloss away with a single shriek. Their tut-tutting mouths had managed to fill the yawning silence that fell after Kathryn struggled out from under the cape. But they could not shine any of their artificial light into the blackness she had in that instant brought into her own world and that would not leave it, ever.

Her mother died two months later, and she had gone to her grand-mother's to live, but the swarming inky edge of another world followed her. It was there whenever she paused and thought, really thought. And sometimes it would leap at her, smothering and infinitely opaque. Like now.

She swallowed hard. Her hand reached out, found the cool stainless steel reassurance of a long cylinder that held four frozen bodies. She opened her eyes, blinked away tears. The shiny steel concentrated the fluorescent's glare, banishing the black.

"Hey, you all right?"

"Yes. Oh yes. Just looking."

She blinked and her composure returned. A quick glance at a shiny cylinder confirmed that her mascara was okay. To her surprise a garland of flowers graced the cylinder's feet. "Relatives?" She pointed.

"Sure. Those were left by the children of the fellow inside. Some-times they talk to the tank."

"How touching."

"No different than a cemetery. Except here we don't let our people turn to dust."

"And this one?" She strolled to another cylinder with a plaque.

"That's Dr. Bedford, first person ever frozen. In 1967."

Kathryn was startled. "Wow, twenty-eight years! He put aside the money to keep himself frozen, way back then?"

Alex shook his head, bemused. "No, his children challenged his will and legal expenses ate up the funds. We're carrying him as a charity case."

"I heard that you did that for several people. How can you afford it?"

Alex smiled ruefully. "Not well, and not often. Really tragic cases—kids with leukemia, say—we try to take. But we're small, and no busi-ness can operate only as a charity."

"Ummm. So not just the rich have a shot at the future."

To her surprise, Alex gave an easy chuckle. "Everybody thinks you have to be rich. Actually, suspension isn't so expensive—bargain base-ment is about a hundred thousand dollars."

"A lot more than I've got."

"Sure, but I'll bet a life insurance policy for that much costs about what you spend on lipstick."

"Hey, that's a necessity."

"So I see."

He grinned and she did not know quite how to take the remark. Talk between them had an oddly delicious quality of keeping her off balance. Before she could react he was off, threading through the huge steel cylinders, and she hurried to catch up.

They passed through the ranks of concrete vaults and steel canisters —state of the art, he said, installed in '90—and into a large operating room. On a pallet lay a handsome Irish setter, its coat bedraggled. She knelt and stroked its gray muzzle. The body seemed to quiver in response. Breathing stayed steady and shallow, she noted automatically as she ran her hands over the thin, bony body.

"What's wrong with him?"

"Her. Sparkle's come back from a long trip," Alex said, unreeling some electrical sensors.

"From . . ." Kathryn studied the equipment deployed around the dog. "You . . . really—brought her back?"

"Days at twenty degrees below freezing," Alex said, matter-of-fact.

"That's"—he gestured, and she took the fluid feeder lines from him and began slipping them into the access sites along Sparkle's body— "wonderful."

They worked steadily then, Alex showing her how to cycle Sparkle's blood. They dialyzed out the impurities still entering the circulation from cells that were cleansing themselves. Sopping up the unwanted residues of low-temperature suspension demanded vigilant attention, to temperature and to electrolyte balances and a dozen lesser chemical details. Within minutes she was immersed in the procedure, registering dials and liquid crystal displays as she adjusted balances, checking the dog's delicate internal equilibrium.

"Can't unload the circulation system too fast," Alex said. "We made that mistake before."

"Her brain waves seem steady."

"Right. Been that way for three days now."

Alex gave orders without seeming bossy. He knew the work well, and under his guidance her initial nervousness dissipated. She found herself learning quickly, free of the anxious uncertainties she had known before when she had been a medical assistant. Alex was a natural, unhurried and utterly solid, the kind of man who lived for and through his labors.

Ray Constantine, another I^2 employee, came in, saw that matters were in hand, and went into the front office to tend to his own job. Alex happened to mention that Ray was vice-president of I^2, and when she expressed surprise he showed her the employee roster.

"Three full-time, three part-time. A small company."

"We're pretty easygoing."

"You humbly forgot to mention that you're general manager."

He snorted. "Which means I get to take out the trash on a regular basis. Including the ecologically virtuous task of sorting into the recycling bins."

Dr. Susan Hagerty called to see how Sparkle was doing, and Alex reviewed matters with her. Incidentally Kathryn learned that this was his fourth straight day here. Sparkle had come off the heart-lung machine well, was unsteady for a long time, and then seemed to improve. But this was all fresh medical territory, fraught with danger. Alex spoke tersely as he worked, like one holding back a gray wall of fatigue. She saw now that what she had first taken as a certain distance, a coolness, was in fact a careful hoarding of reserves.

She massaged Sparkle's legs and trunk to speed the circulation and ease the process of chemical replacement. Then she felt a subtle change, an easing of strain, a curious lightness in Sparkle's movements. She shot a glance at a nearby oscilloscope. Complexity spread through the dog's alpha rhythm.

"Something's happening," she said softly.

Alex bent over his old friend. "Hey, girl," he whispered. "Hey, Sparkle, wanna catch a rabbit?"

Sparkle's eyelids trembled. Sluggishly they rose, like fleshy veils lifting under great weight to show a dark kingdom beyond. The deep amber eyes were bloodshot but unglazed.

"Hiya, girl." Alex's whisper was filled with hope.

Sparkle blinked, and her eyes rolled up, then around, as though the world were whirling for her. Then they steadied, blinked rapidly, and focused on Alex. Kathryn dimmed the lights to lessen the strain, remembering that hospitals did that. Sparkle lifted her muzzle, panting. She whimpered, a high, thin note.

"I wonder if she remembers anything, anything at all," Alex said.

"You think she might have lost all her memories?"

He nodded sternly. "Could be. In some brain surgeries, patients get cooled down quite a bit to slow their metabolism. Their brain waves vanish—they're clinically dead. But when they're warmed up, they come back. Fred is still Fred. And Fred says he just went to sleep for a while— no interrupted visits to heaven, no souls wandering from the body."

"But Sparkle was frozen *solid*."

"Not really solid. The protectants kept her so that the water in her cells didn't actually form ice crystals."

"But still . . ."

"Right." He nodded in sympathy at her incredulous expression. "That's why this is research. Maybe we've revived only the basic bodily processes. Maybe the real Sparkle went down the drain when we chilled her."

As if in reply, Sparkle whimpered. Quivering, she stretched forward weakly and licked Alex's hand.

"She knows you," Kathryn whispered.

"Could be. Maybe she just likes my taste. Good girl! Rest now. Just rest."

The dog seemed to understand. She settled back. Alex patted and stroked his dog for a long time, the two of them looking into each other's eyes. Kathryn could see concern in Alex's thin-drawn lips and narrowed eyes, but he said nothing. He gestured for her to take up the petting herself. She did it gladly, murmuring to Sparkle but letting her hands do most of the communicating. The dog relaxed, snuffling wetly, and seemed to be easing into sleep.

Alex got up quietly and walked a few paces away, out of his pet's line of sight. Softly he called, "Sparkle. Sparkle."

The dog's ears perked up. With visible effort she turned her head, found him, and whimpered loudly, her nails scrabbling at her pallet, tail thumping.

"Good girl. Sleep, Sparkle," Alex said shakily.

"So her memories are still there," she said.

Alex allowed himself a brimming smile. "Knows her name."

It was miracle enough to bring an intact animal back from freezing, she thought, but a further wonder on top of that to have preserved the memories, responses, the self. And she had just walked in, first day at work, and witnessed it.

Kathryn felt an eerie sensation. Cryonics was weird, she was comfortable with that, but if it could actually *work* . . .

Alex ran his hands over his dog, talking to Sparkle warmly, easily. Kathryn could read in the cast of his mouth and the slight misting of his eyes how much he felt. Love for a pet was commonplace, unremarked, but she could see how deeply it ran in him.

"That's the real Sparkle in there," he whispered wonderingly. "I've got her back."

She said nothing for a long time. The machinery hummed and worked around them, a halo of sound around a small knot of simple emotion, so quiet and fragile she did not want to fracture the moment. But at last, after Sparkle had drifted into a calm slumber, Alex looked up, as though emerging from somewhere deep within himself.

"I'll call Susan Hagerty soon as I wash up." His voice was laced with tired satisfaction. "Been a long day."

"A long four days, I'd say."

"Think I might catch some Z's."

"It's not noon yet."

"Why be hemmed in by hidebound convention?" He grinned. "I'm on watch here, but I can sack out upstairs. Ray Constantine can keep an eye on Sparkle."

"Oh. I'll go help Ray in the front."

"Look, I need to fill you in on how we operate. By the time I sleep a few hours, I'll be ready to eat a horse. Let's meet for dinner."

"Mmmmm. I didn't think vegetarians ate horses."

"Only on alternate Wednesdays. I'm no vegetarian, though."

"I haven't been out here long, but it seems like everybody in California is." Actually, she thought of cryonicists as an extreme kind of health nut, so they should be vegetarians, too. They fit right in with the California oddities.

"I don't believe in crank diets."

"Ummm. A cryonicist calling others cranks?"

"What's cranky about wanting to live longer?"

"Plenty, where I come from."

"Where's that? From your accent, I'd say it was one of those midwestern states that starts with a vowel."

"Accent? I don't have any accent."

"That's what everybody thinks."

"Anyway, you're wrong. I came from South Dakota."

"Traditional values."

She made a comic grimace. "Very."

"They have their rewards."

"I agree, but still, I felt claustrophobic back there. A strict South Dakotan upbringing. It took me a long time to realize we were free to go."

Mock horror. "You mean you left the state without raising your hand and asking permission?"

"'Fraid so."

"Good for you. Take some hours off now. See you at seven."

"What? Oh—"

"Little Italian place, great pasta. Just off Harbor in Costa Mesa. I'll give you the address."

"Well, I—"

"And now I'm beat. Got to run down to the end of the alphabet."

"What?"

"Catch some Z's, like I said."

Moments later, when she stood outside blinking up into the dry sun glare, she thought, *Nerd clothes, maybe, but he got that date effortlessly.* And it was definitely a date; subtle signals had thronged the air. Yet there were none of the usual bits of warmup business you can pick up, the little gestures and eye maneuvers while a guy you just met is working himself up to ask.

Maybe there were possibilities here, more possibilities even than the Immortality Incorporated sign suggested.

She crossed the parking lot with a freshly jaunty set to her stride. New job, new guy. Bright sunshine and far horizons. Sure, a weirdo job, but life wasn't all retail sales and oatmeal, after all. And the guy was promising, quite—that evasive female cliché—"cute." Fun to work with, anyway. So in all—

She stopped at the sight of the man in overalls crouched down beside the side wall. He had a small black object in both hands and was pressing it against the grouting between two cinder blocks. He looked up, startled.

"What are you doing?" she blurted out. Something in the man's posture and his sudden scowl told her things weren't right.

"Power company, ma'am." A tight, high voice. "Just checking. Everything's okay, so I'll be going."

He stood and walked quickly toward a gray pickup truck parked at the edge of the lot. A lean, nervous man, shorter than she was. He clasped the black flashlight-shaped thing to his chest.

"But you weren't looking at a fusebox or anything," she insisted. Her impulse was to advance toward him, but something told her to stay put.

No answer. He yanked open the truck door and slid in, and the engine rumbled to life.

Her sense of wrongness condensed into irritation. "Hey!"

He popped it into gear. His constricted face glared at her, the eyes dark slits. The truck peeled rubber, wobbling, and veered off the blacktop. The man jerked at the wheel, and the truck spat gravel at the edge of the lot before he got it back under control. Tires squealed again as they hit the pavement of Santiago Canyon Road, bit hard, and accelerated away with a roar.

She frowned. *Keep driving like that, buster, and you'll have the lifespan of a cockroach.*

Some gawking curiosity seeker? No, there was a stringy tension in the man's hurried walk. She bit at her lip. He had left nothing at the wall. Still . . .

She turned and walked back toward the front door. Best to at least let them know about it. Then it was their problem, even if she was a brand-new employee.

TWO

THE LONG HABIT
OF LIVING

The long habit of living indisposeth us for dying.
—Sir Thomas Browne

1

GEORGE

He marched down the bleached corridors of UCI General, nerves jangling, fingers longing to twitch and grasp. But he kept careful control, did not let any of it break swarming onto his skin surface. Time to be smooth, cool.

Looking for the doctor.

The remnants of his morning awakening still clung to him. If he closed his eyes for just a moment, it would replay on the pink screen of his eyelids.

—The same moist sensation of floating upward, not to heaven but toward a pale sheet of light, the infinitely receding surface of a black lake. Tendrils of waving weed clutched at him, slimy, vainly urging him back, down. But he rose, buoyant, through miraculous fluids running like watered inks. He broke the surface—into a harsh gallery of blaring light, waxy faces hovering, cotton clots billowing in his lungs. Deranged air steamed before his blinking eyes. Needles pin-pricked his canvas skin as he rose toward a ceiling leaking torpid heat. The rotting tiles above split into the wide toothless grin of a hard-boned skull, jawbone creaking as it swung, speaking soundlessly, trying to tell him something ponderous and remote, all while within the gutted eye sockets a black spider slept and stirred, slept and stirred, rustling—

He shook himself, and the tight images shed from him like skin from a snake. The cool clear part of him had been keeping track, following the directions of the front office, counting the room numbers in this anonymous corridor. Here. Hagerty.

He checked himself. Suit and tie, neat and clean, creases razor-sharp. Hair freshly combed.

Knock. No answer. Knock again.

Abruptly the door swung open on a wise-faced woman. Her broad mouth was reserved, her gray eyes distracted. From her no-nonsense hair and lack of cosmetics, he sized her up as a businesslike type, not one to be pressured. Okay, then—the aw-shucks approach. "Doctor? I'm a friend of a patient you operated on in the emergency room? Patricia Olin?"

George made his tone rise upward at the end of each question, properly humble. His face he made open and expectant as Dr. Hagerty's mouth flattened into a severe line. Doctors saw lawsuits everywhere.

"I was a friend of hers, and well, we're all just kind of shocked and shook up. You know? I was wondering if I could talk to you, just a li'l bit?"

Hagerty's mouth softened as he spoke. Women often did that with him. George knew he didn't look half-bad himself, he could sling the words okay, and women appreciated a snappy dresser, too. "Well, there isn't much to tell," she said. "I did all I could, but she had been in that dumpster for hours with a broken neck, the police told me afterward."

"I understand that from the newspapers, ma'am." The *Register*'s headline, FREEWAY PILE UP REVEALS DUMPSTER DEATH, had attracted his attention first thing at breakfast this morning, jerking him out of his troubled state, out of the frayed remembrances of his dream. "Awful, just awful. She was so fine, and for somebody to do that—well, I just wondered, for the sake of her mother, you know, if Patricia was able to say something, anything at all? As a last message for her loved ones?"

Dr. Hagerty frowned. "Her mother was here at the time."

George felt a spike of cold alarm but let none of it into his face. The newspaper said nothing about the mother, of course. He should have taken some other line. Too late now. "I heard, but she's so worked up, you know, I thought I'd take the burden from her, come and ask?"

"The patient never regained consciousness." Dr. Hagerty cocked her head skeptically.

"Now that's sad, real sad. I'll not be able to bear last words to comfort her mother." A mournful downturn of his mouth, then a hopeful jut of his head. "Nothing to help the police find the person who did this thing?"

"No, nothing. And your name is . . . ?"

"Martin Jacobson, ma'am." He didn't like her glinting eyes. "I thank you muchly, and I'll take no more of your time."

Nod, wheel about, walk away. Clean. He heard the door shut behind him and let out a cleansing whoosh of liberating air.

He still had no memory of what happened with the waitress, of what she had done to provoke him so. *A girl notices,* she had said.

And maybe after all she had broken her neck when the dumpster-collector truck racked over onto the freeway. That could be it, despite what all these know-it-all doctors said.

So he was safe. Coming here had been a momentary impulse, and his cool self had voted against doing it, but now he was glad. He was sure, consolidated, able to make his new home here without a shadow hanging like a hawk in the back of his mind. He walked out of the hospital with a springing step.

2

ALEX

For their second date she wanted to go to a cemetery.

"Not just any cemetery, mind you," Kathryn said when Alex looked startled. "The best. The biggest."

"Ah. Forest Lawn," Alex supplied.

Their first date, the week before, had been almost disquietingly successful. The moments when you both realized that somehow, unexpectedly, you agreed about the most remote subjects: favorite movies, interest rates, Stilton cheese. The small realizations that, unaccountably, you simply *fit*. The sudden moments of pulse-pounding possibility, freighted in seemingly innocent phrases. The symphony of unconscious signals had gone on, culminating in a goodnight kiss that started warm and turned quite hot before he broke it off, more unsettled than he wanted to reveal. A kiss, he thought, with a future in it.

"I've heard about it so much. Great day out," she said helpfully. "Not much traffic on a Sunday."

"Ummmm," he said.

"Still no leads on that guy I found outside?"

"Nope. He'd already bored a hole through, and I filled it up with quick-dry cement. Probably he was trying to slip some detector in, maybe a mini-TV camera or something."

"Whatever for?"

"Who knows? Cryonics brings out the crazies."

"Most people think *you're* the crazies."

"Exactly—so maybe he was some sleazoid reporter, snooping for sensational photos. But without license plates to go on—"

"I told you, they were taped over."

"Without anything more, what can we do? The cops, they'd just laugh."

"Well, he looked . . . serious." She bit at her lip, uneasy.

Alex's face clouded. "You mean dangerous?"

"Look, let's forget him." She busied herself with some filing, obviously to break the mood. Alex smiled; already he could read her maneuvers. But he didn't like her undercurrent of apprehension. She had picked up something ominous in the guy, he guessed, something she could not quite convey.

They were sitting in the front office of Immortality Incorporated. Kathryn had "just dropped by" to pick up some paperwork about joining I-Squared. The quiet of the facility was only occasionally broken by a crew moving equipment around in the back. Though there were three full-time employees, much of the labor was done by volunteers on weekends. Company rules demanded that a full-time employee be on duty at all times, to man the phones, top off the liquid nitrogen in the suspension cylinders, and deal with the usual traffic of deliveries and curiosity seekers. They could take short naps at night if they liked, the company's one concession to bodily rhythms. Alex liked to work in long stints, when he could get some repair work done and tinker with the gadgets he kept running. He put in twelve-hour sessions four times a week.

She said brightly, "You're off work in five minutes, right?"

Alex tried to look casual. He was a little tired; as usual at Immortality Incorporated, he had gotten less nap time than he had hoped. "Well, I thought I'd take Sparkle for a walk."

"Let's do it together. Come on—enough of this watchman stuff."

"My job description includes 'maintenance engineer,' I'll have you know."

"I thought that's what they called janitors."

"Right, and garbage is 'postsecondary-use consumer goods.' Sparkle!"

A rusty-brown mass came bounding in from the back room. When she saw Kathryn, Sparkle barked twice, moist nose twitching. A shiver of anticipation ran along her body, and she looked ready to leap up, but her good-dog demeanor asserted itself and she simply licked Kathryn's hand, whimpering. Still, she knew something was up and stood with eager-eyed energy, glancing from Alex to her leather leash, which hung near the door.

Kathryn petted Sparkle's sleek, shiny coat. "Wow, what a recovery." She looked up at Alex with open respect. "Y'know, I thought you were kidding about taking her for a walk."

Alex grinned, glad that his little surprise had come off. "She's come back fast."

Kathryn took the lean head in her hands and made a face. "You're sure no zombie, Spark."

Sparkle's tail whacked on the cement floor in agreement. "C'mon, humans"—Kathryn spoke for her—"let's bomb outa here."

As Alex leashed her, he said, "A real high-tech dog, this one."

Kathryn ruffled Sparkle's fur, blowing in her ear. "I hear some biologists are developing a new breed of dog for the next century. Half pit bull and half collie. It sees you, it rips your leg off, then it runs for help."

"Sounds wonderful. Just the thing for apartment dwellers in Manhattan. C'mon, gal!"

They emerged into a crisp, sunlit day. Alex noted how the dog took gingerly steps going across the asphalt of the parking lot.

"She walks kind of funny," Kathryn said.

"Just on asphalt. Maybe she's forgotten what it is."

Once off the warm black surface Sparkle strained at the leash, whimpering eagerly until Alex let her off. She trotted into the arroyo, nose up, eyes bright, millennia of evolution at work. This *was* a hunting jaunt, wasn't it?

Kathryn frowned. "You think something as basic as that could get lost in the freezing?"

"Sure. We don't know how memories are stored."

"Has she got the rest of her doggy stuff down pat?" She picked up a stick and threw it. Sparkle looked disdainfully at the spot where it landed and ambled on.

Alex picked up a stick. "You don't think she'll fetch for just anybody, do you?"

She gave him a sidelong glance. "Not an easy first date, ol' Spark."

He ignored the implied opening. "Maybe all her TV exposure has turned her head."

"I saw it last night. Pretty accurate."

"They like anything with footage, even if it's just Sparkle giving her patented ferocious scowl."

Kathryn shrugged. "So she hates media people—who doesn't?" She made a surprisingly schoolgirlish kick at a stone and added seriously, "Y'know, if there's any more media stuff, I'd appreciate, uh . . ."

"Keeping your name out of it."

"Well, I'm not one of you."

"True enough. Look, we follow standard confidentiality. Our membership roster is secret, and so is our employee list."

"I remember reading some tabloid about Liz Taylor—"

"Oh God, that! Sure, her and Ronald Reagan, they had a secret pact to get frozen, see? They'll run off together when they're revived."

She looked sheepish. "Okay, I confess, I'm another brain-damaged tabloid reader. But only while I'm standing in the supermarket checkout line."

"Yeah, everybody says they just glance them over there in line, pick up on the 'Space Aliens Raped My Lawn Sprinkler' stories. Makes you wonder how they sell any copies."

"You've got to admit, movie stars and cryonics somehow go together. Very California."

In a way she was right, he thought. The balmy climate erased the season's sway, bringing a calm continuity that silently promised to go on forever. Maybe the cryonic effort to extend life through the veil of what society called death did indeed come unconsciously out of the California weather's reassuring sameness. He found the thought disturbing, as if it robbed the ideas behind cryonics of their stature.

He brushed the thoughts aside. "The real trick with the TV people was not giving away Susan Hagerty's role."

"That's got to come out, doesn't it? The real science, not just the media trash."

"That's for Susan to report. She's working on a paper for one of the biomedical journals right now."

"Better than your big splash in *National Enquirer.*"

"I thought you just glanced at them."

"Your name leaped out at me."

He laughed. "Yeah, I'm there in 'Roy Rogers' Horse Frozen For Future Life' and 'Elvis Joined Club of Immortals.' Plastic fame. The best thing is that after a week the yellow press goes away. They have the attention span of a cockroach."

"Umm, I've noticed the resemblance. Not big on step-by-step progress."

"Or regress." Alex frowned. "Sparkle gives us a chance to test things about memory that Susan couldn't do with lab mice. She used her cryoprotectants on batches of mice, but Sparkle's a big step. I had to talk Susan into making the leap to big animals—because I was desperate."

"I understand." The momentary warmth of Kathryn's hand on his arm was unexpectedly touching.

"Thanks. I—I had to hang on to the old pooch. And as an experiment, it's working pretty well."

"Not perfectly?"

"Sparkle didn't recognize John Flander yesterday."

"Should she?"

"John puts in a lot of time here, helping out. He's known Sparkle since she was a pup."

Sparkle sighted something in a thicket of manzanita and dived in after it. "Go get 'em, girl!" Kathryn called out. "Fresh meat."

"You're sure no vegetarian either," Alex said dryly.

She grinned saucily. "Hey, I agree with Sparkle. If you can die and come back later with your sense of fun intact, who cares about remembering some John?"

Immortality Incorporated scavenged surplus medical equipment from labs and hospitals, which let older but perfectly serviceable gear go for a few cents on the dollar. Finding such bargains, though, demanded long hours on the dulling expanses of freeways; you had to cast a skeptical eye over used goods, not just bargain over the phone. In running these endless errands Alex had learned to keep himself alert by scanning nearby cars for interesting personalized license plates. Somehow he wasn't surprised that Kathryn shared this minor hobby.

Within a few miles headed north on I–5 they spotted KLOUD 9 on a silver cloud Rolls-Royce and B KLEEN on a beatup cleaner's van. Alex said, "Seems to me they give a weird kind of angle into people. We're all sealed up in here, just a few feet away from each other, but no communication."

"Very Californian," she said judicially.

"Cultural chasm. In the East people brag about how little they had to bribe their condo plumber to actually do some repairs. In California we're happy if we can figure out what country our landlord's from— usually from what he had for lunch. The East has bitter, interesting cab drivers, California has these plates. Balances out."

"Look at that one. US GODS."

"Okay, so we overreach a little out here."

"That's a polite word for it. See that one?"

Alex peered ahead at a low-slung sports car with a rear plate reading TOOL MAN. "Maybe he's a mechanic."

"Suuuuure. Catch that Corvette on the right."

JOE COOL. Alex craned to look. "Figures. The driver's about thirty, with a duck's-ass haircut."

"Needless to say, we do not have such creatures in the respectable states."

"South Dakota doesn't have citizens like that guy over there?" The driver of WACKO wore long sideburns and had a copper ring in his ear.

"He'd need a passport to get into South Dakota. And a customs inspection."

They saw a new plate about every minute and began to look for deep metaphors. ALL GIRL wore a glittery sheath dress and had a three-day growth of beard. But HUNG UP was a guy in a porkpie hat, which seemed to fit in with the cosmic order. DSCNT IQ was a lean man with an intense, competitive glare. A healthy-looking woman with too much ruby lipstick on had HIHOPES. Coming into the center of L.A. they saw IHVNFUN and LZYDAZE.

"Here we are cruising through the power matrix of the goshwow Pacific Rim, and that's the best they can do?" Kathryn asked with a curl of her lip. "Come on, L.A.!" As if in answer, NO1UNO zoomed by them, a black Ferrari with night-tinted windows. "Nice," she allowed, "but out here, everybody thinks they're 'Number one, you know.' "

"Not all of us. How do you know that guy's not saying 'No one you know'?"

"Ummm. The symbolism's flying thick and fast." She looked at him skeptically. "Anyway, you say a lot more with your car."

He shot her a questioning glance but was scrupulous about watching traffic. "How you figure? I don't have custom plates."

"You're driving the cryonicists' standard car, a Volvo."

"It's the safest," he said defensively.

"So's a tank. Not too racy, though."

Alex felt unaccountably irked. *Okay,* he thought, *I drive a car so old the 'fifty-five' is highlighted in red, from the Carter days when that was the speed limit. And to get to sixty from a standing start takes a couple of weeks, maybe. Blue-collar guys don't pull down a hundred thou for shuffling paper, so?* Normally the matter wouldn't faze him; he had gone to work for I^2 knowing he'd never cash in a stock option or live at the beach or sniff the all-leather interior of his Beamer. Why should it all of a sudden make him uncomfortable now, with her?

He decided to keep the conversation light, casual. Safer that way. "I saw a Cadillac once with California plates saying NOBODY."

"From the Bay Area," she said definitively.

Forest Lawn Memorial Park occupies one of the best hills in Glendale, commanding a striking view that, unfortunately, the residents cannot see. Neighboring hills were thick with large homes rich in stuccoed swank, but here all was green and silent. Alex drove slowly up the winding roads. They had stopped at the attendant's booth, and Kathryn had surprised him by asking where the grave of Walt Disney was. The attendant peered at his records and then looked them over and announced that they were not allowed to give out "addresses."

"In your face, motha," Kathryn said as they climbed back into his car. "I know where it is anyway."

"How come?"

"Hobby of mine. Addresses of the dead."

Forest Lawn was genteel, circumspect. A map admonished them that no photo taken there could legally be published. Like a Disneyland of the Dead, it had theme sections: Garden of Ascension, Lullabyland, Eventide, Wee Kirk o' the Heather. The lawns slumbered beneath the weight of sunlight that seemed to seep from a blank sky. Raked gravel walks enticed the car-borne into warrens of humus-fed plantings of exotic flora, where shrubs bore small tags, as though just named by Adam.

"Good thing we didn't bring Sparkle," Kathryn said, reading the map. "Dogs have to stay in the car and maintain a respectful silence."

"How about dogs risen from the dead?"

"Today's special, zombie dogs get ten percent off in Poochland."

They went up Cathedral Drive and onto Arlington Drive. Walt Disney was in the Court of Freedom. A majestic marble Freedom Mausoleum dominated the little gardens. Statues dotted the small enclaves alongside rectangular paths: fallen warriors, mourning women wrapped in winding sheets. Alex stopped to study a concrete Indian on bare horseback, legs extended downward in rigid dignity, head bowed to the barrel chest in an expression of dazed sorrow. Alex had to admit the work was good, ushering him into a silent world of contemplation, detailed down to the fingernails. Death was so upscale here, so respectable.

Kathryn strolled around inside the chilly, echoing Freedom Mausoleum as though she were picking out a book in a library. "Look—here's Gummo Marx. Gracie Allen! Larry—one of the Three Stooges. Francis X. Bushman."

"Do you collect autographs, too?"

Disney's grave wasn't in the mausoleum. She led him around to a tiny garden set snugly against a sedately gray brick wall. Alex had to admit the whole thing was done well, with lush green lawns, a low unlocked gate, shaded marble benches, carefully pruned holly and azaleas. A small statue of a girl watched over the cool preserve, her eyes studying some eternal principle just beyond view. Kathryn gestured, and he saw a metal plaque set in the wall. WALTER ELIAS DISNEY was the top name of the eight spaces provided.

Kathryn stared at it for a long moment, her eyelids fluttering slightly, breaths coming in short little gulps. Her lips parted, shaping first a delicate downward turn, as if into disappointment. But then her complexion flushed and her lips drew back, whitening slightly into a severe, assessing expression that contrasted with the sensuality of their fragile fullness. He could see warring emotions in the way she clenched and rubbed her fingers together while holding her arms straight down at her sides, in the tensed lines of her body in the sun-dappled silence.

"Mickey sends his best," Alex said, beginning to get a little jumpy. As soon as the words were out, he knew that he was letting his nerves do his thinking, but to his relief Kathryn's rapt gaze did not alter; maybe she hadn't heard. Still, why in the world would she bring him here? Was Disney a relative? You met some odd birds in cryonics, sure, but—

"I wonder what's behind this?" she asked with fresh purpose.

"Bones."

"I mean behind this wall."

"Say, what's—"

"Come on." She marched off energetically.

He followed, consoling himself with the view of her nicely fitted blue skirt. Places like this always turned his thoughts in that direction, for fairly obvious reasons.

He knew that immediately after experiencing danger people often got quite randy. Reminders of mortality had the same effect. Still, cemeteries weren't considered sexy places—except, he recalled, one time in high school when he and his girlfriend hadn't been able to find any other place. Around midnight you were pretty damned sure of being uninterrupted, and the grass was nice and soft. Trudging along behind Kathryn through the spring heat, he remembered all the weight of prohibition and anxiety that he, like every adolescent, had carried around. Sex was the source of our very existence—yet how many could envision their own parents Doing It? Alex tried for a moment, grimaced, failed, and trudged on. Maybe the fact that we all came from a moment of unthinking passion was too close, too uncomfortable, he thought. It meant conjuring up a time before we existed. And it was just around the corner from the idea that the time would come when we weren't here anymore.

They had circled around the Freedom Mausoleum in the hush of early afternoon. A couple stood on Benediction Slope nearby, looking down at a spot in the great swath of grass, their images rippled slightly by heat waves. Headstones here were tastefully recessed in the lawn, so that from any vantage point this place did indeed seem to be a sunny park awaiting picnickers. Soil from a freshly dug grave was covered with Astroturf, he saw, lest it remind anybody that the dead were going into plain old dirt.

Kathryn marched nearly to the Dawn of Tomorrow section, with its rows of narrow boxes like the tenements of the next world, before doubling back. "Ah!" she cried. "Here."

"Where?" All Alex saw was a mass of bushes beside the road.

"See, you can tell by the geometry that this"—she pushed aside the bushes, revealing a footpath—"leads into the area behind the Disney family's small garden."

"Uh, right."

"Well—come on." She plunged into the bushes, limbs scraping her. Alex followed. The path led to a stucco wall and then along it until they found a wooden door. She tried the knob. "Locked. Damn."

"Let's look." He didn't know what was going on here, but he could seldom pass up a chance to indulge a hobby he had learned in high school. He fished out his big key chain, which had as its sinker weight an ornate-looking steel tool. He clicked it open, deploying a narrow shaft, notched and furrowed.

"You can pick locks?"

"No, I talk them into opening. This just gets their attention."

He could have done this one with a credit card down the door frame. It popped open within ten seconds of fiddling. They stepped into a cool, dank blackness. Daylight from the open door cast shadows among stacks of gardening supplies, rakes and hoes and fertilizer. Alex smelled bare earth. Kathryn nearly tripped over a wound-up hose. "Here, wait." He flicked on the other end of the lock-picker, a pencil-beam flashlight.

They shuffled forward as their eyes adjusted. Kathryn followed a rough concrete wall, counting paces, eyeing angles, and at last pronounced, "It's here. The Disney family garden is right on the other side of this wall."

"So what?" All he could see was a paper towel dispenser of cracked green plastic.

"Well, I—" She stopped, biting her lip, and he saw that she had reached the end of some interior odyssey. She gave him a wobbly smile and slapped the wall. "I wanted to check, I . . ."

"Oh." At last he got it. "The old frozen Disney story?"

She looked sheepish. "I heard about it when I was in junior high. My best friend *swore* it was true, she'd heard it from somebody who lived in Hollywood." She twisted her lips into a derisive grimace. "There were others, too. About how he was frozen in a special chamber under the Pirates of the Caribbean ride at Disneyland. Or that there was a special apartment in a spire of the Cinderella Castle at the Orlando Disneyworld, and he's there. Those stories got me interested in cryonics, in fact. I promised myself that when I got to L.A. I'd check into it."

"So when you saw the Disney marker out there—"

"I didn't want to let go of the story. Not *zip*, just like that."

"So we're looking for the secret cobwebbed lair where Walt swims in his liquid nitrogen, tended by loyal dwarf retainers, guarded by slavering attack dogs and corporate lawyers?"

She giggled, an odd, lilting release in the gloom. "Something like that."

"Well, what say we beat it before the dogs come back and have us for lunch. Or the lawyers."

"I think I'd prefer the dogs."

"Me, too."

He breathed more easily when they were out among the slumbering lawns. A sweetness of distant flowerbeds perfumed the air. As they strolled back to his car, Kathryn told him about her recent research on the old story that Disney had been frozen at death. "I even saw a copy of the death certificate. December 15, 1966. Cause of death: 'acute circulatory collapse.' "

"His heart stopped."

"Right—isn't jargon wonderful? Actually, they were operating on him for lung cancer when it happened. No media coverage of a funeral, no info on disposition of the body."

"So? The family probably wanted privacy."

"Yes, but Disney was a man deeply troubled by death. He made a gruesome seven-minute Mickey Mouse cartoon once, with a mad scientist who tried to cut off Pluto's head and stick it on a chicken."

Alex blinked. "Really? I never saw—"

"I do my research, Buster. He withdrew it years later. Disney was a big technology freak. Monorails, Space Mountain, Tomorrowland, EPCOT. Once he found that he had lung cancer, why not try a high-tech dodge?"

"Reasonable—only he didn't."

She stopped beside a flowering azalea and looked at him forlornly, shrugging. "I guess not."

Her grown-up veneer had miraculously evaporated. He saw in small details—a lock of hair tumbled down, a smudge on her left cheek like a sort of inverted eyebrow, her wry, tilted mouth—the girl she had been. A spirit open to a world of wonder, only to find it shadowed by the grim edge of circumstance. Her mother had died when Kathryn was six, he remembered from the offhand here's-my-life summary she had offered —oddly, even before the fried mozzarella appetizers had arrived at the Italian restaurant. Her father had filled in as many of the gaps as he could, but at seventeen a traffic accident had taken that solace away. Kathryn had finished high school living with her grandmother.

He reached out and ruffled her hair, then patted it into place. She looked at him with wide, luminous eyes, as though some part of her were silently pleading with him for understanding. Without thinking things through, which was his usual policy, he said warmly, "Look. You were a little girl, you loved Disney characters, and along comes a story that says he's still around somewhere, only frozen. It's a comforting thing to believe in."

She reached up and pressed his hand to her temple, a quiet, intimate gesture. Something changed in her face, the openness melting into a smile that brought her back from a great empty distance. "My—my favorite was Pluto."

Alex stared at her incredulously. "Pluto? Now, Mickey, I could see that, a little too sugary for me—but *Pluto*?"

"Okay, who was yours?"

He said primly, "Donald Duck. Angst, anger, plenty of character there. All Pluto ever said was *woof.*"

"Nobody could ever understand *what* that duck said. An obvious psychotic."

"Ummm," he said judiciously. "Sociopath is more precise."

Her face clouded again. "Actually, I wanted to come here to, to, say good-bye to him, I suppose. I was such a fan, I checked the media coverage of his death."

"Ah, your love of libraries."

"Well, you'd be amazed how much you can find out that way. That's how I scoped out I^2 and you, before I even interviewed for my job."

"Touché!"

She frowned prettily and went on, undaunted. "I found out, from reading old microfiche newspaper files, that there was a funny coincidence. The first man ever frozen, a Glendale professor, was put into liquid nitrogen just a few weeks after Disney died."

"Glendale—same town."

"So people probably made the connection. Glendale, Forest Lawn, Disney, cryonics."

"Too bad Disney didn't do it," Alex said with a bitter fervor that surprised him. He hitched his thumbs into his belt to keep his hands from displaying the frustration he felt, an old habit hard-learned.

For a tiny fraction of the wealth the man had created, Disney could have had a shot at walking again in bright sunshine. He had given so much innocent joy to so many, and now he was dust. The immense tragedy of that, of this entire phony place, welled up in Alex.

Forest Lawn equated death with sleeping, the final loss of loved ones with bees and flowers and peace, as if they had just gone off on a pleasant holiday somewhere. But he knew in his soul that it was probably oblivion, darkness, nothing, the end of love itself. "Till death do you part" was not a promise but a threat. Disney and his immense talent had gone into that, and there was not a scrap of hope that he could ever return.

"Hey," she said, taking his hands between hers, obviously sensing his mood and wanting to break it. "Forgive me for this, okay?"

"For what?"

"For talking you into a downer date."

"This is it?" he asked with mock incredulity. "*This* is the date? I thought this was just foreplay."

She looked askance at him. "In broad daylight? Come on, I'll treat."

He said reluctantly, "I've got to do some thinking. Rehearsal."

"For what?"

"TV show. Tomorrow morning this talk show wants me to come on and gab about cryonics."

"Great!"

He grimaced. "Maybe not so great. I've done radio shows, sure, just you and a mike. But this—"

"Listen, the reason talk is cheap is because there's a lot more supply than demand. But for *smart* talk—"

"I don't know how to handle myself onstage." Alex recalled reading somewhere that public speaking was the biggie on most people's list of terrifying prospects. Well, it was reassuring to know that he was an ordinary Joe.

"I'll help you," she said briskly. "Throw questions, stuff like that."

"Well . . ." He knew he should spend the time alone, thinking through a strategy. So why did he want her to talk him out of it?

"Come on. We can test one of Kathryn's Universal Laws."

He brightened at her impish grin. "Which one?"

"The one that goes, 'If you ask the waiter, restaurant fish is always fresh, even in Nebraska.' "

"This is a dinner invitation, I take it."

"My, you're *quick.*"

He sighed. Okay, the day was shot. But he did need some time off, and her sense of humor was infectious. "As Universal Laws go, how about 'The longer the title, the lousier the movie'?"

"Another invitation?"

"We'll call it a scientific experiment. Testing the Laws."

"Gee, and I forgot my lab notebook."

"I've got one in the car."

3

GEORGE

He loved the crisp, clean smell of his new apartment—paint barely dry, carpets exhaling their sharp essence.

The apartment was only the latest in God's gifts to him, and George set to work right away to repay the Lord in the ways he knew how. First, he had to do his homework. Then there would be the real centerpiece of his day, an evening church service. He had found his proper place here already, a clear and certain Calling. Which was yet another blessing to thank the Lord for.

He had put the waitress incident behind him with humble prayer and right Scripture. There was always a biblical passage that explained his own actions to him. This time the Old Testament was of more use, with its righteous rage against the world's harlots. He was sure that the Lord had sealed that waitress Jezebel's lips in UCI General, just as the Hagerty doctor had said.

Yes—time to thank Him by getting right to work, George reminded himself. He was seated at a broad plywood work table, hands resting on the keyboard of his new Zenith 2000 computer, all fresh-bought with a Computerland credit card. He reached into his shirt pocket for the crucial element in his life, the 3.5-inch high-density floppy disk he carried with him always. The Feds had gotten all his gear and printouts in Tucson. But George had been careful to leave no vital files in his hard disk there, files that gave the core data for his network. They lay in this one precious disk.

He slipped it into the disk-drive slit with a nearly sensual joy and booted up the system, savoring the thin little whine that told him 200 megabytes awaited his beck and call. Within twenty seconds he had his spreadsheet running, a lovely multicolored display on the flat screen monitor. A fairyland of wealth and promise, George liked to think of it.

He had arranged the interlocking names into a gaudy technicolor pyramid. The big bank cards—Visa, AmEx, Discover, Optima, Fuji—appeared as solid granite-gray blocks at the base, the firm underpinning of his "Bruce Prior" universe.

Above them were stacked blue and red cubes, representing the money-market accounts where he had a minimum of five hundred dollars on deposit: Dreyfus, Chase Manhattan, First National, Fidelity, a half-dozen others scattered evenly across the country, revealing no pattern.

Soaring above these in the pyramid were the bright red icons of his department store cards—Neiman Marcus, Robinson's, Bullock's, I. Magnin, a dozen lesser names.

George liked the store cards especially. He knew from experience that he could pile up debt there for months without a peep from them. He'd gotten in good with them years before by simply overpaying his bills.

He'd learned that when he overpaid his $1,500 credit line with Neiman Marcus on a combined MasterCard account. He had deliberately sent Neiman $3,500 extra one month, using a momentary cash surplus. They had raised his credit level to $5,000 right away and sent him the usual glad-handing letter about what a choice customer he was.

That was where his computer-hacker skills came into play. With the ID numbers on his balance statement, he had worked his way into their accounting system, using pretty simple search patterns to wiggle in. By modem, you could voyage just about anywhere in the cyber-labyrinths of finance.

He had found that they had flagged him as an especially good risk. The accounting programs at Neiman never forgot what a swell fellow he was, and they let him pile up bills for three months before even beginning to hint delicately about repayment.

Quick like a bunny, he overpaid his others. They had even started inviting him to special closed-door bargain sales and sending him little gifts at Christmas. Yes, he loved the store cards.

George had stumbled upon his profession almost by accident. When he had started out as a mathematics teacher in high school, he had been deluged with charge cards. They had come in the mail, sometimes two or three a day, within a few months after he started work.

He hadn't applied for them, of course. Some diligent computer program had decided a solid citizen teaching school was just too good a risk to pass up.

At first he had thrown away the official, embossed letters on creamy bond, welcoming him to their array of services, flattering him with a lot of gush about how he had already been approved for thousands of dollars in credit. Still, the flattery worked, in a way. He held on to some cards, used a few now and then. He had not mastered the knack of keeping friends, and his new job in Albuquerque had put him in a strange city where he knew no one. In a way, he supposed, the cards were a friendly gesture, a welcome he had not gotten from his co-workers.

Then the trouble had started at the school. He got angry with the kids when they did not do their homework, when they made dumb mistakes in class, when they sassed him. They joked about his praying during the lunch hour and made faces and even imitated the passing of gas when his back was turned.

The principal had taken their side, of course; the sallow-faced man was a jellyfish. When parents started complaining that George had made some mistakes in dealing with them, understandable errors, the principal put him on probation. Then the father of one of the worst boys had come in for a conference, and they'd started arguing, the father shouting and calling George a fool. Somehow George's quite justified rage had turned into a slugging match, and the parent had gone down with a broken jaw, and that was what put George on the street with $235 in the bank and no prospects of ever teaching again.

He had prayed a lot then, sought the solace of his Church. The minister had not been very sympathetic. Walking home from Sunday service, George had passed a Bank of America. He knew the landlord was waiting back at his apartment, hand out for that month's rent.

The letters say these cards are good for cash advances, he had thought. As quick as a greased pig, the teller machine had rewarded him with $800 in less than five minutes, honoring four of his cards without a single question or pause. He had walked away with forty twenty-dollar bills and a new profession.

George had built his system from scratch. The banks very nearly taught him how. He had learned a lot about the "float"—the number of days it took each bank to process and approve a check.

Each box in his multicolored pyramid gave float time, precaution codes, other tips. George moved his mouse to the Chase Manhattan icon and tapped it, calling forth in an instant all his transactions.

He had written a $3,000 check on his Chase Manhattan money-market account in Delaware and mailed it to Colorado for deposit at Rocky Mountain First National. Below this transaction appeared the parallel check he'd written on Rocky Mountain, mailed to the Delaware account. For four days, his program showed, he would run $3,000 in both accounts, earning top grade interest. In the last week he had set $76,000 floating among his dozens of accounts.

The bookkeeping took about ten hours a week to keep straight. Not bad for a decent income, earned simply by passing money around.

But the system worked only so long as the banks kept increasing his credit limits. That let him cover his mounting interest costs with fatter loans.

It had taken him a while to figure out how to make the banks do this. Politely applying didn't work. You got a form letter back saying *nosiree*! and pussy-footing around about why.

Simple, really. He had never gone over his limit and he paid promptly, so to them he obviously didn't need more credit. So he had started playing deadbeat.

He charged more than he was allowed, all in a single day, to sidestep their pathetic phone-in precautions. Sometimes they'd call him and he'd say *Uh-huh, gee, sorry 'bout that, guess I'm a little strapped. I'll make good though, you betcha. And thanks for calling.*

Then he made only minimum payments for a few months, to make their brows furrow. Every time, some assistant account manager had made the same decision: Give the guy more credit. After all, school-teachers are the salt of the earth, right? They never checked on his employment again.

George worked steadily, filling out deposit orders and letting his laser printer spit out the deposit slips and address the envelopes. He had to watch the float, be sure no account got in serious debt. That would make his name spike up on some account clerk's monitor. He liked to work his system so that no human eye ever saw his busy transactions, ever caught on to the transfer of funds that kept him on the street with cash in hand while a shadow debt hovered in the computer banks.

George finished up, licked the envelopes, and got ready for church. His fresh gray suit, just back from the tailor's, fit snugly. He liked the crisp, sharp feel of the best clothes, Oxford broadcloth shirts, silk ties, shoes polished until he could look down and see his broad smile in their mirror shine. Exactness, clean details—that was what had led him to a life of prosperity, simply by following the rules the banks themselves laid down.

On the way he stopped at the Main Street Mall in Orange and mailed two dozen letters to his unwitting benefactors. Most of the big money-markets even gave you stamped, self-addressed envelopes. He stopped at a big bank done in pure Monetary Modern—welded steel sculptures, hangarlike expanses of glass, cantilevered ceiling illuminated by indirect lighting to draw the eye upward.

Like a cathedral, mosaic murals faintly echoing the gospel. A marriage of art and commerce. One of the pleasures of living off these people lay in rebuking such subtle insolence.

He used one of the new extrasmart tellers in a tastefully lit carrel beside the immense steel-and-glass-slab building. A silky female voice welcomed him as he slid in his first card, a First National with an $8,000 limit. Plenty of room on it, his printout said. He hit the card for $400. The woman's voice even gave him directions on how to connect into the different networks for which his different cards were valid, using his electronic fund transfer card.

It was almost like being guided around a bank vault, having the batches of twenties politely pointed out and stuffing fistfuls of them into his pockets. The soft breezes of Orange County ruffled his hair as he worked, like the soft caresses of his mother when he was a boy. He walked away with $1,600 in less than ten minutes.

4

SUSAN

The patient had no hair. Margaret Yamada had lost it three times now from her chemotherapy. Her most recent course had been more severe, leaving her drawn and lined, but her eyes gleamed like black marbles in the pale face, defiant, quick, and glittering. She was a second-generation Japanese-American, sixty-two, with three quiet children who visited every day. Her husband had died two years before of complications following on kidney disease.

Flowers perfumed the air of her sunlit bed as she turned the pages of a magazine, not noticing Susan. Mrs. Yamada's children had gotten her a private minisuite, which she deplored as a needless extravagance. Her children did not want their mother having to bother with the teaching routines of UCI Hospital, but she had adamantly kept her name on the list of patients open to a visit. She seemed to like the idea.

Susan Hagerty finished her furtive glance into Mrs. Yamada's room and slipped back into the corridor. Her memory was often visual, so that just looking at a patient called up associations, previous diagnoses, details. It also reminded her that beneath the thicket of documentation there was a human being, a complex personality, warts and all.

Susan walked energetically into the ward conference room two doors down. The band of interns and subinterns awaited her, clutching Styrofoam cups of coffee like magic talismans that would get them through another morning of "rounds."

"Good morning, gang." She nodded to Robert Skinner. "Mrs. Yamada is first. Go ahead."

Skinner was a slightly overweight medical student with an air of edgy uncertainty. His brown eyes kept glancing down at his notes, which seemed to be in an unreadable scrawl. Susan smiled to encourage him. Skinner was the only person she knew at UCI Hospital who was interested in cryonics, as she had discovered when she met him at an Immortality Incorporated open house a year before. She had seen him around the hospital occasionally, before finding herself acting as his team attending physician. They rarely talked about cryonics at work. The cool antiseptic air of the hospital, with odors of rubber tubing and freshly waxed linoleum, made professional distance easy. Skinner was now a fourth-year student acting as an intern, which meant that Susan usually glimpsed him heading somewhere at a brisk pace, frayed and preoccupied.

The medical students shifted around Skinner as he glanced at his notes, coughed, and fingered the lapel of his white lab coat. As senior staff, Susan accompanied the students twice a week. Clinical teaching took time and had some status attached, but it cut into research work. In the academic pyramid, one rose through the airy promise of original research, not by dogged service to the profession. Susan knew she should probably worm her way out of doing rounds so often, but she actually liked them, the rub of reality.

Skinner stumbled a bit at first and referred anxiously back to his clipboard. Gradually a coherent picture emerged. Mrs. Yamada was an oncology patient of Dr. Blevin, admitted to house staff after a fracture of the right humerus, suffered in a fall. X-rays showed a clean break. The radiologist noted signs of tumor infiltration at the fracture site.

Skinner matter-of-factly dropped the other shoe. "She has a two-year history of breast cancer, with known metastatic disease to bone."

And now she's got a fracture because of it, Susan thought. A reasonable conclusion. But the essence of method lay in testing your quick intuitions.

Skinner ran through her history: a standard mastectomy, lymph node dissection results, early chemotherapy. Tumors recurred as lung metastases six months ago. "Patient reported considerable pain. Positive bone marrow biopsy. No family history of breast cancer. Family close and attentive."

He likes her, Susan guessed. *Maybe he hates seeing a patient waste away on the same chemo that didn't even work well for her before.*

Review of organ systems. "Positive for shortness of breath, skin nodules, constant rib and arm pain, weight loss, and depression. Not hard to understand that last," he added wryly.

"Physical exam revealed a mastectomy scar and multiple indurated areas on the skin of chest and back. Lab data includes abnormal X-rays, a macrocytic anemia, hypoalbuminemia, and some liver enzyme abnormalities." Other than these, there was nothing unusual, only the erosions and oddities of the human species.

Skinner got through it well. He scrambled the details a bit but didn't stall. He threw in some "pertinent negatives," too, particularly some normal vitamin levels that excluded a few specific diagnoses. In Mrs. Yamada's case there were some interesting sidelights, but the central truth was clear.

The mastectomy and lymph node removal of two years before, plus chemotherapy, hadn't caught all the malignant cells. Nobody really knew why chemo worked sometimes and not others; it was a crapshoot. The cancer had spread and now was eating up her lungs, penetrating her bones, even her skin.

Susan held up her hand, stopping Skinner. Time for the quiz.

"Would you recommend hormone receptor studies of the tumor?" she asked Skinner.

"Yes—let's see, they must have been . . ." He thumbed through the thick file and found the results. He was tired, as interns often are, and visibly pleased when his answer proved right. "Here. Negative receptor results."

Susan did not let approval show. "Why give hormonal treatment, then?"

He shrugged. "It sometimes works anyway."

She nodded but kept on. "Why might she be better off if her family had never come to the USA?"

"Uh, Japanese have a low incidence of breast cancer if they stay in the home islands."

He had been doing his reading. She turned to another intern, a woman who seemed distracted. Susan thought it would do medicine good to have more women in it, but that didn't mean she would coddle anyone. "Why the anemia?"

The woman blinked and supplied the right answer.

"Why might the patient's blood cells be abnormally large?"

The intern gulped and stammered, then stopped completely, eyes wide. Skinner came in with the right answer. Fair enough. "What further diagnostic would you recommend, Mr. Skinner?"

"Look at the alkaline phosphatase level."

"How about an ultrasound of the liver?"

"Uh, okay."

He looked uncertain, but she could show no favoritism. "What would you do with the information?"

"Very little."

"Why?"

"I don't think there's much to be done here."

She had to nod. Adroitly, she turned the discussion to illustrate a point about cost containment, the constant problem. Then she led them into a discussion of pain "management" in cancer. After half an hour they were ready to see the patient.

Mrs. Yamada's flowers crowded the little band of medical students into a tight crescent at the foot of her bed. The patient's keen black eyes studied the circle of students with real interest. She was propped up with a book, her right arm encased in an orthopedic brace and sling. She had tugged her soft blue robe tight, as though to ward off a chill.

Skinner made the introductions, following protocol.

"I've been wanting to meet you, Dr. Hagerty," Mrs. Yamada said in a surprisingly high, cool voice.

"We'll try not to take too long."

"I'd like to ask some questions. But I know your students want to put me under the microscope first, so—" She started to take off her robe.

One of the students drew the curtain while Susan helped her out of the left arm of the robe, trying to disturb the right arm as little as possible. As Mrs. Yamada leaned forward the back of the gown opened. They could all see dull red nodules pushing up in her pale skin. First Susan, then the others, ran a finger over the lesions, feeling the hard tumor mass beneath.

"Does that hurt?" one of the interns asked.

"No. They would if a man would come along and make me work hard while I was on my back, you bet," Mrs. Yamada said impishly. The crescent dutifully chuckled.

Few seriously ill patients would talk to interns, especially flocks of them. With physicians, the local gods, they were more willing. Mrs. Yamada's good-natured ribaldry was very unusual.

"What hurts is this." She lifted her right arm a fraction. "And my ribs. A lot."

Susan could tell that this wily woman knew perfectly well what the nodules were. Susan spent the next few minutes asking about reactions to the morphine, her digestion (always a fallback, to give the patient something to report positively), and minor symptoms. As she was helping the patient back into her robe, a voice said, "I see you've met our medical team."

Susan turned to find Dr. Blevin peering around the curtain, apparently making a visit to his patient. He halted, glanced at the cluster of students, flashed someone a distracted smile. Usually other senior staff did not interrupt rounds. She felt a flush of embarrassment, remembering the curt remarks between her and Blevin a few days before. Susan saw now that events had piled up that day, fatigue and worry and sheer overwork weighing like cinder blocks on her, until Blevin had innocently chanced to tip them over. She had been unprofessional, self-righteous. Worse, she'd had no chance to take him aside and heal the breach. She caught his eye and flashed a quick smile, hoping she would see him at coffee break later.

"I wondered who had the chart," Blevin said, moving alongside the bed.

Susan pulled back the curtain. "We're just leaving—"

"Not yet," Mrs. Yamada said alertly. "I don't see anybody very often, and I wanted to ask someone—Dr. Blevin—if I have a pathologic fracture."

Susan frowned and saw Skinner stiffen. Earlier Skinner had said that the patient did not know the X-ray results.

Blevin's jaw jutted out irritably. "I see you have been talking with the house staff." He looked significantly at Susan. "I was about to discuss the X-rays with you."

Susan opened her mouth, but Mrs. Yamada cut her off. "I can read, you know." She slipped a thick paperback out from concealment beneath her covers: *Bantam Medical Dictionary.*

Blevin said, "I'm sure, but—"

"I knew that bone scan was positive—you showed it to me last May, remember? I asked Mr. Skinner, studied this book. When cancer breaks down the bone, you can get a pathologic fracture, right?"

"Well, yes," Blevin said. "We do think you have a tumor where the break is. We'll fix that with a metal rod—the orthopedist just advised me on it. Who's Mr. Skinner?"

"Uh, me. I'm a subintern." Skinner spread his hands in nervous apology. "I may have mentioned pathologic fractures when I was in here yesterday, checking some details. I certainly—"

"Please do not blame Mr. Skinner," Mrs. Yamada said precisely. "I am afraid that I badgered the information out of him. I needed it. He is a very polite young man."

Skinner's lips twitched apprehensively. Susan could not understand why; it was no crime to answer the questions of a bright, alert patient. House staff could pass on diagnoses, too. And Mrs. Yamada was plainly on top of things. Most patients regularly mistook students for interns or even staff; the only difference was a few years in age and a missing "M.D." on the name badges. Patients asked all sorts of questions and usually remembered the answers in garbled form, if at all. Mrs. Yamada had retained the medical term and remembered as well that Skinner was a "Mr."

The rest of the house staff rustled uncomfortably. Susan glanced at Blevin, who was still standing absolutely still in the doorway, head tilted up at a lofty angle. The lights reflected from his horn-rimmed glasses, making it hard to read his mood.

Susan asked Mrs. Yamada, "You needed information? I'm sure Dr. Blevin will describe the orthopedic—"

"My arm isn't the problem. Not the main one, anyway." Her eyes flicked to Skinner, jet-black marbles in a white setting moving so abruptly that Susan half-expected to hear them click. "It isn't ever going to heal, is it?"

No, it isn't, Susan thought. Often patients offered random comments, complaints—usually about the food. But to see clearly through the blur of detail was unusual. Mrs. Yamada was stern and controlled, giving away not a glimmer of self-pity.

"Well, we can't tell," Dr. Blevin said, getting a little more warmth into his voice. "We'll touch it up with radiation, and we still have to finish your chemotherapy."

"Chemo!" She gave them all a twisted smile, feeling her chest with her left hand. "It didn't touch my skin cancer. Didn't keep it from rotting my bones, either. What's next—breaking a leg when I stand up? Or when I roll over in bed?"

Blevin sighed. "I can't say what will happen. We're doing the best we can. Remember how I told you that these therapies are only treatments, not cures? The precise course of the disease may vary—"

"That's certainly clear. So I asked Mr. Skinner here about that new idea, about freezing myself till they have a cure. He knew more about it than any other doctor I've ever found, believe me—and I've been to a lot of specialists in the last few years, plenty of them."

Susan said hurriedly, "You should be aware that such measures are not part of the accepted protocol at any—"

"They all play dumb," Mrs. Yamada said crisply. "More likely, they think I'm crazy. Won't talk. But Mr. Skinner here—"

"Skinner," Blevin interrupted, "is a subintern. Do not rely on him for advice in so personal a matter. This freezing thing is quackery designed to get your cash, nothing else. Save your money. There are always things to be done."

"I asked you about it, remember?" Mrs. Yamada tossed her medical dictionary onto the bed. "*You* brushed me off."

Blevin said stiffly, "I do not believe it is an appropriate alternative."

Mrs. Yamada said quietly, "Should I not decide 'alternatives,' doctor?"

"I can see you're upset. I'll return later, and we'll discuss this entire matter." Blevin looked steadily at Skinner. "I'd like a word with you, if you don't mind." He strode quickly through the crescent of staff, sure that the waters would part before him.

Skinner started after Blevin, but Susan motioned for him to stay. She thanked Mrs. Yamada and promised to see her again soon. The small group, plainly rattled, followed her out of the room and down the hallway. Several looked around edgily for Blevin but he was not in sight.

"Well, a taste of real medicine." This brought smiles of relief. "Disagreements are scientific, not personal. That's crucial to our profession. Think that over, and I'll see you Wednesday."

They all left quickly, except Skinner. "Come on," she said. "I'll go with you. There's nothing wrong with answering questions."

They found Dr. Blevin standing at the main counter of the nurses' station, writing in Mrs. Yamada's chart with a gold Cross pen. He appeared not to notice them, then closed the chart and carefully returned the pen to his breast pocket before looking at Skinner with his head tilted back, horn-rimmed glasses again reflecting the overhead lights.

"Tell me, Mr. Skinner, is this your idea of medicine? Telling patients that they can always get frozen when they die?"

"No, I—well—she asked about what could be done, and I—she had already heard of the idea—even knew the term—and well, I—"

"The term?" Blevin's bass rumble carried heavy sarcasm.

"Uh, *cryonics.*"

"Cryonics?" Blevin said with withering disdain. "And you *recommended* this 'idea' to my patient?"

Skinner opened his mouth, closed it, and in that instant seemed to regain his composure. "I told her about it. I did not recommend it."

"And just how do you know anything about it?"

Skinner blinked. "I've read some literature."

"Is that all?"

"Well—" He licked his lips. "I visited their facility."

"Whose?"

"A company. They had an open house, and I just—"

"A visit. So you feel qualified to discuss this harebrained idea with *my* patient?"

"Well, sir, I—"

"Listen to me, Mr. Skinner. We let students into this hospital, we give them white coats, let them see our patients—because that's the only way to learn. That doesn't mean you're free to do any damned thing you like. There are ethics, responsibilities. You must *think* like a doctor to be one. Is that clear?"

Skinner nodded, eyes on the floor.

Blevin cast Susan a cool, speculative glance. "I'm going to speak to the dean about this. Meanwhile, I believe that Mrs. Yamada had best be cared for by myself alone. House staff will no longer see her."

Again Skinner nodded woodenly. Blevin returned the chart to its rack. Susan said to Skinner, "Later. We'll talk later." Still silent, Skinner left.

Blevin said casually, "You know, I don't really have to admit any of my patients to the teaching service. It's not as though it's less work. In fact, it's more. I have to check orders and sometimes deal with stupidities like this."

Susan took a breath. "May we speak?"

He lifted an eyebrow. "I suppose. I'm headed for my office. You don't condone this action of your student, do you?"

"It's complicated."

"In that case, we do indeed need to talk."

·   ·   ·

Each medical specialty has its character, and Susan found them amusing.

Surgeons, for instance, were active by nature, ready to intervene. They thought that physicians procrastinated, fidgeting over diagnoses and splitting hairs while patients slipped away.

Internists, by contrast, saw surgeons as lightweights, untroubled by ambiguity. They, on the other hand, are the heirs of the noble Hippocrates—while surgeons descended historically from barbers.

And within internal medicine, the specialists who handled the most frail and sick of patients, nephrologists and oncologists, were hedgehogs. They contented themselves with tiny, incremental improvements. So they never saw the larger onrush of medicine, the spreading possibilities.

Susan reminded herself of this as she and Blevin marched in complete silence to Blevin's office. He didn't look at her, just kept walking so fast, she had trouble keeping up. He reached up and fidgeted with his yellow tie visible beneath his white lab coat, but otherwise kept a stony reserve.

At least that gave her time to think. Skinner had been a damned fool to bring cryonics into his remarks to a patient, but it was hard to ignore a direct question. Still, his infraction was minor. She would protect Skinner, partly because she liked the young man but mostly because she knew what a connection with cryonics could do to a budding career.

She hoped that some of Blevin's hostility came from the incident several days before. She knew that she had let her foul mood ricochet crazily off Blevin's sardonic diagnosis of Maria Lowenthal. A few sharp words, culminating in Susan asking him to leave her office. Yes, she could see a minor wound like that festering in Blevin. Well, it was her fault. But she saw also that to open with an apology for the earlier incident would be bad tactics.

Blevin had a good reputation and a curt, all-business style. Very well. She would be all business.

"I understand your concerns," she began before Blevin had closed his door. "But I believe we have to keep our personal reactions quite apart from the students during our instruction of them."

Blevin closed the door smartly, just short of slamming it. He came and stood close to her, not backing away to open any space, not offering a chair. This allowed him to peer down his hawkish nose at her. "I won't have students spewing nonsense at my patients."

Susan studied the determined set of Blevin's chin. His stance was an effective tool, letting her know right away that he was rock-solid, adamant. But physical intimidation only worked if the target absorbed it subconsciously, and Susan could see right through him. She resolved to not let it bother her. Best to try a lateral approach, maybe. "She's a lonely woman. She was probably just talking to him, and out came—"

"They're hard enough to deal with, when they get more bad news every day, without them hearing drivel."

Okay, back off, try another angle. "The chemo—I understand she was having no response?"

He nodded. "The tumor's everywhere, all right. I'm going to try changing the protocol a bit."

"She asked about cryonics before?" Let him talk it out, maybe. Behind the professional face men often just wanted to let off steam.

"Pestered me about it for days. Seems to think it's some sort of miracle cure."

Careful here. "Did you give her a name, a number to call?"

Blevin looked shocked. "What? Of course not!"

Susan stood firm, not backing away, not letting Blevin's greater mass dominate the room. "She's a desperate woman. That Japanese manner doesn't give much away, but look at her eyes. She probably just wants to talk to somebody about it."

"Therapy, then."

"No, I don't mean the usual psychiatric counseling. She wants information, and that may help her to cope with what she's facing."

Blevin's mouth compressed. "You're not condoning this corpse freezing?"

"I'm not taking sides. I'm just suggesting—"

"Look, the issue here is that student. Not my patient, not my handling of her."

"Of course. I was just trying to point out that the student probably just humored her a bit, let her talk it out—"

"That is *not* the task of a student. He's out of his depth."

Time to back-pedal. "Granted. I only mean that Skinner was probably moved by pity for her. She got the diagnosis right, she's no dummy— but her emotions may not be so easily dealt with."

Blevin drew himself up. "*I* will deal with my patients. And I am going to write this up as a formal complaint."

"About his talking to her?"

"No, the nature of what he said. We cannot tolerate students who show signs of bad judgment"—his face reddened—"of outright *quackery.*"

"As I see it, he only—"

"No one should be allowed in this profession who displays such gullibility. To recommend freezing cadavers—"

"Don't you think it might at least give them some hope?" Susan herself hoped that she could derail Blevin, whose face was becoming more congested and tight. He was plainly building himself up into a cold-eyed rage, and Skinner would be the target.

"What?" Blevin blinked.

"Mrs. Yamada. It might provide some solace to her."

"And drain her bank account. We would have those cranks crowding in here, trying to sell her policies."

"That's not the way they work. All I'm saying is—"

"How do you know how they work? We've never allowed anything like that around here."

"I—I've looked into it a little. Anyway, Mrs.—"

"Looked into it? Say, you're not siding with Skinner over this, are you?"

Careful, very careful. "I don't think anybody has to take sides," she said slowly and mildly. "Cryonics isn't the issue—"

"Oh, so you give it that fancy name, too? Pseudoscientific nonsense. I'm surprised."

She reminded herself that keeping cool was always a better strategy, particularly when you did not want to provoke more questions. Under his penetrating gaze she felt uncomfortable, glad he could not see the medical alarm bracelet she wore; it had a small I^2 logo.

"That's what they call it. Who cares?" she asked in what she hoped was a light, casual tone.

"Well, *I* care." Blevin glowered and shot a clenched fist into the space between them. "If those nuts have started to get support among our own students—people who will be our colleagues in a few years— then they're more dangerous to us than I ever thought."

"Look, they're not the point. I'm sure Skinner will apologize to you, to Mrs. Yamada"—*I'll make damned sure he does!*—"and we can forget about this."

Blevin studied his fist as though it belonged to someone else, his jaw working with irritation. "No. This kind of thinking has to be stopped. I'm going to look into it."

"I'm sure Skinner is the only member of the class with the slightest interest in, ah, such matters. I'll speak to him if you like. That will put an end to the whole thing."

Blevin said in an odd, flat tone, "Why are you so sure about the other students?"

She breathed shallowly, time stretching on for two slow heartbeats. "I—I just suppose so. It seems an unlikely subject to interest them."

"Look, you work in cryopreservation of organs yourself. You know how irresponsible talk can get out of hand."

"There's a difference between advocating an idea and knowing it exists, in telling patients—"

"No, there's not—not in this area. Your own research shows how hard it is to keep even a simple kidney or liver preserved for more than a few days at low temperatures. When—"

"That's at temperatures above freezing. Below freezing, with the right cryoprotectants, there's no reason why—"

"Sure, sure, someday maybe. But there are nuts selling trips into the future for dying patients! You *have* to condemn that."

Susan said awkwardly, "I don't believe I must. It is a legitimate hope. You have to allow them that much, at least."

"I don't allow anything, not top—say, you're not defending this craziness, are you?"

Susan said carefully, "I don't have to take a position."

Blevin studied her with narrowed eyes. Then to her surprise he nodded. "I . . . see."

His intent gaze unnerved her. "I—I'll talk to Skinner."

Blevin said with an utterly unnatural calm, "I would appreciate that."

"Ah, good. I'll get back to you."

"Good." He still stood rock-solid in exactly the same spot.

Susan stepped back. Her hands at her sides felt awkward, and she stuffed them into the pockets of her lab coat. "By the way—I was a bit curt with you the other day. I was upset, you see, over several things. I hope you didn't feel too offended."

"Oh. That." Blevin remained impassive, his sallow cheeks unmoved, as though he were thinking of something far away. "Not at all." His words came out robot-smooth.

"Well, then. Sorry. I'll—I'll be going."

She closed the door behind her softly and walked away with quick, hurried steps, as though fleeing a pursuer. Her shoes made a hollow clicking down the hall.

5

GEORGE

The service that evening was hypnotic in its cascading beauty. Seen from the park of pepper trees and gnarled oaks that surrounded it, the great Marble Cathedral shone with alabaster radiance. The lawns and shrubs were pools of ink, like the sunken state of man's daily world. Above them glowed spires of all-consuming brilliance, as though beams of God's own luminosity spiked out from the massive, lofty building. The spotlights anchored along the cathedral's flanks sent great white columns of light sweeping the sky, like the Lord's word piercing the obdurate blackness that threatened to consume all mankind.

George meditated on this immaculate grandeur as he approached. It helped him prepare his mind for the service. This was the first time he had seen the majesty of the marble fortress embedded in the grasp of night. Great slabs of rock rose straight from the ground like soaring spirits. Tall windows sent prickly light beaming outward, the multicolored biblical scenes larger than life and working with jewellike facets. The surrounding oaks were dwarfed by the erect radiance of the cathedral. From their leafy recesses more great spotlights raked the stalwart buttresses and arches.

He was like those solid stacks of stone, George thought. Men like him were the essential underpinning to the glory of the Church itself. They had to do the silent holy labors. He felt himself a member in a stalwart legion, a massive presence unsung but felt everywhere within the airy reaches of this majestic transept and nave.

He let himself enter into the service, as always. The outer shell of himself fell away, the lean and efficient carapace he wore in the world. It was a hard, durable armor, and George carried it like a righteously borne weight.

But seated, letting the vibrant minister's words pour over him like a warm torrent, George felt his shell evaporate, leaving his second self exposed. He was awash in the grand old resonant harmonies, as the choir rose throughout the holy hour to offer up sweet messages that seemed to come not from the white-gowned faithful but from serene, angelic voices suspended high in the lofty reaches of the luminous yet massive stoneworks.

George had always sought solace in church, ever since his sainted parents had died. Weeknight prayer meetings, singing suppers, and the weekly carnivallike atmosphere of Sunday school, with a potluck dinner after—those had made warm, reassuring islands in a cold world.

He had learned something about money then. He was an unruly boy who spent most of his time alone, fiddling with computers at school or wandering the fields and woods. The foster homes that had taken him in then were in it for the state payments, nothing more. For a few coins they went through the motions. The women in them had treated him okay, but there had been no connection, only a casual neglect, and George had early on learned that only the Church offered him any true shelter. The time he had beaten the Childress boy in a fight, bloodied him up pretty bad, not able to stop kicking the kid after he was down— the minister had gotten him out of that trouble, when his foster parents had just handed him over to the cops, turning away. So he'd gotten another foster home, just as cold as the last one. The couple had not been hostile, just indifferent, which was really worse. And they'd lived too far away to ever let him see that minister again.

But here he felt the old currents running in him again. The vast vault of the cathedral had felt cool at first, but a warmth crept into him as the songs rose and George's own voice joined the finer silky ones that filled the humming, gravid air. By the time the collection plate had passed, with George leaving five twenties in it—spread out like a green fan, startling the wrinkled old lady next to him in the pew—he could feel his pulse accelerate.

The commanding voice of the minister was rich and strong, the baritone words reaching down into powerful bass notes as the sentences rose and fell like great waves on a warm, tropical ocean. As the sermon began George listened carefully, absorbing everything, but the point of it eluded him at first.

Then it began to dawn on him: The minister had been in a holy contest on the television, a medium George had little time for.

But the thing this man of the cloth fought! George watched one of the large TV screens mounted along the vestry as the pictures and words rolled forth. A videotape from some local TV news. The dog seemed ordinary enough until he understood. Then the screen filled with the dog's sudden snarl, the black lips pulled back from suddenly bared yellow-white teeth.

A shock of recognition ran through George. He had seen beasts like this in movies, heard their growls in his dreams. One had attacked him when he was wandering on a farmer's plowed land. He had been running away from a foster home, crying as he stumbled along—when the farmer's dog had come at him with that same angry deep rumbling. It had bit him twice, and George had run away. A few weeks later he had gone back to that place, though, and when the dog leaped at him, he had swung the baseball bat he carried behind his back. The crack of connection, his joy, the dog going limp and useless in midair—that image floated before him now as he watched the screen. Here was another hound of hell.

Then the strong voice spoke on, booming in the immensities of the cathedral. The meanings penetrated slowly as he shook off the memories of the farmer's dog.

The very idea of it all took a long, shattering moment to even comprehend. It shook George, outraged him, made him break out in a sudden clammy sweat of revulsion. He had known that California was a lair of baseness, of perversion and dissolution and the decay of souls. But this thing the minister described—the words winding on like glistening snakes, the minister's voice pealing on with full and horrid detail—was beyond mere human evil. It was direct interference with the holy and natural order.

The dog. The dog *was* from hell. A frozen hell. It had been there and returned.

And its ugly black lips grinned—sarcastic, infuriating.

George felt his second self absorb the minister's unfurling, billowing words. They struck into him like blows, staggering him mentally, confusing him, setting his skin afire with prickly rage, knotting his fists tight and hard as he sat in the pew and watched the sway and thrust of the minister, pressure building until he heard his own heartbeats as fearsome, shuddering, ever-hastening hammer-blows.

Other fears shot through him, moments, memories. He caught only fragments. An image of something flat, ominous. Smooth and malignant, like a black lake.

As the minister cried out, "Pity those yanked viciously back into our sad world!" the power of the words made George see it, *feel* it. Floating up from watery rest, into the harsh glare of heartless doctors, their sharp chrome knives gleaming.

Hot disgust rushed into his throat like vomit. The images that the minister called up pounded at him furiously, and he clutched at his jimmy-john in fear.

He could not help himself. George shook throughout the last minutes of the rolling, powerful sermon. Cryonics, they called it. Usurping the rightful terminology of science.

The Reverend would confront these people tomorrow, appear on television. The time and channel flashed on the screen: *Call in after the show! Let them hear the faithful voices lifted.*

George saw that his appointment with a real estate operator next morning would prevent him seeing the Reverend. Okay—he'd tape it. His outer, crisp self set an internal reminder, while his inner self fumed at the Reverend's pealing sentences.

And George would do his own research into this usurping horror, this cryonics. He knew their company name, and from that his skills could lead him on a long path into their operations. Those skills themselves were gifts he could lift up unto God.

The rage built in him, like a tidal flood of searing lava that lapped at the words and scalded them, consumed them. But the minister had turned now to bless the sacrament, and through the roaring in his ears George could make out a bass theme from the big organ mounted high up the chancel walls, its majestic brass gleaming in the flicker of a thousand candles. He realized dimly that as the minister spoke, the lights throughout the cathedral had ebbed away, acolytes moving like silent agents to light ranks upon ranks of milky candles.

Now the service swept on to its climax, a hymn that rolled on through the thumping of his own fevered heart. He rose to his feet, gasping.

Heads turned to watch. Hands plucked at his suit. He batted these away. Turned. Made his way to the outer end of the pew. Walked on thumping legs like the trunks of aged oaks. Left the cathedral.

6

KATHRYN

The host for *Mornin', L.A.!* was a blow-dry blond man with teeth that rivaled the full moon, Kathryn thought, in luminosity, though not in sincerity. His hostess partner had black hair, an obvious dye job, with teeth to match his. She wore a flowery print job that covered a lot but didn't conceal much.

Kathryn settled into her well-padded seat in the audience as the show's canned theme music boomed through the studio, pseudohip synthesizer stuff beeping along in four-four time. There were about a hundred people in the audience, nearly filling all the seats. Amazing, she thought, that people will haul themselves out for a nine o'clock talk show, which meant getting to the studio before eight. For Kathryn, the question of why anyone would bother ranked right up there with riddles like the origin of life, the destiny of intelligence, and why overweight men wore T-shirts in public.

At least I-Squared had the lead-off position, complete with a second guest, some minister. In the third guest slot, after Alex left, would be a guy who had a new trick in real estate investing that sounded like a scam. But then, to most of the people here, cryonics did, too. *Ummm— wonder if that's Today's Hidden Theme?*

Alex came onto the set led by the hostess, who was wearing spike-heel pumps, the heels too high for comfort or her figure. Alex looked cool, composed, but Kathryn caught the little fingering of his moustache that meant he had a fidgety bone left somewhere in his body. He wore his only business suit, a dark blue that she hoped would not come over on TV as funeral-director black. He looked severe amid all the pastels and fake flora of the set, which might be a positive, making him seem careful and sincere. She was impressed at how he carried himself, this man who was seldom out of shorts and sneakers.

The hostess arranged Alex on a russet couch, one of those awful Naugahyde numbers where you lie down to sleep on a summer day and when you get up your skin peels off.

Wendy, the hostess, then sat beside the tanned host. She managed to strike a position so that the second camera would show that she was wearing those tacky hose with the seam down the back, imitating the forties look. Alex managed to notice this, too. Irked, Kathryn imagined Wendy immersed in a vat of hot, salted oil in order to pass the time.

Theme music down. An air of expectancy. The set was the standard neutral background stuff, tan armchairs, plastic flowers heavy on yellows and reds, and two moving cameras. One zoomed in on the host as alert lights flashed in the studio.

He grinned and made a joke about how death and taxes were certain, only now maybe not, due to our guest today, and so on, messing up his description of what he called "cryogenics." Sure enough, CRYOGENICS EXPERT appeared under Alex's camera #1 shot on the studio monitor. The first thing Alex said was, "Hello. I'm afraid you misspoke our field, though. We don't do 'cryogenics'—that's engineering at low temperatures. We do cryonics."

The host flexed his right hand as if to wave away the distinction. "Which is freezing dead people, though—that's right, isn't it?"

Kathryn was relieved to see Alex lean back for just an instant, rather than obeying what she knew was his natural impulse—to hunch over earnestly, frown a little, and rattle off an incisive rebuttal. He actually stretched his arms to both sides along the russet-colored couch, the way she had drilled with him, which made him look far more relaxed and unbothered by the host's opening salvo.

"First, we don't think they're dead. Not in any deep sense."

The hostess said with real astonishment, "Whaaaat?"

"Sixty years ago, anybody whose heart and lungs stopped was dead, period." Alex smiled, showing some teeth, rather than the rather grim, tight line he usually produced. "Then came CPR—cardiopulmonary resuscitation. Suddenly, medicine said those folks weren't really automatically dead after all. Definitions changed. When—"

"But you can't *cure* the people you freeze, can you?" The host gave Alex a sharp, accusing look.

"No, or we would be doing it right now. We're just pretty sure that medicine will eventually be able to cure them." Alex kept his arms extended along the couch, showing to good effect his shoulders and pectorals, she noticed with approval.

Wendy watched Alex warily. "*Pretty* sure? Doesn't freezing these poor people hurt them?"

Alex said, "Well, not literally—they're dead by the usual sense of the term."

"The *real* definition," the hostess shot back.

"No, 'fraid not—the current definition will change, just as it did after CPR came in."

Wendy said, "I've heard these frozen people called 'chillers' and 'corpsicles.' How can you—"

"Those aren't our terms, and I object to them," Alex said sharply.

The host leaned forward earnestly. "But what Wendy said, isn't there some damage from freezing?"

"Sure—freezer burn, you'd call it when you're talking about steaks coming out of a refrigerator. But—"

"Ooooh!" The hostess drew back in revulsion.

Wrong move, Kathryn thought. *Too graphic.*

Alex saw it and held up a hand. "Sorry about the phrase. Medically, I should have said that cells get damaged by ice crystals. Future doctors, if they can cure cancer, can probably fix—well, let's call it fixing frostbite."

"*Sounds* better, anyway," the host said, hugging himself and shivering, looking out at the studio audience and getting a rather feeble laugh to which Kathryn did not contribute. At least Wendy hadn't gotten any humor out of her "corpsicles," because of her timing. Still, Kathryn thought, this host could use a little more class—a dash of Larry King, say, and lose the Geraldo.

At the host's signal they showed footage of Sparkle looking puzzled and then hostile as the cameraman came closer. Alex got in a few sentences about Sparkle's revival, which had stimulated the invitation to come on *Mornin', L.A.!*

When they cut back to the set, the hostess bit her lip, studying Alex as though he had crawled out from under a rock. "You promise people immortality this way?"

"No, we offer a chance at life extension. Immortality—you'll have to ask God for that."

"But even if people can be thawed out—this is wild!" Kathryn saw that unlike the host, Wendy wasn't faking her response. Wendy uncrossed her legs, losing the seam-showing shot, and rushed on. "These people will come out—no assets, no friends, no family, not even skills they can use. I mean, it will be hell for them!"

The host joined in: "Yes, 'way in the future, there might not even be a USA!"

Both of them looked appalled, as though they had never thought of this possibility before. The hostess added with an incisive air, "Sending people into the future—how far?"

"A century, maybe longer," Alex began. "You—"

"That's completely irresponsible!" the hostess said, blinking rapidly. "They'll—they'll be completely lost."

Yeah, no skills, disoriented—they could become talk show hostesses, Kathryn thought.

Alex responded in calm, measured tones. "Wendy, I really wish you wouldn't project your own anxieties onto me. This is the future we're talking about, right? I've got friends already frozen—they might be there for me."

"But I'm sure *I* don't have any of *my* friends in—in—"

The host broke in, "Look, it's a tremendous crapshoot, that's what you're saying, am I right?" He glanced at Wendy, a quick ripple of concern showing in his mouth.

"Of course. Probably—"

"They won't want these—these chillers, these throwbacks to the twentieth century, will they? With their strange germs and ailments?" Wendy licked her lips, staring at Alex and ignoring the host, who held up a hand in a small cautionary gesture.

Kathryn thought Alex would blow it then, go after Wendy with a derisive laugh. She could see the beginnings of it flicker in his lips, but then the drilling they had done together took hold and he turned it into a lighthearted grin, lifting his eyebrows, giving the host a quick glance as if to ask, *Are we playing with a full deck here?*

"Wendy"—*good,* Kathryn thought, *use first names, warm, we're-just-folks-here*—"We spend billions every year to cure people in the Third World. People of different races, creeds. Life is *precious.* I'm willing to bet that human decency will grow in the future—that if they can bring us back from the cold, they will."

"Boy, I hope you're right," the host said. "We'll come at this from a different direction when we return."

They cut for commercials. Kathryn realized she had been holding her breath and let it out. Alex shifted on the set, stood up, and stretched his lean frame, visibly letting out the kinks. He seemed more aware of his body than most men she knew, conscious of riding in a machine that spoke to him in muted, blunt ways. It seemed an almost feminine trait, for she had always felt that women were tied to the rhythms of the planet more firmly, a blood-deep current that ran through their lives.

Another feminine trait rose in her—the desire to go up there and mop his brow (now visibly moist), and pass a few private words, a moment in isolation. But winsome Wendy rose and crossed to him, speaking rapidly, plenty of business with the eyes. Alex took another gander at her legs, plainly noticing the pseudoforties seams. Kathryn gritted her teeth and stayed in her seat.

The audience around her muttered, but she couldn't get any reading on their reactions.

The next guest was tall and bulky, wearing what Kathryn had always thought of as an "ice-cream suit," immaculately white. He was commanding, moving with a casually powerful grace.

The host grinned. "No stranger to our show, I want to welcome again the Reverend Carl Montana. He presides over the largest congregation in Orange County and is widely known as a forthright voice on religious issues."

Kathryn saw why the Reverend Carl was a regular here. His lion's mane dirty-blond hair framed a well-tanned face that broke into a sunny smile, head bobbing slightly in thanks for the host's compliments, one hand waving modestly at the audience.

"I'm powerfully grateful to be here," Reverend Montana said in a rich, well-modulated baritone. He sat carefully at the other end of the couch, adjusting the seams of his pants. Kathryn judged him to be early thirties but with a striking physical presence that made him seem older. His thick wrists gave an impression of strength, while his hands, cupped together in an almost prayerful gesture, conveyed a strangely sensual piousness.

"You were watching backstage," the hostess began, "and I was wondering—"

"I heard it, yes." Montana shifted toward Alex, his mouth turning down sternly. "I must say I am amazed to hear the voice of mindless and immoral technology come right out and say such things."

Kathryn could see Alex's torso stiffen, but his face showed nothing as the #1 camera zoomed in.

Montana's full lips formed an amused, distant smile. "You spoke the truth earlier, though no doubt by accident." A ripple of laughter from the audience. "You said you sell life extension, and that Wendy would have to ask God for immortality. Now, there I agree with you. Absolutely, amen!"

To Kathryn's astonishment the audience burst into applause.

The host moved smoothly in. "You feel that our guest here is intruding into Godly matters?"

"Let me just ask a simple question from a simple man of the Lord," Montana said, not looking at Alex but focusing on camera #2, which had moved in for a close shot. Kathryn could tell that Alex was trying to figure out how to counter this surprise threat. He glanced out into the audience, as if looking for help from her, but the studio lights seemed to prevent him from spotting her.

"You wish to avoid the natural order of life, *not* by curing disease, or even by lifting the burden of pain from these people—am I correct, doctor?"

Alex said tersely, "First, I'm not a medical doctor—"

"*Not* a real doctor?" Montana seemed genuinely shocked. "Yet you believe yourself qualified to send good people, God-fearing people, into your frozen oblivion?"

"We have an attending physician at all—"

"And if God has a destiny for their souls—which from Scripture we are told, many times, is the Lord's divine intention—then what *have you already done* to those souls?" Montana's voice rose in alarm, yet Kathryn had to admit that the effect worked; a man near her whispered, "Why, yes!" with genuine shock.

But Alex had used the moment to take the measure of Montana. "Remember that boy who fell into an icy river last winter?" It was a trap to simply answer your opponents' questions, Kathryn knew, always on the defensive. "He was in there *fifty-five* minutes. When they pulled him out, he had no heartbeat, no breathing—but he's going to junior high right this minute. Where was his soul while he was in that cold river, Reverend? Are you telling me that boy is walking around now, loved by his parents, shooting baskets in the gym—and he has no soul?"

Kathryn clapped loudly, but no one else in the audience did. She glared at the people around her, then stopped.

Alex made a little gesture toward her with his right hand, a grin playing at the edges of his mouth. The host said rapidly, "I'm not sure that's—"

"The Lord knows things you do not, sir," Montana said severely. "He may well have taken that poor boy's soul into his mighty grasp, held it, then returned it."

"Okay, then why can't the Lord do the same for cryonics suspension patients?" Alex said mildly, turning with genuine interest toward Montana.

"Because you are keeping them for years. For centuries!"

"I thought God took the long view in these matters," Alex said.

"You are interrupting a part of life that is as natural as birth. More natural, for it leads to the very gates of heavenly reward."

"I'd say that was supernatural," Alex said, and at once saw his error, eyes darting out into the studio, for *boo*s came from the audience.

The host said, "You do take a short-term profit out of all this, don't you, Mr. Cowell?"

"What?" Alex was peering at the audience and this took him off guard.

"You charge how much to freeze a corpse?" the host asked.

"We regard them as patients—people who can still be saved."

"But how much?" Wendy joined in.

"A hundred thousand dollars to suspend the entire body."

Montana said in a sly drawl, "I'd say that sounds like a lot of money. My parishioners don't have that kind of cash to throw around, I know that."

"It provides for indefinite suspension," Alex said. "In the United States we spend about fifty thousand dollars on the last two months of a hospital patient's life, trying to haul them back from the brink of doctor-defined death."

Wendy said, "So you would rather people spent that money becoming chillers?"

Alex shrugged with an easygoing smile, an exercise Kathryn had put him through repeatedly. It made him look more moderate and emotionally balanced. "I'd never deny anybody medical treatment. But I'm not alone in thinking that we're paying a lot to extend people's lives by just a few days."

"Maybe you fellas would like a slice of that money?" Reverend Montana said with a folksy grin.

"I *resent* that," Alex flared. "I—"

"How much do you make a year, Mr. Cowell?" Wendy asked.

"Twenty thousand," he shot back.

"Not much," the host mused. "Uh, I mean—for a person of your obvious ability."

Not much compared to talk show hosts, you mean, Kathryn thought. *Still, more than I'm pulling down right now.*

"Less than the Reverend here, I'll bet."

Montana shook his head with hound-dog sadness. "I get along on the gifts of my parishioners."

"You expect dying people to come up with that much cash?" Wendy played this line with righteous-indignation special effects, Kathryn noted —raised eyebrows, bulging eyes, accusatory curl of lips, jutting chin.

"No, our clients handle it through an insurance policy that pays off when they die."

The host turned to the audience, "That's called a whole life policy, I believe. I always thought that just meant you paid your whole life long."

This got dutiful muted laughs. But Montana chose to shake his head sorrowfully. "That money could go to the relatives of the deceased, who are in their darkest hour of grief."

"Money doesn't help the grieving very much, in my experience," Alex said crisply.

"That pays for thawing out the chiller, too?" Wendy persisted.

"It pays for indefinitely long suspension in liquid nitrogen at seventy-seven degrees above absolute zero. That's cold enough to arrest all decay."

"But who'll thaw them?"

"We will—Immortality Incorporated of Orange County." *Good,* Kathryn thought, *get in the plug.*

"A fly-by-night chiller company?" Wendy asked incredulously. "They've failed before, I remember."

"Yes, that was a tragedy, an awful, illegal—"

"What you're doing is legal," Montana broke in, "though it violates the laws of God."

Get him, Alex! Kathryn felt such a rush of fighting spirit that for a second she was afraid she had actually shouted the words out. *Hey, you're not a cryonicist, remember?* she reminded herself.

"Reverend, I respect your calling enormously. But might I point out that Jesus gave four missions to his disciples? To heal the sick. To feed the poor. To spread the word—that's your job. The fourth was to raise the dead. But Jesus did not say *how* to do these things. I'm trying a valid, scientifically possible way."

Montana blinked. "That is a *perverse* version of the Lord's charges."

"I take my stand on Scripture," Alex said mildly. Kathryn could see the smallest hint of a smile playing at the corners of his mouth, but he suppressed it.

"You feel yours is a—a *holy* mission?" Wendy asked wonderingly.

"You could put it that way," Alex answered, remembering to lean back and nod agreeably.

"That is a *foul* and deceptive claim. An insult." Montana's homespun veneer fell away. His nostrils flared, and he sat bolt upright, the white suit making him loom large. His reddening face showed a completely different inner personality that looked out on the world with slitted eyes, his eyebrows gathering like thick, dark knots. With some surprise Alex turned as Montana raised a massive fist and shook it under Alex's nose, the deep voice carrying a harsh edge now: "There is only one answer for those who use the sacred word against the Lord's true intent."

"Do you really believe you know God's intentions better than any-body?" Alex asked with real curiosity, staring at the fist hovering a few inches in front of his nose.

He doesn't believe this guy will slug him, Kathryn realized.

"I know the hand of the Black One when I see it," Montana said loudly.

"Go to it!" a man near Kathryn yelled.

"You can't stop ideas with fists," Alex said, sitting back on the couch, spreading his arms out along the back of it. This was exactly the right move, Kathryn saw, because it left Montana leaning forward, threaten-ing, fist hanging in air, face contorted. Montana blinked, seemed to recover himself. He snorted with exasperation and stood up to face the cameras, which had grouped tightly around him.

"I won't pretend to be kindly and civil toward such vermin," he said loudly. "I do humbly apologize to you all, but there are some insults to God's laws that I cannot abide."

The host said, "Reverend, we hope you'll stay for—"

"Good day to you all." Montana waved, and the audience applauded loudly. He smiled and stalked off the set. Some *aahhh*s from the audi-ence Kathryn interpreted as disappointment that a fistfight had not ex-ploded.

Camera #1 closed in on Alex, who shrugged lightly. Camera #2 picked up the host, who said rather shakily, "My, this is an issue that excites people. I'm sure the Reverend was only making his point power-fully, as he is well known to do, and did not intend any real harm to our guest, Mr. Cowell. Now, I—"

"Oh no," Alex said. "I think the only thing that stopped him was the TV cameras."

There were angry shouts from the audience that Kathryn could not make out. Wendy said, "I think, Mr. Cowell, you'll have to expect peo-ple to become rather fired up about this idea of yours. After all, you're saying we've been wrong about death, and our loved ones . . ." Her voice trailed off, as if something had just occurred to her. Her false eyelashes batted, and the host glanced with some alarm at the way her heavily lipsticked lips wavered.

"Well, we promise you controversy here on *Mornin', L.A.!* and we deliver," the host said with bouncy verve, his grin a trifle strained. Kathryn could tell he had detected some unsteadiness in Wendy by the way he projected toward the audience a little too much, carefully not looking at her. The camera panned away from Wendy as she brought a hand up to her mouth as if to hide the sudden emotion written there.

"So I want to thank you, Mr. Cowell of Immortality Incorporated—"

"In Orange County," Alex added quickly. *So they can get the phone number from information,* Kathryn noted admiringly. *He's not shaken up at all.*

"And we'll be right back after this."

Kathryn noticed that Wendy got up and followed Alex off the set, but she did not think anything of it until she got backstage herself, flashing her pass at the guard. There was no sign of Reverend Montana. She would have liked to engage him in soulful discourse, or perhaps simply scratch his eyes out. The man's arrogance and casual power had irritated her. Actually, she had to admit that she was relieved that he wasn't here. Such men struck a chord of fear somewhere deep in her.

Wendy was talking to Alex, her face working with free-floating anxiety.

"But—but if I understand, you're saying that the graveyards, they're filled with people who didn't need to be there." Wendy's voice was high and tight. Backstage workers stopped and looked around at her.

"Well, yes," Alex said uncomfortably.

"You *can't* say that! You don't *know* that!"

Alex nodded, shifting his feet. He hitched his fingers into his belt, which Kathryn knew meant that he did not want to give away his unease. "It's a gamble."

"Those people you freeze, they'll probably never come back."

"We try to give them every chance."

"Chance? What chance can they have, hoping that you'll come around in a hundred years? It'll never happen!"

"It might. Nobody knows the future."

"But—but saying that people were buried and they didn't need to be, that, that—" Wendy's mouth sagged, and her eyes jerked to left and right almost as though she were seeking an escape route.

Alex caught sight of Kathryn with evident relief. He held out a hand, and she grasped it, finding his fingers cold. Kathryn kissed him lightly on the nose. "Winner by a knockout."

Wendy did not seem to register Kathryn's presence. "I mean—how long can a person go, a dead person, before you can't even freeze them anymore?"

Alex plainly wanted to walk away from this stilted, tense conversation. But he turned back to Wendy and said carefully, "The short answer is that we don't know. Memory fades away in brain cells, but how fast— that's a subject for future research. I'd say a day or so."

"A . . . day." Wendy's mouth worked anxiously, but her eyes gazed into the distance.

Kathryn said softly, "You lost someone?"

"Yes, my mother." Wendy turned almost gratefully to Kathryn. "Two months ago. We buried her in—in—"

"I'm sorry," Alex said.

"And now you come here, come barging in, you say that wasn't necessary, that we could have done something." Wendy blinked rapidly, her eyes flitting from Kathryn to Alex and back again.

Alex shifted uncomfortably. "Well . . ."

Kathryn asked, "She had stated her last wishes for burial?"

Wendy nodded, gulping, eyes wavering.

"Then you had to carry them out."

"I suppose. But I didn't know, I hadn't even heard of—"

Alex said kindly, "You did what you had to."

Something firmed in Wendy. She shook her head and stood taller. "And it's just a long shot, that's what you said."

Kathryn was taken aback by this sudden shift of mood. Alex said, "Well, yeah."

"A big gamble. Costing a lot of money."

"True," Kathryn said guardedly.

"I'm sure my mother would have wanted to leave that much money to her children."

"Probably," Kathryn kept her tone flat and neutral.

With an edge in her voice Wendy said, "In fact, that's what she *did* do. Left that money for the living."

Alex said diplomatically, "We have no argument with individual decisions like that. These are very personal matters. Your mother—"

Wendy's gaze hardened. "So there's no reason, no reason at all, to listen to you people try to sell me some scheme to—"

"Absolutely," Kathryn said rapidly. "You did the right thing."

"Yes," Alex added quickly. "Yes, that's right."

"I was doing what my mother wanted."

"That's right." Alex took Kathryn's arm and turned to go. "Thanks for all your help, and we'll be going now."

As they walked out of the studio Kathryn sighed with relief. She was shaken by the raw emotions and by her own reaction. Cryonics was a long, long shot—but the reality of death now seemed far worse, a chasm of no return.

Behind them Wendy called out, "It'll never work anyway!"

In the parking lot outside Kathryn gave him a solid, deep kiss before climbing into his old Volvo. "Forget her."

He grinned ruefully. "She could be right. For some reason we can't guess, maybe it won't work at all."

"No, I meant forget her legs."

"What legs?"

"She was walking around on them."
"Gee, I thought she had wheels."
"Grrrr."

7

SUSAN

She was finishing a difficult sample preparation when a knock came at her laboratory door.

Susan Hagerty called out, "Wait a sec!" and finished flushing the prep zone with argon. Her hands were in flex-gloves which reached into a transparent-walled isolation chamber. This part of the job was finished, and she needed a break; might as well answer the knock.

Seal all the caps. Check the valves. Now do it again. She made herself go through all the procedures. A screw-up here would destroy months of careful labor.

She finished and extracted her hands from the gloves. They felt clammy in the dry, faintly antiseptic air of UCI General. She waved them as she walked away from the isolation chamber, feeling her back muscles speak to her, protesting how long she had been working in a fixed position. *Should get more exercise,* she reminded herself. She had been working solid twelve-hour days for as long as she could remember.

She unlocked the big metal lab door and found a secretary from her department nervously shifting from one foot to another. She was a good-looking woman in a red sheath dress, and Susan vaguely recalled that she worked in the upper reaches of UCI Medical administration. Susan didn't seem to have the time anymore to get to know the steadily swelling ranks of new people; UCI was growing fast.

"Sorry to bother you, Dr. Hagerty." A cool, polyvinyl smile. "Dean Wronsky would like to see you."

"Okay, I'll finish up some of my notes, and—"

"He said, uh, right away."

A small alarm went off way in the back of her mind, as distant as the echo of a pealing church bell in a far valley. Sending a human messenger was part of the message. "I'll be there."

"Well, he wanted me to bring you up."

"I can find my own way, thanks."

She kept her voice neutral, letting the words alone carry all the sarcasm. The secretary frowned, as if trying to puzzle out something, then Susan closed the door.

Some secretaries still felt awkward dealing with physicians who happened to be women. At times they unconsciously slipped into a we're-just-nobodies camaraderie with Susan. Often they automatically assumed that Susan would jump to do the bidding of as august a person as the dean.

When she was ushered into Dean Wronsky's office a few minutes later, she saw immediately how he helped along the secretaries' reverential attitude. The room was startling after the fluorescent and linoleum and shiny enameled surfaces of the hospital outside. Here a jade-green Chinese rug spread like a tranquil mountain clearing, its design of bamboo stalks radiating outward from a center of frosted lime. The rug lapped at the base of well-oiled paneling of tongue-in-groove cedar, which exhaled a woodsy air. An ample Louis XIII sofa occupied one wall of the spacious preserve, upholstered in a pale blue-green that perfectly matched the rug. The sofa led Susan's eye to broad windows that cast a slanted wedge of afternoon sunlight into the hushed spaces here. A polished mahogany desk dominated the room. A broad felt pad of forest-green filled most of the desk top, supporting only a file folder and a brass pen holder, which held two gold-plated pens with ebony crowns. The remaining light in the room came from three copper lamps, one a spindly floor model and the other two on end tables bracketing the sofa.

It was a textured, welcoming space, the lamps shedding buttery radiance in pools. The single intrusion from the hard-edged hospital ambience outside was the plastic-rimmed file folder that lay on the desk blotter. Even that matched the blotter's deep green; she wondered if that was deliberate.

The dean sat in a posture that looked studied, leaning just far enough back into his tall leather chair to be able to place one hand on the folder. He smiled and said, "I'm happy you could join us," without looking happy at all.

"Us" included Sidney Blevin, who half-rose from the sofa in an apparently aborted gesture of politeness.

Susan felt her pulse rate increase. *The Skinner incident last week. I've been so busy, I completely forgot it.*

Dean Wronsky had the affable look of a man who enjoyed life and had, in Susan's judgment, let it take a toll of him. She estimated that he was about twenty pounds overweight, though his beige sharkskin suit was expertly tailored to reduce the usual midriff bulge and narrow chest. His face was slightly pudgy, giving him an air of generosity and calm judgment. A quick intelligence showed itself in his veiled eyes and the guarded set of his mouth. She had met him only once before, at the reception welcoming him half a year before. He had been captured by the administration from Harvard, a coup accomplished by an above-scale salary and certain perks that were only whispered about but certainly included a Lincoln Continental that he parked in a slot bearing his name; she saw it every day on her hike in from a distant parking lot.

Susan followed his languid gesture to a wicker wing-backed chair, sat, crossed her legs.

"I've been reading with *great* interest this most recent quarterly report of yours," Wronsky said. "Good, yes, very good."

"Thanks," Susan said. She knew one of her own irritating traits was an unwillingness to smooth conversations along when plainly the other person was trying to, so she added, "It's the culmination of a decade of work."

"Umm, I'm sure, I'm sure," Dean Wronsky said rather obscurely. He opened his mouth, firming up the thick lips to say something decisive, then frowned, the lips going slack. "I must say I was surprised. To be able to hold a specimen that long, below freezing, and recover it—intact and functional—after weeks. I would not have believed it."

"Yes," Blevin said dryly.

Susan caught the edge in his voice. Before she could stop herself, she shot Blevin a piercing look. "What?"

The dean hurried to intercede. "I read very carefully your description of the actual revival. Admirable use of these new compounds you've spent so *much* time developing, these . . ."

"Transglycerols," she supplied.

"Odd name," Blevin said.

"They perform the same function as glycerol, only better," Susan said. "They raise the transport rate of water through cell walls. As we freeze—"

"We?" Blevin's eyebrows rose.

"I. As I freeze the cells, these transglycerols speed water evacuation from the cells themselves. Before actually freezing, water spreads easily outside cell membranes, easing the pressure imbalances. That lessens the ripping damage if ice crystals do form. It also inhibits harm to enzymes, I found."

The dean gave Blevin a veiled look that Susan could not read. "I gather that you spent years simply developing these glycerol-type compounds. This was your first use on a living specimen?"

"No, I worked with tissue samples first. Then smaller species. Insects first, then mice."

"All done here?"

"Mostly. I have lab space here and on campus."

The dean leaned back, tapping the folder. "Supported by NIH."

Susan nodded. The National Institutes of Health spent a bit for the development of cold preservation of organs—cryopreservation. Saving human body parts was already standard procedure. Surgeons routinely salvaged skin, corneas, heart valves, even human embryos and froze them for later use. In fact, it had been the astonishing saving of embryos, those compact constellations that cradled the miracle of human inheritance, that had first interested Susan in trying for something bigger, grander. She started research in the late 1980s. It had been a long, hard labor. "They've kept me going. UCI chipped in, too."

"Yes . . ." The dean paused, tapping the folder again. "But there is no record of any experiments here on . . . dogs."

Here it came. "I didn't do the dog revival here."

Blevin said sharply, "Where, then?"

"Private lab."

"Private! You know damn well—" Blevin broke off when the dean raised his hand.

"Which laboratory was that?" the dean asked mildly.

"Longevity Laboratories."

"Ummm. Never heard of them."

Blevin said nothing, but peered at her closely.

The dean asked, "Where are they?"

Keep things matter-of-fact, girl, she thought. "Right here, Orange County."

Blevin looked disconcerted. He shifted uncertainly on the Louis XIII couch, his orange sweater clashing so strongly with the subdued colors that she had a momentary, mad fantasy of the couch attacking him, turning into a giant yawning blue-green mouth with a drooling scarlet tongue, and swallowing the offending orange morsel whole, like an exotic fruit. She suppressed the lunatic image and the beginnings of a grin. Time to be strictly professional, yes.

The dean opened the file, which she read upside down: HAGERTY BKGND. *Background on what?* "I could not help but notice that your file in the Register of Animal Experimentation does not mention any work with higher animals."

Couldn't help it, see, somebody forced me to read this specially prepared file. . . . "I didn't go any higher than mice."

"Not *here,* you mean."

"Right."

Because I'd have to go before the whole review board, she thought. The pressure from animal rights activists was incessant. They would want all details, and of course they would be horrified to learn that she had killed Sparkle by freezing. The UCI guidelines on animal experiments did not include such methods.

Yet cooling down was a painless method, leading to lethargy and then a deep sleep well before onset of the conventional definition of death. That fact made no difference to the animal rights types, though, and universities all across the land were careful not to offend their tender feelings.

Susan had some sympathy with the animal rights movement, but she indulged in no sentimentality about which came first, mice or men. To her, "rights" themselves were the wrong way to look at relations between species. In a time ruled not by reason but by lawyers, ideas like rights, which evolved to lubricate human relations, were extended willynilly in all directions. No species had an inherent right to live to a fat old age, including humans. They won that "right" by making it happen. All life fed off other life, down to the very bottom rung of the food chain. And animal rights movements themselves had no affection for cockroaches or snakes or even lowly lab mice, preferring to focus on pets like kittens and rabbits. And dogs.

The dean pursed his lips, sighed. "I am sorry to say that is a violation of our regulations."

She knew it was, of course. Her moves had been thought out long ago. "I did not do the work using UCI or NIH funding."

The dean nodded. "However, in a UCI document you report animal experiments *far* beyond our guidelines."

"True. I believe I can defend them."

Blevin said, "Ah—but these 'transglycerols.' You developed them here."

"Of course. I—"

"Regulations cover use of experimental chemicals developed at UCI," Blevin said triumphantly.

"*Some* types of chemicals," the dean added.

"I can explain my—"

"*And* use in an unauthorized facility may well transgress the regulations as well," Blevin said rapidly, warming to his subject.

He had engineered this whole meeting, of course, and made up that folder. He must have seen her quarterly report, which after all was a public document. Once he saw her mention of Sparkle, it was simple to bring her research to the attention of The Dean. That was how it must have happened. Deans spent their energies managing bureaucratic appetites and getting money, not sipping from the heady wine of research reports.

She kept her voice flat, factual. "Look, I reported the experiments with the dog in a UCI format, sure. Rules require that. But the crucial experiment was done on my own time, away from here."

"That may be insufficient to absolve you," the dean said in an oracular, rolling voice. It was the kind of tone that was useful at fund-raisers, usually at the conclusion of speeches titled "Whither Medicine?"

"Huh? Absolve me from what?"

"From working in areas UCI has never sanctioned," Blevin said mysteriously.

Here it comes. "What areas?"

"Freezing bodies," Blevin said sternly.

Somehow Blevin had found out. Her earlier sharp words with him, the dustup with Skinner and Mrs. Yamada on rounds—that had put him on the scent. There had probably been some speculation about her; every researcher in cryopreservation of separate organs might be a closet supporter of cryonics, after all. She wondered if all this stemmed from her momentary fit of ill temper last week. Blevin's callous, purely technical treatment of her patient's results had pried up the lid on Susan's long-standing irritation at the manner of medical treatment.

I let my fatigue and personal dislike override my own professionalism, she thought. *And this is the upshot. I've really blown it this time. So ends my secret life.*

"I've worked here on cryopreservation for over a decade." She hoped it came out calm, unconcerned.

Blevin leaned forward, his orange sweater bagging. "Preserving organs for transplant, certainly. Not whole creatures."

"I repeat, I did no experiments on whole body preservation here at UCI."

The dean looked judiciously at the file folder, arching his bushy gray eyebrows, an almost theatrical effect. "But you *are* reporting on such work in this document."

"Right. It is a natural continuation of—"

"Natural!" Blevin said. "You're working with those loonies who freeze corpses. Take the money of sick people. Sell them false hopes for a fast buck and promise them eternal life."

Susan said with deliberate calmness, "Nothing's eternal, Dr. Blevin."

The dean looked almost relieved by Blevin's outburst, as though at last all the cards were on the table and he had not had to put them there. "Then you do not deny these further charges."

"What charges? That was just verbal abuse." *Admit nothing.*

"You have carried out research *far* beyond the areas which NIH and, yes, UCI have allowed." The dean steepled his hands in the air and peered at her over them, his mouth becoming a stern, flat line.

"What I've done is a natural extension of my previous work. Once we know how to keep cells from suffering mechanical damage, and how to prevent enzyme loss—"

"You just stated to us that you did this work with something called Longevity Laboratories, correct?" Blevin talked right over her explanation.

"Right." *Maybe if I just answer the questions, volunteer nothing—*

"And what is the relation of this outfit with something called Immortality Incorporated?" Blevin spoke the name with distaste and contempt.

Oh damn. So much for the cover story. "They're . . . connected."

"Using a fictitious company to hide her outside associations," Blevin said triumphantly.

"Not fictitious. They're legally separate entities."

Blevin snorted in derision. "A transparent dodge."

"Longevity supports research in cryopreservation. Immortality carries out cryonic suspensions."

The dean looked puzzled. "Suspensions?"

Susan looked at him soberly. "They freeze patients after they have been declared dead by current medical standards."

"Current medical . . . ?" The dean sniffed. "Dead is dead, Dr. Hagerty."

"No, sir, not in the light of history. *Dead* means 'we're so ignorant, we don't know how to revive this person.' That's all."

The dean said, "Nonsense. After you've lost all heart function—"

"There's cardioversion," she interjected.

The dean's mouth tightened. "Heart function *and* brain function, as I was going to say, well then, the brain quickly sustains neuronal damage which cannot be repaired."

Great. At least the discussion's back onto something resembling medical grounds. "No, sir"—*a humble gesture can't hurt*—"a few minutes without oxygen doesn't impair the neurons. It damages the brain's circulatory system, clogs it. That's why people revived after five or ten minutes, if they've been at room temperature, show brain function loss. They don't get a good oxygen supply again."

The dean frowned and waved his right hand. His Yale class ring caught the yellow sunlight that was slanting lower, reaching into the hushed recesses of the room. "A minor distinction. They're gone, Dr. Hagerty."

"For us, yes. Maybe not for medicine fifty years from now. Or a century."

"See?" Blevin pounced on her words with a quick, thin grin. "Just as I said. She believes all this crap, supports—"

"Are my personal beliefs at issue here?"

The dean looked at her levelly for a long moment. "I believe they must be."

"Only my actions are subject to UCI review."

The dean said judiciously, "Your outside sources of income are, however, also our concern."

"That's not the issue here," she said, "and you know it."

Blevin said, "They must have a hard time finding legitimate medical people to give them a pretense of competence. You provide that—for how much?"

"I receive no money from them."

The dean said slowly, "I'm afraid we'll need proof of that."

"I've kept entirely inside the professional standards—"

Blevin said, "You have involved UCI in this fraudulent, crank—"

"Do I have to listen to this?" Susan addressed only the dean, not letting herself even look any longer at Blevin's reddening face.

The dean's eyes were distant. "No, Dr. Hagerty, but you do have to answer for your intertwining of legitimate UCI research with these—these freezer people."

"Have they been paying you to sign death certificates?" Blevin asked, his voice tight and high.

She still refused to look at him. "Of course not."

"Do you appear at their sales meetings?" Blevin asked.

She had always believed that the person who kept calm and polite in the face of anger won the moral victory. This idea obviously had not occurred to either of these two.

"There are no sales meetings."

"You help them con customers, though, right?"

"You speak out of utter ignorance." She kept staring straight ahead.

"Well, maybe you should enlighten us."

"Why do I suspect that would be pointless?"

"You have abused your UCI association—"

"And *you* have abused my privacy. I—"

"Now, now." The dean held up both hands, palms out, an expression of stern control bringing a certain character to his face. "I don't believe we need to have a preliminary discussion decay into *this*."

Susan asked quickly, "Preliminary to what?"

This seemed to take the dean off guard. "Well, I was thinking, perhaps I should refer this to an ad hoc review committee."

"What will be the charges?" she asked, looking not at Wronsky any longer but over his head, out the window, at the distant slumped peaks of Saddleback Mountain. *Should I explain? Try to head off this committee?* Her judgment said it would do no good. And Blevin, sitting here like a vulture to snap up any gobbets of information, might get some valuable clues.

"Well, I don't think the word *charges* quite describes our customary review process," Wronsky said.

"What does?"

"Uh, I shall ask the committee to review your actions, in light of the standards of our university and our profession, and recommend what sort of discipline is—"

"You've already assumed discipline is called for?"

"No, no, I certainly didn't mean to imply—" Wronsky halted, undoubtedly calculating whether his wording here could be used against him, a landscape of possible, hideously expensive lawsuits looming up in his mind's eye. "I am asking only for a scrupulous review. A thorough one. Recommendations, of course, will be made."

"I see." She stood, her shoes sinking into the thick Chinese carpet. Somehow it was important to stay ahead of the ball on this one, not allow Wronsky to bury everything under a pile of fuzzy, slack sentences. She felt a sharp desire to be quick, lean, sure.

Then it hit her. Her computer log-in had shown an unexplained intrusion. Somebody sniffing around.

Blevin. And no possible way to prove it.

Blevin said, "Wait, I want to ask her—"

"Stuff your questions," Susan said, finally turning to look at him. She smiled bitterly. "To ascertain where, consult your proctologist."

Wronsky rose to his feet, his sharkskin suit falling without wrinkles. "Now, I hardly think such language is necessary—"

"Good day, my colleagues," Susan said, and walked out.

The shock of emerging into the cool, ceramic light of the hospital was refreshing. To be among precise lines and hard facts, after the muggy evasions of that pleasant, soft office, was a genuine pleasure. She didn't even mind the faint antiseptic tinge that invaded her nostrils like a clarifying breeze as she strode energetically back to her office, knowing that ahead lay a protracted hard time.

8

GEORGE

He returned to his cool, sharply appointed apartment as dusk fell upon the sprawl of Garden Grove. He had spent the day setting up a profitable little sideline in real estate, the enduring obsession of Orange County, and looked forward to his rest.

Reverend Montana had called Los Angeles the "Metrollopis" last night, then explained that a trollop was a whore. True enough, George thought, for the women bared themselves here, displayed their carefully tended skins like fine wares. He was still getting his bearings in this concrete-subdued land where a twenty-two-foot tower of wooden beer pallets became an official San Fernando Valley cultural landmark. The palm and eucalyptus trees were imported, but its morality was home-grown. Real estate was the cornucopia here, gushing forth profit without work—California Schemin'. When the developers got through, orange trees would be as rare in Orange County as seals in Seal Beach.

George slumped down before his TV and started the VCR tape recorded this morning. *Mornin', L.A.!* was the usual vacuous stuff, but as soon as the man Alex Cowell came on, George sat up, a bite from his TV dinner forgotten in his mouth.

When Cowell said outright that freezing corpses was a holy mission, George spat food onto the carpet.

When Montana said forcefully, "I know the hand of the Black One when I see it!" George applauded, the claps ringing hollowly in the shadowed recesses of his apartment.

When the Reverend stormed off the show, refusing to abide this man Cowell and his insults to God, George shot to his feet, shouting at the screen.

Cryonics. And their company, Immortality Incorporated—smug Cowell couldn't resist getting in his plug, right at the end of the show—its very name a travesty, an insult to God.

It did not take George long to use his computer and modem to track I² through the labyrinth of telephone logic. Their system defenses were good, but he was better. He had made the most of his special scholarship in Information Science, a fancy name for computers, though the tricks he had learned would not have pleased his professors.

In a few minutes of adroit maneuvering he found the I^2 public records—data that their staff could access from outside. Duty roster, a work calendar, schedules. Easy, using his craft, his offering to God.

His narrowed eyes slid down the work calendar. They had somebody there twenty-four hours, overlapping duty rosters, all neatly arranged. He was about to close out on the file when one name caught his eye. HAGERTY.

Could it be the same? The woman doctor?

Joy rushed into his chest, brimming his eyes with tears. So he *had* been intended to go to the hospital, to check if the waitress had babbled anything about him. After doing that, he had been beset by a buzzing anxiety. His passion-self had done that, going to UCI when it wasn't smart to reveal himself.

Now he saw that the impulse had come from the Divine Shepherd. Not for George's sake, but for the Lord's. As part of a design.

He checked the work schedule. HAGERTY. She would be there in a few hours from now. At night.

He rewound the VCR tape and sat through the whole exchange, fuming, his meal forgotten. Then he replayed it again, listening to Cowell's smug distortions of Scripture. *To heal the sick, to feed the poor, to spread the word, to raise the dead.*

Only God could do that. George quickly found it in Ezekiel 37: "I will open your graves, and cause you to come up out of your graves, and bring you into the land of Israel," he quoted to the inky silences, with Alex Cowell's head freeze-framed on the TV. "And ye shall know that I *am* the Lord!" he shouted.

He replayed the tape again and again. With each viewing the insolent, smirking face of Cowell had another wreath of color surrounding it, filaments of burnt orange, virulent yellow, electric blue, hotblood red. The colors danced and sizzled, as they had around the woman in the alley, around others who had stood in his way before, jimmy-john hard and hot. The Lord's sign.

George watched the tape for another hour, letting it do its slow, sure work upon one part of him, while the other thought calmly and clearly about what had to be done. About the devil dog, a creature of the night that now walked the day.

A wind from the desert brushed his cheek. It was like a warm caress from his long-dead mother, who now slumbered beneath desert sands, where the eternal dry breezes could sing her praises. He had not visited her grave in nearly a year. The thought stabbed him with gray remorse, but the fleeting emotion was consumed in the thudding momentum of his rage.

George made his way along the rocky hillside, trying to pick through the snagging branches of chaparral bushes. The abrasive dryness of the winds made his flesh jump. Not even Arizona had possessed these harsh breezes that rubbed like sandpaper, sending electrical snaps and tingles through him.

He had parked on Santiago Canyon Road and hiked over a ridgeline to come down on the Immortality Incorporated building from behind. It was a mere half hour's drive from the Marble Cathedral. So near, yet such a strange place. The ordinary cinderblock shape was illuminated by parabolas of actinic light at its corners, casting pale blue shadows across the parking lot at the front. Two cars in the lot. Little traffic on the highway.

The self George thought of as his shell, his clear and certain self, could carry him no further than this. His inner self—the true-running and deeper person he was now, the George who could remember the nickel skatekey from his fourth birthday and the heady, swarming smell of the leather in his fielder's glove—that inner George had no plan. He had come to do the Lord's work, and the Lord would provide.

Just as He had always before. There had been that night when George had sat up in bed, sweaty from fitful dreams in which he had been swimming, endlessly swimming through a thick, sweet ocean of something that swarmed up his nostrils, trying to get into his mouth—and he had awakened to the realization that it was blood he had been swimming through, not fresh-spilled and bright red but brown, muddy, coagulating around him as he struggled. That had been a portent, one of the Master's Messages.

And that coagulating night had been like this, the air roiling and spitting with electrical urgencies. George had pulled himself up from that murky dream, rolled out of the swampy-wet sheets, feeling his feet strike the cold tile floor of his apartment—and had known in that sliver of an instant what he must do.

So he had. The next night, after his shell-self had carefully thought it through, he had gone forth. Careful, swift, silent. Clad in black, with dark high-top tennis shoes to smother sounds. Into the rustling gloom.

He had found the right neighborhood, crossed lots, slipped down alleys where momentary whirlwinds churned cyclonic spires of dust. And at last he had stood in utter silence and solemn certainty, safely immersed in pools of inky dark, waiting.

At 10:23 P.M. the back door on a ranch-style house had opened, letting a wedge of yellow light into a back yard, picking out neatly arranged beds of flowers. A man had come shuffling out, one hand filled with the evening's garbage. The Lord had been with George and so the man was indeed the one he sought, not the teenage son he knew this family had. The principal of the school, the jellyfish, had lifted the lid on the battered can, dumped the trash, clanged the lid back down.

With infinite care George slid forward through the shadows. He cradled a smooth, hefty rock.

As George came soundlessly out of the engulfing night, he saw the man's head, the bushy hair lit from behind by the glaring porchlight. A radiant aura, a nimbus of hot colors. Strands of hard yellow and searing gold. Sizzling, sliding markers that he knew came straight from the Lord. The fiery streamers had been a wonderful gift from God, a vibrant sign at the crucial moment, an instant when he might have weakened.

George had struck then, slamming the rock down on the man's neck, feeling cartilage crack and give. The principal had folded with a coughing gasp. George caught him by the shirt collar and held him up. *Receive justice like a man.* Two more swift blows to the temples caved in the skull like tissue paper.

Getting the body over his shoulder had been simple, for George crouched and caught it with one quick muscular motion. A glance at the house. No face at a window, no noise, nothing.

His outer shell had read up on the twisted complexities of the law, and he knew that the crucial element was witnesses. Without them, circumstantial evidence was a thin reed, unable to coax a guilty verdict from a jury.

Swift, sure, silent, invisible—that was the way his outer shell led him. But the deeper, seething caldron fed his engines, drove him forward.

He had carried the limp, heavy body down the alley to the drainage ditch that paralleled it. There were no lights here. A pale glow oozed between the houses from distant halogen street lamps. As planned, he simply tossed the body down into the concrete-lined ditch. The sound of it smacking hard at the ten-foot drop was satisfying. He had scrambled down the slope and found the hefty stone he had left there from his reconnaissance earlier that day.

He had to work in nearly total darkness, too cautious to use a flashlight. He struck the principal as hard as he could in the neck with the stone. The sharp snap was so loud, he looked around, sure someone would hear. But there was nothing afterward but the stirring and rasping of dry wind in the desert brush.

And so it was again tonight. The sighing, rubbing wind.

George made his way down a stony gorge that led into a large, broad arroyo. He had no plan, only a certainty that weighed in his belly, rock-heavy, a solemn duty.

The principal's death had been reported in the newspapers as an accident, but the police had admitted that there were "curious features" to the case. So George had been even more cautious in the weeks and months following his night of retribution. He had built the Bruce Prior identity and several others. And the Lord had seen fit to warn George when the Feds closed in, by the amusing but profound mechanism of the noisy party across the street. Maybe they were after him for his credit card empire, though it seemed to George perfectly legal, or maybe for the principal. It did not matter. The Lord caused His all-searching light to shine down in protection and solace.

But works were necessary to repay this holy favor. Works that could not be done by the ordinary devout. Only a man who stood outside the sheep of His flock, who resembled more nearly a wolf, could do the necessary deeds.

George crouched and worked his way among the fragrant manzanita of the arroyo. He had no weapon, but the Lord would provide. Tonight would be no different. He felt the night wind charge him with purpose, send snapping currents along his prickly skin.

The commonplace, boxy construction of the building ahead was itself like a taunt. Ordinary, innocent—yet here they sundered innocent people, splitting soul from body, so that the spirits of the cruelly betrayed could not find their place in His reward. George wondered if these spirits gathered here, each in agony because of its separation from the Lord. The wind's churning howls sounded like the moaning of lost souls. Could they know that he was here? Would they assist him?

George bent over onto all fours, creeping forward. No sign of movement near the building. Immortality Incorporated—a slap in the face of every Christian. An insult to even the heathen, steeped in darkness but still acknowledging the lesser teachings of Mohammed and Buddha.

He panted with excitement. This was like that other night, when he had struck back at the principal and the corrupt school system. A night ordained for retribution, for destiny working through his hands.

He heard a small thump. Peering through bushes, he saw a woman emerge from the rear door.

Her. The Lord confirmed his faith, her white doctor's smock fluttering like a flag. One of those who banished the dead into a frozen limbo, made them into the word the Reverend Carl had told his horrified congregation—into *chillers.*

George searched for a rock.

9

SUSAN

"Come here, Sparkle!" Susan Hagerty called.

The sleek red-brown mass came padding quietly over to her. She ruffed the floppy ears and stroked the freshly cleaned fur. "Good dog! So smart! Hey, do you know what this is?" The offered meal bone disappeared in a flash.

"She's eating better," Alex volunteered, leaning against a steel-jacketed liquid nitrogen cylinder. This was his night to stay until midnight. When she had come into the Immortality Incorporated building he had been tinkering with a pump assembly in faded, greasy blue jeans.

"Good. I stopped by on my way home, to leave off her test results. Sparkle's in reasonable condition."

"Great. How 'bout the rest?"

Susan sat in a wheeled office chair, feeling her fatigue. Seldom did a thorough workup on a patient bring solely good news. "There are some neurological deficits."

"Neurons she's lost?" Alex's voice tensed up as he stroked Sparkle's head. His Angels baseball cap shadowed his expression.

"Yes. Poor sensitivity in her paws. Some propensity for blood clots, which may reflect an underlying disorder. Some kidney problems."

Alex peered judiciously at the diagnostic report sheets. "Yeah, I caught some of that. Ummm, some of these blood indices look a bit off."

"They are. I've prescribed some things to bring them back into balance. You're getting pretty good at diagnostics."

"I pick things up, but only because you're a good teacher."

Susan felt a nervous, jittery depression steal over her, but she kept her voice factual, almost dispassionate. Alex did not need to know about her troubles at UCI, not quite yet, though I^2 would inevitably become involved in testimony before a review board. Let today be a celebration. They might not have another for quite a while. "That reminds me, Bob Skinner has volunteered to serve as a backup medical technician here. He's the UCI student I told you about."

"Hey, great. We can use the help for sure. Good guy—I met him when he came out to see the facility a few times."

"He and I seem to be getting in deeper with this guy Blevin. That seems to have tipped the scales for Skinner. He's going to sign up with I^2."

"Even better. Hey"—Sparkle was at her feed dish—"she's sure as hell got a big appetite."

"Getting exercise?"

"Practically claws her leash down off the wall."

As if to demonstrate, Sparkle perked up at the word *leash*. She padded over to the hook where it hung and woofed twice. Susan laughed. "Her skills haven't suffered."

"Let's take her for a walk," Alex said. "I was too busy today."

"Fine. You can tell me the inside dope on that TV show. I watched my VCR tape this evening."

Alex looked guarded. "How was it?"

"Terrific! You creamed them."

"Kath thought so, too." A small, pleased smirk.

"Something tells me her opinion matters more than mine."

"Let's say things are going well. She's fantastic."

"You're due for it. You need someone."

"So do you."

She waved this idea away. "Too busy. Too old. I'll miss our Dutch treat dates at the movies, though."

Alex pursed his lips in concern. "Look, you could go with us sometimes."

Susan laughed. "Kathryn would love that. No, I have friends in Laguna I can rely on, through the Episcopal church."

"You're sure? We're buddies, I don't mean for Kathryn to—"

"Perfectly sure. Now tell me about being a TV personality."

Alex raised his eyebrows in rueful puzzlement. "That minister gave me the funniest damned look."

"He's just being tough on the competition."

Alex raised his eyebrows. "We're competition?"

"We're both selling the same product, only his doesn't work."

"You think not?" he asked sincerely.

"I don't have anything against Jesus, but I sure don't like some of the people working for him lately."

"I don't think Jesus is to blame for that."

Susan rubbed her eyes, feeling a headache coming on. *Drat, and I left my medical bag at the apartment.* "I'll ask him when we meet. Come on, let's get ol' Sparkle outside."

"Sure, I—" The telephone rang. Alex made a face and picked it up. After listening for a moment, he made a helpless gesture.

Susan took Sparkle's leash from the wall and whispered, "Sit!" The dog gazed up at her in rapt anticipation, panting loudly, watery eyes dancing.

Alex was the only other person awake in the facility tonight; Ray Constantine was sleeping in the bunk room, before taking what Ray liked to call the graveyard shift. Alex didn't like to be away from the phone for long. I^2 stood ready to send out suspension teams around the clock. There was an automatic telephone relay, but this phone was the command post that separated out the true alerts from the chaff. They could take Sparkle for her walk, trusting to the backup. Susan watched Alex answering questions, apparently responding to yet another in the endless series of inquiries from the curious. This one sounded as if it were prompted by the TV show. From past experience, only one in a thousand of these ever resulted in anybody signing up, but that came with the territory. Alex gave friendly answers. She watched him for another moment, then gestured to the back door. Alex waved for her to go on. She whispered, "C'mon, girl!" and went out the back.

A sliver of moon brought faint silver-yellow radiance to filmy clouds. Warm breezes stirred her hair, reminding her that she needed to wash it, maybe even venture into a salon and get a full reconstruction job done. To Kathryn's dismay, Susan went in for utilitarian cuts, simple and short and with a minimum of curl. Her clothes were much the same, functional and sensible and utterly unlikely to turn heads. That was just as well. Her emotional life was like an amputated limb. Some nights the pain would come back, a hollow absence that cost her fruitless tossing and much sleep. But there was no chance of finding another man like Roger. Life was for keeps, and Susan had played the cards she was dealt.

Susan sighed and walked out into the pool of halogen light cast by the big lamps perched at each corner of the building. Which way? Up the arroyo, yes, but not so far that she couldn't see. Sparkle already strained at her leash, noisily demanding release. She barked and capered, licking her lips.

Susan bent to release the clasp on the leash. Let the dog charge around in the bushes, but Susan was going to avoid twisting an ankle in the dark.

Sparkle bounded off, sniffing eagerly. Susan walked a little way, breathing in the cleansing aroma of eucalyptus. Some gum trees further up the ridge sent a soft tang. The Santa Ana wind carried a medley of smells from the far desert, as if to deny the moist ocean fogs that she knew from the weather report were already stealing ashore ten miles to the west. Their tendrils might penetrate this far in the night, blunting the desert's long reach, but for now a prickly energy ran on the wind and set her nerves to jumping. She tried to make out constellations in the dark bowl of sky and spotted Jupiter's yellow-white dab. She had observed it through a Celestron eight-incher for endless rapt hours as a teenager, knew its banded majesty better than the faces of her co-workers.

Tonight the thin moon cast eerie shadows as striated clouds passed over its face. The arroyo phased in and out of focus, sharp edges lapsing into insubstantial murk as clouds rippled by. Her tired thoughts were equally vague when Sparkle's eager, playful barks changed to sharp yaps.

Susan instantly became alert. Sparkle was a watchdog and not prone to needless noise.

Snarls now came between the quick, fierce yaps. Susan could see nothing among the slender, low trees and clotted bushes. She looked directly away from the bright glow behind her, wishing her eyes would adapt faster. "Sparkle! Here!"

Ordinarily the well-trained dog would come instantly on command, but no guard dog would give up its stance. Susan hurried toward the angry barks. She had never heard Sparkle rage this way.

There, a movement. Someone large was backing away from a quick, darting shadow on the ground—Sparkle.

A man in a dark jogging suit. Crouched, legs far apart and holding one hand out, a hand with something large in it.

She had always known Sparkle as a mild, unexcitable dog, but now deep-throated growls erupted into the sighing breeze.

"Who are you?" she shouted. "Sparkle, back!"

But Sparkle did not even glance toward Susan. Instead she snarled louder and lunged in at the man, then back, and again forward. A little closer.

The man did not follow these little spurts. He did not answer Susan's question. He simply followed Sparkle with his eyes. She could see him better now, his clenched grin with lips drawn far back. He swayed to the side with an easy rhythm, and she heard him humming a deep, low song, a gospel hymn she could not name. He grasped a large stone and moved with quick strength, as though utterly at ease. He had his back to a large mesquite bush, but did not give the impression of a man who considered himself cornered.

"Get away!" Susan took a hesitant step forward, nearly brushing against Sparkle's tail.

Damned if I'll call her off. "She won't hurt you if—"

He laughed. She had never heard a laugh like that, hard and fast, like an immense chuckle coming from deep in the lungs and squeezing through a throat tight with anticipation. It had an odd merry quality on top of an ominous bass energy. For the first time she felt a note of cold fear.

The laugh made Sparkle back away briefly, growling. Then some canine pride asserted itself, and she barked louder. She made a feint toward the man's nearest hand, then another to the side, and an instant before it happened Susan saw that the dog would attack.

The man saw it, too. Sparkle gathered herself, hind legs tucking down. Irish setters are not attack dogs, but Sparkle did not know this. She launched herself at the man.

He caught the snarling mass deftly in midair, swinging hard. The rock in his hand smacked into Sparkle's head. The dog turned over in midair with the momentum of the blow and fell to the ground. The body sprawled limply.

Susan let out a cry of dismay. For a moment she could see only the pathetic, lifeless form on which she had spent so much effort and love. She took two swift steps forward, crying out, "No, no!"

Dry winds stirred Sparkle's ruddy fur. The silver-white moon moved from behind a cloud, and in this fresh radiance she saw the dog twitch just once, staring up at the sky. Sparkle looked at Susan. Her tongue lolled out, almost as though she wanted to lick Susan's hand. Her eyes were confused, silently beseeching—and then the light in them died. She went completely limp.

"You one of the freezers?" a rough, hard voice asked.

Susan looked up in a daze. "What . . ."

"You the one makes chillers?"

The man seemed to fill half the sky. His eyes bulged in the moonlight like monstrous frosty marbles.

"I—what . . ."

"You are. Yeah, you are."

She had just begun to comprehend the look on the man's face, a fixed and glazed expression. *I've seen him somewhere.* Thin lips curled back in an eerie mixture of rage and rapt pleasure. There was a wrecked, warped quality to the way he tilted his head to the right, as if trying to puzzle out some inner riddle.

"You're one. I saw this devil dog before, on the TV. You made it come back."

Where have I heard that voice? "Yes, I did, you—"

A faint scrape behind her. The rear door opening?

Help, she thought. *Get help. Don't try to deal with him.*

She moved back a half-step that she hoped he would not notice. He had heard the door. Sudden, startled fear. His eyes bulged, and his slit of a mouth opened, losing its grim, triumphant set.

Panic flitted visibly through him. There was more white in his eyes. For one who had just clubbed the life from a dog, he had a surprising uncertainty, his arms drawing back almost as if to hug himself.

"Devil dog," he whispered, "from hell."

"You bastard, you'd better run," she said in a swift shift of tactics. *Don't back down,* she thought fiercely.

The man blinked. He still had not taken his eyes off the rear door. Susan glanced back and saw that for some reason no one had yet come through the half-open door, as though they were delayed. *Damn. Hurry.*

She turned back, determined now to face down the man, who seemed frozen in place. But then he moved with startling speed. The rock seemed to swell enormously in the half-light. It rushed at her. The last thing she registered was a hot spark of pain.

THREE

ROUNDED WITH A SLEEP

We are such stuff
As dreams are made on, and our little life
Is rounded with a sleep.
                          —William Shakespeare
                          The Tempest

1

ALEX

A warm wind whipped his hair as he ran into the shadows. Yes—the clump of clothes he had seen fluttering in the breeze was Susan. She lay sprawled near thick manzanita bushes.

Just before Alex reached her he heard brush crackling and peered into the gloom. Someone thrashing through the undergrowth up the arroyo? Impossible to make out anything. Then he reached her and knelt on the sandy soil.

A black smear of blood matted her hair. "Susan!"

No response. He touched her throat and felt a rapid, weak pulse. As his vision adjusted to the darkness he saw her eyelids flutter. Her eyes moved, so maybe there was no concussion.

Her breathing was ragged. He knew just enough medicine to realize that the best action he could take was to go back inside and call an ambulance. Yet something in the murmuring night breezes made him hesitate. Again, a faint scraping from the arroyo. Someone was up there —moving away, to judge by the faint swish and crackling of brush. He felt a sudden impulse to leap to his feet and pursue—and stifled it.

"Susan?"

Her eyes had closed momentarily. Now they opened, but did not focus. "Ah. Ah," she said.

He knew enough to not touch the head wound, even though his hands wanted to *do* something. "I'll get help."

It took only a minute to dash back inside I², call an ambulance, shake Ray Constantine awake, and collect some medical supplies. As he ran back outside, he heard faint sounds of someone crashing through underbrush up the slope.

Susan had not moved. Blood, everywhere. Her scalp wound was pumping it out.

He knelt again, this time with a flashlight. Checking her over, he saw that her medical telltale, worn around her left ankle, had not gone off. It was a microminiature sentinel, primed to beep, flash red, and send a radio telemetry alert via satellite to I^2. Its silence meant that Susan's basics—pulse, blood pressure, blood oxygen—had not veered too far from equilibrium. He felt a reassurance that steadied his hands.

He applied compresses to the long, bleeding gash on her upper left scalp, pulling her hair aside to get good contact. Her skin was clammy and cool. When he tightened the bandage, the blood flow from the wound slowed. Susan coughed, gasped—and looked at him. "What . . ."

"There's an ambulance on the way."

"Ah." She blinked rapidly.

"How do you feel?"

Susan rolled onto her back, winced, closed her eyes. "Where . . . did he go?"

"Up the canyon, I think. Who was it?"

"Man . . . a big man."

"Stay still. Just lie there until—"

"How's Sparkle?"

"Spark—" *Of course. I forgot her entirely.* He stood up and picked his way through inky shadows toward the vague blur he had seen.

Ten yards away the dog lay inert, head framed by a black pool. Alex felt along her scalp, a sticky mass. The skull had a large soft patch surrounded by splintered bone that poked through the scalp. *Don't put pressure on it. Might push skull into the brain.*

But he couldn't just do nothing. He hesitated, then slipped a compress and bandage onto the area, something to soak up some blood. The dark, soaked soil testified to how much blood Sparkle had lost. But he was afraid to tighten the bandage.

"How . . . how is she?" Susan called in the shadows.

"Bad. Bleeding. Lots of bleeding." Alex felt along the body for any other wounds. None.

"Let me see." Susan dragged herself to her knees.

"Hey, no, you stay where—"

Susan began crawling toward the dog.

Alex scrambled over to her and held up his hands. "Believe me, there's nothing you can do."

"Let *go,*" she said crossly, her words slightly vague.

Alex watched helplessly as Susan made her torturous way to the body, illuminated now by a flashlight beam. He turned to see Ray Constantine trotting toward them with a big, bright emergency lamp. He answered Ray's questions with monosyllables as he watched Susan gingerly rest on her knees beside Sparkle, not minding the blood.

Susan paid no attention to the men clustered around her, trying to get her to lie down, to keep her head low. "I'm the doctor here," she said fiercely to Ray when he put a gentle hand on her shoulder.

She took the emergency kit Ray had brought and expertly rebound the bandages Alex had put on Sparkle. Two other staff members came and spoke but for long moments they were all curiously silent, watching Susan give Sparkle an injection, checking the limp body carefully, then cradling the dog's head in her lap.

Finally she looked up. "She's . . . gone."

Even though he had guessed, Alex felt a rush of sorrow, tears trickling down, his nose stuffing up. He made himself say, "We've got to get you looked at, too."

"I'll be all right. I want to start Sparkle's perfusion. Now." She got unsteadily to her feet but waved away helping hands. Her clothes were soaked in blood, hers and Sparkle's. "Take Sparkle's legs."

"Let me get the stretcher," Ray said.

"No point." Susan bent to gently lift Sparkle's head. Alex carried the midsection.

They got Sparkle inside and into a tub of ice water. Susan started on the heart-lung hookups before the ambulance arrived. More people came in, ambulance attendants and I^2, and Alex sensed their distant babble of voices only dimly. He was packing ice around Sparkle when an ambulance attendant said to Susan, "Lady, I oughta have a look at that head of yours."

Susan didn't look up from her work. "Later."

"You oughta be lyin' down, too."

"I am a physician." She still did not look up.

"Well then, you should know—"

"I am attending to a patient," Susan said severely, glaring at the man.

"A dog? It looks dead to me."

Alex could see Susan grit her teeth as she kept working, hands moving deftly over Sparkle's body. "She is."

"Then what in hell—"

"Look, buddy," Alex said, "we love this dog. We're preparing to put it in cold storage, hoping we can save it."

"Cold—?" Recognition dawned in the man's startled face. "You people—you're the ones make chillers, right? My God!"

"Right. Now if you'll just let Dr. Hagerty—"

"Hey, I got to treat her, man, can't you see she's—"

"I bandaged her myself. She has to get this done, then you can—"

"Quiet!" Susan shouted. The operating room became so still, Alex could hear the ice popping as it warmed around Sparkle.

"Hey, you reject treatment, you got to sign a release," the ambulance attendant said irritably. "I don't want anybody saying later that we—"

"Fine, fine. Go get it." Susan did not look up. The ambulance crew glanced at each other, rolled their eyeballs, and walked out.

Susan worked silently for a while, shaving the dog's lower belly and legs and then making incisions in the groin. Carefully she raised and isolated the great femoral vessels and connected them to the heart-lung machine. The ambulance crew came with the release. Susan slipped on a second surgical glove to sign it and waved them away.

Delicately she cleaned the skull, incised and peeled back hide, then lifted out yellow slivers of bone. By now the bleeding had stopped and the pale pink perfusion fluid oozed from the wound.

"I can see a little patch of cortical surface," Susan said with satisfaction. "The pial vessels seem to be perfusing, without much clot."

She looked at Alex as if seeing him for the first time, although he had been applying light pressure to her scalp from behind. "Take over for a while, please."

She was pale and drawn and plainly holding on by sheer will. But before stepping away she bent over Sparkle's head and kissed her cold, black nose. Beneath the enamel-hard light of the operating room Susan looked fragile, her lower lip trembling. "Good-bye, old girl. We brought you back once. We'll do it again. This time . . . it'll take longer." She left quickly.

When Alex came into the small scrub room next door, after leaving Ray to monitor the cooling-down, he found Susan gazing in a mirror. There was damage to her right cheek, a purpling contused area, eyelid puffy, lip swollen. She pulled her lip out, revealing a half-centimeter laceration on the inside, cut by her tooth under the crushing blow.

"Come on," he said, taking her arm. "I'll drive you to the UCI ER."

"Check my blood pressure. I want to stay awhile. I'll rest."

In her dazed state Susan had reverted to a physician's automatic independence. As soon as she lay down, she gave a long sigh of relief and let him minister to her. He was doing a better job on her bandages when Bob Skinner, the UCI medical student, arrived, along with four other I² members. Ray had sounded the general call for help, and now the computerized phone tree was bringing them in, a flat-voiced Paul Revere.

Skinner took over the bandaging just as county sheriff's deputies arrived. After that chaos reigned. The deputies called in help and started questioning Susan. An Orange County sheriff helicopter buzzed the building and bombed on up the canyon, spotlights seeking the intruder. Two deputies with big flashlights combed the arroyo for clues, finding only the rock that had hit Sparkle and Susan. A TV team arrived, undoubtedly tipped by somebody in the sheriff's office. They sniffed after cryonics-related sensationalism, faking sympathy for Susan. Alex put some I² members to work patiently downplaying the whole matter. One of the crew recognized Alex and tried to coax him in front of the camera, but he just shook his head and walked off. Too much was happening at once.

Susan finished talking to the deputies and left for the UCI ER to get X-rays, with Skinner in attendance. Alex went back to work on the long process of pulling Sparkle down into the realms of utter cold. The descent was comparatively simple, a matter of distributing antifreezing agents at the right temperature level.

The warmup process held the great unknowns. There lay the hope of cryonics—that future technology could master the long climb up from the eternal stasis of liquid nitrogen, three hundred and twenty-one degrees Fahrenheit below zero. To cross that abyss of cold would demand a new level of scientific understanding and high-tech craft. As he worked on Sparkle, Alex remembered one of the "chiller" jokes from the media.

Q: How many chillers does it take to screw in a light bulb?
A: None—they just sit in the dark and wait for the technology to improve.

There was some wry truth to that, he had to admit.

By the time deputies came to question him, Sparkle was in good hands, with Ray and two others attending. Alex had already carefully searched his memory of those short moments as he ran out into the arroyo, and so he got through the whole thing fairly quickly.

No, he had not seen anyone. Yes, he had heard somebody crashing through the brush upslope. No, no motive he could think of. A deputy told him that Susan remembered that her assailant was a big man and nothing more, not even what he had said. This was a common outcome of head trauma, Alex knew. Maybe the memory would come back. *Probably not,* he thought.

The ruddy-faced deputy said when they were finished, "With all due respect, Mr. Cowell, you got a funny kinda operation here. Seems to me it'd attract loonies."

Alex shrugged, his mind full of gravel. "Probably a vagrant."

"They don't often attack people."

"Maybe Susan surprised him while he was trying to steal something."

"What've you got back there?"

"Reserve liquid nitrogen, surplus heavy gear, leftovers from our remodeling."

"Not likely anybody'd lift that."

"Maybe he specializes." Alex's sarcasm went by without provoking a flicker of reaction.

"Well, we'll look into this, y'know, but—" The deputy sucked on his teeth skeptically. "Maybe you're right. Maybe she just surprised a bum."

"I'm really too tired to have an opinion."

"Yeah, well, get some sleep."

Alex stayed three more hours to care for Sparkle and secure the building. Susan called from the hospital; her X-rays came out fine—no fractures. The deputies finished up and finally the bays of I² fell silent. Ray Constantine and two others took over the long job of lowering Sparkle's body temperature, negotiating the descent with minimal cell damage. Still Alex lingered, until Ray said kindly, "Hey, it's the early A.M., buddy. Get on home."

Alex put his hand on Sparkle's flank, immersed in a chilly bath. It was already so cold it stung his fingers. "G'bye, Spark. Next time I see you, I'll throw you a tennis ball. Promise."

He knew he was going to cry, but he did not want to do it here. He sniffed loudly, waved awkwardly to the others, and went into the night carrying a leaden lump in his chest.

2

GEORGE

The Reverend Carl Montana received George in a sumptuous study. The Reverend had private quarters, rich in the aromas of leather and wood, in the rambling complex behind the Marble Cathedral. A light rain had swept in during Wednesday-night prayer meeting, and George shivered in his short-sleeved shirt as he was escorted along an outside walkway. Already he had developed the California habit of dressing as though the mild weather could never change.

He followed a young woman through a labyrinth of softly carpeted rooms, noticing despite himself her ample hips and slow, sensual sway. She smiled demurely up at him as she stopped before a large carved oak door. She put her hand on the doorknob, but he pushed it partly open to spare her the effort. This brought him close to her and he inhaled a heady scent of ripe roses. Her breast brushed his elbow, and the soft resistance of it made him lick his lips and stutter his thanks to her. Then she was gone, swaying down the corridor. After a long moment of warring impulses, urges he fought down without letting them come fully into the arena of his mind, he thought to knock on the door.

The Reverend called heartily, "Come right on in."

George found himself in a large room dominated by bookshelves of thick, oiled cedar and high-backed leather armchairs. The Reverend was standing beside a broad desk of polished rosewood. Tall windows of colored glass loomed behind the desk. Though heavily leaded, they let in enough street lamp glow to reveal biblical scenes illustrated in garish colors. Beads of rain trickled down the glass, casting robed figures in a watery-gray light.

Up close, the Reverend was even more imposing. His long hair flowed back like a lion's mane, framing a large head. His face was broad, the features finely chiseled, the flesh deeply tanned. The eyes were piercing steel blue as they peered alertly at George, a glimmer of respect granting the acknowledgment that big men often exchange unconsciously. His snugly tailored blue suit seemed to George like a banker's, but gold cuff links and a diamond tie clasp gave the Reverend an air of both flamboyance and gravity.

The Reverend made George comfortable in one of the deep, soft chairs. "It is truly good to see you among the congregation, George. I remember your speaking to me in Tucson."

"That was a beautiful sermon you gave there."

"Your comments later, at the chicken supper, were insightful. I was pleased that a man of your intelligence came right up to me, engaged in a scholarly discussion." Montana gave a small, self-ridiculing laugh. "So many of these revival socials have to be, well, a little thin on theology."

George seemed to remember that it was the Reverend who had sought him out, not the reverse. George had been too shy, awed by the rolling power of Montana's rhetoric. Nothing could have surprised him more than to have the Reverend approach, speak warmly, and then urge him to visit the Marble Cathedral. That evening shone so brilliantly in George's memory, though, that he was quite prepared to believe that he had in fact thrust himself upon the Reverend, perhaps without meaning to. The man was charismatic, his magnetism a disorienting tug and whirl.

"I came as soon as circumstances let me."

"Perhaps you were answering a Call. Could you tell me a little about yourself?"

The next half hour went by without George remembering much of it, only that the Reverend extracted from him a life history, using murmurs and easygoing questions. The turns of George's life-path somehow seemed to make more sense as the Reverend drew them forth, turning the facets to the light, conjuring a story with meaning and purpose, a path upward.

George lost his self-consciousness and let himself ramble on, a rare luxury. He talked of foster homes, of each new chapter in his early life begun by a visit to the state office—upstairs at the county building, lilac-painted walls, big old-fashioned manual typewriters giving an air of reassuring sturdiness. He remembered the prim foster care specialist better than he could some of the homes he had passed through for a week, a month, and one time just a day. The specialist had been neat, with even handwriting, forms clipped in a folder, boxes crisply checked with pencils she kept in their own thin box. She had worked with the court-appointed doctors, even though beneath her steady, friendly voice he had somehow heard the slow burn of the footsoldier blaming the fools at headquarters as he slogs on. And George had tried to be like her. He had held fast to that crisp order through lean years, through a series of neighborhoods with guard dogs frothing behind fences, of narrow-eyed gangs on corners, of grime and unvoiced defeat.

He thought of that foster care woman as being like his mother, as maybe a way his mother lived on. He began telling about the foster parents then.

"The poor of pocket, the rich of spirit," the Reverend said sympathetically.

"Oh no!" George said, startled out of a blur of remembrance and confusion. "The foster parents, they were nothing like my mother. She was a *saint.*"

"Don't compare others with your mother, George." The Reverend sat up, brow knitted with alarm. "Just let those memories lie."

George saw he had done something wrong. His chest tightened, and dusky memories flocked in a dizzying, hot spin, as if to mock the Reverend's instructions. He resolutely pushed them away, his cool and analytical self coming to the fore. It was hard to deal with the fluttering, shrouded memories, for there were blanks, yawning spaces, slippages from that distant time, the year after his parents' death. George tried to say this, but the words came out in staccato rushes, phrases like machine-gun bursts, and finally he made himself stop.

"It's all right, my friend," the Reverend said soothingly. "There are people here who wish to help those afflicted by their past, like you."

George panted, chest still constricted. "Really?"

"They wish to remain in the background, like so many of the truly charitable. I can serve as intermediary between them and the needful such as yourself. Almost as though they were foster parents, too."

"No, no, you don't understand. Foster parents, they—they—" And then he was off, spilling out the stories. He left out the way he had begun taking revenge on the cold, stern families he stayed with. Of killing their pets and enjoying the discovery, the mourning, the tearful burials in weedy back yards. Or of the other animals surprised on his long walks at night, the bursts of pleasure as he squeezed the life from twisting dogs or plunged his pocket knife into the soft fur of vagrant cats.

He had begun then to see these as missions for the Lord, for only holy powers were allowed to make or take life. In erasing the meaningless animal lives George had assumed a small role for the Lord, and as he had made his way through the filthy, blind world, he had been shown further, higher tasks. Such was his assault only the night before upon the devil dog and its attendant woman, a cesspool woman deceiving the world in her immaculate white laboratory coat.

He did not dare tell even the Reverend of his inner landscape, or of the torturous path he had followed to come to this moment. Still less did he want to divulge his double self, the passions and mission of the inner realm. Only a fragment did he let seep into his tale, a small clue from which he hoped the Reverend would be able to deduce George's deeper nature. He told of his rage when some boys in high school had beaten him, and how he had killed their pets. Once he had started, the words simply burst from him without thought, telling far more than he had planned—all drawn forth by the generous eyes of the Reverend.

The Reverend sat very still then. George felt his stern, judging gaze. For just a moment a look of something like alarm flickered across the tan features. Perhaps even fear. But then the Reverend's broad smile split the gloom of the study.

"We have all transgressed, good friend George. I wish you to know that the Lord is willing to receive your guilt, your pain, your remorse. He is willing to enlist you in his army as a humble footsoldier."

"Yes, that is what I want to be, a warrior for the godly."

"And so you shall be. Forgiveness is yours."

"I—I feel so much better . . . talking about it. . . ."

"You have righted yourself this way, my brother. I understand a man like you."

"You—you do?"

"I have walked in your shoes. I have known the stings of rebuke."

"But I—I—"

"The killing of the animals . . ." Here the Reverend's eyes saddened, his mouth turned downward. "A pity. Yet sometimes it must be that way. The Lord tells us that."

"He does?"

"The animals were put here for our purposes. Sometimes their role is that of blood sacrifice. The Bible recounts such uses—the fact is undeniable to anyone who will but read. I urge you to consult that most wonderful of all books whenever you find moods of sorrow and depression falling upon you, falling like the wings of a dark angel."

George had never seen his tormented teenage years this way. He felt a gust of fresh insight. "Genesis . . ."

"Yes, Genesis speaks of such. You were using these animals to extinguish your own fires. You had to, I know."

"Yes, yes, that's it. I *had* to."

So George was pleased when his story came to his raid on Immortality Incorporated, the dog's death, the way he had been forced to strike the woman—and the Reverend simply nodded, frowning some, but motioning with his ring-rich hand to go on.

"I—I did not really mean to hit her."

"Of course not."

"It was an impulse. I—I have had impulses before."

"With women?"

"Oh, yes, yes, many . . . but not like that. I mean, I know that desire can lead a soul astray."

"True enough, but this doctor woman was not like the young ladies you meet, was she?"

"No, she was older, and—"

"I mean that she was an enemy. And this struggle in which we are enlisted, my comradely friend, it is a *war*." The Reverend smacked the arm of his leather chair, the sound big and startling in the shadowy room.

"Yes, yes."

Montana studied him. "And you—why did you pick this particular struggle?"

"What they're doing, it horrifies me."

"Deeply?" A penetrating gaze as remorseless as the eye of God.

"The idea, freezing people, it calls up terrible images in me."

"What images?"

George did not want to speak of the yawning gray spaces he saw, the air of malignant force. "Unholy ones."

"I see." Montana leaned back in his big executive chair, curiosity satisfied. "Brother, I do not think you need trouble yourself about that incident." A sympathetic smile. "The Lord forgives his soldiers their, as you say, impulses. As long as *you* are sorry for them as well."

"Oh, I am, I am. That woman, she made me turn to the Bible. I found what I needed, just like I always have."

"And the Lord turned your hand to what passage?"

"Ezekiel, the valley of bones," George said.

"Yes?" The Reverend said blankly, shifting uneasily in his outsize, polished leather executive chair.

"It says plain as day, 'And ye shall know that I *am* the Lord, when I have opened your graves, O my people, and brought you up out of your graves.' But before that Ezekicl says over and over that the bones were very dry and white."

"True enough."

"So the bodies must rot first, before resurrection."

"Ah."

"Then their graves can be opened. But these corpse-freezers, they stop the natural process."

"You have hit upon the perfect text," the Reverend said. "I only wish I had done so well on that TV talk show."

"You were wonderful."

The Reverend brushed aside the compliment and returned to George's own life. With nods and small phrases he brought forth more and more. And *forgave*. George felt himself lifted, as if the mass of knotted troubles that he had carried now for years were borne away by bright-winged angels. He spoke of his love of order and cleanliness, of mathematics and numbers, and finally of his profession. Of his search for a mission, and his dawning conviction that somehow *this* time and *this* place held the answer.

When he was finished, wrung out, the Reverend pursed his lips. "You are a valiant warrior, sent at a crucial moment in our struggle. Brother George, I think you should continue this"—the Reverend paused an instant, his large eyes peering up into the high vaulting of the massive, shadowed study—"this harrying of our enemies. It is God's work, indeed."

"I'd hoped you'd say that . . . support the work . . ."

The Reverend frowned again, this time a different, deeper scowl that suggested the weight of unseen obligations upon his broad shoulders. "The cathedral has many tasks." Smoothly, as though to get some distance from George's trembling supplications. "I fear we have little money to help."

"Oh, nossir! That's not what I meant."

"The effort you described, your plans, the harassment of these God-less people—that will require time, perhaps money. I support these ideas fully, but as they verge on matters no Church should undertake, I hope you understand, my friend George, that I cannot publicly support them. Indeed, I cannot even condone them."

"Sir, I only want your blessing for my struggle against them."

"That is freely given, brother. You do understand, however, that we of the cathedral do not oppose true scientific research, including especially the preservation of organs."

"I don't know anything about that," he said uncertainly.

"There are fine companies, one right here in Orange County, devoted to saving organs for transplantation. A Dr. Lomax has achieved much in this field and contributed handsomely to the construction of the cathedral itself. A good man."

Montana peered closely at George, making him uncomfortable. "I don't care about that stuff. That's different," George said.

Montana seemed relieved. "Good. Now, I don't wish to be told of your plans or of your detailed actions."

George nodded. "The Lord's soldiers must keep their own counsel."

The Reverend sat back in the thick brown folds of his chair, visibly relieved. "Still, in doing such works of virtue, you will need to support yourself."

"I can do it through my—my method."

"Method?"

So George told him of his other side, of mathematics and banks and the river of cash in which he swam.

It took a while. The Reverend did not at first comprehend, and then he did not believe it was even possible. But George pulled forth his decks of credit cards, showed the bountiful paper prosperity he had created with them, and the Reverend's face became rapt with thoughtful respect.

After a long, meditative silence, the Reverend said, "You feel that this method of making a living is sinful?"

"Well, it is, isn't it?"

"You can't think in the usual way about yourself, friend. You are not a usual person."

"I never tell anybody about it. I mean, I don't have any relatives to speak of. Not that I'd ever call *them.*"

"Unethical. At least sleazy. That's what you've been feeling that other folks would think about you, isn't it?"

George nodded. There was worse, much worse, but George knew that he was no sinner for killing the high school principal. That was a blood debt he had paid off, pure and simple. But he would not speak of such things now. They would merely clutter this discussion, which had already so lifted from him a burden of wrong thoughts.

"You've been saying to yourself that you're living off other people's money?"

"Well, I *am.*"

"When you get a line of credit from the American Express people— say, five thousand dollars—do you imagine that they take five thousand dollar bills and put it in a shoebox somewhere, saying 'This is George's money now, nobody else touch it'—do you?"

"No, it's just an electronic notation. Still—"

"The only reason you've got that five thousand is because people *think* you have five thousand."

He pondered for a moment, and he couldn't see anything wrong with that argument. One of the things he liked about the Reverend was that this big, important man with plenty to do would sit there and talk to George, letting him figure things through in silence. Most other people hurried you.

"You are not thinking deeply enough, my brother. Now, I know you are a very intelligent fella—shucks, you're way smarter 'n I am!—but you've been fed a lot of media lies."

"But in Corinthians it says—"

"Please don't quote Scripture to me, brother. I could quote plenty more back at you."

"I'm sorry, but—"

"George, do you know how most people make money—*big* money?"

"Sure, they invent something, or get a big salary, or—"

"No!" The Reverend smacked his palm flat on the slick leather arm of his chair. "That's what most people think, but I'm a little surprised, George, that you do, too."

He said hurriedly, "I know there are plenty other ways, movie stars, gold mines—"

To his surprise the Reverend laughed heartily, slapping his hands on his knees and rocking forward. The laugh cut off suddenly, and with theatrical grace Reverend Carl gazed slowly up at George. "How about the banks?"

George hesitated. "Uh . . ."

"They make it off you and me. Off our money. Most of the big guys have always made their fortune by using other people's money!"

He felt a puzzled pleasure spread through him. "The fat cats."

"You betcha—they got fat on your money. And mine. On all the little people."

"You're not little."

"Oh, I am. Born poor. Hope to die poor, too—after giving it all away to others, in the service of Christ."

"Like Jesus."

"Like the Jesus who drove the moneylenders from the temple, George. Not that I compare myself to Him."

He saw the Reverend's point and nodded vigorously.

"I think you don't give yourself enough credit, George. I think you're not a thief. Just the opposite."

"Opposite?" He was replaying the story of Jesus in the temple, see-ing the scene of crashing tables and spilling gold coins, righteous anger blazing from the Savior's eyes.

"Government bigwigs are all the time complaining and worrying about 'consumer growth' slowing down, about recession. *You* help with that for them. You keep money moving, George. Take an advance from

Subitomo, stimulate our economy with it, and pay it back somewhere downstream with a MasterCard. I got to hand it to you—it's a brilliant idea."

"You really think—I mean, I'm not sinning at all?"

The Reverend frowned solemnly and a little sadly, the way he did in the sermon when he got to the really serious part. "The true meaning of a man's labor is which direction it points. You support yourself this smart way to carry out divine purposes. How can work—warrior's work —be sinful? That's the crucial point, George."

A warm and peaceful gratification stole over him like a benediction.

"Money isn't real, my friend. It's not like having land or owning some chickens. It's a figment. A fiction. A story we make work for the Lord."

"I—I kind of knew that. It bothered me a little, but I could feel how important it was to keep going, to be ready for my future missions."

He peered around the big room, its recesses of thick books and biblical sources. There was a Wall of Respect, thickly covered with plaques and medals and photographs of the Reverend with famous people. Deeply tanned movie stars with perfect white teeth. The Reverend Billy Graham. Even two presidents, smiling in big glossy prints, autographed. This was a place of learning and authority and it spoke to him silently with its heavy cedar scent, its smooth leather, its cottony quiet broken only by a grandfather clock's solemn brass pendulum stroke and the faint patter of rain. Here was purpose, weight, destiny.

"Those who freeze the dead and rob them of their salvation are worthy foes for your missions." The Reverend's deep baritone soothed his thoughts and yet quickened his pulse.

"I have friends in the mortuary profession, good God-fearing members of this church. Parishioners who make an honest dollar burying those who have passed beyond, in proper Christian ground. They tell me tales of what these cryonics people do to the bodies before freezing— stories that would horrify you."

"Yes, yes."

"Frozen bodies do not release the soul to heaven. That is the role of decay."

"I see that. Every decent person should."

The Reverend's voice seemed to fill the room. "Even the papists disapprove of cryonics. All faiths are united in this."

George felt a trembling, awed energy within himself.

"These people who make their *chillers,* as the jokes say—those people are far worse sinners than you ever could be, my brother George. And their name: Immortality Incorporated! That is a blasphemy itself."

George nodded, but he could hardly follow the Reverend's words, his mind was swirling so with thick, hot emotion. "My mission—it's very important to me."

The Reverend came from behind his big desk and stood over George, his height seeming to take him soaring up into the gabled gothic ceiling of the study, like the upthrusting columns of the Marble Cathedral, forever yearning skyward.

"Do you know Ecclesiastes forty-one, George?"

"Uh . . . 'Fear not the sentence of death'?"

"You are a scholar. The rest says, 'Remember them that have been before thee, and come after: this is the sentence from the Lord over all flesh. And why dost thou refuse, when it is the good pleasure of the Most High?' It was as though the word were spoken directly to us. To you and me."

The Reverend laid a fatherly hand on George's shoulder. "Your mission is clear. Go forth, brother, and may the Spirit fill you in the service of the Lord."

"I—yes. Yes." The room felt warm, constricting him.

"Go, with Jesus walking beside you."

As the Reverend raised his hands in benediction, a spotlight caught a facet in his gleaming hair. George left blindly, his mind swarming. He registered nothing more until he was outside, walking back to his car in the night of rain and fog, amid moist tendrils and muffled murmurs. His heart thumped hard with longing and fresh power.

3

KATHRYN

The first six melodious notes of a Bach chorale sounded in the large storage bay. Kathryn knew this was the signal announcing a nonemergency call on the main I^2 telephone line, but she kept a firm grip on two guy wires. They held in place a large steel cylinder that was canted at an angle, looming up into the bay.

"Who's got phone duty tonight?" Alex asked, not looking up from his welding job. Bright blue sparks cast strange shadows across the faces of Alex and Ray Constantine as they worked on a seam of the cylinder. Their goggles made them look like underwater divers.

Kathryn said reluctantly, "Me." There was something serene about doing manual labor, a relief from her chatter-clogged day job in retail sales, and she didn't want the mood interrupted. But she secured the lines and trotted into the executive office, catching the phone just before the answering program cut in.

I^2 had an extensive integrated telephone and computer system, and she found it daunting despite all her practice. With some hesitation she punched a blinking button and said, "Good evening, Immortality Incorporated."

"You're the people who were on the TV, right?" A woman, voice thin and edgy.

More fallout from Alex's appearance. "Some of our staff have been on talk shows, yes."

"You freeze people, right?"

Many of their calls were from cranks. By now Kathryn had learned the protocols for dealing with a public that was often hostile and even obscene. Keeping a professional manner was the best defense, but she still had to brace herself for each call. She found she had been holding her breath. "We cryonically suspend them, yes."

This time there was no nasty accusation, no cry of "Heathen grave robber!"—just a long silence, a decisive intake of breath at the other end, and then the distant woman's words came tumbling out as though from a bursting heart.

"It's my mother, Mildred Appleton. I was thinking all the time these last three days, while we were holding vigil at her bedside, after her second stroke, the bad one. I talked to her about it, even. She could still understand what I was sayin' and I told her how I saw your people on the TV and how you looked and all and would she like to try that, and she didn't understand much at first, but when she did, she nodded and said yes. Yes, she would."

Kathryn said carefully, "And how is your mother?"

This brought a wrenching sob. "She's gone—*gone*. Just of a sudden, coughed and spat up this dark stuff, and then they did that, you know, called the code and all, and—heart attack, it was. On top of her stroke."

"I'm so sorry to hear that." Kathryn put all the care she could into her voice to mask her own sinking feeling. She wished fervently that she were back holding the guy lines.

"It was so quick. The doctor, he said she'd maybe even overcome this stroke thing, get some of her left side movement back. He *never* said she would just up and die of a sudden like this." The woman's voice had turned adamant, almost irritable. Like many of the bereaved, she unconsciously thought that there was someone to blame.

"Well, you know that medicine is not perfect, Mrs. . . . ?"

"Fiegelman, Doris Fiegelman, I'm her daughter. But he should have warned us. Told us, you know? I would've called you people right away if I'd even had the slightest suspicion that—"

"How long has she been dead, Mrs. Fiegelman?"

A sniff, a cough. Kathryn glanced at the digital clock—11:27 P.M. "Just, well, less than two hours, I'd say."

It was best to let them down easy. "And where is she now?"

A measure of pride came into the voice. "Right away I got the hospital here to take her down, put her in the cold place."

"The holding morgue?"

"Right, it has these long drawers in it, refrigerated and all, they just wheeled her right in. I made sure of that."

"I see." There was fractured pain in the voice at the other end, a tightening of Doris Fiegelman's throat that forced her sentences to end on a ragged note, as though she were hurrying to get through them.

"So I came up here to the waiting lounge, I asked information, they were real nice, didn't take any time at all, I found your people's number. My brother, he's not so sure about all this, but right off I told him not to interfere."

Well, here it comes. But all she could think to say was, "I see," again.

"So I said I'd wait here for you. It's gettin' late at night, I know, but you people, you must have some arrangements with—"

"Mrs. Fiegelman, your mother never had any contact with us, did she?"

"Well, no. How could she? She was a terrible sick woman, been in this hospital three weeks, near."

The rising tone of the voice spelled trouble. Kathryn retreated into a calm, mechanical manner, telling herself that it was easier that way, really. "First, Mrs. Fiegelman, you yourself, speaking for your mother, cannot give informed consent under these circumstances. You are under severe emotional strain at this time. It simply isn't possible for you to become adequately educated about us or—"

"I saw you on TV."

"—or be objective about cryonics. Not given the emotional pressures and these circumstances. We—"

"Look, I know enough. I know my mother's goin' to go into a hole in the ground unless I do somethin'."

"Of course, and I sympathize with you completely. But when you later understand about cryonics, well then, you could change your mind, couldn't you? That could expose us to serious litigation."

"I'm *not* gonna change my mind, I tell you! I'll sign anything you want."

"The lawyers call that signing under duress, Mrs. Fiegelman. It's reversible, believe me—our company has been through that before."

"Listen, I'm the executor of my mother's estate. I can dispose of her remains. That should be enough for you."

"Even if you had her will right there, Mrs. Fiegelman, we would still be on shaky legal grounds. I—"

"But I said I'll sign any paperwork you want."

"How about your brother? He has an interest in this, and you remarked that he—"

"I'll take care of *him*, don't you worry!"

"I wish we could be sure of that, but our experience—"

"You're actin' like a hospital or something here. Bunch of clerks and lawyers, wantin' to see the charge cards and all before they'd even let her into a bed or anything. I can show you all that same stuff, I got it right here with me, Blue Cross—"

"Medical plans do not cover this, believe me." Stay calm, articulate, neutral. "Questions of legal authority take time, often—"

"Time is what we don't have. I mean, my mother's down there, I had them even pack some ice in around her. She needs you *now*." The voice was nettled, terse. "You people, you should be set up, you know, like the ambulance, come when you're called, on the double."

"We can't be. If you had called a day, even two days ago, there might be—"

"Well, I didn't. We were all so, so worried. I just . . ."

In the long pause that came next Kathryn could think of no comfort to give. The distant woman was spinning frantically, somewhere out above a vast, shadowed abyss. She was suffering through every moment of this call, taking each of Kathryn's statements as another vital moment forever lost, more of her beloved mother slipping away into the inky grave. And against all logic Kathryn rummaged through her own mind, searching for some way to help this disembodied voice out of the night that carried so much squeezed pain. But from training and experience she knew that there was none. The thicket of law and custom surrounding modern death was thorny, breached only by surgical shears of documents and careful preparation.

When Mrs. Fiegelman spoke again, after an audible, exhausted sigh, there was a crafty note in her tone. "It's the money, isn't it?"

"Not at all."

"There's always a way to get somethin' done if you just pay a little extra."

Kathryn bit her lip and said flatly, "Not here."

"I can write you a check right on the spot, at the hospital."

Despite herself, Kathryn's frustration and sympathy began to slide into simmering irritation. "That would make no difference. As I explained, you cannot give informed consent. Legal authority is unclear. Even financial logistics are usually so tied up in probate that—"

"I knew it!" Mrs. Fiegelman said triumphantly. "You're worried about your money! Won't let simple mercy get you past this bureaucratic logjam you keep talkin' about. Seems heartless to me, almost like murder itself, to stand around and do nothin', nothin' at all, while my mother is down there waitin' with the ice all around her."

"We can't do this at the last moment," Kathryn snapped back. "Surely you can see—"

"I can't see *any*thing, not while my mother's dead and I'm losin' her while you talk and talk and won't even help!"

Kathryn let out a long breath. "Mrs. Fiegelman, you have my complete sympathy. I went through what you have, I lost my mother too—"

"Then in God's name how can you—"

"But I won't expose this company to the risks I know will come if we even attempt to suspend your mother. I'm afraid it is simply too late."

"No! You're just refusing me, bunch of damned—"

"Mrs. Fiegelman, I feel that we simply have nothing more to say to each other that would be productive. I'm very sorry," Kathryn said calmly, and hung up.

She leaned against the big steel desk and discovered that her left hand was clenched in a tight fist. She relaxed it and wiped her eyes with a Kleenex.

As she expected, the telephone control board lit up again with an incoming call. It was too much to ask that Mrs. Fiegelman give up right away. Reluctantly, after the third ring, she thumbed the system over to automatic response. The recorded corporate announcement ran, Ray Constantine's dry voice very official and yet friendly. Then a click, and Mrs. Fiegelman shouted from the speaker, "I know you're there. Talk to me! I demand that—" and Kathryn silenced the strident cry of anger that came knifing down from atop a mountain of grief.

She stared at the far wall for long moments, not thinking of anything in particular, gazing abstractly at the photos of the suspended patients who lay only a few yards away in their cold oblivion. She had never known any of them. They had never spoken out of an immense night to her, pleaded their case with breaking voices.

A second call light lit up the board, this time on an unlisted number. Mrs. Fiegelman was still haranguing the recording machine. Without thinking Kathryn thumbed in to overhear. A fast chorus of pips and squeaks told her that this was a data transfer, computers chattering to each other.

Oops, a data line. She still didn't have this system down pat.

Inevitably, cryonics groups were technology freaks, but I^2 held the championship. This telemetry message was probably something to do with the MedAlarm system. Every day I^2 computers sent a message to the little necklace she wore, checking to make sure the device still worked properly, asking it to squirt a short radio beep back to confirm. There were more complex systems running around the clock, too, far beyond her limited command of computers. Her side of cryonics had always been the personal.

Sure, she thought ruefully. *Your interpersonal skills worked just fine with Mrs. Fiegelman, didn't they?*

Death shatters people's carefully composed masks, stripping away the polite cushions that keep us from having to recognize the raw emotions that swim at the core of every soul. When the naked underself bursts out, it rips the pleasantries and manners we have learned to wear like clothes, Kathryn thought, and we all feel exposed before the simple, awful truth.

—And at once the old claustrophobia was back, her aunt Henny's cloying cape falling over her, damp musty stench and swarming dark. She saw her mother's skeleton-thin face bravely smiling at her from the sagging, ill-kept deathbed. Skin so pale, like the thin pages of an old book unopened for a century. In her last months her mother had unaccountably taken to writing letters to the editors of the local paper, so that once or twice weekly there was a short paragraph with her name beneath it. They were usually declarations on local matters, parking and development and elections, calling on decades of experience, referring to minor events now smothered by time. These letters stood out to Kathryn's eyes like bold assertions, evidence of vitality on what her mother already called the "op-ed page," in her newly acquired jargon. As though her mother's pen drained life from her, sucking it onto the printed page, leaving behind a hollow husk of a woman.

And what would your opinion be now, Mommy, of your daughter turning away another daughter? Another who was only trying to do what I so desperately wanted for you—to pull you back somehow, snatch hold of your thin nightgown with the rose embroidery and drag you up from the damp final blackness that I felt opening its arms for you?

She clutched at the desk for her balance. Did she still truly care now what her mother would think? Yes. If only there was a place where her mother *could* think, could have an "op" on the op-ed page and hold forth—as she always had, an opinionated woman. No matter what her mother thought, if there were such a place where she still *was,* even if immobile, beyond all communication but still waiting . . .

Kathryn blinked, sniffed, straightened her blouse, and made herself walk back into the recesses of the long building. She left the blinking message light from Mrs. Fiegelman, promising herself to come back and erase it later so that no one else had to chance upon the venom that was no doubt still spewing through the telephone. She headed for the voices and the crackle of the welding job, its actinic flashes and loud pops, the two men like companions crouching around a cheery campfire on a cold night.

"Who was it?" Alex asked, peeling off his goggles and shield. He and Ray Constantine were finishing the seals on a new suspension chamber. Technicolor stains traced the top and bottom of the long stainless steel cylinder.

So she told them. It was better to talk about it, she knew, yet the words came reluctantly at first, then in a steady, storytelling rhythm, as if by making it a yarn she could gain some distance on it. Yet she heard her voice straining as she went and knew that they could tell.

When she was finished Alex said gently, "Pretty tough."

Ray nodded. "I took one of those last week. Not as bad as that, though."

"You handled it right," Alex added, taking off the leather jacket he wore while welding. She was disappointed; it gave him an agreeable Brando touch.

Their reassurance lifted her spirits more than she expected, brushing away old cobwebs in her mind. "What was yours like?" she asked Ray.

"Guy had his brother in a mortuary. Pretty damned sad. Same thing—only the mortician had already embalmed the body."

"Good Lord." Kathryn blinked. "And you said 'not as bad'?"

Ray was a thin, wiry man with a wedge of nose jutting out over a ragged brown moustache. Pale green eyes peered through a sprouting tangle of ginger eyebrows, and his decayed smile would have brought despair to the sunniest dentist. All this somehow gave him a look of laconic severity. She imagined that in another century he would have been a Jesuit priest, making minute distinctions about the infinite.

"It's easier when there's no hope," he said simply.

After a stretching moment of silence Alex said, "You have to stick by your standards, we all know that. If we take a big legal risk and the relatives of the deceased have second thoughts, we're dead meat."

An unfortunate choice of metaphors, Kathryn thought.

Ray nonchalantly related a case in which CrossTime, the cryonics firm in Northern California, had suspended a retired banker. The banker's son, a lawyer, slapped CrossTime with a suit as an "accomplice" in defrauding his father. The son attacked the trust fund his father had set up to pay for the continuing costs of the suspension. Much of the fund's assets went down the rat hole of an eventually successful defense. CrossTime now kept the banker suspended, paying the liquid nitrogen bills themselves. And they had settled out of court with the son, who walked away with lined pockets and reportedly felt quite good about the transaction.

"We've got to protect the people in there," Ray finished, pointing to the rows of tall cylinders around them. Beneath the high lamps of the bay, the gleaming suspension vessels were like modernist buildings in a miniature city. "If we get into a big legal hassle, we might lose the money they left to keep them suspended. It's for them that we don't take risks like this woman wanted."

"And for ourselves," Alex added.

"Mind you, some say we ought to charge more from people who can afford it," Ray said pensively, "and use that to support last-minute call-ins."

"So people with foresight should be taxed for people who don't plan?" Kathryn asked doubtfully. Through all this she was acutely conscious of the fact that she wasn't signed up for suspension. Nobody at I² ever referred to it, and she wondered what they thought about that.

Alex said with a lopsided smile of amused experience, "I don't know what the path to success is, but I do know the path to failure. You get there by trying to please everybody."

Kathryn nodded, still hearing the tight voice of Mrs. Fiegelman. In a real sense, she thought, everyone alive was in the same state of quiet, unexpressed desperation. Here they were, trapped in an era whose medicine would be outstripped by future research. Someday, if medicine continued on its present paths, it would be able to halt or even reverse the slow but yearly more visible ebbing of the body.

Yeah, she thought, *even this wonderful machine with its trim thighs (fifty leg-lifts a day), flat stomach (endless sit-ups), and pleasing curves (ah, the cream and second helpings and succulent desserts passed up!). Sure, maybe right now you're a bird of paradise in a chicken run, but you'll fade. Even this gorgeous cellulite-free wonder is going to go, kid.*

And none of them here would probably live long enough to reach that life-saving medical help. Just as her grandfather had died of lockjaw, two years short of tetanus injections that were now routine.

But seldom did anybody think of it this way. People forgot that the future will be qualitatively different from the present. Smallpox no longer scars your friends, so you blithely forget how it ravaged your ancestors. Fevers and flu are now interruptions in our schedules, not knocks on the door from the man with the scythe.

For cryonicists, the only alternative was to go on a desperate voyage across a chasm of time and happenstance, a journey against vast but unknown odds, into a strange and scary future. But not utterly alone, no.

"Family," she said abruptly.

Alex and Ray gave her puzzled looks. "How's that?" Ray asked, pulling on the bill of his California Angels baseball cap.

"You talk high tech all the time, but you're really like a family. A synthetic one."

"More like gamblers, I'd say," Ray said, "placing one last bet."

Kathryn was appalled. "No, I'm just catching on to what really holds I^2 together. You're in this together. We've agreed to be a kind of long-term family for each other."

Alex's mouth twisted with mild surprise. "And the first obligation of any family is the well-being of the family."

"Ummm." Ray looked skeptical. "Us versus them?"

"You don't pull homeless bums off the street and invite them in for supper if your own family is going without, do you?" Kathryn persisted.

"No, but your analogy—"

"Or to share your house for the night. Much less for the rest of your life."

Ray raised his hands in mock surrender. "Okay, okay, you've got a point."

"It's important to realize it, too," she said earnestly. "You men never talk about things like this, but you should."

Alex chuckled. "We understand each other better if we just do stuff together and don't say much."

Kathryn snorted. "The Gary Cooper school of communication."

"Yup," Ray said.

Alex grinned. "Yup."

4

SUSAN

Marie Lowenthal's funeral consumed most of Susan's morning. The cancer had already spread by the time Marie had come into UCI. She had declined sharply and refused further chemotherapy. Her family was quiet at the service and seemed stunned, disbelieving. Susan always went to a patient's funeral, but she was never sure that it did any good.

She had a brown-bag lunch of the usual virtuous foods, fruit and grain bars and carrot sticks, and then she sat for the remaining few minutes and looked at the wood-framed photograph on her desk.

Roger. His wryly self-aware smile beamed out at her from a summer day frozen in the frame. Taken five months before his heart attack, it seemed to speak of an era as distant as the pharaohs. She needed him so much now, her chest ached with the longing, like a fist that squeezed her heart—classic heart attack symptoms, she knew, but due to "mere" emotional distress. He still had the power to reach into her life and grasp her inner self. It had been years and yet she still awoke, tangled in sweaty sheets, full of longing for his firm muscles and restless, insistent energy. Sometimes it even seemed that he hovered in the shadows over her, about to plunge down and into her, again and again, and she had cried out more than once, in the long years, for that.

Whoosh! Get that pulse rate down, doctor. Lust will do you no good today.

She stood, adjusted her formal blue suit with conservative white blouse, redeemed by a maroon bow at the throat, and walked across the sprawling medical grounds to her inquisition.

Her old friend Rachel had advised her not to fire until she saw the whites of their eyes—size up the committee first, then play to the members. *Strategy comes out of personality—yours and theirs,* Rachel had said. Susan tended to think in terms of principle—a rather masculine view, Roger had pointed out once—but med school politics was a different game.

She arrived at the committee room atop the principal UCI Medical building with one minute to spare, put her hand on the lever doorknob, and thought, *I hope this doesn't turn out to be the second funeral I attend today.*

Marie Lowenthal's MRI scans had set off her rudeness to Blevin, she remembered, like a pebble that brings on a landslide. Now here came Blevin himself down the astringent light of the corridor. Stonily he nodded to Susan as he approached. She jerked the door open and entered, to avoid acknowledging him.

The committee room was far better appointed than the usual seminar rooms. The thick carpeting and heavy paneling hushed the greetings she received from the dean and two other faculty members. She spread her own notes before her at the end of the long oak-finish table.

The dean took this as his signal to sit at the other end. Blevin and the others murmured together while the dean's executive secretary came in with a valise and set up the recording equipment. The omnidirectional mike and small cassette recorder, once on, created a stiff, subdued atmosphere. Blevin sat on the right hand of the dean and the two other medical faculty—Marilyn Jacobs, a white-haired oncologist, and Jack Aronski, a bald, intense surgeon—sat on the dean's left. Susan was isolated at the other end of the long table.

"This ad hoc committee is convened under my direction, Dean Maxwell Wronsky, for the express purpose of reviewing alleged violations of university medical school standards by Dr. Susan Hagerty," the dean said crisply. His gray eyebrows matched his well-tailored suit perfectly, and he lifted them at the end of his announcement with theatrical effect. "I believe Dr. Blevin has reviewed the case and will present the salient facts."

Blevin rubbed his angular nose with an air of reluctance at having to broach such matters, then glanced at his notes. "As substantiated in documents prepared by me, acting for this committee, and offered as appendices to this report, I maintain the following points: One—Dr. Hagerty knowingly and repeatedly used experimental chemicals developed here at UCI under joint National Institutes of Health and UCI funding, in operations conducted off campus, without authorization. Two—Dr. Hagerty performed experiments on a canine without undergoing scrutiny of her procedures by the Human and Animal Subjects Review Board. Three—Dr. Hagerty knowingly associated activities in her UCI laboratory with those of a firm called Longevity Laboratories, which deals exclusively with the freezing of the dead, an area long deplored by the medical community."

The dean nodded. Susan saw that each member already had a thick binder containing Blevin's documentation. She had gone over the elaborately buttressed files for days, and she had to admit that the case was airtight. Wrong-headed, but tight.

The dean peered at her, using his eyebrows again. His full face gave him a look of solid, grave authority. "And your response to these charges, Dr. Hagerty?"

"I admit points one and two, but I do not believe they contravene UCI standards. Point three is simply sanctimonious drivel. I ask that it be dropped immediately."

The committee looked surprised, as she had hoped. She could not resist the little flare of outrage at the end.

Dr. Jacobs frowned and pursed her lips. The rest of the committee looked at her expectantly. The first salvo was often the one you remembered.

Susan wondered if Jacobs, one of the older women physicians at UCI, would be an ally. No, that was old-style feminism, and good riddance. Women had to stand on their own merits, Susan felt, and she disdained the sorority-sister underpinnings of the usual professional women's organizations. Ruefully she reflected that this, too, might cost her today.

Dr. Aronski asked, "These experimental chemicals, these . . . transglycerols? You developed them yourself?"

Susan said precisely, "They've been synthesized before. Actually, I use the term to cover a mixture of polyalcohols, including butanediols and glycerol. I simply found a usable combination, an extension of cryoprotectant and vitrification work I did years ago."

"Yeeeesss. . . ." Aronski leafed through his folder. "I hear that a local company, Vitality or Vigor or something, does this kind of work, too."

"Vitality Incorporated," Susan said. "They have some research but aren't willing to share results. They have a reputation of being very competitive for patent rights."

"I wish we could get some patent money," Aronski mused. "I must say, you have a fine file here. Harvard Ph.D. in cryobiology, taken before you went into medicine. Then Rockefeller. Boards in both emergency and internal medicine. Most impressive."

The dean came in smoothly, "Dr. Hagerty's diverse academic background was one reason for her recruitment. Now, so we don't waste time, I'd like to take these points one at a time. Does anyone have any questions?"

Susan looked around the table, admiring the way Aronski had built her up, then handed off to the dean. It had an uneasy resemblance to a doctoral oral exam.

Dr. Jacobs asked, "Do you believe we should not be able to control the use of drugs developed here?"

Susan nodded. "UCI's patent rights are fully covered. I was simply using the transglycerols in a test case."

Blevin shook his head furiously, his narrow face compressed by sudden emotion. "My brief is that at a minimum, UCI should have been compensated for use of materials it developed."

"You mean paid?" Susan asked calmly.

"Yes, then UCI could have a voice in *whether* they would be used." Blevin glared at her, then smiled mechanically. "I have no doubt about which way *that* decision would have gone."

Susan shot back, "Nothing in my NIH or UCI agreements gives UCI control over further experimental uses."

Blevin countered, "I believe that matter should be settled by university legal counsel."

"Lawyers don't make policy, we do," Susan said.

"And so we are, I believe," the dean came in smoothly.

Dr. Jacobs peered over her bifocals. "These documents show that you receive twenty percent of your laboratory support from UCI, and the rest from NIH. How much of that goes for the manufacture of these drugs?"

"Very little to *make* the transglycerols. Most are easy to cook up, and Aldrich Chemical will make up anything special I need. Testing them— that's what costs. Even in guinea pigs."

Dr. Jacobs had a kindly look, but her voice was sharp and business-like. Susan knew the manner, for she had used it herself. Women were a rare species here, and they had to show that they could play by the same hardball rules as men. "How much, would you say, for the drugs you used on the dog?"

"Two hundred eighty-seven dollars and sixty cents." Susan rattled it off, having calculated it to the penny a dozen times.

"Trivial expense," said Dr. Aronski. He was quick-witted and ambitious and had been scribbling in a notebook the whole time. Susan suspected he was working on something entirely different, keeping track with one ear cocked, a common practice during committee sessions. That usually meant that he had already made up his mind, but Susan could not read his expression.

"There is also point two," the dean said. "Circumvention of the Human and Animal Subjects Review Board is most serious."

Susan quickly replied, "They approved all my earlier work with mice. The canine experiment was not UCI funded work."

"I have served on the board and believe I understand its guidelines," Dr. Jacobs said slowly, her lined face still impassive, unreadable. "I wonder how the board would rule on higher animals used in such a bizarre manner."

"Issues before the board deal with pain and discomfort felt by animals. I assure you, the canine simply fell asleep from anesthesia. It felt no pain."

Dr. Jacobs said, "And at recovery? Prolonged attachment to a heart-lung machine? It endured having its blood replaced with these chemicals, then the reverse."

"Only while it was unconscious."

"But did you measure anomalous neurological activity while it warmed up?" Dr. Aronski asked.

"Of course. There is always some. We cannot tell if that activity correlates with pain."

"But you cannot rule out that it might have," Dr. Jacobs said pointedly.

"One never can. It is a very remote possibility. Surely that cannot be the standard by which—"

"That is for the board to decide," Dr. Jacobs said, her downturned lip ending the subject.

"A role you denied the board, by simply failing to inform it of your outside activities," Dr. Aronski said, still looking down at his notebook. Was he avoiding her eyes?

Dr. Blevin said with a note of satisfaction, "That covers points one and two. I wish to point out that documentation from the state business registry shows that in fact Longevity Laboratories is a paper shell. It is wholly owned by Immortality Incorporated, the corpse-freezing business we in our profession know all too well. I would point out that there is even a little joke, for the Longevity letterhead features a large L^2." He held up a sheet. "Notice how similar it is to the I^2 on this letterhead. Not very subtle."

Sometimes the playfulness of cryonicists was a bit much, Susan thought. She said quickly, "Surely you don't think that is an argument."

Blevin held up the sheets a moment longer, then said with pinched-mouth precision, "I offer it as an observation."

Events were moving swiftly here, Susan thought—an ominous sign. Neither Jacobs nor Aronski seemed to be deliberating over the issues. Aronski was obviously wrapped up in some paperwork, even taking a few blue departmental memos out of one stack, marking them and moving them to another pile of orange sheets. She wished she had taken the time to use a little political finesse on Jacobs and Aronski, working through colleagues. A quiet conversation over drinks oiled academic machinery better than a barrage of memos. Her recovery from the trauma to her head had been fairly quick, but for over a week the headaches and general weakness, typical signatures of such injuries, had sapped her energies. Preparing her own paperwork justifications had taken all her time.

Susan rubbed her temple reflexively, fruitlessly trying to recall any further details of the attack, then snapped her focus back to the dean. Her attention had strayed—another slow-fading symptom of the blow.

Luckily, the dean had digressed into a matter involving procedures. He had considerable power here, and Blevin's eyes jerked about anxiously enough to give Susan hope.

The dean said with rolling, nearly biblical majesty, "I have been advised by counsel that ultimately some aspects of these issues will have to be referred to the appropriate committees of the Academic Senate. However, I entertain arguments regarding Dr. Blevin's point number three, in hopes that we can keep such matters within the medical school."

Susan said, "I believe this committee can fully well perceive that Dr. Blevin is hounding me out of a misguided sense of medical propriety."

"In my view," Blevin said carefully, looking at each person in turn around the table, "any association, however slight, with an obvious fraudulent scheme sorely damages UCI."

"The key word here is *fraudulent,* of course," Susan said.

Blevin looked down at the table, fingering his yellow pencil, but addressed Susan. She wondered if this was a studied courtroom-style tactic, to express his unwillingness to even see her. "I wonder if my colleague would agree that no leading figure in cryobiology regards your *cryonics*"—he paused, sniffed in lofty disdain—"as serious science?"

Susan replied evenly, "That is merely a way to define *leading.* There are cryobiologists who believe cryonics has at least a chance to work."

"Well then, not wanting to embroil this committee in fruitless definitions, let me ask you to name them."

"I cannot. Their views are privately held. I will not divulge them without permission."

Blevin tossed his pencil onto the table, an eloquent way to convey his dislike without having it show up on the tape. "So—invoking shadow colleagues."

"I think the simple fact that you have successfully called me up before this committee speaks of the reasons why they would remain silent," Susan said, measuring out her words for full effect on the others.

"Tell me, then, does the Society for Cryobiology accept papers on this 'discipline'?"

"No. The governing board decided to avoid publicity."

"Ummmmmm, I see." Blevin was enjoying this, laying a finger to his bony nose in comic meditation. "So we are expected to have UCI involved with elements that the scientific community has ruled out."

"Science lies in the results, not in people's opinions."

"Oh?" Mock surprise. "And your results that you wish to publish— that's how this matter came to light, wasn't it?"

"As you full well know, Dr. Blevin, since you brought my paper to the dean's attention."

"Well, what about your results?"

"I still intend to publish them."

"And the proof? The recovered dog? Where is it?"

She saw which way Blevin was going, as she had feared before, but could see no way to stop him. "It—is cryonically suspended."

"You mean what the rest of us would term clinically dead, is that not right?"

Her anger rose at being cross-examined. "The information lodged in that dog's brain is still there. Damaged by the ischemia and the vitrification process, yes—but *there*." She slapped her palm on the table.

She had not intended to show emotion, but that resolve was wearing down in the face of Blevin's sarcasm. She could tell from their faces, though, that it did not go over well with the rest of them.

"I wish to point out that the dog died in an incident at the Immortality Incorporated facility. The dog was killed, and Dr. Hagerty injured by persons unknown." Blevin produced Xerox copies and handed them around. "I ascertained this from the police reports, which I give you."

He does his homework, she thought ruefully. The rumor mill must have led him to the police blotter. Better head him off.

"This has nothing to do with my case. The man who attacked me was probably just a vagrant we surprised in the dark."

"I must say that having UCI associated with such incidents is troublesome," Jacobs put in.

To Susan's surprise, Aronski raised his head from his papers and said emphatically, "Isn't the death of the dog awfully . . . convenient?"

"I resent your implication," Susan said sharply, but she felt as though she had stepped off a stairway in the dark and found nothing but thin air. Aronski's vote was crucial, and this was his first signal.

"Well"—he shrugged—"miracle dog rises from the dead. I'd sure like to see it catch a ball."

"So would I," she said with sudden feeling. "She wasn't just an experimental animal, the kind we discuss in committees like this without ever really seeing them, much less petting them. I loved that dog."

There was a long silence, which she realized came from the embarrassment of the others. *Well, I'm not ashamed of how I feel,* she thought defiantly.

Though of course emotion was never enough. Susan had not made a big splash herself over Sparkle's revival—though I^2 had—because of nagging doubts about whether she could repeat the success. Her earlier work with lab mice had not been nearly as convincing, because one couldn't be sure the mice really retained memories well. And she needed time to do more extensive dog experiments. Medicine couldn't settle for one test, even a successful one. She felt acutely uncomfortable to be talking even this much about her one case, and she hoped the committee wouldn't misread her unease as a sign of guilt.

The dean raised one bushy gray eyebrow, shifted uncomfortably in his neatly tailored ash-gray suit, and said formally, "I have myself considered Dr. Blevin's point three and feel that it is indeed out of order. I dismiss it."

Susan sat up straight. *Dismissed?*

Blevin blinked, then rubbed his nose to cover his surprise. "I am dismayed that—"

"Further, I believe that Dr. Blevin has acted out of personal enmity." The dean shot Blevin a piercing look.

Blevin gaped. Apparently he had assumed the dean was an ally. "I assure you that my concerns were purely—"

"Just why have you spent so much time assembling this investigation, rather than allowing an independent member of the faculty to do so? Did your professional responsibilities suffer as a result?"

"No, no, I—"

"Be in my office tomorrow morning at nine so that I might discuss your professionalism with you at length, doctor."

Blevin looked as though the dean had slapped him. For a long moment no one spoke.

"Now we should take up points one and two," the dean went on crisply, ignoring Blevin. Susan felt a stab of hope. Was the dean in a mood to minimize this entire matter?

"Further, I rule that Dr. Blevin will *not* vote on these points."

Blevin opened his mouth and slowly closed it.

Dean Wronsky held the eyes of Jacobs and Aronski, lowering his voice to get the full effect of a rich, authoritative baritone. "We have the power to refer these issues to the Academic Senate for disciplinary action, or to dismiss them. I believe a vote is in order. Do you concur?"

Both Jacobs and Aronski nodded, and Aronski even put down his pen.

"Point one, that Dr. Hagerty knowingly and repeatedly used experimental chemicals developed at UCI, in operations conducted off campus, without authorization."

Taking this to the Academic Senate guaranteed some press coverage, Susan thought, and the dean could not want that. Unless it could be taken care of backstage, with what amounted to a plea bargain . . .

"Who favors forwarding point one to the senate?" the dean asked.

Aronski raised his hand. Jacobs shook her head.

"Very well. Point two—that Dr. Hagerty performed experiments on a canine without undergoing proper scrutiny by the Human and Animal Subjects Review Board."

Aronski picked up his pen and held it aloft. A few seconds crept by. Dr. Jacobs looked at Susan and slowly raised her hand, saying in a small voice, "We have to be very scrupulous about the animal issue."

The dean let out a loud sigh. "Very well. You realize that I have not voted. I feel I must retain my distance from your deliberations, since my responsibilities exceed those of faculty. Also, my powers."

All this he said as he gazed pensively at the papers in front of him. Then he raised his eyes to peer directly at Susan. "I shall forward the documentation regarding point two to the Academic Senate for appropriate review. Point one is more difficult for me to decide without further thought. I instead turn to the matter that is solely my province. As dean I may determine the clinical responsibility of each faculty member."

He pursed his lips, and a momentary hardness flitted in his face. Susan sucked in her breath. Now she saw that the quashing of point three had been a neat maneuver, designed to make the dean appear moderate. In tongue-lashing Blevin, he had distanced himself from Blevin's obvious unprofessionalism.

All very clean and cosmetic. The dean would be seen as making the best of a messy squabble. She would have to defend herself in the Academic Senate, a process that could take a year, but the dean could inflict pain immediately.

Medical schools run on the ample grease of money. Faculty can presumably make more in private practice but prefer the intellectual luxury of research and some freedom from the incessant parade of patients. To soothe the financial loss, most do clinical work in the hospital, which often pays more than their purely teaching salary. The "clinical component of salary" was the meat in the sandwich.

"I rule that as a disciplinary measure, Dr. Hagerty be reduced to base salary. Pending the outcome of this matter."

Back to base meant no clinical practice at all. Since Susan was a 2X, earning twice her base salary now, that cut her income in half.

Susan sat open-mouthed until she realized that the dean had not even waited for a reaction from her. He was getting to his feet. She snapped out of her shock and said loudly, "I protest!"

Dean Wronsky studied her owlishly. The others were busily gathering up papers, deliberately looking elsewhere. "You may do so when the Academic Senate takes up your case, Dr. Hagerty."

Hold your temper. Don't give them the satisfaction. "What about the point that started all this?"

"Your choice of outside association?" the dean asked, puzzled.

"No! My paper. I reported the results of the canine revival. I plan more experiments to back it up. You saw that paper, and your office has blocked its submission to a journal."

"I should think you would await the findings of the senate," the dean said patiently, as though explaining to a child. "As you must remember, no work done outside the protocols of the animal subjects provisions can be submitted."

"But that will greatly damage my ability to use the work in my next proposal to the NIH," Susan said.

Blevin gave her a superior, gleeful grin. "Should have thought of that before you got into this mess."

"But . . ." Her voice trailed off.

The committee was leaving as quickly as it could. She saw in their faces the simple truth: They weren't impressed with her case because they didn't believe her. Anybody who took cryonics seriously was pretty doubtful already, right?

Obviously nothing she could say would deflect the professional calamity now descending upon her. At best she could hobble along on half pay, marshaling her arguments for the senate review. She would need a lawyer for that. The whole thing would grow and eat into her time. She could fight that battle with one hand, and with the other try to keep her NIH support going. Clearly, the dean would cut off UCI's customary twenty percent support.

Then she saw it. The dean wanted her to resign.

They all did. That was the simple, elegant way to avoid professional disgrace, rumors, the inevitable sensational treatment in the newspapers. The *Times* would take the high road and broadly hint, while the *Register* would run color photos of Sparkle.

All she had to do was resign. It would all go away. *Poof.*

By the time she saw this and knew that a part of her was tempted by the idea, she realized that she now stood alone in a deserted room, without a soul to see her cry.

5

KATHRYN

"Hey, didja feel that?"

Kathryn froze, one hand on a rack of nylon blouses. "Ummm—no."

"Maybe I'm just a tad hung over," Sheila said. The slim black woman pressed the back of her hand against her forehead and did her warbling southern accent imitation. "Or pahaps ah'm a-havin the vapors, Rhett."

The broad main room of Fashion Circus was crisp, calm, and fresh in the morning sunlight, and then she heard a small tinkling noise, and *this* time Kathryn felt something, a definite jolt that brought pops and creaks from the ceiling.

"Geez, should we—?" Sheila looked around with large eyes, saw that there was really noplace to seek shelter, and started for the front door.

"Stay away from that glass!" Kathryn called.

The shaking was no worse, not seeming to build up into something really strong, and she could not decide which way to go herself. *Is it getting rougher? No, calming down, slower. . . .* A part of her mind tried to put body English on the universe for a moment, as if hoping could stave off a repeat of yesterday's major quake. Then it definitely did ebb, and she let out a long sigh. She looked past Sheila at the street outside, where people stood still, glancing around, while traffic muttered on, oblivious. *A mild little reminder,* Kathryn reassured herself. *A nothing.*

But one man was not reacting to the fading trembles. He stood across the street looking directly at Fashion Circus—peering, Kathryn thought, directly at her. He was husky and seemed a bit out of place in a blue serge suit, like a banker going for lunch who had lost his way. But it was only eleven o'clock.

Sheila said, "Y'know, gal, I haven't been *that* scared since I was stuck in traffic and remembered that for breakfast I had three cups of coffee and two bran muffins."

"What about yesterday?"

"I was drivin' on the Santa Ana Freeway. Didn't feel a thing. Life's dangerous enough there—nobody notices li'l quakes."

Kathryn had been walking in the Mile Square Park. She had learned that earthquakes are a threat only to civilized man; we fear the fall of our own constructions. In the park, spindly eucalyptus had swayed with stately grace, and Kathryn had simply sat down until the shocks passed.

By the time she walked home, past a traffic jam generated by people who seemed to think there was someplace safer to go, the media blitz had started. The TV coverage showed the same collapsed freeway overpass and sprawling buildings over and over, as if hoping to see a survivor crawl out at any moment. None did. In all only fourteen people died, the same as a slow weekend's toll in traffic accidents.

There were tiny *tsunamis* in hot tubs, and a news spot about them. Platoons of shrinks appeared on the tube, talking about After-Shock Emotional Care, with workshops to be announced. Nobody recommended a magnum of cabernet sauvignon, Kathryn's favorite therapy. A ferret-eyed Freudian said the earthquake was primarily significant as an "internal event" and that it gave him a sense of "existential anger." Old friends called her from South Dakota, where the week before tornados had killed a dozen people, to ask "But aren't you *afraid*?" This morning on the way to Fashion Circus she saw a man wearing a T-shirt that said I SURVIVED THE EARTHQUAKE MEDIA COVERAGE. She had given him a thumbs-up and called, "Right!"

Kathryn said, "I hope that wasn't a bigger quake, just farther away than yesterday's."

Sheila shook her dreadlock curls adamantly. "You immigrants, you don't know the dance steps at *all.* That one was sharp, God slappin' the earth. The ones a long way off, they come in as rollers, waves. They've had time to spread out and ease into their rhythm by the time they get here, see?"

Kathryn puzzled this out. "So if it's a quick jolt, but not really powerful, that's good news."

"Ri-aight. We'll turn you into a native yet, girl."

The normal buzz returned to the street outside as people took up their lives, ignoring the sudden intimation of mortality. A couple came through the door, first customers of the day, and Kathryn went to help. The Fashion Circus was two blocks from what the legislature called California State University at Fullerton and what everyone else called

Cal State. The area was a litter of boutiques, small cafés, a photocopy shop, a dance studio over a Danish modern furniture store, and three trendy jeans outlets. They were two doors down from a fried chicken shop ("Chicken Parts! Buy the part you like best!") and across the street from a Victoria's Secret outlet, which led to what the manager termed a "diverse clientele." An example now came clumping through the big front door.

They were full-bore punk—black clothes, both sporting three-color mohawks that looked like lurid, frozen explosions. Each had what was obviously a carefully chosen assortment of earrings and safety pins in their ears. The woman wore dead-white Kabuki makeup with bright red eyelids.

Fear not the weird, Kathryn reminded herself, *they make life interesting.* These were true punks, not the young teenagers trying to look all of sixteen who betrayed their sullen, supercilious air with sudden giggles. The woman had a leathery look. To Kathryn's surprise, they proved to be polite and well-mannered. They wanted sheath shirts and Brazilian leather belts, which were in stock, and in black, too. The man called Kathryn "ma'am" and spoke precisely, both showing such diffidence that by the time they left, she felt like creeping out to buy herself a walker.

"Yeah, punks're like that," Sheila said when they had left. "Maybe since they look like the Four Horsemen of the Apocalypse on a bad day, they figure they should talk like *Leave It to Beaver.* Keep the straights off balance."

Kathryn had been working here only three weeks, but she already felt as though she had known Sheila all her life. The slim, quick-eyed woman was a blend of seemingly incompatible traits, from her meticulous vegetarian diet to her reflexive drinking of caffeine-heavy diet drinks, from her street savvy to her offhand knowledge of things like the Four Horsemen. If anybody had shaken Kathryn awake in the middle of the night, she would have guessed that the Four Horsemen were an old shoo-bop group, but in bright daylight she vaguely recalled that they were the classical image of bad news.

"Hey, whatcha think of these?" Sheila prompted, beginning their daily game.

They shared the conviction that customers' buying patterns were obvious the instant they stepped into the store. "Sorority girls," Kathryn gave her snap judgment. "And I use the word *girls* on purpose."

"Right. See the circle pin on the one in the red sweater? Cashmere, I can tell from here."

"They're going to stop at the lingerie counter, I'll bet you a dollar."

"No sale, Dr. Watson," Sheila said in her Sherlock Holmes imitation. "They betray far too obvious a predilection for the scuzzoid."

The two blondes were nearly identical in soft sweaters and pearl combs that held back waterfalls of obviously bleached hair. One had on jeans and the other culottes. "Slumming. Bargain-hunting for undies," Kathryn assessed.

"Tsk-tsk. De*cid*edly poor economics."

"How do?"

"Skimp on the lingerie, your boyfriend gets halfway home and he hits the bargain basement. Gives a gentleman a poor impression."

Kathryn nodded. "At just the moment you want his pulse rate to climb."

Both the girls picked up cheap, frilly white bras and looked around for help. "Betcha they never use any verbal lubrications," Sheila observed.

To Kathryn's raised eyebrow she answered, "Y'know, like 'please' and 'thank you.' We're spear carriers in their opera."

"Ah so." Kathryn tipped her hands together and made an Oriental bow of respect. "I shall check your theory, honorable one."

Sheila proved absolutely correct, and the two went on to a predictable pattern of collecting armloads of blouses and dresses, liking none of them, and leaving them in piles on the fitting-room floor.

"Hey, you'll pick up the signs once you've been in the business," Sheila said at their midmorning break, sipping a Diet Pepsi and eating stalks of broccoli.

"Ummm. I've done retail before, but it was usually upscale clientele."

"Ri-aight, ladies lookin' for some clothes that Make A Statement."

"We get all walks, don't we?"

"Near enough to Santa Ana to get some gang members. We pull in some matrons who're maybe down on their luck, husband laid off or could be facin' slim days after a divorce. Even see the occasional fast-lane trophy wife, comin' down from the Orange hills looking for something hubby'd get a laugh out of."

"Like those old bomber jackets with Pacific mission tags?"

"Exactly. Gotta be real if you want over a hundred bucks for them. The search for authenticity, I call it."

"Authenticity? But it's somebody else's jacket."

"You aren't perkin' this mornin', girl. Authenticity is a *commodity*, y'see. Like the hooker joke."

"Which one?"

"Dude asks for somethin' special, and she says, 'Sure, and sincerity will cost you ten extra.'"

When Kathryn smiled, Sheila said deadpan, "Hey, girl who told me that story said it was for real."

"Well, *my* sincerity costs more."

"And here I been giving it away."

"Spreading it thin, the way you tell it."

Sheila made a mock-indignant face with arched eyebrows and jutting jaw. "Just because I apply the principles of democracy to my social life?"

"I couldn't help but notice that your date schedule book is broken down into half hours."

"That's so I don't miss any soap operas in between assignations."

"Your life *is* a soap opera."

"Tsk-tsk, is that envy I hear? Anyway, you know full well that ladies like us, we may have lives that look like rerun soaps from the outside, but they have all the sweep and grandeur of *War and Peace* from the inside. And how *is* old Abe, or Arthur, or whatever his name is?"

"Alex. Now I know why you have that fat date book—you can't tell the players without a scorecard. He's fine."

"Stayin' cool?"

"That's what cryonicists do," Kathryn countered.

"You hear the one about why the chiller guys are so sad?"

Inwardly groaning, Kathryn looked quizzical.

"All their women are frigid," Sheila supplied, and Kathryn made the required face. But then Sheila said hesitantly, "Y'know, Kath, this stuff —I mean, it sounds just plain bizarro. Could it work?"

She had to shrug. "It's a gamble. A long shot."

Kathryn could see that Sheila had been thinking the matter over and was slow to come to terms with it. She had seen this often, a reluctance to ponder the darkness that surrounds each tiny life.

"You believe any of this after-death experience stuff?"

To Kathryn, such experiences were a last-ditch stand by the mind against the onrushing abyss. Perhaps the inner self held off insanity with this last invention, a hallucination of a bright light welcoming it into immortality. But she didn't *know* that, and no one ever would. So she said, "Could be. Me, I'd like some insurance."

Sheila paused in an uncharacteristic meditative moment. "I can see that. I bought my ticket, might as well see the whole show. So far I've had Birth, Childhood, and Hideous Adolescence. Coming up are Midlife, Plastic Surgery, Futile Regrets, then Death Or Whatever."

"Go for Whatever, I'd say."

"I've got time to fret. My problem isn't Dr. Death—it's bozo boyfriends."

"Say, want me to bring some stuff by about cryonics?" The instant Kathryn heard her own words, she knew that Sheila wasn't ready to think concretely about it. The standard problem: how to lightly talk about a heavy subject. But it was not really *her* problem, she reminded herself. She wasn't a convinced, signed-up cryonicist, after all.

"Thanks, but I'll just go home and relax and worry about my shrinking ovaries."

Predicting people's purchases from what they were wearing, Kathryn mused, was easier than guessing their reaction to cryonics. Sheila would mull it over, she knew, for a long time, never truly able to put the idea completely from her mind.

"Uh-oh." Kathryn looked out at the main display areas. "Looks like the noon rush is early."

An hour passed in a busy blur. There were college guys boisterously trying on unlikely hats and gaudy shirts—and finally leaving with goods that looked like what they already wore. Then a pair of what Kathryn thought of as Helgas, big and blond and shouting to each other across the store, excited by their discoveries. Asian tourists lusting after Hawaiian shirts. Japanese searching out 501 jeans with the coveted black "E" tags. Aged hippies, gray and long of tooth, seeking Indian cottons. A man who was nearly bald and had carefully combed the last few black strands across the dome of the head to make it look worse. He bought a Panama hat.

A rumble in her stomach announced a need for lunch, and Kathryn hurried to finish putting new filmy blouses on the racks. She slipped on her reading glasses to fill in the inventory form.

Fashion Circus was a fill-in job until she could get a position that used her bachelor's degree, but she reminded herself to do the best work she could here, anyway, as a matter of principle. Despite Sheila's slangy derision, Kathryn knew that the black girl felt the same way; pride in your work kept you steady and prepared for the next step. She was nearly through when a deep man's voice said, "Could you help me, ma'am?" and she turned to confront a wall of blue serge suit. She tucked her reading glasses away.

"Well—yes, what did you . . . ?" Her voice trailed off as she studied the mail-slot mouth that smiled with a strangely cold confidence. The man was broad and yet athletically light. Despite his white-on-white shirt and black tie with thin red stripes, which she had to admit worked quite well with the serge, he did not seem remotely like a banker.

"Say, you look better with your glasses off."

She suppressed the urge to reply, *You look better without my glasses on, too,* but said, "You were looking for . . . ?"

"Some ties," he answered, more businesslike now.

"We don't have very many. Our selection is a little depleted." She was still daunted by his bulk and by his outsize hands that hung from thick arms. She noticed that even hanging at his sides, his fingers curled back to touch his palms.

"Just something simple," he said, not taking his eyes from her face.

She had violated one of her own rules, playing down the stock even before showing it off. She put on a bright smile and spun the lone tie rack. "We have some good conservative knits. Are you looking for something close to what you have on?"

"No, something different. Something that will catch the eye of a woman who knows how to dress, like you." He smiled again, the edges of his mouth pulling up but somehow not changing the straight, tight draw of the center. His lips were full but bloodless, and his face seemed shiny and stretched taut over strong cheekbones. He was starkly, provocatively handsome.

"How about a deep red, maybe burgundy?" she said cheerily, offering several ties.

"Lemme see," the man said, his pronunciation roughening as he reached for the ties. His extended arm showed thick wrists and ropy muscles beneath the white shirt sleeve, a hint of concealed power. "Kinda nice." As soon as his attention focused on the ties, his diction suffered, she noted, a southwestern twang coming in.

"Will you be wearing them with a formal suit like this one?" she asked smoothly, the bright customer patter coming from years of part-time work to get herself through university.

"Maybe." He worried the ties around a little but hardly glanced at them. Instead he looked steadily at her.

She plucked three shades from the rack, turning away from the inquiring eyes. "Perhaps these will help you think about the differences."

He tossed the first ties onto a glass counter and laid the three across his arm. "Ummmm."

Kathryn knew when to withdraw from a customer and let the product itself do the selling. But this duck simply tossed the three aside as well and looked back at her expectantly.

"Maybe something in a green? That would go well with—"

"I need somethin' that will catch a lady's eye, y'know?"

"Well, a bright color will do that."

"Yeah, bright." But he didn't look at the tie rack.

"How about a brilliant red, then?"

He glanced down at the choices she offered and shook his head. "What I really need is a lady who'll show me how they work out with my clothes, y'see."

"Well, you could bring in the suit you have in mind—"

"No, I mean with a whole lot of my clothes."

"I—"

"See, I'm pretty particular about my stuff. I don't have a good eye for colors, though."

"There are several shades here that will go with just about any—"

"If you was to give me advice like that, I'd sure appreciate it." He turned toward the ties.

Kathryn found this a welcome relief from his penetrating dark gray eyes. She slipped her hands under several ties to make them stand out, while saying something automatic about color pairings, then saw that he was not truly following her proffered wares. Instead, he was focused beyond the counter, and as she followed his line of sight, she found herself staring straight into his eyes, reflected in a display mirror. He was studying her from a different angle while seeming to be following her routine discussion. A cold sensation swept across her skin.

He saw her answering stare in the mirror and turned toward her. "In fact, I really am kind of more interested in you than I am in the clothes. I can buy plenty of ties, but a fine woman like you is hard to find."

"Well, sir, I—"

"It's about noon now, and I figure you could stand some lunch. Let me take you out, just to get acquainted."

"I really cannot."

"Anyplace you want. I'm just tryin' to be friendly. Got a brand new car, we could shoot over to one of the fancy spots near Main Place."

For an instant she thought that a quiet hour in a pleasantly darkened, atmospheric restaurant, away from the bleached light of Fashion Circus, would be agreeable. He was ruggedly handsome, and his rough manner had a certain animalistic charm, she had to admit. Not that this guy could replace Alex, who had a musky maleness about him as well. Alex could be a touch unpolished, he promised a certain rugged zest in the more intimate contests, *and* he got his grammar right. But a woman was free to do a little window shopping in the Mating Mart, was she not?

As she hesitated, she saw him make a little grin, a preliminary hint of triumph, sure that she was going to agree. He stared hard at her. Where had she seen that?—and then she remembered the man on the street outside earlier, during the little tremor.

Had it been this one? Had he seen her before and come back now, just before lunch? He might have been that attracted by the angle of her jaw, her pert nose—but from across the street?

No, not enough to come back with timing perfect for a lunch invitation. *Something funny here.*

Women have a finer sense of hazard, and Kathryn's made the decision.

"No," she said decisively. "I really can't."

"Well now," he said, in what she had to admit was a classic aw-shucks ingratiating manner, "I'd sure appreciate it if you would."

"I can't. Thank you for your invitation."

"I'm new here in town. Maybe I could take you out to a proper dinner, then. What time you get off work?"

Uh-oh. The persistent types she was well versed in brushing off. Ever since a neighborhood boy had kept after her for weeks when she was fourteen, she had developed a set of hardline retorts for men who thought they could simply wear her down.

"I have a policy—no dating customers. Sorry."

"But, hey, I'm not a customer. Not yet, anyway." He spread his big hands with boyish innocence. "Haven't bought nothing."

"That is precisely what you *will* buy, sir," Kathryn said sternly. "And you can forget about talking to me when I get off work."

"Ah'm sorry you feel that way." He cocked his head to the side in studied puzzlement. "Real sorry."

"I have work. Excuse me."

As she turned away, a glint came into his eyes and his mouth returned to the mail-slot severity. "I have a feelin' you're gonna be sorry, too."

Something in the steely coldness of the words propelled her away from him, her high heels clicking rapidly on the tiles as she fled to the rear of the store. Sheila was in the clerks' tiny back room, already eating a brown-bag lunch beneath the time clock. She raised her slim eyebrows when she saw Kathryn's face.

"Hey, you have trouble out there?"

"Ummm." Kathryn was still trying to sort out her emotions. She had felt a real attraction to him, had very nearly accepted the lunch date, and then a powerful pulse of alarm and outright fear had run through her. Her intuition was odd that way—it seemed to lurch from one reaction to another. "It—it was ugly. Strange."

Sheila shrugged. "Don't get in fights with ugly strangers. They got nothing to lose." She told her a brushoff technique, one she had learned in high school: "Just give the guy your phone number, only when he dials it, he gets Acme Pest Control."

"Subtle girl," Kathryn said, her voice rickety.

She sat down on a fold-out chair, her knees suddenly wobbly. Her alarm signals were still clanging, but she did not know why. There was really no rational reason for her becoming so alarmed. After all, the guy had only asked her out to lunch. A car ride, some pasta—big deal, right, girl?

But her nerves were so jangly that day, she didn't end up eating lunch at all.

6
GEORGE

The dream had been worse that morning.

He had squirmed upward through cool water that tasted flat, metallic. Thrashing. Bubbles spurting from his aching chest. Through warmer layers, then a chilly, heavy wedge squeezed his ribs as his legs pumped wildly, driving into a sudden layer as warm and startling as freshly spilled blood.

Radiating down to him from the shimmering silver sky above, unreachably far, came long, slow waves of absolute malevolence. Something massive and malign waited there.

Then there were the voices shouting to him, the plastic faces that stretched and yawed and droned, trying to pull him into their world, their horrible blaring lights and cutting smells.

Then the white creatures with their twisted faces had jerked away, shouting, dissolving into the dawn glow.

Awake, his dreams were like the dried husks of cocoons, their moths flown away, or the split husks of seed pods. Dead shells at the edge of some primitive sea, empty, their slug life already crawling farther up a gritty beach.

He had ached from the dream this time, his joints rolling sluggishly in their bony beds, his throat like #4 sandpaper.

Luckily, even though he knew that his dreams were in some warped way the Master's Messages, he had been free of them for days. This new one was worse, though. Smeared plastic faces trying to pull him out of the metallic waters, into their blistering light.

He thanked the Lord that it was His day. The Sunday cathedral service had been a wonderful pageant—busloads of the faithful from all over Orange and L.A. counties, women in cream dresses with crinoline, and men in shiny dark suits showing hanger marks at the shoulders.

Sister Angel had sung alone, her voice clear as a sunrise. In her white robes she was the embodiment of spirituality. He loved the enveloping, motherly air of the cathedral and its flock. It reminded him of the dimly remembered times when his real father and mother had lived. It helped erase the cold years in foster homes. He had seized a chance to exchange veiled greetings with Reverend Montana. The Reverend's rousing sermon against both the corruption of government and the corruption of values represented by cryonics had fevered the crowd. Montana's TV assault on I^2 was swelling cathedral attendance, bringing more back to the simple truths of faith, when confronted with the horror science had wrought.

That brief contact had energized him anew to his appointed task. The congregation was excited, eyes bright, and he had talked for hours to others, staying for the buffet supper featuring roast beef, gaining conviction as he heard the righteous outrage in the voices of so many good people.

He felt the prickly fire in his belly, knew how to keep the embers banked and glowering red, ready to burst into righteous flame—but only when his cool, certain self gave the signal. Just as a man walked on two legs, each catching the fall of the other with every step, so did his dual nature work.

So after the day's services, George sat down to work. Once more he blessed the minister who had gotten a shambling orphan boy into a special Information Science course.

He set about doing a deep recon of Immortality Incorporated. No creeping about—he would save that for tonight. For the moment he was content to dive into the dense thickets of computer programs that told more about I^2 than any eye could see.

He had broken into their systems before, the night when he killed the hell-hound. That was nothing compared with the several days he had taken now to penetrate the shell around the I^2 computer files. He still reddened when he remembered his first outing.

He had entered the FINNet system, since he knew that electronic financial labyrinth well. Then he had made a routine payment to Immortality Incorporated, and from the receipt tag he got the corporate financial codes. A quick zig-zag through some directories yielded the I^2 telephone numbers, which carried data. So far, so good. But then a FINNet system manager had spotted his activity. On George's screen popped up

I HAVE BLOCKED ALL YOUR TRANSACTIONS PENDING
IDENTIFICATION.
SUBMIT PASSWORDS AND ID IMMEDIATELY!

He had been so frightened at this nearly instantaneous trouble that he turned off his computer and sat in shock for a full minute. Then he had realized that he had to go back into FINNet, under a legitimate purpose—because even an instant turnoff left his log-in signature behind.

This worked—he had erased his footprints.

Now, days later, he was ready to try again. He had researched the myriad gossamer pathways that webbed North America, searching for I^2 tendrils. Their weak spot was their system of medical bracelets. Each member had tied their bracelet code into the I^2 mainframe. That gave him a thread to follow.

He had gotten the idea from his background work on the woman he had attacked. It showed that she was at UC Irvine. To learn more and also to cover himself, he developed an indirect routing through the UCI mainframe, a big IBM.

This was the blanket he needed. UCI had numerous connections to communications satellites. So did I^2. They used the STARFIND satellite system to locate a medical bracelet instantaneously when it sent an alarm.

George typed, COPY SYS.MANAGER:MEDALARM{OVER-RIDE}.DAT[SUPP]. Side-slipping the security precautions took a few delicate moments. Finally, onto his screen leaped the background files on all medical alarm bracelet holders.

HAGERTY, SUSAN A., 22123 CASTLE ROCK ROAD, LAGUNA BEACH 92651.

The woman God had brought to him, who had treated the waitress, and who hid her chiller works behind the honorable shield of UCI. The Lord had pointed His finger at Susan Hagerty for him, as part of His unfolding plan.

Her UCI address followed, with BitNet code and information on doctors. There was even a list of the medical procedures Hagerty had set up for when she was in terminal condition.

Curiously, there was a footnoted entry:

TRAVIS, CANINE, ANCILLARY. SEE: 3282A.

Could that be the dog he had killed? He had to search further.

George had to be cautious now. This was big-time hacking here, on a playing field as broad as the planet. He had gotten this far by a variation on the Trojan horse gambit. By simply patrolling the waiting list for clients, he had found the name of a UCI user who generated a lot of simple-minded programs; that minimized the chances that his tinkering would be noticed. Then George simply logged into UCI using the user's access code, asking for help running a fresh program. This time the system manager readily helped—probably because he had done so for the real user many times before. So under the system manager's imprimatur George's program ran, free of the usual defensive checks. It swiftly awarded George privileges in the operating system. SYSOP OK, the screen assured him.

Now to work. The connections into I^2 led from UCI's bulky IBM through a twin-Cray array. He found there lightly protected internal I^2

files and broke in. The actual routines for locating bracelet holders were in a VAX machine located in Los Angeles.

George called up the VAX on his modem, using a parallel telephone line. He asked for the system manager's name, then departed. Typing swiftly, he set up an account in that same name in a lesser system. Then he entered the VAX system again, using a different NET connection. He tapped his fingers anxiously on the work table as he waited for the VAX to process his requests—and the screen said

ACCORDED SYSOP ACCESS. INFORMATION BEING
RETRIEVED.

Now he wore the system's own skin as a disguise. He made three typing mistakes in his eagerness to send in commands. First, the Hagerty woman.

To the VAX operating system he *was* Immortality Incorporated, asking for a routine position check on its client. Within two seconds the order flew to a distant satellite, which in turn transmitted a narrow frequency search wave, looking for Hagerty's bracelet. An answering *ping* came up from the coast of California. The satellite measured the bracelet's location to within ten yards, squirted the information to the VAX. There a program matched this data with a topographical map.

On George's screen appeared a grid and contour lines. Northern Laguna Beach, El Morro Bay. He wondered why she was there, when her home lay out in Laguna Canyon.

COWELL, ALEX M., 29850 SILVERADO CANYON, ORANGE
COUNTY

The tracer showed him to be at I^2 on Santiago Canyon Road. Or was he? George leaned close to his flat screen monitor and called up the general locator flag for I^2.

Cowell's telltale came from a few hundred yards back into the arroyo behind the buildings.

He frowned. This satellite grid was supposed to be more accurate than this. For a moment he considered how he might complain about this failure. *I'm illegally penetrating your files and want to gripe about the resolution.* Sure. If he was to use this effectively, though—

As he watched, Cowell's blip moved back toward the I^2 marker. So he *was* far back in the arroyo.

Did I^2 have another installation tucked back there?

Or more likely, maybe Cowell was just out for a walk.

Of course. That was where George had met the Hagerty woman and the devil dog. It had been no coincidence. Godly signs echoed down through his life, and here was another. He had escaped clean and free from the arroyo, and here a Sign pointed there again. He would meditate upon the significance.

George put that aside, lit up a Camel, and thought at last of the girl.

He had followed her two days ago from I² to Fashion Circus. He had made a move on her on impulse, and it had nearly worked. He liked the pursuit, the bursting joy of watching the prey up close, even though it was risky to let anyone see him. Something electric had swarmed in the air around her. He felt it the moment he had casually sauntered into the clothing store. It had seemed to radiate from her, like deep pulsing waves unheard but felt through the press of his sweaty skin.

Something had put her off at the last moment. He didn't know what it was, but that didn't matter so much as the simple fact that she had gotten a good hard look at him. And he didn't even know her name.

Not yet. But the I² background data files were excellent, including photo ID. He ran the entire directory, flashing digital photos on the screen at high speed to get through the hundreds of "clients." There—

SHEFFIELD, KATHRYN J., 37454 WOODFERN,

TUSTIN, 91707.

An employee entry. She was making chump change, he saw.

That did it for him. He had been willing to give her the benefit of the doubt, a young woman with a fresh smile, new to the cryonics blasphemy, probably involved with that Cowell guy, falsely led into it by him. George had been willing to allow for that.

But she worked there at I² a lot. He had seen her car there. With Cowell, probably wrapping long legs around him, her knees drawing up, the hair patch there dripping and smelling, spreading to receive his thrusts—

He caught himself, smothered the carnal fever. He would *not* let his jimmy-john rule him. Especially when he was doing the Lord's work. He stubbed out his Camel and let his pulse slow, getting the better of it, putting his cool and analytical self back in control.

She had turned him down for a lunch date, peering at him with those inspecting eyes that laughed. He was not sure what he would have done if she had gone with him, just as he was never sure which of his natures would manifest itself with women. Generally his cool outer shell was enough. It dealt with them well, kept them at a distance. But he had felt his inner self was pressing close to the skin in that clothing store, surging for release, and maybe she had sensed it, too.

She was of *them* and had rejected him with her mocking, tart tongue and so would have to bear the consequences.

He breathed deeply, studying the screen. Hundreds of I² members, all believing in the foul heresy. Which ones were essential? He could not strike at them all.

He entertained the idea of setting some bugs loose in their computing system. He remembered when he was a boy, and someone had sent the infamous Naked Ladies program into the Macintosh he used at school. It appeared innocently in your directory, and if you tapped it with your mouse, sure enough, it showed you naked ladies. He had done that and been hot-faced with embarrassment when he could not stop the flow of fleshy images while his classmates gathered around, the girls tittering, his rage building. And while the computer had showed him the disturbing pictures, it had systematically erased every program he had in the directory. Retribution. A lesson.

No, that was too simple, too obvious. He could slip in a Trojan horse, pillage their software without ever leaving this chair. But that would not stop the heresy.

Only action could stem this tide.

George came out of his mesmerized concentration slowly. The window was dimming with sunset. He lit up a Camel and let its pleasure seep into him. Soon it would be time to begin.

He spent a full hour under the truck. In the darkness at the edge of the I^2 parking lot, there was little chance that anyone would spot him, but the time ticking by heightened his nervousness.

His reading in the Garden Grove library, together with experiments on his own car, had promised that disabling the brakes would be easy. But the Ford flatbed had enormous brake drums and disc rotors, well sealed and rugged. He had to use most of his tool kit just to loosen them and get to the dual hydraulic system.

The vulnerable spot was in the brake fluid lines. He cut them, tying the plastic tubing off with clamps, and reconnected them into a single reservoir. This added plastic cylinder had a membrane that would hold the line pressure—but only for a while. When the membrane broke, it would drain both the front and rear hydraulics.

It took more time to adjust his depredations so that they would not be immediately obvious as soon as someone used the brakes. The many hours he had spent in auto shop in high school at last paid off.

He slipped away into the shadows, passing up the chance to damage the telephone wires or sabotage the equipment that stood by the rear loading dock. Minor stuff.

He needed to concentrate his energies. That meant research, care, endless dedication. Energy strummed and pulsed through him, seeking an exit, a use, a cause to match his roiling interior desires.

He would find work for this seethe within. Labors of the night.

Castle Rock Road snaked up from the humming traffic of Laguna Canyon. The Sunday-night exodus from the beaches ground along in the outbound lane, and George had to cut across them on a left turn to enter the oak-shaded drive. He parked at the base and walked up the steep street, studying the yellow windows tucked back among bushes, many betraying the frosted gray flicker of TV. He found Susan Hagerty's rambling frame home of Douglas fir sheltered under a stand of eucalyptus. The planking and beams were so weathered, they gleamed like silvery slabs in the moonlight.

He circled the house in the rough hillside terrain. A sudden loud bark from the back porch startled him, and he slipped back among some manzanita just in time to gain shelter from a gray shape that came rushing forward, yipping and snarling. It stopped at the thicket edge and barked angrily. George turned and crashed through plucking, stinging branches. He broke free and ran up the hillside, scrambling, clutching at rocks to keep his balance.

The dog below stopped at some invisible boundary and continued its woofs and howls. Neighborhood dogs set up a chorus of yaps and yelps. George finally stopped a hundred yards up the rough hillside and sprawled beside pampas grass, puffing. He had kept up his rigorous routine of weights and running, circling the Mile Square Park three times each day, and his heaving chest came more from fear than exertion.

As a boy he had always feared the big dogs that snarled and bit. But once he had conquered a small one, a thin Cocker spaniel, he knew then that God had given him dominion over all, just as God gave to Adam.

That had been a great flowering moment. He had then taken to nightly wanderings from his succession of foster homes, confronting and defeating the animals he met in fields and parks. Usually he needed no cleverness to bring them within arm's reach. There was never anything about it in the newspaper, though he constantly checked. No one ever saw a link among the sad little bloodstained patches, the wrecked carcasses left in wayside ditches.

But the blurred gray shape had surprised him just now, sending heart-stopping gasps through his chest, shooting sparks of the old hot fear. He lay on the hillside and burned with self-loathing. It took a long time to still his labored panting, to notice the warm stain on his blue jeans where he had wet himself.

Slowly the iron self returned, borne on a wedge of rage and disgust. Stupid, yes, *stupid* to not anticipate that she, who had made a dog of damnation, would not have a pet. This was the TRAVIS, CANINE entry he had seen and forgotten to track down. She intended to take that pet dog with her, have it frozen for companionship, in the icy citadel of the damned that she had been put on this earth to bring about.

Something about this discovery brought a steely coldness back into him. He stretched out on the hillside and faced the fears that etched at him. He squeezed his eyes tight and heard the scuttling things that peopled the dark, that chirped and rustled and squeaked at the edge of hearing, sounds that had filled him with hot terror as a boy—of scaly creeping lizards and things with ropy tails and slimy red-rimmed eyes. Presences prowled the air.

He withstood them and mastered himself. When at last he opened his eyes, he saw the skyshine brimming at the horizon toward Irvine, the collective illuminations of a million souls offered up like a glowing benediction to the infinite abyss above. He heard the strangely reassuring hiss and slur of weekend traffic on the canyon road below.

He sat through the night, letting it seep into him, thinking, planning. He clasped his hands in his lap, like a boy in church. A wad of beef jerky in his pocket provided some flicker of strength.

An orange flare rose above Saddleback Mountain, and to the west the dark retreated, leaving gray. The city lay snuggled against its hills, an artist about to wake up to the usual beautiful beginnings.

He lurched to his feet, rumpled and rough-chinned, feeling a queasy slosh as he crept carefully down. He let no stone slip away to announce his coming. Halfway down to Hagerty's home, he saw movement. He hid. Dr. Susan Hagerty pulled out of her ramshackle garage and coasted down Castle Rock Road, tires spitting gravel like bacon frying.

Just as well. He could get closer to the house if she were gone. Homes here were hidden up narrow driveways, but sound carried well. Not a good place for him to operate. He passed a Jehovah's Witness Kingdom Hall nestled into the foot of the big castlelike rock formation. The Jehovah's people were on the Lord's side, of course, but unable to see beyond their narrow doctrines, like so many. He could not count on them for help.

As he patiently edged toward the house a mockingbird trilled in the cool shadows. Hagerty's dog came trotting out to give him a suspicious look—a keeshond, looking smaller in the pale light, one of the Dutch dogs with peppery coat and glinting eyes. It went into a teeth-baring attack stance.

"Here, Travis," George called. "I'm just lookin' round."

Travis growled. He kept up his soothing patter, squatting in a relaxed way. Travis's throaty rumble slowly ebbed.

The dog shrewdly kept its distance for a full ten minutes before it sniffed at and then accepted the offered scrap of beef jerky.

It took ten more before the skittish creature allowed George to place a hand upon it. He gave it half an hour of crooning and petting, sitting among the pungent scents of eucalyptus as the morning dew evaporated. He rubbed the dog's belly, and Travis happily jiggled his legs in appreciation, tongue lolling.

More than once his hand strayed to the dog's throat, felt gently deep into the downy coat, found the cartilage there that he knew would crumble under one swift clench.

But he held back, fought the quicksilver desire. He needed this animal as a friend, not as another in the long trail of crushed, discarded lumps.

The dog by this time would run and fetch a tossed stick, even jump for it in the air. But it would not let him approach the old wooden house. Very well; he did not need to. What he did need, he had already gained here.

George walked away, past a neighbor's giant satellite dish that seemed like the discarded brassiere of a giantess. Among the aging cottages were some fancy gothic and French country constructions, giving the aroma of instant antiquity.

He felt a solidity of purpose settling into him in this pearly morning, a sensation of his gathering power, and of human lives as the inhalations and exhalations of God.

FOUR

NEW EVILS

He that will not apply new remedies must expect new evils, for time is the greatest innovator.

—Francis Bacon

1
ALEX

He slammed shut the tailgate of the truck and climbed in beside Ray Constantine. "First call, Multitech Labs," Alex read from his clipboard. "Big game hunt—an automated blood chemistry analyzer."

As Alex cranked up the engine, Ray asked, "Up for salvage? Think we'll get it?"

"It came in on SalNet last night. If we're quick, we might sweet-talk them."

Ray squinted at the clip board. "A 1992 model—still worth something."

"Not much."

"We're nonprofit, so if we show up first—"

"They squint at us and say, you do *what*?"

They laughed as Alex backed the truck out and nosed it onto Santiago Canyon Road. He headed south toward El Toro, among hills thick with chaparral. "I remember one time we showed up for an ultracentrifuge that a research lab had used on a navy contract. They had put it on the list of surplus gear available to nonprofit groups, but the clerk wouldn't even speak to us."

Ray leaned back and folded his lanky legs against the dashboard, wedging himself in securely in case the opportunity should arise for a doze. Slanted morning sunlight heightened the creases in his face and gave him a brooding air. "No surprise there. Once I had a woman go out and spray paint GRAVE ROBBERS on the truck while I was inside trying to get some freebie gear."

"Damn. Actually, that's not so bad as the fish-eyed ones who stare at you as if you were Zombie Nazis From Mars. I—"

The truck slewed sidewise, tires screeching. Ray sat up in alarm. Alex had swerved to avoid a motorcyclist who had come out of nowhere from behind them, passing, zooming back across the divider with only inches to spare just before an oncoming car arrived. The biker was a heavy woman in a leather jacket, no helmet. With an insolent blatt, she roared off down the highway.

"What's she trying to do, surf on the waves of traffic?" Alex was aghast. "Geez, people get crazier all the time."

"The county's nearly packed to the rafters," Ray said meditatively, watching the motorcycle race away, blond hair streaming like a flamboyant farewell affront. "So to get a taste of freedom, they hit the last few open roads and jazz their wheels awhile."

Alex let out a long breath. Sudden, lancing danger brought its delayed thumping increase in pulse rate, the prickly surge of adrenaline. He mentally cursed the woman who had so cavalierly brought them all so close to a nasty accident. He remembered all too clearly that limitless, zesty bravado. Everyone knew that bravura zest when young, and most survived it.

The thought brought forth a dusty recollection in a tingling flash. It had been a similar cool morning, one almost swanky in its richness of sun and scented air. He had been driving to a part-time TV repair job, one that had met the bills until he figured out what he was really going to do with his life. He had just broken up with his wife, and some bile had pooled in his mind, souring the comics in the *L.A. Times* for him, including even *Calvin and Hobbes,* his favorite. In a vexed, caffeine-saturated, lip-chewing mood he had sped toward a traffic signal near a high school. He saw a student in jeans and T-shirt quite deliberately slouching across, against the light, aiming a haughty, buck-toothed grin at him. As Alex had neared the hatch-marked pedestrian crosswalk, the boy had slowed his disdainful stroll even more—and then with languid grace, given him the finger. Without thinking Alex had sent his Volvo angling sideways. He had picked up the kid on the right fender, a kiss of the chrome, a brush with the paint just enough to send him sprawling.

It had been an instant gut reaction, no mind between the impulse and the act. The kid spun off in a wild, arms-flailing whirl of bug-eyed alarm, reeling away, tripping on the curb, crashing into a hedge, banging down for an inglorious landing on his ample butt.

Alex had stopped. The kid jumped up and began cursing him, quickly joined by several of his friends. The kid's nonstop swearing assured Alex that there was no injury except to the vocabulary, which had already started to repeat. He suddenly realized that what he had done was probably a felony and jumped back into his Volvo.

Speeding away, Alex had felt quick remorse and, to his surprise, deep anger—an instant rage that the kid had been so *oblivious,* so cocky. Paradoxically, mixed in with the shame that came later, he had felt a tart pleasure in reminding the kid, in yanking him back into the real world where the Dark Trickster always waited, infinitely patient.

The seemingly solid world was fragile and could be shattered by a moment's idle carelessness.

Alex shook himself and stabbed at the radio button. A bright, completely phony woman's voice bloomed over the speakers, chatting approvingly of the latest way to save precious water—pee during your shower. "You save a whole flush—five gallons!" the perky woman gushed. "Whatcha think of this new idea from the Water Control Board, folks? Call in your opinion right now to station KFGH—"

Alex snapped the radio into silence and realized that the motorcyclist had released some free-floating anxiety in him. Something was not right, but he could not pick up the elusive blip at the edge of his screen. As he thought of that image, Ray's conversation intruded into his self-absorption, and he realized the man had been talking for some time about the I² computer systems.

"Thing is," Ray continued, "we can't tell if it's a glitch or a sniffer."

"Uh—why do you think it's a sniffer?" Questions were the best way to cover your inattention.

"Because it's moving around. One time it fuzzes up our personnel records, then it's in the MedAlarm, next day we're getting error statements from our longtime archives, for chrissake." Ray had given up hope of a doze and now produced a toothpick, sticking it at a frustrated angle between his teeth.

"Does it do damage?"

"A few times, yes. But mostly it's just there, reading files or something, then gone. Our protection picks up little whispers from it, then it leaves."

"A moving glitch?" Alex knew just enough computer lingo to skate through.

"Could be. Some systems ghost, dancing on the data."

"How about vandalism?" He turned onto Lake Forest, a boulevard with no visible lake or forest.

"It could do a whole lot more, scrub whole directories, if it wanted."

"Sounds like the opening for a creep feature to me." Ray squinted at him skeptically and Alex went on imitating the hard-sell voice of a TV producer: "See, first the tortured beings floating in the liquid nitrogen try to make contact through the computer, pushing defenseless electrons around. Got it? Then the frozen souls appear as ghosts, only real icy ones, so they freeze *solid* anybody they touch. Then—"

"Awwww, that's so bad, it just might get made," Ray admitted.

They slowed to find the MultiTech Labs address and passed a crowd of scruffy Latinos bunched at an intersection. This was one of the city-approved pickup points for day workers, mostly illegals. Lined, dusky faces with hooded eyes, a patient endurance. Worldwide economic integration had leveled workers. Symbol-manipulators were doing well, and in-person service industries held their own. But the unskilled of all nations now earned pretty much the same meager minimum. And all varieties seemed to end up here.

In L.A. the cultural conflicts were east-west; in Orange County, to be different, they were north-south. Money, influence, the sheen of the new —all gravitated southward, bumping against rock-ribbed San Clemente. The upper tier of engineers and managers peered over the collective heads of the immigrants and minimum-wage replaceables. Alex said, "Y'know, to those guys, what we're doing is absurd."

Ray studied their faces. "Trying to hold on, never knowing whether you'll work the next day or go hungry, sending money back to Mexico for people who're even worse off—" He chuckled ruefully. "And here we are, helping people try for a second life a century down the road. Seems unreal sometimes."

Alex liked Ray's crooked grin, his western accent that had no sharpness and sometimes reflectively softened into a drawl. Ray faced the world square and still retained the incredible, head-spinning optimism any cryonicist needed. As vice-president of I^2 he could summon up a tough shell when the occasion demanded it, as they soon found.

The clerk at the loading dock of MultiTech sneered when he heard the name Immortality Incorporated. "You guys think I'm going to hand over this expensive piece"—he gestured toward a big pine-frame crate— "to the likes of *you*?"

"I don't see as how you got any choice," Ray drawled.

"Well, I'm foreman here, and I'm to tell you I got plenty of choice," the man said, shifting around to display his broad shoulders face on, in what appeared to be a show of bluster. The effect failed because a lot of his chest had slumped into his belly, held in by his huge American Eagle belt buckle.

Alex had considered running a tough-cop-versus-sweet-cop routine on this guy, but that didn't look promising. The shrewd mouth and veiled eyes suggested a motivation beyond simple dislike of cryonics. Without saying another word, Alex turned and walked through the MultiTech dock and staging area, ignoring the "Hey, you can't—" from behind.

Ray was with him as they tracked down the divisional super and explained matters. Economically, I^2 was a bottom feeder. A rain of half-used gear filtered down through the twilight of a technological society, settling onto the shelves of salvage sheds.

"We usually ask maybe a penny on the dollar for this stuff," the super said skeptically.

Alex held out his clipboard. "Here's your Receipt for Beneficial Donation, all filled out and signed."

"Well . . . I dunno. A broker I know said he might be able to place this blood analyzer someplace."

"Your tax writeoff will beat his price," Ray said.

"Well . . . if that's so, how come the foreman didn't just sign off on it?"

Alex gave the super his best innocent smile. "I think he gets a kickback from your broker."

The super didn't know how to take that, but he signed anyway. He even accompanied them back to the dock and waved the foreman off. Alex gave the foreman an ironic, exaggerated salute after they forklifted the crate onto the truck bed.

They had a long drive next, up the 405 to the town of Fountain Valley, which was flat and dry and not in a valley. They saw some good personalized license plates, including EARXPRT, N2WORRY, LOV U LA, PAR T, the inviting PHYS MS, CUTE4NR, and MSMARVL, and the perhaps insulting FORK U. He wondered if ILL GAL was sick or just from Illinois.

Reality chose that moment to blind-side him. He glanced leftward and saw his ex-wife buzzing by on his left, a silvery Japanese sedan zipping along in the fast lane. He gulped, chest knocking as though somebody had jump-started his heart.

Just a glimpse, but he was sure. The wasted years came flooding in again, salt-sour in his mouth. He peered after the dwindling car. This was yet one more facet of divorce he had not anticipated—the way a mere moment could yank you back through time and pain. Somebody had said that marriage was like a long meal, with the dessert first. His had opened with a short sweetness, sure, but then stopped halfway through the salad, and the vinegar was still on his lips, ready to sting.

After a moment he realized a second shock. His ex looked a lot like Kathryn. Now, what the hell did *that* mean?

He forced his attention back on traffic and saw a plate stating GOD IS. It prompted him to wonder aloud, "Is what? Dead? Even if God just plain ol' *is,* what are we supposed to do about it?" The chunky man driving the Chevy looked like the type who never entertained such questions. Not that the seven spaces available on a plate left much room for philosophical niceties.

Ray said reflectively, "I'd be happy just to understand that bumper sticker up ahead."

Alex saw one of the HONK IF YOU LOVE JESUS stickers on a Toyota in front. "With all our digitized this and computer that, you'd think we'd do better at communicating."

Ray chuckled and managed to fall asleep just as Alex followed LZY LAY off the 405 and onto Beach Boulevard, a street name that delivered on its promise. He went east, though, and found Modern Supply. Medical warehouses had to discard sterile supplies that ran past their use dates but that were still perfectly useful on people whom medical science had abandoned to the tender attentions of the worms. Modern Supply let them cart off packages of compresses, pads, and special tape. Alex liked the work of hauling, simple labor that popped major calories.

Their third target was a waste of time; somebody had gotten to the small contract research lab first and made off with a surplus blood pump. Heading back to I², he took a shortcut out through Lemon Heights and over Loma Ridge, beating the noontime traffic. He had to work the stick shift on the upgrades. He and Ray rode in a comfortable silence that still communicated between them, something he had read about in old married couples but that grew between men who had become friends by shared work they believed in. Ray was telling a new chiller joke as they came down the long slope of the highway and headed east with Rattlesnake Park a froth of green in the distance, and Alex never did get to hear the punchline because as their speed climbed above sixty, he eased down on the brake and it wasn't there.

The pedal mashed down smoothly to the floorboards, and nothing happened. Their tires howled on the curve. Alex shouted to Ray and grabbed the emergency brake. It came up, held firm—then snapped with a loud *spang.* "Damn!" Alex pulled at the brake lever frantically, but it was utterly dead.

"*All* the brakes gone?" Ray said disbelievingly.

"Here—" Alex tried downshifting, but they were going too fast by now and he couldn't get it out of neutral. "Damn!"

"Weave, gotta weave," Ray said.

Alex sent them rocketing back and forth across the two lanes available. This lost some kinetic energy and gained time, but at the price of slamming them back and forth in the cab. He tried to think. "Damn! Damn!" was all he managed to say.

Ray shouted, "Look for a turnoff."

A scenic vista or just a fire road would give them a chance to slow down. There were none. As they picked up more speed going down the long slope, the valley floor beyond spread as if to welcome them.

Alex wrenched the truck across the solid yellow center line, using road friction to steal a little velocity. Oncoming cars honked, startled and angry faces going by in a blur, and he remembered the foolhardy motorcycle rider. A warm wind whipped through the cab.

"Chapman Avenue—it's at the bottom of this hill," Alex said. "We'll shoot right through the intersection."

"Never make it," Ray said, his eyes jerking in a drawn face. He leaned out the window to look around the long curve of the highway. Alex fought the wheel. They were going fifty-eight.

Ray leaned back in. "Chapman's coming up. No help that I can see."

Time slowing, thinking hard. "We've got to ditch."

Ray's voice was thin, fear-filled. "Where?"

"Away from the edge."

"Okay." Ray gazed grimly at Alex. "You pick the spot."

Alex pumped the brakes. Nothing.

Ray quickly checked Alex's safety harness, then his own. For the space of a heartbeat Alex swore at himself for not getting air bags retrofitted into the truck. I^2 had decided they couldn't afford it.

Ahead the highway grade lessened for about a hundred-yard span. After that it steepened rapidly, running down in a deep cleft. The road seemed to sink into a groove carved in the beds of sandstone. At the base lay the big, busy crossroads.

Alex imagined the Chapman intersection and knew that they would be doing over seventy by the time they got there. It was tempting to hang on, hope for a break, but he felt with leaden certainty in the pit of his stomach that there would be none.

"Hold on," he said. "Hard."

They were already at the easier grade. His calculating time was over. They had left all traffic behind.

He slewed the truck across the highway and got a look downslope. Nobody coming. He swung them back into their lanes, tires screaming, and he thought of the damned air bags and remembered from his old physics class *velocity in a gravitational field varies as the square root of the distance descended,* and the right tires hit the gravel with an angry clatter.

He lost control for a split instant and the wheel jerked away like a living thing. They veered close to the edge. The right fender banged into the safety railing. Metal screeched. The tan valley looked as though it were directly below them.

They shot along the safety railing, striking a shrieking sheet of yellow sparks into the air. That helped him get the wheel under control. At least he had the power steering to help.

He swept them back across the highway again. They shot over and struck the gravel. Tires splattering rocks into the undercarriage sounded like the *brrrrttt* of a machine gun.

They went into a skid and struck the dirt berm. A brown shower erupted along their left side. Momentum slammed him into his safety harness. The wheel fought him. Noise exploded around him. Dust swarmed into his nostrils. He choked. Pebbles smacked the windshield. He could hardly see, but he wrenched the wheel to the right.

The truck wrestled free of the hillside, steel protesting, and shot across the highway. He could still see the sleeping sunny valley beyond and knew he could not stop the truck from going over.

The right tires left the highway again and clattered into the gravel. They ripped across it. As he stared out the side window, a wall of rock reared up. Sandstone.

They had reached the cleft. The road was now a gouged-out path with no choices left in it.

Better rock than air. It's a long way down.

The right tires blew, *pop! pop!*

They scraped along the rock face. Grillwork and shards of twisted metal sprayed back onto the windshield, peppered the hood. Alex grunted with the effort of pulling the wheel back toward the center again.

With what seemed to be majestic slowness, a big chunk came out of nowhere and starred the windshield. At the center of the spider-web pattern he saw a smashed plate of glass pop out and hit Ray's knee. Through this hole gravel spattered. A pebble stung his cheek.

They rebounded from the sandstone wall. Spinning now, out of control. Axles screeching on the asphalt.

The world slipped sideways and whirled about, and here came the other side of the highway, more rock to slam against.

Alex stared at its approach almost abstractly. He still vainly leaned into the steering wheel, which failed to respond. Pieces of the truck flew away from them, as if abandoning ship. Bangs and clatters frayed the air. There was all the time in the world to blink just once.

They struck the rock solidly. The windshield exploded. When Alex opened his eyes again—hands at his sides, now just a passenger—he saw that his vague plan had actually made them ricochet between the stone walls. Robbing them of energy. But at a cost in pain. Ray was slumped over in his safety harness. Blood ran down from his scalp and neck.

They clanged and rasped their way down another few hundred yards of highway, confined by the rock that at each fresh collision shredded steel away from them like a giant petulant child tearing the packaging from a Christmas gift.

All this was to Alex quite abstruse and distant, events played out in hollow air. He was concentrating on his left shoulder, which hurt rather badly.

And . . . was that the oily smell of something burning?

2

KATHRYN

The annual Immortality Incorporated turkey party was always held at the spacious Craftsman-style home of Boyd Zeeman, which crowned a tawny hill with angular slabs of wood and glass.

Compared with the coastal cities, a home at the eastern edge of Orange County typically had twice the lot size and square footage for half the price. Throughout a century's tides of go-go real estate, this simple rule had held. It was as deep an article of faith as the county possessed.

Boyd was the only I² member who could conceivably host the throng. By tradition, the mob began arriving at dusk and soon spilled out onto the ample lawn.

Kathryn pulled Alex's Volvo into the long swooping driveway and stopped at the top of the arc, beside a splashing fountain. "Boyd recycles his water onto his lawn," Alex said, peering rather glassily at the stand of jacaranda trees that lined the walkway up to the house.

"You sure you're up to this?" Kathryn asked.

His mouth stiffened. "Sure. Good to get out. Flap the wings."

He lifted his left arm a few inches, all that the white sling allowed, and imitated a wounded chicken trying to fly. His left shoulder had broken in two places in the accident. The orthopedist had kept Alex on the table three hours rebuilding the socket with steel pins and doing rotator cuff repairs. After a week at home Alex was going buggy, he said, and needed a party.

"Let me know if you start enjoying yourself too much," she said, helping him out of the passenger seat.

"I'm off the pain-killers," he said, starting up the walkway. "Think I'll try some other anesthetic."

He strode ahead, attacking the slope like a test on this first outing. His off-white shirt looked a bit baggy from the weight the operation had taken off. The tan slacks still fit nicely, she noted, particularly in the most important area, the rear. She had never liked pleated trousers on her men and so had been happy to note that Alex favored slim hopsack cottons with a slight bell-bottom flare. They were coming back into fashion, but she suspected his were holdovers from the last cycle of lean-jean popularity, at least a decade back. So he was thrifty; no character flaw there. But the Indian leather belt—the kind of thick, byzantinely worked thing bought in an airport gift shop when your flight had been delayed yet again, and then unaccountably never given up—that had to go.

"So you can have a glass of wine," she said, catching up. He was puffing slightly from the little climb. "One."

"I am captain of my own chemistry," he said sardonically.

"Ummm! You're getting downright surly, sitting at home."

"Daytime TV. It clouds the mind."

They passed through the broad double doors and into Boyd Zeeman's expansive arms. He was a big man, gruff and barrel-chested and wearing a western tie with a turquoise clasp that exactly matched his eyes—accidentally, Kathryn deduced, since his pink shirt and twill trousers clashed.

Boyd swept them up with an ample air, bombarding Alex with questions about his accident and giving Kathryn a conspiratorial wink that said, *Let's look after him together.* As unpaid president of I² he somehow made the job seem like managing a football team.

He steered them to a couch like a scalloped-out flower, saying, "Rest here and the whole damned party will pass by, shake your paw. Too bad you don't have a cast to sign."

"I'd just as soon not, thanks," Alex said. "As it is, I'll be in this rig for weeks."

"How's Ray?" Boyd asked.

"He'll be here," Kathryn said. "In a wheelchair, though."

"His leg'll be okay?"

"So they say," Alex said. "I had to wrench it some to get him out of the cab."

"You didn't have much choice."

Alex shrugged. "The gas had started burning. Anyway, Ray says he's all right otherwise."

Boyd nodded reflectively. "Damn lucky, you ask me. Those highway patrol guys report yet?"

Alex and Kathryn accepted glasses of chardonnay from Boyd's wife, Evelyn, who exchanged quick greetings and flitted away into the crowd, the busy hostess. Alex sampled it and murmured approval. "They just filed. The brakes were so smashed up, they had trouble. The way I ping-ponged us off that rock, the front end took a beating. The brake fluid lines got all burned away. Looks like routine failure."

"Can these experts explain why the emergency brake failed?"

Alex shrugged again. To Kathryn, this feigned indifference verged on macho posturing, but he had a vulnerable quality in his face that belied that.

"It came loose some way," he said. "The insurance guys are listing it as an accident."

"Think it was?" Boyd asked, mouth skeptically skewed.

"Dunno." Alex started to shrug and winced, rubbing his shoulder. "Damned funny accident."

Boyd said, "Maybe I'm just suspicious, but . . ."

Kathryn shook her head in disbelief. "You honestly believe people hate you that much?"

Boyd grimaced, gazing moodily off into space. "I've had relatives slug me, protesters splash blood on me, strangers sling garbage, neighbors throw me out of their parties."

Kathryn spotted Susan Hagerty and exchanged light conversation, but Susan was quiet, probably depressed by the harassment she had suffered at UCI. Women bonded with blab, and men through sharing work or sports, but Kathryn felt a certain connection with Susan based on their link through I². They strolled through Boyd's home, which sported great walls of worked granite, well-oiled cedar planking, and huge oval windows looking down on the sprawl east of Anaheim Hills. Gazing out over the city, Kathryn reminded herself that the night inverts things: swaths of light brim with activity but are concrete playgrounds; the dark patches—fewer every year—are in fact alive, the realm of plant and animal. Man's works look best in the night.

She stepped onto the vast, wraparound patio and caught the dry valley breeze, fresh and smelling of reasons to live. The I² crowd was as varied as any she had seen in a state noted for the offhanded bizarre. Most people, when they first heard of cryonics, assumed that the members were palsied, scared old folks grasping at a last chance. But the house was packed with people in their thirties and forties though, many bouncing to pop music or diving into the kidney-shaped pool. These were the on-call laborers who made I² work: suspension team members, willing doers of scut-work, seldom seen at the facility but vital.

There were a lot of intelligent-looking men; somehow, cryonics appealed less to women. Ladies seemed to feel it was unnatural—and of course it was, just like the smallpox vaccine and indoor plumbing, two other activities that had lengthened the human lifespan.

Sic transit, Gloria, Kathryn thought, strolling in a bemused state back into the house. After a leisurely talk, skirting around major stuff, Susan left early. Kathryn wandered again. Most talk was about the perpetual legal battles I² had to fight in the courts, against the mortuary lobby or the local coroner. Two or three of these conversations were quite enough.

Many here were computer specialists. It was easy for them to see their personalities, their identities, as software programs running in the hardware of their brains and bodies. Since their software selves would be trapped in the fast-decaying body-hardware when they died, what was more natural than freezing the hardware to save the self?

This dispassionate way of viewing themselves—*dem ol' mind-body duality blues,* she reflected—was probably why men took to cryonics better. Women were more tied to their times, their friends and family. The idea of being ripped out of their social network and awakening into a distant future, all alone—that was nearly intolerable. They'd literally rather die. Even though, of course, the first time they had come into this world, they hadn't known anybody either. . . .

"Kath babe!"

Sheila had just pulled up into the driveway in a car that looked like a traveling scrap heap. Kathryn was glad to be tugged out of her meditative mood; she walked down to greet her. Sheila's Ford bore the undoctored wounds of at least three separate collisions and sported a bumper sticker GEEZ, IF YOU LOVE, HONK US.

"Your friends may be crazy, but they got the bucks," Sheila approved as they went into the house.

"You were whining so much about your boyfriend, I thought this would broaden your horizons."

"That's boyfriends, plural. Never know when you'll need a spare."

"Not very romantic."

"Ro*man*tic?" Sheila snagged a glass from a passing drink tray and arched her purple-tinged eyebrows in comic alarm. "Romantic love sounds to me like clinical depression. Self-inflicted delusion."

"Well, this party will give you a whole new hunting ground."

"Ummm." Sheila looked around. "I've got house pets better dressed than some of these guys."

"They're techies. Not of our tribe."

"The Folk of the Freezer?"

"Okay, so they're not wearing spandex."

Sheila grinned. "Even better, they're not insecure surburbanite guys in logger boots or navy pea jackets or army field gear or beatup cowboy boots or A2 leather flight getups."

"There are more important things in the world than clothes."

"Name two. Without bringing sex into it, I mean."

"No deal. Anyway, clothes and sex are the same thing. Say, try these mushroom caps." An appetizer tray drifting past perfumed the air with luscious advertisement.

"No thanks," Sheila said grimly.

"Still on a diet?"

"Sure. This one lets you have anything you want, but you have to eat meals only with naked fat people."

"You're starting to look like a concentration camp victim."

"My goal is to not pay the IRS any taxes because I'll be so thin they can't see me."

"You always had a practical side."

"Hey, can I—?" Sheila waved an unlit cigarette. "I've gotta have one, even if these white-wine drinkers disembowel me for it."

"Come on outside. They might."

"Be worth it."

The smokers were outside and, in an added show of civility, on the downwind side of the rambling house. Cryonicists divided sharply between the health nuts and the technophiles. The nuts were veined by exercise, flensed of fat, encased in sleek ivory-white skin and scrupulously short hair, like monks. Some had abdominal walls ridged with sharp rows of muscle and wore running shoes, marathoners mentally ready even on a night out. They munched their raw broccoli appetizers and spilled their words out with bright, lively smiles.

"On the other hand, these are the technos," she said to Sheila, doing an imitation of a museum-guide voice. "They sport pot bellies and deep suntans and visibly enjoy their cigarettes."

"God's people, except for the bellies."

"They figure they'll get all their damage fixed up when they're revived a century or two down the timestream."

"I notice I'm the only black here," Sheila said. "Future going to be all white?"

Kathryn smiled. "By the time science can repair the damage from freezing, girl, they'll be able to change skin color."

"Wowee. I dreamed 'bout that since I was just a little thing."

"About being white?"

"No, blue. Gotta be a guy somewhere with a fetish for that."

"Yeah, but he'd probably want you to have twelve toes or something."

"Zat, mah dear, can be arranged." A flutter of eyelashes. "Still, y'know, for such a wild idea as this freezing angle, I thought this would be a pretty swift crowd. Not exactly the Prep H set, but *some*thing."

When Kathryn didn't get the reference Sheila looked aghast. "Where you been? Preparation H is the item most often shoplifted in drugstores. At first folks thought it was because people with the problem it was meant for, well, they were just too embarrassed to face a clerk and buy it. Turns out the nose candy crowd was liftin' it."

When Kathryn still looked puzzled, Sheila said, "Cocaine addicts glom it, see? Stuff some up their noses. It soothes and shrinks all those membranes they been abusing."

Kathryn felt the familiar Out Of It sensation that Sheila often induced. Looking for Alex, they wandered into a room dominated by a huge flat screen prickly with random colors. She watched a thin, intense woman wearing a button saying CRYONICS IS COMING BACK flick through channels. The screen jumped among cable stations.

"Digitized bread and circuses," Sheila said with disgust. The screen showed a cathedral interior lit by splintering crystal light. A congregation swayed and sang. They formed concentric circles, and at the center was a lone man.

"Hold there!" Kathryn called. "That's Montana."

"Ah," Sheila said, "guess I'll never get to heaven. He's not my type."

An organ pealed out long notes, and the congregation in the huge hall turned, feet slamming the floor. Slow, solemn, in lines, but not a snake dance. Spin. Stamp. Whirl. Sing.

The camera played across the upturned, rapt faces. Sweaty, glistening, eyes unfocused, singing.

> Running Lord, leaping, soaring,
> Brimming, loving, flying, joying,
> Yes Lord now and yes forever
> Joyful singing love together.

"Yes, but can you *dance* to it?" Alex said behind her.

"Want to try?"

"For folksy, I prefer the Virginia reel."

Kathryn introduced Sheila, who gave Alex a frankly appraising eye. "Yum. I approve."

Alex grinned. "Suggestions for improvements in our service are always gratefully received."

"I was looking for something in blue."

Alex didn't understand why Kathryn chuckled, but before she could explain, Reverend Montana started his sermon. Alex said seriously, "This Montana guy has got some of the old-line Protestants on the run around here. They've got something for everybody. Redemption of your ancestors, like the Mormons. Evangelism with spin."

"*And* weird dancing," Sheila added. "But if you look on Channel Sixty-two you'll find Brother Jim preaching against Montana. Same as Sister Elaine on Channel Eighty-five."

Kathryn blinked. "You're up on this?"

"Just 'cause I'm a hip black girl with an attitude don't mean I don't believe."

"Uh, I see," Kathryn said. She had a faith in the sense that the church she did not attend was Catholic.

"The All Evangelical Conference condemned Montana's group last year, y'know. He's a fringe type. He surely doesn't speak for folks like me. I'm a Baptist."

Alex seemed as surprised as Kathryn. "Well, what do people of your faith think about us?"

Sheila sat back in a web chair. Her words came more slowly, and Kathryn sensed a quick intelligence that usually masked itself with fast patter. "You got to be middle-class white to even consider it, seems to me. You guys aren't worried about using up money that could be helping other people, or taking up room from the next generation. The old ought to get outa the way of the young, I'd say."

Kathryn nodded. "It *is* their money they're spending, though. If they used it to build big mausoleums, nobody would gripe."

"God might. You're getting in the way of natural processes."

"So does a heart transplant," Alex said, a stock answer.

"And a lot of folks like me think we shouldn't be spending big bucks on those transplants when children go hungry."

"Nobody asks society to pay for cryonics," Kathryn persisted.

"Oh yeah?" Sheila smiled sardonically. "You never talk about who's gonna pay to defrost you, do you? Suppose you chillers stack up like cordwood. There's *plenty* of you. Hundred years from now, who pays to do the Lazarus number?"

Alex pursed his lips and said nothing. Kathryn said uncertainly, "The economics of the present are taken care of. The future—well, they'll have to decide."

"You don't sound so sure about that," Sheila said.

"Well, I'm not really a cryonicist," Kathryn reminded her. *Why do I feel this impulse to defend them, then? Or am I defending Alex?*

Sheila said, "They'll need some reason to foot the bill. Think they'll warm you guys up just 'cause you got wonderful personalities?"

"Who can guess?" Alex said. "Wouldn't *you* like to talk to somebody from the past?"

"Abraham Lincoln, sure. Joe Frump, nope." Sheila grinned. "Maybe Malcolm X, yeah."

"Maybe they'll need me for fashion tips up there in the future," Kathryn said.

"Right on—a future with everybody wearing plaids and stripes together. They rush over, pop you guys out, put you in charge of the Good Taste Police."

"Well," Alex said seriously, "I think you have to have—"

"Faith," Sheila supplied. "That's why you guys and us Baptists, we're alike."

"You're not serious!" Alex protested.

"You have to believe somebody's going to develop the technology to defrost you—and then will pay the bills! Hey, at least *my* faith depends on somebody more reliable than people—good ol' God."

Kathryn laughed. "She's got you there."

Alex seemed stunned. "I never thought of cryonics as a matter of faith."

"Now, I don't mean it's *that* kind of faith." Sheila pointed at the big screen.

Montana's face beamed forth, ten times natural size. He began to speak about hellfire.

"—and the opposite sin, the greater. *Coldfire,* I say unto you. *Coldfire.* The unholy clinging to the body—to the worn-out carcass—when we should be rising to the Lord. Hellfire, my friends, for the sinner. Coldfire, my friends, for the special sin of *arrogance.*"

"Y'know, he'd be funny if he weren't so scary," Kathryn said.

"Man looks like he could use a little shakin' up," Sheila said.

"He's been attacking I^2 daily on this show of his," Kathryn said. "He really *believes* that stuff."

Sheila said, "That man needs a good laugh."

Alex scrutinized the screen. "Good idea. I'll work on it."

Kathryn punched off the sound. "I can't understand how anyone can keep telling deliberate lies—"

"Malt does more than Milton can," Alex saluted the screen with his wineglass, "to justify God's ways to man."

"Malt? You should be drinking beer to say that," Kathryn said. "And who did say that, originally?"

"A dead English poet with a long nose," Alex said grandly, and she realized he was getting tipsy.

"Uh, maybe you should sit—" but by then he had walked away.

Sheila whispered, "Good guy. Have you ravished him yet?"

"Have mercy. He's been recovering."

"Best medicine in the world is yours to provide."

"I'm a little cautious."

"He's not the diseased madman type, trust me. I should know."

"I like to get to know a guy."

"Who doesn't? Me, I hold out for the last name *and* his address."

Kathryn laughed. "Wow, an old-fashioned girl."

"How long you two been going out together?"

"Um, a few weeks."

"My Lord! Even the *Pope* doesn't play that hard to get."

Kathryn grinned and followed Alex into the next room. He had sat down at a grand piano that looked out upon the city lights. With his right hand he suddenly began playing a familiar classical piece, fifteen seconds of one-handed magnificence. The entire room stopped chatting and turned, enthralled. Just as abruptly, he stopped.

"Go on!" several called.

"That was great, Alex."

"Play the rest."

He turned with mock solemnity. "I can't. That's all I know."

"No! Play it," Kathryn said.

Alex held up his right hand. "That is all this hand has in it." Then he got up and walked back into the screen room.

"What was *that*?" she asked when she caught up with him.

He sagged into one of the net-loungers. Montana mouthed oracular points soundlessly on the screen—*like a weird street mime*, she thought.

"I once was terminally shy," Alex said with boozy carnestness. "I tried to find some way to stand out at parties, y'know? So I learned to play the opening of that Chopin piece. Practiced it for months. It sure worked. Got everybody's attention."

"And you can't play anything more?" Kathryn asked, somehow shocked.

"Nope." He grinned impishly. "Not a note."

There was something oddly confessional about this, a way for him to open up to her this odd side of him, that warmed her. "Well, I liked it." She leaned close to him and delivered a long, passionate kiss. Sheila would have approved, but she had wandered off somewhere.

This made him actually swoon for a second, something she had only read about. He eased back into the netting and she sensed his vulnerability in the soft shadows, his shirt bunched where he had lost weight in the hospital, eyes strangely brooding, as if asking her to understand him. The brush with death had shaken him but he could not easily talk of it. He was like so many men in their yearning to reach out, to penetrate their own reluctance to show weakness.

He exhaled deeply, peering ahead of him as though he half-expected his alcohol-laden breath to hang like a separate, substantial cloud, unmixed with the usual air. Then he hiccuped and wearily lifted his glass toward Montana's enormous head, which had sweat gleaming on the high forehead. "Make a joyful noise unto the horde."

"Ummm, good pun. Maybe we'd better get you home," she said.

"Sheila's right, y'know. Need to loosen up the good Rev."

"Think about it tomorrow."

"I have a plan, too. Loosen him up."

"Alex, am I going to have to carry you to the car?"

"Bugs. The secret is bugs."

"Why do I always get the guys who are buggy?"

"Woman, you seek to take from me my secret," he said in a surprisingly good Boris Karloff imitation. Drink did open the man. "I have the

knowledge of eternal life. But first"—a comic, leering roll of his eyes—
"I must have . . . your bod-ee. . . ."

She laughed. "Okay, it's a deal."

"And don't let me forget the bugs. We'll have a little fun with this
Montana. You game?"

"Uh—sure."

"Good. Now—your bod-eee."

Which was the way it worked out.

3

GEORGE

He got out of his new Chevy and strolled casually over to the view-
point above Ortega Highway. Smog lay like greasy gravy over the midsection of the county.

A hawk slid down the warming wind. It cruised along the dry wash of
a broad creekbed and then dove suddenly into a stand of tan pampas
grass. George imagined a fleeing mouse down there, scampering among
the dry stalks and their comforting shadows, not knowing what veered
on the air above. Then a flicker in the sky, and the mouse would run,
dodging, bright fear snapping in its veins. It knew only the two-dimensional geometries that had let it elude the snakes and ground predators.
The swoop and plunge of three dimensions brought a sudden shadow, a
tiny squeal of blind panic, and then the sharp hard pain that prey had
always known was coming for them.

He made himself close his eyes and breathe deeply three times. The
sweat on his skin cooled.

Something had called up the dream from this morning. The same
dream, every night. He had floated up from some blood-shrouded place,
into blaring hard light. Twisted faces peering down at him, judging him.

Working on him. Their sharp tools flashing with cruel reflections.

He made himself think about the dream. They were the Master's
Messages, just like that reverend had said, and suddenly he knew what
the dream meant.

Chillers. The Master was showing him what it would be like to return to the world of the living as a chiller, still sunken in the corruption that flesh is heir to. Returning to horror and raw chaos. Not immaculate, white, like the cleansed bones of the decently dead.

That atrocity had to be avoided. George felt long, slow waves of absolute malevolence welling up from far within himself. He would heed the Master's Message. This work today, it would contribute to his Calling.

Then he shook himself, emerging back into the rasp of the real. He needed his carapace self now. The quick, analytic self.

He shook a Camel from its pack and lit up.

"Mr. Goff," a man's voice said behind him.

George turned and made his usual smile. "Mr. Miller." The real estate agent wore jeans and a T-shirt, just as George did. No need to attract attention in this remote spot by sporting a business suit. He had made sure the man understood the importance of even small details.

"I've got the last bunch of paperwork," Miller said, showing a brown valise.

"And?"

"Well, the cash, of course."

"Of course."

"You come well recommended by your friend in Arizona."

"He spoke well of you, too." George used his flat, standard American accent for business. It took some effort. A southwestern twang came into his words when he wasn't minding it.

"These deals are a little bit delicate . . ."

"Sure are."

For some reason Miller wanted to start off with an edgy civility, and that was all right with George. He had followed some earlier contacts from his Arizona work, and it had taken only a couple of weeks to set up this little number. All done by telephone and fax and modem, but there was no clean and untraceable way to move the money. People don't like to work with ghosts, either, so at least one meeting was essential. George knew all that, but he didn't have to like it.

He followed Miller to a big blue Cad, and they sat in the front seat. Miller had left the motor running for the air conditioning even though the day had not gotten warm yet. They went over the papers, and George took the time to read the main parts. He had used his Bruce Prior identity on this deal, and he wanted to be sure no minor screwup endangered it. The banks had wanted a thorough background, and Bruce Prior was the only paper persona that could stand up to that.

George was building up the Charles Goff persona, the one he used with Miller. It was about time to get a cheap apartment for Goff, some reality behind the paper identity. It could be useful in his holy work, too.

Miller consulted his spreadsheet printout and poked a finger at some lines. "Chase Manhattan okayed you, just like you said they would."

"That got us through the week?"

"Yeah. The owners, they loved that."

"They ask about closing dates?"

"Hot to trot, yessir."

"What'd you give them?"

"Like we planned, twenty days."

"They bought it?" George smiled, thinking of the owners of the big ranch-style house in Rancho Santa Margarita, sitting in the barnlike place with fresh carpet just laid down and no buyers.

"I told them the whole thing was looking pretty fine. The guy went ahead and moved out."

"Where to?"

"Boston. No way he's gonna run back here, check things out. He's got a brand-new job to deal with."

"So what's next?"

"That's why I wanted to talk. Fuji waffled on us."

Miller was a medium-size man in his early thirties with a way of wetting his lips and then smacking them when talking about money. Beneath the round face lounged a pudgy body. All appetite and no real work, George thought. Shave your percent from somebody else's property and stuff it into your gut.

"So? I told you they wouldn't go all the way."

"Your frame's still holding, that's okay."

A slight anxious grin flickered across Miller's face, a placating reflex. Afraid his whole house of cards would crumble too fast. His imagination watching the bucks fly away. And all the time not knowing that he was helping out with the Lord's work, through George.

"So let it ride."

"Uh, I'm wondering if you got a backup."

"I might."

You had to let them come to you. George took a long drag on his Camel and let the smoke trickle out through his nose. This made Miller sniff and readjust the air-conditioning vents.

He'd learned this sideline in Arizona. It was easy to front for a real estate agency, on properties that could make a quick score. Executives needing to move, disoriented widows and widowers, impending bankruptcy cases squeezing out of a property before the court grabbed it. Bruce Prior would make a bid on the house, showing proper financial backing—assets and liabilities in order, a clear TRW credit check, no civil litigation outstanding, no liens or judgments against him. The escrow would go smoothly until the last minute. By that time the homeowner had made arrangements, probably bought another house, maybe had already scooted.

Then a problem would show up in Bruce Prior's financial profile. Surprise, surprise, excess debt. Usually buried down in a few personal loans that he hadn't listed; after all, nobody can remember everything when reporting all that paperwork, right? Tsk, tsk. The deal would fall in escrow.

George never saw the people involved, never even walked through the property. He just acted as a foil for the paperwork machinery. He pocketed half his fee when the deal was signed, the second half when it fell through. Within a month or so, the homeowner would be desperate. Then the real estate firm could slide in with a lowball offer. The mark would snap it up. By that time, the agency would have a client ready for a quick sell at a slight markdown.

This had worked in Arizona for a while, until the market busted. But southern Orange County was rich, dumb rich, and George stood to get an easy twenty thousand here. He'd heard that a lot of the upscale mansion market down here was cash freighted out of the insurance crisis, so these people were basically in the same business he was. Fair game.

And perfectly routine. No crime in making a bid, right?

There was no way to tie George to the realtor company. Not even Fuji could work backward from Bruce Prior to him.

"My boss, he's jumpy."

"Slip him a Valium."

"The Fuji paper, it'll stand how long, you figure?"

"Maybe another week."

"You sure?"

George turned sideways in the Cad bucket seat. His jeans caught on the decorative buttons in the fake leather and popped one off. He loomed over Miller and looked at him for a long moment, taking a drag on the Camel. "I'm sure. That's all I guaranteed."

"Yeah, I remember." Miller looked around nervously, but there was nobody else at the view point. A hawk spiraled by at eye level, a thousand feet above the canyon floor. Being seen together was a bad idea, and George had not wanted this meeting. Guys like this could never stick to a plan.

"You want another week, I might let you have a Dreyfus backup."

"You could? Listen, I'd really appreciate a favor on this."

"It'll cost you."

"Oh." Miller blinked, coughed, but didn't say anything about the Camel. George figured he was already in heavy with his boss on this and the waiting was making him jittery.

"Look," George said with his friendly voice, "Fuji's slow because they still haven't got their patterns set up with Tokyo. Language problems, some accounting stuff."

None of this was exactly top secret; he had read about it in a banking trade magazine, right off the shelf at the UCI library. But hardly anybody read those. Guys like Miller wanted the inside play but never did their homework.

"How much for the Dreyfus?" Miller's voice was tight now.

"Y'know, pal, I can see this is bothering you. So I'll give you the Dreyfus."

"Huh? You will?"

"Sure. Next time we do business, remember that."

"Oh, I will. Hey, I will, Charles."

"I'll fax you the details. A money-market checking and a tax-free bond. Carrying about twenty-five thousand."

"Great. That'll give us some margin." A big phony grin.

"You bet."

George got out of the Cad and walked away. He didn't like spending any more time with contacts than he had to. Better to run the money transfer game from home. But he needed to build up a cash reserve for what was to come, and a real estate scam was a fast way to do it. He needed time to think and plan and the cash to do it with. Miller seemed square enough to count on, too. Not really smart, but probably too scared to cheat.

Thank you, Lord, he offered to the sky. Things were going right for him now. The truck accident hadn't worked as well as it might, and on top of that the news item about it hinted that maybe they knew it was no accident.

Better not try anything like that again. Somehow he had always known it would have to be a serious, solemn undertaking. He was sure the Reverend knew that, too, although he understood that Montana could not implicate himself with even a telling word. Very well. That was how it had to be for those who would soldier in the secret legion of the Lord.

He watched a hawk balancing high on the clean wind. It took its effortless time, hovering, waiting for the right moment. Then the plunge, arrow-straight.

George dropped the Camel and ground it out with his heel.

Thank you, Lord. With this money in hand to pay for his computer intelligence work, he could devote himself with full and deliberate energy to his Calling.

4

KATHRYN

By night, the Marble Cathedral resembled an abrupt mountain bursting from the murky ground. In the park around it the trunks of gnarled oaks seemed like a twisted gloomy forest, stooped below the vast peak.

Kathryn followed Alex into this foreboding, inky woodland, wondering just why she was doing this. He had been decidedly odd this evening, bursting into laughter in the middle of the restaurant, talking fast and telling jokes, and then making her drive by the UCI biology department on a mysterious errand, and now here.

"No," she said, and stopped beneath a pepper tree.

"Huh?" All his attention was on the plastic picnic cooler he carried with his free hand. "Come on."

"I said *no*—not until you tell me what's going on."

"Shhhh!"

"Don't *shhhh* me. Where are we *going*?"

"Around back, to the big dining hall." He hurried on and she had to follow him into the shadows or lose him for sure.

Piercing white beams artfully lit the cathedral from below, bringing out the soaring lines. She had to admit it was striking, in a kind of tacky way. How did such lofty works come from such small minds as Reverend Carl Montana's? She knew the answer—donations of tens of thousands of hopeful people, "love gifts" from folks who needed a sense of place and mission in life, relief from the raw edge of the world. Montana reached through the phosphorescent fairyland of TV and plucked forth a rain of little gifts—only a five- or ten-dollar bill in each envelope, but a torrent of envelopes every day. There was a believer born every minute.

"See any guard?" Alex whispered.

"Uh—no. Is there one?"

"Wouldn't be surprised."

They had reached the edge of the shadowy grove. Beneath the pale moonlight lay long, rambling two-story buildings with wide concrete walkways connecting them.

"That's the dining hall on the left. We head right. See those low windows?"

He started walking quickly before she could respond. She dashed after him, trying to look in all directions at once. They reached the windows, which were mercifully shadowed by a spreading old walnut tree. Hulls crunched under her feet. The broad windows were used to slide groceries in from the driveway, she guessed. She looked anxiously around, liking all this less with each second, and heard a tinny pop.

"There. Knew my prankster days weren't a total waste." Alex put a shim in his pocket and raised the window smoothly. Grunting, he stepped through it, finding the floor with his foot. "Piece of cake."

"It seems to me your prankster days are still going on," she whispered, but his head had already disappeared into the blackness beyond.

Her eyes flicked over the still, moonlit scene beyond. It now seemed brooding, ominous. Not a place she wanted to stay while he had his loony fun inside. She stooped and slid through the window.

A hand touched her arm. "Here, hold the penlight."

The faint beam revealed a standard institutional kitchen. An aroma of pine-scented disinfectant. Steel cabinets, wide wooden counters, big grinders and slicers and blenders, chromed appliances, massive supply bins, deep steel sinks.

"Down at the floor!" he whispered when she raised the beam to look around. "In here."

He led her into a long gallery-style preparation area lined with wooden cabinets. "This is a good place. Help me with the cooler."

She knelt. Alex grinned at her, put his hand on the cooler lid, and yanked it up.

Inside were—cockroaches.

Not the small, black creatures she knew and hated. These were immense, the size of her hand. Nightmares straight out of her childhood fever dreams. Giant horrors that seemed to move sluggishly as her flashlight hand trembled.

"Ah! Oh!" She jerked to her feet.

"Quiet! They can't hurt you."

Alex put both arms around her, and somehow that stilled her instant impulse to run back to that window, flee screaming across the cathedral grounds—guard or no—find the car, drive to the airport, and fly to the other side of the planet. But just barely.

"They're *harmless,* believe me."

"*No* insect is harmless. Not *that* size."

"They're asleep."

"Cockroaches *never* sleep. Ever walk into your kitchen and turn on the light? They're *there*. Waiting."

"Geez, I didn't know you'd have such a reaction."

"To insects from Mars?"

"South America. They're giant cockroaches from South America."

"That's crazy."

"Nope, it's brilliant. A good ol' buddy of mine at UCI was telling me about some he had left over after he'd finished some studies on them, and at the party the other night Sheila said just the right words, and—tadaaahh! Science strikes again."

Her heart had ceased its attempts to escape her chest and run away on its own. "They're . . . hideous."

"You're not giving them a chance."

"Alex, you are a madman."

"Look, they're beauties."

Her flesh had also stopped trying to crawl off her body and start a new career. After all, Alex had a Ph.D., he knew what he was doing, right?

Mind whirling, she made herself look into the ice chest again. The huge things were not black, like regular cockroaches. Each had a technicolor swirl, intricate markings arcing across the carapace. In full daylight they might even be gaudy. A few stirred, antennae wobbling.

"Okay, they're not completely horrible. So you have a box of giant insects. So?"

"Touch them."

"*Touch?*"

"Notice that they're not moving much?"

"If they had been, I'd be in Iowa by now." She gingerly put a finger on one of the hard shells and felt biting cold.

"I stacked them in on top of ice. Easy way to control them. At that temperature they're immobile. Standard insect defense against a cold snap—hunker down and wait it out."

He lifted two out and popped open one of the kitchen storage cabinets. "Guess what we're going to do?" he asked, grinning evilly.

She awoke in the predawn stillness, and for a moment didn't know where she was. Then memory flooded in, and she felt Alex's warmth next to her. His arms enfolded her, and he snuggled against her spoon fashion, an endearing position. Maybe his shifting had awakened her.

She let her mind glide back over the night, sailing across soft memories of passion aroused and sated. The number and ferocity of her own climaxes had shaken her. And they were *different,* too. One she recalled like a flash of lightning, unexpected and crackling. Another built slowly, almost against her will, as if her body had a hunger she did not know and was going to fulfill it no matter what.

And that had been the second night, not the first. She had to admit that she had a pattern with men, a tendency to lose the fervor of the first lovemaking. She found that they settled into a routine, using the same set rituals and approaches. That robbed the act of its spontaneity and undercut the tingling thrill of it.

But not this crucial, second night. They had been great, each eager and accommodating. Somehow the exhilaration of planting the bugs on the Reverend Montana's sacred soil had translated, back in her apartment, into trembling eagerness. *Am I so blasé I only get turned on by danger? A risk junkie?*

But no, that had merely gotten them started. Their wondrous silky couplings, the artful work of hands and mouths, her own gloriously sought impalements—those had come from some deeper wellspring. Someplace splendid and powerful beyond words.

Having to be tender with his broken arm had somehow helped. It gave them a game, wounded soldier and accommodating nurse, which they made jokes about but that somehow quickened every response. She sighed, luxuriating in the loose contentment of her body.

A distant, muffled scraping. There it was again.

Instantly she knew that this was the sound that had awakened her. In the trusted warmth of her own bed she knew the familiar sounds of her neighborhood. This was not one of them. And intuition told her that it was close.

Lightly, reluctantly, she slipped from the sheets. Her feet sank into the cool carpet, and without searching for something to throw over herself she traced a half-seen path through the gloom and into her living room. A distant street lamp cast eerie silver-blue blades of light through the far window. She stood listening. Nothing.

Then a shadow slid across the window. It was moving as though from the side of her bungalow. A sharp shadow, which meant it was close.

A man. The head and broad shoulders shifted, and she knew with a corkscrew chill up her spine that he was looking at the window, into this room, at her.

He stood unmoving for three thuds of her heart. A solid, monolithic silhouette. Utter silence, hanging in the air. Then he turned, and in profile she glimpsed strong features, impassive, and the specter slipped across the window, and he was gone, speeding away as he left.

Her chest hurt and she realized she had stopped breathing. The whole long moment had frozen her in place. She heaved a gulp of air into her lungs and the world started up again. She felt the cool night air and heard again the faint ticking of the kitchen clock.

Slowly she crept to the window and looked out. Nobody. The silent street of parked cars and well-trimmed lawns told her nothing. The man must have sprinted to be gone so quickly.

She stood for a long time studying the street and trying to explain to herself the sense of foreboding that coursed through her. The shadow had summoned up deep fears from far back, memories of rough boys in high school who had once terrorized her, of the squinting gaze of men on street corners, of all the casual small dreads that a woman encountered in her passage through a world of hovering threat. *Was that it? Just a trill of feminine caution at a passing shadow?*

No, the specter had been something more. A prowler, maybe. She tried to reassure herself that he had been just another random intrusion of the chaotic world. A symptom of Life In The Big City.

But it wouldn't work. Something ominous and utterly implacable had flitted across her mind when she saw that shadow. Something somber and brooding. It would not go away.

Something familiar, somehow.

She shivered and walked quickly back into her bedroom. With relief she slipped into the sweet-smelling, musky embrace of Alex, who had not even awakened.

"Watch," Alex said. "That's all we do."

He jammed his hands in the pockets of his jeans and made a show of sauntering down the broad sidewalk. They were a block from the Marble Cathedral. It towered above the Garden Grove rooftops like a cooled extrusion from a subterranean volcano.

"Great breakfast," Alex said, twirling a toothpick in his teeth. "I love that restaurant."

"You eat like a farmer," Kathryn said. "Steak and eggs. Heartattackville."

"I was rewarding myself," he said blandly. "Man's got to do that."

"I thought that was the dainty woman's role."

"Different department. You took care of that last night."

"You had a hand in it, as I remember."

"More than a hand, lover," he said with a warm grin that tilted her heart.

"Ummm, and barnyard humor for dessert, too."

They approached the cathedral grounds. It seemed smaller and innocuous in morning light. A big digital display board bordering the street said

FELLOWSHIP BREAKFAST. ALL WELCOME IN THE HOUSE OF THE LORD.

The crisp morning air lent sharp detail to the cathedral's sheer heights, its wooded grounds and vast parking lots. It was almost like a tiny, independent province, Kathryn thought, a pleasant glade of rest. The shrouded gloom of last night had evaporated.

She had never felt the emotional tug of organized religion—indeed, the term seemed a contradiction, for her immediate sense of reverence extended to the whole natural world, and organizing it into boundaries and beliefs was as pointless as learning the names of all the flowers without taking the time to smell them. But this morning's sunlit glow spread through her like a luxuriant fluid, and she was willing to accept the vast need others had for the company of like-minded folk in the face of the infinite. What she could not accept was their relentless campaign against those of other persuasions.

"I wonder if this is really a good idea," she said, her stomach tightening as they got nearer.

"I couldn't stay away," Alex said. "Not now."

"You're really sure the cockroaches will wake up?"

"Tested it in the lab. It's a natural defense mechanism. Cold weather comes, they slow down until it's warm again."

"Like that girl who fell into the lake, ice skating?"

Alex gestured amiably with his free hand. "Different—we can't actually hibernate. Sometimes it's not so great being human, but it's always fun being a mammal."

"Ah, so *that's* what you were trying to demonstrate in bed last night?"

He laughed but would not be deflected. "That kid came back to full function after nearly an hour in the water, stone cold dead by any clinical definition."

"Dead by clinical definition," Kathryn said.

"Right. Which really only means they don't know how to save the structure that makes up who the person is."

They turned off the sidewalk and ambled among a line of willows. Through the trees and brush they could see the long cinderblock church buildings. A breeze carried faint murmurs of many conversations and the cloying sweet scent of scrambled eggs and syrup. Kathryn's stomach knotted. She felt conspicuous, sure someone would guess.

"Should be about now." Alex said, his eyes bright.

She saw suddenly that he needed this. Although he could not speak of it, she had felt in the last two nights a fierce animal drive in him—the desire to prove to himself that he was alive, brimming and bursting and exuberantly alive. The accident had brushed him with black wings.

And she had gone with him last night, into a world they made together—that fierce, demanding jungle where only a thin layer of skin separated two minds that suddenly desired to merge, blend, and fuse in a blaze of furious heat. They both carried an unspoken deep reservoir that had finally broken open, spilling years of tensions, draining them away.

Alex said, "That's how researchers keep those little guys inactive in the lab, y'know. Ice them down. They wake up good as new, and the first thing they want is breakfast."

The distant mutter of talk rose. Kathryn turned and impulsively embraced Alex, awkwardly putting her arms around him and his bound-up left arm.

A window shattered in the dining hall. A can of tomatoes tumbled out onto the lawn.

A woman's high shriek. Then another. Quickly, a chorus of screams and shouts.

A woman ran out the side door, hands in air, shouting incoherently. She ran five paces and tripped over a curb and crashed into the lawn, still babbling.

From inside, bangs and clatters. A splintering crash of glass.

The main doors flung open. Men and women bolted out, mouths agape, howling.

A panicked babble arose from the building, and for a moment it seemed about to explode from the rising din. Torrents of people in their Sunday best fled like waters from a burst dam. Another window smashed.

"Why, something seems to have occurred," Alex said innocently.

"It does indeed," Kathryn said. "What's that?"

A gray, official-looking Ford sedan pulled into the parking lot.

"That'll be the inspector from the County Board of Health," Alex said, glancing at his watch. "Right on time."

5

SUSAN

Mrs. Yamada was in pain, but she gave Susan a joyful grin. "Welcome to the flower show."

"Ummm." Susan sniffed at a gorgeous fountain of irises. "Does one of your sons own a florist shop?"

"They'll have paid for one by the time this is over."

There was a subtle difference between Mrs. Yamada's laugh lines, earned in life's battles, and the thin crinkles that now told of gnawing aches. She had chosen to endure rather than yield up a scrap of herself to drugs. The menu of chemical consolations was seductive, but this wry woman permitted nothing to blunt her world.

Susan admired the scentful clouds of day lilies, roses, vibrant baby's breath and moist orchids, then perched on Mrs. Yamada's bed and chatted amiably for a few moments. When the right moment came by, she said softly, "I'm afraid that I won't be practicing here any longer."

There; careful and neutral. This was Blevin's patient, after all. But it didn't get past the gleaming black eyes. "Blevin's pushed you off my case?"

"Out of the hospital, actually."

"He can *do* that?"

"It's not about you."

"Oh, yes it is. Cryonics, right?"

"It's over my research. Not about the student who spoke to you, Mr. Skinner."

"That started it, though." Mrs. Yamada's mouth twisted into a scornful line and she crossed her arms with absolute conviction. "I put him on the scent."

"You are not in any way responsible." It would be reprehensible to load any of this onto a patient. Particularly one who would need every resource, and soon.

"Well, I'm going to look into it anyway. And I'll get somebody other than that Blevin."

"You are free to have any physician you like. Not me, though. I'm sorry."

"All right." A sigh. Some of the starch went out of her. "Did you get a look at my latest tests?"

It would be smart to say no. "Well, yes."

"It's eating away at me, right?"

"I'm afraid that seems to be the most probable implication of all the diagnostic results."

With an impish grin, this time momentarily free from pain, she said, "You don't have to be like the rest of them. You could just say yes."

Susan laughed. "Uh, yes."

"Well, you play the cards you're dealt."

There didn't seem to be anything to say to that, so Susan simply took Mrs. Yamada's hand.

"Are the rest of the doctors here like Blevin?"

Susan knew she should not really even be here, but she let herself answer, "In what way?"

"Stiff. By-the-book types."

"Not all."

"Are they all against freezing the patients they can't save?"

"Probably. We've never really discussed it."

"Shouldn't you?"

"This is a conservative institution."

"What's more conservative," Mrs. Yamada said sharply, "holding on to as much of the patient as you can, keeping them, hoping you might find a way to bring them back? Or burning them to a crisp?"

"Your family favors cremation?"

"Oh yes. People are dying to do it." The mordant wit came without even a smile, as though a gesture toward gallows humor were a purely social obligation, something the dying did to get the living through an awkward moment.

"I am ending my clinical practice here. I cannot properly give you detailed advice, but—" On impulse she reached out and firmly clasped both Mrs. Yamada's hands. They were worn smooth by a lifetime of labor. "You have a terminal condition. Cryonics is a slim possibility. No one knows how slim, but it's probably quite small. You should follow up the process *if* you feel it is compatible with your own personal philosophy. Think about it, Mrs. Yamada. I'm not pushing."

Mrs. Yamada squeezed back with surprising force. Tears welled up in the marble-hard eyes. Susan saw that the impassive stoicism was a veneer, perilously thin. "I'm going to. I promise."

"Good. Very good." Susan blinked rapidly. Doctors did not run their mascara.

"Good-bye." Mrs. Yamada gave her a hug.

Other physicians had always been better at knowing when to let go. It was part of the clinical attitude. Still, Susan left the room feeling oddly cleansed, at having put some small matter right, at least.

She could not reasonably involve herself in the paperwork pyramid Mrs. Yamada would have to climb, while fighting her illness, to arrange for cryosuspension. Courts frequently found terminal patients to be mentally incapable of executing legal matters properly, especially if relatives claimed any "duress." Susan would be a prime target of any such litigation, and she could not give such potent ammunition to any of Mrs. Yamada's sons. They looked like dutiful, unassuming men, but inheritance law makes ogres of the meek.

She made her way to her hospital office and resumed the stale task of boxing up her books and notes. She would haul them over to her medical school office, but didn't plan to unpack them. In her bones she felt that her clinical days were over. Her UCI time might be quite short, too, if the Academic Senate acted swiftly.

She tried to focus on the many issues she would have to deal with, but her heart was not in it. There had to be a way to leave a dying patient's bedside and cleanly go home to your own troubles, but she had never mastered it. And there had to be some professional method to take Mrs. Yamada's impending fate with the right level of seriousness, and yet still have some intensity for her own predicament, for her friends' passing troubles, for the daily parade of discords that were, in the end, life.

She resolved to by God be ready for anything. But she was not prepared for a visit by Dr. Marilyn Jacobs, who swept into Susan's office in a severely tailored gray suit.

"I wanted to have a private moment with you," Jacobs said. "I feel I owe you an explanation."

Susan cleared some files from a chair, and the white-haired woman went on briskly, as though this speech had been prepared. "I voted against you in the committee because I thought Dr. Blevin's charges had some foundation. And I feel we must watch very carefully for animal abuses, or the rights activists will crucify us in the media."

This didn't seem to require any answer. Susan gave none. She reflected that it was interesting how, with nothing left to lose, she could simply watch events unfurl like a spectator at a play, safely sitting in the darkened audience.

"But I have since come to feel that Blevin is continuing to conduct a personal campaign against you. As a colleague and as a woman, I had to tell you." Marilyn Jacobs looked down at her hands, which were knotted together in her lap.

"This is not exactly news," Susan said dryly.

"I did not understand the depth of Blevin's feelings."

"Weren't they pretty obvious?"

"I took them to be in the heat of the moment. But now he is spending a great deal of time gathering support against you in the Academic Senate."

"I expected that."

"He wants a quick judgment and your formal ejection from the faculty."

Am I being cynical? Susan inspected her feelings. *This sounds like just another way to hustle me into resigning.*

But Marilyn Jacobs seemed genuinely vexed, her face lined and pale. In contrast with the neatness of her freshly pressed formal suit, her makeup clung to the crow's-feet spreading from her eyes and there was a haggard roughness to the skin that creams could not banish.

"I'll have to move fast."

"Do." The thin woman's voice was tight and earnest. "We've hushed up problems in the med school before, but in this case the dean is playing his cards, shall we say, under the table."

"By reprimanding Blevin but letting the charges against me go to the Senate."

"He's cut Blevin's clinical income, too—but not by much. That way he looks even-handed. And he can divorce himself from Blevin's private accusations."

Susan had figured out most of this, but she no longer heard any corridor gossip, of course. "Accusations?"

"That you were using UCI's reputation to make money, dirty money, and to do illegal experiments."

Susan had been cultivating a bemused detachment, but this rankled her. "That's obscene."

"You have this, uh, entanglement with Immortality Incorporated. And you haven't reported that experiment with the dog yet."

"Because I'm not through analyzing it."

"It would be smart to get something out. Call a press conference, announce your results."

Susan shook her head. "That's not my style. I need to run some more tests on my lab mice population, and then—"

"There isn't time!" Jacobs was flushed, becoming more animated. "While you're refining your results, going through the scientific journals, Blevin will crucify you."

"Executions always draw a big crowd, don't they? If only I could find a way to get through to my own colleagues here. . . ." Susan gazed out her sole office window, toward a tawny hillside.

"A lot of people think what you're doing is, well, immoral."

Susan laughed. "I see—Immorality Incorporated?"

Jacobs looked uncomfortable, as though struggling with her own inner arguments. "I've heard some faculty say it is simply unprincipled, to spend money on people who are already dead."

"It's their money. How does paying to suspend yourself differ from setting up, say, a nonprofit foundation to spend your estate?"

"Because it's for yourself, not others."

"Sounds like forced charity to me."

"There's more to it than that. If the older generation hangs around, even just in liquid nitrogen, it's not getting out of the way of the young. Every generation deserves a fresh start, don't you think?"

"Descendants inherit the gains of the past, all the knowledge and creativity. That doesn't mean each generation gets to dispose of the past as it likes."

Jacobs looked genuinely concerned, as if she had been struggling with these issues herself. Probably she had been defending Susan in coffee-break gossip circles, and these ideas troubled her. "What about the ethics of overpopulating? What if everybody docs this and it works?"

"I don't think there's danger of people jumping on the cryonics bandwagon. Just the opposite," Susan said wryly. "And even if they did, so what? The industrial countries are the only ones which could afford to, and they're not the breeders of the planet. The increase comes from Asia, Africa, South America. That's where we have to fight the battle."

Jacobs looked at her hands, still vexed. "Ron Miller, the bioethics fellow, said something about that. But he questioned the emotional elements of refusing to accept death."

"Sometimes I wonder if talk about the wisdom of acceptance and so forth isn't just making a virtue of necessity."

Jacobs gave a weak, worried chuckle. Susan tried to read the concern that knitted her brow. Physicians tried to be superrational, but constant exposure to death kindled deep emotions. Many people entertained the consoling fantasy of themselves peacefully sleeping in their fancy sealed coffins, unchanged through the ages. And even Joe Sixpack could envision the "discomfort" of spending a century as a frozen, naked statue in a giant Thermos bottle.

Susan said softly, "Something else bothers you, though."

"Well, yes." Jacobs bit her upper lip. "I think you're being treated shabbily, but still—this *feels* wrong. If I did it, I might reawaken in some strange place, without any of my family, my friends, no job."

Susan nodded sympathetically. "Women feel that way, more than men. I call it the neighborhood argument—you're really saying 'I am my neighborhood.' That you can't live outside your present context."

Jacobs nodded jerkily. "It's a horrible idea to me."

"Me, too. Until I realized that I came into this world pretty much that way. I had family, true—but there'll be your descendants in the future, remember. When you and I started out as babies, we knew nothing, nobody."

"But now we have friends, family we've known so long. I would hate to lose them."

"If they elect to be suspended, they can go, too."

Jacobs blinked, as though she had not considered this. "Oh, I don't think they would."

"Maybe they won't. It's the most deeply personal choice anyone can ever make."

"But I'm *used* to this time. Who knows what the future will be like?"

Susan shrugged. "Nobody. And no matter how much you love this time, you can't hold on to it. The world changes. Sometimes for the better."

Jacobs brushed at her cheek, and Susan saw a tear. She had been involved with cryonics so long, at times she forgot the deep emotions this kind of discussion called up. "Look, it's perfectly natural to react this way," she said. "We women are more communal, we relate to others. These ideas, the first time we hear of them, it pulls the rug from under us, emotionally."

Jacobs took out a tissue and dabbed at her eyes. "Men don't seem to."

"I've noticed that," Susan said, trying to be a bit upbeat. "They're more loners than we are. They like long hikes, getting away, exploring. Most of the great male myths are about that, like *The Odyssey*. Cryonics has that same feel for them, a big journey to a strange place. Deep down it's okay for them. Us, it frightens some."

Jacobs said reflectively, "I'll have to think about it. A very strange idea."

"A wholesale shift in the paradigms of medicine," Susan agreed. "But that's not why Blevin and the dean are acting this way."

"They think you're in this for the money."

Susan leaned back and with studied calm put her feet up on her desk. It was definitely unladylike, and she saw what men got out of doing it. She hoped her shoes—sensible, heavy-soled for long days of clinical work—would scar the maple desk top.

She said, "I remember my father saying that Republican scandals were always about money, and Democrats got into trouble over women. I never knew why that was true, until I went to university. Here the scientists and physicians have money misery, and the humanists, they stumble into sex scandals."

This brought a flicker of a smile from Marilyn Jacobs. "Why?"

"Because that's what they really care about. Or maybe it's just what they can get."

"Well, it's still unfair. The dean should keep Blevin on a leash."

"Can he?"

Jacobs leaned forward earnestly. "We have had physicians giving experimental drugs to patients without going through the Human Subjects Review protocols. We have had disputes between physicians, in which one published data—remember that idea about warming up HIV patients' blood to kill the AIDS virus?—even though his co-workers disagreed. Every time, *every time,* the dean finessed the dispute through committees without raising a ripple in the school large enough to attract outside attention."

"Why not this time?"

Jacobs puffed out her cheeks and sighed with puzzlement. "From corridor gossip, I think it's something emotional that neither the dean nor Blevin will admit."

"About death?"

"They *hate* the idea of what you call suspension. I really don't know why."

For a moment Susan felt a certain sympathy for the dean. He was a man of ordinary ability trying to ride a technological tiger. A ripe zoo of possibilities opened up as new crafts flowered. Companies were patenting viruses and bacteria made in the lab. Specially genetically engineered mice were on the market for research use. Most of it dealt with the beginnings of life. Fertilized eggs in a freezer. Gadget-assisted childmaking at ten thousand dollars a pop. Hospitals rated by their "take-home baby rate" after artificial fertilization. Champions of fetal rights who wept over fertilized cells so small you could see them only with a microscope—but did full constitutional rights depend on size? Hot-eyed advocates who saw most of the fertility technology as further evidence of a male conspiracy to enslave women, keep 'em barefoot and pregnant. Fish gotta swim, birds gotta fly, men gotta oppress. And on the other end, women who longed for children and worshiped physicians who might make that possible.

With birth so uncertain, she thought, it must be comforting to confront death with, well, dead certainty. But science was seldom soothing.

"We have a funny relationship with death," Susan said, coming out of her reverie. "At least it tells us when to stop trying."

"With Blevin it's deeper than that."

Susan nodded. "Academics always underrate the importance of the irrational in human affairs. Especially their own."

"I feel bad about this. I'm sure some of it comes from the fact that you're a woman, doing something radical."

Her colleagues thought she was radical, and to Mrs. Yamada she was conserving . . . She smiled. Which made Dr. Jacobs look even more troubled. "I'll see my lawyers tomorrow. My friend Rachel said I shouldn't have gone into that ad hoc committee without one."

"She was right. If you could just publicize your results, a lot of your colleagues would rally around."

"I'll try to hurry up, but I'm not going to rush results and get something wrong."

"So it's up to the lawyers."

"Lawyers and worse," Susan joked. "I'm afraid I have to do this by the house rules now."

Jacobs accepted this soberly, sighed, and left. Susan was oddly touched by her visit. She left the hospital lugging a cart of her papers and looked back at the imposing edifice from the parking lot. She thought she could catch a glimmer of what lay behind Blevin and the dean.

Most people live inside the patterns of their era. They accept current standards and designs as natural phenomena sweeping over them, like massive, oceanic waves. They can't imagine that their basic assumptions are forces emerging from their own genes and from their times. Yet much of their thought reflects deeply ingrained needs, artful evasions of a simple point: We all have to end.

Before such an elemental truth, most can only flee. Or hide.

6

GEORGE

The Laguna Beach Library was small but airy, and homeless bums filled most of the seats. There was a rent-a-cop on duty to control the bums, but the librarians looked nervous.

George found that they also had a good hookup to the main Orange County library facilities, and within half an hour he was reading the reference material he wanted.

The librarian he asked for help took him on a tour of the whole reference system, her ample breasts touching the keyboard of the computer as she showed him access codes. She had full lips free of lipstick, which pursed with attentive, dewy interest as he described how he was doing a term paper for a night class in criminal justice at Saddleback College. She seemed oblivious to her breasts beneath the plain blue blouse and to her hips that bulged hourglass-fashion below her broad shiny black belt.

There were a lot of women like her here, showing off themselves. They pushed their breasts at you with those special bras and wore skirts that either clung or shaped but certainly didn't just leave their bodies alone. He would see them on the streets and they would usually look right through him, eyes only for the window displays in the splashy fashion places, the ones with the *e* in *shoppes*. Plenty attention for the clothes but not for what they were doing to the men on the street who had to live with the everlasting enticement but do nothing about it until one of the rouged harlots gave the nod. Or more likely, smiled coolly and flicked the fake eyelashes and brushed him off. That was the game they were all playing, the newspapers and TV screamed it at you, never giving a minute's peace. But none of them would admit it.

His jimmy-john spoke with its heathen voice, and he willed it to subside. His chest itched, too, with the fresh tattoo he had dedicated to his mission, words in inch-high lettering across his chest: GOD IS.

George watched the librarian call up the directory of U.S. government publications and track down background titles. He gave her his aw-shucks routine, and pretty soon she was getting the stuff faxed down from the main county library. He could have done this at home with the modem. It gave him a laugh to get the system to oblige him, though, to cater to a cause they would find horrifying if they could understand it but that in the end was the Lord's.

As usual, government was anxious to spill its beans. The FBI Behavioral Science Unit stuff was funny and useful. The way they sliced and diced the world, so sure that by defining everything they could understand it. So murder wasn't just bloody death, no. There were types: single, double, triple, mass, spree, and serial. Like a Baskin Robbins, take your choice, flavors for all. With a topping of experts on each, like candy sprinkles.

So was he a spree killer? No, because though he had killed at two or more locations, he also had an "emotional cooling-off period" between them. That made him a serial killer. The FBI had a whole subunit assigned to computer analysis and psychological team studies of "a new phenomenon that has baffled law enforcement officials and mental health professionals."

But all these smart guys in three-piece suits—there was a group photo in one of the background pieces, and a piece in *Psychology Today* —hadn't figured that one of their subjects would read up on *them.*

He speed-read through pages of clotted, official prose. Then some words made him stop breathing: "He thinks he will never be caught—"

His skin rippled with a prickly, itchy wave. He glanced around, for an instant convinced that people at nearby tables could sense his reaction, knew what he was reading, saw him clearly for what he was. But the drowsy air of the library carried no such electricity. His eyes dropped back to the page: "—and sometimes he is right."

Yes. "A serial murderer controls the events. Spree killers may barely control what will happen next." Right. Spree killers were just loonies. It was an insult to be associated with them.

The scientific papers had titles like "Criminal Profiling from Crime Scene Analysis," written by a half-dozen experts apiece. A whole platoon of beady-eyed nerds, blind men grasping at the elusive elephant. Their "profiling inputs" and "offender risk analyses" and breakdowns of killers into organized versus "lust murder" were earnest, remorseless, comic. Plenty of attention lavished on details, none on the real issue.

Spree types kill just about anybody they run into. Serial killers stalk victims because they are red-haired women or look like their mother. Demented, obvious patterns.

"Serial killers display powerful inner direction." That was a small piece of it, but they missed the essential. They could never understand him.

He wasn't a serial killer, he was a *serious* killer. He worked not out of blind passion but from scrupulous service to the Lord, as revealed by the dancing many-colored auras around his victims, and as the Reverend Montana had ordained him.

This was *war,* the Reverend had said. Holy war. George had sensed it all along without being able to find the right way to say it. The Bible had made it all clear. You just had to know how to read it. King David had killed many, even his girlfriend's husband, and was still beloved by the Almighty.

He had always wanted to fight for the Godly against the unholy. Now he would, freely. Even the waitress in that dirty alley, she had been part of the struggle. If she had succeeded in her obvious plot to draw the police to him, he would never have been able to do this good work now.

He spent the afternoon carefully reading the inert prose of the papers, then checked out the major work on the subject, Joel Norris's *Serial Killers.* The case studies and grisly lab reports did not move him. They were like newspaper accounts of distant wars, tales of moral confusion far over the curve of the sleeping earth.

And through all this they never spoke of the obvious point: the experts could study cases only if they knew the crimes were murders.

George could avoid all this relentless analysis and attention if he did what these "experts" said was impossible—change his pattern. The high school principal, the waitress—those had been obvious. His beginner's mistakes, really. Cops were looking for separate, single killers for those.

Time to change. He should operate the way he had as a boy, with the trusting dogs and cats in the safe cloak of night.

Accidents. They must look like accidents. No witnesses. Do it at night, far from prying eyes. Not easy in Orange County's urban sprawl.

No killing in one place and moving to another; the forensics labs could build a story from a single slender carpet fiber, a dime's weight of mud, an invisible thread of DNA like a chemical fingerprint.

No autopsy. That was crucial, too. George knew little chemistry, but he had respect for the intricacies of the human body. It was the work of God and could tell many tales, to the unbeliever and the saved alike. At all costs he should avoid any suspicion, for that would bring the autopsy, the experts with their test tubes and microscopes and calipers. And the FBI Special Unit on Serial Killers.

No, he would be a serious killer. A stinging retribution that would go as unnoticed here as the salty ocean breeze.

He left the library and walked the streets. It was a lazy day beneath a pale sun that brushed his face with rewarding warmth.

He stopped before a pet shop and recalled the Reverend's rage about the cockroaches. Two women had twisted their ankles and a man had cut his hand in the scramble. They had found one of the insects dead with some ice caught around its legs, and so they knew it was the chiller fanatics who had sent them. They had left a clever sort of calling card.

The county health inspector had harbored a grudge against the Reverend for some past matters, something about serving so many from the cathedral kitchen. The inspector was the kind of man who would have applied rules and regulations to Jesus's multiplying of the bread and fishes. Once he had the cockroach setup, he used it to cost the cathedral fines and trouble.

The Reverend had summoned George and showed him the hideous insects, grotesque things like a biblical scourge. But the Reverend could not speak out publicly and blame them or seek any legal action. That would link the Reverend too strongly with the chillers, in case George's activities became known. The Reverend was strong on this point, and George readily agreed. He was to be a secret soldier for the Lord. So retribution was up to him.

Just reflecting on it brought a slow burn into George. Standing at the pet-shop window he watched a rainbow parrot in its cage and suddenly recalled how as a kid he had thrown a parakeet into a fan and laughed at all the feathers twirling around the room.

As he would laugh today.

Three times now he had approached Dr. Susan Hagerty's house and made friends with the peppery gray keeshond. She followed a predictable pattern of work and exercise, seldom straying.

It was late afternoon as he walked up Pacific Coast Highway and stopped to watch the sun send tongues of yellow-gold through the decks of cumulus. How could people witness such splendor every day and yet remain unmoved by the wonder of God's works? Did they not know that some greater force had created all this for mankind?

The beauty of the natural world contrasted so profoundly with the ugliness of the men he saw here, the primped and coiffured queers who flounced in the sand. At a nearby coffee house, Zinc's, the moneyed sluts advertised their insulation from the moral world. He felt like bursting into a torrential sermon right on the boardwalk of Main Beach, like the great prophets of old. Instead, George shoved his hands in the pockets of his double-weave gray slacks and brushed past the sauntering male couples. A Hare Krishna group chanted by the lifeguard tower, a grotesque parody of what these doomed souls truly needed: not eastern fog, but the stern hand of biblical justice.

George would never understand these people, perched on the edge of the continent. The palms nodded with a malarial indolence in this attempted Eden. Laxity suffused the balmy air. He walked past a bookstore named for a temperature and sporting a huge mural on its side depicting whales. THE WHALING WALL, it said, another scornful toss-off of a great biblical site. Arrogant irreverence was just a joke here.

His car was squeezed into a slot on Coast Highway. He reached it with a sense of relief. The view of the ocean troubled him. Its infinite perspective stretched away toward Asia, flat and ominous for a reason he could not name. Beneath those mild waters lurked shadowy recesses, forests of seaweed, the cold black spaces.

A shudder lanced through him, but not from dread at what he was about to do. Something more. Something dark and cold and deep within.

He shook off the strange, seeping emotions. He must be a warrior now. Silent warrior of the Lord. He carefully checked to be sure he had everything ready, righteous energy snapping in his trembling muscles.

7

SUSAN

Straightening up her office took most of the day. After the discussion with Marilyn Jacobs, she had pondered her lab notes for a while. They were in good order. There were some points she would have to recheck. A measurement or two to perform again, to be sure. She disliked leaving any point not firmly nailed down. Still . . .

If she pulled a few all-nighters, she could get out a short paper on the revival of Sparkle. That would send a few ripples through the medical-scientific world. Maybe enough to upset Blevin's little boat. Worth a try, anyway.

The decision lifted her spirits. On the way home she decided to stop at Immortality Incorporated in late afternoon, enjoying the winding drive through canyons rippled by the warm puffs of a fitful Santa Ana wind. Her skin jumped with prickly energy. The natural world could always draw her out of herself, remind her that the laboratory was a deliberately antiseptic lie that managed to tell deep truths about the sprawling, mad reality of nature.

Physicians fight against nature's slow insults of age, the hardening arteries and Alzheimer's and silent cancers. People accept the signatures of crow's-feet and sagging jowls, have another beer, and forget about it. But research showed that aging is a comparatively recent invention of evolution. Ancient, primitive organisms like rockfish, bristlecone pines, and the queens of lowly anthills all keep their youth. Maybe man's ejection from the Garden had indeed cost him immortality. Still, humans did better than nearly any other mammals, lasting up to 120 years, whereas Susan's lab rats had palsy and cataracts at the age of two. Somehow the genes ordained all this, plunging forward by their own designs. Fretting over mortality was a property of complicated soups like humans. Genes were ferociously single-minded. Seen from their view, a chicken was an egg's way of making another egg.

Susan inhaled a crisp eucalyptus zest in the air and parked at Immortality Incorporated. As usual, there was only one car in the lot. The company was running on a shoestring.

Alex waved greetings to her with his free hand, and they had a cup of coffee together. It was pleasant to sink even momentarily into the consolations of simple friendship. Perhaps the little speech she had given Marilyn Jacobs, about men liking cryonics better than women because it was like an exploratory voyage, was truer than she knew. Maybe women were more dependent on community than men. She seemed to need a lot of it lately. And she got it here, not at UCI.

Alex nodded at her theory. "I fit that, sure. After my divorce I went backpacking in the Sierras every other week. If I didn't, I started putting away a bottle of wine a day."

"Ummm, so it's women who drive men off on their voyages?"

"Could be. Hey, Odysseus took off for the war with Troy, and a woman sure started that."

Susan laughed. One of the best things about the war between the sexes was that it would never be over.

There was work to do here, too. As always, her double life at UCI and I^2 created a tangle of details. She went through the I^2 computer files, searching out the paper house that legal help had erected around Susan's research here. They had known the ground beneath their feet was tricky, liable to spring open with any distant tremor of jurisprudence. Now her survival at UCI would turn upon piles of paper speckled with *whereas* and *wherefore* and *thereupon such that.* Formalisms were useful, she knew. Medicine abounded in them. But the study of law seemed to sharpen minds by narrowing them.

When the work was done she walked back through the main bay, among soft shadows cast by the big steel canisters. A valve clicked open automatically and fed liquid nitrogen into one of the great Thermos bottles. A brass fitting snapped as the nitrogen cooled it. It was composed and restful here. The required big notices of HUMAN TISSUE and HIV POSITIVE MATERIAL were taped to the sides where the lights would always strike them, a point the state inspector had made.

She stopped before a particular cylinder and gently rested her hand on the cool sheen. *The grave's a fine and private place,* she recited, *but none I think do there embrace.*

"Hello, Roger," she whispered.

She stood for a long time thinking of nothing, ridding her mind of the day's distresses. He rested only inches away, utterly inert. For a while in the first year she had imagined that she could *feel* him in there, sense some faint aura or emission from him that came into her as a soothing presence. Logic and science told her this was nonsense. She did not in fact believe in it, in the sense that she understood belief. But she came here regularly still.

The cells that contained memories and instincts and character and self—those drifted in lazy eternity. Damaged, surely. Ripped and gouged by the rude intrusions of sharp-edged ice crystals. But still carrying some fraction of their initial meaning.

How much of Roger had truly glided through these nine dreamless years no one knew. But there was something. At least there was hope. And it did not suffer time's rub.

"Good-bye, lover," she whispered.

A final stroke of the smooth, frosty metal. Then she walked out through the steel cluster and was back in the world.

She exchanged some small talk with Alex, picking up some printouts. He was just leaving for a date with Kathryn, which Susan gathered would be mainly spent in bed, and not because Alex was still recovering from the broken arm. This heartened her in the way that fresh love always strikes a vibrant chord in those who have known it. She wished him the best of luck with Kathryn and gave her seal of approval, administered with a firm, warm kiss planted in the middle of his forehead.

Then she headed for home, looking forward to an exhausting, cleansing run on El Morro Beach. If she beat the traffic down Laguna Canyon Road, she could catch the sunset, with her dog Travis racing at her heels.

A salty, zestful romp. There were few moments in her day that brought more pleasure. She hurried.

8
GEORGE

He drove north on Coast Highway, away from the sunny evils of Laguna Beach. He passed Irvine Cove, with its enormous houses perched on tiny lots, the upper storys bulging out, like ladies lifting their skirts to avoid a mouse. Aromas of blacktop highway and fragrant honeysuckle warred in the slanting rays of approaching sunset.

He was driving against the commuter flow of tired executives fleeing southward into the endless pseudo-Mediterranean bungalows of south county, so he reached the bluff above El Morro Beach in plenty of time. The parking lot at Reef Point was deserted. Hotels and homes inland caught the sun's descending glow. Few tourists ventured down to this long beach between Laguna and Corona del Mar, and locals departed with the sun. He changed into a dark blue jogging suit that he had never worn before and never would again and sat in an inconspicuous gully looking down at the beach.

The sun seemed to speed down the sky and kiss the sea with ripe orange streamers. Darkness closed in. He had marshaled his resources for this last ten days, and his reward was this oncoming gloom. No moon at all, just as the Farmer's Almanac said, and a steady autumn breeze bringing moisture from the slumbering sea. As the land cooled, the air mass moving in might condense out a touch of its vapor into coastal fog.

He began to worry that today she had deviated from her pattern. Sometimes she parked inland and ran up Muddy Canyon instead. But that was when the surf was high, and now the tides were mild, the waves rolling into sheets of white foam.

He stood up and looked south toward Abalone Point, where a house of jutting wood and glass dominated the wave-weathered rock. Below it a line of run-down beach cottages were trapped between the churning waves and the Coast Highway, seeming to shrink back from the ocean as far as they could get. They were eyesore shacks, their cheap plywood battered by the winter storms. A few runners padded along with the usual agonized/distracted air. Traffic on the Coast Highway buzzed, and he wondered if she would hazard the left turn across the streams of commuters.

But then he saw her unassuming Buick sedan pull into the lot scarcely a hundred yards from his own car.

He had planned this moment for so long, seeing every gauzy possibility. Now the unfolding, matter-of-fact reality had a piercing, razor-sharp exactness. She got out with the keeshond and let him off his leash.

"Come here, Travis boy," George muttered. "Gooood dog." The sharp sea breeze snatched the words away, and George ducked back into his hollow.

Dr. Susan Hagerty trotted down the ramp to the beach, wearing a dark blue jogging suit.

Excellent. Her usual suit. A week before she had run earlier in the day and gotten hot. She had left the jacket top on a rock and ran on to Corona del Mar. Before she returned, he had checked the label and taken a few threads. Creslan, an acrylic fiber, Sears Active Wear. Now George was wearing exactly the same.

Travis followed her, barking happily.

This was a state park, no dogs allowed. The Hagerty woman flaunted the law and society itself, smiling as she went.

Now his work would bear fruit. The vicious prank played on the Reverend had finally confirmed that these people would stop at nothing, not even at the defiling of a house of God with filthy insects. On such transgressions the Bible was quite explicit. George had listened, aghast, as the Reverend described the terror struck into his parishoners' hearts. And in the Reverend's grave, iron-hard face there had been a silent message. For George. For George alone, who could move as a swift knight through the swamp of this society.

The last dregs of sunset drained from the sky as she hit the sand. George had been so focused on her that when his eyes shifted out to the west, he was surprised to see a sullen line of mist hanging off shore.

His heart sang. Was it moving? Yes—drifting shoreward, a thin vapor thickening into a white sludge as the sun's buoyancy left it. An ally. A sign.

She turned north, as always. George began to trot along on the high bluff that shot straight up from the sand.

Here he could watch her on her daily round and yet be unseen from below. Anyone in the parking lots would just see a man out for a jog. Along the miles of beach ahead of her he saw a single runner, also headed north. The warm yellow lights of Corona del Mar twinkled weakly through the gathering gloom.

She was a good runner. Wiry, with the strength that comes from steadily working at it. He huffed along and watched the fog roll in. She rounded Reef Point and made good time.

Crystal Cove was a tiny group of beach cottages, a time-honored assembly permitted to remain, as this last virgin stretch of coast in the entire county was transformed into what the real estate guy had called a profit center. The important thing was that few people lived there, except weekends.

That was his first worry, and the second was the runner ahead of her. As she picked up speed George had to run faster. She seemed more energetic today, and he hoped that meant she would go the full distance, not turn back at Crystal Cove. George prayed, muttering through his panting, that the guy ahead of her was not out for a long slog. Timing, that was the thing.

And method. *The general rule is that a brutal facial attack means the killer knew the victim,* one of the journal papers had said. But their rules didn't matter if the injury looked natural.

The fog loomed closer.

George was prepared to come back here night after night from here on, prepared for little things like the male jogger or even one of the Coast Guard helicopters to get in the way. But he had chosen this moonless night as the best time to begin, and God was saying to him now, with the fog, that this would be *it.*

Not a slap-dash job like the high school principal or a sudden impulse like the waitress. More like the pets: clear command.

The waves sent their soft rumble up the cliffs, and George ran faster, drawing even with the woman as her dog fell a little behind her. Darkness came settling in. Through the first tendrils of light vapor, he saw the guy ahead turn off into the jumble of Crystal Cove cottages. His heart leaped.

A sudden, blitz style of attack usually indicates a younger killer.

George laughed. Their dull-witted categories, their smug assurance.

Now for the crucial moment. There was no easy way down to Crystal Cove here. He ran alongside the Coast Highway for a moment, pulling the cowl of his running jacket up to hide his face from the oncoming headlights. Then he slipped by the Shake Shack, its doors of chipped paint sealed shut. He pushed himself to his limit to gain distance on her as he plunged down the winding narrow road that snaked toward the cottages. Suddenly headlights pierced the dark. He crashed aside into high bushes as a motor gunned and a sports car lumbered up the road.

The guy who had turned in, this was him. The car growled, spun its wheels in sand, and then caught. The headlights swept past George's hiding place.

He let the taillights dwindle and then ran on. No lights in the cottages. No dog barks. He sped among the rickety cabins and by the clock mounted near the beach, the one that always said the right time here was 1930.

He reachcd the sand. Glanced left.

Nobody. The surf boomed.

Looked right.

There she was.

Hard to see in the bank of fog that came seeping in along the slick sea. Moving well for a woman. The dog not far behind her.

She had followed her pattern. Now she would have only two choices open to her on the long stretch of beach ahead. And he knew with granite certainty which she would take.

Bloodred patches flashed in the air around her running figure. Colors strobed and popped like flashbulbs. He gasped deeply, building up his oxygen for a hard dash. Colors worked through the air like bulging veins. Crimson streamers played among the fog.

A person who covers up the body with clothing, or hides it, is saying that he feels pretty bad about what he has done.

Fools, fools. George laughed with immense release and loped after his prey.

9

SUSAN

She heard him coming.

She had been watching the swells die on the beach in ghostly phosphorescent fans, letting the salty tang reach into her nostrils and leach away her bitterness. Raspy breaths and thudding heels had often drawn sour depression out of her, and tonight she hoped it could again.

She had often shared this lonely sweep of beach with other fitness nuts. When she picked up the faint splashing rhythm, slightly faster than hers, she glanced back over her soulder. A large figure moved with the familiar grim purpose, barely visible beside the curve of luminously foaming surf.

In pursuit of the running high, she thought wryly. Exertion makes the body squirt endorphins into the brain. *Cheaper than booze, and better for you.*

The peptides of pleasure, Roger had called them. And the man had known a lot about pleasure, both the giving and taking of it. She let herself slide into a pleasant reverie, sensual memories slipping through her. Exercise made her sexier, just as it had for Roger. Often they would do their beach run, dash home, shower, and let the toweling off—always very detailed—turn to something more.

Then she shook her head and put the memories back in the soft nook where she kept them. Travis was demanding attention, bounding along beside her, his energy building as hers leveled off. Travis loved a long run.

She debated turning back now, but a small thread of competition laced through her. This guy behind her was big, sure, but he looked a little too heavy. She had seen a lot of them take the first mile easily, then end up puffing and hawking and stumbling before the next one, eyes hollow and mouth sagging.

Susan grinned. She would do some hard distance, see if the man fell behind. She quickened her pace.

Pearly fog slid across the stars. White billows closed around her like the lacy fingers of a great fist. She liked its moist, cool touch, the sensation of running in a cottony pocket universe. She felt sheltered amid muffled breakers and crunching sand that tugged at her shoes.

The splashing footfalls behind grew louder. Faster.

She turned again, puzzled. Despite her burst, he was closer.

Near enough now to see that he was not running on the clear sand. Instead, he splashed through the shallows.

Why would anyone do that? To build up the calf muscles? Fitness freaks . . .

Then something sent a sharp alarm through her.

Something about the dim profile, the bulky shoulders and broad head. He was tall and came lumbering across the damp sand, splashing into the surf to cut a slight angle off the curve of the beach. Intent. Remorseless.

Her heart lurched. She suddenly knew with absolute conviction where she had seen that profile in the night.

Outside Immortality Incorporated, in seeping shadows.

A spurt of fear jerked into her muscles. She had slowed to turn and look, and now she lowered her head and gave herself over to the sudden impulse to flee. She sprinted, bringing her knees up high and building speed without thought of endurance.

The lights of Corona del Mar hung yellow-warm, two miles away. There was an easy path up the cliff there.

Could she outrun this man over that distance? She had no choice.

The beach was narrow. Slippery rocks bordered the foot of the cliff. She could not possibly reverse direction, slip around him, head back to Crystal Cove.

Her years of earnest jogging would now have to save her. She knew that she was running for her life from a man whose motives she could not guess but whose relentless steam-engine stride told all.

The fog that had seemed, only a moment before, a sheltering moistness was now a cloak that kept anyone on the bluff above from seeing her.

Travis bounded after her. The beach sped beneath her churning feet, and for several minutes she scarcely thought at all. She became slamming feet, plunging thighs, heaving gasps. She stretched for distance with each stride. She ground and labored and finally fought the sand for every extra foot.

Then her years and the gnawing fear began to eat at her. The fog's gathering grip blotted out the cliffs. Her breath rasped. A burning fatigue stole up her calves and into her thighs.

She looked back once again, just a quick glance thrown over her shoulder. He was closer.

The face. She was right. Him.

She could make out the slitted mouth drawn thin across the broad face by muscles stretched tight. A mouth without meaning or emotion.

She ran on. His low grunting followed her.

There was another sound, a regular, hoarse moaning, and it took her a moment to realize that it was her own agonized cry.

The lights ahead were still glimmering, dancing, distant. She knew she could not keep this pace that far. And she was in her forties, while this man behind her seemed twenty years younger.

This man who ran in the shallows. Not on the sand.

A slight breeze thinned the pearly fog. In the last faint glow of dusk she could see the cliffs.

It took her a moment to register the smudge of gray—a ramp that wound up to another parking lot. She was just passing it, too late to turn and try to make a burst for freedom. But that gave her the idea of using her knowledge of the bluffs. Up ahead lay Pelican Point. Maybe she could outlast him to there, then get to the next ramp beyond. But waves already broke over the outer rocks, foam glimmering through the murk. The rocks would be slippery, and he could overtake her.

She was trapped. She had to find some way up.

There—materializing out of the gloom. A narrow dirt path, a track used by surfers in the old days. Loose soil and worn sandstone. The man would have to slow to keep his footing. His weight would be a liability.

Beneath the bluff were jagged rocks that buttressed the cliff and acted as a sea wall against high tides.

She had been wrong to think she could outrun him. He would catch her at Pelican Point if she tried. Here was a second possibility, far closer than Corona del Mar.

What were the chances that someone would be in the lot above? Not good, this late.

But beyond the lot lay busy Pacific Coast Highway. Traffic.

She turned toward the bluff. It loomed up out of the pearly fog and she dug in, calves clenching. Gasps roared in her throat.

Help was only a minute of hard running away. She heard the clashing of nails on smooth rocks as Travis followed.

And the harsh, heavy panting of the man. Close, close.

The slope was steep and her lungs burned. She willed each leg forward, heaved back to gain momentum. She thrust as much as she could without losing her footing. Pure agony forced her up the incline.

She was gaining on him. *Yes. Yes.* Then she slipped.

—but caught herself, staggered, and pushed on. Near the top now.

With a final burst she broke onto the brow of the bluff. The path led to a knobby platform above the beach. She decided to sprint across it. Once on flatter ground, she could work her way inland through the chaparral.

Rough panting behind. She turned her head—

A hand seized her shoulder. Spun her around.

He shoved her roughly. She sprawled. Almost went over the crumbling edge. Caught herself.

He stood confidently on the balls of his feet, looking at her with interest. Sweat soaked his dark blue running outfit.

It was almost a relief to stop. Susan felt a rush of nausea, her mouth flooding with sour spit.

Travis came laboring up the incline. *Why doesn't Travis attack him?* she thought.

Travis yapped angrily. He circled both of them, excited. Susan gasped, "Travis . . ."

The man squatted and held out a sliver of beef. "Travis, good boy."

Travis hesitated, eyes jerking with anxiety, tail bushy.

Then the man knelt and Travis came to him. He stroked the dog, and she saw with dawning terror that Travis snapped up the beef and then licked his hand. *Friends.*

Susan cried, "Travis!"

Travis jerked. Glanced at her, confused.

Deftly the man reached down on the dog's blind side and grasped its neck with both hands. He gritted his teeth, and she heard a sharp crack as he snapped the neck.

Travis went limp. His claws rasped against the broken sandstone and then stilled.

"Man's best friend."

Susan gasped, "You . . . bastard . . ."

"You see," he said, "I have thought of everything."

"Who—what . . ."

"You wanna bring the dead back," he said, voice suddenly grating. "The walking dead, when what God desires is the valley of redeemed bones."

"I'm a doctor. I help people—"

"Why not just join them?"

"What? Who?"

The cotton fog swirled restlessly about them. She could see the beach below and the distant winking lights of Coast Highway, infinitely far away in a preoccupied world, and there was no one to help. She thought of slipping by him, but he caught her glance and his slow mirthless grin showed that he was set to grab her if she tried.

She looked down. A steep, impassable jumble of sharp rocks.

"The dead."

"Join . . ."

"You're keeping them from their holy appointments."

"Join them? You mean to kill me." It was not a question any longer. The man's wide, bloodless mouth made that clear.

"I was angry before. I was disorganized." He said this earnestly, as though reciting in school.

"At Immortality Incorporated?"

"Yes. But now I am a serious killer."

Quickly he stepped forward and bent. She wrenched away, but that was what he wanted. From behind he snatched at her collar with one hand and her belted waist with the other. She slammed her elbow at him, but he ducked, chuckling.

He yanked her backward and her running shoes lifted from the ground. She felt his other arm take her weight. He had her firmly supported from behind. She tilted farther back and was looking up into the ominous fog.

Angrily she flailed at him, reaching awkwardly behind her. "Aaahhh!" she yelled in frustration as her hands grasped only his jogging suit. She ripped his sleeve, but he shook off her grip.

Briskly he hoisted her up. He took her full weight, pressing her up. She gasped.

She hammered her fists at his head. He grunted hard, shifted his weight, and raised her higher. Her hands found nothing in the cool air. He inhaled deeply, lifting her above his head in one smooth movement.

She twisted to look over her shoulder. He was peering up at her, eyes distant, cheeks puffed out in exertion. His face was as unconcerned as if he were lifting weights in a gym.

Beyond him, the rocks.

"Bless you," he said. "May you rise in the valley of bones."

She flew out in an arc that seemed to hang suspended for a long moment in the chilled salt air.

Weightless. Then plunging.

She saw him standing above, hands clasped together as if in prayer.

Falling.

Hard.

Sharp.

Black.

FIVE

THE DREAMERS
OF THE DAY

All men dream, but not equally. Those who dream by night in the dusty recesses of their minds wake in the day to find that it was vanity; but the dreamers of the day are dangerous men, for they may act their dreams with open eyes, to make it possible.

—T. E. Lawrence

1
ALEX

The MedAlarm on the bedside table beeped. Alex felt a spark of irritation. Of all things that cannot survive an interruption, heartfelt kisses ranked near the very top. Erections, more so. "Aaargh!" His head flopped back on a pillow.

Kathryn blew an exasperated puff of air upward, feathering her long hair. "Technology strikes again," she said. "Just when our little seminar was getting interesting."

"Seminar? This is an advanced lab."

"Well, maybe this will give us a chance to eat some of the fabulous little appetizers I brought along."

"I thought *you* were the appetizer."

"I'm the main course. Go on, make your call."

Alex felt no particular concern. A lot of MedAlarm alerts were just to keep him informed. A patient entering the hospital with chest pain would bring I^2 to a state of moderate readiness, in case the situation worsened. Alex hit the key on his telephone that dialed the emergency I^2 number.

Within a minute he was glad that their preliminary short-breathed tussle on his bed, which had shown every sign of turning into the main course without benefit of appetizers, had not gone so far as to leave him undressed. That saved time as he hurried Kathryn into his Volvo.

"*Susan?*" Kathryn gaped as he pulled out onto El Toro Road. "*Our* Susan?"

"Yeah. I saw her less than two hours ago."

"Traffic accident?"

"Might be. Gary Flint's on watch and called me from the paramedic ambulance. He said our satellite fix puts her right on the coast, between Laguna and Corona del Mar."

"Coast Highway, then."

"Could be. That's within the error bars of the satellite locator, he said. Gary called UCI Emergency. They can come down McArthur and reach her faster than we can."

"What did the MedAlarm say?"

"Danger signs, but she's alive." He ran a yellow light that turned to red before he was halfway across Muirlands.

"Does that tell you what's wrong?"

"The MedAlarms monitor electrocardiagram. As long as it's regular, no trouble. Susan's is wild."

"She could be, well, exercising. Walking on the beach."

"Running's more her style. But exercise increases heart rate in a regular fashion. Hers is erratic. So the first thing the MedAlarm did was look for other problems. Her oxygen saturation is down and skin conductance way up. The MedAlarm program went bananas and blew the whistle."

"Might be a traffic accident, then."

"We'll see," Alex said grimly.

El Toro deadended on Laguna Canyon Road. The rush-hour traffic was ebbing away, and even though the Canyon Road was one of the much-ballyhooed "superstreets" of Orange County, the flow speed was barely thirty miles per hour. Alex fidgeted and looked for every chance to weave through traffic. He passed on the right, zooming down the bike lane. When that got blocked he darted into an opening between two vans. He swore at them as he floored the gas and squealed across another lane. "Van drivers! Biggest, slowest hogs on the highway."

He noticed Kathryn staring at him, white-faced, and he had to laugh. "Thought I was Mr. Cautious, huh? Drives a Volvo, wants to live forever."

"Well . . ."

"Notice I put my seat belt on first."

"That makes me feel *so* much better."

"Got yours on?"

"Uh, no." She reached for hers.

He ran the red light at Canyon Acres and shot past the Festival of Arts. Coast Highway was clear going north, and with difficulty Alex kept himself from pushing the Volvo over fifty. "See any police blinkers up ahead?"

Kathryn peered out. "No. It's getting foggy."

"Can't see more than a hundred yards."

He did not slow down, though. He began to wonder how he would know exactly where they were. He tromped down and sped two miles along the Coast Highway. A car came off a feeder street from the big hotels inland, slowed slightly, and turned right without looking, even though the light was against it. "Tourist!" Alex swore vehemently and swerved around it. The lights of Corona del Mar appeared over the curve of the road, murky in the mist, and he saw nothing on the highway.

"There!" Kathryn pointed at a cluster of police cars and ambulances, behind them and far over in the parking lot of the state park. Banks of white vapor wreathed the winking reds and yellows, making pulsing spheres in the mist.

Alex hung a vicious left in front of an approaching brigade of cars, stomped the gas to make up the distance he had overshot, and nearly lost the rear end as they hit gravel on the turnoff into the parking lot. They left skidmarks behind the police black-and-whites.

Alex trotted toward the big UCI ambulance just as two paramedics appeared, rolling a gurney. They were sweating as they reached the top of a concrete path that led down to the beach. Alex knew well enough to step back, giving them plenty of room. Susan rolled by in a full neck collar, eyes closed, her body listless and somehow vulnerable on the stiff white sheets. Swiftly they got her into the ambulance with great speed. Only when the orderly slammed the door did Alex say, "I'm her friend. What happened?"

"Fell down the cliff," the woman paramedic snapped, and rushed for the forward door. The ambulance swiftly pulled away into the pearly fog.

Alex turned toward the cliff, and there was Kathryn. She had found Gary Flint, a sandy-haired man in his early forties. Gary had on a checked work shirt and jeans. The I^2 ambulance stood well to the side of the police cars, its logo deliberately subdued.

Gary said, "We'll follow them right now, Alex. Susan's in pretty bad shape."

"What happened?"

"Don't know. We got here a few minutes after UCI. All I could do was watch the emergency crew work on her. She'd been pretty badly messed up on the rocks. Deep bruises, a contusion. Her pupils are unequal in size and inactive. She's breathing, but low and slow. Pulse jumping all around. Blood pressure high but starting to come down."

"What's your guess?"

"Certainly concussion. Brain damage, maybe."

Kathryn said, "Oh no," with a sinking tone.

"Where did you find her?" Alex pressed.

Gary gestured into the billowing fog. "Cops are all over it."

"Looks like she may need us," Alex said. Distantly he listened to his own voice, flat and factual. That was the best way to be when you had to make clear decisions, not about a stranger but about one of your friends. But that wasn't why he responded this way. Events had simply compressed him, switched him over to automatic.

Gary nodded. "Looks like. Hope to hell not, but . . ."

The heavy-set man shook himself, but not because of the clammy fog that now thickened around them. It was the way Gary worked off the stresses of being on the emergency team, giving vent to his need for physical action when there was really nothing to be done. Yet.

The police cars yards away were visible only because of the diffuse winking halos of their lights. Behind the occasional rasping voices over the police radios and the idling engines, Alex heard the perpetual mutter of the waves.

The moment of silence between them passed. "Look," Gary said, "I got Pete with me in the unit. We'll go on down to UCI. I'll check in with the staff, check on the legal angles."

Alex gritted his teeth. "Not the best place. They've been giving her shit lately."

"I heard. That won't make any difference at a time like this, will it?"

"I'd rather not find out. Any chance we could transfer her to Hoag in Newport?"

"Her patient's directives specify UCI if at all possible."

Kathryn said, "That paperwork is from better days, though."

Gary nodded. "Nothing we can do, I'd say. We're stuck. We've never done a suspension with them, or even met with their ethics committee."

"Right." Alex grimaced. Though UCI General was one of the nearest to I^2, it was only a few years old. Hospitals usually took a while to work the idea of cryonics through the bureaucratic labyrinth. Sometimes they never did. "We'll come along. If we split up the jobs—"

"No, stay here. The cops need some background on her."

"They can fill out their forms later. Right now—"

"They've got some doubts."

"Huh? About what?"

"Whether it was an accident."

Kathryn's eyes widened. Alex felt a leaden apprehension in his stomach.

"That's why you should stay." Gary looked significantly at Kathryn. "Both of you. Don't let the cops get you alone, get you rattled."

Alex nodded slowly. Gary was an old hand in cryonics. He had dealt with some dicey suspensions. Once the police had arrested him for interfering with an investigation because he wouldn't buy their suspicions, and worse, wouldn't shut up about it. The charges had been dropped, of course, but it would be a good idea to keep Gary away from any cop with a long memory.

"We'll stay here," Kathryn said. "When we're done, I'll go back to I^2 and help with communications."

Alex was pleased with how cool and quick she was. As Gary left in the I² ambulance, they walked cautiously down the concrete path. At the brow of the hill the police had yellow-taped it off. Two officers stopped them, and Kathryn used her nicest voice to get through to the officer in charge. He was a thin man with an earnest look who immediately told them to stand where they were and not to walk around.

For fifteen minutes this was all the attention they got while some plainclothes police arrived. Alex's mind churned with possibilities, plans, fears—just as they always did when a suspension might have to start soon, with no preparation time. But this time Kathryn was there and he found himself rattling on, not editing his thoughts into presentable form, just letting them gush out. It was a fresh sensation in the midst of the free-floating anxiety he so often felt at these times, and as the words tumbled out he realized that he was calming, thinking more clearly. On impulse, in midsentence, he kissed her. None of the cops noticed.

Then for long minutes he stood with his arm around Kathryn and watched the soldiers of the law at work. He had crossed swords with them before, as was inevitable in cryonics. He could still clearly remember a car accident scene years before, when he had helped carry out a cryonic suspension in the face of obvious distaste from the police. But that was not what had troubled Alex.

Cops spent their lives in a world ruled by the worst impulses, peopled by vermin. Constant reminders of mortality flourished. They became cynical, inured to calamity. "You're not staring at a person," an obviously veteran detective had said calmly at the car crash site, making notes on his clipboard. "The suffering is over, and that's just something that got left behind."

A healthy way of dealing with accident, maybe, if you had to face it every day. But, he reminded himself, at least for a while, it was wrong. Even if Susan died this instant, the structure of her would not be inescapably lost for several hours more.

A flinty-eyed plainclothes detective nodded at them. "I'm Detective Stern, county office. You know the woman?"

"Yes," Kathryn answered promptly, while Alex, still amid his memories, stayed deliberately silent. "She is Dr. Susan Hagerty, a physician on the faculty at UCI." She rattled off Susan's address and other details from memory, which Alex found impressive. It was another sign of how thoroughly she had taken over the I² office, getting it into crisp shape after years of volunteer casualness.

"Know why she was down here?"

Alex said, "She went running here nearly every day. I've gone with her a few times, when she took her dog out."

"She usually took her dog?"

"I"—a little caution here, Alex thought, though he did not quite know why—"I don't know. Sometimes."

Stern squinted, but not because of the harsh white spotlights that officers were setting up on the pathway. "A jogger. Pretty agile?"

"She was in her forties and stayed in good shape. But if she ran this far from El Morro Beach, I'd guess she might be tired."

"How'd you know she started at El Morro?"

"I didn't. Just seemed logical. When I was with her we started there."

Stern nodded. "We found her car parked in the lot down that way."

Kathryn said, "She probably ran here on the beach, and—"

"We know she did." Stern led them down the path, by some investigating officers, and stooped to pick up a plastic bag holding two running shoes. "We've matched her prints down below."

As Stern led them down the path, Alex firmly kept his anxiety in check. He had never been much of an actor and his wariness was bound to come through to Stern. Better to say as little as possible, he decided.

They reached the beach and stood beside a stretch of sand sliced out of the shrouded dark by piercing spotlights. Two plainclothesmen were taking pictures. A third seemed to be making plaster casts of footprints.

"She left a clear track coming from the south and up this ramp. There are other prints, too." He pointed at several different tread marks. One set was deeply gouged into the sand, as if by a big man running hard. Alex couldn't help but follow them into the distance with his eye. They followed the same curve up to the path as Susan's.

Stern said, "Those tracks run into the surf, so we're pretty sure they were made much earlier, when the tide was out."

Alex nodded, and then he saw the dog prints. They ran roughly parallel to Susan's.

Stern was watching him. "What kind of dog did she have?"

"Uh, one of those Dutch dogs. They were bred to live on barges, I remember her saying. A keeshond, I think they're called."

"We'll keep an eye out for it. Though you'd think it would stick around." Stern looked casually puzzled, in a way that instantly reminded Alex of that television detective who always looked confused and slow-witted. Columbus? No, Columbo. Life imitating art, and not very well. Okay, then. Alex could play dumb, too.

"We can walk around a little and call it."

"What's its name?"

"I . . . don't remember."

"Um. Do you suppose many people knew she came here every day?"

"I don't know that myself. I said she came here pretty often, that's all. She's a physician, totally wrapped up in her work since her husband died. I don't think she has many friends."

"And how do you know her?"

Alex started to shrug, then thought maybe that was too casual a gesture, too obvious a mockery of Stern's manner. "She consults for our company. We struck up a friendship."

"So how'd you get here so fast?"

"My friend, Gary Flint. He called me."

"He was the guy in the other ambulance?"

"Right."

"Now why would he do that?"

"We're part of an emergency team."

"At UCI?"

"No, Immortality Incorporated."

Stern did not even blink. "Ah, I've heard about you. The chiller people."

Alex knew better than to explain. Stern had this easygoing, just-routine manner down pat. He was fishing for something, but Alex didn't know what. Stern looked at Kathryn and asked, "You're part of the team, too?"

"I work for the company, yes. I came along because they might need help."

Stern seemed completely relaxed. He tugged his black tie up to cover his unbuttoned collar, getting chilled in the fog. Alex, too, felt the damp cold settling into his legs and hands, silent, steady, cloaking the night with thick mystery.

"Well, let us hope your Dr. Hagerty does not need your services," he said amiably. Then he looked squarely at Alex, his face still betraying nothing. "Or mine."

2

KATHRYN

The University of California at Irvine General Hospital had an imposing, metallic sheen. In contrast with the settling, damp night outside, frosty brilliance flooded the emergency room. Kathryn escaped the enameled warrens as quickly as she could after finding out from a stiff-necked clerk that Susan Hagerty had been moved down to CAT scan. UCI was organized into clinical research units rather than the usual hospital plan, and it was confusing. Half an hour later, she discovered that Susan was in the intensive care unit, and that was where she and Alex found the I^2 emergency team cooling their heels.

The waiting room was designed to soften tensions, Kathryn noticed. Modern paintings, highlighted by concealed spots, made big bright explosions on the walls. A complex metal sculpture sat on a low pedestal, so that a lamp shaped like a ballistic missile threw its looming shadow on a wall. Two I^2 members sat in the waiting room, biding their time out of long experience. They were kept in reserve, resting for what might be a wearing wait. Cryonicists had learned to pace themselves, letting only a fraction of the team deal with business at a time. Dying could be a lengthy affair. They nodded to Kathryn and went back to paging through magazines.

Gary Flint was a complete contrast. Fidgeting, he paced outside the big doors of the ICU, absently scratching the back of his neck. In the bright corridor his oil-splotched checkered shirt and torn, faded jeans stood out against the scrupulous orderliness. She was quite sure that Gary had not taken up the torn-jeans look as a fashion statement. She did remember that he liked tinkering with pre-1960s Thunderbirds. Alex had told her that despite appearances, Gary was an experienced surgical technician. He looked relieved to see them.

"Susan is stable, but pretty bad off," he said. "I tried to see her, but of course they'll only let in close relatives."

"Susan hasn't got any close relatives nearer than the East Coast," Kathryn said. "I remember that from her file."

"How are her vitals?" Alex asked.

Gary's mouth twisted. "Not well. In a coma, looks like."

"Damn," Alex said.

"All from a fall, they said."

"Yeah." Alex bit his lip.

All three studied each other's faces as if looking for answers. They made frustrated comments and for several minutes let the news chew at them. This time, she sensed, was different. They would be standing by for a close friend.

Training asserted itself. Alex asked, "What're her numbers?"

"Pulse rate and the rest are steady, the head nurse says."

"What is the head nurse's attitude? You told her why we're here?" Kathryn had never seen a suspension, but she had read all the I^2 protocols. They were clogged with details, and Alex had asked her to rewrite them so that the main ideas stood out plainly. She could remember him saying, *These aren't going to be read by a graduate student interested in exact drug dosages—they're crisis guidelines. Make them read that way.* Now she was going to get to see how they played out.

Gary held the loose-leaf binder labeled EMERGENCY INSTRUCTIONS FOR

STABILIZATION OF CRYONIC SUSPENSION PATIENTS in his hand. He nodded, his light hair slipping down to shade his eyes. "She's guarded, maybe a little horrified—but she seems fair, so far."

"We haven't been through any paperwork with UCI," Alex said. "I don't think anybody's even been over here to talk to them."

Gary shrugged. "We can't cover every hospital in California. I'm pretty sure they got the usual letter asking them to consider how they would react to us in case something like this came up."

Kathryn had seen that form letter, too. It had a blissful naïveté about it, as though a hospital would get involved in correspondence about hypothetical situations. A waste of time, she had thought.

Gary went back into the ICU office, and when he came out he held up a sheet covered in dot-matrix type. "She gave me a printout. No skull fractures. Proteins are normal, too, so maybe there's no cerebral hemorrhage. The CT scan didn't pick up anything in the head, but it looks like she has a broken neck at C4-5."

"Why is she in a coma?" Kathryn asked.

"Concussion. She's starting to come out of it, they think."

Alex asked, "How you figure we're doing with the hospital administration?"

Gary sighed. "We should have come by on a goodwill visit when they opened. Cryonics is a whole new ballgame to them. The head nurse, Dowell, gave me a blank stare."

"We should go to the medical director," Kathryn said, remembering the I^2 protocols.

"I asked for him, and to see Susan's physician of record," Gary said. "Nothing so far."

"As I understand it, even though we aren't relatives, we have some standing," Kathryn said.

"You're right, the patient's directives document," Gary said. "But it's at I^2."

Kathryn looked around. "Where's a phone? I'll get her file faxed over."

"And I'll pound on a few doors," Alex said.

There was a pay phone around the corridor corner. Kathryn got through on the I^2 emergency number and set up the fax transfer, using the ICU number. Then she asked one of the volunteer standby staff, who had moved into place once the alarm went out, to bring the originals of Susan's file over by car. By the time she got back to the ICU entrance, Gary was talking to a tall man in a white coat.

"This is Dr. Anderson," Gary said, "Susan's physician."

Anderson nodded and went on in a warm, reassuring tone, "I knew her only slightly, of course, and I'm happy to say she seems stable at the moment. We'll know more in the morning."

Kathryn recognized the smooth, meaningless phrases. "Something could happen tonight, though."

"Well, yes, that is a possibility. I assure you, however, we do not anticipate that. Many such cases that begin to show progress this soon after head trauma do well. Before—"

"I'm sorry, sir, but that's why we're here," Gary said mildly. "Some cases die, too, and nobody can predict when."

"True, but uncommon. I think you're reacting too strongly, to request this."

"If she dies, your job's over. We'll have to act immediately."

Kathryn could see that Gary was never going to go into the diplomatic service. Dr. Anderson stiffened visibly. "I assure you, if Dr. Hagerty does in fact pass away, none of your efforts will revive her. What's more, they are quite outside the bounds of procedure allowed at this or any other hospital I know."

"We aren't here to interfere with medical practice, doctor," Kathryn said quickly, before Gary could respond. "We certainly won't get in your way. But we aren't going to try to revive her at all. We simply limit the damage done to her after death and freeze her for the future."

"Oh." Anderson blinked, his mouth twisting into a distantly sardonic curve. "An even more absurd idea. I'm afraid you'll get no cooperation from me."

Kathryn readied herself to respond with the soothing sentences that women were supposed to be better at than men, when Alex's voice said over her shoulder, "With all due respect, doctor, isn't that a matter for the Ethics Committee?"

"Well, yes, I suppose. You are?"

"Alex Cowell, part of this team. I'm told the medical director has reached the hospital and will see us all in his office."

Anderson nodded vigorously, as though relieved. Kathryn imagined how they must look to him—crazies in street clothes who showed up in the middle of an acute case, claiming a legal relationship with one of his own colleagues. *Damn right he should be suspicious,* she thought.

They left Gary and the rest of the suspension team at the ICU, just in case Susan suddenly worsened. Kathryn had the faxed documents with her when they reached the medical director's carpeted, neatly appointed office. The director introduced himself with easygoing informality, shaking hands all around, even Dr. Anderson's—maybe to defuse the obvious tensions in the group, she guessed. "I'm Irwin Wright," he said to Kathryn, "and I suppose you're another believer in this, ah, cryo—"

"Uh, not exactly," Kathryn replied uncomfortably. "I work for Immortality Incorporated, that's all."

"Well, they have good taste in employees, at least," Wright said, settling into a big leather armchair that dominated a cozy arrangement of two couches. Indirect lighting, heavy polished walnut, lots of earth-colored fabrics—very reassuring. Kathryn judged that he did most of his real work here, negotiating. A teaching hospital like UCI was a grand opera with a surplus of prima donnas and few who wanted to be spear-carriers.

Alex gave a quick, incisive summary of their position and the cooperation I² would like from UCI. Wright asked Anderson how he felt about this, as attending physician, and Anderson bounced the ball right back to him, saying it was clearly an issue for the Ethics Committee.

"Um," Wright said, stroking his lined face. He wore corduroy trousers and a brown cotton work shirt, exactly the sort of thing executives slipped on to relax for the evening. It was 8:27 P.M., and she was sure he was thinking fondly of another armchair at home. Alex sat forward on a couch, hands gripped in a ball, elbows on his knees almost as though he were prepared to jump to his feet. Anderson sat back, legs crossed, his mood betrayed by his upper leg, which bobbed with nervous energy. Both of them gave off the kind of prickly stubbornness that born compromisers like Wright avoided.

So she was not completely surprised when after a long moment of thought, he turned to her and said, "You understand that I cannot, as a practical matter, call an emergency meeting of the Ethics Committee to consider this matter."

"Of course," she answered. "We simply want to be allowed some access to Dr. Hagerty."

"I'm afraid I do not have time to consider the deeper issues here." He fanned the I² documents Kathryn had given them. "I do not quite understand the exact legal position we are in, and whether these agreements between your company and Dr. Hagerty do in fact act to constrain this hospital in any way."

"Well, professor, you will note that we specifically exempt you from any—here, I can quote it from memory—'from any and all liability in the post-mortem handling and transfer of the patient's remains.' That lets you off the hook."

Wright's eyebrows lifted pleasurably at this, but then descended into a frown. "I appreciate that, but I still feel I am too unacquainted with this entire idea to pass judgment on such grounds alone. I am troubled, indeed, that Dr. Hagerty is in fact so deeply connected with your—uh, enterprise. You may know that she is under review by the Academic Senate for her professional actions that were, I believe, related to you. This deeper connection will not help her case."

Alex said sardonically, "If she passes beyond your justice, we'll be the only ones who can help her."

Wright did not look as though he understood this clipped sarcasm, and Kathryn decided to not give him enough time to puzzle it through. She said rapidly, "We only want a few simple things, believe me. She may need them at any moment."

"Um. What things?"

Anderson opened his mouth, but Alex jumped in with, "We want to bring up from our ambulance a heart-lung resuscitator, a gurney that carries a blood pump, a membrane oxygenator, and a heat exchanger."

"Why?" Anderson asked, annoyed. "That's the sort of equipment one would use to revive her."

Alex said patiently, "We want to minimize the loss of oxygen to the brain."

"Well, I'm afraid all this is beyond easy resolution. I realize I don't know enough about it, so I've asked a member of our faculty who has looked into this to come over after he finishes dinner." Wright nodded significantly at a flashing light on the telephone at his elbow. "I suppose that's my secretary, announcing him."

Kathryn had a sinking feeling. Sure enough, the Dr. Blevin Susan had described turned out to be a stiff-faced man in a baggy red sweater with a hooded, closed look to his eyes. He was flushed, as though he had hurried.

"I was shocked to hear the news. How did it happen?"

"She fell from a cliff at the beach," Kathryn said, going on to introduce herself. Blevin listened carefully to Alex's quick discussion of the accident and her symptoms, then interrupted, "I really believe I should hear from the physician. Dr. Anderson?"

Anderson had been notably quiet ever since they got to the director's office, and Susan saw why. Susan's case before the Academic Senate made her treatment in the ICU a potential bombshell. Anderson betrayed this in his hesitant delivery, confining himself to strict descriptions of tests, vital signs, and the patient's history. It was almost as if Anderson were reciting for a grade, and Kathryn suddenly saw that indeed, the man had reverted to the hedged-in, minimize-possible-damage style that medical students use. She had seen this sort of thing on TV hospital dramas. Anderson fit perfectly: *And the first of all the commandments shall be, Cover Thy Ass.*

After Anderson finished his just-the-facts report, Wright said conversationally, "Do you think she may die within the next few hours?"

"Well . . ." Anderson glanced at Blevin. Kathryn did not have to see a staff chart to know who was the senior figure here. "I don't think so. The spinal trauma is serious, but she is intubated and controlled."

"Can you be sure?" Kathryn asked.

"No. In cases like this, with multiple injuries, widespread hematoma, and of course the severe spinal trauma, one doesn't know."

Wright said casually, "I'd like to ask you, then, Dr. Blevin, to comment."

Blevin gathered himself, measuring his words. "I have from the beginning suspected that Susan Hagerty's involvement with these people was more extensive, and more insidious, if I may put it that way, than was obvious."

Kathryn said, "I don't see why her arrangements for the disposal of her remains after death should enter into your medical school catfights."

Wright glanced sharply at her and then got the message. "I want to assure you, Ms. Sheffield, that I shall allow no such linkage."

It was a pleasant, vague denial that she did not believe for a minute. But she kept her bland half-smile in place and listened as Blevin went through a catalog of his griefs and grumbles about "these corpse-freezers" and the way they defrauded the ill and dying. They were a blot upon the respectable medical community, raising utterly false hopes, draining dollars.

"I had wondered about that, too," Wright came in, stroking his chin. "I mean, as a strictly moral issue. Do people have the right to spend money to keep themselves, ah, as you people would say, 'suspended'? Rather than pass assets on to their family?"

Alex said flatly, "It's their money, isn't it?"

The director said mildly, "Yes, but not after they die."

Kathryn said, "Not at all. Susan Hagerty could have left a will directing her estate to build a giant pyramid and bury her in it. After all, the pharaohs did."

"And they believed their mummies would live again, too," Blevin said acidly.

"But they—and Susan—had the right," Kathryn said. She noticed Blevin's face congesting, lips drawn white.

The director made a cathedral of his fingers before his face, gazing into it. Kathryn saw he was treating this as a rarified issue, as though this were a seminar on medical ethics. But three floors below them Susan lay damaged and weak, her body struggling with ripped nerves and smashed tissues, far beyond cool, neat abstractions. She felt a sudden rush of pure anger at these smug, comfortable authority figures in their warm offices—and at once felt close to Alex, who let his impatience show too baldly, but at least was close to the deep truth of all this.

Wright said, "Still, her personal pyramid—for I must admit, Ms. Sheffield, that is all I feel it to be, a big, pointless gesture—her pyramid involves letting you invade our ICU, disrupt it, use our resources."

Kathryn could see Alex pause for an instant and knew he was tempted to launch into a spirited defense of Susan's own research, of the results in reviving Sparkle, and how they would vindicate her in

UCI's coming inquiry. But this was certainly not the place or time, and after a breath he said, "We will be quiet. We will use nothing of yours."

"*Nothing* of ours?" Blevin finally erupted. "You're taking our reputation!"

"If your patients die, it's not our fault. We just try to hang on to the structure remaining in them and save it for the future."

"You empty their bank accounts, you mean, in return for snake oil. Dr. Wright, you simply cannot allow these misfits to use our hospital for their fraudulent—"

"Careful of your words," Wright said mildly, holding up a single finger. "They are actionable."

Blevin shook his head and snorted in exasperation. "By condoning this, you—"

"Don't worry," Kathryn said. "We're not here to cook up a lawsuit. We're here to save Susan, if that's necessary."

Blevin said sharply, "Irwin, I appeal to you on behalf of the medical faculty. We are united against this kind of thing. I had hoped that Susan Hagerty's being brought forward to the Academic Senate on charges would alert you to that. Apparently it hasn't. I suggest you consider our wishes in this matter, particularly in view of the way the media will view this entire incident. You know how we dislike such outside perceptions."

This struck Kathryn as a well-reasoned threat, couched in high-minded tones but just obvious enough to remind Wright that he was, in the end, elected by the physicians who worked here. Blevin was biased but not dumb.

Wright registered all this with a flick of an eyebrow. His sallow face hardened. "I wish you hadn't said that, Sidney. To take your position would then make it seem like giving in to in-house pressures." A thin smile. "You know how I dislike such outside perceptions."

3

ALEX

It was a relief to release his pent-up energies in a flurry of activity. As soon as he reached the ICU with Dr. Anderson, Alex began to pepper the man with questions.

"Can we move Susan into that area down at the end?" he gestured down the long, machine-thronged room, which was partitioned into ample spaces around each bed.

Anderson looked at the head nurse, the muscular woman named Dowell. "That's farther from the nurses' station," she said.

"I appreciate that, but then our work won't bother your other patients as much, either." He studied Dowell's stony face for an instant and added, "I'm thinking of them. We'll do as much as we can to minimize the disruption."

"I should hope *so,*" Dowell said, rolling her eyes skyward, apparently because Anderson was going to be of no use whatever in warding off these crank invaders.

Alex ran through the checklist in his mind, with Gary standing next to him, eyes on the loose-leaf manual. Doing things by the numbers saved time and, long afterward, could be the touch that kept lawyers off your tail. "Dr. Anderson, will you or another physician be available all tonight, to pronounce legal death?"

Anderson frowned. "Normally, no. I have other duties, other patients."

"Could you let us know when you're in the hospital?"

Anderson's mouth worked, annoyed. "I suppose so. You can reach me on my beeper, through my office. I go off duty at two o'clock. You'll have to talk to my replacement physician then."

"We'll be happy to, sir," Alex said briskly.

The ICU outside the nurses' station murmured with the whispers and gurgles of machines, the music of medicine. There were five patients in the ICU at the moment, each the nucleus for a web of tubes, wires, catheters, lines, and other unsubtle invasions. The price of survival is inevitably an utter exposure, a nakedness before the brute fact of the physical self that reduces a person to a machine. That is the philosophy of modern medicine, and it works.

But the whole person has properties beyond the underlying machine, facets like passion and gossamer-thin intuition and a certain instinctive resonance with other life. Usually our minds work on, party to airy dreams, while our bodies labor in ancient silence. Here the roles reversed. Susan lay inert and her body held the stage. Modern medicine could pull her body back from the abyss, yet lose her self to the oblivion of coma.

Alex was no poet, as some cryonicists were, rhapsodizing about immortality. He was here to save whatever he could. This head nurse was not his enemy, though she undoubtedly thought herself one. Compared with the touchy-feely brigade, the health faddists and cult figures and gurus, he and Nurse Dowell were soldiers in the same small army.

"Nurse Dowell, you've got IV lines, bladder catheter, some other diagnostics in the patient now. Could you please leave them in for our use, if Susan dies?"

Nurse Dowell frowned, looked exasperated for a moment at this intrusion into routine, and then turned to Anderson without saying anything. A savvy nurse deferred to the physician, if possible. Anderson nodded.

Alex asked, "Before we look at her, I wonder if the hospital has any ice on hand?"

The nurse's mouth twitched with irritation. "We have a perfectly good morgue cooler."

"Of course, but we'll need a lot of ice. We want a steady temperature held a few degrees above freezing."

Nurse Dowell said sharply, "I thought you people *wanted* to freeze her."

"We do it under controlled conditions. Look, I'm hoping we won't need to use the morgue at all. Gary, could you and Kathryn go down and check with the morgue people?"

This was actually a good way to hand off the problem, keeping relations smooth with the ICU. A big hospital resembled Eastern Europe, with balkanized fiefdoms presided over by lordly, capricious technicians. Gary nodded and left to get Kathryn from the waiting room outside. Director Wright's guidelines allowed only two I^2 staff in the ICU unless Susan died.

Gary was following a protocol in the manual. Morgue attendants were the lowly of hospitals, essentially charged with disposing of its failures. Brought into the loop, they could speed movement of a patient when time was most crucial.

Alex asked for permission to view Susan. Anderson and Dowell shepherded him cautiously through the sliding curtain partitions. Despite his training, he was shocked. Susan's face was chalk-white, glassy, grossly swollen. She breathed shallowly through a tube, and the video monitors showed a steady, slow heartbeat. He remembered her as determined, always in motion. Here she was inert, seemingly less alive than the humming devices surrounding her.

Alex put a hand on her arm, an instinctive act that he found reassuring. He was here to help her, but he ached with the hope that he would prove unnecessary, that he would see her sunny energy again.

"Anything more, then?" Nurse Dowell demanded briskly.

Jerked out of his mood, Alex clicked into automatic again. "Uh, yes. We've got two E cylinders of oxygen on our cart, but we'd like to save them for transport. Could we tap into your oxygen line?"

"Well . . ." Another glance at Anderson, who was playing a cagy, quiet game. He nodded again. "I suppose so."

"Thanks very much. I brought a DISS fitting for the adaptor. I'll just check it out, and—"

"Mr. Cowell?" One of the other nurses had stuck her head through the curtains.

"Yes?"

"There's a Detective Stern outside to see you. He says it's important."

Alex glanced at the clock as he left: 9:14 P.M. Three hours ago he had been in Kathryn's arms. Life was a cabaret, right.

Stern's face seemed furrowed with fatigue beneath the unforgiving bleached light of the corridor. He was talking to two other men, both in rumpled gray suits. They had the same steady hardness about them and Alex instantly knew they were cops, too. Stern finished talking and nodded to Alex. "Come on, let's go in here," Stern said without preliminaries and led him into a small conference room down the carpeted hall. One of the other plainclothesmen came back, bringing Kathryn from the office where she had been discussing Susan's legal papers with the staff.

"How is she?" Stern asked when all three were seated around a plain table.

"Stable, but not good."

"Too bad. I came by to ask you a few more questions."

"I don't really know much more about her."

Stern looked sour. "Come on. She worked out there with you guys for years."

Kathryn said, "We knew her well enough to know she didn't have any enemies."

"How about right here?"

Kathryn blinked. "What?"

"At UCI. Seems she was up for some kind of trial. Accusations of illegal operations, that sort of thing."

Alex kept his voice flat, noncommittal. "She had a dispute with another faculty member. We just saw him here, in fact. It was a scientific matter."

Stern sniffed, rubbed his nose with his hand. "Not the kind of stuff people kill each other about, you'd say?"

"Of *course* not," Kathryn said.

"So she was a workaholic with few friends? Who liked to run on the beach with her dog?"

"Well, yes," Alex said guardedly.

"We checked out her home. Nothing unusual there, near as we can tell."

"Oh," Alex said.

Stern made a thin, mirthless smile. "But no dog." He gazed steadily at Alex. "You were the last person to see her, near as we can determine."

"I suppose so."

"She say anything about the dog?"

"I think so. About taking it for a run."

"You're sure?"

"Not really. A lot has happened in the last few hours."

"Sure has. We spent an hour trying to find that dog down on that cold, foggy beach."

Kathryn said firmly, "So probably it ran off."

"Could be," Stern said. "Seems unusual for a pet, though."

"Did any witnesses see her on the beach?" Alex asked.

"We haven't found any. Weather kept them away, I expect."

A sharp knock at the door startled Alex. He was intent on not giving away his own suspicions. Acting concerned, but not too much, was the hardest part. And how could he bring up Susan's earlier incident with the vagrant, without arousing Stern's suspicions? He had to play a cagy game here, in case the worst happened.

Alex opened the door and there was Dr. Blevin, hands tucked into his loose-fitting red cardigan. Alex had a sudden impulse to slam the door in the man's face, a hot urge so strong, his arm twitched. But that would earn him nothing, and he made himself say, "This is a private conversation, doctor."

"I know precisely what it is. I want to see the detective."

Alex stepped aside, thinking furiously. He couldn't imagine how Blevin could mess this up, but he could see from the hard, flat line of the man's mouth that Blevin was there to try. He watched as Blevin went through introductions with a sudden air of warm sincerity—a bedside manner on a switch, he supposed. "Do you know Frank Olenberg in the

DA's office? Old buddy of mine," Blevin said, ignoring Kathryn completely.

Stern said, "Yeah, we have lunch now and then."

"Great guy. I heard you were in the building and thought I'd stop by."

"Why so, doctor?"

"Well, I'm sure these two"—a contemptuous wave—"have been filling your ear about the dispute between Dr. Hagerty and myself."

Stern said politely in a just-making-conversation voice, "Oh, that was you?"

"Regrettably, yes. It was over her research, some violations of university standards."

"Involving what?"

Blevin seemed truly surprised, his mouth hanging slightly open. "They didn't tell you? Over this cryonics stuff. Susan was using university facilities, university funds—all to carry out crackpot research for these people. I was pretty sure she was getting some money under the table for it."

"That's a lie!" Alex erupted. "We didn't pay her a dime for research."

Stern turned his gaze lazily to Alex. "You said just a while back, as I remember, that she did some consulting for your company."

Kathryn said, "That was for other services."

Blevin shook his head with thoroughly believable sadness. "I understand that you cryonics people refuse to accept death. I see it every day, and I guess I know how you feel. But surely you can see that conservative medical practice cannot go along with your claims. Somehow you enlisted poor Dr. Hagerty in your beliefs. She was under a lot of strain, and I suppose I feel responsible. I had public and private disagreements with her—maybe I should have simply taken her aside, tried to get her therapy, maybe even apologized. The last time I saw her she looked so depressed."

"Tired, not depressed," Alex said. "She's been working hard to get her research written up."

"The mysterious revived dog?" Blevin raised an eyebrow. "That's somehow dead again?"

"The dog, Sparkle, is well documented." Alex knew that Blevin had the weight of authority on his side here, and Stern was the audience for both of them. They weren't really talking to each other at all. "She has earlier work with mice, too. A fair hearing will clear her of your attacks."

Blevin remained collected, his voice reasonable as he turned to Stern, conspicuously ignoring Alex. "She admitted at her hearing—you can check this from the transcript—that she did some of her experiments at this corpse-freezing firm. Under a fictitious corporate screen, of course, a phony name. She was clever. No one ever accused Susan Hagerty of being dumb, not at all. My dispute with her was over—well, ethics."

"You're misrepresenting her work," Alex said sharply. But even to himself it sounded weak.

"I wanted to come by and clear up any suspicions you might have, Detective," Blevin said evenly, ignoring Alex.

"Suspicions?" Stern asked.

"Well, Susan is hurt, I've had a feud with her, I suppose you could say—the line of logic is clear."

"But wrong."

"Of course. I was home with my wife all evening. But I bring up our past associations and differences because I do believe them to be germane. I believe Susan may have tried to commit suicide."

"Suicide!" Alex blurted.

"No. No no no," Kathryn said.

Stern raised his eyebrows. "Why?"

"Susan faced expulsion from the university—a near certainty, to my mind, once the full facts were known. She would find difficulty in obtaining another post. Certainly no major research institution would touch her."

Alex shot back, "You're exaggerating—"

"*And* frankly, she was something of a depressive sort already, in my estimation."

Alex made himself say stiffly, "I wasn't aware that you were a psychiatrist, Dr. Blevin."

Blevin gave a self-deprecating smile. "Well, of course I'm not. However, any physician receives some training in that area, enough to recognize obvious symptoms."

Alex had been struggling to hold his temper. He recognized his own symptoms—the room seemed too warm, his breathing was fast and shallow. But he judged that Stern liked hard evidence, coolly stated opinions, so he kept his voice flat and factual. "I don't think your opinion of her mental state has any validity. You're her enemy. You're biased as hell. I knew her, and I saw no depressive behavior. She kept herself in good physical condition. As I recall, that's seldom the case with suicides."

Blevin narrowed his already hooded eyes. "I don't believe any credence whatever can be given to the medical opinions of laymen."

Stern held up a hand, a world-weary signal for them to stop. "It's an interesting idea, anyway. An unusual method, though. Women usually choose sedatives. You'd think a doctor would go that way. Men like guns. Jumpers are rare for either sex."

Blevin said, "She may have acted on impulse. And remember that suicides often occur at night."

Alex sputtered in exasperation. "Look, anybody who knew Susan—really knew her—knows she wouldn't kill herself."

Blevin said adamantly, "In my opinion she never recovered from her husband's sudden death."

Kathryn said, "She spent years trying to *do* something about that death. She didn't mope around, she worked."

Blevin pointedly turned away from Alex and Kathryn and addressed Stern. "I believe you will agree that suicide is a plausible hypothesis."

Alex's caution blew away in a sudden spike of anger. "You're bringing this up out of spite!"

"I have information relevant to Detective Stern's business."

"You're personally involved."

Blevin gave a long-suffering glance to Stern. "And you are not? I am being objective—something you wouldn't understand."

"You know damned well that a suspicion of suicide demands an autopsy."

Blevin shrugged. "I don't make the law."

"If Susan dies and the coroner believes your claim, he'll section her brain, maybe keep some of it. That will erase the memories lodged there. It'll destroy any hope of reviving her."

Blevin spread both hands in a we're-professionals gesture to Stern. "You can see that they're fixated on this preposterous corpse-freezing idea, to the exclusion of any other considerations."

"Gentlemen"—Stern sighed—"I am trying to find out the truth here. I haven't got time to referee between you two."

"My point is that Dr. Blevin is trying to use your investigation to get at us."

Stern smiled. "And you? You were trying hard to convince me it's an accident, so I won't turn the case over to the coroner if she dies."

Alex hoped his face gave nothing away. He had hoped that Stern wouldn't think of that, but he should have realized that was a futile wish, once Stern had some knowledge of cryonics. "I *do* think it's an accident. Nobody had anything to gain from—"

"Honestly, Detective, you cannot believe anything these people say about Dr. Hagerty. They—"

"You deliberately came down here," Alex spat back, "hoping to—"

Stern again held up his hand for silence. "I've already called in the coroner's office."

Alex froze with shock. "What? You can't mean that—"

"I want some technical help. The coroner's deputy and one of our guys are going over Dr. Hagerty's clothes and body right now. All without any risk to her, believe me," Stern added when he saw expressions of alarm from Kathryn and Alex. "It's a standard procedure when we suspect evidence will be lost in the hospital."

"The men outside," Alex said dumbly.

"Yeah."

Alex sat back, his mind churning fruitlessly. A sickening dread yawned, a black certainty that events were turning against them, against Susan. Abruptly he stood up, so furious that he did not trust himself to say anything. He slammed the door on his way out, except that it had one of those damned self-closing arms and only eased shut, depriving him of even that. He stormed down the corridor outside the big ICU doors, reached the end, and came back, trying to think. Kathryn emerged from the conference room and joined him, walking more rapidly to keep up his pace.

"Even after Susan's descriptions, I didn't think Blevin could be that bad," he said.

"A four-star bastard," Kathryn said.

"I wonder if Stern will pay attention to him."

"He's probably amused, actually. We were being so careful with him, he must have guessed why."

Alex glanced at her sharply. "We were trying to keep him from getting sidetracked."

"How do we know his questions about her friends, about her dog, were sidetracks?"

"Well, of *course* they were. He's looking for a murder here, and there isn't anything. Zero, zip, *nada.*"

"We don't know that for sure."

"C'mon, who'd kill Susan? The dog is a red herring."

"Mixed animal metaphor. To Stern, the dog's a red light."

"He's overreaching."

"And he hasn't had time to dig."

"Dig for what?"

"Have you forgotten that Susan was assaulted a couple of weeks ago?"

He snorted with exasperation. "No, but that was a random incident. No connection to this."

"You don't know that."

"It's probable as hell."

Kathryn blinked, her lips pursed with surprise. "You're more concerned with the cryonics angle on this than with whether she was attacked."

He bit his lip in exasperation. "Listen, the main thing is her care, and that's out of our hands. But if the doctors fail in there, then everything comes down to us. Got it?"

"But she's our friend, and maybe somebody—"

"Maybe, crap. I've got to prepare for my job, if I have to do it. That means keeping Stern off our backs."

Kathryn frowned. "As soon as he finds out, he'll get mad at you for not telling him."

"The county sheriff's office is a paperwork operation, not really computerized yet. I^2 has dealt with them before. He can't just call up a cross-check right away. That gives us a window, maybe a few hours."

"He'll get mad, and—"

"Okay, so he'll get mad. I'll say I forgot Susan's bang on the head in the excitement here."

"Do you think he would order an autopsy just on that basis?"

"I don't know. He's paid to be suspicious." Alex paced. He could see that his argument hadn't really convinced her. She didn't sort out things into compartments so easily. He consciously put aside his concern for Susan to prepare for the worst, separating out the issue of whether she had been attacked again. That could come later.

Kathryn stopped his furious pacing and put her hands on his shoulders, peering into his troubled eyes. "Lover, we're trying to put body English on Stern, sure. That's your job, I suppose. We have to let Stern do his job, too."

Alex said stiffly, not allowing himself to be mollified, "You don't feel the way I do. You're not a cryonicist, after all."

Kathryn's eyes flickered, and he knew he had hurt her. After all, he thought, he was simply stating a fact. She wasn't signed up, so she wasn't really one of them. A flat, hard fact.

She blurted, "Damn it, I don't know all this legal and technical stuff, but I can still feel!"

Kathryn's nose twitched in annoyance, but she did not take her hands from his shoulders. Instead, she drew him closer. This unsettled him. He had wanted a quarrel, some sharp words that would take away his anger. Abruptly he remembered his ex-wife saying, *Don't take it out on me!* and it was as though years had peeled away. He had made this mistake before: gotten into shouting matches with a woman he loved. Become so involved in *that* spat, he forgot the ire that had started it off.

The clarity of it was like a cold splash in the face. He blinked. Stared at Kathryn. Opened his mouth. And closed it, not knowing what to say.

Okay, face it. It's a habit, a mode you've gotten into. That doesn't mean you have to keep on doing it. He nodded, confirming it for himself.

Kathryn looked puzzled. He realized that he looked dopey, or crazy, or both, nodding to himself. He opened his mouth again, and again did not know what to say. So he laughed. A deep, ironic howl that came up from his gut and threw his head back in explosive relief.

Kathryn looked even more puzzled. He grabbed her firmly and planted a full, wet kiss on her astounded lips.

When he had made good work of that, he tilted his head back to look at her quizzical half-smile. "Thanks. I needed that. I love you."

Uncertainty left her face. "You big dumb brute, I love you, too."

"I've been meaning to say that."

"You sure picked the nonstandard moment."

"It's my way. Creative romance."

"Whatever it is, it's all your own. You are a strange man."

"I suppose so," he said, reflecting.

4
KATHRYN

"Ms. Sheffield? Mr. Cowell?"

It was Detective Stern, eyes averted slightly, seeming a little embarrassed to approach them while they were standing with their arms around each other. Kathryn caught a closing in his face that told her that he had seen a lot of mayhem in his line of work but not much affection.

"Yes?" she answered in her best business voice.

"I've got some preliminary results here from the technical people. I thought I'd go over them, see if you could add anything further."

She noticed Blevin entering the ICU down the corridor and was thankful that they did not have to endure him again. On the other hand, he was probably going to spread his acutely logical venom in there now.

Stern held out a clipboard and read from it. "These three-sheets are a mess to read, but—"

"Three-sheets?" she asked. She had resolved that she was not going to let jargon cascade by her in all this, or else she would never understand what was going on.

"The third carbon copy of the arriving officers' reports and the technical team reports. Like reading hieroglyphics." Stern waved a clipboard of his own notes. "So I talked to the docs before they left to do their workup."

"You can get the radiological and CAT-scan data right here," Alex said.

"Already have. That lady is really banged up. Multiple contusions, a big one on the lower rear skull, but no evident pattern of blows in them. So those and the bruises probably are from the rocks, all right."

"Wasn't that obvious?" Alex asked.

Stern paused just long enough for Kathryn to see him resolve to not get irked by Alex. It was a reflex obviously built up by long practice. She had solid respect for Stern.

"We check everything, Mr. Cowell," Stern said with a slight ironic precision. "The officers took threads from beneath Dr. Hagerty's fingernails. Preliminary analysis says they are of the same color and material as her jogging suit."

Kathryn said, "So she might have gotten them from her torn clothing?"

"Quite possible, but the lab will have to dot the i's and cross the t's on that one."

Alex nodded vigorously. "How about the blood workup?"

"Got a quick one, just preliminary. The part we're interested in, the drug screen, is a bunch of goose eggs. No drugs, nothing funny. Pretty rare among doctors, by my experience."

Alex smiled. "Any chance I could get a copy?"

Stern pressed the clipboard to his side, face inward, firmly drawing the line. "This was a courtesy, Mr. Cowell, not an invitation."

"We thank you," Kathryn said quickly.

"Hey, we appreciate it, yeah," Alex followed along.

He's finally catching on, Kathryn thought. *Feeling you're on the moral high ground makes for lousy diplomacy.* "Does this influence your conclusions?"

Stern pursed his lips. "I don't have to conclude anything just yet. There are certainly no obvious signs of—"

"Mr. Cowell?" It was one of the ICU nurses. In her flushed face and the web of lines around her narrow mouth, Kathryn saw trouble. "Dr. Anderson said to come right away. All of you."

By the time they reached Susan's partitioned-off space, it became obvious that Anderson was covering himself thoroughly on this one. He was not going to violate the medical director's order that I² be present, but at the same time he wanted the detective there. Kathryn herself was swept in on the tide, along with Gary and the other two in the I² team.

Kathryn stood behind the team and watched Anderson. He called "Clear!" and fired the electric-paddles on Susan's chest. The body heaved. On the monitors above a spike appeared, then lapsed into the same yellow flat line as before.

He did it again. And again.

"That's all," he said at last. "She's gone."

Kathryn felt numb, stark disbelief. All through these hours she had never really thought that Susan would die. It had been a bad fall, but after all, Susan had lived through the impact. And now here it was, a simple few words, and all hope fled.

For a long, quiet moment the crowd around Susan's dwindled form said nothing. They looked at each other, pensive and with small expressions of surprise, even on the faces the nurses. There was a moment, Kathryn thought, when one of us departs and the others left behind know with a deep, sure shock that their time will come, as well.

Then Alex said in a quavering tone, "You will sign the death certificate?"

Anderson was peeling off rubber gloves. "Why, yes."

"Fine," Alex said, his voice sounding forced and under strict control. His jaw muscles clenched rhythmically. "May—may we take over now, Dr. Anderson?"

Anderson stood absolutely still. He returned Alex's gaze as though confronting a demon that had only this second sprung forth from the earth. "I—I don't know."

"I might remind you, doctor, that we have a legal obligation to comply with the patient's wishes."

"I—I know that, but—"

"Your job is done here, sir. Now please let us do ours."

Anderson's eyes fidgeted around the room, searching for someone—anyone—to hand off this problem to.

"If you will simply stand aside, then, we will do for the patient what we can."

Anderson hesitated for a long moment. In the tense quiet Kathryn could hear a *snick* as a nurse slid the shock paddles back into their gloves.

Kathryn said quietly, "I have here copies of Dr. Hagerty's authorization of anatomical donation form." This was a big legal hammer, one the police had to enforce on the spot.

"Oh, all right." Anderson turned and led the nurses out of the area. *Thank God Blevin isn't here,* Kathryn thought.

She noted the time in her notebook: 11:47 P.M. Susan had not quite survived the day.

A phrase rang in her memory: *At least death tells us when to stop trying.* Susan must have said that, in one of their talks. Now that conventional medicine had let go of Susan, a well-drilled team went into action, bringing fresh technology to bear. She stood to the side, took down notes on the Transport Data Collection Form, did odd jobs. She had never seen a suspension before, and despite her reading about it, the reality was far more intense, busy, with critical procedures carefully carried out, than she could have imagined.

Cooling down a body had seemed such an obviously quiet, serene event. She was unprepared for the chug and wheeze of the "thumper"— a heart-lung resuscitator that sat over Susan's chest and kept blood flowing to her brain. The energetic way Gary moved in to begin working on Susan startled her. His medical assistant training must have been thorough, for he operated with speedy assurance. The team packed blue plastic bags of ice around the head. Surgery began. They opened arteries to get access to Susan's circulatory system. Gary mentioned to Dr. Anderson—who stood nearby, asking questions—that they were making the same incisions as surgeons did when setting up artificial circulation for patients undergoing open heart surgery.

Kathryn didn't have much time to watch. The paperwork blizzard began. Anderson signed the death certificate. Under "cause of death" he listed "cardiac arrest" and "shock." Head nurse Dowell wanted copies of the I^2 "hold-harmless" form, of Susan's directives and will, and there were hospital releases to fill in. A clerk brought these and took Kathryn into the ICU nurses' office to get them done. As the blood pump began its steady work of flooding Susan's tissues with the protectant she herself had helped develop, Kathryn noted down times, medications, dosages, flow rates. She charted the input of a sophisticated soup of preservation drugs, entering terms like "nasogastric tube" and "Streptokinase" as Gary called them out—all without knowing quite what was going on.

Ordinarily I^2 had a team member for this job, but he was a volunteer, away on a business trip. The company ran on part-time and unpaid labor. Actually, "ran" was an overstatement, she thought. "Limped along" fit better. She had to admit they were crisp and professional, even though spread pretty thin.

Alex had been right, she saw, to get Susan moved to this far, isolated end of the ICU. The I^2 gear took room, especially when they brought in a Siremobil 2U C-arm rig to X-ray Susan. Gary studied the X-ray and said slowly, "Looks like a saddle embolus blocked her pulmonary artery. Agree, Dr. Anderson?"

Anderson did and made an added note on the death certificate. By this time, the team had begun readying a long box filled with iced water, a Pizer transport vessel.

So Susan had died of a small glob of clotted blood, fruit of one of her bruises. It had detached from the wall of a vein and glided along with the rushing slosh of lifeblood, bumping into elastic walls, resisting the body's attempts to dissolve it. Then it had reached the great pump itself, the Times Square of the circulation, and snagged at a crucial turn. Spasm, blockage. The vital thumping coughed, shuddered, stopped. Just a clot.

For Kathryn, it all brought swarming back the memories of her mother's death. She had worn out her knees until they were constantly sore, kneeling and praying for the great God to make her mommy well. The days and weeks had waxed on, draining everyone. After a while, her prayers had shifted, until they were pleas to take the dried-up, shrunken husk of someone who had been a big, full mommy—take the husk away so that the pain in the hollow face was gone, the moans and sometimes outright screams would stop. But the battered instrument of God's will proved strangely strong. White as bleached bones, it had lasted and lasted and lasted. By the time the emaciated vessel died, Kathryn's religion had, too.

The memories coiled through her like smoky dreams as she mechanically noted down the slow, measured processes. Gary called out the procedures.

Prevention of coagulation, to keep the protective drugs circulating through arteries that threatened to squeeze shut. Adjusting metabolism. Administering calcium channel blockers. Expanding blood volume. Protecting against molecular free radicals. The intricate play of technology.

Time wore on. The ICU nurses were purse-mouthed with disapproval. A burly man appeared, bringing a hundred-pound block of ice. This was the morgue attendant, who turned out to be buddy-buddy with Gary after only a few minutes of talk, earlier. He even helped chip chunks from the block for the Pizer tank.

They were moving Susan into the iced water, wrapped in protectant plastic, when Kathryn saw Blevin and the medical director appear at the far end of the ICU. They conferred with Nurse Dowell, frowned, studied paperwork.

Look at those bulldog eyes, Kathryn thought, watching Blevin. *He's not the kind who gives up.*

At 2:53 A.M. they carefully rolled Susan from the ICU. She was immersed in water rapidly descending to near-freezing temperatures. Her cells were well permeated with cryoprotectants. The team had done the crucial part of their job, and now there remained the drive back to I^2, where Susan would continue her descent into the depths of a cold where all decay arrested.

Kathryn was weary, but her nerves danced. They didn't need her now so Alex drove her home with exaggerated care born of fatigue. She peered out into the enfolding night, thinking of the absolute stillness where Susan now dwelled.

"I can't believe she's really gone," Kathryn said.

"I know. It always takes a while."

"Finished. So fast. Lose your footing, and—"

"You leave a hole in people's lives. One that takes a while to fill in."

"Sometimes it never does. Wounds heal, but the scar's still there."

Kathryn studied his lined face in the streetlights. The fog had thickened into a light rain, giving the asphalt a shimmering hide in their headlights. "You were close to Susan, weren't you?"

"Yeah, as close as she let people get."

"How well did you know her?"

Alex glanced at her, heavy-lidded, face drained of color. "We were buddies, I suppose you'd say. She would bring a pizza by my place sometimes, and we'd just talk, maybe take in a flick. That's all, in case you were wondering."

Kathryn blushed. "I didn't mean—"

"Oh, sure you did. That's okay. Natural curiosity. Like pacing off the perimeter of a piece of land you're fixing to buy."

"Maybe just rent," she said, retreating into coquettishness.

"The payments are easy but frequent," he said sardonically.

She opened her mouth to top that and stopped, aghast that they were bantering so soon. "God, listen to us, will you?"

He gave an easygoing shrug. "Sex is the flip side of death. Susan would approve."

"She probably would. I keep thinking of her in the present tense, still."

"She's still present, in a sense. Just shut down, really, awaiting repairs."

"Despite everything, I . . . think of her as off in heaven somewhere. Classic cartoon stuff, I'm afraid. Sitting on clouds, listening to harp music."

"Despite everything? What's that mean?"

So she told him about her mother. "I don't really believe anymore, but somehow it builds up, and every year or so I go to church. Catholic. The whole thing, confession, the works."

"Whatever helps."

"Do you believe in . . . anything?"

"Sure. Just because I think it's smart to hang on to the structure of a person, the organization in the brain, doesn't mean I'm an atheist. The good Reverend Montana would be shocked out of his boots to hear that."

"What's a hard-line cryonicist like you actually believe, though?"

"That it's a big universe, with infinite possibility. That this little planet is an interesting experiment, still running. Maybe it's a failure. Maybe it's a success, so far. The nearest we get to something really big, I suppose, is when we open ourselves to possibility—embrace that infiniteness."

"Well, religion tries to do that."

"Sure it does. I just never liked those formal rituals, the rules and regs. It's like"—he gave her a telling glance—"like learning love from a manual. Other people seem to need it. Fine. I just don't take to the idea of marching lockstep into paradise."

"Ummm. I took a while to recover from my mother's death. Finally I realized that it was dumb to blame God for disease. But by that time, church was just going through the motions, for me. When I go back, it's beautiful and distant. Like paging through your high school annual. There's a young woman back there—one who was serene and sure and sort of sweetly naive—and that's the only way I can visit her, now."

He smiled warmly. "No, she's still there. I can see her peeking out sometimes."

"She has a shell now."

"Don't I know it. A very hip shell."

"The best kind. You have to keep it polished, though."

"Really hip people aren't nostalgic for their earlier faiths."

She watched the neon consumer gumbo stream by outside. "I guess not. They don't still fret over why there's evil in the world, either. Why Susan should die from a simple misstep."

"If I was being a complete cynic, I'd say that evil is just our name for things we don't like."

"Like weeds? They're simply plants we don't like."

He nodded, earnestly keeping his eyes on the road to make up for his fatigue. "Good analogy. And pornography is just erotica that some people don't like."

"Why does this conversation keep straying back to sex?"

He grinned devilishly, though on his haggard face it gave him a certain rogue boyish quality instead. "Guess."

She leaned over and kissed him. "Fine, but you have to stay over. Tonight I want to be held. Close."

"Try to get away."

After he parked in front of her apartment he immediately took her in his arms. His kiss was warm, soft, demanding. But even as she let him work his magic upon her, she peered over his shoulder at the street outside, which was dark with something more than night.

5

GEORGE

Entering the Reverend Montana's private quarters behind the Marble Cathedral was like returning to the warmhearted clasp of his dim childhood memories. The hushed, sprawling rooms, thick carpeting, a broad brick fireplace with gleaming brass fittings, aromas of walnut polished with linseed oil—all pierced George with a longing for permanence and solidity, for the certainties that lay behind this solid, almost achingly familiar place.

"Come right on in," the Reverend said in his slight country accent, leading George into the shadowed stillness of his personal study. Montana seated him in an ample chair near the study's fireplace. Logs snapped and popped. A prickly heat soothed the air, a caressing glow that freed George of his swooping, skating anxieties. He was back in the reassuring embrace of the church, and he felt himself easing into the simple pleasure of giving over to something greater than himself.

The Reverend stood for a moment, one hand resting on his polished rosewood desk, as though he knew what a striking figure he cut there. His mane of hair caught the firelight. A hand-painted red tie, obviously made by a parishioner, fit in well with his dark blue suit and diamond cuff links. Through the tall stained-glass windows distant lights gave a sheen of blues and yellows to the flat planes of his face.

"I'm overjoyed with your success, my friend," he said. "The news has been tragic, of course, and yet I know it is God's will. The woman was the key to their misguided so-called science."

"You know?"

"Of course. I keep close watch on all my flock, George. I knew that you were carrying out your mission in your own way, under divine guidance."

"Believe me, sir, I have given it all my attention. I'm not a well-educated man, but I've studied them. That's how I knew what to do."

"But of course you're educated, in the ways that matter. You are a scholar, George, a student for the Lord."

"It was your sermons that told me what to do, Reverend. I—"

"Please, call me Carl. And which sermon was that? I give so many, both in the cathedral and on the airwaves, that I—"

"The one about transgressions."

"Ah, yes. Violating the conventions of the secular abyss, the fallen world, in order to uphold the holy."

"The way you put it, sir, about hewing to a finer, a higher word—that was beautiful."

"The truth was written for us by God, if we can but see how to read it."

"I do read it, I do. But the way you say things, that's what makes it all so clear."

"I am most humble for whatever I can do, my friend. You have plainly harassed these Godless people who profiteer from the grief of others, and for that I owe you great thanks. I am sure your efforts contributed to this woman's end."

"You . . . know?"

"I understand your nature."

"I'm so relieved. I've prayed and searched, wondered if I was wrong to do it. . . ."

Montana's brow glistened with perspiration, and George saw that the man was frightened. Yet Montana's jaw clenched with resolution, as though an inner battle had been waged and won in George's favor.

"I can see the hand of God in many events. The good professors of the University of California have done the lion's share, of course, by ferreting out this woman's illegal acts. There's been plenty about that in the papers, background on her. But your own works have helped, of that I am sure."

George had not known how to tell the Reverend what he had done, or of the troubling dreams he had, the plans, the shooting hot desperation he felt in his dark moments of depression. Now he saw that he did not need to tell him at all. The Reverend *understood*. Deeply, without being told, those profoundly wise eyes could see into George's soul with a searing gaze of piercing love.

"The Lord's soldiers must keep their own counsel," George said automatically. The words rolling forth into the scented air sounded strange, for though he had repeated them thousands of times since his first interview with the Reverend, he had not spoken them aloud. They were his mantra, the resolute code that calmed his inner storms.

"Amen, brother. I—"

"Their bones shall be dry and white. 'And ye shall know that I *am* the Lord, when I have opened your graves, O my people, and brought you up out of your graves.' So their bones must be cleansed by holy rot."

"You are a true student of Scripture, George. I do hope the Lord gives you the strength and courage to continue on with your works."

"I am full of His joy."

"Harrying the un-Godly is a thankless task, as I hope you realize."

George was aghast. "Reverend, I will *never* seek credit for this."

"Your silence shall place you even higher among the exalted, brother. There shall be no public touting of your struggle, for a minister such as myself cannot embrace it before the cameras of our benighted world."

"I understand, I *know.*"

"This woman—do you believe what my friends tell me? That she was forced to commit suicide?"

"What?" George blinked, the sudden question pulling him back from a gossamer realm of quicksilver images.

"That is what a friend tells me."

"Suicide?" Troubling emotions struggled in George. He could feel them flicker in his face. Tried to control them. Could not.

"Now, I don't say you are to blame. Dr. Hagerty was sick in her soul and ended her personal pain without accepting the Lord."

"But, I mean, it came over me, did I have the right—"

"The pressure you exerted was righteous."

"I—I see."

"And it shall be rewarded."

The Reverend pushed a button on his desk. George's mind spun. Montana had seemed to know that he had killed the Hagerty woman, but never said so, exactly. Deniability—that was it. The Reverend had to always be able to say that George had not told him, that he had not known.

George sat back, accepting the principle, letting his gaze drift to the Wall of Respect, where past presidents beamed vacantly out at the camera while shaking hands with the Reverend. Purpose, gravity, destiny. The Reverend said something, quoted Scripture, his powerful baritone booming up into the shadowy recesses of the steepled study ceiling, and George did not register the massive oak door as it squeaked open. He caught the swish of a long skirt on the carpet and looked into the pool of orange light thrown by a tall lamp, and there she was—the woman who had first led him to this study, a few weeks ago, on a rainy night.

"I want you to meet Karen Bocelin, George. I have told her of your devotion, your works."

He shot to his feet. "I—I'm awfully proud to meet you."

"I admire you, Brother George," she said in a soothing, soft voice. She did not accept his hand to shake—which made him grateful, because he could feel his fingers trembling—but instead grasped both his hands, bringing them together with her own soft touch. Skin like silky promises. Something in the gesture carried a moist, clasping intimacy, warming his face.

"I wanted you two to meet. Karen here is a student at Chapman College."

George groped for something to say. "That's a good school, I hear."

"She is one of our scholarship students, as well. Vitality Corporation pays her tuition and a stipend."

"Oh, good." George rummaged for words but could think of nothing. He looked to the Reverend for some clue of what this was about. "Vitality . . . ?"

Karen said enthusiastically, "It's a wonderful company that does research in many areas. It's run by a genius, and I get to work with him sometimes."

"George is a man of intellect as well," Montana said. "In fact, I wanted you to be here, Karen, when I present him with this." The Reverend held out to George a small cut-glass cross on a gold necklace.

"Ooohh. A crystal cross!" Karen exclaimed. "How lovely."

George took it wonderingly. Only the elders of the Marble Cathedral and prominent members of the congregation sported these. He was touched. Karen fastened the thread around his neck, and George felt a rush of pride, washing away all doubt. He thanked the Reverend profusely, and conversation went on for several minutes without his really paying attention, until Montana said, "Like you, George, Karen was brought up in a foster home."

Karen smiled, her teeth perfect, brilliant. "Except that I had only one set of foster parents. You had a much harder life, the Reverend tells me."

"The Church saved me," George said, which was for him the simple truth of it.

"He is a man of resources," Reverend Montana said.

Karen still held his hands between her own, slightly uplifted, as if the two of them shared a private prayer. She went on for a while about foster homes and how much she had loved hers, but George was acutely conscious only of the heady fragrance that blossomed outward from her, enveloping him. Her high-necked white linen blouse did not conceal the ample swell of her breasts, and her full-length black skirt, severe in the Marble Cathedral manner, nonetheless hinted strongly at the flare and curve of her hips. The room pressed in thickly around him, the crackling fire talking like a separate brittle voice. He was acutely sure that she knew the thoughts that rose up in him, making his face hot, his eyes dart.

"—do you believe?" Karen finished, and looked at him. George blinked and tried to recall what she had said. His mind whirled, stubbornly blank.

"Oh yes, oh yes," he said helplessly. This seemed to answer her question, and Karen rewarded him with a demure smile.

"I believe George here works a bit too hard. He could do with a bit of feminine company, Karen," the Reverend said. "Perhaps you two will stay for the cathedral supper this evening? There'll be a choir performance, too."

"Oh, I'd *love* that," she said.

"Uh, sure," George stuttered out. In the Reverend's glance he saw a silent exchange. George had earned this introduction, the Reverend's eyes seemed to say. This reward. This benediction.

George pressed the woman's hands with sudden fervor. Images swarmed in his mind, black fears, fiery impulses. *No, no,* a part of him cried, but he forced that part of him down and put on a mask he had learned long ago, a stiff and bland smile. He would do as the Reverend guided, despite his fears. A man conquered fear, or else it stood final victor over him.

He took her hand. She squeezed it. The Reverend and Karen led him from the shadowy study and out into the majesty of the cathedral, their talk flitting around him like darting, artful birds. Words were light, quick, hard to catch. And all the while something new had entered him, a sullen weight that pulsed in his belly, a midnight-black foreboding.

6

KATHRYN

She woke up while making love. Drifting from fuzzy sleep, into slow, sliding rhythms. Her legs entwined his shoulders, and her fingers found two tight bands of muscle in his neck. She rubbed there as he brought heat into her, and she felt the tenseness dissolve in him as well. She sighed and caught his pungent musk. Moist. Urgent. The valley formed by the muscle ridges of his neck resisted and then flowed away. His mouth was quick, impossibly fluid. Her own knotted confusions focused in a silky thrusting, and then he was all over her, huge in the morning radiance.

Here was the true center of them both. So soon, they had found an almost courtly cadence. He acknowledged the sweetness and slumbering strength of her with tender kisses, a kind of long knowing and dwelling on the tiniest crevices of her, and on the sounds this called forth. He *knew* her, meditated on her ample territories and secret dominions, all without rushing anywhere else. And after their slow turn-taking symmetries, there came the time when he displayed his power and deep force. Not aggressive, vicious and dominating—unless she summoned that herself, as sometimes she did—but showing his fervor and even ferocity, displayed for her appreciation. Beast in the jungle, lion-fierce and growling, biting, he rolled over her with his protective vigor. Then she answered with her own savagery, with snarls, scratches, hisses, fierce nips —showing, too, her capacity to contain and finally tame his vitality, by giving him hers. It all had a magic momentum, an inevitable tide that swept both before it.

Then she was waking up again, fuzzily free of time, and she dimly realized that she had drifted down from orgasm to woolly sleep. Alex was sitting up next to her, studying the play of morning light on the window shade. A memory flickered, of a shadow looming across a window in the night. The image yanked her up from warm lassitude and then dwindled, trickled away, leaving a troubled, skittering echo of fear.

Alex whispered, "You asleep?"

"That's high on my list of classic dumb questions." She rolled over and buried her head in her pillow, banishing the thin wedge of dread.

"Oh yeah. Like, 'Where'd you lose it?' "

She tossed about again. "My favorite is, 'Promise not to be mad if I tell you something?' I always say no and watch them struggle with it."

"Cruel woman."

"I try to be."

"Interesting philosophy of life."

"What's yours?"

He arched his eyebrows ruefully, rubbed at his beard stubble, and she saw he took her lazy question seriously. After a moment he said, "Don't take sides." He paused, mouth tightening. "But keep score."

"Ha. 'Don't take sides'? For a man who works untold hours on cryonics, a belief that most people think is repulsively wacko, that's a little odd."

"Oh, I left out part: 'Never be consistent.' "

"Now it makes perfect sense."

"Cynic."

"I just love this postcoital sweet talk."

She did. Somehow she felt that she knew this man better than she had any of the others in the long legion of Mr. Mightabeens. It felt so *right.* Sometimes we were just nets of nerves, she thought, snatching up the zinging call of our pheromones on the first ring, while our professed sensitivities and fastidious morals cooled like an unread novel on the nightstand.

But this time, everything clicked. He had that swampy something that made her breath catch, and as a bonus, he could complete a sentence. Okay, he liked modern jazz, his closet looked like World War I, but he showed up for dates on the button—a metaphor with some resonance, since their dates recently both began and ended in bed.

While she had been blithely mooning on about him, the man had been at work. His hands glided lightly over her breasts, but his face was distant. "Isn't it a wonderful accident?" she asked.

"Huh? What?"

"How mine are exactly the same size as your hands?"

"Uh, yeah."

"Another snappy comeback. And here I thought I was sleeping with Oscar Wilde."

"I was thinking."

"About what?" She hoped it wasn't Susan. He had these flashes, somber and pensive.

Alex sighed. "I dunno, memories just come into your head sometimes. A while back, right after the divorce, I was taking a late-night flight. Plane half empty, had a couple drinks. Noticed a really striking blonde in the seat next to me."

"It took that long?"

He ignored her amused jibe. "She was a stewardess, off duty, flying to meet her boyfriend. So we started talking, had some more drinks— she got them for free."

"Why don't I like the direction of this story?"

"Calm down. It was one of those moments that can happen while you're traveling. Strangers in the night. Big plane, passengers nodding off, only us talking, as if we were alone together at thirty-five thousand feet. I start wondering can I make a pass."

"She had a boyfriend!"

"But no ring. Hunting season's still open, I figure. So we're hitting it off, and then she asks me if I'll do her a favor. Couple days before, she says, she had an operation. Cosmetic. Her breasts enlarged."

"Are you sure this isn't the opening of a dirty joke?"

She was instantly sorry she had spoken, because his eyes had a mournful quality. He simply shook his head, his neck muscles bulging as he tightened his throat against some suppressed emotion. "Surprise for the boyfriend, she says. Did I like them? So I look closer and tell her, sure. Then she says yeah, they're just what she wanted for him, but she's a little worried. She wonders if they, you know, feel right. To a man."

"So . . . would you—"

"Right. And I did. They felt perfect."

"Another triumph for technology."

"I know it sounds funny, but it was really, well, innocent. There were tears in her eyes when I said they were okay. I realized I had no chance with that lady, ever."

"True love."

"It was. But now we know that some of the implant material can degenerate, maybe cause cancer. Silicone can get out into the rest of the body. I think about the woman sometimes. Things we do for love, they can turn out funny."

In some eccentric way, she saw, this story was a shadow of his divorce. But it was also about them. Falling in love was taking chances. Sometimes ones you never suspected.

"Oh, Alex . . ."

His hands moved lightly over her nipples. Then he grinned devilishly. "Hers were the same size as my hands, too."

She rolled against him and covered his mouth with a wet, sloppy kiss.

Her doorbell rang.

Alex gave her a quizzical lifted eyebrow.

She was the sort of person who could let a telephone ring incessantly if she did not feel inclined to talk, but she always answered a doorbell. Physical presence somehow made an unavoidable demand. She pulled on an off-white terrycloth robe, automatically checking the disarray of her living room as she passed through, but nothing short of a major sweep-and-destroy would help much. She had been at I^2 most of the last two days, helping with the suspension of Susan. The ruins of last night's dinner—Gourmet Takeout of Laguna—sprawled across her broad glass coffee table.

She cracked the door an inch, letting in sharp sunlight that rebuked her disorder, and saw Sheila. The black woman wore a denim blue sheath dress with a matching silk scarf, shiny black high heels, and flecked hose. The top flaunted orange stitching and brass wrist buttons.

"Ready to hit the avenue?" Sheila asked brightly.

"Uh-oh. Is that today?"

"Sure is, gal. We were gonna do the fashion dance, strut through a few dozen stores, remember?"

Kathryn's mind stalled, refused to provide a solution to this small social dilemma. *Well then, play it straight.* "I'm running a little behind. Come in."

"You look like you just woke up. I guess you weren't just scammin' when you called in, said you had to be at that chiller place."

"Coffee will repair the damage. Uh, there's somebody else—"

"Hi, Sheila," Alex said, walking in as casually as possible from the bedroom, tucking his lumberjack shirt into denims. Sheila took one blink to catch on and then smiled broadly. "Glad to see you haven't been wasting *all* your time, girl."

She had felt a spark of irritation at Alex for being so blatant, but then saw that speaking straight was the best way with Sheila. They weren't alert enough to bring off even a minor deception. As well, she felt a spark of elation that Sheila now knew. First chance they had alone, Kathryn could now share some delicious secrets. "Let's say the chiller job has its compensations," Kathryn said wryly.

Sheila grinned. "*I*'ll say. Wish I could get work like that."

Alex ambled into the kitchen and found the coffee pot. "Boyfriend trouble?"

"Can't have that kind of trouble anymore, 'cause I got no boyfriend."

Kathryn's mouth pursed with concern. "Really? Fred, wasn't it? He seemed very nice."

Sheila's eyebrows shot up in mock surprise. "That's it—I *knew* there was somethin' wrong with him."

Alex said, "Speaking as an official Nice Guy of America, I take umbrage."

"I thought umbrage was a color." Sheila found the coffee grinder and started pouring beans into its snout. "Kind of dark blue."

They had moved into easy synchronization, waltzing around the galley kitchen as though they had all been making breakfast together for a thousand years. Yellow sunlight slanted through the warming space. Kathryn got out some raisin bran muffins and put them in the microwave. "You'll get another right away," she said. "No doubt about that. What's your all-time record for going without male companionship?"

"Ummm. Three weeks. Watched enough TV to puke."

"Three whole weeks," Alex said. "Practically a nun."

Sheila winked. "More like a monk. Monkey business was what I had in mind."

The telephone rang. Kathryn took it, and Gary Flint's clipped voice asked for Alex. *Geez,* she thought, *maybe I should take out an ad announcing that we're having an affair. Just in case a few people in the Western Hemisphere don't know.*

Alex took it, and she went to change clothes. When she emerged from her bedroom, wearing a simple pastel cotton that would not get her arrested but would keep Alex suitably involved, he was still on the telephone. He listened, then said, "Uh-huh, uh-huh. I've got all the paperwork in the car. We'll do it now. Right. G'bye."

Kathryn bit into a warm muffin and chased it with aromatic coffee. The world began to improve. Alex stood for a long moment, staring into space, and then focused on the kitchen, the women. Kathryn did not like the gray pallor that had come into his face.

"The coroner's office just called I². They want to know why we haven't come in to file the death certificate and a VS-9 form."

"Because we have three days to do it," Kathryn said.

"They want it done now."

"Immediately?"

"Right now, Gary said. I've got the paperwork in my car. I was planning to drop by there today anyway."

Kathryn sipped her coffee to suppress a gathering sense of alarm. "Sounds funny."

Alex said, "I'd better get over there."

"I'll go with you," Kathryn said on impulse. She would fret until she knew what was going on.

"Girl, we've got a lot of shopping to do," Sheila said amiably.

"Oh, I'm sorry. This won't take long."

"Okay. I'll meet you at Smithson's, on Euclid."

"That's the leather place?"

"Yeah, they got a permanent tap on my paycheck. But gal, you're dressed a little too alive for the dead folks place."

"What? Oh." Kathryn looked down at her cotton dress, for which "well-tailored" was perhaps an understatement. "Okay, I'll change."

When she came out of her bedroom again Alex was coming through the front door, shaking his head. "Damned Volvo."

"What's the matter?"

"Won't start. Battery's okay, though."

Sheila said, "What's the problem? You can go in Kathryn's."

"Mine's in the shop," Kathryn said.

Sheila made a disgusted face. "Don't tell me we're all members of the Clunker Club?"

A charter member, bucking for lifetime, Kathryn thought ruefully. She was going to have to go deep into the plastic just to get hers back out of the shop.

Alex shrugged, his eyes a thousand miles away. "Poverty sharpens the mind." He blinked when both women laughed.

Sheila dropped them off outside the gray concrete coroner's office, near the Orange County jail. A receptionist let them wait the required five minutes, then ushered them down an antiseptically lit corridor. Kathryn could glimpse along side hallways the steel gurneys bearing white-sheeted burdens.

There was a curiously neutral smell to this place, as if its business must at all costs be kept matter-of-fact. People used to say they knew death both as an enemy and as a friend, she remembered, because it sometimes at least brought an end to suffering. It came right into the house and sat with you for a while, stayed for supper, and left its calling card, an empty space where once somebody you loved had been.

Those days were gone. Loved ones and friends went off to scrupulously clean emporiums to die, as politely as being ushered out of a play. And if your case caught the eye of the coroner, you made one last stop here, to contribute another digit to the world's all-consuming curiosity.

The receptionist left them in a crowded office. One wall was covered with framed citations, medical degrees in pathology, and photos of the coroner, Miles Wellington, shaking hands with the Board of Supervisors, with Donald Bren of the Irvine Company, and with similar local luminaries. Their smiles had a rigid cast. Quite fitting, Kathryn mused; they were all involved in the dying away of the best in Orange County.

Dr. Wellington nodded to them but did not shake hands. Kathryn had noticed that none of the police did either, apparently to keep some psychological space between them and the public. On Wellington's big oak desk was an outsize coffee mug, with bloodred lettering stenciled in: DEAD CERTAIN.

Dr. Wellington's sense of humor did not reach as far as his stiff, downturned mouth, however. "I have some questions about this body, and your treatment of it," he said.

"We have a copy of the death certificate, a VS-9, and other forms here," Alex offered.

"I'm sure you do, and all filled out. You people have always had your paperwork in order." Wellington's clipped voice had an edge, as though he were savoring this. "But I have other issues in mind."

Wellington pressed a button and into the office, led by the receptionist, came Dr. Blevin and Detective Stern. The shock of both appearing left Kathryn speechless. A tart dread soured her mouth.

Blevin and Stern sat on a long couch. Each nodded to them but said nothing.

Wellington sat back in his leather lounger, plainly pleased with his theatrics. Coroners were basically politicians in Orange County. "Dr. Blevin called me to express his own suspicions that Dr. Susan Hagerty's death was in fact a suicide. Studying the photographs and other evidence, I find the circumstances do warrant such a preliminary hypothesis. As a physician, Dr. Hagerty would have realized that such a fall of approximately fifty feet would probably be fatal, but people have survived such heights before. Physicians more often use drugs. Therefore I was interested to find that under further study her urine sample showed traces of fluoxetine."

"What's that?" Alex asked. Somehow he seemed calmer under pressure than he had on the drive over.

"An antidepressant."

"At what concentration?" Kathryn asked. Wellington looked like the kind who would grant you some respect if you got into the technical details a bit. She was winging it, actually; she had no idea what was an important amount. She tried to remember the drunk-driver level for blood alcohol. A tenth of a percent?

"A tenth of a microgram per milliliter. Also triatolam at 0.1 microgram per milliliter. The hurried lab analysis at UCI failed to turn these up."

"No wonder," Alex said, giving Kathryn a grateful look. "Those sound like trace amounts with no pharmacologic effect."

Wellington was unbothered. "True, but they are indicative."

"So she was taking an antidepressant and a sleeping pill. So what?"

"This is a physician prescribing for herself, perhaps indicative of a problem. If Dr. Hagerty was experiencing depression, there is a chance that it suddenly got the better of her."

"While she was out jogging?" Kathryn asked, incredulous.

"Mood swings are difficult to explain," Wellington said. "We are some years away from procedures that could yield psychological profiles of the deceased through neurochemical analysis. Such measurements could perhaps tell us whether she was depressed, suicidal, even angry or homicidal. But even without such certainty, there are grounds here for suspicion."

"Given her behavior the last few weeks," Dr. Blevin said in a flat, professional voice, "there were more than mere suspicions."

Kathryn could not stop herself from snapping, "What's that mean?"

Blevin gave her a cold glance. "She was plainly self-destructive. If she had confessed right away to her doings, perhaps even thrown herself on the mercy of the dean, then—"

"She intended to fight you all the way," Kathryn shot back. "That's not depressed or suicidal. It took *guts.*"

"I hope you don't think you are qualified to pass judgment on a clinical matter," Dr. Blevin said sarcastically.

Kathryn reminded herself that the real power here lay with the coroner, not Blevin, and said nothing. She had to bite her tongue to do it.

Dr. Wellington glanced at Blevin and said, "I am not certain whether an autopsy would give us any further evidence of suicide, in any case. But of course, that is what an autopsy is for—to reveal the unsuspected."

Alex said earnestly, "Look, I don't for a moment think Susan threw herself off that bluff. That's not *her.*"

"Your concern is of course understandable," Wellington began, clearly launching into a set speech. "Still, you surely must see—"

"But even if it was, so what? A determination of suicide would just move her from one column of statistics to another. I know your job is looking after those statistics, but this is a *person.*"

"California Code, Section 27491, makes this office responsible for investigating the circumstances, manner, and cause of all deaths other than natural," Wellington recited.

Alex leaned forward. "You're not listening. The bodies that come in here, they're really gone, dead. Susan isn't. The structure of her body—and her mind, her *self*—is preserved in liquid nitrogen, at minus three hundred and twenty degrees Fahrenheit."

"I'm not responsible for that," Wellington said. "You are."

Blevin said with professional smoothness, "This hope of regenerating tissues after they have suffered that much freezing damage—well, it's a fantasy. An absurd scheme used to separate suckers from their cash."

"We can't revive them now, sure," Alex said. "But fifty years from now? Who knows? Not you, Dr. Blevin. Meanwhile, thanks, we'll hold on to what we can save—and that means not letting Susan get cut up. That's what you plan, isn't it?"

"A complete autopsy, yes. The law requires it." Dr. Wellington had kept a mild composure, Kathryn noticed. His eyes said that he knew a deep secret: that they would all be the same, once they stopped breathing.

"Doing that would destroy all of Susan that remains," Alex said. "All to find out if she committed suicide? You know, sir, how hard it is to tell if somebody jumped rather than slipped. Hell, it's *impossible*. The body isn't going to show you anything."

Dr. Wellington nodded, still quite calm and resolute. "There are further grounds. Detective Stern?"

Kathryn had wondered why the detective was here at all. Now his angular features lost their reflective cast, and he said sardonically, "You two didn't mention the fact that Susan Hagerty was assaulted a few weeks ago. Right on your own company property, too. I had to turn it up from the county sheriff's blotter."

The silence that followed was just long enough to be embarrassing. Kathryn's memory rang with what Alex had said when she had brought up that uncomfortable fact: *That was a random incident. No connection to this.*

"We forgot it in the excitement, that's all," Alex said. "It was just some transient. He knocked her down and ran away."

"The sheriff's office listed it as 'assailant unknown,' though," Stern said.

"Because they didn't try any harder," Alex countered.

Kathryn said, "It was a minor injury."

Stern said tightly, "But now, along with this fatality—"

"They're unrelated, I tell you!" Alex was at last breaking open.

"We don't know that," Stern said flatly.

"You can't mean that you'll destroy her, just to—"

"She is *dead,*" Blevin said sternly. "Your silly dreams about reviving her do not carry any weight here."

Kathryn said, "But all you've got is *suspicion!*"

"Not all," Stern said. "Her dog, remember? It hasn't turned up."

Alex gritted his teeth, and Kathryn said quickly, "It ran off. It was frightened. Maybe somebody ran over it on the Coast Highway."

"It's another detail that doesn't fit," Stern said.

"You're not seriously proposing that someone killed Susan, then stole her dog?" Kathryn asked.

Stern shrugged. "I don't propose anything. Not yet."

"That step follows after all the evidence is gathered," Dr. Wellington said, "which I intend to do."

"Look," Alex said rapidly, "I *know* the cause of death. We took X-rays while we were suspending her, to see how the glycerol was circulating. The embolism was very clear. I've got them right here." He held up a manila folder.

Wellington accepted them, glancing quickly at the prints, nodding, and for a moment Kathryn felt a spurt of hope. "These will be useful, but *we* shall determine the cause of death."

"She's not really dead, not in the full sense," Alex said, his voice thin and desperate. "Her structure is still there. You're going to destroy that, just to satisfy your curiosity?"

"What nonsense!" Blevin spat back. "Dead is *dead,* and surely the coroner knows this better than some jumped-up crank—"

"Death is a continuum," Alex said loudly.

He's going to lose it completely, she thought. He spat out the words. "Every time a little girl is pulled out of a snowdrift, declared clinically dead, then revives—every time that happens, dead is *not* dead!"

Kathryn had a moment of split loyalty as she watched Alex's face give way to anguish. She understood these officials; after all, they were following the conventional definition of death, and the hallowed traditions of the law. But she saw, too, that Alex was fighting to preserve a last, small possibility for his friend.

And neither side was going to give ground.

"We are carrying out the *law,* Mr. Cowell," Dr. Wellington said severely. He flicked a glance at his big Rolex imitation, too fast to actually read the dial, to show that he was a man whose time was precious.

"To warm her up"—Alex's anger had dissipated, or burrowed inside somewhere, for he now seemed dazed—"without any technical measures, that will rip her cells completely to pieces. Do irreparable damage. You can't, you just can't."

"We will do our jobs," Dr. Wellington said. "Just as Dr. Blevin has, bringing his ideas to my attention. And as Detective Stern has. We will have to account for the fractures from the freezing in liquid nitrogen. This will be a technically difficult autopsy, one that will break new ground in forensic pathology."

"I don't suppose that fact has colored your thinking?" Kathryn asked mildly.

"What?" Wellington said, startled.

"It's a nice little career enhancer, isn't it?"

"I object to any such insinuation," Wellington said, standing up briskly. "And I'll thank you to leave."

They got out of there fast. Down the bleached glow and astringent smells of the long corridors, Kathryn holding Alex's arm protectively. A sheriff's deputy told them there was a cab stand down the block, and on the way there she said soothing things, meaningless things, any words that might get through to Alex. He stared straight ahead, saying nothing. His face was tight, distant, working with small flickerings in his eyes, his lips twisting—echoes of inner conflicts.

Then, just as they got into a yellow cab, he looked directly at her. "We're not going to leave her out in the warm," he said. "We *won't.*"

7

ALEX

He tossed some cash to Kathryn and jumped out of the yellow taxi before it had fully stopped. She paid off the cab while he ran into the Immortality Incorporated facility. The front door was locked, a precaution they always took when they were low on staff. Alex opened the door and went through the front office, then trotted into the main bay. Gary Flint was there with the medical student from UCI, Robert Skinner. Alex shouted, "How's the nitrogen filling going?"

Gary looked up from a silvered blue sleeping bag that lay on a gurney. Inside was Susan Hagerty. Gary saw Alex's wild gaze and answered with deliberate steadiness, "We're about ready to start."

"Good. Change of plans. *Big* change. We've got to use the emergency storage."

It took several minutes to explain to Gary and Skinner what had happened at the coroner's. They listened in stark, open-mouthed disbelief. Kathryn came in, her face flushed, hands clamped around the envelope holding their forlorn, rejected paperwork.

Gary nodded decisively. "Blevin, he's the one. Stern's case is all guesswork, but Blevin and his suicide theory—"

"That's what's so awful," Kathryn said. "They have two incompatible theories—suicide and murder—and we got sandbagged by Stern while we were defending against Blevin."

"Never mind that," Alex said. "We've got to get Susan into emergency storage."

Gary nodded again. "We're ready for nitrogen staging."

"Move her first," Alex said, "then nitrogen."

The human body has considerable mass. For the last three days Susan had been immersed in a silicone oil bath, cooling to a temperature of −77 degrees Centigrade. Alex checked the seals on the shiny silver-blue, precooled sleeping bag into which the team had recently slipped Susan. For a moment he wanted to peel the bag back, gaze once more down into Susan's composed, resolute features. She would have known what to do in this crisis. He missed her steady judgment, her sense of the many vectors society brought to bear. Was he going off half-cocked here? Should they all talk it over a little? Or was speed essential?

"We could let the lawyers hassle this out," Gary said uncertainly.

Skinner blinked owlishly. His face was drawn and pale from the long, tedious hours of cool-down. "Yeah, get an injunction against the coroner to show cause, or something like that."

"That will take days," Kathryn said.

Alex glanced at her. Her mouth was set firmly, all her lipstick licked away by her fretting tongue. He said, "Right. And the coroner won't carefully warm Susan up. He'll probably put her under heat lamps or something. She'll be gone by the time our lawyer gets in front of a judge."

Skinner bit his lower lip. Alex could see the implications dawning on him. Skinner was in the most trying, crucial years of medical school. In a while he would apply for a license to practice medicine. A gaudy, public association with cryonics—particularly amid a case of "body-snatching" —could wreck his life.

"Look, Bob," Alex said, "you can bow out of this."

Skinner worried his lower lip some more, eyes seeing nothing.

Gary said, "Yeah, go home. This is going to get messy."

Skinner nodded, not at Gary's remark, but to some inner voice. "No. No. I'll stay."

Gary gently patted Skinner on his shoulder. "Okay. We get her to safety, then."

"So you figure to do something right now," Skinner said. "Make her be missing."

"Damn right," Alex said.

"How?" Kathryn asked.

"Come on." Alex waved them toward the back of the bay. "Let's get Susan lashed on here." He drew the straps from under the gurney.

"What are you going to do?" Kathryn asked.

Alex had said nothing specific to her in the taxi. He loved her, sure, but she was not really a cryonicist. She might not fathom all this, and anybody could get rattled if they had to handle too much at once. Let her stay ignorant a little longer, then. "Could you stand guard? Stay in the front office. Start the telephone tree, call in some members. We're going to need them."

"What if the sheriff shows up?"

"Stall them. Ask to see papers, warrants."

Kathryn waved her hands, exasperated. "But I'm not an officer of the corporation. How can I—"

"You're all we've got. Move!"

Alex turned and ran through the towering ranks of steel cylinders and out onto the polished concrete loading dock. The new I² truck—a used Ford with an extended flatbed—stood nearby. He unlocked the wall-mounted security box and grabbed the truck keys off their hook.

As he trotted over to the truck, he noticed that they hadn't had time to stencil the company logo on it yet. Just as well; less conspicuous. He had never really liked the company name, anyway. They didn't promise immortality. At best, cryonics was a second chance at life. Right now those chances didn't look very good, either.

He backed the truck to the dock. Gary Flint and Robert Skinner brought Susan out, rolling her carefully on rubber wheels. They carefully slid the stretcher onto the truck bed and lashed it to the securing hooks. Alex got in the truck cab—an act that still called up memories of the crash, the flames, no matter how he tried to suppress them—and slammed the door. The two men behind rolled a dewar of liquid nitrogen across the dock and directly onto the bed. Alex was putting the Ford in gear when Kathryn appeared in his window, standing on the running board. Her hair was touseled, her mouth awry with excitement.

"Hey, what—"

"Ray Constantine showed up. On crutches, no less. His shift is just starting. And he is an I² officer."

"Damn."

She grinned impishly, enjoying this. "Now you've got to cut me in on the secret."

He said grimly, "Climb in." She laughed, which startled him further.

He pulled carefully around the edge of the I² building, halfway expecting patrol cars to come slamming into the front parking lot. But there was nothing there except their own cars. Nor was there any traffic visible at midday on Santiago Canyon Road. He waved for the two men riding in the bed to lie down. The truck surged powerfully onto the highway, went a hundred yards, and then turned off onto a weathered dry track. Alex clunked the shift into low, and they roared up a barely visible trail. It petered out in another hundred yards and they ground to a halt.

"You're going to hide her out here?"

"Help them with the brush. Gloves are in the glove compartment."

"I always wondered why they called it that." She climbed out and helped tug big tumbleweed bushes out of the way. The surface root systems of the plants made it possible to pull them away from their natural growth patterns and hold them back while Alex drove through the temporary opening. Then the three dragged the towering dusty-tan bushes back into place.

Kathryn climbed back in, puffing. "So you had this all planned."

"Not for Susan specifically. It's our emergency backup." He took them forward at a slow crawl over rough ground.

"You've been here a fair amount."

He blinked. "How do you know that?"

"Look at the tire tracks. It hasn't rained in weeks, and I can see four separate sets."

He stopped the truck and leaned out the window. "Bob, can you run back and cover our tracks beyond the bushes?"

They snarled forward. Alex was conscious of the truck's noise. They were angling back into the arroyo. What if a sheriff's deputy heard them?

The possibility of pursuit, of deputies yapping at their heels, brought the old horrors welling up.

He knew what the coroner would do. It would all transpire on tiled surfaces gleaming under bright fluorescents, with strong suction hoods to spirit away unwanted odors. The sterilized, stainless-steel glaze would flood the space with merciless glare, the precision, promise and hope of modern medicine. But he had seen the analytical, careful way an electric vibrating saw cuts a thin line around the head, just above the earline. Then they lifted the top of the skull away, like taking off a beanie cap. They cut away the membranes and arteries holding the brain in place. It took some work with the fingers to free the brain until it lifted out. About fourteen hundred grams of wrinkled jelly, the essence of Susan Hagerty. Memories, personality, hopes, and dreams—a lump of matter that with a few applied volts could laugh or cry, ponder and plan, could know inexpressible joys. They would then cleanly slice it into sections, inspect it for hemorrhaging or lesions. There would probably be some blood clots, some explanation for her coma. And then they would toss the now-useless, decaying mass onto a sideboard, where it would await the trash collector's red plastic bag.

The truck lumbered and dipped through a narrow path in the chaparral. Alex wrestled with the wheel and forced his mind back into the present.

"Boy, we really need the four-wheel drive," Kathryn said. He was somewhat surprised that she didn't pepper him with questions. Instead, she studied him with disconcerting interest.

"We didn't smooth out the track any. The fewer signs, the better. Hold on, here's the gully."

They lurched into the dry wash at the bottom of the arroyo. The Ford slid in the sand, wheels whirred angrily, and then rolled up the incline.

"That's the footpath over there, right?" Kathryn pointed.

"Right. We cover it with the same tumbleweed trick, at five different spots."

Kathryn nodded. He liked the way she figured things out for herself. It was a risk, he supposed, letting her in on this most closely guarded I^2 secret. But he was sure of her, with a solidity that he knew sprang from his love rather than from his sober judgment. Well, he thought, all that judgment had done him no good in his marriage, so how much real use was it?

They worked up through several twists of the dry streambed. "The mystery spot is somewhere near here."

"Right. Bet you can't see it even now," he said as the truck stopped.

Kathryn searched the worn sandstone slopes on each side. "I can't even see any footprints."

"We brush them away when we leave. Come on."

Alex held up his hand for silence after they all got out. On the whispering breeze the hum of a car on Santiago Canyon Road rose and ebbed. No slamming doors, no squealing tires. Just the lazy warm wind. They nodded to each other, and Alex fetched forth a new set of keys. He watched Kathryn, feeling a small measure of pride, as they walked up a slope crowded with manzanita bushes, rounded a split sandstone boulder—and stopped at a jutting wall of conglomerate rock. Or so it looked.

"Concrete." Alex rapped it. "We copied the technique from Laguna Beach."

"I remember." Kathryn ran a hand over the pebbled surface. "They blend it in with the bluff rock."

Alex fitted keys into two small crevices in the rock. "Right here, for the door, the concrete's only half an inch thick. Ray did the work."

The heavy door swung out on thick steel bolts. Alex flicked on battery lamps and stepped inside. The single room ran twelve feet into the soft stone and housed a single glistening steel cylinder. It smelled dry and cool.

"Let's move her," Alex said.

He was uncomfortably aware that even in her insulated bag, Susan would slowly climb up the steep gradient of temperature. Each warming degree might bring further cell damage. Organisms suffered wreckage of membranes, enzymes, and untold chemical subtleties when they rewarmed. Nobody quite knew why. The riddle awaited a future generation of biological research. *One with fewer Blevins around,* Alex thought bitterly.

The four of them carried Susan up and into the narrow facility. She slid into the cylinder, inside the shiny sheets of aluminized Mylar layered to cut heat transfer. Stainless steel withstood deep cold without becoming brittle. There was a vacuum gap between inner and outer skins and thick insulation. Wire leads at both ends were ready to send an alert to Alex's beeper, if the liquid nitrogen level got low.

"You did all this and kept it secret," Kathryn said.

"And hoped we'd never need it," Gary said somberly. "Finished it just a few months back. Sure didn't think it would get filled so quick."

Alex secured Susan in the cylinder. He started to swing the end cap shut and paused, peering in. When all this madness was over they would —he hoped—be able to move Susan to one of the big cylinders in the main bay. But for now, this was good-bye. He noticed that the others stood quietly, heads lowered. He reminded himself that he wasn't religious. But that did not erase the deep, human need for some ceremony to mark Susan's passage.

"God rest you, Susan. I promise you, I—we won't let you down."

He wanted to say something more, but the words would not come through his tight, agonized throat. He remembered Sheila at the party: *You guys and us Baptists, we're alike.* The memory sent blurred, troubling thoughts skating through his mind.

He coughed to cover his unease. "Okay, now let's lug that nitrogen in here," he said gruffly.

8

KATHRYN

She slipped from behind a stately stand of eucalyptus and walked with what she hoped was nonchalance toward the loading dock of Immortality Incorporated. The roundabout route of the truck had been deceptive; the emergency storage site was only five hundred yards from I^2. Now she knew why Alex had taken Sparkle for walks down the long, rugged arroyo; he had been finishing the outfitting of the hideaway and needed a cover. Few in I^2 knew about the site, and certainly Kathryn, as a noncryonicist, had to be kept in the dark. She had to give him credit; the guy could keep his mouth shut and lie while looking like a blue-eyed saint—a vivid contrast with the man she was discovering in bed.

She had already circled far enough around to see the sheriff's patrol cars parked at odd angles in the front lot. She told herself to be calm, not to betray anything, and most of all to cover any evidence of their hasty departure. But that did not make her stomach stop fluttering. It felt as if it wanted to take wing on its own.

There was nobody in the loading area or the cool recesses of the main bay. She heard loud voices from the front office and steeled herself. Head held high, she walked in briskly. She faked mild surprise at the four sheriff's deputies grouped around Ray Constantine.

They wore irked expressions, but at least they were not the thick-necked glowerers she had expected. Ray was sitting with his arms crossed, face set, saying nothing beyond the obvious, as she had told him. Detective Stern was talking on a telephone. When he saw her, he spoke rapidly into the receiver and hung up.

"Where are they?"

"Who?" she answered mildly.

"Cowell, to start with."

"I believe he went home."

"You were with them, weren't you?"

"With who? I came straight here from the coroner's."

Stern's face reddened. "They took her—and you helped."

Kathryn was going to say *Took who?* but the man's jutting chin warned her otherwise. Men who routinely stayed calm in the face of mayhem were doubly dangerous when something did manage to arouse them. "I don't know anything about corporate business policy. I'm hired to handle this office, that's all."

"They told you to say that."

He was quite right. She said blandly, "It's only the simple truth."

"We're going to search this place. An unfriendly search."

"You have a warrant?"

"Damned right we do. For Susan Hagerty's body and supporting evidence."

Stern held up a clipboard of papers. He came closer to her and stood taller. A typical cop mannerism, she thought. Probably unconscious.

"Why are you involved? I presume these other gentlemen are deputies dispatched by the coroner's office?"

Most likely she was overplaying this, but she liked being precise and even amiable in the face of obvious, bullish hostility. Miss Manners had taught her well.

Stern blinked and lost his brontosaurus body language. "I came along to see that strict rules of evidence are followed." He spoke more conversationally, with less stiff-necked intimidation. *Score one for civility,* she thought. "We've got to be careful. This is a bizarre case."

"*That* I can agree with."

"And I nosed this was going to play strange."

"Nosed?"

"Smelled. As in *rat.* From the way you two left the coroner's. Now, where's that Cowell?"

"I thought he said he was going to play basketball."

"I'll bet."

"Detective, I don't make it a hobby to keep track of—"

"This guy Constantine tells us the Hagerty body isn't here."

"I'm sure he is correct."

"Where is it?"

"I only work here." Better to evade than to lie.

"So where did they take it?"

"I don't know the details of Susan Hagerty's will." Another evasion, but Stern didn't seem to notice.

Stern snorted in frustration. "They can run, but they can't hide. Not with a frozen body."

Kathryn took some pleasure in reflecting that this was exactly what they *had* done. She suspected Stern already knew that. Until the three men were well away from the emergency storage vault, though, she had better stop Stern from thinking along those lines. He might order a search of the surroundings. Worse, he could call in a helicopter. It would see the truck.

She said, "I would like to inspect your warrant."

"Sure." He handed her the clipboard. "Our friends will be along in a minute or two."

"Friends?" Kathryn studied Stern's sardonic smile, but he was giving nothing away. The search warrant was a barely readable carbon copy that seemed correct, though of course she had never seen one. It allowed removal not only of Susan's "remaining remains" but also I² patient care records (including "personal photos and patient diaries"), records of members, and "misc. records dealing with the described remains, procedures of treatment of the remains, equipment used, and attendant matter as so implied."

"Pretty inclusive," Kathryn said.

"We try to be," Stern said grimly.

"What's this 'equipment used'?"

"Just what it says."

"That's pretty broad."

"So are you," Stern said with a thin smile. She wondered if this was a teenage-level pun: *You're a pretty broad.* A last show of macho intimidation? She suppressed a sudden impulse to laugh.

Kathryn went to photocopy the warrant in a side office. With the door closed she telephoned five more I² members, following the crisis alert procedures outlined in a loose-leaf notebook she had helped type up herself.

When she returned chaos had descended. Overlapping male voices came from throughout the building. Deputies swarmed everywhere. Three uniformed UCI police were poking through the equipment racks. To her disbelief, a dozen Orange County SWAT team members methodically searched the rooms, brandishing automatic rifles and covering each other as they flung open doors. They were mechanical, well-oiled. She would have laughed at the surrealism of it, but the men scowled and glared so ferociously, she became alarmed. She realized that they were pumped up for this, knowing nothing about I² and expecting hardened grave robbers to bound out of any cranny. She had to keep moving out of the way of the hubbub, and it was some time before she could find Stern again.

"This is stupid," she began. "You won't find anything—"

"Come back here." Stern's tone was again clipped, nearly threatening. He led her into the main bay. Deputies were reading the ID plates on the tall stainless steel cylinders. "How do I know these are marked right?"

"What do you mean?"

"Maybe Susan Hagerty is in one of these."

"No! Our other patients are in there. You—"

"Yeah? How do I know?"

"Every suspension vessel is sealed and dated. Your muscle men have probably dumped the files for all the documents into your vans by now."

"Maybe we'll just open a few of these for a look."

Kathryn could not imagine how anyone could be this stupid. "Go on, stick a hand in."

"Oh, we'll drain the bubbly stuff first."

"Empty the liquid nitrogen and you'll endanger the patients."

Stern chuckled. "Patients, huh? These are dead people."

"Their attorneys will sue you for more damages than you can earn in a lifetime. And so will ours."

"You're going to be busy looking at felony counts yourself," Stern said.

"For what?"

"Interfering with a police investigation. Destroying evidence."

"What evidence?"

"The body."

"The *last* thing a cryonics firm would do is destroy a patient. Go to a mortuary for that, mister. They burn their clients, or else turn them into worm food."

Stern put his hands on his hips and smiled. "My my, I finally get to see some temper."

Remember Miss Manners. "You'll see a fat lawsuit if you open those vessels."

"To nail you guys, we don't need to do that. There's a little count of grand larceny, too."

Events were moving with blinding speed for Kathryn, but this stopped her. "Stealing?"

"I noticed all that gear with UCI stickers on it."

"That's why the UCI police?"

Stern nodded. "We alerted them. They're here to check it out."

"I've been over the inventory lists. That's part of my job. Every piece here we bought from UCI Surplus and Excess Property."

"We'll just look into that."

"This is harassment!"

"Only doing my job, lady." Stern looked at her with piercing eyes. "Now, if you'll just tell us where the Hagerty body is, we can drop all this other stuff."

"Good grief! Even TV cop shows are subtler that this."

"I guess they have to be. Difference here is, we mean it."

"Mean what? That you'll prosecute me on moronic charges unless I tell you where Susan is?"

"Lady, you're implicated in a lot of felonies here."

The deputies around them nodded sagely and studied her with cagy alertness. She swallowed hard and thought, *All this for a part-time job?*

What's happening, girl? After all, Susan *was* dead. Bringing her back was a long shot at best. Did she believe in cryonics, really? More to the point, did she believe in anything enough to risk doing major time in the slammer over a frozen corpse?

Kathryn had thought through the cryonics arguments, pro and con, with indecisive fascination. Now the issue was framed in a way she had never anticipated. Part of her screamed, *This isn't your fight!* and another answered, in a severe, almost prissy drone, *You owe it to Alex.*

The first voice was steely and probably more intelligent. The second was less articulate, moody, dutiful. But then a third chimed in. *You* love *Alex, dope. You might scamper out from under all this, but he can't. Stand with him, or you'll all go down together.*

Maybe, she thought desperately, the one thing I never understood about cryonics was just that—love. Devoting yourself to an off-the-wall cause like this came out of a kind of love she had never known before. Alex had it. Was that the element in him she found so mysterious, so pulse-quickening? Beneath that endearing, focused man lurked an expansive spirit. Yes—the thought was startling—that was part of why she loved him. A different brand of love, sure, eros rampant—but the real thing. And street-savvy she might be, but love was worth pain. Through all the blizzard of arguments about cryonics, at least she now knew that.

She gave him her best arched-eyebrow gaze of disdain. "Detective, I don't have the slightest idea what you're talking about."

Stern's mouth drew tight and bloodless. From the bitter twist of it she knew he was going to deliver some stinging sarcasm, but he stopped, eyes focusing across the bay. She turned and there were Alex, Gary Flint, and Skinner, ambling easily in from the loading dock. "Hey, what's happening?" Alex called.

Stern's mouth broadened into a smile. *Now he can stop beating up on this brassy broad and get into something more interesting,* Kathryn thought. *Fresh meat.* Despite knowing this, her heart leaped at seeing Alex. She started toward him. He grinned back, something passing between them in his look that caught her breath. He opened his arms and hugged her, lifting her heels from the floor.

"Handcuff them," she heard Stern say grimly. "Not her, though—she's just a flunky. I'll Miranda them myself."

9
GEORGE

The Reverend finished his benediction. The vast bass notes of the Marble Cathedral organ swelled up, pealing forth great resonant chords of glory and majesty, almost drowning out the powerful choir. George suppressed his impulse to applaud until the red lights of the TV cameras winked off. Then he clapped his hands heavily, grinning at Karen Bocelin, as the music rose still more, reverberating in the stately recesses of the cathedral, becoming a weighty presence itself in the immense volume overhead.

The stage lights faded, the organ stopped abruptly, and the broadcast was over. The Reverend accepted congratulations from several in the choir, from parishioners, from the producer of the show. Smiles, tanned faces, sleek grooming, a heady electricity. Then he came over to where George and Karen sat in the first pew.

"That was profound," Karen said. "Truly."

"I loved it, the way you brought the show together at the end," George said.

The Reverend shook George's hand and patted Karen on the shoulder. "I owe a great deal of that to you, brother. It was you who pointed out the passage from Ezekiel, you'll recall."

George beamed. "I didn't know how to relate it, to use those words."

"And the jokes you made about chillers," Karen said. "So funny! But horrifying, too."

The Reverend dipped his head with winning humility. "Friends tell me those jokes. They're not mine."

"But the way you used them together with the news. About their stealing that poor woman's body, leaving her God knows where." Karen's voice held deep indignation. "Denying her proper burial! Why—"

"That's what was so beautiful about the words of Ezekiel," George blurted. "The way you wove them in, it—it made me weep."

The Reverend's expressive face beamed with solicitude and gravity.

"I only hope we can reach the great viewership with that message, George. With *your* message."

"Oh, I'm sure you have," Karen said. "It was stunning."

"Let me say that I was especially happy to see you two sitting there together during the service and sermon."

"We have you to thank for introducing us," Karen said, squeezing George's hand.

"Y'know, I have tickets to a film here." Reverend Montana fished them out and handed them to George. "I surely do not have time to use them, and they say this new Disney film is a true inspiration. Why don't you two see it together?"

George had planned to work tonight on the endless detail of tracking the I^2 personnel, but he saw in the Reverend's face a clear command. He reached for the tickets. Karen beamed.

George felt a sudden spurt of strange, tilted joy. This was the world of solidity and purpose, the sanctified path. He had pressed himself against the window of life for so long, peering into the warm, well-lit interior. Now the window cocked open, letting out a thin slit of that yellow glow. A soft aroma like perfume wafted out into the cold rain that fell upon him, frigid in the night that had swallowed him for years. He could wine and dine this woman. She would appreciate Burrell's, the country restaurant where he liked to belly up to a three-egg breakfast with grits, stewed cinnamon apples, cornbread, and link sausage. He'd treat her to barbecue that would melt in her mouth.

The tickets loomed in his vision, emblems of the ordained path, and the great cathedral whirled around him, the air warping with fractured colors, splintered sounds that came to him as if from a vast, hollow distance. He closed his hand upon the tickets.

"Oh, thank you so much," Karen said.

George could scarcely breathe. He held the tickets aloft, like a holy scepter, and found that he had crushed them.

Karen lived just off Brookhurst in a residence court of small, attached bungalows. Twenty of them formed a hollow square. He drove in beneath an ornamented arch done in rococo Spanish style. A sign announced VISTA VILLAS in heavily looped script, though there was no view at all. The courtyard sported dead rosebushes around an empty concrete fountain. In the dim nightlights he saw tiny dry yards behind low iron fences.

"Isn't this drought terrible?" Karen asked as he parked in front of her pale tan stucco bungalow, number nineteen. "It just makes my *skin* jump."

"Yeah, zephyrs of the night." This was a quotation, but George could not remember from where. The Bible? Except for technical stuff, that was just about all he read. Overhead sea breezes churned a line of eucalyptus, clattering the branches.

Automatically he noted the cars parked beneath dim night lights nearby. A beat-up Nissan pickup, one tire nearly flat. Probably day workers, illegals, a dozen crammed into a sweaty one-bedroom. Two recent sedans, a Pontiac Grand Am, all clean, chrome polished. Symbols of pride and upward mobility. An aged, battered VW van with a mural spray-painted on the side, lurid and without a trace of creativity. Warmed-over hippies, probably, drug-stupefied, barely getting along. A fairly typical crowd for middle Orange County, some on the way up, some drifting down. He wondered which Karen was. Scholarship student. You had to respect that. This seemed like the wrong place for her.

There were few windows in the small rooms of number nineteen, and he guessed they would be depressingly dark by daylight. Karen conducted a bright-voiced tour of the living room and kitchen. The furniture was mostly Sears Modern with flowered slipcovers. Tall floor lamps had elaborate imitation Victorian shades. Karen effervesced, chattering with delight over the Disney film and then over the Reverend's broadcast. This let George relax into the ambience of the small living room as Karen served coffee and fluttered about, straightening knickknack items on a sideboard, arranging cushions, and then finally coming to rest next to him on the sofa. She began to ask him about the work he did for the Reverend, not being pushy or anything, and he gave a little ground without revealing much. To deflect this he asked, "You got the scholarship through the cathedral?"

"Oh no, through the Reverend himself," she said brightly.

"You must be smart. Chapman's a good school."

"I was never any big brain." Her eyelashes flickered low, a pretty embarrassment. "Just C pluses, really."

"But your coming from a foster home . . ."

"That helped, sure it did. I got a job with Vitality the week after the scholarship, too."

"That was fast."

"Not many girls are lucky enough to get a real job right out of high school."

"Know anything about computers?"

"Oh no, do you? I can't seem to think that way."

"So what do you do for Vitality?"

"Oh, I'm sort of a personal secretary to Dr. Lomax. Just part time, though."

"Dr. Lomax?"

"He's the president of the whole thing. A very intelligent, distinguished man. I met him through the Reverend."

"So you work in their office?"

"Oh no, that's in Huntington Beach. I don't go there much. They've got it all fixed up so that I can do most of my work right here."

"Personal secretary? How can you work here?"

She dimpled. "I guess I kind of exaggerated a teensy bit. I really just keep track of Mr. Lomax's accounts and billings. Part of the energy conservation thing, you know? Work at home with computers and faxes and modems."

"Sounds like an important job."

"I like it." She leaned toward him, her voice a sliding whisper, her scent again steaming up into his nostrils with pungent sweetness. "I get a look at how *really* wealthy people live."

For a moment he wondered at this abrupt shift from the demure, religious girl he had expected. Then, as she went on about Dr. Lomax's accounts and how much he spent for clothes and cars, all under the Vitality Corporation expense blanket, he saw that she had the simple, awed respect that so many did for the sheer accumulation of wealth. Mammon rampant. And in Southern California money inevitably connected with fame. Lomax knew some show business personalities, too.

"He took Amanda Palmer out to dinner last month—can you believe?" Karen said, eyes round. "I had to call him up to ask how the bill was to be categorized, and he told me all about it."

"Uh, Amanda Palmer is . . . ?"

"You don't *know*? She's the big new star of *Fool's Hill,* that great comedy. The one set in a fire station? Well, Mr. Lomax says Amanda isn't at *all* like her TV self. Really, she's shy and kind of quiet. She wears simple little frock dresses, too, not like those glitzy ones they make her use on the show. Can you believe? So then I asked . . ."

George let her go on, burbling happily about the lives of people she knew only as sheets of phosphor dots on a screen. Her guileless gush was a symptom of the times, he saw, an age when shallow actors loomed as immense as Zeus and Athena, as distant as the clouds, shakers of the video earth. It was electronic idolatry. But beneath her innocent fan enthusiasm he sensed something more, a sharpness and withheld assessment. He caught that only glancingly, for her aroma and warmth were coiling up into him, suffusing the air between them on the sofa with a heavy incense of unspoken energies.

"My, you don't know *any*thing about the world, do you?" Karen chided him coquettishly.

"I've been about the Lord's work. And my regular business, real estate, that kind of work." His voice sounded stilted and square even to himself.

"That's a very difficult field, a hard market."

"It takes concentration, sure." He was having trouble concentrating himself, with her beautiful eyes swimming so close.

"Here, I'll show you some pictures from my album."

"What?" Her presence made it hard to think.

"Photography's one of my hobbies. Here are some girls at school. And my foster parents."

"T . . . very nice."

"Here I am at the beach. Do you like swimming?"

"No, I don't do it." The idea alarmed him. He stayed away from the swimming pool in his apartment complex.

"Oh, I love to fool around in the surf. Living here, it's practically required."

"Required?" Swimming. Cold waters, fears of childhood. So much he couldn't remember from those years, but some memories danced like dust in a summer twilight.

"Oh, you'd like it if you gave it a chance. We should go to the beach together this weekend."

The conversation was veering so fast he felt a centrifugal sense of dizzying velocities. He put out a trembling hand, as if to balance himself, and it cupped her breast. Succulent. Soft.

He stared dumbfounded at the hand as though it belonged to someone else. It moved with a will of its own. The fingers caressed the peach-colored silk blouse, feeling a tingling excitement in the soft resistance. He could not speak.

Her lips parted, letting out a sweet, long gasp, and her eyes lost focus.

George leaned forward. His lips met hers in a touch at first satiny, a supple brush that hardened into a pulse-quickening collision. She seemed to surround him. Abruptly he remembered from long ago a girl, red-haired and freckled. She had given him a sheet of paper, fetching it forth from the back pocket of her jeans, still warm, so that it carried the ample curve of her rear as he spread the sheet. His hands had felt the warm paper, acutely uncomfortable, but filled with strange wonder.

It had been a Xerox of a diagram from their Sunday school teacher, titled "For Girls Only." In detail it showed what parts of her body a girl could allow a boy to touch, and the conditions that allowed such intimacy. A dotted line at the throat and below the lightly sketched breasts; Zone 1. You had to be going steady for that, the girl told him. *Did that mean he could unhook the bra and everything?* he had wondered. Zone 2 was everything below the waist, and it was shaded out. A legend below it said that you had to be engaged before anything happened there, and then not that one thing they all knew had to happen, once you got started this way.

His mind whirled, snagged in the past. The long-forgotten sketch had been a kind of release, so that he finally knew what was allowed him. Startled by the memory, he squeezed her hand. Karen gasped.

He blinked. "Oh, I'm, I'm—"

"You're so strong, George. I like that."

"I'm so sorry."

"No, I—listen, I want it that way. But first, I want, I need to . . ."

"What?"

"Get to know you. Believe me, I'll just feel better later, you know, when we do it, if I've had a chance to"—she frowned prettily, searching for words—"to really find out who you are."

Bewildered, he mumbled, "Maybe, I guess . . ."

"Here, I'll show you my life, right here in pictures. See? Here I am in the Vitality offices. That's my boss."

George gazed down at the ordinary office setting, flat lighting, grinning faces. One face snagged his eye, and he could not look away.

"Here, let me take your crystal cross." He had forgotten that he was still wearing it from the Marble Cathedral service. He had gotten used to its reassuring weight on his chest. She lifted it over his head.

But George hardly noticed. Something about the office photo struck a cold knife into him. A thin man, giving the camera a grudging smile. Dressed in a gray business suit, trimly tailored.

"Oooh, what *did* you do to deserve a cross?" Karen swung it, gleaming in the yellow lamplight, swaying from its golden chain, the long arcs steady, beating, piling up, resounding in him.

"I—who is . . ."

"Oh, my boss. You really should meet him. Let's look at some more pictures, I can show you my—"

"What does he do?"

"He runs everything, you know, everybody is very respectful. Here, we'll just snuggle a little, and then you can have what a man ought to have."

"Ought . . ." The Xeroxed sheet flickered in his mind. *What was expected of him.*

"What did you do to deserve this, George?"

The chain swayed. The tall floor lamps caught the greasiness of shiny metal, sending the glow refracting endlessly into his eyes. The soft, soft breast. "I, well . . ."

"I know what you want. I know that man was meant to rule, George. As the holy book says. As every woman knows. I understand that as well as you. Scripture says so. I want to be ruled. The others, they knew. Men in the back seats of cars, boys I went with in the pews of the church late at night, because we had no other place to go, they all knew. I welcome that. My, just look at this wonderful beautiful cross."

George saw the barren alleyway, the leering waitress, *don't want a guy like you to get away.* He let himself go into the oily oscillations of the cross, so slow, so slow.

"—as the Lord intended, the man in charge, the man on top."
She smiled. Something sprang into his mind.
Splintered light.
Silence thick as cotton.
He was spinning down into something cold and wet and streaming with gray light, *currents making his legs heavy,* something coming up at him from far below, *hands numb,* moist, clammy, *balloon breasts, mother soft, pink vast nipple suck* fat slimy fingers reaching out for him, into him, *parents bodies rotting, the smell* and behind it a great enveloping mad redness, *cat twisting on the point, steel blade gleaming, catching the street-light glow in a grimy alley* everything coming together in a vortex whorl *the black lake* that seized his chest and squeezed until a tormented, despairing cry burst from his lungs and shattered the warm, clasping air.

10

ALEX

For some reason there was a small videocamera in his cell. It hung high in a corner inside a wire mesh cage and watched him sit and pace and sleep and get bored. He hoped somebody was having fun watching.

The cell door was shiny steel, padded on the inside, with a square observation window and a slide port through which came bland, starchy food. The cell was painted neutral light brown and smelled bitingly of disinfectant.

The guard had told Alex that this was comparatively the penthouse luxury suite. Felony cases got the best. Orange County jail was so crowded with those whose ambitions had gone awry that the "holding facility" had stopped taking drunks entirely and most cells held four inmates.

Alex's suite at the Ritz had two bunk beds in it with gray sheets and two gray blankets that were neither clean nor dirty. The mattress was maybe an inch thick over crisscross metal slats. *A firm sleep,* he thought moodily. Except that last night he had slept little, and when he had, his dreams were of endless pursuit through swampy murk, with something unnamed and implacable hounding him as his feet grew heavier with thick, clinging mud and his lungs labored. The unseen thing following him was a shifting shadow, formless and moving, restless and hungry, always coming toward him with a steady, relentless pace.

There was a small washbasin, paper towels, and a steel toilet. Until the preliminary hearing, Alex got to wear his own clothes. After that, a trustee told him, he would wear jail denims. No shoelaces, no tie, no belt. Alex had asked him if this was to put a stop to any kinky sex in jail, and the man had simply given him a stolid stare.

It was day so the lights were on. When they had first put him here, he had recalled reading somewhere that guilty suspects fell asleep immediately in their cells, relieved that the suspense of whether they would be arrested was at last over. Innocent suspects were incensed, worried, and so stayed up. The cops knew this and used it so he lost some sleep, defiantly glowering at the TV camera. There was nothing to read, and since his cellmate had left this morning, he had plenty of time to run over the events that had led him here and to examine each for the possibility that somewhere, somehow, he could have avoided this. It would be better if he could talk to someone about it, particularly Kathryn. He had seen the I^2 lawyer only briefly. Ever since the deputy had put the cuffs on him, the sheriff's men had devoted care to seeing that none of the three arrested—Alex, Gary Flint, and Robert Skinner —talked to each other. A proper precaution, Alex realized: They might have polished their stories.

He was glad they had kept the cover story simple. Skinner and Flint had been out in the truck running errands. Alex had gone home, and then Ray Constantine had called with word that the deputies were already at Immortality Incorporated. He had tried to start his Volvo and failed, so he called Skinner and Flint on the truck's phone. They had picked him up on their way back to I^2.

It sounded moderately reasonable, and Alex liked the part about the stalled car. The cops could check that—probably already had, since Immortality Incorporated's lawyer reported that the sheriff had more warrants to search their homes—and it was a small detail that a liar in a hurry wouldn't include. Or so Alex had thought. He had imagined that he was handling the whole thing pretty well, considering, but a day here in this gray sameness had underlined how out of his depth he was.

He was ready for interrogation, but he had not figured on just sitting. Which meant that the I^2 lawyer was having trouble getting them out.

Suspended, he thought. That was the word cryonics used to describe their patients, but it applied well here, too. Jails held you in a neutral, gray grip.

He had always thought jails were places where men yelled, banged on the bars, and ran spoons or cups along them to make a racket, and the guards rushed in to club the prisoners back. That was all TV cliché. Jail was really like being kept in a box with nothing to fight against, nobody who cared remotely about your case, not even any primary colors to stimulate the eye. Even his cellmate had listened to Alex's tale of his arrest with what seemed to be interest and then at the end had said, *"No comprendo,"* rolled onto the lower bunk and dozed off. The trustee who had led the man away said he was an illegal alien from a car theft ring.

Alex was reviewing how he had gotten here for the nth time when a deputy popped the slot aside and said, "Comin' in." The man was brisk, efficient. Alex submitted to handcuffs. He remembered how the cuffs put on him at I^2 had hurt, his hands going numb in the squad car, and how long they tingled and stung afterward. These were looser, almost pleasant by comparison. The deputy looked around the cell and asked, "Any personal stuff in here?"

"Just me," Alex said. "I'm as personal as I get."

In two minutes he was sitting in a soundproofed interrogation room with Detective Stern and a heavy-set man named Detweiler. More minimalism: a desk, a tilt-back chair behind it with Detweiler rocking slightly back and forth, two straight-backed chairs and a Mr. Coffee machine on a small table against the wall.

Stern took off the handcuffs, looked through a file, and opened up with detailed questions about the Hagerty body. Alex stuck narrowly to his story. No embellishments, no clever added details. When Stern ran out of steam he looked at Detweiler as if he were calling in the marines. Detweiler sat with his shirt sleeves rolled up, showing thick muscles under pale skin. Detweiler was as bald as a brick and looked at Alex as if he were a piece of furniture, just something in the line of sight. He drank coffee from a cardboard cup and not quietly. He finished the coffee, staring through Alex, and then wadded up the cup and threw it over his shoulder without looking.

"Dumb story," Detweiler said. "Everybody at this company of yours says they dunno where the corpse is. We're supposed to nod and go away?"

"I'm not one to tell you how to do your job," Alex said.

"Damned right you aren't," Detweiler said.

From the look on Stern's face Alex could see that Detweiler was going to run things now. Alex had always assumed that the law was paperwork and arguments by guys in three-piece suits, but Detweiler looked like something from a gangster movie, and not one of the good guys. His nose had been broken and he held his hands like blunt instruments. His muscles had started to turn to a thickening at the middle but his face was bony.

"You stole the body, and that's felony obstruction. We'll nail you for three to five, easy." Stern nodded in agreement, but Detweiler didn't notice. His eyes fixed on Alex.

"I tell you I don't know who took it," Alex said.

"We got evidence that one of your company trucks took a little run down to Mexico yesterday," Detweiler said. "You got a place to stash her down there?"

"Absolutely not." It felt good to be able to tell them the flat truth and see the scornful disbelief in Detweiler's face. The truck dodge had been Ray's idea.

"I could work on that with the Tijuana authorities," Stern said with no enthusiasm.

Alex hoped Detweiler would go for that, waste some more time, but Detweiler waved the idea away. Alex sighed and repeated, "I don't know who took it."

"Yeah, I heard." Detweiler snorted. "Just what I'd expect from Captain Cockroach."

"What?"

"Think we'd miss that? A little kiddie prank that hurt some people. Well, this time it's no prank."

Alex shrugged. Detweiler said, "The health inspector traced those bugs back through the UCI lab. It was in the background file on your company. We couldn't figure out how to use it, but now I think there's plenty grounds. Plenty."

"I don't know what you're talking about," Alex said automatically.

"Pattern, that's the point," Stern said. "Any judge would accept evidence of prior misdemeanors."

Detweiler waved that aside. "This guy's a flake, that's easy to prove. But he's covering a murder."

Alex blinked. "What?"

"You and your friends were real anxious to get that body away from UCI," Detweiler said.

"I should've done more background checking, Skipper," Stern said. "But I did turn up that assault on the Hagerty woman."

"Yeah, after they'd had plenty time to work on the body," Detweiler said with disgust.

"It looked straight at the time," Stern said evenly.

"Sure, if you're blind. These creeps are crazy, I told you that first thing."

"Look," Alex said, "we didn't do anything to the body except—"

"Freeze it and steal it," Detweiler spat back. "You think we're stupid? Somebody at this body-freezing business wanted to get hands on the evidence. Probably you."

"That's nonsense," Alex said. "We were carrying out Susan's expressed wishes. We—"

"Why are the cuffs off him?" Detweiler said to Stern.

"Well . . ." Stern saw the look on Detweiler's face and got up. Alex held out his hands and Detweiler said, "No, behind the back."

Stern cuffed him while Detweiler got two more cups of coffee. Alex sat on the hard chair and wondered how long it would be before he saw his attorney again.

"I don't wanna see his elbows," Detweiler said, rolling his chair closer to Alex and sitting erect.

Stern nodded and tightened the cuffs until Alex's arms were straight behind him. "Get some bite in them," Detweiler said.

Stern tightened them again, and Alex felt his fingers start to go numb. If this was the old good cop/bad cop act, both these guys were competing for the same role.

"Let's hear a straight story now, Captain Cockroach," Detweiler said.

"I don't know anything." Alex leaned a little to each side to test his balance. He wondered how long he could sit like this without falling off.

"Tell us about the cockroach caper," Detweiler prompted.

Alex shook his head. Detweiler said sarcastically, "Come on, make us laugh, creep. I bet you thought it was real funny."

His hands were numb, which was better than the pain, but he would pay for that later. And if Alex made noise later, Detweiler could say the bruises were from the arresting deputies. The I^2 lawyer had checked Alex over for marks when they booked him, but the bruises could take a while to come out. Not something a smart cop would do, but the contempt shown Alex here fit in with their general attitude—a corpse-stealer didn't merit respect or constitutional niceties.

Alex sighed. He had let them talk, hoping this little chat might compromise any future court action. Most of what he knew about law he got from TV shows, and of course the I^2 attorney had told him to just clam up, but he hoped he could turn this little discussion to his advantage. Questioning him this way could blow the case, bring about a major career move for Detweiler into mall security at Fashion Island.

But he had taken about as much as he could from these clowns. "I want to see my lawyer again."

Detweiler made a thin smile and gripped his cardboard cup of coffee. "People are hard to find in this place sometimes. Could take a long while for a trustee to locate you while your lawyer sits on his ass and charges you couple hundred bucks an hour for it."

"And cops wonder why people think they're scum," Alex said.

"Talk, creep," Detweiler said. The muscles in his jaw jumped, and he gripped the coffee cup so hard, Alex wondered if he would crush it.

"There's no murder here. Some people—I'm not saying who—just want to give Susan Hagerty a chance at a second life."

"Some jerko killed her, and you con artists are covering it up. Like maybe it's the jerko I'm looking at."

Alex glanced at Stern. "Have you got anybody here who knows the law?"

"A lawyer lover, huh?" Detweiler said.

"If you were halfway professional—"

Alex caught the tightening in Detweiler's eyes and threw himself sideways. The coffee cup came at him, but then he was on the floor, landing on his shoulder with a sharp stab of pain. It was the shoulder he had broken before, of course.

The coffee was all over the chair, and the cardboard cup bounced onto the floor near his nose. He wondered if this could rebreak the shoulder.

Beautiful gesture—get smashed up while heroically avoiding coffee stains. But he was damned if he was going to let Detweiler get the better of him.

Stern helped him up. His arms had started to hurt above the wrists now. Detweiler shoved him hard back into the chair. He felt moist warmth along his legs. *So I get my pants stained rather than my shirt. Terrific.* But his shoulder felt okay now, or at least no worse than his arms.

"What a stinking piece of shit," Detweiler said. "Get him out of our clean jail."

Alex looked at Stern, who seemed almost sympathetic. He suddenly saw that Stern was just marking time here, a smart cop under the command of an old-style, meat-ax superior. But even Stern didn't seem to have any clue what to do next.

"Don't guess we need these," Stern said, unlocking the cuffs. "Your lawyer's downstairs. Preliminary hearing."

"How long has he been there?"

Detweiler grinned. "Long enough for you to spill some coffee on your pants." He already had another cup of coffee in his hand. *Maybe that's his weapon of choice,* Alex thought. He debated giving Detweiler an obscene gesture, shrugged, and turned to Stern. "Can we post bail?"

"Yes," Stern said. "The DA won't let us go for a murder charge. Not yet, anyway. So if you got the bucks, you'll spring."

"Don't tell that shit anything," Detweiler said, but Alex had already headed for the door.

11

GEORGE

He burst into the Reverend's study without knocking. The devils that had been tormenting him had clamped their claws around his throat, making breathing hard. They had clouded his vision for so long that only now did he see that he had to go to the one place where he knew he could receive comfort. The massive oak door swung open with a squeak, and George plunged through.

"Reverend, Reverend, I need—"

But the Reverend was not alone.

Two strange men sat in the deep, soft chairs. Both looked at him, startled. The Reverend Carl Montana stood, stately and unhurried, his face showing only mild, fatherly concern.

George stopped and struggled to breathe properly, normally. So much had happened. He wanted to let it all out now, to deliver all his turmoil into the hands of the Reverend. But now the Reverend's face wore a severe frown and drawn lips told him to hold back, keep it within. George opened his mouth, gasped, swallowed.

"I see you have heard the news," Reverend Montana said.

"Yes, yes, I—"

"Please come in." The Reverend's voice swelled with reassurance.

George did not dare speak, sure that from his mouth would form only a pitiful squeak. He came forward on wooden legs, passing among the shadowed comforts of the tall study. The stained-glass windows rose behind the Reverend, like bright angel's wings. George sank into one of the large chairs, his bones aching.

"This is Detective Stern, George. And Detective Detweiler. Detectives, George—"

"Goff," George interrupted. "Though in business I use my real first name, Charles."

The Reverend betrayed no surprise. "I've already told them a few things about you. What a fine man you are." The Reverend sat back, his hands steepled before his solemn features.

The smooth baritone notes soothed George, and he could feel his other side, the analytical self, swell and grow strong within his mind. He would have to think hard now, hard and clear and fast, and yet let none of it into his face. Most of all, he would have to be Charles Goff here, put them onto his paper persona.

Momentary panic grasped him. His legs tightened with the sudden desire to flee. He made himself cross his legs casually.

"They are the detectives assigned to investigate this morning's terrible news about Karen."

Stern was studying him closely. He had better respond. What would be right? "Karen," George said numbly. "This morning."

Stern said, "She was killed last night, Mr. Goff. I understand you took her to a film."

"I . . . yes. Sure. It was that great new Disney one."

"I gave them the tickets," the Reverend added. "A fine couple."

Detweiler's voice was a sour rasp. "Which showing?"

"Uh, the early one. Seven o'clock. At the Edwards in Main Place." Detweiler made a note in a pad. He was phlegmatic, almost sleepy, but George sensed in him the resting power of a man who liked to use his body. Stern, on the other hand, seemed sharper. He had better watch out for both of them. Cops often ran this Mutt and Jeff act to catch you off guard.

Stern said, "What time did you last see her?"

"Oh, early. I drove her straight home."

Detweiler nodded, made a note. Then he sat back and looked at Stern, as if turning this boring procedure over to the other man.

Stern's face was angular, concentrated. "Did you go inside?"

"Well, yeah, for a few minutes. She was tired."

Detweiler said craftily, "Bad date?"

"She was tired."

"Not want to, y'know, play ball?" Detweiler glanced at Montana.

"This was just a friendly date, Mr. Detweiler." George tried to sound politely offended.

Stern asked in a flat, routine way, "When did you leave?"

"Nine, nine-thirty."

"Did anyone see you?"

"No, gee, there wasn't anybody else there."

"Then you drove home?"

"Yessir."

"Where's that?"

He gave the Santa Ana address of the Goff persona. Then he had to show ID. When he handed Stern his driver's license he included some credit cards, apparently by mistake. Stern gave them a good look, then copied down one of the card ID numbers, not bothering to conceal it.

"She was alone when you left?"

"Yessir."

"What was she wearing?"

"Uh, a black skirt and a peach-colored silk blouse."

Stern nodded. "That's what we found her in."

"Found her where?"

"In a dumpster behind a Vons Market. She had been hit in the head, her skull beaten in."

"My merciful Lord," the Reverend said. He did not look at George.

Stern asked, "Did you know her well?"

George shook his head, his face still showing astonished grief. *Dumpster.* "That—last night was our first date."

"They left from my service, Detective," the Reverend said. "I gave them two free passes myself, to encourage them. I'm afraid I've always been something of a matchmaker."

"Neither of you have any idea why she might have gone out for a walk?"

"None," the Reverend said. "Especially since she lived in a rather rough neighborhood."

"She didn't have a dog or anything—no reason to go out for a walk," George said.

Dog. Don't mention dog, he thought too late. But then he breathed out, the constriction of his chest clearing. There was no connection of Karen to the Hagerty woman. He had to keep that in mind. This detective was the same one mentioned in the newspapers, assigned to the Hagerty case. Was that an accident?

Stern asked, "Did she jog?"

Why ask that? Because the Hagerty woman was jogging? George wiped his brow, then regretted giving any sign of the turmoil within him. "Uh, I dunno."

"We thought she might have gone out to run an errand or something," Stern said. "There was jogging gear in her closet."

"But you said she was dressed in the same clothes as I saw," George said.

"Right," Stern said. "I'm just looking for a reason for her to be in that particular alley. Did she say anything that might suggest why?"

He's just fishing, maybe. "No, nothing I can recall."

"Could be she just went to the Vons to do a little shopping," Detweiler said.

With a slight edge to his voice Stern said, "She would have had to walk over two miles."

George wondered what tension there was between the two detectives. Stern was cool, Detweiler was sarcastic muscle, barely restrained by the Reverend's presence. Then George snapped his attention back to keeping calm, thinking ahead. He could not allow his drumfire heart-beat and short, scraping breath to betray him.

Cool and casual, Stern said, "That dumpster was the same one where we found the body of a waitress a while back."

George froze. Last night was one howling nightmare, events stacked atop each other, images fever-hot and garish, and he could not make sense of them. He remembered a grimy alley, yes, inky shadows, carrying the body in a sheet. . . . *The same alley?*

Gaping vacancy. Blanks.

Until this instant he did not know that he had gone to the site where he dumped the waitress. *Pattern. They look for patterns the killer doesn't see.* He had read that somewhere. Someplace buried far back in a swamp of memories.

"Mr. Goff? Did you remember something?"

His face must be giving him away. *Cover.* "No, no, I just . . . which Vons was it?"

"The one at Santa Ana and Lacy. Why?"

"Just wondering. It's such a shock."

"You live nearby?"

"A few miles."

"I'm afraid we have a serial killer on our hands here, and Karen had the awful luck to come upon him somehow," Stern said reflectively. "I had hoped that maybe you gentlemen would know of some connection she had, some way she met him."

"Maybe she didn't." George felt a lump of fear in his throat even as he said it. "Maybe he just grabbed her on the street."

Detweiler shook his head derisively. "Nope."

"That's unlikely," Stern said. "It would not fit what we know of the previous murder."

What we know. George could not make himself speak, ask for more. And they undoubtedly would not give it anyway. He sensed that they knew something important. And he had to sit there while they looked him over, tantalized him with it. He had never hated cops more. Not even before, when he was running from them.

George listened closely, thin-lipped. Stern went on, trying to pry some tidbit of information out of him and the Reverend. Details, times, people she knew. George kept himself alert, tried not to think, not to let his mind spin above the abyss within him. Stern kept asking, but the Reverend shook his large head sadly, answered in mournful tones, and after a while George saw that the detective was just going through the motions.

George realized that the logic of serial killers now played on his side. There was no visible connection between the waitress and Karen, except the neighborhood. Therefore, the killer was probably a local, not tied to the Reverend.

The talk went on. He could see that the detectives had dismissed him for the moment. Serial killers never linked themselves closely with their prey.

But if they got the scent of him, they would close in.

Stern stood, handed the Reverend and George each a card in case they thought of anything further, and left with Detweiler. He shot George a speculative look, but nothing more.

When he was gone, George stood for a long moment in the shadowy softness of the study and did not have the courage to meet the Reverend's stare. The leaden silence stretched. George felt the solemn weight here, the heavy ranks of engraved books that rose into the recesses above. Soft glows flickered through the stained-glass windows, speaking of the chaos of life outside, while within here a grave, cottony hush prevailed, broken solely by a grandfather clock's somber brass pendulum stroke.

"We both know there is more to this," the Reverend said at last, his voice powerful and resolute, the same voice that he used to end his sermons.

"Yessir."

"And we grasp that this hour is fraught with peril."

"Yessir."

"I want to be sure of you, Brother George."

"I am steadfast in the Lord."

"Yea verily, but that is not enough. Standing steadfast is only the beginning."

"Yessir."

"I hope you understand why I did not press that officer of the secular law with any misleading details."

George stood ramrod straight before the Reverend's polished rosewood desk, face as stiff as a soldier's. "I can tell you what happened, what—"

"I do not wish to know. I am sure you had some intimacy with Karen, but that is beside the crucial point here, George."

"Nossir, I didn't—"

"I do *not* wish to know." The Reverend slapped the desk, his eyebrows knitted together. Then he rocked forward, head in hands. "If I'd known—if he'd said—that it could come to this—I didn't—" The words cut off with a strangled sob.

George could not guess what the Reverend meant, but the man's pain was obvious. The big shoulders shook with silent sobs. George did not know what to do, could not bring out of his own deep confusion any words of solace.

A heavy silence stretched until George began to feel like praying, or maybe just going away, ashamed of all he had brought down on the shoulders of this man. The Reverend sighed gravely. He sniffed, sat up. His face was composed again. He stared at George for a long moment and finally scowled. Mournfully he said, "The task we share is to keep the cathedral untarnished. That means I shall hear *nothing*"—his big hand smacked the desk—"of what went on between you last night. For by truthfully saying that I do not fathom such matters, I keep the skirts of the mighty cathedral *clean*"—he slapped the desk loudly—"of the soil of gossip, of innuendo, of the nay-sayers all about us."

George was terrified of the wrathful countenance before him. Still, he ventured to say, "I need to talk about—"

"Talk is not your task, my friend. You and I are bound together in a holy alliance. We cannot be caught up in some side matter. Terrible though Karen's death is, it should not reflect upon the cathedral. Upon our deep connection to the good works of Vitality Corporation. Upon *your* good works, too, George."

"Vitality?"

"They are a great benefactor of ours. Working always behind the scenes, in ways great and small."

"I have heard you speak well of them, sir, but—"

"Scholarships, charitable works, donations—they are a Godsend. I will not have them blemished by this girl's unseemly passing."

"I don't see how we—"

"Her church connection need not be stressed, that is my point."

"If anybody asks—"

"No one will. Those detectives are going on about their business, running after some serial killer. Very well."

George felt confused, his head congested by impossible pressures. "If he gets more evidence—"

"He will then move further from us," the Reverend said with soft-spoken confidence. "But that is not what I fear, George."

"It isn't?"

"I fear you."

"What?" His shock made the cool air seem to churn with whorls of pale phosphorescence. "How?"

"I fear that you are our weakest link."

"I am the strongest!" George shot back with injured pride.

"So you seem. But if in your future works you run afoul of someone, there will be those who cast a sharp eye at your ties. Ties to me."

"I won't say a thing."

"I must have a pledge, George."

"I do solemnly pledge that I shall never say that you had anything to do with—with my Calling."

"That is what I want to hear, George. Repeat it."

George spoke the words with gravity and a strange sense of liberation.

"Then let us put this ugly incident behind us. I believe it would be best if you did not attend any further services, George. Come see me here, if you need. I will lead you in simple worship. I will give you my private telephone number, and you may arrange with me for spiritual guidance. The world will be watching."

He nodded. The Reverend began to pray. George mouthed the words with a helpless sense of letting go, of acrid fluids draining from him, leaving a slack and empty carcass.

Only the Reverend's determination could fill him now, could cut through his fog of lurching emotions. He let the other man's certainty enter him, invading every vein and fiber, a firm possession and a delicious release.

12

ALEX

He had spent the morning playing basketball on the half courts at Main Beach in Laguna. The action there was worth the drive from his apartment in Irvine. Guys in their twenties turned out to sweat and grunt and suck in the sea breezes. On the small courts you ran less and maneuvered more. There were dunks galore—double-pumps, spin shots, classic alley-oops. Shouts of glory, high-fives, back-slapping, grins and glowers.

Alex kept up, but he wasn't there to shine. It was enough to pour himself into the game.

Everybody had the moves. Trick dribbles, footwork fakes, the collapsing full-court press. The fine art of the slap steal, the squeeze, the trap. And the one-on-one sparring—blocking, getting in the other guy's face, hitting the outlet man on the fast break, maxing your free throws.

He was winded in thirty minutes, staggering at the hour. *These guys aren't* that *much younger than me,* he thought, leaning over to let sweat drip off him, lungs heaving. He bowed out of the next game and cooled off with a walk on the beach. That made him think of Susan, though. The contrast of her icy stasis with the surge and sweat of lunging bodies made him reflective, moody.

Some called this Silicone Valley, but the meat in this market was real. Deeply tanned athletes parked their jeeps with giant tires in handicapped spots, muttering, "Only be a sec." Lolitas in string bikinis rollerskated by gawking men and then spun to a stop, glaring and indignant at their audience's open-mouthed attention. The body reigned here.

He wondered if he was souring on California. Lately it seemed that personal prosperity depended less on Adam Smith's Wealth of Nations and more on the Health of Nations. The life sciences commanded the metaphors of innovation. It was an ideology of hope, craving choices. Bionarcissism, the conspicuous consumption of "health" as a commodity: plastic surgery and diet for the skin's pesky folds and wrinkles; lasers to clear blurred vision; pills galore to erase pain, amplify energy; clever genetic engineering to tailor away chronic ailments and defective children.

The beach, despite its lazy sun worshipers, was a battleground. Roving eyes compared slim thighs, bunched pecs, ribbed bellies. Stay slim, live right, last forever. Try the fad treatments. And if you couldn't see eating like a lab rat for 130 years, or smearing yourself with sheep placenta daily, or nipping and tucking each new skin fold—well, just change the definition of old. The sinful Older Woman, Mrs. Robinson in *The Graduate,* back in the 1960s, was thirty-six-year-old Anne Bancroft. But the yuppies and baby boomers had aged, and Bancroft might get away with that kind of role even now.

Alex yanked himself out of his mood, ducked under the public showers at the beach, and changed clothes in his Volvo. It was running okay again after replacing the starter, and he took a back route to work. There were few remaining orange groves in Orange County. He drove slowly through the biggest, savoring the thick aroma of blossoms that swarmed through the windows and up into his head, lifting the melancholy clouds in his mind.

How did we lose all this? he wondered. By inches. The developers, the eager immigrants, the boundless plenty of sunlight and sharp air—all conspired to wedge in just one more condo, another street, a minimart to shave seconds of convenience from myriad lives.

The mood at I^2 was no better than the one he brought. Ray Constantine and Bob Skinner were tending to the perpetual small jobs. Alex talked with Skinner about their legal problems for a bit while helping clean up some of the mess left by the sheriff's deputies. They had taken most of the emergency electrical cart, returning the gcar banged-up and messy. In the guise of searching, deputies had opened sterile tubing packs at random, dumping them anywhere they liked among the storage shelves. Perfusate chemicals had been opened and tested for cocaine, then tossed aside, usually so they would drip onto shelves below.

Skinner had just come up before a UCI Intern Review Board hearing. They wanted to know about his involvement with I^2.

"Guess who brought up the question?" Skinner asked with a wan smile. "Three guesses."

"Blevin, Blevin, and Blevin."

"Bingo."

Alex snorted in exasperation. "The man never rests."

"I think I have some chance of charging him with conflict of interest."

"Why?"

"He's getting some flak from the med school. The dean has distanced himself from Blevin since Susan died."

"Good news, but too damned late."

Skinner nodded. "His pushing that suicide idea backfired. People figure he drove Susan to it."

"Bull. Susan didn't kill herself. But if the idea hurts Blevin, great."

"So I think I can maintain that he's just trying to push his own agenda, bringing me up before the board. If I—"

A hooting alert sounded through the bay. Alex jumped up and ran into the main office. Ray Constantine had already called up the trouble onto the main display board. "It's Susan," Ray said.

"The nitrogen," Alex said with a sinking feeling.

"Looks like."

"Damn!"

"It's running low. Maybe four hours left."

"I thought that fill-up was supposed to last through tomorrow night."

Ray rolled back in his wheelchair and consulted a smaller screen where numbers wavered in yellow phosphorescent columns. "That feeder system we rigged has got some heat leaks in it."

"We wrapped more insulation around it," Skinner said.

Ray grunted. "The sucker still boils off way more nitrogen than it should."

To minimize damage to Susan's cells required that she be lowered slowly down the three-hundred-degree slope in temperature. Automatic valves bled liquid nitrogen into her vault. The system had just sent a radio cry for help.

Alex looked out at the shimmering morning sun. "We can't wait for dark?"

"No way."

"We could take a big slug of nitrogen out on the truck."

Ray frowned, said nothing. Skinner bit his lip, face clouded. Alex sensed in them a natural reluctance to face another risk, another round of the bad luck that had plagued them.

"Right, the truck's too conspicuous," Alex said. "I'll carry a small dewar on my back."

Skinner nodded, relieved. Alex realized that Skinner must have been weighing his options a lot lately. Getting further implicated in the now-infamous Missing Body Caper would not help him.

It took a while to rig a backpack to carry the cylindrical dewar. When it was filled, Skinner helped Alex swing the dewar up and settle the straps on his shoulders. He felt the bite. "Good thing I don't have to go far," he said to Skinner.

They checked to see if anybody was pulling into the parking lot outside. All clear. He went out the loading dock and trotted into the shelter of the trees.

He moved with extreme care, erasing signs of his passage. He avoided vegetation where possible and slid through bushes so that stems bent but did not break. This was crucial, for a broken stem cannot be fixed without careful cutting and even so, a sure reader of signs would catch it. Leaving stems or branches pointing the way you came was bad, too. They had to be gently urged back to a random pattern. His adventures in the Boy Scouts, pretending to be Indians, were paying off. Stealth spelled safety.

The whispering wind calmed him. He caught the soft rustle of the life that underlay all fervent human busyness and felt himself relax into it. Everything in the land fled from his footsteps. Lizards scattered into the nearest cracked rock. Quail hovered in shadow, hoping he would take them for stones—but at the last moment they lost their nerve and burst into frantically flapping birds. Mice evaporated, doves whispered skyward, rabbits crazylegged away in a dead heat. A coyote had melted into legend, leaving only tracks and dung. The heart of the arroyo was pale sand, a field whose emptiness exposed life here for what it was: conjured out of nothingness, and bound for it, too. Desert plants existed as exiles from each other, hoarding their domains of water collection done silently beneath the sand by single-minded roots. For a plant, neighboring vacancy was life.

He had not seen Susan's refuge in daylight since they had brought her here a week before. There was no time to let his mood fasten on this place, though. He quickly switched the dewars, checked the fittings, started the trickle of bitter cold into Susan's cylinder. He permitted himself one moment, while he was waiting for an automatic valve to pop open. His hand rested on the cool metal. *Rest easy, old friend. We're still fighting for you.*

He hefted the empty dewar onto his back, then stopped. It was blatant evidence, after all. He rolled it into a corner and then stripped off the backpack carrier and left it, too. Quickly he resealed the entrance.

He was intent on erasing his footprints, walking backward down the sandy slope and using a whisk broom. He did not hear the helicopter until it came hammering over the ridge line above.

"Halt!" a cutting, amplified voice barked down. "Do not move!"

Slowly he shaded his eyes with one hand and read OC SHERIFF on the helicopter. With the other hand he slipped the whisk broom under his shirt. Then he stood and watched the excited, scowling faces above. Wind and noise buffeted him. A deputy came trotting up the arroyo. Only then would the chopper depart to land in the I² parking lot. Its *whump-whump-whump* had deafened Alex, and it took a while to understand the deputy.

"We'll just stay right here, mister," the deputy insisted.

"I didn't know taking a walk was illegal."

"No smart mouth. You wait."

Alex sat down and tried to look bored. Depression settled over him. Had the cops positioned someone out here to track him, send up an alert? He should have thought of that. He felt hollow.

Detectives Stern and Detweiler came slogging up the arroyo with a corps of sweating deputies behind them.

"You trying to run?" Detweiler grinned slyly.

"I didn't know you were coming. I would have put on some coffee. In case you wanted to ask me any more questions."

Detweiler frowned. "We're going to throw a lot more at you this time, creep."

"Are you guys just out for a hike, like me?"

"The hell you're hiking. You heard we were coming."

Alex was startled and tried not to show it. He turned to Stern. "What's the story?"

Stern said evenly, "The grand jury returned an indictment against you for obstruction of justice and a few other charges. They authorized another search for the body."

"I want to be there when you ransack my home again."

"You will be."

"Are Skinner and Flint included?"

"Sure," Detweiler said. "A regular li'l creep roundup."

"Okay, let's go inside. I've got to go down to the jail, right?"

Stern said, "Later. We'll search here first."

"I hope you don't think you're going to open the suspension cylinders."

Stern shook his head. Detweiler said, "You give us any lip, I'll pop the seals on those corpsicles of yours."

Alex gritted his teeth and said nothing. Stern looked around. "What were you doing out here?"

"Taking a walk before my shift starts."

"Uh-huh." Stern's eyes narrowed, and Alex felt his heart lurch.

"There are a lot of deer up in these hills," Alex said. "Over that way there's coyote tracks right behind the deer, and what looks like a cougar."

"Yeah?" Stern was interested. "Show me."

Detweiler stayed behind with the others, talking loudly into a walkie-talkie. Alex spent some time going on about the tracks and Stern nodded, crouching to look at the sandy soil. Alex had led him off to the side so that the strokes of his brush were not visible.

Stern straightened up and looked at Alex for a long moment. Then he turned and called to the other men, "Spread out. Search this area. Report anything that looks funny."

Alex let nothing show in his face. After a long moment he managed a shrug. "I know you've got to go through the motions, but do I have to stand out here? I'm late for work."

"You're going downtown again."

"My hourly will get docked. Can't you—"

"Move it."

The worst of it was the waiting. He managed to delay awhile at I², expecting at every moment to hear hoarse shouts of discovery. None came. Then they loaded him into a sheriff's cruiser, complete with the wire cage back seat, and took him into Santa Ana.

Paperwork. Waiting. The I² lawyer. More bail. More money to juggle. His checkbook was getting riddled. Already he had taken out a short-term loan, paying surrealistic interest, and now he saw he would have to go back for more to get through the month.

If anybody would give him, infamous body snatcher, a dime.

More waiting. More paperwork. More legalese.

But the worst was the battery of reporters, videocams, and snapping cameras as he emerged into the street with Skinner and Flint. The indictment had created a bloodlust in the media. Microphones thrust into his face.

You've got her, haven't you? What would make you give up the corpse? Do you deny that you're a member of a Satanic cult? What have you chiller people really used the body for, anyway?

He got back to I² as fast as possible, brushing aside the media feeding frenzy. Flint and Skinner went off to tend their own gardens, the three shaking hands solemnly, comrades in a cause they could scarcely speak of directly, for fear of being overheard. But there was a quiet steadiness between them, a peace almost like the slow silences he had felt when he had walked, in better days, back in the arroyo.

He walked into I^2 with tingling apprehension. Stern was in the main bay watching two deputies methodically cataloging gear on the shelves.

"Are you finished in the arroyo?" Alex asked casually.

"Maybe," Stern said, eyeing him closely.

He let into his face no hint of the sinking feeling that washed over him. Small triumphs went unheralded in this game. "What happens next?"

"We toss your apartment."

"Okay, let's go."

Crime wasn't exciting at all, he thought wearily. He would have to remember that when he thought of future career moves.

Kathryn came over and helped him put the place back together after the deputies left. They had been thorough, polite for a change, and seldom put anything back right.

He took her out to dinner at Rumari's, an Italian joint in Laguna. They walked on the beach and came back to his place and made love, all without speaking very much. There seemed no need.

Late that night, after Kathryn had left, he took out the garbage for the early-morning trash pickup. He didn't mind sorting plastics, aluminum, glass, and newspapers into their proper recycling bins; at the end of a day that hadn't yielded much accomplishment, a touch of civic virtue was a welcome afternote.

As he rattled the lid on the last can he heard the rush and whoosh of rumbling menace. An inky figure hurtled toward him. He leaped back to the curb as a teenager shot past on a skateboard, rasping into his turn, steel wheels swooping with casual ease across and down the street. The boy passed beneath a yellow streetlight, and Alex could see in the smooth, turned face a glaze of oblivious pleasure, eyes fixed upon an infinite perspective. He felt a peculiar pang. When was the last time he had done anything so blissful, so unthinking, so much fun? The boy sped away on the street's steepening slope, *rrrrrrrr* in the sharp air, blithe freedom passing him by without a wave.

13

GEORGE

There are many tricks in the computer world, and George knew most of them.

He had started as a cracker, one of the legion who infiltrate systems to filch credit card numbers or other data. Typical teenage bozo stuff, he saw now. Making calls out of pay phones, with an acoustic coupler clamped on the mouthpiece like a plastic parasite. Tapping in with a cheap Taiwan laptop computer, so that if he was discovered, he could dump the gear and run. A can of Jolt cola, "all the sugar and twice the caffeine."

He had quickly graduated from such easily caught invasions and began planting worms. These were illicit accounts in bank systems that gently transferred funds out, into a labyrinth of dummy accounts, and finally into one that George could tap with one of his many credit cards. Tricky, risky, but profitable.

When he went to work on the extensive I^2 files, he had at first considered installing a logic bomb. This could be a mere few lines of insinuating orders, nothing obvious. But the shrewdly stated commands could go berserk later and destroy vast realms of existing computer software. He had gleaned several crafty logic bombs from his thousands of hours at the keyboard. He enjoyed exchanging secrets with other hackers through the message boards available by merely dialing a number.

But today he decided against that. Too obvious. He needed a Trojan horse, some malign software disguised as an interesting, friendly program. Slip it into I^2 files, let it lie in wait.

That took him most of the day. The procedures were subtle, and someone at I^2 had erected fresh defenses. But he got through.

While he skated joyfully through the I^2 networks, he stopped to check the positions of his quarry. That premed guy, Skinner, was at UCI. Alex Cowell was at I^2 itself.

He thought about Kathryn Sheffield and her tight rounded ass and wished he could track her. But she wasn't a signed-up member of I^2, for some reason. She had seen him once, got to be careful about that. *She liked me, appreciated the way I dress, the suit and all, sharp woman. But she works for the chillers, and God has ordained her fate, there's nothing I can do about that.*

They deserved it, they all did.

He was just doing what was necessary, acting out God's will. They had brought all this on themselves by not reading the Lord's word and knowing about the bleached bones, or how important the vision of rising skeletons was. The divinely risen dead would dance merrily at the end of time, animated by sweet celestial music, skeletal grins wide beneath the waning red sun, their bony feet stirring the dust of uncounted generations long passed.

The grand vision swept whistling through him.

George sat back and puffed cool air in and out, waiting for his heart to stop thumping wildly against his ribs.

Enough. The dance at the end of time faded.

His shoulder muscles protested against his hours at the keyboard, but he willed away their pain.

Time for a little fun, then, before saying good-bye. He had spent a good deal of his real estate income on computer costs, fashioning programs that could insinuate themselves into the I² systems. He started the timer of his Trojan horse. Many hours from now, during a quiet time for the Immortality Incorporated computers, the Trojan would come out to play.

He checked again his taps on the I² telephone system. Delicately he opened the line to their phone in the bunk room. Nothing, not even background music. He jumped to their storage bay line, where the chillers were.

Eeeeeep! George jumped. Going through the local Tustin switching center, a three-step electronic handshake had to occur. Sometimes that backfed a chirp of noise into the line. He hoped there was no noise on the storage bay line, but if anybody picked up the receiver, curious, he would just hang up.

Evidently nobody did. He listened to a conversation between two minor I² volunteers, rambling on about the Dodgers while they did routine tasks.

Still, it worked. Someday he would need to eavesdrop. He had programmed his portable car phone so that he could patch through the Tustin switching center in seconds. He could park his car near I² and approach on foot, listening to them talk inside.

That was for another day. He slid neatly out of the I² system and fled, exploding the dummy telephone numbers he had used to mask his entrance. Anyone who tried to trace him would find a handful of puzzling leads to pizza parlors and sporting goods stores.

Now for the more difficult game. He tapped in digits with trembling fingers. Last night he had culled information from a small, tightly knit message board group, one he had spent a year getting to know. He had used a *nom de Hague,* of course, making electronic pals, trading insider dope, generous with dialup numbers and passwords that he no longer needed.

But the dialup he needed cost money, on top of the network friend-ships. This single telephone number, plus access code words, had cost him ten thousand dollars.

On his shimmering green screen appeared

J00TR01 333 0000

0000

LEN 24 125 893

002 000 000 000 000 000 8

This was what the expensive telephone number looked like to the switching system. The LEN was the line equipment number that gave access to the true hardware, opening digital doors.

For tense minutes he tiptoed through protocols, guards, filters. His breathing came in shallow, tight gasps.

"Bonanza! Bless you, Lord!" he cried out as the screen cleared, giving him access to the Orange County Sheriff's records file.

Detective Stern was an orderly type, he saw. The files on the Karen Bocelin case were logged under a special action brief. Detective Det-weiler had logged in hardly anything. That confirmed George's percep-tion of Detweiler as a muscle mechanic, out of step with modern police work. But still dangerous, he reminded himself.

George patrolled through high-security files, popping them open with hacker tricks, digital burglary tools. There was a cross-correlation chart that connected details of Karen's case with the earlier waitress file. He pounced on it.

Data, reports, text—all slid by as he scrolled through the richness, feeding. Heart thumping. Skin cooled by drying sweat.

There was a file on him, on the Charles Goff persona. A fabric of numbers, Social Security and credit and the address of the crummy Santa Ana apartment George had rented for his nonself. He ran his real estate work out of there. That helped give the persona convincing de-tails.

The file said Stern had already searched it. Fine. They got nothing. The leads would trickle away into the morass of shady real estate.

No hint in the report that anybody suspected the apartment was a blind. They had checked the credit with TRW and found him to be a fine fellow, a solid citizen of the data universe.

They were sniffing around, getting close. But so far Charles Goff was nothing special to them. A suspect, sure, but with nothing more to go on, they would have no great interest. Perhaps. Until they wanted to talk to him, of course, and found that he never stayed in the Santa Ana apartment.

His hands gripped the table until they turned white. Excitement fretted the pale air. He did not dare let his shaky hands linger over the keyboard. A momentary impulse might make them do something stupid, act on their own. George felt his body shiver with feverish fancies, wild, darting ideas.

Control. Planning. He had to hold his other half in, not let it seize him.

But joy spurted through him, threatening his control. The cross-correlation chart confirmed George's hopes.

He could recall pieces of that night now, and they matched what the cops had found out. He had wrapped Karen in a sheet from her bedroom closet. The dim lights outside number nineteen had been easy to reach; he had unscrewed the bulbs. He waited half an hour, wiping his fingerprints from every surface he could remember touching, and letting anybody nearby who was curious about the failed lights get bored.

The worst part had been carrying her to the trunk and rolling the body in. That had taken five excruciating seconds in which his heart didn't beat. Then he was gone, his Chevy purring down Edinger in the solemn night.

Nobody behind the Vons. One glance around, just one, because furtiveness drew attention to itself. For an instant he regretted his GOD IS custom plates; too easy to remember.

Pop the trunk. Biceps bulging, getting his legs into the lift.

She came out easily. Up and over. He kept the smelly, urine-stained sheet and threw it into a trash can miles away.

He called up the police report on the site. Jargon, boilerplate paragraphs, then a note that jarred him.

Vons worker Marco Cardena found dead dog in same dumpster "a week or so ago."

The dog.

Blank.

He could not remember what he had done with Susan Hagerty's dog.

Of course he took it from the beach, of course he dumped it. But where? He had no memory.

Blanks.

There were many of them. Small details he could not call up, as if they had been stored somewhere in his head and then when he went to get them they were gone, stolen, had never really been memories at all.

The year when he was eleven. That was a big, yawning abyss. A blank that drew him back to that time, against his will.

His parents, rotting. Their stretched faces, blurred and hollowed by putrefaction. Waxy skin, staring empty eyes. The stink.

His mind rushed away from the images, his analytical self gradually getting some control of his racing mind.

Nothing more. The events following his parents' death were lost, erased by God's merciful way. He had gnawed at that missing chunk of himself for years. It never yielded.

It was as if he had started to blot out parts of himself then. He would find that a football game he *knew* he had watched last week, could remember anticipating—had dissolved. Blank.

It was always something he *felt* about. His memory for numbers, details, or names was flawless. But emotions—the swirling currents, freighted with fire and rage, brimming desire and hopeless yearning—those moments fled, vanished. Deleted.

He must have brought the dog back to that same dumpster.

Why? Some deep, reflexive pattern?

He grimaced, his heart racing. *Pattern.* He was showing an unconscious pattern. And that was how they caught serial killers.

I'm a serious *killer,* he thought chest tight with anguish. *Karen was a mistake. Something happened to me there.*

Something buried in the gray spaces beyond memory.

Blanks.

They floated like thick snowstorms in his mind. Evaporated moments, condensed into opaque, pearly fog.

George's hands trembled as he typed out commands, copying a few of the documents, getting them stuttered into his modem. Then he dropped out of the sheriff's records. Again he covered his tracks, burning his bridges behind him in the Pacific Telesis webbing.

He stood and paced around the apartment, trying to stifle the shrill alarms that rang in his mind. He gazed down at the courtyard of the apartment complex, and the blue slick surface of the swimming pool licked at something inside him, bringing old fevers teeming up into his nostrils, forcing a strangled gasp from his throat.

Wet. Dark. Cold. The black lake. He whirled away from the window.

Blanks.

Gray spaces skating through his mind.

Karen? *The same dumpster?*

He lurched over to his exercise machines. A sweaty workout would make him clean again. He tore off his clothes and threw himself on the chromed bars.

14
KATHRYN

"There." She decisively signed the last document.

Ray Constantine stacked the inch-thick paperwork and ceremoniously shook her hand. "Welcome."

"When do I get my bracelet?"

"I'll phone the order in. A couple days."

Kathryn sat back, feeling as though a trumpet should sound somewhere at such a big moment. The I^2 stereo system was thrumming with a Dixieland number, ignoring her mood. She blew a puff at wisps of hair that had tumbled down before her eyes. "I'm not quite sure why I did this."

"Fastest signup on record," Ray said neutrally.

"I borrowed the money for the insurance installment from a friend of mine."

"At your age, it doesn't come to much."

"Okay, you can cut the Gary Cooper act. When a lady makes a leading statement, you're supposed to ask what she means."

Ray blinked. "Leading statement."

*"No*body can be this dense. Ray, doesn't it strike you as odd, my signing up as an I^2 member so quickly?"

"Me, I wonder how come everybody doesn't."

"Just because I worked for you guys didn't mean I was convinced, you know. But seeing Susan suspended, how much it takes to buck the system—it made me choose sides."

"You did a damned fine job through all that mess." Ray struggled visibly for words. "You've got guts."

"Well, thanks." Ray was not a man to hand out compliments like party favors. Still, she could see she would have to go to Sheila for some real talk.

"Don't think I don't know what you're feeling," Ray said, smiling ruefully, "just 'cause we don't dwell on it."

She laughed, stood up, and gave him a kiss on his tanned forehead. *"Vive la différence,"* she said, and went back to her job. So much for grand moments.

She had devoted several hours of her shift to signing up, and now that it was done, she needed something to occupy her mind. Ray went back to checking the liquid nitrogen connections. She took refuge in her skills.

She pointedly didn't listen to radio or watch TV. The incessant media circus had permanently cured her of that. Even print journalism, from the circumspect *Los Angeles Times* down to the *National Enquirer* level, was like a steady, distracting drum roll. A moronic inferno of hateful insinuations. And some rasping, abrading truths.

The truth wasn't pretty. They *had* spirited away a body, and Kathryn was implicated. Stern had made a snap judgment that the three men, ambling into the main bay, must have done the job—and only that had kept her out of jail. Stern simply had not believed that Kathryn would take part in such a ghoulish thing, probably because she was a woman. Well, sexism had its uses.

Kathryn herself had trouble believing she had done it. She had acted out of instinct. Alex had needed help, so she had given it. A path ordained by tradition. How had that old country and western song put it? "Stand by Your Man." So she had.

It had gotten her into a bad spot, and then gotten her out. After all, she owed her freedom to a certain gentlemanly reluctance to think that a lady would do such things.

Take your gains with your losses, girl, she thought moodily, sitting at the main desk in the Immortality Incorporated office. *What was that Alex had said? Don't take sides, but keep score. Well, so far we're losing. Losing big.*

Kathryn dragged her attention back to her work. She had put in her time at Fashion Circus, scurried about on I^2 business, seen Alex as often as she could (considering how much time he had to put into talking to lawyers)—and still she felt restless. She logged into the autosecretary and concentrated.

First, a list of incoming calls, arranged by category. They were tagged by the voice reader for individual I^2 employees, but most ended up in the "general public" column. Which meant they were mostly pest calls, rumor-mongerers.

Second, electronically transferred utility billings, flagged for the I^2 bank accounts. General Telephone, SoCal Edison, water, trash. She would check them over for errors, and if, as usual, there were none, she would forward them to the accountant for electronic authorization to pay.

Third, news items culled by their electronic clipping service. It surveyed print and visual media, and the list ran down through three full screens' worth. Kathryn surveyed a few and groaned. CASE OF THE CORP-SICLE. CHILLERS PUT THE CHILL ON THE LAW. WHO STOLE SUSAN HAGERTY?

Fourth, personal messages. Ah, a please-call-back from Alex. Her day brightened. She would have preferred something short, sweet, romantic, maybe mildly dirty, but he had been distracted these last few days.

She remembered that the memorial service for Susan was only two hours from now. And here she was, swarming with carnal thoughts. Well, perhaps the service would be a useful boundary for them. They should go away somewhere for the weekend.

She tried his home number. Busy. She stabbed repeat call and said "Silky Thighs" with her voice low and musky. The tape would add that to the beginning of the English-accented "is urgently trying to reach" message that would now try Alex's number every minute. Romance by the numbers; who said there was no such thing as progress?

She rewarded herself with a new technotrick that had been installed in the autosec. She had spent yesterday trying out the new voice-writer, writing a letter of protest to the *Los Angeles Times*. She thumbed it up on the main working screen.

```
                                            four
How does this part work? Oh, it's already on for
             Eye     right                  fore
VoiceWrite. I got it write the first time. Okay, Dear
         Eye          too     strait    you're
Editor: I am writing to set straight your incorrect
                          two
reporting of incidents involving Immortality Incorporated.
Their                         Eye   knot sea
There were numerous errors. I did not   see any of the
                      you're
"deceptive behavior" your reporter said that I² employees
                        too         O
carried out. In fact, you failed to report—oh, this is
     eye                    two             write
where I should use the Contextual Option key, right. That's bet-
ter.
```

From there on the program had simply assigned the most probable-sounding word. To start off the program yesterday she had pronounced a few minutes of vowels and words, following instructions. From what the monitor called her "variations in idiom, adjacent and verbal modalities," the program had gotten nearly everything right, cleaning up most of the mistakes.

She worked through the rest of the letter, polishing it even though she knew the *Times* probably wouldn't run it anyway. As she printed it out the thought suddenly struck: *This is what my mother used to do. She was a maven of the op-ed page, a walking bundle of opinions, sensitivities, ferociously worded arguments. Every week, a fresh volley in newsprint. All from a frail, worn woman with parchment skin who was lying in her deathbed and knew it.*

She shivered. The afternoon sunlight outside slanted low, bringing an autumn gloom.

Quitting time. She had asked to leave early, to attend the memorial service for Susan Hagerty. She kept her copy of the letter and sent the text electronically to the *Times* number. If she didn't save a hard copy, there was a good chance that the entire message would never be more than gossamer phosphors on a screen. Unless they published it, the entire matter would have been carried out through dancing electrons on cathode ray tubes, words without weight. She liked a certain solidity in her world.

Maybe I need more of it, she thought, getting into her car. *I wonder if that's what Alex means to me? He has his own fragile side, but he's rooted, steady.*

She had never seen him wear stripes with plaid, either. The man had many pleasant aspects.

15

GEORGE

He steadied himself with fifty one-handed push-ups, then some weightlifting. Lats and pecs and biceps. Straining, grunting. Bulging ropes of muscle reflected in the plates of chromed steel.

The gray spaces in his mind faded. His analytic self spoke clearly now, telling him what to do.

Muscles oiled by sweat, he sat down and went through the things from Karen's apartment. Scraps, paperwork, items he had taken on impulse, out of urges his mind would not recall.

The whole time there was now a chalky, vacant zero. But he had the records.

Why? Until this moment he had not thought about these scraps. Now he saw with a sharp jolt that—*of course!*—they were strong evidence against him. How had he forgotten them?

Blanks.

Scattershot colors fractured the air at the edges of his vision. His head jerked around, muscles knotting, trying to catch the fleeting traceries. Finally he calmed himself.

Karen had said something about being the personal assistant to this Mr. Lomax, and here were his routine billings. The Saddlery. Neiman Marcus. Boutique International. Pascal's. Lomax had running accounts in dozens of the best shops and restaurants. The man got around. Vitality Corporation must be prosperous.

Something caught at the edge of his mind. He was making mistakes, he knew that. Whatever had made him kill Karen was now working on him slowly, silently. Bringing flashing, discordant images into his mind. Fretting his sleep with vibrant dreams. Snatching him up from slumber into hoarse-voiced hysteria.

But now he forced that side of him back down. He exerted the rule of his analytical self. The exercises helped. After some leg lifts he had himself under control again and was ready to begin thinking, planning, readying himself for his next task. His Calling.

He began by replaying tapes from the news coverage of I². Shots of the crowds, the smug faces of the cryonicists, their self-advertising speeches. He could look at them now with cold, patient hatred.

So arrogant, so blind. So rich, from selling their damnation to the desperate. Rich enough to skip off on a Hawaiian holiday.

He went into the kitchen, feet like wood thumping on the Formica. Popped open the refrigerator. Cartons of Mexican takeout, moldy tacos and burritos, half-eaten during the endless hacker hours. He threw them out, clearing the ground for his analytical side.

Then he took from the freezer the cyanide-carrying compounds he had ordered through a St. Louis pharmaceutical firm. He had ordered them through a dummy address, using the Bruce Prior identity. Extracting a stable dilute solution of cyanide in water was tedious, requiring care. *The Chemical Handbook, The Merck Manual,* and a college text told him just how to do it. The work calmed him, set him square with the world. Once he had it done, he felt better. The Lord's peace descended upon him.

But a sudden impulse drew him back to Karen. The hot moments between them. Fragments of sentences. Shards of memory.

Lomax. Vitality Corporation. The itch in his mind would not go away.

No listing for Lomax, even in the unlisted directory he could access through Pacific Telesis.

There were many ways to trace a man, but most left a trail. No one must remember George, or be able to trace his telephone line equipment number. Money would insulate Lomax. The rich and famous had their Maginot lines; George remembered trying to call Billy Graham once.

Boutique International gave him a Ms. Neal in accounting. He used a well-rehearsed accent. "This is Walter Davidson of Shea and Davidson, Ms. Neal. I'm having to clean up after a regrettable loss which occurred in the accounting of one of our clients, Mr. Alberto Lomax."

"I see. Shea and Davidson?"

She was probably looking in a directory. She would find that Shea and Davidson did indeed handle most of Lomax's financial management, and they had offices in Orange. George had gotten all that from the letterhead on a note to Karen. If Ms. Neal was shrewd, she would hang up and call back, using the number from the yellow pages.

But she was merely cautious. "I see. We usually work with a Ms.—"

"Karen Bocelin, yes. She passed away, and I—"

"Oh yes, I read about that. Terrible, to be just thrown away like, like . . ."

George wondered why it made any difference to this woman where a body was found. He said brusquely, "It has created difficulties for Mr. Lomax, in that his files are in disarray. I am calling to find his present credit balance with your firm."

"I suppose you want the exact amount. It is nine hundred fifty-six dollars, thirty-three cents."

"Thank you. Could I have your billing address on that?"

"We send bills to the trust department, Wells Fargo, Santa Ana office."

He thanked her and within a minute was speaking to a frosty-voiced young man, Mr. Hamblin, who said "trust department" as though it were the Vatican. George had worked with such people before, the precise, cool, and withdrawn personalities who could be entrusted with vast assets.

"Mr. Hamblin, I am Mr. Fitzhugh of the Saddlery. I am forced by extraordinary difficulties to trace back on a billing to Mr. Alberto Lomax's account. We show a balance of nine hundred fifty-six thirty-three. Could you verify that please?"

"Hold, please."

George could see in his mind's eye the neat, circumspect man calling up confidential files on a video terminal. Personal services through a bank's trust department ensured privacy and care. The bank totaled it all at year's end, took a percentage charge, and forwarded the entire ledger to Mr. Lomax's tax people. Among other conveniences, it was a smooth way to make personal expenses look like investment costs.

"I check that, Mr. Fitzhugh. We settle accounts the final working day of each month, so—"

"Oh, I am certainly *not* calling to ask payment of Mr. *Lomax's* account. No no." He hoped he had the right tone of prissy pretension, subservient yet proud. "He is one of our most valued customers. No, I'm afraid I have to confess that the problem lies with us. A clerk who is no longer with us, if you get what I mean, took a special tailoring order from Mr. Lomax. But somehow this person did not note down which address to send the garment. Now it has come in, and I know Mr. Lomax wanted it right away. I *could* simply send it to his business address, but I *know* he wanted it for a special function, and I was just wondering, perhaps you would know which address would be speedier. If necessary, we will hand deliver."

Mr. Hamblin paused a few seconds. George could imagine the war between the desire to serve and the instinctive caution in Mr. Hamblin. Service won. "Our most recent communication shows that Mr. Lomax is currently at the Tustin estate, I believe."

"Oh, this dreadful computer. We've got this new kind, they say it's really the best, but I can never seem to call up what I want. I *think* we have that number, let me see. . . ."

"It's 1421 Meadowlark Drive."

"Oh yes, we often send things there. Wonderful."

"Will that be another billing to this account? I can just add it in now."

"Oh no, that is very kind, but please don't bother. The paperwork will be along." They were buddies of the budget now, the unsung elves who made the world work. Might as well use it a little more. "But he will be there long enough to receive a delivery?"

"I think so, Mr. Fitzhugh. By the way, Mr. Lomax does not normally use it, but he is actually Dr. Lomax."

"Oh. Well, many thanks."

He had used the formal, exact voice he had practiced for years. It took a few minutes to come out of that cast of mind.

He burned the papers from Karen's, a yellow pyre in his bathtub. Said a prayer over them. Breathed in the hellfire fumes, which liberated him from that mistake. Set him free.

Detective Stern might find out where he really lived, after all. Stern was smart and would come here with a technical team. Detweiler would swagger through and see nothing. They would scour the apartment, George's car, even his clothes. He was a logical suspect, especially if they penetrated his Goff persona. But they would find nothing here.

He got back into the telephone net and used some log-in account information. He had gotten the Orange County property record codes from that real estate agent, Miller. They had both made some fast, big bucks from George's scams. Miller had been pathetically grateful. He had given the password for the county's blueprint files to George, in the Goff persona, for free.

He slipped in easily. With the Meadowlark Drive address he got everything the county had. His laser printer spat out the plans of the Lomax estate. Grounds, landscaping, rooms, basement, sewer lines, the works. It looked like a fortress.

Still, he felt the constriction of time's sliding moments.

Lomax. Blanks. Why would they not go away?

The digital clock on his computer screen winked at him, seconds spooling by.

He had to keep track of the chiller people, look for their hidden weaknesses. And now this Lomax thing, pulling at him. So much.

Time's steady tightening. He had to act.

16
KATHRYN

One of the signs of how Alex was working his way into her life was his habit of noticing personalized license plates. She had picked it up. On the way to the memorial service for Susan she saw a Cadillac sporting UP YRS, an XDORMAT that promised an interesting story, NICEGOY, X RATED, ACTU LEE, RM 4U QT. At first she thought A24KLDY might be a two-fork lady, then decided was another brag—a twenty-four-carat lady. That morning she had seen BANKRPT on a new Mercedes, SX CEE driven by a woman who looked like a typical suburban housewife, and HONK4ME, which luckily nobody did.

She wondered if the jerko in front of her now was going to the same place. He had a personalized plate that said GOD IS and drove as though he were paying more attention to his rearview mirror than the road in front. There was a tight look to his movements, and though she could not get a good look at his face, she recognized something about him. At least she could be sure he wasn't one of her old boyfriends, she thought. They were burned into her memory. *Maybe he's a cop,* she thought, alarmed. *Doing some savvy forward tail?* She wasn't out of the woods yet with the sheriff's office, she knew. *Well, let him stick to me. I'll bore him to death.* The man turned off when she reached Laguna Beach, though, and she lost track of him.

She met Alex outside the church. He had been out getting some exercise, he said, with the phone off the hook. "I'm getting an unlisted number," he said grimly.

"Did Silky Thighs get through?"

He brightened. "Yeah, just as I was going out the door. I tried to call you back."

"I had some news." She smiled demurely and told him that she had signed up with I². The quick waves that flashed across his face—surprise, delight, wonder, and then warm affection—made up for Ray Constantine's tongue-tied performance. He gave her a deep, moist kiss, serious enough to provoke polite coughs from others outside the church. Kathryn patted her hair, pleased, and they went in.

She held his hand throughout the service. The Episcopal verities had a classic, King James Bible roll to them, and she let the words wash over her without questioning. She had only been to one other funeral service since her mother's, and that had been for Aunt Henny, the bearer of the all-swallowing cape that had given her nightmares for years. Aunt Henny's service had verged on nightmare itself. She had been a Baptist, and the funeral featured wails and sobs from the audience, loud enough to make her suspect they were encouraged. Her relatives had carried on about the wondrous things done to Aunt Henny, including a final wash and set, extensive "cosmetizing," even a new pair of shiny black shoes that laced up the back.

They got through it all fairly well. There were many cryonicists, UCI faculty, and several of Susan's family from the east coast. Three photographers stood at the back and took pictures until a vestryman shooed them out.

There had been no time for sorrow when Susan died. The suspension team had repressed it. Now she saw on the faces of Ray Constantine and Bob Skinner and the others their delayed reactions. And felt it herself. She caught her own tears in her handkerchief and watched Alex brushing away his, mouth unsteady and eyes fixed on infinity.

At the reception afterward, Kathryn and Alex passed through the receiving line and Kathryn was surprised to learn that Susan had been a regular churchgoer here. "Why, yes," the solemn-faced minister said, "she was a devoted parishioner. She worked with the homeless and was here every Saturday, helping make lunch for them. Her specialty was the soup—*won*derful soups. Especially the split pea."

As she shared some pound cake and coffee with Alex, she said, "Funny, huh? I never knew she believed in religion."

Alex was an unbeliever and looked edgy here. "Neither did I."

"I'm going to talk to that minister."

Before Alex could catch her arm, she marched over to the big man in his tasteful robes and asked, "Did you ever talk to Susan about . . . her interests?"

The minister gave her a sad-eyed smile. "Cryonics, you mean?"

When Kathryn nodded, acutely conscious of Susan's family members a short distance away, he said, "Of course. She wanted to be very sure that she was not violating the charge of Scripture."

"And she convinced you that she wasn't?"

He chuckled. "*I* convinced *her.* She came to me with misgivings. Especially after Roger, her husband, died."

"*Susan?* Misgivings?"

His eyes crinkled with amusement. "Surprised? She was troubled by the usual misunderstandings of Scripture. It is difficult to avoid them."

"Well, sir, after all the biblical quotations this fellow Montana has been throwing at us—"

"Try Matthew ten-eight on him. Christ commanded his disciples to 'Heal the sick, raise the lepers, raise the dead' in no uncertain terms."

Kathryn blinked. "Susan never mentioned any of this."

"She saw no need to, I'm sure. She knew that God is the Physician of Physicians."

"You supported her?"

"I support all the activities of my flock that are Christian in spirit."

Something devilish made her say, "You don't mind, then, that her body is . . . missing?"

"Her body is unimportant. If you people extend the human lifetime a century, even a thousand years, I do not doubt that even such a span is but a moment in the totality of God's plan."

In wonder Kathryn mused, "She never said a word."

"The Bible promises resurrection, whether in the body, or in the grave, or in a frozen casket."

"Then you actually support cryonics?"

"I did not say that."

"Well, what *do* you think?"

He gave her a shrewd look, eyes pouched with weighty experience. "I think the idea will never work. It is a complete waste of time."

"You, uh, trust in the—hereafter?"

His eyes flicked almost shyly downward. "Terribly old-fashioned of me, but yes—though I don't venture to define precisely what that is."

"And Susan?"

"With God's grace, she somehow managed to trust in both."

"There may not be a contradiction."

"True. I always wonder about the fear of death, the lack of symmetry."

Kathryn frowned. "Symmetry?"

"We fear a day when we will be no more. A future time. There was a vast expanse of time like that already—before we were born. Yet we feel no emotions at all about that."

Kathryn blinked and had no idea of what to say.

17

GEORGE

The ample estate of Alberto Lomax crowned a rugged hill. Dry gullies gave the hillside the look of a weary, lined face. Chaparral thronged the lower reaches.

George puffed as he worked his way through the raw land cut by erosion. He wore goggles that amplified night vision, bought that day from a surplus store. Barely used, the clerk had said, left over from the Iraq war.

The enhanced night was eerie, a shimmering land of pale greens and blue-tinged shadows. The cooling soil bristled with detail. Working his way here on foot, he had watched a neighborhood dog marking its turf, leaving a faint lime artist's signature with each lift of its leg.

Ahead he could see clearly the glowing blank wall that ringed Lomax's estate. Massive, ten feet tall and rimmed with broken glass. He had studied it through binoculars, planned, and bought the equipment he needed this afternoon. Time was running against him now, with Stern and Detweiler looming in the background, and his own skittering urgency driving him on.

The chiller people had all flocked to their memorial service for the Hagerty woman. He had watched them walk right straight into a church with the bald-faced gall of heretics. They would probably be consoling each other tonight. Maybe they held their own chiller rites or something foul like that. Anyway, tonight they'd give him no lead on what they had done with the Hagerty body.

So that left the Lomax problem. Pulling at him.

Ten minutes before, he had seen a heavy delivery truck admitted through the wrought-iron gates to the Lomax estate. That might provide a diversion, a loosening of security. Time to move.

He angled up the hillside, watching for electronic trip wires. They were unlikely this far out, but as sin spreads, bringing the inevitable worsening of crime, the rich grow ever more cautious. He chose a spot by the wall that was shaded by the tall eucalyptus and oak. As he stood next to the wall, it looked immense.

He unwound his climbing rope and checked the grappler hooks. He had done this once on a church outing, learning to secure lines and wear a harness, rappelling down sheer cliffs in the desert. This would be easier, maybe, but he had to avoid noise.

The night goggles trapped his sweat, fogging the night. They seemed to make the air itself glow with a smoldering radiance, as though visited by angelic hosts. He had to stop and mop his face, let the mist leave the lenses. Carefully he listened, standing in the moonless gloom. A rustle of a field mouse, maybe, over to the right. Distant hum of traffic. Nothing else nearby.

The wall was concrete faced in stucco. A thick lip jutted out at the top, making it hard for anyone climbing up.

He uncoiled the loops and swung the rope. One heave sent the hooks flying over the wall. He tugged. Hooks scraped. He felt them catch, then come free. The rope flopped back down.

A second toss. Again the rope came thumping back to earth. This time he heard a tinkle, a glassy clink.

His third throw caught. He hauled back on the rope and heard the tink of breaking glass again.

So the wall was rounded off on the inside and thick with glass. Very professional. Dr. Lomax looked after himself.

He worked along the wall until he was near the big shadowy oak that dominated this area. The best tree to throw into, sure, but whoever designed the security setup would know that, too. He would have to be careful of the top of the wall. There might be razor wire, set low into the concrete and impossible to see from a distance. He had run into some long ago, during one of his teenage night forays, cut his hand on it bad.

He swung the rope around his head, getting speed, and threw the grappler far up into the air. It came down through the oak foliage, making small thunks, then stopped. George put all his weight on the line. It gave about a foot, then held.

He looked around, edgy, sure that someone must see him in the bright emerald noonday glare given by his goggles. Distant houses smoldered in their lime-green heat, but they were hundreds of yards away, on other hillsides.

No point in delaying. He put his full weight on the line. It held. He put a tennis shoe against the wall, pulled himself up. The line bit into his hands as he walked up the wall. Halfway up, he thought about the line sawing across the embedded broken glass above. That made him hurry. Getting over the top lip was tricky, but his long legs helped. Cautiously he stepped onto the broad flat top, keeping the line tight, feeling his way with his shoes.

Razor wire. He stepped between the shiny gleaming lines. There was room among the sharp glass teeth to stand. *Fine. God is with me.* The dry night held him in loving, divine hands.

Holding the line for balance, he tried to look through the oak tree. He could see only a dim glow of windows in the house itself. At least that meant they couldn't see him, either.

What to do with the grappler? If he jumped down with the rope in his hands, he might not be able to get the thing free, up in the branches.

He yanked on the rope. Leaves rustled, branches swayed.

Another yank. *Careful.* Another—louder, too loud.

Time for a calculated risk. He whispered a prayer and stepped off into space, hands wrapped in the rope. It creaked as he swung down and in. Leaves rustled, branches popped. Just before his feet hit the ground, he felt the pressure go on the line. He let his knees take the fall and rolled forward, curling his shoulders, going all the way over. He flopped onto thick grass, face up. Something flickered across his enhanced vision and thumped down by his right knee. It was the grappler.

George got unsteadily to his feet, thinking about how close the grappler had come to driving its steel hooks into him. But divine grace had prevented that, would shelter him here.

Now the thick lip on the outer wall was a help. In two tosses he got the grappler secured on the lip, tested it with his weight, and left the line dangling. He measured with his eye the distance from the oak, so that he could find the line at a dead run if he had to.

George stood in the shadows of the oak tree and studied the big, rambling Spanish-style house. Blueprints did not capture the impressive mass of it. Tile roof, heavy wooden beams, deep walls. It spoke of money, ease, stature. There were several smaller side buildings, probably for servants, and a garage near the driveway. Bushes crowded the lawn here. What he wanted was in the main house. As he started toward it, his mind swarmed again with questions.

What had drawn him here? Why?

In the days since Karen's death he had been skating over a deep pit of fear and dread, panic welling up in his throat, bitter tastes invading his mouth from his churning belly. But he had to keep on. The Lord was driving him, had taken George's tiny life into the great stream of His plan.

He studied the house, ticking off details he knew from the blueprints. His mind tumbled with skittering thoughts, and he almost missed the sound.

A low gruff grunt. Nails scrabbling on a stone walkway. Something running fast.

It came around a thick bottlebush that had hidden its approach. George saw the bunched muscles and sleek skin as its stubby legs ate up the remaining distance. It was all muscle and bone, white teeth bared beneath an ugly nose, a snarling pit bull.

For a slice of a second a terrible fear seized him. The dogs he had killed as a boy had seldom fought. When they did, he had learned to deal with them swiftly, for there was a moment when an attacking dog was vulnerable. The memory flashed in his mind. Then the fear washed away. He felt his own power gather. He set himself, balanced on the balls of his feet.

The pit bull might go for his arms. George drew them back, at the same time crouching slightly to bring his face down. Dogs lined up on an outstretched arm. A pit bull would go for the throat if it could. It wanted to bowl him over, slash open the jugular, rip and shred in the vital seconds before you could recover your surprise.

The pit bull gathered itself, a bundle of swift sinew. It leaped. This was the instant when it was committed. And open.

Its forepaws stretched out before it, first to arrive. George pivoted on his left foot, bringing both hands up to grasp the dog's right foreleg.

He threw himself to the side, grabbing the leg hard, his hands only inches from the jaws. The dog's own momentum carried it around, helping the tight pivot.

George fell back, yanking hard. The sudden snap slammed the dog forward. It could not get its head around and down to close on his hand.

The leap, the pivot and swing, the heave—all combined in a centrifugal whirl that slung the dog over George as he himself went down. He felt something snap in the dog's leg. He let go. The pit bull sailed over him with a startled, small yelp.

George slammed into the grass. He heard a solid thud, a clack as jaws snapped shut. A soft thump as the dog hit the grass.

He scrambled up and to the side, fished for the knife on a scabbard at his belt. His breath whistled with a cold fear.

He crouched, knife forward and low. Ready. But the pit bull did not bound back up, turn, and charge again. Sweat had filmed his eyes, and it was a long moment before George could blink away the moisture caught by the goggles to see that the dog lay at the base of the oak tree.

He approached it, rolled it over. The skull was dented in. Clear fluid oozed out. It had hit the oak tree square on.

He stared at the ghostly image of the dog and thought about his childhood terrors. Things with teeth and claws that come at you out of the night. He had defeated those horrors by venturing into that blackness, finding the foe, gutting it. And yet now here it was again, still coming at him, unrelenting, Godless, still horrible.

Into his mind crowded the image of Susan Hagerty's dog, and of the devil dog he had killed at Immortality Incorporated. They were all agents of dark forces, like this one. He had conquered them. This had been yet another test. A challenge to his Calling.

This man Lomax took a stern view of uninvited visitors. There might be other dogs, maybe a mate for this one. That shook him. He had managed to catch this one just right, kill it without even much noise. He wouldn't be so lucky the second time.

There might be worse waiting. He let this thought strum through him, echoing. Grimly he got control of it. *Think.*

The dog's body was too close to his grappler line. If anybody—or anything—found it, they would locate the rope, too. Be waiting when he returned.

He did not like touching the dog. Its bowels had let go, cutting the air. That left a smear behind as he dragged it fifty yards along the wall and dumped it in a plot of cactus.

Swiftly he trotted across the broad lawn, taking advantage of the bristly bushes. Adrenaline popped through him. Every time he stopped, he looked back and memorized landmarks. He might have to return this way on the run.

Most windows in the big house were dark. A group on the ground floor blossomed with rich, yellowish light. He was in a heavily gardened area of the estate, and there was a thirty-yard swath between the last bush and the walls of the house. The goggles made the windows blaze with a strange, superheated glare. He took them off and let his eyes adjust. Still he could see nothing through the windows from this angle. Somebody could be standing in there, a few feet into the room.

He looked the other way and saw a one-ton truck pulled up to a side door. Parked, engine off, nobody nearby. He wondered why a heavy truck was making deliveries to a house.

He knew it was dumb to delay. Caution would crowd in on him, taking his edge away.

He ran across the space and flattened himself against the wall. Peeked in a window, just a second's glimpse. A big dining room, polished mahogany table, high-backed chairs. Nobody. He ducked beneath that window and stopped at the next. This gave a view into a small tiled bathroom. Deserted.

Next were two tall French doors. Gauzy curtains like clouds of heaven framed the tall side panels. He squatted down and bobbed his head around the bottom pane.

A sumptuous den. Deep leather armchairs with upholstered footstools. A desk of black wood, absolutely clear except for a slim white telephone. Cedar bookshelves soaring into a vaulted ceiling. High up among the thick beams, broad wood panels were crowned by a black skylight. In the exact center of the room sat a man wearing a maroon dinner jacket and sleek gray slacks. His lightly frosted hair framed a pale face dominated by bushy white eyebrows. He was engrossed in a leather-bound volume.

Something in the jawline, the eyes. . . . Had he seen him before? Was he related to someone George knew?

He felt his heart thud with leaden dread. Yet he knew he had to go into that room and stand before that man.

Why? His mind answered only with a gray blank.

To his surprise the French doors were not locked. He closed them behind him with a slight click. The man looked up. Surprise flickered in the shrewd face for only a moment. Then he looked back down at the volume, slid a leather bookmark in place, and put it aside with care.

"I see," the man said in a deep, almost hoarse voice.

"Dr. Lomax?"

"Since you have managed to get by my guard and my dog, I expect you have taken the trouble to learn my name."

"They weren't hard." No need to tell Lomax anything more.

"I expect he's watching television somewhere," Lomax said sardonically. "There is a delivery in progress, and he takes every opportunity to shirk his duties." A sigh. "I expect you are here to take, not to deliver."

A whirlwind roared through George, but he could barely get out his cramped words. "Can—can I ask you some questions?"

"You already have."

George stepped closer. Lomax's calm unnerved him. "You told Karen Bocclin something about me."

"Yes."

"How come you even know who I am?"

"I am a good friend of the Reverend."

"Good friend? Why—"

"Your struggle against the heresy embodied in Immortality Incorporated is a holy battle. My company deals in the good side of this technology, the freezing and recovery of tissues, even whole organs such as kidneys and livers, for purposes of transplantation. I have a great deal of pride in my company's work, and I despise the empty promises of the cryonicists. You are a hero to me, George."

The masterful voice drew him forward. Lomax's words were like warm, liquid reassurance, lapping around him.

But vagrant images pestered him. *Moist. Dark. Cold.*

He shook off the sensations and suppressed a sudden, yearning moan that caught in his throat.

With unsteady step he came closer, hands open and held up, as if about to receive a benediction. "I—I thought Reverend Montana was going to keep this just between the two of us."

Lomax rose with athletic grace. He was shorter than George but possessed a compact energy. A thin smile illuminated the pale face, then was gone. "I am no danger to you, George. The Reverend saw in you the ideal person to act where he—where I—could not."

"But he told me—"

"Circumstances change, George." Lomax gestured amiably at a sideboard crowded with tall bottles bearing an elaborate silver brocade. "Drink?"

"I don't touch alcohol."

"Pity. If you don't mind, I'll have a little something."

Lomax went to the sideboard with obvious relish and selected a bottle. He poured amber fluid into a squat crystal glass, sniffed it, and sipped. George could smell the opulent aroma from five feet away.

"I don't get it, how you and the Reverend—"

"It is really quite simple. I stand with him in opposing this corpse-freezing heresy. I fight it as I can, because it gives my entire profession a bad name. Through Vitality Corporation, I support research at respectable medical institutions—UCI, for example. I also had some men I hired keep track of I^2, but they were inept. One nearly got caught when he was trying to plant a miniature television snooper in their facility. Such people are unreliable and too easily traced back to me. You have been much more steady, though the Karen matter . . ."

Lomax let his voice trail away significantly. George had come to terms with the Lord over Karen, and he shrugged off this man's insinuating manner. The heat of this room curled up around him, making it hard to think. Better counterpunch, to keep the initiative. "Look, fella, how do I know you're not freezing people yourself?"

Lomax laughed. "You mustn't think that everyone interested in the preservation of organs is the same, George."

"Yeah? How do I know?" Stifling in here.

Lomax fiddled with the tinkling bottles and glasses. He sipped the liquor again, turned toward George with an assessing gaze, and said mildly, "With the same certainty that tells me that you killed Karen."

George gaped. He saw Lomax's sharp, cold eyes and then Karen's breasts, soft slopes alive with heat. And an instant later, flaring in him, the blaring light and waxy faces of his dreams—

He did not have a chance to say a single word before Lomax lifted a slim steel cylinder. *He must have had it hidden among those bottles,* George thought quickly, starting to move.

Lomax pointed it carefully at George and sprayed him in the face with a hissing cloud.

18
ALEX

Amid the chaos of legal matters, Immortality Incorporated had gotten word that a long-term member was terminal. Alex was unavailable, so Ray Constantine, Bob Skinner, and several others in the backup team had done the job. The patient lived in Lahaina, Hawaii. The Kaiser clinic there wanted nothing to do with cryonics. So the wan, brave old man had to spend his last days wasting away in a distant hospital, Maui Memorial.

Their patient had finally fallen to the liver cancer that had shriveled him. He had not been rich, a brilliant philosopher, or a saintly philanthropist. Some critics of cryonics, when not maintaining that it was impossible, seemed to believe it should be available primarily to the unusually deserving. Alex bristled at such sentiments. The long-shot promise of cryonics required pioneering resolve, not the admiration of society. It was a right, not a privilege, Alex thought—but it had to be won, by taking action while you were alive.

The suspension went through without a hitch. The team got their patient into a subzero traveling case, through the long flight back and the skeptical shipping department at Los Angeles International, and then into one of the "bigfoot" liquid nitrogen cylinders in the I^2 main bay. Job done.

Alex stood now, looking up at the cylinder and the fresh nameplate on its side. He touched the cool steel, wondering idly. Ray Constantine came by, on a single crutch now. Alex said, "Get some rest."

"Yeah. Did Bob Skinner go home?"

"Nope, he's bunked down in the back. Too tired to drive." Immortality Incorporated had a three-bed dorm squeezed into a side room for tired teams during the lengthy cryonic suspensions.

"How're things going for him at UCI, you figure?" Ray asked.

Alex frowned. "He doesn't say much. Without Susan to advise him, I think he's headed for trouble. That guy Blevin could hound him pretty bad."

"Damned shame."

Alex sighed dreamily. "The luck's been running tough lately for all of us. Still, we saved one more." He rapped the smooth steel cylinder. "When do you figure anyone will come back out?"

Ray shrugged. "A century? Hard to say."

Alex thought of the inconceivable cold that waited only inches from his palm. A century or more? An immense, uncharted ocean of time. "Geez, I hope things go faster than that."

Ray grinned. "Don't count on the inevitable march of history. I read somewhere that a guy named Hero of Alexandria demonstrated a model steam engine sixteen centuries before James Watt built a practical one, but everybody ignored it."

"How come?"

"Thought it was a toy, I guess. But medicine's just as bad. Arabs were using anesthetics way back in the Middle Ages. Christians thought suffering was good for the soul—y'know, brought redemption—so we didn't get even laughing gas until about a hundred fifty years ago."

"Well, okay, but once it was discovered here—"

"The medical authorities brushed it off. After all, *dentists* discovered it—not even real doctors."

"You're depressing me." His faith—he ruefully realized now that Sheila was right, cryonics did demand a kind of optimistic creed—lay in technology. But people judged technology, and they could be wrong. Society ran on good yarns, not on research reports. Frozen zombies made a better spot on the eleven o'clock news than a dry exploration of the possibilities of preservation. So the gauzy future might just ignore the possibilities of cryonics, refuse to spend the money or time or thought.

"Sorry, man," Ray said sympathetically. "Hate to bring you down and all."

"That's okay. Every time we do a suspension, I wonder if we're like those shipwrecked clowns you see in cartoons, putting messages into bottles."

Ray chuckled. "Sure we are. Steel bottles, frozen messages, in a sea of liquid nitrogen."

"Have you ever picked up a bottle on the beach and found a message in it?"

"Nope. But if you're stuck on an island—an island in time, I guess—you might as well try it. What's the alternative?"

"Right. Right."

"Hey, you been hassling legal stuff all day—why don't you head on home? I'll finish up here."

"Nope. It's past midnight. Good time to run some more nitrogen out to Susan."

"Okay." Ray shook his head in wan frustration, his shaggy hair giving him a brooding presence. "Wonder how long we're gonna have to keep this up."

"Hiding her?" Alex realized he had not really considered how this could end. "Years. Until they get tired, I guess."

Ray leaned against a tall cylinder, taking some of the load off his feet, letting his crutch idle. "Somebody once said that for a new idea to take hold, it's not enough to persuade the older generation. You have to wait for them to die."

Alex laughed. "Die and not get frozen."

"Yeah. Hey—" Ray was impatient with talk, preferring action; he brushed away the subject. "By the time you're back, that Chinese take-out will be delivered."

"I've got better than that being delivered," Alex said with a hint of pride. "Kathryn's coming by to pick me up."

"Fine woman you got there, to come get you this time of night." Ray looked awkward, and Alex knew he wanted to talk about something else.

"Don't think I don't know it."

"She came to me, said she wanted to sign up right away."

What was there to say about something so big, so deep? "Yeah, she gets like that."

"Sent in the insurance money and everything."

"She's amazing. Changes her mind faster than her underwear."

Ray chuckled. "She did it for you, y'know."

"Yeah, I know."

The two men looked at each other for a long moment, and Alex felt the wordless companionship he valued so much with Ray. The man just *knew,* and that was worth far more than the endless shallow gab that passed for communication these days.

Alex put his hand on Ray's shoulder for a moment and then was all business again, crisp and sure. He got his backpack ready and looped his tool holster into his belt. The fittings on the regulator needed some looking after. He grunted as he hoisted the nitrogen dewar onto his back. "Say, could you call Kath in maybe fifteen minutes, tell her I'll be back by the time she gets here? Uh—and that Chinese stuff, what did you order?"

"Garlic chicken, spare ribs, spicy Mongolian beef."

"Why have your body saved when you're doing all that damage to it? That stuff will burn right through your stomach lining."

Ray snorted derisively. "What's the point of living if you eat like a rabbit?"

This was their usual exchange, and Alex knew he would dig into the chow anyway, even if he did think that garlic was the ketchup of the intellectuals. He clapped Ray on the back and set out through the loading dock.

The night was moonless, the dry arroyo cloaked in ink. He waited for his eyes to adjust, thinking of Kathryn. Her signing up was a stunner. It touched him in a way he could not have expected. She was saying to him, yes, I'll share your dream.

She would be sleepy when they got back to her apartment. He longed to slide into her bed's warm sanctuary and snuggle up to her, spoon fashion, for a swift descent into blessed sleep. They clung to each other now, were inseparable outside work.

She even gave him his distance when he wanted it, too—one of the reasons his marriage had failed—and with a wry, tolerant smile, to boot. She hadn't bugged him about how downright dumb the cockroach caper had been. The gut-twisting story of the collapsed marriage she let him tell in bits and pieces, over time, and cut him plenty of slack about details. She endured his regular little lectures about signing up for cryonics. She had invented a new term for the dead—the "metabolically disadvantaged"—that had become their private joke with earnest cryonicists.

Distracted, Alex wondered what it was like to *be* Kathryn—to toss that marvelous buoyant hair, to live behind the deep, swamp-rich eyes, to feel the lift of breast and thigh. To take short steps on hard wood in high heels. To feel the swoop and plunge of a body that tapered from one wonder to the next. What was it like for her to take a bath (women liked them so much—why?), to know the simple mysteries of the toilet? He was immersed in the swarming implications of delicious difference.

He still brooded about Susan, though, and with the blossoming love with Kathryn came a further revelation. As his life wore on, his mind had returned again and again to that moment in the Tokyo airport. He had met death there, seen its rictus grin. His boyhood had made a shattering collision with that most brutal finality humans can know. It had driven him forward into a life that circled ceaselessly around a desperate gamble, an escape hatch from the foe that others simply mutely accepted.

And now the landscape had shifted for him. His dread of death was evolving, transfigured into something strange and yet mysteriously hopeful. His own end seemed a minor issue now. Towering over that weathered fear there loomed the far worse possibility of losing Kathryn. Sweet, enigmatic, deftly amusing Kathryn. The fresh fulcrum of his world. Without *her,* he would be devastated. She was the sole reason he had been able to get through this last month.

And it dawned upon him that this must be how it was for many people. *We fear the deaths of loved ones more than our own.*

He had to smile wryly at his own thoughts. *So this is what it's like to grow up. Or at least to start.*

19

GEORGE

The fretful night teemed about him. Streamers forked and furled like the heat lightning of distant boyhood summers. Yet he knew the night was darkly sullen, moonless, and that not even the light-enhancing goggles he wore explained the fretted filaments of incandescent excitement that arced about him.

George moved silently through the head-high brush. He had left his car on a dirt byway off Santiago Canyon Road and hiked in over the ridge line. He navigated by the emerald glow of pools where chaparral and manzanita helped hold the day's heat, giving forth a wan radiance.

He had come at least two miles, and his body burst with anxious forces. He was a man transformed, a man propelled forward again by erupting energies.

He could remember little of what had occurred this night—only that it was after midnight now and that something glorious had happened earlier, something that had exploded through him and filled his mind with rapturous joy.

Fragments flew through his mind, shadowy birds winging through slumbering murk.

Something about a dog. Cold fear, savage victory.

Something about a house. Big, Spanish. A high wall.

About a wise man, wanting to know—

Blank.

He had set out to discover something, find out some information, yes —but that was long ago, receding through a swamp of time, a detail swallowed in the jubilation that now poured hot energy into his legs, his arms, his strumming senses.

Cowell. Cowell, giving the finger to God.

The precise topographic map that the satellite locator provided—all through unsuspecting agencies, dummy telephone numbers, blind accounts—said he was out here. Working, walking, it didn't matter. Alone, probably.

He had planned this weeks ago. An attack in the open, as before. Now he seethed with a deep passion for it, an act of completion, the Lord's wrath plunged into the heart of the living foulness that crawled upon the earth.

Up ahead. A metallic clank. Movement.

George crouched, duck-walked forward, dry soil crunching under his shoes. He stroked the crystal cross that hung about his neck, letting its smoothness calm him. The diffuse blush of lime-green light showed a narrow arroyo angling up. He was not far from I^2, maybe half a mile. Cowell's telltale signal had come from here. George had sped through the engulfing night to get here, hoping that Cowell would still be there.

He was. Again, a metallic ring. The steaming green night jittered with flecks of blue shadow, fleeting shards of light.

He moved up the arroyo, turning his head slowly to scan every detail. And there it was, up ahead.

A rectangular shadow. An open door.

Whoever was inside worked with little light, for there was no flood of brilliance that would come from an ordinary bulb. Only a wan radiance spilled from the open doorway.

George stilled his lurching lungs. Why hadn't he guessed? This must be where the Hagerty woman was hidden.

Thank you, Lord. By following the proven path, he had come to this fulcrum moment. Cowell *and* the Hagerty corpse together. In one stroke he could avenge and correct the perverse course of the past.

He crouched and moved forward, running shoes silent on the sand.

A rattle from the doorway.

A long, sliding moment. George held his breath.

A clank.

Cowell's head appeared at the doorway, silhouetted in the dim gleam from within. He stepped out, pebbles scattering, a shiny dewar strapped to his back. A holster of tools dangled from his belt. The heavy door clunked as Cowell tugged it.

George leaped forward, a terrible swift angel from the forest of the night.

20

ALEX

His only warning was a flitting shadow. The inky moving bulk hit Alex and slammed him hard against the rock face of the arroyo.

The impact nearly knocked the wind out of him. The empty dewar was light but large, and it took some of the brunt of the collision.

Alex spun away from the rock wall, trying to get away from the mass that hit him hard in the stomach and then tried to get its hands around, grab, find a grip. Elbows jabbed, a fist caught him in the left shoulder. It was like being mauled by a line backer in high school football, a moving appetite for violence.

Alex punched at the shadow. He connected with surprising softness. A strangled gasp. *Got him in the neck,* Alex thought with a spurt of pleasure. He backpedaled two steps, tried to get his bearings.

The figure threw a left jab, missed. The right grabbed, got only air. *Strong, but a tad slow. Got to get this dewar off.* Alex stepped back again, got his right hand under the shoulder strap.

A fist caught him in the chest. The shadow muttered angrily.

Alex swung the dewar free. Dim light raked across the scene as the door swung lazily open. The big man shifted left, eclipsing the rectangular glow. His silhouette swung heavily with his right fist, and Alex spun opposite to it, bringing the dewar around over his left shoulder. The fist clunked into the dewar.

A meaty crack.

"Ah! Oh! Lord!"

The figure lurched back, clutching his right hand. Alex swung the dewar around and got a firm hold on its straps with both hands. The silhouette backed away. "Ah!"

Alex stepped forward carefully. If the man had a weapon, the dewar wasn't going to be of much use. He tried to see. Could this be a cop? Detweiler was this big. But why rush him in the dark?

His eyes were adjusting now, and he was startled to see that the man's head was distended, bug-eyed. Deformed? The hairs on the back of Alex's neck stood at attention. Crazy-wacko-psycho?

The man was staggering, confused. Hunched over. Clutching his hurt hand. The bug-eyes veered skyward, as if the man looked for something. Help from above?

Try to spook him. "Run, you little shit, or I'll bust you open."

Wrong move. The figure straightened. The backbone returned.

The shadow wore a dark jogging outfit and tennis shoes. He shook his head as if to clear it. Then he reached up and snatched at his face and pulled away the bug-eyes. A strong, lean face, big nose.

Goggles? What kind of a guy wears—

Night-vision goggles. A systematic guy. Careful. Determined. *Not going to run away.*

"You broke my hand." A gravel voice. Not Detweiler. Strain lacing through it.

"I'll break your head if you don't—"

"Damned chiller rich from Hawaii think you own the world defying God's word bastard."

"Huh?" Hawaii? Following them, then. Planned this.

"Wanna bring back the dead from *Gawd* you bastard unholy rich sinner, walking dead you want to keep them from their holy appointments when *Gawd* wants white bones released redeemed when *he* says *rise again* not when *you* do, chiller bastards insane with your dirty science spitting on *Gawd*."

Crazy. Worse, crazy-smart. Organized. Big.

Fast. Without warning the man rushed him. Alex brought the dewar around to club at him, but he ducked sideways and slammed into Alex's shoulder. Alex reeled away. Hands snatched at him. Yanked at the dewar straps. Got it away, hurled it into the blackness. It struck with a clunk. Heavy breathing.

Alex drove his fist straight into the face that loomed up in inky silhouette. Smacked home. The man took it, staggered. "Uh." Came back.

Alex scrambled away. The figure spread his hands, blocking flight down the arroyo.

He'll corner me. Big and crazy-fast. *Need to even things up. A weapon.*

He glanced around. In the dim glow he couldn't see a rock big enough. No sticks, nothing.

The man took a step forward. Another. Alex felt the tool belt hooked to his belt. He yanked out a flat-headed screwdriver, plastic handle cool to the touch.

Do I have to kill this guy? It suddenly struck him that this strange figure had killed Susan. In an instant he knew it as a fact, some corner of his mind putting together the threads. *Yeah. I have to kill him.*

Alex held the screwdriver out in front, low. Standard six inches long, a pathetic substitute for a knife. Maybe the man would mistake it for one in the dark.

The figure came at him carefully. For one long moment Alex studied the contorted face, trying to read the expression. But there was none. The wide slit-mouth showed no emotion. The eyes peered out from some far, empty space. They stared right through Alex. Toward infinity. Fixed eyes in a rigid face. Vacant.

The man reached into his pocket and pulled out a gun.

Alex tensed. He would have to move fast, not let the guy get a smooth shot at a running figure, dodge as much as he could in the damned narrow arroyo, dodge while running uphill— *Wait. Something funny.*

The pistol caught a gleam from the open doorway. Yellow. The pistol was yellow. Alex had never heard of a gun colored that way, and an idea leaped into his mind. *Plastic. It's not a real gun.*

Before he could react there was a liquid squirting noise, and something lightly touched his chest. He looked down, saw nothing, and a heavy vapor swarmed up into his sinuses. *My God! Gas!*

He breathed out. Coughed. Rasped out the last of his air. *Don't breathe in.* An acrid taste stung his mouth, invaded his throat. *Bitter. Almonds.*

He lurched away, legs wobbly. Uphill. Away. His eyes stung, and he ran for ten seconds before his lungs convulsed and he sucked in sweet dry night air.

Pebbles scrabbled away under his feet. He fought the racking pain that shot through his head, spiked through his throat. His lungs would not work right. They felt as though a rope were wrapped around them, twisting. Spasms shook him.

He looked back and could see nothing. Just blackness. Blue dots danced in the hot dark.

A crunch of steps. Feet coming up behind him.

He gasped and scrabbled at the crumbling dirt and soft sandstone. Years ago he climbed up this way when the idea of the emergency storage site was just a half-formed notion. There were caves up here, but they were too obvious, too easy to spot from a distance because of their height—visible from the air, too. Maybe he could hide in one of them.

His hands clawed upward, closed over a smooth lip of worn rock. He still had the screwdriver. He jabbed down with it, got some purchase. Pulled himself up. Rolled onto a flat area.

This must be the plateau. Alex scrambled forward. Got to his feet. Pink fireflies danced in his vision. He shook his head to clear it. The fireflies buzzed and whirled, mad darting insect luminosities. He looked out and saw sheets of yellow glow brimming on the horizon. Orange County, burrowed deep into its fitful night. Making ready for the next day. Civilization cast little glow here to guide him and from behind came the scrape of pursuit.

Almonds. Bitter almonds. Somewhere he had read that executed prisoners smelled that in their last moments.

He ran forward into nearly complete blackness. Find a place to hide. Or else try to outrun this guy.

Hiding seemed like a better idea. He tripped, stumbled, smacked his head. Scrambled up, charged on. A stick rolled out from under his shoe, and he went down, banging hard on his right knee.

Soft slaps of running shoes behind.

He turned and saw the big silhouette blotting out the pale sky glow. The man's head turned, sweeping the view methodically, radar-serene.

He has the goggles back on. His head spun with this realization. Hiding would be impossible.

Run, then. He ducked low, hoping that would help, and trotted along the brow of the worn rock.

Footsteps behind. Coming fast. Sure, steady, able to see the way.

A dark mass to the left. Alex veered away from it and hit something hard. A boulder. It knocked the wind out of him. No time to recover. He slipped around the rough sandstone and walked, unable to see his footing. No sound from behind. Then a crunch, very close. He dodged right, and a hand struck him hard on the left temple. Pink fireflies.

The squirting noise. Droplets spattered his face.

Bitter almonds.

Choking pain. Needles spiking his throat.

"You scientist chiller bastards know about cyanide don't you?" Voice rasping the thick air. "Dilute solution, fifty milligrams per liter. Taste good? Bastard heathen corpse-kisser, taste good? Makes you easy to do, not enough to leave a trace. God's science, chiller asshole."

Through a dizzying haze of pain he swung wide at the voice. He could not see the man at all. The screwdriver cut only the air.

A scuffling to the right. He jabbed. Struck solidly. Jabbed again. A startled cry. A fist grabbed the screwdriver, yanked it away.

Alex fought to not breathe, but it made no difference. His head raged with red pain. Steel teeth raked his chest. He felt himself teeter, fall. Stone slapped him in the face.

Hands caught him. Swung him with lazy gravity toward the brim of rock. Lifting.

Up into the chill night. Below lay consuming blackness.

"Bless you," the hollow voice said.

A distant grunt of effort.

Arcing up toward the sky glow.

Weightless.

Falling.

SIX

DEATH, BE NOT PROUD

One short sleep past, we wake eternally,
And Death shall be no more; Death, thou shalt die.
—John Donne
"Death, Be Not Proud"

1

KATHRYN

She had worked late at Fashion Circus, and her feet were only now beginning to feel like true, loyal members of her body again.

Earlier, they had protested being encased in high heels for what felt like half the age of the universe. She had changed into petite white walking shoes when they had finally closed the doors on the Annual Thank You Sale. "Thank you and *good*-bye!" Sheila had boomed out, slapping the bolt lock shut. They had fueled up with some fast food and Cokes, and then dived into the annual inventory. The manager, a phlegmatic woman with a whim of iron, had kept them at it until after midnight. Kathryn had barely gotten home to receive Alex's call, and now she could look forward to a few soul kisses to increase her pulse rate.

Kathryn crossed the 1^2 parking lot, a dry wind tossing her hair, her reflection a pale ghost in the mirror wall. She remembered the day she had come here to report for work, and was surprised to realize that it was not even two months ago.

Yet it seemed that her life divided into two eras, with After Alex much the better part—a long, warm epoch of discovering him, and finding surprises about herself, too. He had made her see that she kept most people at bay with her crisp, brittle persona. He had put up with it only so far, and then he had joked and kidded and soothed her out of those moods. He was quiet, even shy—except in bed—and really completely ruthless, never letting her get away with a glossy superficiality or offhand bit of easy cynicism. Two months! And they had a whole lifetime left. What could this man do for an encore? It was going to be fun finding out.

She used her key and walked into the main office of Immortality Incorporated. Ray Constantine was sitting at the central computer crescent, frowning at the big control screen. "How did it go?" she asked.

Without taking his eyes from the screen, Ray said automatically, "The patient is in guarded but stable condition."

"Ah, the cryonicist's classic claim. At least things don't get worse."

"Hey, it's the truth."

She dropped with a sigh into a roller chair and fought down the impulse to prop her feet up on the desk. Accumulated mail and paperwork covered half the desk. She retreated into it, disposing of the junk mail and doing blessedly mindless routine.

"Damn this software," Ray muttered.

He and Alex and several other I² members had been working for weeks with the computer system, battling unseen antagonists who lurked in the byzantine network. Ray sighed. "I found another Trojan horse in the MedAlarm system yesterday. Thought I had it fixed. Now it's fritzing again."

"Trojan horse?"

"A program somebody plants in your system, looks innocent. It just sits awhile, then bursts open, lets these little damaging programs loose."

"Who would do that?"

"Hackers, maybe. Pranksters. But this stuff looks too sharp, too specific to our system architecture."

She knew Alex and Ray had been fighting constant incursions into the computers, and a trickle of suspicion ran through her, a cold apprehension. "What's wrong now?"

"Got something funny." Ray stabbed a finger at the screen. "Alex's MedAlarm just came on."

"Are you guys checking the system?"

"No, this looks like an honest alarm."

"Isn't Alex here?" She felt a spike of concern.

"He took nitrogen out to Susan."

She was on her feet without thinking about it, staring at the screen. *This is an error. A dumb mistake. Please.* "Find him."

Ray called up the satellite locator program. It filled the screen with a topographical map, curving nests of green lines on a black background. Ray tapped a subprogram and blue dots appeared, the perspective zoomed in, and a bright yellow flashing icon pointed: I².

The map exploded a portion of its grid until she could make out the contours of the ridgeline behind I². Beside a wedge of green lines, indicating a steep slope, a red dot strobed.

"That's got him tabbed all right." Ray pointed. "That's not far from the emergency storage."

"But what could—I mean—there can't—"

"Let's go." Ray tapped for a printout, but Kathryn beat him to the laser printer. Three copies came out, the color ink gleaming, and when she looked up Ray was gone.

Bob Skinner shuffled out of the dorm room, blinking. Ray was pushing him along, walking by using a single crutch. "What's up?" Bob said blearily.

"Something's happened to Alex." Kathryn felt her words burst out, the awful solidness of them giving weight to her tight, rising anxiety.

"Huh?" Bob blinked. "Damn." He took only seconds to scan the MedAlarm status report on the big screen. "Ummm. Rise in skin conductance, heart rate erratic."

"Oxygen?" Kathryn asked.

"A little low, and falling."

"Couldn't that be from exercise carried out while he's tired?"

"Doubtful, but possible. These diagnostics aren't perfect."

Kathryn felt a jolt of elation and searched Bob's face for more, but he wore a medical student's dispassion. "What's the location?" Bob asked, his mouth twisted with uncertainty. Ray showed him the map.

Without a word Bob turned to a gray cabinet of open shelves, marked EMERGENCY, and snatched up a medical care backpack. "Take this," he said, handing both of them a kit.

Kathryn opened hers and checked the flashlight and radio phones inside. Their verifying lights went on reassuringly. By then, Bob had his shoes on and a red windbreaker. They went out through the loading dock, each clutching a copy of the topo map. Bob grabbed a fold-up cloth stretcher from the I^2 ambulance.

Ray kept pace, his face lined. "Shall I call paramedics?"

They stopped in the rear parking lot, the same thought striking simultaneously. "Damn," Bob said, startled. "We'd lead them to the emergency storage. To Susan."

Ray said, "The locator says he's near the facility, but not in it."

Kathryn said, "Maybe if we're careful—"

Bob shook his head. "If we get a team stumbling around out here, maybe a helicopter, too—they could see it. For sure."

Kathryn said, "But if we don't, and something's really wrong—"

"Look, take the truck," Ray said quickly. "You can work your way partway around the ridge. You know that dirt path. Faster than on foot, for sure."

"You mean you won't call the paramedics?" Kathryn demanded.

Ray looked at her steadily for a moment that seemed unendurable, but passed in a heartbeat. "Not yet. Let's see what's going on first."

"But if Alex—"

"We'll reach him long before paramedics could," Bob said.

"They're trained. They—"

"I'm almost a doctor. And I'm here."

Ray said flatly, "Enough talk—let's move it."

Kathryn drove. She had used the truck several times now and knew most of the route. Bob knew the rest. He checked through the medical backpack, rearranging things. They jounced into sandy ruts, catching the tailgate in dips, the engine grinding. She slewed too hard on a left turn and the tires spun madly, nearly getting stuck. Branches whipped the windshield. Her nose wrinkled with a sour smell, and she realized it was herself, a sharp bite of sweat and fear.

She concentrated on weaving along the barely marked track but could not keep out of her mind the images of driving with Alex in this same truck through a night like this, racing toward doomed, crumpled Susan. So long ago. Yet only two weeks. A time crowded with legalese and grinding anxiety. But looming larger now were the quiet yet grand moments with Alex. They had watched the late-night news together, greeting the sensationalized coverage of I^2 and Alex with catcalls. She had never realized how TV news teams were a pseudofamily, with jokester weathermen and solemn daddy-figures and concerned, earnest moms. The lightweight team member always handled the I^2 items, playing them for macabre laughs. Kathryn guessed that many forlorn viewers tuned in not for news but for an echo of family warmth. It was all rather sad, revealing a vast, unspoken loneliness.

The path ended. She slammed to a stop. Bob checked the topo map and pointed to the left. "Instead of going up by the facility, let's follow along the base of the hill. It looks like the signal's from over there."

"How far?"

"Couple hundred yards, looks like."

She rummaged in the truck seat. "Damn it, where's that hand-held locator?"

"I've got it."

She jumped down from the truck and ran through the scrub bushes. Beyond the headlights the night swarmed in on them in dry embrace. Bob fell behind. She held her flashlight tightly and barreled ahead, not feeling the twigs that snapped off, the thorns that plucked at her skirt and scratched her arms. She plunged through the slightest opening in the brush if it would shorten her route, crashing through and making a lot of noise and not caring. Like a jittering small sun the flashlight beam threw giant shadows from inconsequential mounds, brought ropy tangles into stark relief, and bored forward through a pervasive gloom. She ran without thinking, navigating by keeping the rock face as a looming presence on her right. A huge stand of prickly pear cactus towered ahead, and she cut around it, trotting slightly downhill. She saw an opening in the broad pads, a narrow gap between sharp needles, and turned sideways to slip through without slowing. She ran smack into a man.

He had been hiding from view, crouched down, and she spilled over him, arms flying. Thumped onto the sand. Sprang up.

He was big and even in a sweat-stained jogging suit she could see he was heavily muscled. But he scrambled away with agility, got to his feet quickly. He was white-faced, his mouth a pale slit. His legs trembled. He reached convulsively for his belly, where the jogging suit was blood-stained.

I've seen him before.

The shock paralyzed her. Questions reverberated through her, but she knew she had no time to think. *Who is he?*

His eyes jerked feverishly from her to the menacing wall of cactus. Gasps shuddered from heaving lungs. Thin lips worked, but no words came forth, only strangled shards of sound. This man was teetering on the verge of some abyss she could not glimpse.

Later there would be time to understand. Now only Alex mattered. Whoever this was, he was slowing her down. She had to push this massive obstruction out of the way.

The strained bulk of his shoulders, bunched neck muscles, flexing fingers—all spoke of panic. But his eyes now became more rapt, fixed on her face with blazing intensity. Emotions fought across his face. She sensed that he was balanced between fight and flight, and in another heartbeat would decide.

She consciously willed herself to take a step forward. What could she say? She remembered her emergency kit. It was clipped to her belt on the left side. She turned so that he could not see it, then reached with her left hand for it, as though for a weapon. She held the flashlight forward, throwing her left side further into shadow.

She put as much authority as she could muster into her voice. "Freeze. Right now."

He gaped, the big mouth open so wide she could see his tongue. "N-no, no."

"*Freeze,* I said!"

He bolted. Swiveling, lurching among the soaring cactus. A barb snagged him, and he gave a startled cry. He yanked his torn sleeve free and plunged into the brush beyond.

She let him go. It would be impossible to catch up to him. Darkness swallowed the running shape. A crackling of snapped branches faded until she heard only the hammering of her own pulse. The confrontation had taken perhaps five seconds.

She took a deep breath and sprinted along the curve of the rock slope, angling upward. In a few moments she saw another beam bobbing to her left. "Bob!"

"Locator says it's this way." She scrambled after his voice. In the inky shadows Bob moved more slowly, encumbered by the medical backpack and fold-up stretcher. He carried the hand-held transmitter that gave a homing vector on an active MedAlarm within a range of a hundred yards.

She struggled up a rough slope, slipping on gravel and banging her knee. Branches and cactus seemed to reach out of the blackness and pluck at her. She caught up to Bob in a narrow gully. A dark mass filled half the sky to her right, the steep slant of the ridgeline.

"Here!"

She reached him as Bob shone the flashlight into Alex's white face. Bob began checking all over Alex for trauma. Alex lay motionless. The eyes were closed. The chest fluttered. The right arm was caught under him at a wrong angle.

"Is he . . . ?"

"Pretty bad," Bob said, slinging his medical backpack to the ground and fishing for equipment. "Here, hold the light where I'm working."

She watched helplessly. Bob carefully inspected Alex's neck and spine with deft fingers, moving the body as little as possible. Only when he took his hands away and wiped them did she register the sullen red and notice that blood stained the sand around Alex's head.

"What's—what's—"

Bob ignored her and worked with an elastic bandage, fixing a tourniquet. "We've got to get him to help. I've stopped the bleeding, but there's plenty of other trauma."

"His arm—"

"Yeah, but that's secondary. He's in deep shock. That's the big problem."

Alex seemed shrunken. The small cone of the flashlights held him within a precarious zone of weak light, while all around them an immense dark wrapped its sullen cloak. "Do you think—"

"Lay the stretcher down here."

"We can carry him out?"

"It's not the best, but I think it'll be okay."

"We can carry him back to the ambulance, then—"

"Faster to carry him in the truck. We'll immobilize him in the back."

"We've got short-range radio. If we call Ray, he can get a helicopter."

"Too slow. If we'd called when we started, maybe so."

"We can have paramedics waiting—"

Bob looked up at her for the first time since they had reached Alex. His face was deeply lined, ash-gray in the flashlight glow. A stark desperation narrowed his mouth. "Remember Susan. She's not far away."

"But she's *dead,* and Alex—"

"I'm the physician here. Help me."

Kathryn opened her mouth, felt a sudden rush of piercing fear. Everything was coming at her with screaming, headlong velocity. She had to *think*, see a way through this, understand—

"Kathryn! Get the stretcher."

She closed her mouth and got the stretcher. Helping Bob carefully slide Alex onto the stretcher consumed all her attention. "We've got to move him right or risk more trauma to the spine. I don't think that's the big problem, though, feels not so bad. But that's just a prelim inspection. It's the shock we've got to get a grip on."

It was comforting to listen to Bob as he put an IV into Alex and began administering a solution. It helped still her inner confusion, and she realized that was why Bob was talking like this, telling her exactly what to do, how Alex was.

She had time to think again while they carried Alex back along the contour of the hillside. Bob found a narrow path that made progress along a gentle slope. This time they knew where they were going, beckoned by the truck's headlights. She was intent upon keeping Alex level and steady, watching her footing. The truck's brilliance seemed to shoot out of the cloaking night like a stabbing bright beacon, surprising her. She concentrated on Bob's voice, on following each step. They got Alex fixed onto the flatbed of the truck, using the guy ropes and stays.

She rode beside him on the slow drive back. Alex showed no movement, no eyelid flickering, nothing. She felt his face, his swollen arm, more to seek reassurance than for any medical purpose. She had no clear idea of how to interpret his cold hands, the strange inert quality of his slack face.

Are you there? she thought. *Alex? Fight it, darling. I'm here.* She whispered into the dry night, "Don't leave me. Don't."

They parked beside the ramp of the loading dock. Ray had the tailgate of the truck down before she could get out. He got around amazingly well on one crutch, and she filled him in briefly on what had happened.

"A man? What man?" Bob asked as they slid Alex out of the truck bed and onto a mobile gurney.

She described her encounter by the cactus, and the men peppered her with more questions, but then they were in the operating room and talk ceased as they transferred Alex to the central operating table. Bob began treatment, calling out orders in a flat, methodical voice that heartened her with its matter-of-fact professionalism. She fetched supplies, instruments, helped Ray, all in a blur. Minutes stretched into half an hour, then more, and she had begun to breathe normally again when suddenly Bob said, "Heart's stopped. Give me epinephrine."

Time then compressed into wafer-thin instants. Procedures. Instruments. Diagnostics. Jagged emotions. Shouted orders. Her fingers fumbled as she tried to follow Bob's barked commands.

Her hands slipped and wavered, and then she understood that she was not seeing properly. The bleak light of the operating theater diffused and melted around her. She had been crying for some time without knowing it, the world gauzy and glowing.

She and Ray ran to get the "thumper" from the ambulance, her feet hitting the floor like wooden pegs. They slid it into place over Alex's chest. It came on, *pock-pock-pock-pock-wheeze,* maddening in its remorseless energy.

Alex's chest labored beneath it, a puppet driven to a parody of life. Moments slid by. Astringent medical smells bit the air. Words flew by, technical, quick, pressing.

She finally saw there was nothing to do. Bob said no more, just watched the monitors, and finally shook his head.

"No," she whispered.

"I'm afraid so," Bob said.

Ray smacked his palm on the operating table. "Damn. Damn."

"Look, there's nothing more to do. If I was at UCI, I could try a few things, but frankly—"

"Then let's take him there!" she cried.

"It's too late. UCI is half an hour away."

"But he—he can't go just like that, so fast, so—"

"He can." Bob's lined face seemed to collapse, crinkling into despair. "He has."

Kathryn stared in disbelief. "What happened, what—"

"Circulatory failure, major trauma, massive hemorrhage."

The three of them gazed across Alex's body, the overhead lamps etching their drawn expressions.

Ray said, "Look, this is terrible, but we can't rest. We've got to start his suspension. *Now.*"

"Suspension?" Kathryn simply could not comprehend the word. The room itself swam, watery and remote. Their voices came to her through a thick, cottony distance.

"That's all we can do," Bob said, his eyes fixed, as though he listened to an interior voice.

Ray said tentatively, "You have to pronounce death, sign a certificate."

Bob shook his head. "I can't. Not legally qualified to."

"Then if we suspend him," Kathryn said shakily, "it's—it's . . ."

"Technically, maybe they could call it murder," Ray said.

"The medical examiner," Kathryn said desperately. "Would he be satisfied with a set of samples Bob could take?"

Bob thought, inhaling deeply. "I could draw blood through a femoral stick, so the ME could run a toxicology screen."

"That would be enough?" Kathryn asked.

"Sometimes it is, to rule out foul play by poisoning. But this is clear trauma. I could document that with photographs, which might help, sure, but—"

"We can all testify that Alex was dead."

"That won't stand up," Bob said.

Ray nodded grudgingly. "Prob'ly not."

"But if we wait for an ambulance, for the cops, it'll be way too late," Bob said. "The ME will do a complete autopsy."

"We can't let them!" Kathryn exploded.

Bob's face was ashen, jaw muscles clenching. "Right. Alex, he dedicated his life to this. To let him slip away . . ."

"We got to choose," Ray said quietly.

Kathryn held her breath. She could try to persuade them, but she sensed that words would do little good now. These were the kind of men who could not be herded with more talk.

Ray scowled at Bob. "I know it's a big risk for you."

Bob's mouth drew into a tight line. "For all of us."

Kathryn studied Alex's face. It was calm, unworried, with only a single curved scar under one eye that had crusted over with brown blood. She had to struggle to get the words out. "Yes—yes, but he would like that—want that—"

For a long moment they studied each other's faces. Somehow a sad but determined confirmation passed among them.

"Let's go," Ray said.

Bob began working, assembling materials. Ray swung a basin around Alex's head and started filling it with water and ice. Kathryn noted with numb incomprehension that the ice was all ready, prepared by Ray sometime when she had not noticed. Had he done that while they were out there, finding Alex? It would be like Ray, covering all the possibilities. But not calling an ambulance, she thought. Not endangering Susan's precious frozen self. She felt a spurt of anger, a cutting red rage that shot through her and forced open her mouth, but all that came out was a sharp wail, a forlorn note of hopeless grief. Ray embraced her, the room whirled, and she sagged against a counter. She sobbed as convulsive gasps wracked her. It seemed to go on a long time, a boundless time of utter despair.

And then, seemingly without transition, she was packing more ice into the tank that had somehow come to envelop Alex. There was no memory of anything in between, and she could breathe again without the sobs breaking through anymore. She realized that they were well into the suspension process. Time had passed, and she had no memory of it. Bob had opened arteries to gain access to Alex's circulation. Alex was now the focus of IVs, lines carrying dark red blood, paraphernalia that seemed to bristle from him. She could no longer see enough of his face to read his expression. *I didn't get to kiss him good-bye,* she thought. *He's really gone.*

Kathryn found herself with a clipboard, noting down medications, dosages, flow rates as Bob and Ray called them out. Everything focused to a narrow sphere in which she followed orders, wrote, held tubes, fetched. And it was all under glass for her now, hollow sounds and sights and smells from far, far away.

2

GEORGE

The great Marble Cathedral towered against a pale sky just beginning to ease open with the glow of dawn. George hurried under the twisted trunks of the oak grove. The gnarled trees were peaceful in day's bland light, but now in the diffuse hour when shadows began to melt, they seemed like hunched-over, malevolent spirits, casting a waxy gloom. He shivered. Cutting pain laced through his belly. He had tied a crude compress over the places where the screwdriver had stabbed, but they kept oozing something. He would tend to that later. Now he had to still his mind, regain the analytical side of himself. Only it could deal with the host of torments that dogged him.

He angled along the long brick flank of meeting rooms, past the cafeteria and a warren used for Bible classes. He had spent many a fine hour here, keeping fellowship with others of the cathedral flock. It had been a quiet honor to sit among them, to share their singsong prayers and fried chicken dinners, all the while knowing that no one suspected that he was a special warrior of the Lord. A fighter who would look after the little ones while busy mothers fussed in the kitchen, who would help out with some quiet generosity when a church member was down on his luck.

The Reverend's private residence was dark. He felt the huge steel cross soaring above the complex as a rebuke, a frown. But he had to get help, some balm to soothe his turmoil, and the Reverend himself had said that George was to come to him in time of affliction.

Guilt clung to him as he slipped alongside the Reverend's quarters. The door he usually came in was Douglas fir, deeply stained. He had always admired its solidity and without even thinking about it had remembered the standard lock and safety chain. Now in the ebbing shadows he did not need to see it clearly to know how it worked. His gray guilt ebbed as he got out his equipment. Doing a job got his mind away from the raucous clash of feelings.

The lock was easy. His pick popped it open within moments. He had learned that as a boy, but the next part he had worked out on his own, practicing on his own apartment door. He had learned a lot of things a man needed to move silently and shrewdly through this world, and most of it from books that the libraries were only too happy to lend him.

He fished rubber bands and thumb tacks from his jacket pocket. All his tools were innocuous, easy to carry and arousing no suspicion, even if he were stopped here by police. The door swung open without a squeak and thunked against its chain. He had just a narrow crack to work in. In the gloom he had to do it by feel. A thick rubber band, looped around the thumb tack, right. He used tacks with broad heads because the usual ones slipped through his thick fingers.

It was a little tricky reaching as far around the back of the door as he could, and then mashing the tack into the Douglas fir. He tugged at the rubber band, getting it snagged right. When it was firmly trapped, he stretched it back and looped it around the knob on the chain. Good— the distance was right, the rubber band stretched nice and tight.

He eased the door nearly shut. In the morning stillness he heard the faint clack as the rubber band shortened and the knob slid along its track. He stopped, the door nearly closed. The knob was sitting at the end point of the channel. He jiggled the door a little. The chain clattered as it fell out of the track.

This was better, yes, much better than banging on a door, calling attention to himself. Swift, sure, a shadow. The pain in him had cleared his head some now. He was ready to report.

The soft carpets made him soundless as he slipped along the corridors he knew so well. From outside he had figured out where the Reverend slept, and sure enough, the door he had guessed swung open upon a king-size bed.

"Reverend?" He advanced into the shadowy recesses.

"Uh?"

"Reverend?"

"Wha'? Who . . ."

"I had to come, to tell. The hurt's bad, but I held it."

"Who's that?" This voice was different. A woman's voice.

"The hurt—" George stopped, open-mouthed. Two forms sat up from the bed. A lamp snapped on. Light flooded across the Reverend and a woman, a woman in a white silk nightgown, a woman he knew.

"Sister Angel." He stepped back.

She always looked so regal and pure and remote in the choir, sweet songnotes spilling forth from her lovely mouth. Here she was frowsy, heavy-lidded, hair a tangle, lipstick smeared.

"What the hell are you doing here?" the Reverend demanded.

"I—I came, you said—"

"Haven't you the decency to *knock*?" Sister Angel crossed her arms over her full breasts, though they were covered by a filmy nightgown.

"I thought the Reverend, he would be . . ."

The Reverend said sternly, "Outside, George. Out."

The minutes standing in the hallway were miserable. George brushed away tears and tried to regain the calm he had attained only moments before, but sobs came welling up from his chest and had to get out. The pain got worse, too. When he looked at the bandage it was sticky, bloody, a foul matted mess that made him ashamed again.

He heard the Reverend's deep tones from behind the bedroom door, but no answer from Sister Angel. He thought of how he had worked with the sister at church gatherings, admiring her without being able to say much of anything to her, tongue-tied and awed. Was she listening now to the Reverend apologize for George? The Reverend spoke again, short murmuring phrases, and George realized that he was probably talking on the telephone, probably alerting the guards, if there were any.

He had just thought about this when the bedroom door jerked open. He caught a glimpse of Sister Angel standing beside the bed, face dark with anger, her breasts heaving against the white silk. The door slammed shut. The Reverend stood fuming, scowling at George. He wore a red satin robe, arms folded across his chest. He gestured curtly toward his study and strode ahead. George followed. In the heavy silence George heard the *snick-snick* of the Reverend's legs rubbing the silk, a soft sound of wealth. When they reached the solemn, shrouded room, George felt some comfort from the aromas of wood and leather.

"You should *never* violate a sanctified dwelling," the Reverend said, standing tall beside the desk. Dawn streamers lit the stained-glass windows behind him.

"I never thought, sir, I mean, you and Sister Angel—"

"You do not need to think of that. Your mission lies elsewhere."

"I don't mean to criticize, honest, I—"

"You will have to apologize to the lady."

"Yes God yes I will."

"You were very unwise to come here this way."

"I had to. There's something, I don't know what it means."

"What's wrong with you?"

George looked down at himself. The stain had spread on his sweat-suit, and his hand came away bloody. "Nothing, I'll get it fixed up."

"You got into trouble."

"I was doing good work. I went there, I found the Hagerty woman."

"The . . . corpse? Where? Have you got it?"

"No, but I found their place, back on the ridge behind their building."

"Very fine, very fine. But they injured you?"

"Nothing to it. I got one of them, though. That fellow who rebuked you on the television."

"Cowell? What do you mean, 'got' him?"

"I killed him. Same as before."

"Killed?" The Reverend gasped.

"You said I was to smite them."

"But—before?"

"Hagerty. I did him same as to her, smote him, threw him down."

"Threw?" The Reverend's mouth worked, but no sounds came out.

"You knew about the white bones, how they are God's necessary."

"Bones . . . ? I did not—tell you to . . ."

"Reverend, I didn't plan it out right this time." His voice was high and plaintive, a boy's plea. "Something's happened, something that made me kill Cowell before I meant to. There's this Lomax—you didn't tell me about him—and I, Karen, she was in with him somehow, so after I felt so funny from her, you know, I saw Lomax, and then this other thing, with Cowell, it happened fast, so fast I couldn't think. That's what I want the help with."

The Reverend sagged against his desk, pale and vacant-eyed. "Help?"

"I don't *understand.* Dr. Lomax, something from him, I can't remember it. Made me do this thing. I can't keep straight and true now, my hard half, it needs to come out, I can't go like this, sir."

"Lomax—you didn't hurt him?"

"Oh no. No."

"Thank God. But . . . Cowell."

"Well, yessir. I saw it was right when you spoke to me, the chillers and all."

"As . . . before?"

"Well, yeah. But that was before I found you and my Calling."

"And Karen, too?"

"Now that was where things started to go wrong. I honestly do not know why that happened, sir. I don't even recall most of it."

"But you did it. I gave you her, and you slew her."

"I knew you didn't want to know the worst of me."

The Reverend's face collapsed into a haggard mask. "I—I never let you tell me outright. My way of . . . keeping a distance, I suppose."

"I kind of guessed what you wanted."

"I was able to tell myself that you were just making trouble for them. I had it on good authority that you were all right."

"What authority?"

The Reverend's eyes became veiled, wary. "The Church fathers in Arizona."

"I *am* all right. I had to, the white bones and all, only Karen—"

Reverend Montana pressed his face into his hands, swaying, and for a moment George thought the man was going to topple over. "My God, yes . . . Karen."

"That's what bothers me so, sir. I did that, and then I couldn't stop, I had to find Dr. Lomax because of things that kept coming into my head, things I couldn't shut out. I prayed, I did, powerfully hard. I played the tapes of your services over and over, I did, I have every one, nearly. Made me furious mad just thinking about the chiller assholes, pardon the expression. But your sermons, beautiful sermons, still they didn't do for me, it didn't stop me wanting."

The Reverend was sweating, but his mouth became a thin hard line and he now had a cool expression, as if he were looking down from a high place. "I thought you could be relied upon to do holy work, warrior work. But following instructions. Instead you have run amok on me, George."

George made a strangled cry. "I didn't *mean* to!"

"Nonetheless, you did. And you may have embroiled me and this Church, this spiritual rock, in your madness."

"Don't—don't *say* that."

"A minister must speak the truth, the one truth."

The words came heavy and mournful, and George felt his head swim with the hot currents he had felt before, down through the cascading hours of this night. The pain in his belly punished him again with hell-fire, and he fell to his knees. "No, please."

"You have blemished this Church."

"I was doing the Lord's work, please, don't—"

The Reverend's voice was once again smooth, sad, glorious. "You were to do the Lord's work, not to mesh me in your madness."

"I was doing fine, I was a serious killer like the Lord wanted. But then you sent Karen to me, and something she did, something, it made me hot in my mind again, a way I haven't been in so long. I couldn't help it."

"Do not blame your transgressions upon others. Accept the sin. That is the only way to be free of it."

George opened his mouth but could not speak for his sobbing. The study that was so comforting swirled about him, and he felt himself let go, his belly pain cutting him again. His head struck the floor.

He was trying to lift it when another voice, a stern voice he recognized from somewhere long ago, said, "I agree, George. Accept what you are."

Then he knew who had been on the other end of the conversation in the Reverend's bedroom. In the shadowed reaches of the room he saw Dr. Lomax, standing with the silver cylinder in his hand.

3

KATHRYN

She watched the man who had brought warmth into her life as he descended through a terrible, keeping cold.

Kathryn sat on a hard bench beside the cooling vessel and monitored Alex's temperature. He was drifting down, one lonesome degree at a time. Beneath the icy fluids she could barely see his outlines. He lingered with her, a shadow presence.

Once, while she dozed, she had heard his voice. It was definitely, defiantly him. The strong notes were freighted with a softness in the vowels, so that even when being firm, his sentences carried a certain rounding. The voice had murmured, and she had thought for a moment, drifting up from fitful dreams, that he was there. She had reached out to shape herself to his contours, and then felt the cool, deserted sheets all around her.

After that she could not drop back into sleep's oblivion. She had gotten up, joints aching. The sheets were on a narrow I^2 bunk bed. Sips of coffee now brought a faint spark of interest back into the world.

Alex's digital temperature readout winked down one more notch in his slow approach to freezing, with the cryoprotectants developed by Susan now safely diffused through his tissues. She knew she should feel something. Instead there was numbness, a dry nothing, just sights and sounds and passing moments, each like the last, unending. Valueless, flat. She made another entry and looked up as Bob Skinner approached.

"Kathryn, you need more sleep."

"Had some."

"A few hours, and that was around noon. It's five o'clock. You can go home."

"Don't want to."

"Look, you're no good if you're completely shot."

"We're short-handed."

Bob sat down and let out an exasperated sigh. "I know. But it's a long process now, running him down. Takes a half day before transfer to liquid nitrogen, first vapor and then liquid, so—"

"I know. I'm not going anywhere."

"Then get some sleep, for chrissake."

"Don't feel like it."

"Kathryn, we did our best. There was nothing anyone could have done to—"

"I know. I just want to be here with him."

"Understandable." Bob lowered his face into his hands and rubbed. "We're all pretty flattened."

She forced herself up, out of the gray lethargy that had been stealing over her. There was a job to be done here, and if she fell asleep, it might be too late by the time she awakened. Ray Constantine was already asleep, but Bob was the crucial one. She had been waiting to talk to him alone.

"I want to do some thinking, too, Bob. We were so frantic, I never thought to call the police about that man."

"Yeah, we got plenty of cleanup to do on this one."

She sat looking at her hands, and slowly blocks of logic collided in her mind. "Wait a minute, Bob. Have you filled out the death certificate? The VS-9 form?"

"No, I'll get to it. We've got three days to file."

"Don't."

"Huh?" He lifted a startled face from his hands.

"Alex died the same way Susan did—a fall. And I saw that man. The police will autopsy Alex."

Bob thought, nodded. "Of course. Finding him out there, it looked like a simple fall."

"I let you believe that."

"Look, we were rushed. I didn't really process what you said about the man. How could I have been so dumb?"

"Not dumb—just busy."

"Doesn't matter which. We've got to stop cooling Alex."

"Why?" she asked carefully.

"The coroner will want him. There's nothing we can do."

"We can't let them have him. That's—that's *Alex*."

Bob looked puzzled, then annoyed. "But we have to file in three—"

"We can't file at all. Don't you see? They'll take him."

"Listen, Kathryn, I'm a physician. Well, not quite, I'm not through my internship yet. But I have legal obligations."

"What about your obligations to Alex? This is his only chance."

"Look, this man you saw, it being another fall—it all points to murder."

"Of course it does," she said crossly. "I've known that since last night."

"I didn't put it together, I guess." He straightened up, gazing off into the distance. "If I had, I wouldn't have gone through with the suspension."

She felt a spark of irritation. *Men, always getting on their high horses about principles and laws, when* people *are what matters.* She made herself say calmly, "But you did the suspension. That's a felony, I believe."

"What? What felony?"

"Concealing evidence in a capital crime. Interfering with a murder investigation."

Bob's mouth formed an O in shock. "But I didn't think there was a "

"With so much to suspect? The sheriff won't buy that."

Bob scowled, muttered. His hands fidgeted. He had the classic look of a person who doesn't want to face a fact, Kathryn thought. She knew the symptoms well.

"If I just go in, tell them all of it—"

"They'll get you for conspiracy, too," Kathryn said.

"Conspiracy? To do what?"

"To hide Susan's body, and now this."

"I did that for Susan without knowing there was any murder. This time, as soon as I—as *we* understand there was a crime here, we'll come to the sheriff and—"

Kathryn smiled without humor. "And they'll get Susan and Alex and all the evidence they need for a big, delicious media crucifixion."

Bob's head slumped onto his chest, and she felt a pang of guilt at being so cruel with him. The sheriff might not go that far, but she thought it was a good bet. No matter. She wanted to scare Bob, and it was working. He was the weak one, she had always suspected that. He had every reason to be, too. He had seen close up what the medical profession had done to Susan, and Bob was at the crucial moment of his career, the time that decided whether he even had a career. He was already deeply embroiled. Anything further would destroy any of his remaining dreams. He would be lucky to end up working as a hospital orderly. Or maybe, if he was properly contrite and turned state's evidence, a dialysis technician.

"I don't see any way out," Bob said vacantly. "No way."

"So you have to dive in deeper," Kathryn said mercilessly.

"Deeper?" He still seemed dazed.

"Don't file a death certificate on Alex. No VS-9 for interment of remains either."

"That's another crime."

"Right. Failing to report a felony."

"This is—this is *awful*. If I do the right thing, I'm finished."

"Felony jail time," Kathryn said coolly.

"But if Alex is gone, they'll search for him."

"You and Alex and Gary have grand jury indictments hanging over you. So Alex simply skipped town. That's what the sheriff will believe."

"And us? Gary and me?"

"Without Alex, I think they might drop charges. He's the one they want."

He shook his head. "No, they'll keep after us."

"It's worth a risk. Their evidence against you isn't nearly as strong."

"Do you really think so?" he asked earnestly.

The note of hope in his voice wounded her. She cared very little about Bob's prospects right now. Grief drove her, not charity. Inside her burned a deep urge to hold on to something of Alex, any hope at all.

Fairy tales ended with "and so they lived happily ever after." But everybody knew that nobody lived ever after, happily or not. It was a vast, unspoken lie.

In all the times she had thought and talked about cryonics, she had never felt this massive emotional need to believe it, to grasp at anything. In the end, cryonics was about love, not death.

"Sure. Sure I think so."

4
GEORGE

Dr. Lomax stepped from the shadowed recesses near the study door. A long silence lay heavily on the still, cool air of early morning. A Victorian lamp high up along the Reverend's Wall of Respect cast a blade of pale blue light across Lomax's face, bringing out creases and folds in his pale skin, a web of lines tightened with annoyance.

George dragged himself up from the rug where he had toppled. He grunted as he rolled into a sitting position. The steady, throbbing pain in his belly was like a separate, sluggish heartbeat. He looked down and was relieved to see that the stain in his sweatsuit had not spread further. His crystal cross dangled from its golden thread, and he watched it pulse as though with its own inner life, facets winking with his ragged breath.

Holy soldier. Endure. He glanced up plaintively at the Reverend Montana. "You called him?"

"Alberto Lomax is a generous man who has had a long-standing concern for your welfare, George. He has a right to know if you are in distress." Montana's wary gaze swung between the two men.

"I came immediately." Lomax's voice was gravelly, the vowels sharp. He wore a pair of flannel slacks and an olive windbreaker. "You promised me that you were going home to think things through, George."

"What? No, I—I—" George moved unsteadily on the thick carpet, unsure of his balance, using his arms to brace himself.

"You look awful. Have you slept?"

"No, I *did* go home, I *did* what you said. It all came clear. The bleached bones of Ezekiel, God's necessary condition."

"The what?"

"Holy soldier duty. I studied on it. Read my Bible."

"Look, I only suggested things to you. That's all."

"I went to the chiller place, and I *found* their lair. I used my God-given talents. I got into their MedAlarm system, slick as you please. I traced the Cowell fellow with their own satellite locator system. I *did* it."

The Reverend's voice was leaden. "He killed Cowell."

"Damn. So soon, they'll connect it with the Hagerty woman. How?"

George was puzzled at the lack of surprise in Lomax's face. He tried to think about that, but his mind was churning like a great singing merry-go-round, the bright faces of the painted horses zooming by beneath slanting orange lights, veering toward him and then away, their shiny wooden faces grinning, always grinning. He shook off the sudden vision, tried to focus on the still silence in the study. Answer. They were waiting for an answer. "I . . . threw him off a steep drop."

Lomax's face twisted. "You repeated your method! The police will know now."

"Know?" The Reverend was still standing rigidly beside his broad desk. His red silk robe made him look like an opulent Christmas package.

"That it's the same killer, of course," Lomax snapped impatiently. He slammed his foot into an armchair and kicked it over onto its side, letting out an exasperated grunt.

"He told you about his killing? Last night?" the Reverend asked.

Lomax's thick white eyebrows lifted in slight apology. "I was going to go into that with you later. Too chancy to bring it up on the phone."

Annoyance flickered in the Reverend's face. "You only said he had broken in, killed one of your dogs, and that you had calmed him down."

"That was all you needed to know," Lomax said sternly.

"I have a right to—"

"You couldn't have done a damned thing with him. Only I can—and this." Lomax held up the silver cylinder.

A shiver of icy dread coursed through George at the sight of the cylinder. It brought the room rushing in on him again, whirling, the merry-go-round with its blaring glare and painted wooden horses, grinning with mad, empty eyes. He managed to choke out, "I don't remember—I want to know—"

"I'll say you don't remember," Lomax's rough voice was cut through with sarcasm. "No, not your strong suit, George, never has been. But no fault of your own. You lost a lot of it way back there, and if you're smart, you'll leave it lost."

"Lost? I have trouble, can't remember—"

"You've done plenty you better forget."

"Who are you to—"

Lomax waved away the words with a curt jerk of his hand. He looked at the cylinder, then put it in a pocket of his slacks. "I won't need this. You seem in reasonable control of yourself."

George felt a radiating power in Lomax. His analytical self struggled to understand. Could this feeling come from that cylinder? A chemical this man could wield like a whip? That implied that Lomax had resources George could not fathom. He felt a seething resentment of so much power in such hands—but before those emotions could rise into his tight throat, he felt another impulse. His other half. A bubble of remorse formed in his throat, pressing away all other thoughts. He burst out, "I'm sorry if what I did was wrong. I truly am."

"I think you should realize that only through following God have you avoided this until now," the Reverend said carefully. "The Lord contained your sin."

"Yes, yes, I do know."

"With a little help from your friends," Lomax said sardonically.

"Friends? The Reverend, yes, truly, but who else?"

"Me, George." Lomax's rugged voice had taken on a mild, soothing quality now. Lomax walked over to one of the deep leather chairs and sat, but his body still bristled with contained energy. The high overhead light laid bare his vexed features, the high cheekbones like blades. "I've been your friend for a long time."

"I don't remember you at all."

"Something led you to me. Recall Karen?"

"Oh my God—yes . . . she was so soft . . . beautiful. . . ." George suddenly saw Karen's breasts, felt their supple wealth.

"She said something, did something. You couldn't tell me last night. Can you now?"

"I—no . . . there was so much. So much."

"Try harder."

"I was sitting—the picture . . . she showed it to me."

"A picture? What of?"

"Something . . . flat. Cold."

"Ah, I see." Lomax's rugged voice took on a note of brisk efficiency. "We're getting somewhere. She showed you a picture of—"

"Water, flat water. Cold. Blue." The image seeped into his mind, a chilly surface that stretched away into the distance, ominous and hugely impersonal, as though it were waiting for him somehow. Then it dwindled into a smothering blackness.

"Good. I told that stupid girl not to try anything so intrusive. She got what she deserved."

"She didn't deserve me," George said with vacant despair.

The dark feelings were welling up within him now, and he had to fight to keep them from clenching his throat, forcing the breath from him. He wanted to cry, to throw himself on the mercy of these men, these judges who alone could lift the seething guilt that would give him no peace.

"Nor did I," the Reverend said bitterly.

Lomax's head jerked up, steely, threatening. "You've done damned well. Stop bellyaching."

"You're going to have to tell him," the Reverend shot back.

"So I will." Lomax flexed his fingers together and crossed his legs, considering George with assessing eyes. "I'll have to go all the way back to the accident. Remember it, George?"

"Accident?"

"Good. There are some traumas it is better that the mind erases. You had a severe accident, George, and I saved you."

"When?" George had always kept an interior image of time. It was a long scroll that slowly unwound, so that his early years were distant and slanted by perspective. Each year lay between neatly ruled lines on the scroll, so that he could judge time by the length between events. His mind rushed down this long, unfurled scroll, so scarred and littered with his life. He had often wondered if this was the way God saw time, all arranged before Him, each moment open to His inspection. George hurried through his memories, searching for some garish red mark that would be the accident, some trace of pain and anguish. But he found nothing. There were blanks that he could not see into, yawning stretches of gray nothingness, and he felt a hollow, seeping dread at what might lie there.

"The accident was shortly before your twelfth birthday. You were—" Lomax searched for the right word. He had the precise look of a man who liked accuracy, yet there was about him a coarseness, a considered, brutal directness. "You were badly hurt. Your mind has blotted out the details. That's good, really, because the accident isn't important, except that it was how I came to know you. Your parents were both dead by then, of course, and you had not been working out well with those relatives who were taking care of you then. I paid your medical bills, through charity. I helped find you a foster home, working with state agencies."

The Reverend said, "Dr. Lomax was a generous man. He took a decisive hand in your recovery."

"Were you there, too?" George asked wonderingly. His past seemed to grow and unfold before his inner eye, mysterious events added to the scroll.

"Well, no, but I know your case. I have seen the records of how Dr. Lomax helped relocate you. He thought it was best to start you over fresh, far from the place of your earlier troubles. It was he who placed you with the foster home in Arizona."

"Them. I *hated* them!"

The Reverend looked offended. "That was not his fault, George. He acted out of a spirit of Christian charity."

"Those people only wanted the money. They didn't care about me, treated me worse than that dog of theirs." George ground his teeth and then smiled without humor. "That dog. I took care of it, all right."

George caught a quick, severe glance that passed between the two men but did not understand it. The tall, slanting room was warping, the towering bookshelves threatening to topple inward on him if he gazed up at them. He had to hold on to the carpet, digging in with rigid fingers against the sickening sway.

Lomax said, "It was unfortunate that the home did not work out. Believe me, I tried. I like to remain anonymous, so I acted through intermediaries. That's why you have not seen me, George. But I was there, in the background. I found you another foster home." He sighed. "And then another."

Memories jarred George. He took a deep breath and the reeling room receded. "Them. They barely tolerated me."

"You don't do them justice. You had severe adjustment problems. They tried to deal with those and failed," Lomax said precisely, his clipped vowels clear and impatient.

"They were Godless," George said, "Godless money-lovers."

"I tried to arrange better, believe me I did. But then the Arizona authorities found out about the arrangements I had made—better than they provided, of course, much better. But not done according to their bureaucratic rules. So they took you away from the home you were in—"

"The Cranshaws."

"Ah, you remember well. Surprising, considering that you were only with them two months."

George's chest was tight, and a stiffening ache stole slowing up into it. He breathed shallowly and with concentration could stop the room from spinning with slow, remorseless gravity, the shiny merry-go-round bringing the tall bookshelves whirling with stately weight around and around. But it was important to remember, to summon up facts, dates, faces. He knew this without question but did not know why. "Then—then the Randolphs."

"The Randolphs. Nasty people. They didn't keep you for long after you killed their pet cat, did they?"

George gritted his teeth and held on. *How does he know?*

Lomax said sardonically, "After that little incident the state agency wouldn't talk to my people at all. Not a word about where they had placed you. I honestly thought you might be dead."

The Reverend said, "Only the Lord looked after you. He brought you into the fold."

"Indeed," Lomax said with a skating touch of dry sarcasm. "Only when you surfaced in that congregation in Phoenix did we pick up your trail again, nearly a decade later."

"Providence led you," Montana said, glancing sternly at Lomax. "You had been a religious boy under your true parents, may they rest well. I suggested that the Lord would shelter a soul such as yours in the goodly community of a church. I was the one who found you, when Dr. Lomax asked for my help."

"That was two years ago," George said.

"You were hard to find."

"Why didn't you come forward then?" George asked.

Lomax made a tent of his fingers and gazed into it. "I confronted new problems. I am a busy man, heading a firm that has had its own troubles. Competition in the medical sciences is intense, quite intense. I've had to keep Vitality moving. Immortality Incorporated had solved many problems that Vitality could not, and I was deeply concerned. Their program of freezing people was attracting attention."

"That was the beginning of our collaboration," the Reverend said. "The chillers. Alberto here thought that once people truly knew what the chillers were doing—"

"They'd stop it," George said woodenly.

"You are enough of a technical man to appreciate the enormity of the problem we face, George." Lomax spoke abstractly, his face distant and strangely intent beneath his lightly frosted hair. "The Immortality Incorporated fanatics have gone blundering ahead of real science, poisoning the atmosphere for the rest of us. For the real scientists who want to study the deep issues of biochemistry. They've ignored the orderly processes of research, brought ridicule on the entire field of organ preservation. I was dismayed when I learned years ago that Susan Hagerty was using university support to attack problems I had imagined they would never address. Vitality has been working on those problems for a long time, George, nearly since the time you were born. Preserving kidneys, lungs, livers. But we do not promise anyone a path to revival."

"That's the difference between heresy and science," the Reverend said firmly, using a phrase George had heard before in several sermons. "Dr. Lomax proceeds with his eyes on God's blessing, not on the prospect of false immortality."

"Yet the Hagerty woman was discovering some amazing processes. Cryoprotectant techniques that were hard to patent. Worse, some of her papers drew attention to the field. In the long run that would make for more competition."

The Reverend leaned against his desk and folded his arms. Dawn's growing glow cast a golden nimbus about his great mane of hair, and he brought forth the powerful, rolling tones of his commanding voice. "So I visited that church of yours, George. Spoke to you. Invited you to come and sit among my congregation, should you be in the vicinity. All very open and hospitable."

"You gave a wonderful sermon."

"I didn't bring up the chillers then. Too soon. I had to get a better sense of you." The Reverend spoke volubly, his expansive gestures scooping the air. "I knew you would be a soldier for the Lord, but it would take time."

Lomax said, "Time for you to work your way through your difficulties."

George nodded, feeling the room flex, spin, sway. He fingered his glinting crystal cross, hoping it would give him enlightenment to comprehend all this. "I—I had some trouble. The police."

"We know that," the Reverend said warmly. "We understand and forgive."

"Oh, thank you. *Thank* you."

Lomax said, "Your past, your transgressions, are safe with us."

"I *felt* that, some way. So when I had to leave Tucson, I came here. To you."

"And happy we were, my brother George. You came at the propitious time."

"The chillers were shouting out their claims. It was time to act." Lomax crossed his arms grimly.

George felt a brimming warmth steal over him. These were *his* people. He had found a refuge at last. They accepted him. Took him in with Christian charity, even though they knew his misdeeds, his dark sins. The dim ghosts of his parents wavered before his eyes, and he could hold back his tears no more. He gasped, sobbed, and then the room warped and spun, warped and spun, revolving about his hot mixture of sorrow and strange gladness. "Thank—thank you . , , I don't deserve fathers like you . . . I don't —"

"Oh, but you do," the Reverend said, putting a hand on George's shoulder. "You found where the Hagerty corpse is. A great victory. We can now reveal that, and the chillers will pay for their crimes."

"That'd do the job, all right," Lomax said agreeably.

"I did—I did, but—well, the woman."

"Woman?" Lomax asked.

"The Sheffield woman. She works for them. She ran into me while I was getting away."

Lomax and the Reverend froze. "She saw you? In the dark?"

"She had a flashlight. I tried to hide, but she ran right straight into me."

The Reverend's eyes widened. "He's tied to me. If she knows that—"

"Can't happen," Lomax shot back. "He was just a face in the dark."

"Good, good. But damn it, I told you from the beginning, if any of this got back to me—"

"Wait a second," Lomax said, waving off the Reverend, staring intently at George's chest. "Wait. George, did you change clothes after you saw her?"

Blinking eyes, a confused mouth awry. "No. No, I didn't."

"Then she saw you wearing the crystal cross."

George looked down and saw the cross dangling there, his pride.

The Reverend gaped. "My Lord."

"I—I'm sorry," George said plaintively. His cross was now a witness, a dagger pointed at the heart of the Marble Cathedral itself. The pain in his belly spread, sucking him into it.

"She may not have noticed," Lomax said.

"And she may recall it, nice and sharp," the Reverend spat back bitterly, "once she has a chance to think."

Lomax said nothing, chewing at his lower lip. George watched the two men, unable to tell what they might be thinking, unable to suppress the growing weakness that seeped up into his chest and squeezed it, until finally a moan escaped him and he fell on his side. Then the others were around him, pulling up his sweat shirt, exclaiming at the mess that he had become, pressing cloths on the matted pus and blood and sour fluids there. George was embarrassed, trembling, weak and fevered, and much of what they said battled through a distant roaring, like water smashing down from a great height.

"He's too hurt to tend him here," Lomax said somewhere.

The Reverend said, "I can have some of my people—no, damn it, that would link him to me, a clear tie after this crime."

"Stop worrying about your ass for a minute and—"

"If I'd known he would go loony—"

"I told you it might get rough," Lomax shot back.

"To start killing—"

"You knew what he was like."

"I know your ass is on the line, but I was just helping out, I don't deserve—"

"Shut up. Look, I can patch him up, give him some biphetimines."

The Reverend asked slowly, "Why? He needs rest."

"We'll never be in the clear on this unless he finishes the job."

"What? We can't—"

"The *girl*—that's our problem."

The Reverend said, "True. Not much time to fix it, either."

Water all around him, and he could not resist. It flowed into him and through him, and he recalled suddenly, *the black lake*—and chilly, ancient fear squeezed his chest with steel fingers. He sucked in thin air, throat working with a hoarse cry.

And then the other dream, the Lord's message. It swamped his mind. Awakening into blaring light, twisted faces staring down at him.

What it would be like to emerge as a chiller, the dead restored to once-frozen flesh. The Master's Messages had shown him that, guided him. The horror of it gripped him, and he made himself think instead of the bones, the white dancing bones.

Through blurred eyes he saw the Reverend nod, and then Lomax turned and looked down at George and said something, the words snatched away, lost and floating amid the rushing, storming waters. Lomax pressed something into his face and a short hiss came. A soft breath, like a silvery kiss.

5

KATHRYN

She awoke from drugged, clotted sleep. Sunshine seeped through the blinds of her bedroom and spilled slivers of golden promise onto the carpet. Bleary images coasted through her. For a long moment she drifted and then the crushing weight of memory returned. She rolled over and buried her head in a pillow, but it did no good.

Remembrance was insidious. She could force away the full mass of it, but snippets and fragments kept poking through, cutting and quick. Last month they had been waiting in line for a movie, and as usual nearly all the rest of the audience was teenagers. Alex had said, "Hard to breathe, with all these hormones spicing up the air."

She had said, "Yes, you're probably the only guy in this line who's past his sexual peak."

"Thanks, I hadn't thought of that yet today."

And she had laughed out loud, earning a lot of what's-this-old-fart-up-to? looks from the line.

The memory was a faint note sounding far away, like a love letter you wrote as a teenager, found in a drawer after your second divorce. Anger was red, she had learned, and despair was black. But they tainted the same sucking vortex. Reject one, and you get the other, its twin. She had oscillated between outrage and despair through the long, aching two days in which they suspended Alex. Now, after a long sleep into late afternoon, she had hoped to revive. But this world looked even more bleak. She had awakened in this bed with Alex and now never would again. He had brought smiles and moist sighs here, gasps and guffaws. Passing moments, no less sublime for their momentary passing. They would hang in her memory now, permanent exhibits in her Hall of If Only.

She tried to fall back into the fuzzy world of half sleep, but her body wasn't having any of that. Your sense of yourself followed your strumming senses, she thought irritably. It didn't just sit at home in the head that was processing those senses. The world seized you. At the moment the principal siren call of reality was pressure in her bladder. She got up, perched on the seat—and thought of how often she had blundered in here and plopped down onto chilly porcelain. Her revenge had been a loud whoop, waking the culprit, who never remembered to put the seat back down.

A tear splashed on her knee. She got up and knew she had to stay away from the bed now. Better to stir around, letting busyness fill in the moments. She pulled on stretch denims and a red cotton blouse, wryly noting that maybe the colors would keep her mood out of the basement.

She padded into the kitchen in high-top sneakers, nearly stepping on a cockroach, which scuttled under a baseboard. She poured low-fat milk over raisin bran and filed a mental note to get some insect spray, and then thought about the Technicolor South American cockroaches that had terrified her a thousand years ago. She did not fight the spiral of memory, but instead let its vortex whorl draw her into something Alex had said only a week or two before, while mulling over Susan's death.

We kept feeling ourselves as individuals, he had said, *bottled up in bodies.* But the natural world treated us as a species. Our survival depended greatly on what countless ancestors had done, only a bit on what we did. People of the distant past had died early of inheritable disorders and so had eliminated themselves from humanity's gene pool. In a sense, those ancient deaths had protected us against diseases, against the errors of errant kidneys or lungs. And what was The Lord thinking during all this?

In the cool eye of Dr. Darwin, after all, primates were no more significant than a trillionfold cockroaches. Species were myriad special cases that all looked the same seen from above. Nothing special about that old one-note song, *me me me me me.* How could there be, when there were such a multitude of species, and each one held so many individuals? The sheer masses of souls overwhelmed her imagination. An afterlife for humans—a place beyond death? Preposterous. She would love to believe it now, but the numbers alone swamped the concept.

Kathryn remembered Alex and his mad cockroach caper. A trillion cockroaches, cast into the rude world, all so that the Idea of Cockroach shall live, O Lord? What waste! Cockroaches and humans alike, the quirky specialness of us died by the zillions, felled by grand catastrophe and invisible microbe alike. Did cockroaches die so that their Idea will be made manifest somewhere down the timeline? Will the cockroaches inherit the earth as part of some Divine Plan? Or are they a side note, a minor irritant to us—us, the Crown of Creation, Inc.—so that when we barged into our kitchens, there came that quick scurrying retreat, to remind us of the Idea of Cockroach?

Kathryn sniffed, brushing away tears, not knowing how long she had been crying. She had loved Alex's quirky, loony logic. Now she found that her own mind ran in his eccentric channels. A sadly comforting legacy.

"Hey girl, you look kick-dog *down*."

Kathryn jerked her head up and saw Sheila grinning through the open kitchen window. "Uh . . ."

"Okay I drop in?"

"Sure, uh . . ."

"This time of day, I figured prob'ly wouldn't be interrupting something big, like that time?"

While Sheila walked around to the side door Kathryn had pulled herself together enough to ask, "That time?"

"I came strutting in, all bright-eyed, and the two of you looked like minks in heat."

Kathryn hoped the pang she felt did not show in her face. Sheila obliviously busied herself, saying, "I got off the early shift, feeling full of talk and empty of coffee."

"That's Brazilian, pretty good."

"Gal, you *are* down. Your voice sounds like somebody stepped on it."

"I—I've been working hard."

"For those chillers? Creepy people."

"They're different, that's all. They've got guts, too."

"Terrif, but this hiding bodies, that's creep stuff."

Kathryn opened her mouth to defend them and realized the gulf that now separated her from Sheila. Only two days ago she had been cutting up with Sheila in the stockroom of Fashion Circus, trading chiller jokes, hip and swift and tart of tongue.

"They had to. The coroner was going to—"

"I know, you told me the skinny, remember? Me, I don't want somebody dragging my body around like that. Death's bad enough without having to move all the time, too."

"I don't think Susan minds."

"Hey, who knows?"

"Next you'll tell me you want your casket lined with velvet padding."

"People snatch at anything, when they're grieving."

"Quite true," Kathryn said stiffly. *And why am I talking about this? Pleading for help?*

"Well, freezing people, it sounds like throwing a drowning swimmer a strand of barbed wire."

Kathryn took an offered cup of coffee and sipped on it eagerly. Even an artificial lift to her spirits was welcome. Sheila said, "You been sleeping all day?"

"Just a little."

"That's as believable as slippers on a fish. Girl, whatever you been doing, you need a remake just to cover the major damage."

"Things have been rough."

Sheila said shrewdly, one eyebrow arched. "Trouble with Alex?"

She suppressed a mad laugh. Her chest felt tight, and the enormity of her situation finally struck her. She had to grieve for him in silence, forever. In a few days people would notice his absence, and she would have to say nothing. She fought away tears and sipped coffee.

"Ah, it *is* him. He been stepping around on you?"

"No, look, I can't go into it right now."

"Any connection with those bucks you borrowed from me?"

"No, that was something else," Kathryn said guiltily. Sheila had given her the first installment on the insurance policy tied to her suspension agreement with I². "You were sweet about that."

"Hey, friend needs cash, I'm here."

"I'll tell you about that, too, but—"

"I know, I know—Real Soon Now."

In the hard light of day her gallant gesture to Alex, signing up in his cause, looked pathetically irrelevant. Kathryn simply didn't feel up to facing Sheila's probable reaction—eye-rolling disbelief.

Again the impulse to bray with despairing laughter. Her emotions were lurching all over the landscape. Kathryn stood up shakily. "My mother used to say, a good meal sets things right."

"Ummm." Sheila studied her. "Your mother didn't have a Nazi diet like mine."

"Come on, I've got a refrigerator full of stuff that will just go bad unless we use it."

There were some foods that held the Americana Good Vibe images, and without noticing it, Kathryn had been stocking her refrigerator with them. Against the tensions of her recent life she had shored up homey provisions. Snap beans, with their flavor of farm kitchens in the afternoon. Cornbread. Pie mixes. Somehow peeling spuds or gutting chickens didn't do it. Shucking corn did, or homemade ice cream, or patting out tortillas. They cooked and baked and ate, and Kathryn had to invent a spat with Alex, manufacture dialogue, and then sit through Sheila's cool-eyed appraisal, finishing with racy suggestions for a reconciliation. That was the worst of it, not being able to tell a good friend while pain pierced her heart.

But she got through it. She turned in a credible role and ushered Sheila out as dusk closed a murky hand over the lawn outside. The air was sharp with a desert chill, and even in twilight the nearby trees had the clarity of a good idea. Sheila sensed that Kathryn was not coming across with the whole story, though, and as she was leaving gave a snort of exasperation. "You're hiding something for sure."

"I'll tell you someday."

"You look pushed out of shape, whatever it is."

"Someday. Someday."

Sheila rolled her eyes heavenward. "Lord give me patience—and right *now*."

She could not sleep again, not so soon, though fatigue dragged at her. She found herself climbing into her car and was halfway there before she knew she was going to Immortality Incorporated. The night slipped by, rimmed in neon. She wondered at all that had happened to her in the last few months, the move here, Alex, cryonics. They were all woven together. Take away one, and the others seemed improbable.

An idea like cryonics could only flourish in a place like this. There used to be lots of nicknames for Southern California, she remembered Alex telling her. Somebody had called it Moronia. Then it was Smogville. Some press agent labeled it Double Dubuque, for its provincial natives. Forty Suburbs in Search of a City, Lotus Land, Nowhere ville, Capital of Kitsch, the LaLa Land of mindless weightlifters and suntanned bleach blondes. Angeltown. L.A. was handy and definitive. St. Louis wasn't S.L., San Diego wasn't S.D., New York wasn't N.Y. Somehow L.A. made music in the ear, easy and evocative. So did the Big Orange, though there were damned few of them left. *Maybe now we should call it Gridlock,* Kathryn thought grimly in the grip of commuter traffic, but then she was gliding down Silverado Canyon and the old severe California of brisk air and lean vistas was there again, waiting patiently behind the billboards and consumer goulash.

Once, when she was in one of her fretful moods, Alex had said to her, "Don't live *for* the moment—live *into* the moment, on your toes, eyes bright." Good advice, maybe, but she could not even consider a world without Alex in it. To face the crushing guilt and stress of her deception and go on without him was so dark and horrible an idea that she knew she would have to come upon it slowly, by not looking ahead at all. What had Alex said, back when they pulled that demented cockroach caper? "If you keep your eye on your goals, you're not keeping it on your ass."

Well, yes. Surely he would understand if she kept her mind focused on nothing beyond her next step. Her interior fantasies, so warmly confident only days before, now rang with hollow irony. "Till death do us part" was not a vow any longer; it had been a prediction.

She drove through blackness and wrestled with the spreading dark within her. At least Alex had not gone the way she had seen others go, she thought. Some of her elderly relatives lost control of wits and bowels long before they quite got the hang of dying. *We all plan on being gallant and lucky and carrying on. We call ourselves "middle-aged" when we're pushing sixty, as though we planned on living to a hundred and twenty.*

Alex didn't die that slow, humiliating way. She remembered a funeral she had attended as a teenager, and the whole litany of preparation. They gave the deceased woman a final wash and set, all part of the fixed price, yet another benefit of "the quiet trade," as some called it. At least it wasn't a cremation. While people thought of being burned to a crisp as more neat and sanitary, she knew that in the early days of that profession the morticians had added solemn organ music to the service. Atmospheric, tasteful, and it did cover the sounds of the cremation. When the head had reached the boiling point of water, the skull exploded with a loud pop. Finicky mourners found this disturbing.

She had learned the circumlocutions of death then and instantly hated them. She remembered her gathering outrage at the "she's better off now" talk from a priest. Only later could she see that the priest had made her angry to start her through her grief.

But the idea—*better off dead*—was still a profound insult to humanity, unnoticed by most only because the horror was so commonplace. Sure, death was natural. More certain than taxes, which you could cheat on. Nothing was as sure—not human causes, the world's unending crises, even the whirl and gleam of stars, which would eventually gutter out, too. In the end there was only the triumphant tick of time, sounding alike for elephants and sea turtles and the giant silent sequoias.

Brace up, girl, she thought as she passed a car with a license plate that made her blink: GOD IS. Where had she seen that? The memory would not come.

Forget it. Focus on the present. Don't let the weight of depression fall on you, she lectured herself as she swung into the Immortality Incorporated parking lot.

One car in the lot. Inside there was only Ray Constantine, standing watch, haggard. In the cool, bleached fluorescent light he told her that Alex's suspension was complete. She listened to the details of the final cooldown. Made some entries on the suspension log. Carried on a desultory conversation, words echoing behind a sheet of gray glass.

Yes, they would have to let some other I² personnel in on the secrets.

They should discuss what they should do in the long run. Their primary loyalty had been to Alex, and now they had to think long term. Yes, they would take responsibility, maybe doing jail time. Yes, they had to think about the man Kathryn had seen, what their responsibility was there. All dense, unsettling questions.

"No one'll have any chance of reviving if the company itself goes under," Ray said wearily.

Kathryn became alert. "You're—I mean, we're—that shaky?"

"We're small. The California Medical Board keeps inventin' new ways to hassle us in the courts. The media think we're a creepy joke. Sure we're vulnerable."

Ray went on, detailing how few people they could really rely on, and she was stunned to realize that the core of cryonics was really only a few dozen. Without them, I^2 would wither.

Alex had been one of the truly vital ones. His loss crippled I^2, endangered Alex's own chances of revival. There was much more at stake here than one man's life.

Kathryn said suspiciously, "You went along with me on suspending Alex because you saw that a murder would sensationalize cryonics forever, swallow it up in tabloid scandal."

Ray squinted at her, eyes wry and wise. "That was part of it."

"And the rest?"

"Somebody kills your buddy, you do your best for him."

"That simple?" she asked doubtfully.

"That simple."

"But if this gets out, never mind all the legal charges we'll face—it could kill cryonics."

"Right. And rob Alex and Susan and all the others of whatever slim chance they have."

She felt obligation descend like an inert weight. Now that light had dawned, she saw that even if Ray and Bob had other reasons to go along with suspending Alex, that didn't mean they were less reliable. They had been looking long term, while she was wrapped in her own shock and grief.

She sighed and paid attention as Ray settled some details of the suspension. Maybe men were better at separating emotion and logic; she would have to get better at that, too. Being tired didn't help. Little details threw her off. The telephones made a small popping noise, but when she picked one up, there was only a dial tone. Ray's voice droned on. She realized she was nearing the end of her inner strength.

Ray was, too. His eyelids began to droop. She summoned up a burst of caffeine energy and cajoled him into one of the dorm bunk beds. He dropped into exhausted sleep before she could gently close the sound-insulated door.

As she passed by one of the telephones, it clicked. She picked it up, but the line was dead. No dial tone. She replaced it, filing away a mental note to call the phone company.

That could come later. She was alone now with Alex. In the silence of the big bay, she knew that this was the real reason she had come tonight.

He rested in a gleaming stainless steel cylinder, one of a long row in the main bay. His was eight feet tall and mounted on wheels. If—*no, when,* she admitted to herself—the truth came out, they might well have to move him quickly, hide him with Susan in the arroyo. She laid her palm on the cool reassurance of the steel. She was certainly a cryonicist now, she thought with bitter irony. She believed—because she had to. This was the only chance, remote though it might be, that Alex would ever walk this earth again, peer into her with those oblique, knowing eyes.

She walked out onto the loading dock and switched off the lights. Time to close up, set the alarm system. The night sky leaped at her, stars behind a thin layer of haze, glowing like jewels in oil.

The whole world spun beneath the same twinkling stars. Somewhere elderly couples planted vegetable gardens, never sure they would see them yield fruit. Fighter pilots climbed into cockpits, eager for the flight that might turn to fight. Teenage athletes fell into deep slumber, muscles tired and sore from hours of practice, readying for competitions that most of them would, inevitably, lose. Thousands were falling into heady, delirious love. Legions of women strained and sweated to bring forth the fruit of good marriages, which would look at first like unpromising little monkeys. Millions more were laughing securely with friends. Young boys labored over equations in still rooms. Girls wrote poems in spiral notebooks, and some of those lines might last a thousand years. The world not only went on, it lusted to do so, leaning forward like a runner at the blocks, ready to sprint into the unknown.

But she had no choice. She had to go on, because the battle for Alex's slim chances—and Susan's, and dozens more—lay ahead. In a very real way, she was the one without hope, the one left behind.

A hand closed on her left shoulder. Another snatched her right wrist, thrust it behind her back. It forced her arm high, bending her over.

"Anybody else awake?" a hard man's voice asked.

He grabbed her left arm and wrenched it behind her back. She struggled, and he rammed her hands high behind her back. The pain cut off her breath. She could not shout.

"Never mind, I know there's not, you sassy bitch. I heard every word in here."

"Ah—ah—" she gasped.

"Wonder how? Think you chillers got all the secrets? Well, I got ways of listening in on your phones."

The man's voice was almost conversational. She knew she had heard it before. "I walked straight on in. You're so sure of yourselves, you didn't even set the burglar alarm." His laugh was like a series of grunts.

How did he know so much? He force-marched her to walk back inside the main bay. Something wrapped around her wrists. She had to shout to Ray, get him—

A greasy cloth gag covered her mouth. It tightened, thrusting between her lips, covering her clenched teeth. A grimy stench made her throat clench. She tried to shout. Only a muffled moan escaped.

Hands jerked her back a few inches and then slammed her forward. Her forehead smacked into a polished concrete wall. Splintering pain made everything reel. He spun her around.

"You turned me down for lunch once, 'member?"

Him. The man in the night.

He had come on to her at Fashion Circus, too, weeks ago. All this time he had been out there, watching, waiting. His stiff, concentrated face froze her thoughts. The eyes. They were utterly unmoving, as if he were looking straight through her at some imagined ideal.

"Real cool chick, you were."

He spun her away from the wall, forcing her wrists high, and pushed. She had to walk forward or else fall over. He levered her against the big cylinders. Her face smacked against the cool, slick surface. She could see her warped reflection in the gleaming steel beneath the high lamps.

"This is 'bout right. These valves, they got a simple default switch."

In the curved steel she saw his mirror image lick his lips. The eyes were jumpy, as though he were on drugs. "I can be cool, too, y'know," he said with a flat, threatening tone.

She felt him twist her left foot. He jammed it into a narrow space between two metal support struts. Then he wrenched her around and pinned her shoulder against the cylinder, eyeing her.

"Looks good. One more touch." He pulled a short length of rope from the pocket of his exercise suit—the same one he had been wearing that night. He looped it around her neck and lashed it to the support struts. She thrashed but could not move.

"I untie you later, maybe the chillers will get stuck with this one, too," he said, bemused. His deep voice was detached, as though he were talking to someone she could not see. "Cops'll swarm all over this place. They'll find that hideout of yours for sure." He jerked her constraints to test them. "Set free the dead. Send them to the valley."

She guessed that he was trying to make it look as if she were accidentally caught here. "I'll just disconnect this safety alarm, too," he said, pulling leads loose at the top of a large liquid nitrogen delivery dewar.

Metal scraped her left ankle. What was he planning? She worked her tongue against the greasy gag. That only moistened it, bringing a foul taste gushing down her throat. She tried to pull herself free. Standing on one foot, hands bound, she could not get the leverage to yank her left foot out.

"Firm stuck," he said, standing back with a jagged smile. "Ummm. More convincing if you dropped your equipment. Right about here." Tools and wires clattered at her feet.

She saw what was coming and thrashed against her restraints.

He swung the metal pipe connector from the top of the liquid nitrogen dewar around. Aimed it at Kathryn.

"You chillers never thought about the soldiers of the Lord, did you?"

Kathryn murmured and lunged against the rope. Her ankle shrieked with sharp pain.

With a single twist the man unscrewed the round valve at the top of the dewar. An eerie howling resounded. Gray mist shot from the end of the pipe, three feet from Kathryn's face. The banshee wail came from nitrogen vapor forced through the pipe. It took several seconds to chill down the metal, and then the liquid would flow freely. Frost formed instantly on the pipe, and a gust of intolerable cold washed over her face.

She tried to brace herself for what she knew would come, but it was no use. With a gurgling *whoosh* a full volley of liquid nitrogen shot out, fraying into droplets that burst over her, every splatter a piercing pain.

"May the Lord rest your soul," the man said solemnly. Then, his mouth twisting, "Tell my mommy and daddy that I love them."

He folded his hands before him and bowed his head.

Kathryn twisted, banging against the steel. She could not jerk her ankle free. The vapor clouded the air, cutting off her view. She tried to shout, but her lungs were full of cottony lumps. Liquid nitrogen spurted over her. Intense pain sheeted across her skin.

She got out a moan. Then she could feel nothing in her lips, her mouth, except the stinging that raged like liquid fire and shrieked into her mind, blotting out everything.

Fall. Get away from it. She let her right leg go limp. Veering, she slumped sideways.

Something thumped hard against her. The man was standing out of the vapor, pushing her into the spray with a length of pipe. At this angle the spray spattered more fully across her face and neck and chest. Her nose had turned chalk white.

She thrashed left, right, trying to shake off the pipes, to fall. To get away. Her face struck the shelving, a hard rap that rang in her skull. Her nose broke off. It flapped across her face, held by a shred of iced skin.

She wrenched her head around, trying to flee from the monstrous pain. Her nose bounced and tumbled below her eyes. The skin flap stretched. Her chest exploded with burning torment. Her nose broke away, tumbling into the nitrogen vapor clouds.

She shut her eyes. Agony shot through her, banishing thought. Her lips were rigid in the effort to scream. Frozen.

Pain was an immense gray ocean that opened to receive her. Her last thought was of Alex.

6

GEORGE

The Reverend spun around, surprised. "You!"

"Evening, Reverend."

"I thought you were to go to see Alberto when—when . . ."

George stepped into the Reverend's study with assurance. He had slipped in unobserved, the midnight shadows enfolding him like an ally. "I decided different. Those drugs he gave me, kept me under two whole days. Fixed up the wound. But they gave me ideas, too."

"Ideas?" Reverend Montana looked uneasy.

"I've finished the chiller work. Time to think about what comes next."

"You . . . got . . . her?" the Reverend said distastefully.

"Sure. I knew they'd be off guard."

"I want you to know I never thought all this would work out so— so . . ." The Reverend's voice trailed away. He collapsed into his big lounging chair, his face gray and drained.

George was getting tired of Montana's moods. "Why'd you help Dr. Lomax?"

"Because he's my brother," the Reverend said with a sigh.

"You never said you had—"

"We kept it quiet. I helped him, he helped me. Gave me the startup money on this whole cathedral operation."

"You don't seem much like him."

"I'm not, I suppose." The Reverend stared into space, as if vainly trying to look inside himself. "Alberto does many fine things, mind you. Church work. He donates to UCI, too, supported research there for many years."

"An impressive man," George said neutrally, sitting down in a deep leather chair.

The Reverend looked worried, as though casting about for some angle. "And he did save you, George. Remember that."

"I know what he's thinking now, though," George said flatly. He was seeing the Reverend in a fresh light now, as a man caught by his own limitations. Certainty flowed through George, his analytical side sure and quick. Maybe the stimulants Lomax had given him helped. They suppressed the pain of his wound, gave him a tingling, jittery energy. And they had made him cool and decisive in dealing with the Sheffield woman. Now they would have to get him through this.

"What do you mean by that?" the Reverend asked guardedly.

"The chillers, they're hurt bad. Real bad. So I've done my job."

"Indeed—but at a terrible cost."

"You told me it was my mission. Now I want to pass on to other things."

"Other—" The telephone rang, two short pulses and a long one. Obviously a coded call.

"I'm not here. Tell him."

The Reverend's eyes got large. He licked his lips and picked up the receiver. "How did it go?"

A pause. George tried to read the conflicting emotions that swept over the Reverend's knotted face. "No, no sign of him here. Maybe he's waiting for the right moment."

The Reverend swallowed hard, glanced at George. "I don't think that's right, Alberto."

George could not help but smile. The Reverend said, "No, no." His words came out flat and quick.

Certainty settled further in George, bringing bristling strength to his arms and legs, the places where powers lurked. "I'll call, of course." The Reverend hung up.

"He's got a little party waiting for me, hasn't he." It was not a question. The Reverend looked away.

"You were going to just sit here, let Lomax do what you knew he would."

"I never intended for this whole thing—"

"Skip the theory. I've done the chillers, now Lomax does me. Logical."

"He isn't really like this, you don't know him. He's shaded the law, sure, plenty of times. But this, it's not like—"

"Maybe Lomax is in further than he ever got before, further than he thought," George said, tired of the softness in this man, "but he'll follow his logic."

Reverend Montana leaded forward and buried his face in his hands. His voice was hollow, haunted. "How did I ever—"

"Skip it, I said." His analytical side had more in common with Lomax than with Reverend Montana. A clarity, a sharpness like the gleaming blade of a blue-steel knife. The soft side, the one that needed the Reverend, that part of him was only a small, hushed voice now.

A long silence. George let it do some work for him. When Reverend Montana slowly looked up, there was a wary, gray cast to his sagging mouth. "What are you going to do with . . ."

"With you?" George smiled again, enjoying this. "You're going to get me away, far away. Where your brother can't find me, and neither can anybody else."

"But I don't know how—"

"You'll tell him you never saw me. I'll just disappear."

"How can I—"

"Your sermon about the mission work in Brazil, Colombia, places like that. Lord's work—simple and good, you said."

The Reverend peered at George as if through a fog. He realized that this curiously shrunken man was seeing him true and hard for the first time, witnessing the analytical self who hid so well.

It was pointless to tell the Reverend that George had taken the precaution of hiding some data files deep in distant computer banks. The files would point at Lomax if any legal types came snooping. But the files would lie dormant, sleeping like the noble dead—unless George roused them with a simple dialup command.

Just the kind of precaution that Lomax, the smarter one, would respect. So George had left a tickler in Lomax's computer inventories, too. It would tell Lomax the dangers of trying to strike at George, even if he could find the trail.

Such clean logics eluded men like Montana. The Reverend only now saw before him the inner George, who knew how to cut through the softness of the world, how to act. All along, Montana had not understood what it truly meant to be a silent soldier of God. When swine like Cowell gave God the finger, only George could show God's fist.

A troubled fear worked itself across Montana's face. He did not like or understand the true warrior who stood before him.

George chuckled. Energy flooded through his bones.

We meet at last.

SEVEN

THE COMING HOUR

Marvel not at this: for the hour is coming in which all that are in the graves shall hear his voice, and shall come forth; they that have done good, unto the resurrection of life; and they that have done evil, unto the resurrection of damnation.

—John 5:28–29

1

SUSAN

A chilly pane of glass. Ice crystals speckled it.
She blew on a spot. Hot breath.
Blue-white crystals dissolved. A dark dot grew.
She leaned closer. Through the spreading dot she saw beyond a black wintry night, immense and frigid and forever.

Striations of pain.
Flickering warmth.
Blunt thumps. A hiss. Thin purrings.
Splinters of light that converged. Blobs, moving. Yellow. White.
Floating. Distant rubs.
Time, time. A spike of hot. Then gone.
The glows trembled, faded. Blackness again.
A warm touch. Moving across her. *Like licking,* the thought came. She rummaged for it, but even the words dissolved.
Sooooo. The whistling came from far away. A chilly wind blowing down from mountain canyons.
Soooo. Closer. A soft sigh in the winter night.
Sooo. Annn. So. And. So and so and so.
Hiss. Click.
Crisp. Sharp. She . . . felt motion? Rising? Falling?
Sooosssaaann. Sooosan. Susan.
A strumming heat. *Susaaan. Dooo yooou heaaarrr meee?*
She felt a spurt of surprise. *Susaaaan.* It was a voice, the words coming fast enough to recognize. But no background sounds, except those hisses and clicks before, now gone.
Ah, good. Do not try to talk.

What could . . . ? She had been on the sand. Salty air. Travis beside her. Waves crunching into the surf.

It seemed somehow far away. Dwindled. Like photos in an album. Winking shards of broken glass.

Some sort of accident?

I can sense that you are there.

Where? Was she trapped?

Coasting blackness. A moment of awful silence, profound and frightening.

Do not try to move. I will return muscular control later.

Had she had a stroke? A sudden bursting of cerebral hemorrhage? Thrombosis? Embolism?

Tumbling onto the sand, tongue lolling, helpless. Hemiplegia. Paralysis. Cortical sensory loss. Oh God, no, please.

Deep coma could last days, months.

Years.

I want to check a few things. Can you hear this?

She caught a whisper of sound. A tapping.

Ah, I see you can.

So she was getting some of her abilities back. What had he said about motor control?

She heard the hiss again. Then a humming. Footsteps?

Ummm. Looks good at higher levels, too.

Looks good? She was blind, paralyzed. Disoriented. Terrified. She had seen innumerable stroke patients at UCI, and in many ways they were the most forlorn of all the ill. They were heartbreakingly close to functional, brains still working, missing only sections of the intricate web that directed actions. Yet that failure encased their spirits in their own rebelling bodies. Their haunted eyes peered out from a profound prison.

A prison for which medicine had no sure key.

Now will you please try to open your eyes.

It took a conscious effort of will. How *did* she open her eyes?

The unthinking reflex now took some hard thought, as though she had to search around for it among an old drawer of a forgotten cabinet, numb fingers feeling for the odd lumps there and trying to recognize what they had once been. How had she . . . ? There was a certain flicker of movement, so natural, so obvious when you did not have to *think* about it—

A blaze of hard white light.

Too much, step it down.

The brilliant eruption faded.

Looks like she's getting images, though.

Infinite space. Small dots measured the expanses of it, black specks lined up neatly and marching away forever.

Something moved across this space, and her perspective shifted and it was a head. A human head. Blue operating mask. Blue eyes glittering with excitement. It spoke. "Susan. I am Dr. Eusivio Fernandez. I wish you to go through some exercises for me, please."

She felt a leaden depression. A cerebrovascular failure, then, and a bad one. Hands, arms, legs—no sensation. She willed her arms to move. Nothing. No distant tugs, as though muscles moved but she could not feel them. Complete shutdown. A gray jail of the body.

She fluttered her eyelids in agreement. It was the only way to answer.

"Good. She's registering, all right. Susan, if you understand, answer yes by blinking once."

She thought in despair, *Oh God.* Carefully she gave a slow blink.

"Good. Try two blinks to say no, okay?"

She blinked twice.

"Excellent. Don't worry, everything is going to be fine."

Sure, she thought bitterly. *I'm just paralyzed, is all. I hope my bedside manner is better than this. Was better.*

"Now, Susan, I am going to return sensation to your upper chest." The head turned, nodded to someone beyond her field of view. "Close your eyes and keep them closed if you feel pain."

What? Return sensation? What could— She blinked, startled at the abrupt, intense feeling of her lungs swelling, pushing, midway through expanding, her ribs rising. The elastic resistance, minute stresses, the satisfying savor of surging air. It felt wonderful. Whoosh, rest. Whoosh, rest.

And no pain. She kept her eyes resolutely open, not even blinking.

"Excellent. Remember, if at any time you feel pain, simply close your eyes. All right?" Behind his words she picked out a soft sigh and whir of machinery.

She blinked once. The man's head hung above her like an enormous moon, orbiting against the infinite white space.

Uncertainly, groping, she tried to take a deeper breath. Nothing changed. Whoosh, rest; whoosh, rest. Her lungs were running on their own.

A tremor of cold fear trickled through her. What was this? Nothing in medicine accounted for this treatment. The vast white space overhead was now clearly just an ordinary operating room ceiling, but this was no operation she knew. How did they do this, keep her lungs running, but no heart-lung machine astride her chest, slamming into her? No drug in the world could do that.

"I am restarting your neck and facial perceptual net. Again, report any pain, please."

A fierce itching across her forehead.

Pungent disinfectant smell. A prickly urge to sneeze.

Warm breeze caressing her cheek.

"That seems stabilized." The head swung above her. "It's going a bit better than I expected," he said to someone beyond her view. "How's the global?"

Another man's voice said, farther away, "Cardioculatory five point two liters per minute, steady. Left ventricle one twenty. Broncho-spirometric ratio fifty-three right, forty-eight left."

"Test those mid perifs again."

A faint woman's voice said, "Still getting some current jitter."

"How large?"

"Point one three microamp RMS."

"We can live with that. Should settle down." The head looked down at her. Brown eyes, narrowed with concentration. "I'm going to turn on your upper sensory net. Close your eyes to signal pain, please."

A pause. She studied the ceiling, unable to think.

A click somewhere.

Itching across her chest.

Rub of cloth at her waist.

A suffusing warmth down her arms, into her hands.

"Better watch the levels," the head said. "Don't want to go over the peak into saturation."

"Backing off a little," the distant woman's voice said.

"Feedback stabilization within parameters?"

"One point seven two."

"Great. Great." The head studied her intently. "Susan, it's going to take us a while to get the rest of you up and running. Your legs will take some work. But the boot-up is holding steady. Welcome back."

She blinked furiously.

"What? Sorry, it will be at least a day until we can turn over function management to you. Your throat is a little raw anyway. We'll paint it, get it smoothed out. Can't let you talk until then. And there's a long line of people who want to speak to you. Look, we're excited here, this is a tremendous success. You're going to walk this earth again, Susan, believe me."

She blinked energetically again. Someone murmured insistently.

Frown lines above the brown eyes. "Oh, hell, I never remember the protocols. Sorry. Susan Hagerty, you have been cryonically suspended following a severe injury. You are now revived. We welcome you to a new life."

Later, she would wonder how she could have been so thick-headed. Probably it was the drugs, in part. Still, it came as a complete surprise, a massive freight train thundering out of blackness.

2

GEORGE

The boy Manuel found him deep in the moist forest. The great heat of the day now ebbed, the air no longer brimming with infesting warmth, the first whispering breeze bringing a curious hush.

George was fixing the solar panel drive on the peak that people here called the Fortress, because it reared like a lone, aggressive castle, a battlework of sharp granites towering above the jungle canopy. The panels needed to track the sun to store enough energy for the new microwave dish. The receiver and transfer net filled the knobby summit, a giant ear cupped to hear a satellite far out in chilly vacuum. That such a remote, desiccated and silvery craft in the empty sky could be locked in electromagnetic embrace with this place of leafy heaviness, transfixed by sweet rot and the stink of carrion, was to George a mute miracle, to which he humbly gave his tribute and aid.

Manuel yelled at him in Spanish from a ledge below. "Mr. Confuelos says to come! Right away!"

"I'm nearly through."

"Right away! He says it is about the Reverend."

The word spun George away into a morass of colliding sensations, memories, fretwork pains. He stared off into infinity. Toward him flew a rainbird, flapping with the mild breeze off the Atlantic, a murmuring wind that lifted the weight from the stinging day. The bird's translucent shape flickered against big-bellied clouds, and George thought of memories ancient and wrinkled and yet still coming forth. Bruised shadows of a distant time, floating toward him now across the layered air.

It was not over. It would never be over.

He waved to Manuel. "Go on back. I'll come soon."

He finished wiring the feedback, letting the cool and precise part of him do the job. He had to force down the welter of confusions that wanted to take him over. He struggled to insulate the calm, unsettled center of himself so that it could work on the final circuit, test it out.

The big solar panels caught more power if they tracked the sun, so George had dug into the specs and figured a way to build a feedback mechanism. It used an old motor from a refrigerator and some breadboarded microchips salvaged from a broken-down Ford truck. He switched on the rig and watched it swing back and forth, seeking the maximum sunlight, and then lock on. To test it he held a palm fan over the panels, and the circuitry responded sluggishly, tracking around to seek the sun like an ungainly, flat flower. Slow, sure, but it worked.

Coming back down through kilometers of jungle took him through terrain that reflected his inner turmoil. Rotting logs shone with a vile, vivid emerald. Swirls of phosphorescent lichen engulfed thick-barked trees. Nothing held sway for long. Hand-size spiders scuttled like black motes across the intricate green radiance. Through the decades George had come to know this exotic vitality and how to slip through its myriad threats, spot its traps and viper seductions. He sidestepped a blood vine's barbs, wisely gave a column of lime ants their way. Rustlings escorted him through dappled shadows that he knew held a million minute violences. Carrion moths fluttered on charcoal wings in search of the fallen. Tall grass blades cut the shifting sunlight, like swords upon which jungle giants could impale themselves with a stumble.

He came into the mission church, tired from the day's work, but contented with the roll of muscle in his shoulders and gut. The straps of his pack tugged him with a reminder of another fine day's work done. He was graying now, but still had a flat belly and sinewy legs. He had seen a lot pass here, the press of overpopulation on the lush land. He disliked how the town of Santa Isabella sprawled like a tan fungus and now nearly enveloped the church camp. When he had first come the concrete-block building that became his home had stood in pastel-painted loneliness among the jungle's riot of emerald invention. Now a dirt road wound by it, puddles from the morning rain mirroring the iron cross over the entrance gate. Ramshackle houses and one-room facto-ries lay toward town, soiling the air with greasy diesel smoke. Clattering generators labored, coconut shards and crushed aluminum beer cans littered the walk, and the usual crowd of worn men waited for the church supper to start. They slouched against a stained yellow wall, scrawny and raw-boned and faces slack with fatigue. They were sour twists of men, *maraneros* from the jungle, a machete their single tool, sporting once-jaunty tattoos of wide-winged eagles and bulls and grin-ning skulls. Tough looking, but George had done in quite a few of them in the Lord's cause, stamping out the drug runners and thieves.

"George! A moment," came a stealthy voice. Señor Confuelos tugged him aside, into a side room of the cafeteria building. The gaunt, swarthy man beseeched, "I've been treating you all right, have I not? I make sure you get your injections and good work and even the nights in town, remember? I allow you those nights."

"*Sí, señor.*"

"Now you're not to tell anyone, this Reverend person, about the nights, understand?"

George's mind struggled, his analytical side rusty and resistant. "You just be sure that anybody comes by, you don't know where I am."

"He has sent us the support money for so long now, it would be a tragedy, George, if you communicated to him—by surprise, I wish you had warned me!—if he learned, well, things not to the liking of a high-minded man like him." This came out in a whispered rush as Mr. Confuelos mopped George's brow with a kitchen towel.

"I'll keep quiet." George was sharpening himself inside, but he still felt amusement at this man's anxieties. He frowned and said, deadpan, "He won't like Angelina?"

"No, *no,* do not mention her."

The sweetness of her seemed to swarm up into his nostrils then, blotting out the disinfectant smell from the cracked linoleum. He could see his thrice-weekly walk down to the Salon Maria, a pastel-pink clapboard box three stories tall, where Angelina was always waiting. She was younger than he but not by much and was short and sturdy in the durable manner of the coastal women. Her electric black hair tumbled like roiling smoke about her shoulders, spilling onto her full breasts in the wan candlelight. After a tough day he would lift her onto him, setting her astride his muscular arch. The hair wreathed them both, making a humid space that was theirs only, musk-rich and silent. She bounced and stroked and coaxed from him the tensions of time and later would fetch him dark rum laced with lime. Her eyes widened with comic rapt amazement as he told her about his work, always the work, her deep womanly eyes reflecting the orange serenity of the languid candle flame.

"Now, the Reverend, he is not to know that some of his tithing, it goes for that."

"That?"

"The Salon Maria."

"I never knew it did," George said with feigned innocence.

Genuine shock spread across the vexed face of Mr. Confuelos. "I could not take *Church* funds for it."

"*Sí, sí.* But aren't you just taking it from the Reverend's Church, instead?"

"You must not think so!"

He tired of toying with Confuelos. "Let me see my messages."

"You said I was to call you if—"

"I didn't say to read my mail."

George pushed past him, by a plywood door into the main kitchen. Past steel counters, old microwave ovens, and women in greasy aprons wearing beatific expressions. He strode into the mission office and slammed the door in Mr. Confuelos's face.

The gray computer screen held a WOrldNet news item, letters shimmering. George's program had fished it out of the torrent of news, and it confirmed the worst of his fears: The Hagerty woman had made it through.

His requests for a search/scan on the Reverend Montana had turned up news items buried in the Orange County *Register,* recent but routine. Confuelos had gone snooping, seen them, and spooked.

He sat a long time at the fly-specked Formica table, staring at the remains of Confuelos's lunch, a chipped blue plate with rice and beans and a gnawed crescent of green tortilla. George felt the old swirl of emotions, unleashed as though they had lain in waiting all this time. Incoherent, disconnected images propelled him down musty corridors of self. Words formed on his lips but evaporated before spoken.

"Glory. Glory be to God," George got out finally. His destiny and mission were once again sharp and sure.

He banged open the office door and strode out onto the bare stone patio. The town lay beyond, a crowded shambles. Decades of work, and the problems just got worse.

Work. That had been the best of it, a life dedicated to these mud-brown people steeped in eternal confusions. He had loved roaming around the province in the old Chevy truck, fixing water pumps for the cooperatives that dotted the steep mountainsides. But he had known his time here was drawing to a close. He had even helped it happen. He had helped install the fiber-optic link that brought WOrldNet into the village. "Making all the world WON," the propaganda said. He looked up at the cobwebs bridging the transom of a speckled window. Webs everywhere now. He had used his phone hacker knowledge to keep up on computer stuff, getting free access to the international electronic fabric. That let him keep track of events in California, keep watch like a lonely, distant sentinel.

But that same net would find him now.

A Godly sign, yes. The Hagerty woman. WOrldNet closing in on him.

Here he had a routine of solid work and healthy living. It kept him in what Mr. Confuelos called a native state of grace. He had a reputation as a fix-it man without parallel, willing to undertake any job, in fact liking the tough tasks best, the ones that gave him a workout with meaty arms and legs, that brought a shine of honest sweat.

That contentment was over. His larger, ancient legacy called.

3

SUSAN

They kept her in a milky fluid that seemed to insinuate itself into her skin like a cloudy memory. With her head propped up above the thick, cool liquid, she lay in her drowsy, slow-motion world. The fluid vibrated sometimes, tingled others. For a while she thought they had rolled her outside, for there were green hills in the distance. A river nearby had pebbles and boulders, dry and white in the slanting sun, and the water was leaping and swift near her but blue and deep further along. A wind murmured, stirring a cottonwood nearby. That blew white motes into the moist air, and some drifted down to the river and the spray claimed them.

She slept and then watched the river with its fresh smells and slept again. Only after that did she see that the walls of the room came awake when she did. The next time they were a sea scene, big booming waves crashing on a black reef, plumes jetting into the crystalline, salty air, foam hissing onto a gritty beach.

Dr. Fernandez was there several of these times, and she knew somehow who he was but paid him no attention—until abruptly he leaped into focus. She registered him sharp and clear, like a television picture that balloons into life. He was in the middle of an explanation of the milky fluid's healing properties. Fernandez was precise and deliberate, already describing some neuron repair mechanism, but the chemistry of it eluded Susan, and she watched the big waves beyond Fernandez some more. Afterward she remembered that the milky stuff duplicated many of the body's own cleansing mechanisms, only better. How she had learned this she could not recall. She watched the beach, waiting for nightfall, and as soon as the ruby sunset trickled away, she fell asleep.

Then she came in on the middle of Fernandez talking again. She was sitting up in a soft bed that massaged her with patient skill. A man in a blue scrub suit was rubbing a mottled, stiff jelly into the back of her neck and upper spine, squeezing it from a giant orange toothpaste tube. Fernandez talked straight through this, and it was all very interesting, but she could never remember what he had been saying for very long.

"When do I get these back?" She held up a hand, which had pink flesh where her fingernails should be.

"Frappo, I told staff to paint those." Annoyance momentarily roiled Fernandez's calm surface.

"What happened to my originals?"

"The primitive perfusion technique didn't get to them. Uh, sorry, I didn't mean to derogate your achievements, Dr. Hagerty. I'll have a nurse paint on some triot later."

"Triot?"

"Oh, a salve that makes the underlying cells express the appropriate repair mechanisms."

Just like that, she thought fuzzily. Dab on miracle goo, goose the body's innate fix-up squads. Let Mother Nature do the grunt work. She was trying to imagine how it worked, and the immense changes Dr. Fernandez's casual comment implied, when she dozed off.

She awoke again into a dark room, and the walls and ceiling gradually eased into a night sky, its horizon rimmed in stately spires that after a while she saw were trees. Then she was awake again and Fernandez was talking, but this time she could follow it very well and he introduced a Dr. Blyer. This was a short man with intense brown eyes who kept glancing down at a square pad on his knee. When she turned her head, she saw a thin cable leading from the pad and around, out of her field of view. She turned further and felt a tug at the base of her spine. They explained that the cable was socketed into her so they could check on some diagnostics, and when she asked what kind, the description quickly got away from her, and by the time she started registering things again, Blyer and Fernandez were discussing the spinal membrane, the meninges, as though she had asked an intelligent question about it.

"But do go on with your story," Dr. Blyer said, falsely casual.

"Story?"

"You were telling us your life story," Fernandez prompted.

She was in a large square room packed with odd equipment. A canned hospital astringency flavored the air, and the walls had a peculiar shine to them. How she had gotten here did not seem terribly important beneath the glossy, calming glow of the fluorescents.

"Oh . . . yes. After finishing at Harvard and Mass Gen I did a turn at Rockefeller. By accident I got interested in the problem of cryoprecipitates in long-term preservation of blood samples. The high factor eight content seemed to me to imply a three-step process, taking place at four degrees centigrade, that you could intervene with. I worked out the steps and then saw that perhaps I could extend the range of operation down, to below freezing, where intervention would be harder and slower, but could affect other reaction rates, too."

Fernandez nodded. "Your early ideas, yes. That led to the trans-glycerols?"

"Well, I didn't get into those effects until I—until I—met—"

"You can skip over that," Dr. Blyer said gently.

"I met—where?—met—where is—?" Her lungs lurched, breath rasping in her throat.

"We'll come back to that later," Blyer said smoothly. He looked down at the pad on his knee. With two fingers he tapped on the pad, as though he were entering something on a keyboard.

Susan felt a subtle change in herself. Now her breath came smoothly, her mind cleared. Something had bothered her just a moment before. What was it? An idea, a memory, like a massive fish in the gloomy shallows of her mind, slippery. Darting. Gone.

The vexing thoughts dwindled. She gazed at the wall screens and felt a soothing quiet descend into her mind.

Dr. Blyer leaned forward and held her gaze. "I hope none of this procedure disturbs you, Dr. Hagerty. Of course no such methods existed in your era, but I assure you they are no more intrusive than absolute necessity demands. They leave no detectable trauma."

"I don't quite understand what you're doing."

Dr. Blyer put his pad aside and leaned forward earnestly, clasping both hands together. Both men wore standard white lab coats, which Susan found reassuring amid all the curious elements of her room. Half the equipment surrounding her was completely unfamiliar. "This work is exploratory, really. Research with laboratory animals came before, of course, extensive tests, but humans have so many complex higher functions, such marvelous overlapping nets in the cerebral cortex, that we must proceed with a set of checks, of safeguards."

"Against what?" she asked.

"Against psychological strains that precipitate physiological ones."

Dr. Fernandez put in, "Remember the old divisions of computer functions of your time? Software, that is programs, ran on hardware. Well, that applies to our minds in a crude way. We are trying to see if you have sustained any hardware damage that has software implications."

"I'm afraid you've lost me."

"See, that phrase, 'you've lost me.' It's actually a rather involved metaphor for confusion," Dr. Blyer said. "That's a talent for replacing one kind of thought with another. So we say that time runs out like a fluid, or logic is like a path you can get left behind on. Your language centers fetched up that metaphor right away. I'm glad to see you doing it, because that implies that you have suffered no significant loss in several different areas of the brain."

Susan sighed. "I seem to go asleep at the switch a lot, though."

Dr. Blyer smiled. "Another metaphor. Dr. Hagerty, minds are simply what brains do. The principal activities of brains are making changes in themselves. That's what memories are, of course—they change the way we later think. But to revive you completely, we have to be sure your brain is truly reintegrating your memories."

"I thought you were checking to see how much I can remember."

Dr. Blyer nodded. "But the *effect* of that is to make your mind sort out problem areas. Let me put it in computer lingo. See, the *you* who is listening to me say these words is like a software program."

"I'm software?" She hoped she ran better than the word processor in her office. She could never get the spell-checker to work right.

Blyer shrugged good-naturedly. "It's an analogy. When that software program needs to recall something, it hands off to a memory program, something like a tiny librarian. The librarian goes and fetches the information. The mind maintains that sense of *you,* that self-awareness that we've pulled up out of the liquid nitrogen after thirty-eight years, and—"

"What? Thirty-eight?"

Dr. Blyer blinked. "Well, yes. I thought Dr. Fernandez took you through the protocols."

"I did," Fernandez said. "But it might not have registered. She was still reintegrating."

Blyer was startled and irritated. "She's still having gaps?"

"Apparently."

Gaps. While Blyer shot quick, technical questions at Fernandez, Susan thought about the gap of thirty-eight lost years, friends gone, the press of incessant change while she slept. She felt as though an abyss had opened in her tenuous reality.

Rather than struggle with it, something made her simply watch Blyer get it under control and go back to his bedside manner, his mouth losing its irked twist. He was good. "I see. Dr. Hagerty, I must apologize. You may be experiencing disconnections in your awareness, in your memories. Please bear with us."

Susan smiled. *As if I had any choice. I can't go back, can I?*

Blyer said, "All our memories are processes that make the various agencies inside our minds act in much the same ways that they did at some time in the past. In your case, that past is—"

"It's been thirty-eight years? That's all? I thought cryonics would take a century, maybe more, to get this far, to revive people."

"Perhaps it would have, but for your research. And of course, your case."

"My case?"

"You are a famous woman, Dr. Hagerty. But we don't want to rush ahead into that."

"But what's happened? I need—"

"We're helping you to understand that," Dr. Blyer said soothingly.

She recognized the bland, reassuring manner and resented it. But she could do nothing about it, she soon learned. Blyer and Fernandez adroitly eluded her questions. She was slipping into a soothing fatigue. The two men slipped away from her questions. Usually she had found it fairly easy to tug information out of men by supplying a receptive audience. Physicians particularly liked to go into their lecture mode. Something to do with the kind of people who went into medicine in the first place, she thought vaguely. That fact hadn't changed in thirty-eight years.

But she felt an ominous foreboding. Something was wrong, somewhere at the shadowy edges of her mind.

4

GEORGE

The creamy Buick Riviera George rented at LAX was his first surprise. Small, electric, it buzzed easily through the surprisingly thin traffic easily, its motor sounding like a hornet. He went down the 405 to the Garden Grove Freeway without a single jam or even a slowdown. Off on Euclid, just like the old days. The route had more trees than George remembered. There were no hookers on Harbor Boulevard, no illegals loitering sullenly around the 7-11s.

He pulled over near the Marble Cathedral grounds. At first he thought he had taken a wrong turn because a large yellow sign said THOMSON DAY CARE. Most of the grounds were filled with new buildings. Bright yellow seesaws, slides, and jungle gyms dominated what had once been expansive lawns.

But the majesty of the marble slabs was as powerful as ever, rising straight from the ground like soaring spirits. Buttresses and arches suggested the slumbering strength of the faith within. The stained-glass windows still shone with their immense biblical scenes, alive with jewel-like refractions, though the inner lights seemed dimmer, casting little of their radiance through the early evening gloom and into the surrounding oaks.

No one on the grounds. Usually there would be a fellowship meeting or choir or something going on every night of the week. The outer buildings and the Reverend's residence seemed unchanged, though in need of a paint job. He slipped through the shadows that had always been his ally. The lock on the side door was new, but he picked it and went through. No chain lock this time, either. The hushed, sprawling rooms smelled musty in the pressing darkness.

Down the carpeted corridor. A spill of light from the Reverend's study, the massive door slightly ajar. No voices from inside. George stepped in, and the Reverend was sitting at his desk, talking on the telephone. Reverend Montana's eyes widened.

"Hang up."

The Reverend froze.

George strode quickly forward, snatched the telephone away, and slammed it down.

"You . . . My God . . ." The Reverend sank back in his chair.

"I know about the Hagerty woman."

"I thought it was over. So long . . ."

The Reverend stood suddenly and came around the desk. He walked with a hunched-over gait, head down, his plain brown suit flapping about him. George caught him by the shoulder and spun him into a worn leather chair. Touching him made George realize how much good the decades of solid work had done him. His traveling suit, bought on the way to the airport, fit a bit snugly over his broad back and tightly clasped his thighs. Montana was shrunken and thin beneath his clothes.

"I came a long way, I expect some hospitality."

Montana went ashen. His mouth gaped, twisted, closed. "All—all right."

"Anybody else in the building?"

"I don't believe so."

"Sister Angel?"

The Reverend overcame his alarm and replied automatically. "Oh, her. She was not the woman I thought, my friend. Not at all."

"I remember you being real close," George said deadpan.

"Oh yes. So long ago." Montana's eyes narrowed with remembered pain. Then he snapped back into a stern, officious pose. The seasoned performer. "That moment when you discovered us, it was an aberration for me. A thing of the moment. For her, I later learned, it was but one in a long series. Very long."

The shadowed stillness of the large study held the same rich scent of leather and polished wood, though. George sucked it in, letting the memories come in like old friends, while the Reverend recovered, blinking. The soft warm glow of the brass fixture cast long shadows upward into the bookshelves that stretched to the black skylight. A passing car cast a sheen of blues and yellows among the leather-bound volumes there as headlights passed across the stained-glass rear windows.

"Why have you changed the cathedral?" George asked conversationally, to give Montana time to recover.

"What? Oh, we had to bring in the Thomson Day Care people to help out a little."

"Help out?"

"Well, attendance has been down a little lately."

That helped explain the tired air of this man. Montana seemed to gather himself, though, and asked cautiously, "You know what's been going on?"

"I have watched from a distance. I have waited."

"Waited? For what?"

"For some new soldier to take up our battle."

The Reverend spread his hands helplessly. "The scientists, they've changed everything. What could I, one man, do?"

"Fight them, as before."

"My friend, that was long ago, and—"

"The dead shall remain in the valley of bones until the trump of doom."

Montana started to get up. "Well, I know, but—"

George stepped forward and shoved him back into the chair. "Our work is not done."

The face that peered up at him seemed to shoot forward through shrouded years, lighting up its passage with vibrant memories. The firm chin had weakened, the handsome mane had thinned. From the robust jaw a flap of skin now dangled, stealing strength from the face. Compared to the squat peasants George worked among, this man was pallid, his eyes watery.

George said, "I kept my skills. I saved my money in case I was called again. But you *didn't call.*"

Montana cowered, his papery skin drained of vitality.

"Then this WOrldNet came in."

Montana said hollowly, "I saw something about it. 'How the World Was WON' was the title. WOrldNet, WON. I—"

"In my village they're already giving away WON identification tags.

Coded with retinal patterns and fingerprints. Things I can't fake. Things there are records of here, with the foster homes people."

"A health thing, isn't it? Everybody gets a number, buried in your skin. So you can carry your vaccination records yourself."

"And plenty more. A global ID network, fingerprints, the works."

"A blessing, truly so," the Reverend said automatically.

George spat back, "*Think,* Reverend. I'm a gringo, hard to be inconspicuous. If anybody comes looking, WOrldNet will tag me for sure."

"But why would they . . ." Montana's whispery voice trailed away as he studied George's face.

"You and Lomax, you're clear. But if the chillers remember, they'll know my face. And they are an abomination on this earth."

"I think it's unlikely, after all this time—"

"An abomination!" George shouted. He jerked the Reverend out of the chair and lifted him up, making the man dance on his toes. "We have work. My life's task is not finished."

5

SUSAN

First thing the next morning, she asked for a newspaper.

But the specialist nurse brought her a funny leather-bound thing that opened like a book and only had two pages in it. She asked the nurse what this was, but he was already gone. She remembered thinking once that it was too bad every intern could not be given a short bout of a major illness, just so they would know what it was like, being treated as just another problem in someone else's schedule, a disposable difficulty.

At least he had shown her how to control her walls. She tuned it for soft winds sighing through pine trees, with scents to match. They had left nibble food, crunchy stuff like fried oatmeal.

Okay, time to face the future. The book's spine was a fat cylinder labeled *Los Angeles Times.* She opened it, and the page, which felt like thick paper of high rag content, leaped into life. DROUGHT WORSENS, GOVERNOR STEPS IN. Beneath the banner in blue was *May 11, 2033, 13:46.* As she watched it winked to 13:47.

She thought about decades unfurling as she held stiff, unchanging, in immense cold. Her first thoughts while recovering had been of peering out through a windowpane webbed with blue-white ice crystals. She had blown on it. A spot warmed and spread. She had peered outward through a black night. A night of thirty-eight years.

Something beckoned, something immense and sorrowful. Tears ran down and off the tip of her nose before she noticed them. She was awash in a sea of feeling, but somehow the images and meanings behind the curtain of forlorn ache would not resolve, would not come to her inner bidding. She had lost some memories, but the terrible weight of it was that she did not even know what memories were lost. She felt gray clouds descend in her mind, blank walls of nothingness. Crystals, ice-hard. But no way to blow upon them, to warm them into opening.

A tear splashed onto the thick paper, and she brushed it away, embarrassed, afraid she would mark the paper. But the page did not absorb the tear. Moisture beaded on it, a millimeter above the crisp black type of DODGERS SKUNKED IN DOUBLE-HEADER. She could see the letters refracted through the water. The type was buried in the page, the way an image hangs behind a TV screen.

As she turned the sheet she saw the type of page one wink out. Pages two and three lay beyond, but when she flipped the "paper" back, page four appeared where Page 1 had been. She guessed that somehow the newspaper was in fact in the tubular spine of the book and projected onto the page.

The center two pages held further mysteries. "BEVERLY B" RACES FOR BIRTHING BONANZA seemed to describe a woman who was trying to beat the world record for childbearing. GAME SHOW "STRETCHES LIMITS," SNYDER DECLARES. The lingo of TRIPLE-DIP RULED BINARY NONCONFORMING proved that lawyers were still carrying out their guerrilla war against the English language.

MOON SHUTTLE DELAYED Hydrogen Leak Termed "Minor" seemed clear, but OCEANSIDE BANS EATERIE WARPOS "Find 'em and 'Fess 'em," Says Chief seemed to be about "warpos" who wore offensive clothing. It seemed that if the wearers sat down in a restaurant, they left behind the waste materials that their clothes—"snug-rugs"—had excreted, after digesting the sloughed-off skin, dandruff, and other unsavory elements of "human dander." The story implied that some snug-ruggers were letting their living coveralls digest other unmentionable aspects of human physiology. "Walking, stinking biocycles," the outraged mayor charged.

There was an advertisement for "Grab-Grass Home Security Aid"— a lawn that apparently rolled up to trap intruders. Crime was up—as always. Nasty racial incidents. High unemployment. IMMIGRATION CRISIS WORSENS. By the time she had worked her way through to MEDITERRANEAN SEA "DEAD" SAYS FAYEED and FEDS INVOKE "UNCLE SUCKER" RULE Economic

Downturn "Unfixable" on page four, she had learned how to call up sidebar text on background stories. It would overlay the other stories until she tapped a button on the book's lower spine. The overlays helped explain the snug-ruggers, but not the "bioverts," which the newspaper apparently thought everybody knew about.

A big picture of a sleek jetliner landing on page four moved when by chance her hand passed across it. Smoke plumes puffed behind the wheels as the plane landed, and she learned that it had returned from orbit. The action sequence was in three dimensions and ended with a "movid" star coming down the passenger stairs, looking more green than the grass in the background.

When she turned back to the first page, it flickered and then gave her further pages in the *Times*. The book had only two projection-sheet pages in it. Touch commands could take the reader through the entire paper at varying speeds. She popped open the thick spine and saw a small crystalline rod held by clamps, with the date fluorescing along it. Probably tomorrow the intern would insert a different rod and throw this one away—or recycle it. The book remained the same.

She managed to get it back to page one by tapping a corner of the buffed leather jacket, but she could not figure out how to find an index or table of contents. There might be a piece about her, if she was famous. She fell asleep looking for it.

The next morning was brilliant, all walls giving a real-time view across the Grand Canyon. A hawk wheeled lazily on the thermals, and it was a while before Susan noticed that she was no longer in the reassuring clasp of the milky fluid. Instead she lay on a kind of sculpted water bed. A nurse brought her breakfast, which stayed warm in its plastic case even when she became distracted by the Grand Canyon view. Her true hunger was to be outdoors. *What an arrogant word,* she thought. *Outdoors.* As though all of nature fell into the category of being leftovers, beyond our dwellings.

Breakfast was crisp and tasty and unrecognizable. A digital panel on its side said it was "ocean product fajitas." Seaweed, she guessed. But it had the heft and swagger of steak.

A nurse appeared, collected breakfast, and did not look surprised when Susan wanted to go to the john on her own. The nurse was a big man with enough brawn to scoop her up if she needed that, and to Susan's delight she did not. Her muscles held without trembling, joints worked without a pop. She was so proud of herself that she took a stroll around her room. Most of the medical equipment she could figure out, with some help from the nurse, but the biggest surprise was the carpet. She had dropped a fragment of ocean product fajitas on it, and now the carpet rippled, moving the bits along toward a slight depression under her bed. *Like the cilia in lungs,* she thought, stooping to see the slight dip absorb the garbage.

"Oh sure, saves a cube of work," the nurse said, still hovering to catch her. "Sweeps up just fine. There's one of them new hungry rugs down the way, eats what it can."

Susan gingerly maneuvered back into bed, more tired from her trip than she wanted to let on. "What happens if I toss this bed dress on the floor?"

"It'll try to move the dress awhile and give up. Too big."

"It's alive?"

"Yeah. Smart grass, I call it." The nurse showed her how the carpet cilia hung on to her shoes to stop her from slipping.

"How about cockroaches?"

"Ummm, the favorite dish around here. Only now that the rug's been gobbling them up, we don't see anymore."

She thought awhile about a rug eating the fur off a dog while it slept, or making a banquet out of socks that weren't picked up right away, and wondered how a biological engineer designed against such malfunctions. She thumbed through her wall screen image inventory, asked for a lawn scene, and was startled to see a bed of poinsettias that were gold and magenta. What looked like an olive tree flaunted not the small black fruit but pendulous scarlet things like flagrant eggplant.

She was slowly putting together a picture of how different this world was. The nineteenth century had been dominated by the science of chemistry, the twentieth by the many products of physics—airplanes, atomic bombs, rockets, computers. This twenty first century, barely a third over, was clearly the era of biology. As a physician, she was plainly out of work.

She fell asleep and dreamed of the eggplant-olives.

But a vagrant silhouette flitted through her troubled visions, a wisp of dark memory she could not catch.

6

GEORGE

Dr. Lomax was haggard and grizzled. His deep tan had turned upon him, and now his skin looked like old boot leather.

"All these years I figured you for dead," Lomax said without preamble. His voice was still gravelly in the soft silences of the Reverend's study.

George smiled. The idea of something stopping him, killing him, before he completed his mission, was so absurd. "I took a little rest."

"And my brother knew all along." Lomax's lips pinched thin and white in controlled anger. Barely controlled, George judged.

The Reverend started to say something, but George overrode him with, "He's a good man. He covered for me."

Lomax glared at Montana. "I kept worrying you'd turn up, blow the whole thing. And all the time, *he* knew."

Best not to tell Lomax that his brother had even sent the mission occasional money for George. Not that he had needed it; there were ways of earning something extra and serving the Lord, too. George had killed people in the cocaine trade, both for the cash and to strike a blow for righteousness. No one had ever suspected the quiet gringo missionary worker.

George stood in the exact center of the room, facing Lomax, who was the key to this. "Wouldn't have done you any good if you knew where I was. I got friends there, fine people. Fly down there, come snooping after me, I'd know before you got dust on your shoes."

"Why would I pursue you?" Lomax asked with convincing candor. George had to admire how the man gave no hint of what he had surely planned—to kill George. It had made no sense not to.

"Maybe to spray me with that little cylinder of yours."

Lomax grimaced and sipped at a glass of wine. The Reverend had tried to put a veneer of politeness on this meeting, even setting out little dishes of macadamia nuts. George spent the night here, resting up for the trials to come. The place needed a paint job, but it had prompted him, in the way that smells and photographs conjure up long-dead moments, to remember how Lomax had controlled him.

"That was necessary," Lomax said curtly.

"I was on *your* side, remember?"

"You had also done some unwise things."

"Things you damned well wanted done."

Lomax got up, his legs lacking the springy quickness George remembered, and began to pace. His face bunched with fitful energies, his cheeks were lined, and crows'-feet fanned from his eyes. He sported a pencil-thin black moustache that flexed as his mouth worked. "True. Still, I had to be careful. You were experiencing dissociative disorders."

"What's that?" George hated jargon and people who used it like a crutch.

"Memories of traumatic experiences get locked away," Lomax lectured, "particularly severe childhood events. In the most extreme form, these memories are available only to one of the several personalities that the person sustains. Memories are rewritten, distorted, misunderstood."

George gritted his teeth but kept the rage inside. This kind of quackery infuriated him. "Yeah?"

Lomax was startled by something in George's face. "I didn't mean anything by that, really. I—I expect you were just under strain."

This last part did not ring right. Lomax edged uneasily away from George. He was hiding something. Despite George's self-control, remembered anxieties played like bright striations in him. He closed his eyes and saw blue-white lightning dancing on zig-zag legs against a bleak horizon, the landscape of a fretful mind.

"Don't try anything like that cylinder business again."

"Fair enough," Lomax said briskly.

"What was that stuff you sprayed me with?"

"They were a very sophisticated set of neurotransmitter inhibitors. Quite specialized, a Vitality Incorporated product, and very expensive. But I can see you do not need any of the consolations of chemistry now, George."

"No other tricks, either." Lomax had seemed relieved to rattle off some technical detail, so that wasn't what he was concealing.

"The serpent turns," the Reverend said obscurely, settling behind his desk. He leaned back in the big leather chair, which squeaked, and put his feet up on the bare mahogany. The surface was marred and had circles of water stains here and there.

"I have the information you wanted," Lomax said, moving on with executive crispness. "Once I give it to you, I never want to see or hear of you again."

"I make no promises."

"Well then, I don't—"

"I got enough to sink you if I want. Stop stalling."

"What? What evidence?" Lomax's eyes were like slits.

"I think you know."

This was mostly bluff. George had a lot of threads but not a whole piece of cloth. Certainly Lomax had some interest in the chillers, probably some research angle. Setting the police to sniffing around would be bad for Lomax. Something in Lomax's jittery pacing had made George take the risk.

It worked. Lomax glanced at the Reverend, chewed his lip, and visibly made up his mind. "I used my contacts, got the information. The company that holds the three chillers—to use the old word—has revived one. Hagerty."

"She's fully conscious?"

"My source says she is."

Resurrection outside God's plan. Vagrant impulses whipsawed him. The news media had not divulged any details of who was being revived. To hear Lomax say it flat out—

A pounding in his ears made the study seem to vibrate. The stained-glass windows seethed with broken radiance. *Dissociative disorders.* He gasped, as if rooms were popping open in the worn estate of his inner self. When he looked up at Lomax, he saw muscles bunching in Lomax's lined jaw. He felt his analytical self shudder. To his rising fright he saw that the muscles were not causing it at all. A lump seemed to crawl beneath Dr. Lomax's skin, down from the weathered cheek and along the hinge of the jaw. The jutting mouth worked with its own energy; Lomax was saying something, but George could not hear. The tight ball crept along the jawbone, a knot as thick as a thumb, picking up speed, slithering now with crablike clenchings as if small legs drove it forward. It slid off the jawbone and down into the neck, merging with the loose wattles there, easing into the soft flaps of fat. As this eerie slug worked its way across Lomax, the man himself kept talking soundlessly, and then there was a wet, strangled gurgling in George's ears and the room snapped back into solid focus again. Lomax's voice returned, sandpaper rough, and George understood that it had all been some kind of delusion, a mirage.

Or a sign. A sign from God that would take time to fathom. He sucked in the deep scent of aged cedar and oak paneling and tried to make sense of what Lomax was saying.

"—can't get solid information because the whole damned thing is under max security. I'm retired and that makes it harder. Never thought I'd have to tend to *this*. But I've got my contacts going, used some of my friends. It looks like the Hagerty woman is doing okay. She was the easiest, so they tried her first of the three. Her personality framework is intact. They're getting so they can try revivals from that era of early transglycerol technology. She's the initial case from then, after the experimental animals worked. We can—"

"Three?" George whispered.

"Huh?" Lomax stopped his pacing and glanced at George irritably. "Oh, I forget. Kathryn Sheffield was frozen, too."

Cold, seeping revulsion. "Her? How?"

"Constantine. He hid her, too. Then managed the whole thing just right. You didn't hear about it?"

George had lain low for years, wanting to forget the chillers. His work there had been done, well and true. "I was out of touch."

Lomax flicked a sour glance at Montana, who was somberly staring into space. "The mystery angle tickled the media's nose just right. Swamped our Reverend here."

Montana's eyes narrowed. "I did as I promised."

"You lost the media battle. A sharp, businesslike campaign could have—"

"I do not *hire* my followers." Montana's eyes flashed with the energies George remembered. "I build them, from troubled souls."

"I should never have relied on you to harass the I² operation," Lomax said bitterly.

"You had to," the Reverend countered swiftly. "Who else could? Your lawyers?"

"You let him"—Lomax jabbed a finger at George, voice going scratchy and strained—"got out of hand. That girl, Karen—I told you not to use her to calm him down. That kind of therapy—"

"She worked for *you*, remember? I thought she knew what she was doing."

"I trusted you to work with him, keep tabs. Instead, he got on my trail, broke into the estate, damned near found—"

"Oh yes," Montana said sarcastically, "that heavily protected fortress. George went right through it."

George realized they were oblivious to him, two aging men bickering over ancient aggravations. Lomax spat back at Montana, "And *I* took care of it!"

"I've brought in some of the best clients, don't forget—"

"Shut *up!*" George shouted.

Both men blinked, startled.

"You two are here to do what *I* say now. Got it?"

Montana nodded, his face becoming sober and reflective again. George had liked the momentary glimpse of the fire-eating Reverend he remembered. Now the weathered man of the present returned. "My older brother here can be exasperating at times. For all our differences, we have always helped each other."

"Admirable," George said, meaning it. He had never thought about Montana's family, somehow. The Marble Cathedral had been family to them all. "But you couldn't stop the chillers? After all I did?"

Lomax said, "We worked together to clean up the messes you left, George. The police were already working on the girl's murder, that Karen. They were after you. If they made any connection between that and the Immortality Incorporated cases—"

"They couldn't," George said vehemently.

"They tried to find you for years, picked over my congregation something terrible." There was a sad, worn note in Montana's deeply modulated voice. It would still hold an audience in thrall, George judged, but there was a slackening of once prodigious energies. "Hurt attendance."

Lomax nodded. "But we got by. And with Sheffield gone, we were safe. I figured Immortality couldn't hush up anything, so all the bodies would be warmed up for autopsy. I *never* figured that Ray Constantine guy would go public, make it into this big 'mystery.'" Lomax stopped and threw up his hands in disgust, sarcasm lacing his gravel voice. "So the media got it and that stimulated the whole field—I^2 and Vitality and a half-dozen other firms."

"A circus," Montana chuckled bitterly. "And after all, George just gave the chiller people what they wanted—freezing."

"And your method, covering the Hagerty woman's death so it looked like an accident, that was smart." Lomax eyed George. "Odd how that fit in with *her* aim—to get frozen without an autopsy." He stopped pacing and studied George pointedly. "Funny, huh?"

What was Lomax hinting? George felt welling confusions warring within him, could not find words to give them voice. "Funny? I figured out how to be a serious killer, and then those chiller people, they messed everything up. Now we got to fix them for good."

He slammed a fist onto Montana's desk. Both men jumped, and George saw that they feared him. They tried to keep a calm face, but these were two weak, time-worn men.

The Reverend said softly, "If these chillers remember you, you think this WOrldNet will find you."

Lomax nodded sourly. "No place to hide in the world anymore. And the chillers have erased all that about the statute of limitations. The Supreme Court already ruled on that last year. Resurrected witnesses can testify. Crimes don't have a time limit."

"A God-sent moment," George said forcefully. "I'm going to do it *right* this time. God abhors these walking dead."

Their cowed faces told George that he could get the help he needed.

To unravel the loom of chance and circumstance. To again be of steely resolve, forged in the flames of rectitude.

"You got me that job?" he asked Lomax.

"It cost me plenty, but—yes."

"Then let's get going."

Lomax slapped at his armchair, an old man's gesture of irritation. The leather was ruddy with wear, the arms gone thin and ripped. "I've done enough. You—"

"You're going to train me," George said.

He studied the two men. Obviously they had bought for themselves all the antiaging medical advances George had read about. Still, they seemed a lot older than he was. They should carry a weight of years and authority, but it was all hollow now. They would do nothing—*had* done nothing—about the chillers.

Lomax nodded bitterly. "We can begin tomorrow."

George shook his head. "The chillers are coming out. We start *now*."

7

SUSAN

When she awoke the walls were treating her to a light summer rain, seen across shimmering rice paddies. Farmers stooped over their patient work in the foggy distance. Amid them sat a man talking to Dr. Fernandez. The walls were so good, it took Susan a while to realize that the men were not in the landscape.

"I want to introduce Captain Stern," Fernandez said cordially when he was quite sure that Susan was awake. "He has remained on your case, even though he retired from the Orange County Sheriff's Department."

Stern matched his name. His angular features seemed to stretch his parchment skin over sharp bones. Bright eyes moved with birdlike quickness. He seemed excited, a man who had not let the years get the best of him. "I'm honored to meet you."

Susan listened to Stern begin reciting the history of her "case" and felt the tilt of unreality. She still had trouble getting her mind around a vast shift in perspectives. Despite this man's intent gaze, she could not help but laugh. "Let me get this straight. You're talking with me, the victim, about a murder case you've spent thirty-eight years on? Without solving it?"

Stern looked sheepish.

Susan said, "How is it murder, if I'm now alive?"

Stern shrugged. "Well, some definitions are going to have to change. I leave that to the lawyers."

Dr. Fernandez said, "This is too hard for attorneys. You'll need a licensed semanticist."

Susan had spent long hours approaching up to this moment in her mind, but she still did not wish to face it. "I suppose I should be grateful for your efforts," she said.

"I got interested, and then, well, after all that happened . . ." He looked down at his hands, then back up, his mouth twisted into a thin, beseeching curve. "I still don't know what happened back there."

"It has been a long time. Isn't there a statute of limitations?"

"Not on murder. Although maybe this isn't murder anymore."

Fernandez said jovially, "In this case, it is a pleasure as a physician to hand your profession a new problem."

Stern had to smile. "Thanks. But what I really want is, well, to know who, uh—assaulted you."

She found the truth oddly embarrassing. "I don't know."

Stern blinked. "Why? Did he hit you from behind?"

"I don't know that, either. The last memory I have is of going down to the beach for a run with my dog."

Stern's mouth worked soundlessly. Susan could see the shock sink into him. Fernandez had explained how Stern had dogged the case, kept it in the back of his mind for decades. It had eaten at him, and now she had dashed his last hopes.

"Nothing? Nothing . . . at all?"

"Sorry, no. I've tried."

"I'm afraid this is not really so surprising," Dr. Fernandez said precisely. "And not only among cryonics revivals, of which we have done quite a few. Even ordinary trauma often obliterates memory. The mind does not have time to process an event into long-term memory storage before, uh—it is unable to do so."

"Before the victim dies," Stern said absently.

"It could perhaps have been recalled when she was first revived," Fernandez went on pedantically. "But then the reviving mind was bombarded with so many fresh things, the layers of perception and thought restarting and sorting themselves out. It must have been like strangers trying to find each other in a fog. We have no research about this phase, but I am not surprised—"

"The dog," Stern cut in. "You had your dog with you."

"Yes, definitely."

"We traced it later. The Animal Services people pulled it out of a dumpster. They IDed it from a chip implanted in the skin."

"A subdermal, yes. I had that put into Travis. It carried his full medical records, vaccinations, American Kennel registry, my name—"

"Animal Control ran a data reader over the body. The same procedure we use today on people, now that everybody has a chip embedded. So eventually Animal Control got around to sending a postcard to your address. That's how we linked it with a serial killer operating up in Santa Ana. He killed two women and disposed of them. Same dumpster."

Susan felt a strange, stabbing mix of anger, fear, oblique hope. To her Travis was a bundle of romping enthusiasm she had seen only a few days ago. Then she had awakened in this distant place, and here was a detective describing a serial killer nearly forty years before. And Travis was dust. She shook her head, as if that would clear the blur. But the yawning gray vacancy, the simple disbelief that her familiar era had been utterly blown away by the winds of change—that would stay with her a long time. "Look, I'm having trouble following this."

"I was the investigator on your case. At first I thought you had simply fallen off the cliff near Crystal Cove. Your cryonics friends were leaning on me all the way. I went along with them, they froze you down. But then other evidence turned up. I—I changed my mind."

Susan gave him a piercing glance. "You wanted to autopsy me."

"Well, yes." Stern chewed at his lower lip.

And whoever thought he would have to sit here and explain to me? She waited in silence, not trusting herself to speak.

"But we couldn't. Your friends hid your body."

So that was it. Fernandez had not told her this part. She felt her surprise show in her face, though she struggled to suppress it. "Ray, Alex . . . I owe them a lot."

"You knew they had a facility for that?"

"I helped build it." She gazed off over the rice paddies veiled in silvery rain. The *plip-plop* of droplets sounded real, immediate, and she tasted fresh-turned earth on the mild breeze. "I never thought . . . I would use it."

Stern related what had happened, and she tried to see the bizarre events in her mind's eye. It was like being in a play, scenes moving on while you were offstage. Alex's death, the same way she had gone. Then Kathryn. Each brought a stab of pain, of loss, of building catastrophe.

"Why didn't they see a pattern?" Susan burst out.

"Why didn't you?" Stern asked quietly.

"What? I told you, I can't remember—"

"The man who attacked you outside Immortality Incorporated?"

"What about him? He—"

A ricochet of cold fear cut through layers of memory. The shadowy bulk. A stiff, rapt face, eerily impersonal. Blank eyes. Had she seen it more than once? On the beach? "I remember that. Was it connected? Was *that* him?"

Stern shook his head with frustration. "I don't know. That attack on you—it was just a couple of sentences in a sheriff's report."

"It's been so long," Susan said distantly. But it didn't *feel* that way. Time was a telescope, collapsing perspectives.

"Right. Plenty of deltas since then."

"Deltas?"

"Big changes. Otherwise, I wouldn't be talking to you."

"And why *are* you? The deaths—I mean, suspensions—happened so long ago. The killer must be dead."

"Not necessarily."

"You couldn't even prevent him from killing Kathryn?" She had been appalled when she heard of that.

Stern scowled. "I couldn't see the pattern because I didn't know Alex was dead. There was no obvious link to the Santa Ana cases."

"What a horrible death she faced! How was she suspended?"

"Raymond Constantine was asleep in the facility. He heard something, found her. He called Skinner, the intern, and they suspended her."

"Skinner, of course." So many people, crowding into this strange world and time. "But with a sudden freezing, no perfusate, the damage would be worse."

Stern shrugged. "So Constantine told me. But they had no choice—just like with Cowell. Suspend her or lose her completely."

"They did the right thing," Susan said so emphatically that both Stern and Fernandez looked a bit startled. Of course; they lived in this time, where the ideas of cryonics were commonplace. She was like a zealot arguing that airplanes could *too* fly, in 1950.

"After a while Mr. Constantine and Mr. Skinner came to me and laid it all out. Immortality Incorporated couldn't keep three people hidden back in that little canyon forever. So they negotiated with the district attorney's office. We agreed not to thaw out the bodies for autopsy, even though we knew there was a serial murderer at work."

"In return for what?" Susan said cautiously.

"For testifying, giving us every lead they could."

"Why couldn't you catch him?"

Stern looked down at his hands again. "Nothing added up. He never hit again. No subsequent murder fit his pattern."

"Could he have changed it?"

"We don't think so. Serial killers don't, usually. But Kathryn Sheffield's—well, that was funny. Not like the others. Risky—but it worked."

"Perhaps he was desperate."

"Maybe so. She was alone, maybe she surprised him when he was snooping around."

"You do not seem to have turned up very much in thirty-eight years," Susan said gently. The fact made its own point.

"He disappeared. Very atypical for serial killers."

"This interview, before I see anyone else—that was part of your deal with I², wasn't it?"

Stern looked surprised. "You're a quick lady. Yeah, I got that written in, all right. Just on the wild chance we might be able to use it someday."

Susan smiled wanly. She knew a thing or two about obsession. "That *you* might."

"Well, yes." Stern seemed respectful, shy, almost reverential, despite the fact that he was considerably older than she was now. Or rather, older in true age. While her birth certificate said she was eighty-two, the mirror in the bathroom showed her a face in its forties.

"I'm not the only one who wants a solution to this case. It's famous."

"Now, that can't be true. I saw nothing in the newspaper about it."

A quick glance between Fernandez and Stern told her much. "Ah," she said. "That's why I couldn't find an index in the *Times.*"

"I felt it would be traumatic," Fernandez said with a touch of professional stiffness she recognized. Physicians automatically hid personal decisions behind a facade of specialist authority. "You have no idea how this entire matter has been blown up by the media and distorted. I hoped to shield you from that for a while."

"I understand. But I have to know everything if I am to help you."

Stern nodded vigorously. "I'm hoping that as you recover, you may remember more. I can go over all the evidence with you, see if anything booms down."

"Booms . . . ?"

"Becomes clear. We can do that over the next few days, while we're waiting for the others."

"Others?"

Stern covered his surprise, but still shot a glance at Fernandez. "Cowell. Then Sheffield, if Dr. Fernandez thinks it's okay to go ahead. This new set of techniques he's worked out really is a miracle."

Susan was not prepared for this. She pursed her lips, feeling circumstances accelerating with wrenching thrust. So much to learn—

"I believe this is enough for now," Dr. Fernandez said kindly. "Susan, you should rest."

"Wait—they'll come back? Soon?"

Stern spread his hands. "This is the most famous unsolved case in the world. The public has been waiting decades to see if we can nail this guy. Here's our first chance. Do you have any idea what kind of pressure that creates?"

"I see."

Stern smiled mirthlessly. She saw how all this had chipped away at him, hounding a conscientious man through his entire career. Two women in Santa Ana. Three victims at Immortality Incorporated. A distant sympathy swelled in her. "And all your leads have been cold for a long time," she said.

Stern's eyebrows registered ironic pleasure. "Yes, doctor."

"I don't really feel tired at all, Dr. Fernandez," she said, getting more strength in her voice than she felt. "Not at all."

"Still, I do think that—"

"What comes after Captain Stern? I've satisfied my obligation, haven't I? Don't *I* get to direct my own affairs now?"

Fernandez said reluctantly, "Well, there is . . ."

"What?"

"Another visitor."

"Who?"

When they led in the old man, she at first did not recognize him. Then the quizzical turn of mouth, the sharp nose and glinting eyes gave her enough clues. *But he's so old!* she thought, but did not say. Gray hair, mostly gone, scrawny arms that had once bulged with muscle, brown spots on hands and across a lined forehead.

"Ray," she said. "Ray Constantine."

He said something, but it was swallowed in a sudden sob that burst from him. He had lasted out these years, tending to the suspended patients. A long labor with no promise of success. For her, too, the image of a once-familiar face warped, became watery, and slid in diffuse light as the tears came.

8

GEORGE

Lomax got him safely through the security people with their veiled eyes and funny-shaped weapons. This was a big facility, crisply run, but Lomax's authority still counted for something. He had the right metallic identity-plates, IDs, the works. But then Lomax hung back.

"Come on," George said, striding across the broad lawn beside the creamy buildings. He felt the air zing with energy, promise.

"This is enough." Lomax turned back toward the gate.

There was nobody nearby. George grabbed his arm and twisted it roughly. "I need you to show me around some, straighten it out with the staff."

Lomax's face went gray with pain and fear. "I don't—"

"March." They went across the grass and along a utility road. There was a ragged band of people carrying signs beyond a chain-link fence. ZOMBIES HAVE NO RIGHTS, one said in violent red. $ FOR THE LIVING! They wore their hair sculpted into wings and were well dressed in tight pants and breechcoats. Respectable people, George thought, protesting this madness. He should be with them. Only he knew that just marching around like that got you nowhere. Only true soldiers could stop this. Just like thirty-eight years ago. He had left the battle then, and just look what had happened.

"Look, I got you in with one of my people, McAndrews. He'll do right by you and keep quiet." Lomax smiled, clearly hoping this would get him off the hook.

"There'll be things I won't pick up on. You're going to pay a visit to the processing center, the operating rooms, that stuff. Draw me a map."

"But if I'm too closely identified with you—"

George had his hand around Lomax's elbow and he gave it a savage wrench. "You're in, like it or not."

Fretwork colors played in the corners of his vision, but he kept up a quick pace, bristling with energy. This corrupt place was smooth and clean, but it reeked of sin. There were plenty of troubles in this world of runaway biology. Folks not knowing what the hell was natural and what was literally a God-damned abomination. Creations of atheists swarmed everywhere. New plants. Even "better" animals. A putrid hell on earth.

"What's the name of this company?" George demanded.

"Didn't you read the paperwork?" Lomax was panting with the effort of keeping up. "It's a big medical conglomerate."

"Not Vitality Incorporated anymore?"

Lomax looked startled, frightened by something new. "Well, we have several partner firms."

"Chillers. All of them, chillers," George muttered, bile seething in his mouth.

"Look, there's been a complicated reorganization—"

"Never mind. You get me the plans, the equipment manuals."

"Okay, okay." Lomax held up a placating hand. "Only don't let anybody see you with them. Janitors aren't supposed to have any of that technical—"

George grinned. "Yeah, janitors are dumb. Nobody pays them any attention. And they go everywhere."

9

SUSAN

She had a strange moment upon awakening. A sound bubbled up into her lazy half-sleep, a wet, strangled gasp. She thought it was a last ragged remnant of a dream. She opened her eyes in the twilight her room assumed when it sensed that she was asleep. Awakening eased the lights slightly higher, following some therapeutic routine. In the dawn-like glow she saw a hospital orderly leaning over her.

"Ummm . . . what?" she asked.

The man's breath rasped, but she could not read his expression, since he wore the surgical mask all attendants did near her. Above the whiteness his eyes danced, jerking from her to the equipment that surrounded her bed, then back to her again.

"What is it?"

The attendant blinked rapidly and raised his hands. They hovered in the air, indecisive. She could see his gloves trembling. The eyes swerved, taking in the machinery around her, veering back to her face, then darting away again.

She was vaguely exasperated, still woozy from sleep, and no doubt assisted by a sophisticated mix of pharmaceuticals.

"What's going on?"

The man's breathing was unnaturally loud. Sharp intakes, followed by a harsh, irregular panting.

She felt a faint alarm. He was wearing the standard coverall, and his hair was cut close to the skull, showing plenty of gray among the brown. And now his eyes were rapt, fixed, as if he listened to some interior voice.

She sat halfway up and opened her mouth to say something severe.

Abruptly the man moved away, backing into a bank of monitoring equipment. He bumped heavily into the panel of subdued green lights, hands still held up before him, his posture rigid.

"Ah!" The collision startled him out of his trancelike fixation. He jerked away from the monitor. His hands came down. For three heartbeats he stood looking at Susan.

Then he swiveled and marched away, legs moving in a curiously sticklike, choppy stride. He reached the other end of her room and without looking back slipped through the positive-pressure door.

Susan lay back. What *had* that been? A fresh orderly, somehow unnerved by a real, live patient? Her years of instructing interns had taught her that medical people were just as moody and unpredictable as anyone. She put the matter out of her mind and settled snugly into her incredibly comfortable bed. The room seemed to sense her mood, easing the lights down. She dozed off within a few moments.

10

ALEX

When he woke up he was dead.

No pressure on his skin. Deep silence. A terrible, blank blackness.

No scents. Not even the bland, moist taste of his own mouth. His nerves were like an open circuit, bringing in nothing.

His mind spun alone in vacancy. What was this place? What had happened to him?

He had been working in the arroyo, yes. Started back toward I² . . .

Running in the darkness. Scraping his knee. Cold stars, so far away. Struggling up a slope of gritty sandstone.

Then a long silent drifting time, and out of that seeped a voice. A woman's, dry and monotonous. ". . . blood decomp going flat . . . neuroelectric fluctuation . . . point two seven milliamp . . . getting plateau . . . registering malfs in channels three and sixteen . . . bypassing . . ."

Other voices then, men and women, hollow musics coming down from an unseen sky. He remembered floating in a warm sea, caressed by tropical currents, tasting salt, wondering why he could not see the sun on such a day.

But there had been no day, only the vast voices.

He focused on the memories. There had been a background rustle of steps, instruments clicking, electronic hums, the purr of cooling fans.

Someone had talked to him. A man this time, with a slight, melodious Spanish accent: "You're all right. Don't worry, you're out of danger. We'll need a little time to work here. We just wanted to know if your sensations were okay. They're registering fine. Try to sleep."

Gradually it came back to him. He had not slept. Instead he had clung to consciousness, though the warm sea he floated in dulled him with gentle insistence. Gradually, the voices lapped around him, and he understood. He was in an operating room. They were pulling him back together after some accident.

But that had been long ago. He had finally slept. Now he was awake, but there was no lukewarm, nuzzling bath. No buoyant sense of weight-lessness. Nothing.

He felt a rush of cold fear. Loss of senses. That meant severing of the major nerves where they wound up through the spine.

But then why had he felt and heard before? Why was all that gone?

True, he could not remember actually moving then. Maybe they had him floating in a fluid to support his spine? He knew of no such surgical procedure.

Slowly, vague memories seeped through the haze in his mind. He had been hurt. A blurry constellation of pains lay back there, associated with a cool night, with running, with the rasp and bite of falling on sandstone.

Confusion rose in him. He pushed it away. He didn't know what had happened, but remembrances coiled through his mind like tendrils of fog. He felt something ominous, bruised clouds scudding in from a far horizon.

The only explanation that made sense was that he was experiencing some new procedure. Maybe some drug had dulled his senses. Maybe the smart thing was to just lie here and wait for it to pass. Or for sleep.

No. Something was wrong. He *knew* it.

A voice. He had half-heard it, not long ago. Murmuring, low. It had filled him with a prickly sense of dread.

But he could not attach any name or face to the dimly heard voice— only a blank terror that had dragged him up from sleep.

He concentrated, stilled his own mind, tried to sense beneath the scramble of thoughts.

And felt something. A weak, regular thump. His heart?

Behind that, like a background rustle, came a slow, rhythmic flut-tering. Breathing. His basic functions, plodding on.

He strained for more, but that was all. The human body wore its nerves like clothes, all for the surface. Internal senses were thinly spread, giving only blunt sensations. He caught a dim pressure that might be his bladder.

He tried to move his head. Nothing.

Open an eye? The same blank blackness.

He fought against a bitter, growing despair. Maybe he had some motor control, even if he couldn't feel? He didn't know enough about the neuromuscular system to even guess if that was possible. None of this made much sense to him, but he knew that the only way to hang on to himself was to *do* something, not just lie here like a numb doormat.

He willed his legs to move. If he had sensed the sweet ache of his bladder, maybe a moving leg would bring a pressure somewhere, a signal.

Nothing. That meant his lower motor control was shut off.

Something told him that control was *shut* off, not destroyed. The huge voices from before had talked about him as a system, a wiring diagram, not as a helpless victim. He did not know why, but he felt himself as a labyrinth of connected parts, an intricate web. Some zones of him were not reporting in. This way of thinking was odd and yet somehow automatic, seeming to arise from his body itself. The idea came as a jittery forking in him, soft summer lightning.

He was afraid, of course, but it was a strangely cool fear. No adrenaline surge came automatically, no answering chemical symphony of the body.

He had to try everything. Eyebrows? He urged them upward, but felt nothing.

Mouth? Smile, kid. Not even a slight flicker.

Talk? Maybe somebody would come. He made himself go through the steps. Constrict the throat. Force air out. Move tongue and lips.

No faint hum echoing in his sinus cavities to tell him that muscles worked, that breath stirred his vocal cords.

Despair gathered in him like a weight.

Arms. Left, first. No answering shift of inner pressures. Right? Again, no response—but wait.

A smattering of tight pain. Welcome pain.

He had gone through life with instant feedback from every fiber, anchoring him in his body. Every gesture suggested the next, an ongoing song. Now he had to analyze precisely: How *did* he raise his arm? Some muscles contracted to pull one side of the arm, lever at the shoulder. Others relaxed to let the arm follow.

Pull. His arm could be sticking straight up in the air, and he wouldn't know it.

He tried again and again. Did he feel a reply? Faint, so faint. Maybe his imagination.

Was he a candle glow of a mind, trapped inside failed machinery? Despairing, he lost his concentration.

And felt a thump. His arm had smacked into something.

A table? Certainly not a warm bath.

So his right arm worked, even though his senses were nearly gone. The nerves were there, they took orders. They just weren't reporting back very well.

He felt a slow tingling on his right side. The movement must have reawakened some nerves, kindled them.

He wondered what could have happened to him. Turned the question over, inspected it, and then set that aside. *I think, therefore I am.* At the moment that was just about all he knew. That, and how to move his right arm.

Okay, use that. He willed the arm up again. Careful, slow. Maybe his hand worked, too. Remembering how to do it, he lowered the arm, rotating it.

A meaty thump. Harder than the last one. The arm had fallen. Balance was going to be hard.

He practiced rotating the arm without raising it. A slight feel of sliding, as if on slick steel. Some moves felt right, familiar. He worked without feedback, trying to summon up the exact moves that turned his right hand. Sliding the arm. There, an edge. Faint, remote impressions. The lip of a table. He dipped his hand. Over the lip. Working the fingers. Senses were coming back now, dull and thick. He had an image of the Pillsbury Doughboy, with fingers fat and spongy, hard to work with.

What now? If he was in tact some kind of basket case, he might hurt himself this way. But something remote and foreboding said *no,* go on. Fog-tendrils of dread drifted through him, and he knew he could not give up.

He worked his fingers, feeling distant details. Stubby protrusions. Switches? It was like trying to read Braille with sausage fingers. He managed to get the plump index finger to jab at the switches.

Nothing happened. He fumbled, sensing a regular array of jutting buttons.

Abruptly a woman's voice sliced through the background noise. "Anybody in the bay? Julie? Hello in there? Hell, she probably left to help O'Hara."

Her tones were slightly flat and tinny. Alex realized he was hearing something piped in, probably from some kind of control room. He was apparently lying in the "bay" listening to a high-quality intercom.

A man's voice answered, also with the narrow tonal range. "Patient looks okay on the visual monitors. Just lying there, no motor functions."

The woman said, "I've got him on electrosuppressants and—hey, somebody's been fiddling with the settings. Bet it was that Julie. Always thinks she has a special empathy with the patient."

"She wouldn't fool with the neurofunction board," the man said.

"Well, somebody has."

The man's voice carried a clipped anxiety. "O'Hara says they need us on team three, pronto. I sure as hell wish we didn't stack patients like this."

"Want to keep costs down, we can't just sit around holding their hands and singing lullabyes through the whole warmup." The woman sounded bored, as though this were a standard conversation.

"This final tune-up stage, he's out of danger. Fernandez popped him up into consciousness, and everything looked okay." The man seemed harried. "Look, let's let him run on auto."

"Ummm. Think so? O'Hara gets nasty if we don't come running right away."

"Yeah, he's a wart. I vote we just let the last of those blood scavengers work, clean out the patient a little more. Can't hurt. When we come back, we'll polish up the neurological systems."

The woman answered with something technical, but Alex's attention riveted on a third voice, rising from the background as though it had just come into the room. A strong voice that struck alarm into him like a knife. "You got some used ultracleans in here to go?"

"Huh?" the woman asked, distracted. "Oh, yeah, that bag there."

"Bioactive?"

"Yes yes, the yellow bin."

Instantly Alex knew he had heard that voice before—as he swam up from unconsciousness. The man had been muttering to himself, reading labels or something. The memory came back clearly. The same flat tone of the intercom. So the man had been in the control room before. Not talking directly to anyone, just reading out loud.

That voice had conjured something deep within him, a terrifying buried memory, deep and unquestionable.

The people were still talking. The others—could they help him? Only that one voice threatened him. Alex did not know whether to make a sign, try to communicate. Just as the thought spun through his mind, he heard sounds of papers shuffling, a door banging—then silence.

Not quite. Over the intercom came a thump, a scraping of a chair leg, a low grunt. Someone was left in the control room. And somehow he knew which voice it was.

He had to get away. He willed his right hand to action again.

He grasped something round. A knob? He envisioned his wrist turning, and that helped make the movement. The knob rotated. He felt a new sensation, far away. The knob went no further.

No sounds from the intercom. What would the man in the control room do if he found out Alex was awake?

Alex desperately punched at the buttons. A tremor ran up his right calf. Spiking pain. Cold.

His leg was in spasm. He felt it jerk in a sudden rush of sharp agony. It was flopping on a hard slab. Flailing, like a crazed animal.

He could not stop it. *At least I can feel something.* But what was happening? What could turn him on and off? Something shadowy skittered at the edge of memory. Somehow all this made sense, but he could not stop to let blurry notions come into focus. He stabbed at the buttons again.

A welling coldness in his belly. He poked his fingers again.

More bitter cold, this time in his right foot. Again. Again.

A tracery of itching on his lips. Moving to his cheeks. Then all over his face, as if a dozen feathers tickled him. He longed to scratch it.

Without thinking he brought his right arm back toward his face, then stopped. Okay, he could stand the itching. First he had better get as much of himself back as he could.

He tried more buttons. There, a clear sense of the rise and fall of his chest. He felt only the right side. Breathing, fast and shallow. Fear.

He fumbled and punched, fumbled and punched. Patches of his skin seemed to leap into being, flooding him with sensation. But still no vision, no sounds.

He spent a moment getting his leg to stop flopping around on the slab. The spasms eased into a steady trembling.

He made himself stop and think. The enormity of what he had now guessed would not bear inspection, so he pushed it aside and focused on a smaller problem.

There were no sounds over the intercom, but that meant little. His body lay here helpless. He could only rely on himself. So he had reached some switches that could turn on his neural networks as though they were parts of an electrical diagram. And of course that was exactly what they were, though he had never really thought of them that way, of himself as a huge wiring board.

Okay, accept that. He was fumbling with his right hand for switches that controlled his right side. It was a good bet then that the left side switches were on the left side of the table.

Think it through. What would happen if his right hand poked the button that turned off the hand itself? He would lie here helplessly. Waiting for . . .

Again, the foreboding dread. He did not know where he was. *Or when,* he thought, explicitly acknowledging for the first time his suspicion.

But even facing that huge possibility did not dispel his shadowy apprehension. *Back to work.* He had to get his left side going somehow, before he ran any more risks with his right.

He brought his right arm back to the slab. His motor control had to extend into his upper chest and shoulder to let him do that, but without any feeling from there he did not know how much he could make work.

Still nothing from his left side at all. Meanwhile his right side nagged him with tremors and fugitive itches. He felt jumpy and disoriented and for a moment almost wished he were dead again, feeling nothing.

He willed the right arm to reach over to his left. Fingers crawled over smooth metal and found a lip. They scampered down further, and there were buttons, two knobs, the same layout as on the right side. He started punching buttons. Pain leaped into his left side, each province shouting at him. Slabs of muscle shook violently, sending agony rippling up from his left leg and into his belly.

His breathing lurched. He concentrated on methodically marching his fingers over the buttons, punching each. More pain.

Then light poured in on him. Dazzling brilliance.

He had hit whatever controlled his optical nerve net. A gaudy red universe. He realized his eyes were still closed. He willed them open. Bleached white flooded in. Colors strobed. Pulsed. Steadied. He was staring at a mass of equipment. Digital readouts, oscilloscopes, chassis faces in duraplastic and buffed aluminum.

He got the crisp smell with the next button. Then more sounds: a thin mechanical clanking, distant buzzes. No voices.

He was lying on a white slab. When he had finished with all the left-hand side buttons, he rolled himself back over, pushing with his left arm. It was a lot easier and his balance seemed to be okay. The stings and aches were ebbing, too, probably some transient effect. He got his right side up and running pretty quickly. Then he just lay on his back, staring up into white fluorescents, and gave himself over to an orgy of scratching. The itches faded. He began to feel halfway decent.

But anxiety skated through him. His heart thumped, driven by unknown fears.

He felt a persistent itch at the back of his neck and reached for it. His hand went the other way.

He stopped his hand over his face. Something was wrong. He moved his fingers. His arm was coming from above his head, reaching down . . . but that was impossible. He brought up the other hand, the left. It came into his vision the same way, from above.

Something was very wrong with him. He closed his eyes to think. Nothing came. Immense questions ricocheted everywhere.

He opened his eyes and rolled over onto his right side. There was a blank yellow wall with a tan door in it. The door was upside down, reaching to a white tiled ceiling.

The whole world was upside down. That was it.

He remembered reading somewhere that when your eye took in light and cast it on the retina, ordinary optics inverted the image. But you didn't see things upside-down because the brain set the image right side up again.

He looked at a sign at the foot of the door and managed to read its inverted letters. It said VI² STEPCOM.

Something was wrong, some step in the process all screwed up. It had the feel of somebody getting a detail backward.

When he tried to sit up, a wave of awful dizziness hit him. His stomach reeled. Bile rushed into his mouth.

He lay back down. His senses were telling him that he was on the ceiling of a room. Gingerly Alex felt around the base of his skull. There was a lump there. It bulged out about an inch, as wide as his neck. A cable came out of the crown. It led into the table itself.

He wasn't going anywhere with this thing attached. It must be the lead-in, the avenue into his entire nervous system.

But his skating anxiety would not let him just lie there. His breath came fast and shallow and his whole body wanted to move. He lifted his head, feeling the cable tug at him, and tried to study the upside-down room. After a minute of nausea he began to sort out details. The EXIT door, a lot of equipment he could not fathom, some work tables littered with instruments, and another door on an opposite wall.

He sat up further to see the whole room, and *pop!*—the cable came out of his neck. Instantly a hot, diffuse throbbing spread up into his skull. It felt like a massive toothache as big as his hand.

So he was free, by accident. A simple pressure release connector. Did that imply he was nearly ready to get up and move on his own? Well, so he would.

He sat up very carefully. Braced himself. Swung his legs over the side of the slab. Every move had to be calculated, because his eyes showed him his lap reversed. He was naked. Thin, pale, almost scrawny.

There was a work cart pulled up near his slab. He reached out to it for support, preparing to step down. His hand missed, swiping at air. His brain was directing his arm, always correcting in the wrong direction.

It took four tries before he could override his own reflexes. He got a good grip on the cart and lowered himself to the white tiles. Tingling pain shot through his legs. He had not been walking for a long time.

He took one unsteady step and had to stop, let the world quit pitching and swaying. Cold tile floor. A digital display on a nearby monitor gave upside-down numbers that seemed to be medical information: blood pressure, concentrations, heart rate. The display shifted, heart rate rising a little, as he watched. How did it keep monitoring him?

His next adventure, he decided, would be to reach the closest door. His first few steps taught him to keep his head tilted down toward his feet. He had to move his eyes the opposite way to shift his field of vision. He bumped into the cart and nearly fell. Each step brought twinges. A lancing pain in his left side made him suck in a sudden breath. He pushed the door slightly ajar.

Another room. The equipment was hard to recognize upside down. Chairs clung steadfastly to the ceiling. Somehow, confronting a new room, his head reeled. His eyes told his brain that he was standing on the ceiling. Deep in his brain, alarms struggled to be heard.

He held on to the doorjamb and made himself look at each object in the room beyond. First, no people. Good. An open chest of drawers, holding something like surgical instruments. A washup station with air hood yawning like a thin-lipped mouth. Electronics gear.

A prep room? He eased into this new frontier. He reached the surgical drawers. It was easier to open the drawers by moving slowly and closing his eyes, going by feel. Too bad he couldn't walk that way. In the third drawer down he found a funny curved kind of scalpel. He palmed it.

Sounds from his left. He went right. He was getting the hang of things better now, could walk without the stomach-fluttering sense that he was about to take a dive into the ceiling. He reached a corner and stepped around—

And stared straight into a surprised face. The man gasped. Alex figured out the inverted features as the man stepped back—older, deep suntan, sandy hair, mouth half open. Surprised?—or something else? Eyes big, showing a lot of white.

Do I know him? From where?

Before Alex could react, the man's face whitened and he brought his hands up, palms out. "No. No no."

The hard voice slapped him with a gush of memory. Cold stars. Sandstone.

"Lazarus! You don't—can't—"

Alex worked the scalpel forward in his hand. His voice was rusty. "Who are you? What—"

"You're not—they said—you wouldn't be awake!" The man's lined and roughened face twisted. "But now—like Lazarus. But you've been there, you must know you belong in the valley of bones. I have to—"

The swarming confusion in the man's face hardened. His fingers clenched and twitched.

Alex felt weakness flooding through him. He had only seconds. He held up his left hand to draw the man's attention. An instant later he stepped forward and swung the knife up. It struck the man's left arm, going in only an inch. The man flinched away, face white, grunting in amazement.

Alex drew back to strike again.

"Lazarus! Am I wrong? What did you see?" The man's mouth worked with unspoken emotions. Tears welled in his eyes. Abruptly he turned and lunged away, his lab coat flapping behind him.

Alex gaped, stunned. Shards of recollection winked in his memory, like broken glass seen glinting when he turned the flashlight of his attention on them. Then they faded, just as quickly.

The fear, the anger . . . they ebbed in him. Was he really sure of anything? He wobbled. The scalpel clattered on the floor.

So tired . . . a wall caught his woozy descent.

He was trying to sort out memories when he noticed that he had slid down the wall and was sitting, bare skin on cold tile.

Fast footsteps. People in lab coats. It was funny, in a way, watching them run along on the ceiling, jabbering and pointing. They seemed very excited about something, but in the silky light he wasn't in a mood to listen just then.

11

SUSAN

She had not expected to enjoy her bathroom so much. Dr. Blyer had encouraged her to indulge herself, to focus on the present. Good therapeutic advice, and also fun. Bathrooms had grown up.

The shower had a dozen settings, from MASSAGE to STIMULATE to CLEANSE. STIMULATE released blue gouts of ions that perked her up. MASSAGE made her so slack-jawed, she needed a nurse to get back to bed. The shower had no door, nothing to crash through if she fell. Its padded walls spiraled in on a tight curve, so that no water sprayed out. Even the toilet had attachments, converting into a bidet with one turn of a knob. When you flushed, it first offered an arcing stream from the water tank, to wash your hands, then recycled that water to do the flushing. Susan liked standing over the whole-body blow-dry, which Dr. Fernandez had been very strict about; her skin was too delicate to rub with towels. This felt better, anyway, like a desert wind that knew how to kiss. She lingered in its warm and decidedly erotic caresses and watched the real wonder of the bathroom—something beyond these pleasant gadgets, profound yet subtle.

The bath mat was cleaning the room. At least it *looked* like a bath mat. Its thin cilialike fibers reached out like sluggish fingers, inching along, sopping up droplets, tissue shreds, the debris of grooming. The nurse had said it lived off "human dander," sloughed-off skin and hair. Susan was watching it crawl partway up the shower wall to engulf a spatter of soap—she had gotten a bit playful under STIMULATE—when a chime announced a visitor. She slipped on a royal blue terrycloth robe and sat in a recliner chair before thumbing the room control unit in the chair arm. She wasn't prepared to see Dr. Fernandez and Dr. Blyer push into the room a wheelchair carrying Alex Cowell.

"Alex—they said you were—my God, you look wonderful!"

"Not half as good as you do." His expression of joy turned to awe as he reached out, touched her face.

"It's just old me," she said.

"You look younger."

"So do you."

"And . . . happier."

"So do you."

"But we've both been . . ."

She could see that despite his proper cryonicist training, now so long ago, Alex had almost said "dead." She provided, "Suspended."

"Right. Stored."

The ice broken, they fell into eager conversation. But even as she enjoyed it, Susan felt herself at a slight remove, for reasons she could not quite understand.

She knew intellectually that this man had seen her through what was called death at that time, so for him this was in a way a more convincing, immediate miracle than his own resurrection. It was damnably difficult to truly believe you had died, had been still and stiff and cold, when you could still scratch your nose.

Dr. Blyer had spoken to her about this meeting several times, and she had even rehearsed what she would say. This was a new area of therapy, of course, largely uncharted. Surprisingly, Blyer had said that Alex would have a harder time with this first encounter than she would —because he had seen her die, while Susan remembered Alex as hale and hearty. Mourning someone, then seeing them newly reborn—chattering away, embracing life's minute-to-minute delights—was a profound shock. They had prepared Alex for it by letting him see Ray Constantine. Meeting an old friend at an advanced age was less troubling than witnessing the "dead" walk.

Blyer had mentioned obliquely that the emotional disturbance was even greater for those who had mourned a loved one, and then gotten over it, going on to take up a new life. Meeting a long-lost love reopened old wounds. Feelings buried and forgotten burst anew into consciousness, erupting through the mind's emotional equilibrium. The entire discussion with Blyer had unsettled her, sending her mind reeling into strange, murky turbulence. She had understood the ideas well enough, but thinking about them had made her heart race, and vagrant impulses flitted in her mind. She would catch glimpses of faces, hear fragments of remembered conversations—then they would flit away, sucked into a blank abyss. They were shards of her past, but she could not seize upon them long enough to assemble a coherent picture, to even see what they were about.

The effects seemed to disperse throughout her waking moments, like ripples in some interior pond. Once, standing over the whole-body blow-dry, she had experienced in quick succession a tingling erotic wave, then a jolt of guilt, and finally an inexpressible, sad longing. Yet she could put no name to her feelings, could not tie them to any memory. It had been like groping through chilly, dank fog, searching for a reassuring glow, for homefires in the night.

Even the recollection of her confusion took her out of the present, mired her in vague, troubling sorrows. She shook herself free of the thoughts and concentrated on Alex. He was showing off his skin, which was, as he put it, "as smooth as a baby's ass" one of the benefits of the revival tanks.

"I never thought it would be like this," Alex said.

Susan laughed. "Who could?"

"We *made* it."

She knew what he meant. "Thirty-eight years, gone in the blink of an eye."

"But there are things I can't remember."

"That will clear up with time," Dr. Fernandez put in.

"We can sift over the past later," Susan said. Best to get Alex off the subject; his mouth had turned down in the moody way she recalled. She glanced at Blyer and said brightly, "I have no idea of what it's like outside, but just staying in this room has made me love this place. I won't ever have to shave my legs again—there's a simple smear-on for that. No more sniffles, either. Anybody who can repair the damage freezing did to us, can cure a cold. Dishes here keep your food at the temperature it had when it was served, even if you have a cold salad and sizzling steak on the same plate. Bathroom mirrors don't steam up, even hospital clothes don't wrinkle—"

She stopped, realizing that she was babbling. Dr. Blyer smiled and nodded. "That's fine. Go on."

"My God, I sound like a complete airhead."

"You sound like a woman who is recovering excellently."

She knew as well as Blyer that she didn't know how to act with Alex, but she banished her uncertainty and plunged in. "Tell me what happened," she said. "To me, I mean."

This broke through the last shell of awkwardness between her and Alex. The surest way to get anyone to talk was to let them tell a story, the deeply human way of framing experience. He had been somber and distracted, but now he blossomed. As he talked, in her mind's eye she could see him and Kathryn battling the coroner and police, sneaking her body away, fending off the media. It felt peculiar to hear a yarn with yourself as the pivotal piece, the McGuffin in a Hitchcock thriller.

Then it sank in that Alex had risked prison for her, withstood the police, damaged the credibility of I^2 itself—all out of his intense faith that they had to hang on to the slender promise of pulling Susan back from the dark gulf. She felt a burst of deep affection for this man. She had been led into cryonics by her research, but he had pursued it for deeply human reasons—compassion for the afflicted, black rage at death's brutality, a deep longing to bridge the abyss between souls.

A vagrant thought skittered like heat lightning through her mind. More than the serene curiosity of research had led her. Something else—

A wedge blocked the thought, a black barrier rearing up like thick granite walls erupting from the shrouded earth.

"So then I died," Alex ended suddenly. "Don't know how."

"It was very much like Susan's death," Fernandez said. "A fall from a height. Quite similar traumas."

"How did you fix it up?" Alex asked.

"Microtech," Fernandez said with the touch of relish that a specialist has when he sees an opportunity to hold forth about his life's work. "We had already deployed cell-size repair agents to repair freezing damage, and losses from oxygen and nutrient starvation."

Susan asked, "What solvent did you use?"

"Tetrafluoromethane—it stays liquid down to minus a hundred thirty degrees centigrade. We introduced the line-layers then, workhorse cells to spool out threads of polyacetylene."

"For electrical conductors?" Susan asked.

"Right, to power the next generation of molyreps. Then—"

"Uh—moly what?" Alex frowned.

Fernandez said, "Oh, jargon, sorry. Molecular repair agents—smart cells, really. Like, uh, the smart bombs of your era."

"Except your molyreps bombed ice crystals?" Susan asked.

"Gobbled them up, cleared your blood vessels, then laid down the electrical power lines."

"To run what?" Alex asked.

"The programmed cleanup crew. They stitched together gross fractures. They were like good servants dusting a room, clearing out the dendrite debris and membrane leftovers that the big scavenger units missed. They had to move some of your molecular furniture around—to dust under it, sort of."

"At a hundred thirty degrees below freezing?" Susan asked. "How long did that take?"

"Weeks. We had to be sure we didn't let the molyreps work too fast, or else they'd heat you up all on their own, before we wanted it."

"But all that detail—I mean, how did they get the damaged stuff back in place, once they'd fixed it?"

"We have special units—little accountants, really. They recorded where all your molecular furniture was, what kind of condition it was in. They look over the debris, tag it with special identifying molecules, then anchor it to a nearby cell wall. They file that information all away, like a library. Then we slowly warmed you up."

Susan was trying to visualize the designer molecules Fernandez was so blithely describing. Hordes of microscopic fanatics, born to sniff out flaws and meticulously patch them up. An army that lived for but one purpose, much as art experts could spend a lifetime restoring a Renaissance painting. But the body was a far vaster canvas than all the art humanity had ever produced, a network of complexity almost beyond comprehension. Yet the body naturally policed itself with just such mobs of molecules, mending the scrapes and insults the rude world inflicted. Humanity had simply learned to enlist those tiny throngs. That was true, deep technology—using nature's own mechanisms, guiding them to new purposes. A miracle to Susan, but simple fact to these men.

She asked, "Warmed us up? Until you could get good circulation in the cells again?"

"Well, not good—just sluggish is enough. Brought you up to about minus a hundred degrees centigrade. We sent in the third team then, to bond your enzymes to cell structures. They read that library the second team had left and put all your furniture back into place. Just like the upstairs maid."

Susan realized Fernandez had given this same homey little Introduction to Molecular Repair for Poets lecture many times before. "How long did that take?"

"Months. Fixing the hemorrhaged tissue, mending torn membranes, splicing back together the disrupted cellular connections—that was almost easy, but tedious."

Alex shook his head as though dazed. "You guys must've put the surgeons out of business."

Fernandez blinked. "But we *are* surgeons. Our tools are simply a million times smaller than a scalpel, these days."

"Cutting with chemistry," Susan said. It was still hard to believe, to get her mind around such a huge yet simple fact. Medicine could now do what the body already knew—repair damage at the molecular level, but faster and better, with deft control. What kind of outside world did that imply?

Blyer, who had been sitting quietly, said, "Thanks to Susan's transglycerols, there wasn't a lot of freezing damage in either of you."

"We were easier?" Susan asked.

"Yes, because of your own work," Dr. Blyer said. "You pioneered our entire approach."

"How many have been revived?" Susan asked.

"Several hundred. Those frozen only a decade or two ago have less freezing damage, because our techniques got better. Some of those we can now cure, just like you."

"Several hundred." Susan blinked. She had always thought that cryonics was a path into the distant future at best. But a working program, in only thirty-eight years! Then without warning, the stifling sense of being blocked swept over her again. The black granite barred her. It was like groping for something you *know* is there in memory, buried, yet so palpably close that you can sense its tingling presence. The sensation resembled times when she could see a face in her mind's eye but could not recall the person's name, or caught a smell and could not place the cause—but amplified a thousandfold, into a wrenching sense of being restrained by bonds only dimly felt, but cloying, smothering. She grasped for something related, for a path out of the constricting press. "I—I saw my treatment chart," Susan said, feeling beads of perspiration break out on her forehead.

Dr. Blyer frowned. "You're not to bother yourself with details yet, doctor. This program is still experimental, and while we have some confidence in our medical procedures for revival, I'm afraid our therapy is still very tentative."

"There were serotonin-derived neurotransmitters in the treatments I'm getting. Why?"

Dr. Blyer looked uncomfortable. "These are experimental—"

"I realize your psychopharmacology is far advanced over what I knew, but I don't see the need for those chemicals, doctor. My guess—just from their names I glimpsed on the nurse's working clipboard—is that those are blockers."

Blyer covered his discomfort with formality. "Well, yes, they inhibit the switches in brain chemistry associated with emotional states."

"And that cuts off the memories correlated with those emotions, correct?" Susan bore in.

"Yes, generally," Fernandez broke in. "You should not be bothering with those details right now in your therapy. I suggest—"

"We want your memories to focus on the events surrounding your death, doctor," Blyer said sharply. "You may not realize it, but the series of killings at Immortality Incorporated is a major reason why this center exists. The public demands that your cases be solved. Whatever we need to do—"

"That doesn't give you the right to tamper with my own memories, damn it!" Susan said. "I—"

"I'm afraid it does," a voice came from the doorway. Susan looked up in surprise. The struggle within her had blinded her to the entrance of Detective Stern. He fetched a rolling chair and sat down, looking tired. "We have to clear up some things here. And right away."

12

ALEX

He was still feeling a little rocky, wan and passive, but Stern's arrival jerked him into alertness. The hard-edged energy of the man was still there. The detective radiated a bunched, coiled energy as he intervened in the conversation with Susan.

He had seen Stern already, once his inverted vision was straightened out. That whole incident was now foggy, like a dream. The specialists were still muttering about his temporary failure to store short-term memory. Alex wanted to forget it, to get on with this bizarre life.

He had talked with Stern, then Ray Constantine. Their seemingly instant transformation into aging, heavier versions of themselves had been a jolt. But beneath the sagging jowls and graying hair of each lurked the same intense character he remembered. Ray, of course, had been overjoyed. He had lived through the rise of biological technology and had seen cryonics move in the public mind from being a crank, macabre pipe dream, into the sunny reality of an accomplished fact.

Ray had broken the news to him of Kathryn's death, too.

That had rocked him. He had plunged into a black vortex of despair, until Blyer had administered some drugs. That had hauled Alex up into a sort of neutral, dazed calm—though murky currents swept through him, just below the surface. By then, Stern had finished his questioning and Alex had gotten irritated. Now they were finally letting him see Susan, and here was Stern again.

"Look, can't this wait?" Alex asked bitingly.

"No." Stern gave him an appraising look, eyes glittering. "You don't understand the avalanche of public interest these revivals have brought down."

"Screw public interest. We're patients, not prisoners. I want to talk to my old friend."

"And that's exactly what I'm here to monitor," Stern shot back.

"Why?" Susan asked mildly. Or so it probably sounded to Stern; Alex had caught the clipped edge in her tone.

"Because memory is tricky. The two of you meeting again, it may trigger—" Stern turned to Dr. Blyer. "What was that term?"

"Spontaneous recollection," Blyer supplied. "We have noted it in dozens of prior cases. The brain sometimes needs a visual or aural cue—such as meeting old friends, hearing their voices again—to provide a context for associations."

Stern slapped his knee in vindication. "Right. Look, we haven't gotten anywhere on this case, and that's what the public cares about."

Alex said sourly, "What public—the tabloid readers? Let 'em wait."

Stern shook his head. "You're shielded from the media here because we don't want your memories influenced. So you don't realize that you're the crucial witnesses in the biggest unsolved murder story since Jack the Ripper."

"Why so big?" Alex scowled skeptically. "There are plenty of unsolved cases."

"It's the only one where the victims were suspended."

"Despite you," Alex added.

"Yeah, okay." Stern spread his hands in rueful dismay. "Look, you guys broke a lot of laws. And—hell, it was a different age."

"There's another element, isn't there?" Susan asked.

Stern eyed her cautiously. "Right. The killer obviously targeted you all because you were cryonicists—but why the two other women in Santa Ana? Decades later, we still don't have a clue."

Alex gritted his teeth. Maybe this guy thought the past was history, but to Alex the trouble with Stern and Detweiler was as fresh as last week. "I told you already, I can't remember anything about who attacked me."

Stern nodded. "Post-trauma lapse, they call it. But something could come back. Especially when you two talk. After all, this guy hit you both. There may be some common element that will come out—"

"Look, we're just recovering." Alex hesitated, then decided he had better get everything out in the open. "That panic I had, that should prove to you that you can't rely on us to clear up your case."

"Panic?" Susan asked.

Alex sighed. Might as well face up to it. "I went a little crazy while they were reviving me. I guess I'd been okay, responding to questions and all. But I woke up on a slab and, well, got into these . . ." He groped for the right word, but like most people, a hint of even momentary insanity was deeply embarrassing.

Dr. Blyer supplied, "Delusional structures."

"Uh, yeah. I thought somebody was after me. So I got myself up, fumbled around, grabbed a scalpel to defend myself."

"My my," Susan said cheerily. "You always were one who went through obstacles, not just over them."

"It was quite an accomplishment," Dr. Fernandez said in measured tones. "We were not finished reorienting his sensory inputs, but he overcame that. It could have been very dangerous."

"What triggered it?" Susan asked.

Alex licked his lips, feeling a familiar clammy sensation. Whenever he tried to focus on that incident, he felt the same fearful currents, a gnawing, cold dread. "I don't know. A voice, I think. One of the attendants talking, maybe. But I can't get it straight, can't—can't—"

"No need to fixate, Alex," Dr. Blyer came in smoothly. "We have had such trauma-induced hallucinations before in cryonics revivals. They probably arise from associations the mind makes between deep memories and simple cues—a sound, say, or a snapshot. During rebuilding of the neurotransmitter structures in your brain, some of the connections may get crossed."

"Um." Alex pushed away the skating sensations of chilly unease. "Like telephone calls that get hooked up wrong?"

"Yes. You heard a voice you thought you recognized, and that linked to some constellation of emotions—fear, free-floating anxiety. But it was an error. You were in no danger, lying there in a postoperative transition room."

"Suppose it happens again?" Alex asked apprehensively.

"It shouldn't. Your own mind will sort out those mistakes." Dr. Blyer patted Alex paternally on the shoulder. "That's one of the major tasks of the subconscious. It edits your daily memories that way, every night. Then it stores the results in your long-term memory. We all do that, just by sleeping."

"Then why do I have these dreams?" Alex asked. "Bad ones."

"They are a natural method of setting things right. They should go away soon."

"You're not—well, inducing them some way?"

Blyer looked offended. "Our methods are ethical, I assure you. We do not force interior states upon a patient."

Alex swallowed, finding a lump in his throat. Somehow this conversation, theoretical and distant though it was, had called up those emotions again. He felt a prickly unease, as though someone of malevolent intent were watching him.

He glanced away from the others, let his eye rove over the peaceful scene projected on the walls. Oak trees swayed in a gentle summer wind, tossing their leaves in celebration against an eggshell-blue sky. He tried to let the image draw him away from the turmoil inside him, but the thin thread of anxiety persisted.

It had returned again and again in the days since he had collapsed in the prep room. He never escaped the sensation of being *watched*—as though a thousand eyes hid in the shifting wall-views of his room, in corridors, in clinics. A classic symptom, of course, and his rational mind dismissed it immediately. But it returned, chewing at him. Something here had triggered a deep-seated alarm, one that clanged whenever he let his attention deflect its way—yet one he could not call up to conscious memory. Something nearby. Something wrong.

"You aren't doing anything to our mental states now, then?" Susan asked.

"Well, there are some continuing medications, of course," Dr. Blyer answered cautiously.

"What are their effects?" Susan's voice sharpened with more than professional curiosity.

"I'm afraid fully describing them might well obviate their impact."

"As a patient, surely I have the right to know the probable effect."

"I would rather not discuss this until we are a little further along in therapy."

Alex could see the signs as Susan dropped her tactful manner—compressed lips, narrowed eyes. "I'm not asking for details about dosage. I want to know what you're doing to my—"

"I have to take the blame here, Dr. Hagerty," Stern said. "Part of pursuing this case is to not disturb whatever memories you have. That means we can't have you going through too much turmoil at once. We need to focus your thinking just a bit more, and then—"

"Then you'll let me have my mind back?" Susan shot to her feet, hands knotted at her sides.

"That's too extreme," Blyer said. "I am operating within the scruples and standards of psychodynamics."

Susan shot back, "That includes lying to your patients?"

"We are not lying. We are simply withholding." Blyer looked pained, his mouth twisted in a regretful curve, as though he felt a deep professional conflict but was committed to staying his course.

"Withholding *what*?"

"Dr. Hagerty, I understand your concern," Dr. Fernandez began in a conciliatory tone. "Still, I believe you must leave your full recovery from this enormous trauma you have suffered in our hands, even though—"

"Look, I can help out here," Stern cut in. "We all want this settled, one way or the other. Either you get more memories about the crimes back soon, or else they won't come at all—right, doctor?"

Blyer nodded. "That sort of traumatic event—I'm afraid so."

Stern said in a flat cop's voice, "Don't think the media won't hound you once you get out of here, though."

Alex smiled sardonically. "Let's see now. I've been beaten, tossed off a cliff, killed, frozen, unfrozen, revived by miracle-midget molecules, had my whole body put back together like a Tinkertoy set. Yeah, I believe I can withstand a TV interview."

Stern smiled. "Me, too. Point is, we've only got one more move left. You two have drawn a blank, so now we go on. Dr. Fernandez here, he's been working night and day, and we're about ready, he tells me. Dr. Blyer thinks so, too. It was a very difficult technical problem, I'm told."

Alex felt his apprehension rise. "I don't want—"

"I think you do, Alex," Stern said, coming off his official voice and sounding a note of real warmth. "You do. They've brought Kathryn back."

13

GEORGE

Clouds flowed and churned across a dusky, leering moon. Gusty winds stirred the air with sweeping, sudden gales, playing with the sullen moonlight, making the world go erratically dark and bright. George wondered if God deliberately raked the clouds with windy fingers, like a small boy plunging a stick into an anthill to see what he could stir up. Then he felt a spike of guilt. That verged on blasphemy. A skittering dart of remorse laced through his already fevered mind.

He stumbled in a sudden moment of darkness, and his shoulder slammed into one of the gnarled oak trees that fringed the Marble Cathedral. Pain spiked from his stab wound. Wind harassed the trees, lifting branches high like the rasping legs of giant insects. George remembered long ago the huge bright cockroaches Cowell had brought here, and something in these tossing limbs, now awash in piercing moonlight, made him lurch and stumble again. Something stirred his senses. The giant cross above had an orange halo, great bars of light glowing and vibrating against the roiling sky. The thrashing oaks threw sharp scents at him, cutting in his nostrils. The showers of worried leaves had veins of iridescent silver-green, and the rough-barked trunks swarmed with emerald luminosities. Winds howled among the flying buttresses and high arches of the cathedral.

George staggered away from the whispering oaks, groping through another bout of darkness. Trying not to pay attention to his ribs, where he had smashed into a wall, fleeing from the VI^2 facility. He leaned against a railing at the entrance to the Marble Cathedral, drawn by the soft yellow glow from within, and caught sight of his hand—lumpy, thick fingers like ripe pork sausages, blackened nails, calluses that rasped on his cotton shirt.

Winds whipped his hair into his eyes as he roughly shoved open the big panel doors. Through the antechamber, then into the descending hush of the cool, incense-scented interior. People were milling about the Reverend, who was in the pulpit. They were like shifting blobs of heat and color to George, and then he blinked, and they were only people again, oddly soft and vulnerable beneath the masses of cold stone and glass that towered in swooping grace above them.

He pressed down the main corridor. With its worn carpet it was like an empty spine to which attached the pews, polished wood that sprouted to each side, going by him now, *rik-rik-rik*, George counting each as he passed to put his mind in order, to call up the distant and analytical self that he knew he carried and that he would need now. But that side was a puny thing, pale and dwindled somehow by the decades that had slid past now and would never come to him again. He burst toward the altar, and faces turned like spotlights to transfix him in their baleful stares.

He ignored them, bored on toward the Reverend—who acknowledged his primacy, his weight and momentum as a warrior for the Lord, by turning from the soft others and registering surprise. Then the Reverend's broad mouth curved up in a fixed smile, and he spoke quickly to the others, dismissing them.

George said nothing, just stopped and stood by the tarnished brass railings near the altar. The fixtures here glowed with warming light and plush velour absorbed the harsh edges of words. George remembered the enfolding comforts of his many hours here. He ignored the soiled headrests on the Holy Seats, the tattered satins where once Sister Angel had led the congregation in throaty hosannahs, the bedraggled ruby carpet along the side aisles. Then the Reverend was speaking to him, ushering him aside into the warren of vestry rooms, the smooth words slipping by George like a mountain stream over worn pebbles. They went out the back door and across the concrete walkway, beneath a sky stirred with vagrant light and angry clouds. A storm front was now slamming in from the ocean, and the cleansing cut of rain made the air pregnant with fresh weight.

Nothing registered with George until they were once more in the cedar-scented study, safe from the rising turbulence outside. Sitting in a pool of light was Dr. Lomax, working on blueprints laid out on the Reverend's broad mahogany desk. The leathery man's head jerked with surprise, his thin pencil moustache warping. "You don't get off shift for two hours," Lomax said by way of greeting.

"I couldn't stay there." George stood in the exact center of the Reverend's large oriental carpet, seeking some midpoint in all this, willing his warring senses to calm, to stop showing him a world stretched and seized by shifting smells and visions.

"Why not? That supervisor, McAndrews, he'll keep a sharp eye on you. I had a lot of trouble getting you in that close."

"I know, I appreciate, truly I do." George felt the words tumble out of him without restraint.

"You tried for Hagerty first?" Lomax demanded.

He decided to lie. The truth was too hard to explain—the clashing images called up by the sight of her face, leaping at him out of shadowy memory. "Yes, but it wasn't right. Too many people around."

Lomax shook his head. "Too bad. I learned that the police are talking to her. She's coherent, they say."

"Yes, uh, she is."

Reverend Montana stood to the side, hands folded piously in front of him, blending into the cedar bookshelves. "And Cowell?"

George gathered himself, became crisp. "I tried for him next. I got in, collecting trash in the post-op section. First time I got into the control room, I could see Cowell on the monitors. Out of that molecular bath, unwrapped. Lying flat with a bunch of leads going into the back of his skull."

Lomax nodded briskly. "They're on schedule."

"First time, I got maybe a minute alone. I tried talking to him, seeing if there was reaction."

"What did the acoustic diagnostics say?"

"Spikes on all channels, looked like. He was up and running, so he should have heard me. I spoke real slow, asked him if he recognized my voice."

"And?" Lomax demanded irritably.

"How could I tell? He couldn't talk. Couldn't move or anything. You didn't tell me how to read those other diagnostics."

"Because I don't know how. There's a limit to—"

"I checked the situation board. They were holding him in 'neurostasis,' it said."

Lomax slammed his palm on the blueprints, scattering paper that fluttered to the floor. "That's not the usual procedure! They're doing something new."

Alarms ricocheted through George, anxieties exploding like crimson flashes, jangling his nerves. He hated his failure, having to admit it like this. And he had concealed his perfectly fine opportunity with Hagerty. The fabric of his will shredded into tremors and darting dreads.

"The board said Cowell was having something adjusted in his eyes. They shut him down while they worked out the trouble."

"Worse damned luck." Lomax grimly stared into space.

"So I came back a little later. The team got pulled away for some other case, and I got time to look at things. Then I checked the television monitor and he wasn't there."

"They moved him?" Lomax asked.

"I met him. In a prep room."

"What?"

George shuddered at the memory. "I think he knew me."

"By himself? Why would he—"

"He looked scared and woozy. Maybe it was a side effect of what they were doing to him."

Lomax shook his head curtly. "No, there's no procedure that would make a patient get up off that table and walk away. It was something *you* did."

"I just talked to him, like you said."

"He *knew* you." Lomax's pencil moustache twitched. "You scared him, and he went into a fight-or-flight response."

"Look, I just did what—"

"It's bad news," Lomax said bitterly, "damned bad. But at least we know for sure now. He recognized your voice. He'll be able to identify you."

The Reverend's voice came out of the shadows, heavy with pontifical sadness. "Which places you in severe threat, my friend."

Lomax said carefully, "A voice identification isn't convincing evidence, even if they somehow get a lead on you."

"Cowell had that vision problem—maybe he won't be able to recognize me."

"You mean, if the company starts looking for the employee he saw?" Lomax thought. "Well, maybe."

George finally let his desire to confess burst forth. He turned to the Reverend. "I—I could have killed him."

Lomax gave him a sharp look. "Why didn't you?"

"I don't know. He looked like Lazarus," George said, and knew inside himself that this somehow explained it.

"Anything you could do quickly wouldn't be permanent, anyway. Injuring someone in a hospital these days"—Lomax waved the idea away—"no point. They'd save him."

The Reverend said soothingly, "I am sure you did the right thing, George."

"There's the Sheffield woman, though," Lomax said. "They're reviving her next."

George's throat tightened. He swallowed against a painful lump. "Maybe she won't remember, like the Hagerty woman."

"We don't *know* that Hagerty won't recall you later. But there's no chance Sheffield won't." Lomax tapped the desk top with a pencil, his eyes glittering. "She saw you good and clear, right after you did Cowell, days before she died. She's got your picture right there in long-term memory storage."

George felt power slipping from him, sucked toward Lomax's forceful presence. He felt a whirling sense of events outstripping him, of this strange new world narrowing down to desperately few choices.

"George, once they make the connection to the cathedral, the whole affair will unravel." The Reverend moved solemnly into the pool of radiance at the desk and stood with grave demeanor, staring down forlornly at his lined hands. "This entire congregation will squirm beneath their legal bootheels."

"And something's going to break, I can feel it," Lomax said sourly. "This is too big a deal. The company is pushing—"

"The company!" George erupted. "That's what I want to know. You should have told me that your own business, Vitality, is now *part* of Immortality Incorporated!"

With alarm Lomax glanced at the Reverend. "Look, I can—"

"I saw that logo at work—VI², Vitality–Immortality Incorporated. How could you—"

"I *had* to." Lomax was on his feet, face congested. "With all the publicity, that 'cryonics versus crime' stuff, I² took off. They got research and development money from all directions. They were leaving Vitality in the dust. I had no choice but to go along with a de facto merger. My own board demanded it. We had some patents they could use, which got us in the door. It was the best strategy in the long run—kept our hands in."

"But to *help* them, to—"

"There was no choice," Lomax said coldly.

"The valley of bones—*that* is the proper place for the righteous."

Lomax frowned. "What?"

George saw it suddenly, the broad and sunny land between majestic peaks. The great mountains soared to snow-crowned glory, with the same sweeping grace as the Marble Cathedral. Between two proud peaks lay the expanse of aromatic earth, and from that holy soil came a humming, a throaty chorus. The earth split open ripely—here, there, then throughout the great sprawling valley. The bones that Ezekiel foretold, very dry and white, crisp beneath the new sun, were ripping free of the rich loam. *When I have opened your graves, O my people, and brought you up—* And so they would come, bones leaping into the air with mad abandon, liberated by the golden glow that beat down upon the holy valley. The bones would hover in air, click and snap and lock into place. Whole skeletons would collect to make full cages of ribs, long femurs and clavicles finding their places, too. Then they would dance, the bodies now passed through the astringent cleansing that was necessary and right. They would frolic beneath the beaming radiance from above, clacking bones now shaped back into people, truly and forever resurrected.

He opened his mouth to say all this and saw that it was too much for these men, too precious. They were looking at him, worry deepening the lines in their faces. George explained, "Don't you see? Dr. Lomax, you are a man of science, but you opposed the chillers then, didn't you? They are still bent upon this path. I don't know what their science has discovered in all this time, but it cannot change a moral truth."

The Reverend said softly, "Quite right, George, quite right."

"You've got to realize, a lot has happened," Lomax said warily, holding his hands up in a placating gesture, as though he had seen something in George's face. "A different world."

"How is it possible that people have come to this, that so many permit, so many seem *happy* to let the dead rise?"

"It is an age of spiritual malaise," the Reverend said gravely, the spotlights from above lighting the broad planes of his still rugged face. "An age beset by fleshy rewards."

Lomax eyed George and said, "I'm afraid we've learned technology without learning wisdom. Even the Reverend is having a hard time."

"I hope it is not so hard," George said, remembering the threadworn carpets, the tarnished brass.

The Reverend smiled with an echo of the old confidence. "Now, don't go giving George the idea that we're so bad off. The cathedral is about to launch a big new TV campaign, get back on the airwaves in a big way."

The Reverend's confidence had a hint of hollow bravado to it now, but George said respectfully, "Wondrous news."

"That's what you busted in on, the meeting out there in the cathedral. We're going to come back bigger than ever, you bet."

It had seemed like a small crowd to George, puny and threadbare, but he smiled to reassure the Reverend, beamed with a confidence he did not feel. Inside himself the image of the golden valley of the joyous resurrected yielded to darker currents, a swampy sensation of being dragged under. Abruptly a clattering sounded through the high recesses of the study, and the three men turned as one. The tall panels of stained glass worked with refracted images as rivulets of rain ran down them. Hailstones struck the glass, clicking and rattling, and a distant light seemed to shimmer and contort as the wind whipped branches around, throwing stretched shadows across the running colors of the glass.

Hail. Cold and wet, and abruptly George saw a plane of soft black, cold and infinite, stretching away to the horizon. Something dropped into it, and he saw the spreading ripples—*the lake*—and felt cold dread seep up into him. *So cold.* Then rising up toward bleached hard light, the waxy faces over him, a face he almost knew even though it was twisted. The terror of reawakening in mortal flesh, not immortal bones that the Lord would make whole on the day of the Rapture. The blaring, coarse light spiked through him, and he saw a face coming—

"Are you all right?" The Reverend was beside him, hands holding him up.

George guessed that somehow he had slipped or something, lost his balance, and to cover his embarrassment he gave a little laugh. It came out wrong, hollow and forced, almost like a cough.

"Look—he's been hurt," the Reverend said.

Lomax inspected the cut Cowell had inflicted. It was unimportant, George knew that, and he did not resist the shot the doctor gave him. It took effect immediately, and he felt himself giving way. They made him lie down, and he dozed off for a while. The years were adding up. As he came to on the Reverend's sofa, he heard Lomax saying, "We've got more to block now. It's coming closer to the surface. Even with the new neurotransmitter inhibitors we can't always—"

"Quiet, damn it." The Reverend's face loomed close to George's, sincerity and concern in every line. George wondered what they had been talking about and then relaxed, feeling again the enduring comfort of this place, warm and close, a secure bastion against so much, a sturdy frame he had needed so deeply ever since he was a boy. He had that here, and he would do anything to keep it from harm.

He would be resolute, swift. Soldier of the Lord. He gathered his energies and sat up. A little setback, that was all this amounted to. He had faltered before both Hagerty and Cowell, sure, but that had been surprise, nothing more. He was over that now. "I got to get to them. All of them."

"True enough," Lomax said, all business. "I don't believe you understand quite how difficult it is to kill someone and have them stay truly dead these days."

George grinned without humor. Lomax was smart, but he was older, weaker. He could be used, and George saw that in the worn, veiled face. Lomax held secrets, probably dirty little matters of money, but they were unimportant to George's task. His entire life was defined by this mission, like bookends at the beginning and end of his days. Now came the completion he had sought. "You find a way. I'll make it happen."

Lomax said, "I've already got you a postdated labor history at VI^2, says you've worked there for months."

"I'll need a job that lets me move around."

"Look, what I've done took a lot of slick work, believe me—getting into coded data files, tricks I'd nearly forgotten. But yes, it can work. Everybody will think you're a transfer from another subsidiary of the firm—it's a big, growing enterprise now. In a few days I can get you into a new job."

"Do it." George thought a moment. "I don't suppose I can carry a weapon in with me?"

"No chance."

George said, "Then you'll have to rustle up something in the lab, some way to keep them dead."

Lomax grinned suddenly, eyebrows arching in thin lines that matched the moustache. "I like technical problems. They're so much cleaner than human ones."

George nodded, and Lomax went on, talking details. He was calm again, filing away the information that Lomax laid out. Disconnected, analytical. Inside him, great sullen masses moved. He felt them as deep, coiling presences, slumbering beneath a surface that had been calmed in Santa Isabella. But the smooth plane was deceptive. Cold and waiting, flat, the moist chill of it hung in his storming mind even when he closed his eyes. He did not tell them of it, could not describe the unforgiving air of silent menace. He caught glimpses of something moving like an immense beast beneath the apparent calm, something that dwelled in shadowy depths and robbed all color from the dim, filtered blades of wan sunlight. The cool, seeping grays and somber blacks of the scene would not leave him.

But the other side of himself listened carefully to Lomax with a strange, impatient relish.

14

KATHRYN

She insisted on going outside. The walls of her spacious room gave wonderful, utterly convincing scenery—but you still knew it was only a crafty illusion, and that drained the comfort of it from her, somehow.

She asked Alex to push her wheelchair. He had told her gruffly that it was foolish to do any more than she had to, that she should follow the doctors' advice, that the sanitized comforts of her room were far better for her—and finally she had given in. She knew very well he would deny her nothing, but it gave her a mischievous thrill to see him hold out for a while, frown and bluster and paw the ground a little. The same old Alex, she thought, and somehow that recognition brought slow, seeping tears.

Great glass panels, tinted blue against the sun's ultraviolet, slid aside for them. Alex said something about this being a precaution against the ozone layer depletion, which was still pretty bad, but she ignored him. Her first indrawn breath of fresh air carried a crisp, sweet scent of the far mountains—chaparral, manzanita, eucalyptus, sage. The San Bernadino peaks towered in far, white-crowned majesty, just as they had so long ago. Every jut, valley, and seam was the same as before. A human lifespan, she realized, was just a single snapshot in the slow sway of geology.

It was May. The tangy newborn season caressed her cheeks, kissed her hair. She let her head loll back in the wheelchair as Alex pushed her to the edge of the broad-beamed Douglas fir decking. Sunlight and scents seemed to seep into her, calling forth slumbering pleasures, searching out with their warmth the last recesses of deep cold that lingered in her mind.

This was life. Not the mere sighing of lungs, the thump of heartbeats, electrical skitters in the brain. She had endured enough this last two weeks of medical lingo, of solicitous technicians, of injections and tests, of canned air and phony landscapes. Life was the rub of the real, and every fiber in her yearned for it.

"Lord, you look wonderful." Alex's head loomed overhead, a beloved moon against a creamy blue sky.

She started to smile and abruptly jerked her hand up, holding it over her face. For a moment she had forgotten.

"Come on, I don't mind," Alex whispered in her ear.

"I know . . . I know . . ." *But I don't believe you,* she truly thought, though she said, "I don't like to show it out here."

He gently tugged her hand away. She cringed from his gaze. An artfully sculpted, skin-tinted pseudonose blended into her forehead. More of the same fleshlike stuff spread around her neck and disappeared down her blue hospital blouse. This high-tech mask concealed the ugly damage beneath—sore, purple tissues engorged with blood vessels, bruised planes, twisted brown scabs, and warped, tough cartilage. Fernandez allowed her this mask for a few hours every day. The rest of the time she had to expose her ruined self to a series of salves and radiations, plus the healing air.

Alex had seen it all, when the doctors insisted that she let it heal in the air. Only Kathryn's sensitivity had convinced them to allow her this cover. There was no concealment for the rents and grooves carved in the rest of her body below, savage ruin left by the sudden freezing of her murder.

"You're looking great," he said, and kissed her soulfully on the lips.

Hesitantly she returned his pressure, creating an acceptable, C-plus-grade kiss. He gave her a quizzical smile and returned to pushing the wheelchair. She rebuked herself. She knew she should cast aside her shyness, her mortal embarrassment, but something in her could not. She felt wounded in her most vital center.

"I love this sun." She tilted her head back, feeling the welcome sting. She had emerged chalk-white and hairless from suspension, like an albino alien. Her wig helped her forget that further discomforting fact. The blinding radiance beckoned like an immense, elliptical promise. She would have to be careful not to burn.

"You sure know how to lean on Fernandez," Alex said, plunking himself down in a deck chair next to her. "Talking him into letting you out so fast. I couldn't get out here until two days ago, and I'm weeks ahead of you in recovery."

"Must be my winning smile."

"Seems weird, doesn't it?"

"What?"

"We come through a miracle, something that blows us away—and soon enough, we're caught up in life's little details, wangling—literally—for a place in the sun."

She folded her hands over her blue hospital pajamas. Not a great color for her, but who said the future would be perfect? Then she chuckled at herself, allowing a smile to flicker across her lips. They were still a tad swollen but were beginning to feel like hers again, unlike the nose and even larger chunks of her below.

What he was trying to say was spot-on true. She and Alex now talked about the little things, precisely because you could not speak much of the big things—huge, immutable truths that were easy to state but carried enormous wallop when you truly felt them. Such as, *It's good to be alive.*

So you approached subjects obliquely, easing into them. She didn't feel like a heavy-browed session right now, though. "Ummm. Too philosophical for me. I think I'll just wallow."

"I'm glad to see your talent for self-indulgence was not lost to the liquid nitrogen."

"You should complain? If I remember right, in bed at least, *my* indulgence was *your* indulgence."

"Now who's too philosophical? But that does introduce a good subject."

"Bed?"

"Right. Nothing like the awareness of death to bring out—"

"I think I know how this argument goes. You sound like a bumper sticker."

He grinned. "Which one?"

"cryonicists stay stiff longer. Remember?"

"Oh yes, I saw some at the I^2 party. How can I remember that? It was nearly four decades ago."

"Time is relative, somebody said. I wonder if people use bumper stickers anymore."

"They must," Alex said wryly. "There's still plenty to gripe about. The economy's down, a war somewhere in Asia—"

"Ummm," she mused, "this is where I came in."

"Yeah—but look at that air, sharp as a knife. They've solved the smog problem. Maybe there aren't cars anymore. Or bumper stickers."

"No, I saw some cars in the news. Little boxy things. Maybe they don't burn gas, though."

Alex looked skeptical. "Come on, it's only been thirty-eight years. What could replace oil?"

"Hey, you're telling me things don't change so fast? A few months ago we were both solid ice."

He leaned forward, settling his chin into his hands. His hair was growing back in quickly, and he looked like a marine from the El Toro base. Or did they have marines anymore? Some things were eternal; it would take more than a mere revolution in technology to make them unnecessary. "I wonder if we owe a lot of this to the Crunch," Alex said.

"What's that?"

"Oh yeah, you haven't had time to go through all the orientation stuff. Talk about homework! Near as I can tell, the Crunch was a big crisis in just about everything, stretching from around 2011 to 2018. Then things got better."

"What solved the problems?"

"I dunno. The terms they use now—what's a 'sociologus'?—just don't translate."

She gazed out over the broad green lawn. Orchards dominated the nearby hillsides, leafy bowers that shimmered in the refracting heat. "I did see somewhere that the greenhouse effect is easing off."

"Yeah, in the newspaper—though it isn't paper anymore. I dug into that, found out they stopped it with a big tree-planting program, plus some neat trick to start patching up the ozone layer."

"Is that why I see so many orange trees?" Kathryn inhaled the perfumed air. It felt sweet and weighty in her chest.

"Could be. Me, I'm going easy on the homework. Let's just enjoy all this first."

The grounds of Vitality–Immortality Incorporated were vast, with graceful gravel walks curving across the breast of the rolling hillside. A gardener squatted nearby, ceaselessly rooting out weeds. A bee buzzed by. Gossamer willows brooded over a wide pond downhill from them, and oaks fringed the distance. The grass here was some new type just laid down, darker green. A few patients strolled along the walks, with friends sometimes helping them. Revival was expensive, Dr. Fernandez had told her—and a lot of people were pretty burned about that. Probably a generation would pass before the procedures became common and people could be routinely saved this way. But it was coming. There was a quiet momentum in this place, a feeling of working toward a future only barely perceptible over the far horizon.

"I thought I'd find you here," a familiar voice came out of the sky.

Kathryn blinked, realizing she had nearly slipped into delicious, cozy sleep. Susan grinned down at her, wearing a sensible sun bonnet. "I heard you threw a temper tantrum to get out here."

"Let's say I learned a little method acting in my youth." Kathryn held up a hand covered with purple-brown scabs, wreckage from liquid nitrogen burns. Susan gripped it. All three of them kept their conversation light, matching the sunny day, but with glances and silences they conveyed things that could not be spoken. They were voyagers on a strange sea, and they kept their spirits up in part by not treating everything as if it carried enormous weight. As Dr. Blyer had pointed out, laughter releases some emotions better than crying. Kathryn used a liberal dosage of both; it felt right.

"I thought you might like a friend," Susan said, placing a big Persian cat in Kathryn's lap. Kathryn gasped with delight. Alex smiled—part of the conspiracy, she saw, to surprise her.

"It's wonderful!"

"He—*not* it—is an entertainment consultant, under contract with the therapy center. He will allow moderate petting and will deign to eat certain specific foods if properly served."

"My, what a pretty thing." Kathryn stroked the silky, aloof creature with agreeable results for all concerned.

"He likes being taken on drives, too," Susan said. "Let's go."

"Already?" Kathryn blinked lazily. She really would rather lie in the sun, but the sweet currents wafting up the opulent hillside tempted her. She reminded herself that she had spent decades inside a steel cylinder. Time to get out a bit, yes.

Alex bundled her up, treating her like a fragile flower—which pleased her more than she would ever admit. He pushed her wheelchair down the ramp and onto a smooth path. Susan chattered on about how surprisingly rapid Kathryn's recovery had been, throwing in medical detail that Alex lapped up but that all seemed beside the point to Kathryn, who inhaled the honeyed air like a blissfully drowsy child. She felt their conversation more than heard it, and it was like a mellow background of reassurance.

This was a strange world, awesome in its almost casual capabilities, but she had friends here. She was not alone, the way she had been when Alex had died. That life without him, only a few days of it, had been more terrible than anything she had ever experienced. It had taken everything to hold herself together, to get him safely suspended, to convince the others of what they must do.

She honestly wondered how she would have weathered the years that came after that—years without Alex. He had come into her life, caught her up, and then spun away from her just as she had finally opened, given herself the way she had imagined it could be, a blossom bursting its husk. Perhaps her shadowy murderer had done her a weird, inadvertant favor, sliding her across the decades of loss and longing, to arrive here.

She shook herself. That was all gone now, swept away by what was to her a mere flicker, a passing moment that had been thirty-eight years wide.

She took her gaze from the distant horizon and admired the flowers. Alex was pushing her down a smooth path and then onto the odd new emerald grass. The pond further downhill played host to a few fat ducks, quacking over some dispute. Two men were studying the ducks intently. Alex took her past a long fringe of impossibly bright poppies, a riot of yellow and orange peppered by the vibrant blues of rosemary. A gardener looked up sweating from his weeding—

—and her heart lurched.

Weathered, deeply tanned, with a crinkling around the hooded eyes, deep webs of concern at the mouth, hair thinning—but yes, *yes,* the face leaped out at her.

"Ah! Ah!" she managed to get out, shaking.

"What?" Alex asked, bending forward, concerned.

The gardener's eyes widened. "Lord Jesus, no!" he wheezed, a rasping whisper.

The voice. It was the same voice.

Thirty-eight years evaporated in a jolting instant.

His face swelled to fill her entire vision. And then the man moved, quick and sure, getting to his feet and reaching for something at his equipment belt, and the air became clotted and close as a sudden frosty hand squeezed her chest, dragging her brutally into the past.

15

SUSAN

The storm of two days ago had cleansed the land. Susan drew in the honeyed air and chattered at Kathryn and Alex. Probably they wanted to be alone, but this ripe morning was too freighted with quiet joy to hold Susan back. These were, after all, the only close friends she had in the world.

They ambled down a pathway, heading down the gently sloping hillside toward a wide stand of eucalyptus trees. Far away she saw guards at the VI^2 buildings, and others at the gates. There was a big demonstration outside, shouting, chanting over a bullhorn. *Homo sap* was a cantankerous species, she mused, and no technomiracles would change that.

She was telling them about the oddments of the media she had come across, the telltale signs of glacial shifts in the ways people thought. Political talk no longer used the traditional division between left and right, she had found. There seemed to be a two-dimensional picture that everyone used matter-of-factly, arraying liberals and libertarians in entirely opposite patches of a grid. She could not understand what the two axes meant, but the appeal of it was obvious—left versus right was an entirely too simple, one-dimensional way to view a complex world. She could tell from their expressions that Kathryn and Alex found this matter less than thrilling, but Susan could barely restrain herself. The day was warm and full, and she felt expansive. She shifted to music, and was telling them about mistaking the latest pop songs for static on her audio player, when Kathryn suddenly cried, "Ah! Ah!"

Startled, the Persian cat leaped from the wheelchair. Susan started after him and saw a gardener pulling what looked like a large spray can from his belt. The man wore tan work slacks, a blue shirt, and a Dodgers cap. He leaped from the flower bed onto the grass and the cat darted between his legs.

Susan gasped. The man was older but robust, tanned. The contours of his face brought memory rocketing into her mind, from a time when she had seen those fevered eyes peering at her.

Fixed, fanatical. Among the shadows behind the Immortality Incorporated building.

Time had blurred his body, softened the slabs of muscle, but the intent gaze and the fixed thin line of the mouth were the same.

Recognition came instantly, and a jolt of emotion struck her like a fist. Fingers of fear spiked through her, but even stronger was a profound, buzzing anger at the insult of it—how could *he* be *here*? A ghost of the dark, lost past, now running lightly along this strange, slick grass in bright sunlight—as clashing as a tarantula served up on bone-white china.

"You! You're—him!" Susan shouted uselessly, rage tightening her throat.

His large head swiveled. The eyes were still strangely calm, his face lined by strain. He brought the spray can up and thumbed it. Susan turned in confusion and saw Alex bending over Kathryn, concern knitting his brow. He had not noticed the man at all.

Outrage boiled over within her. She understood none of this, but by God this bastard wasn't going to get away.

She threw herself at him. The spray can spun away as she slammed into his chest. Her fists thumped him. He grunted in surprise, chopped at her, slipped free. His baseball cap tumbled away as his head veered back and forth—jerky, reptilian.

He's not trying to get away at all, she realized. Confusion danced in his eyes. He crouched to retrieve the spray can.

"Hey! You!" Alex's alarmed shout came behind her.

The cat. It hissed and spat, its back arched.

The man seemed transfixed by the cat. His hair fretted in the slight breeze, tufts like exclamation points above eyes now wild.

Alex shouted, "Who the hell—?" and then she heard his strangled surprise. She knew what it meant.

So this man had killed Alex, too. A twisted logic was playing out.

But there was no time to think. The man stood up, lips whispering in what seemed to be a prayer. He trembled, eyes darting from them to the cat. Across his face played a struggle she could only guess at, as the man's lips contorted, his caterpillar eyebrows clenched.

She took two steps toward him and the cat jumped away, howling. The man brought the spray can around. With a small *pop* a slug of yellow spat out. It smacked into the cat's head.

16

GEORGE

He stood dazed and irresolute on the hillside, ignoring the stench and biting fumes rising from the cat.

A strange fog frayed the sun's blaze and sheared the air, condensing with the suddenness of a new idea. Images sprayed like shrapnel before him, mingling with the mustard vapor smell. Everyone moved as though underwater, torpid, and he knew he had plenty of time to catch them. Shoot them with the compound that would erase them forever.

But he had to fight away the memories beating like moths at him, past days fluttering their wings madly in his face.

The Sheffield woman had shouted, her eyes holding a bleached white terror. Then the doctor, Hagerty.

Screams of rage. Pain. Retribution. Now Cowell, silent anger twisting his face.

All looking young, powerful, as they had then.

While time's slow work had stolen clarity from him, had left wrinkles and twinges.

Somehow George could not look directly at them. He had faced each long ago, carried out the solemn tasks a soldier of the Lord must do, and so he should be able to do it again. But whirling insect confusions made him blink, shudder, and force down the bedlam within him.

He really should keep on. That was what a soldier did. Plan, prepare. Then go forward, no matter what.

But this had gone wrong. Lomax was supposed to tell him when they were coming out. George would remain hidden, then hit them. A good plan. But where was Lomax?

He had been immersed in his weeding, sure the guards were not making their usual rounds, were instead dealing with the noisy band outside. A minute was all he needed, anyway. There was some slim hope that he might even get away from this, after the deed was done. But George knew the odds were bad, very bad. He did not truly care. Kneeling in the warm earth, he prepared himself for his fate once he had rounded off his life's work. He was talking to God about it.

Then the damned Sheffield woman had screamed. They were there, all three, sudden and solid.

She should not have even glanced at a gardener squatting down. And Lomax had not warned him that they were coming! But he could overcome the disarray that burst within him. Now it would all be done. His work could finally come to a consummation, devoutly to be wished.

He dealt with the Sheffield woman first. Like a banshee she wailed. He struck her heavily.

But the woman's face. It pulled away as he struck it.

Beneath the mask of false flesh she had hidden the signature of the grave. Twisted, purple skin. A shine of rot. Slime, scabs. And through the bridge of her nose he had seen the white slabs of bleached bone. For him to see.

Bones of Ezekiel. These people still had their lattice cages of calcium rods, white hard beneath their sinew, could still someday rise and dance on the final plain, clacking in the valley of dry bones beneath the whispering wings of angels.

All three seemed razor-sharp in the cutting noonday glare.

Each he had faced separately. Each was a chiller, a perversion of the natural order. Yet together, they sent shuddering waves of apprehension through him. Their accusing lantern eyes. Their lips curled in tight lines of loathing.

This should not be. He had sent them on to God. But now they walked again, and God was not here to help him. Only he faced their silent rebuke.

His stomach shot through his throat a sour mouthful of bile. His hands trembled. He found that his legs were moving, taking him back and away from their lancing eyes. But his legs were like bulky logs, wading knee-high through a syrup swamp.

"You! You!" the Sheffield woman screamed and sobbed.

A weight shifted within him, a liquid as heavy as mercury but dark, bitter, sloshing with its own grave momentum. Tipping him. He had to act, to draw down the curtain here, but something opaque and swelling slowed his hands, like a stone lodged in his brain. Filmy scarlet striations shredded the air. He backed away.

Cowell's hoarse shout alerted him. He heard the fast footfalls behind and gave himself over to the sure physical sense he had learned in the jungle.

Slowed. Waited a thumping heartbeat. Swiveled and caught Cowell hard and sure.

He aimed with the spray tube and fired directly at Cowell's stunned face. But the head dodged and the gob splatted across the bill of Cowell's Dodgers cap.

Dr. Lomax had said these chemicals needed to find flesh, work their way fever-quick into the skull, eat the brain. His hands trembled. He fired again. Missed.

It had been easier, long ago, in the dark. Their faces were shadowed then, not raw and real in the glare of day.

He aimed at Cowell and saw the Hagerty woman picking up a rock. It rattled him, and he jerked the trigger on the canister too hard. The yellow plug passed over Cowell's head without him even noticing it.

George started to turn back toward Hagerty and felt a blinding pain in his right temple. The world veered, teetered.

His feet broke free of the anchoring earth, dull snaps of disconnection reverberating up into his chest. He lurched away into the trees. A beckoning forest, moist and enclosing, like the years in Santa Isabella. In fevered fear, he headed toward the two men who could help him through this, down there, beside the pond.

Flat, cool, the pond.

Gray water stretching like an infinite plain.

The Hagerty woman was running at him with furious energy. Cowell was slower, his clothes still smoking with sour fumes.

He could not deal with them all at once. Better to draw them after him, then turn on them. He ran into the cool shadows beneath the eucalyptus. Out of view of the guards, which might give him precious extra seconds.

Here he would make his stand.

17

SUSAN

The corrosive fumes bit into her nostrils as she plunged after the man. Running past the wheelchair, she saw that Kathryn was hurt but not badly. And Alex was wobbly but had managed to get the yellow goo off him.

It was rage, not calculation, that threw her forward after the man. Here was death itself, and she hated its rigid, fanatic face. She would love to claw this man's eyes out.

Susan followed him into the trees and down the gentle slope, shards of eucalyptus bark snapping beneath her exercise shoes. The man slowed, recharging his heavy canister. Susan gained on him. He glanced over his shoulder and then quickly back.

Of course. He would let her get within range, whirl, snap off a shot right in her face.

As she thought this, she veered to her left. The man turned, brought his hands up, carefully cradling the canister—and saw that she was not where he thought.

Susan dodged behind a tree, grabbed it to stop herself, and abruptly dashed back the way she had come. A *pop* told her he had fired, probably expecting her to emerge from the other side. Scrambling, she plunged through a thicket. He muttered angrily behind her. She reached another old, thick eucalyptus and stopped behind it. The man was only ten yards away. She heard his crackling footsteps in the eucalyptus bark. Moving to her left.

She crouched over, took a deep breath—and bolted to her right, face turned away from his direction. If he hit her, at least she wouldn't take it full in the face. There might be a chance of wiping it away, the way Alex had.

Pop. Something acrid whipped by above her head. It smacked into a branch behind her. White smoke puffed past her nose.

The next big tree seemed far away. She straightened up to run, thrust forward—and her left foot went out from under her. She slipped, started to go down. *Slippery bank all the way down.*

Shot out an arm and turned the fall into a roll.

Downhill, tumbling, keeping some speed. *Be a moving target.*

She let her downhill momentum carry her for three complete rolls, sure he would not try such a difficult shot. Dry dirt in her nostrils. Her head smacked into something hard. She ignored the spike of hot pain and turned her roll into a sprawling, desperate scramble down the slope. No time to look back, see where he was. She could hear sounds of him coming through the undergrowth, bushes whipping against his legs.

Shaky, she got to her feet and spun away from sounds of pursuit. Anger with herself seethed in her throat. He had turned the tables, suckered her into this sheltered place where he could do his job.

She dodged behind a tree and saw a fallen limb. Crashing footsteps behind. Close.

She snatched up the brittle limb and turned, thrusting it out. He was right behind her.

He ran into the limb, coughed with surprise. It knocked him back, and his feet went out from under him. He sat down, face red, puffing. He still had the canister.

His shirt had popped its buttons, split open. Across his chest was a faded tatoo: GOD IS.

"Eternal life to you," he said between gasps of air.

He lifted the canister and paused to aim in a curiously solemn gesture. Susan hit it with the limb. He would not let go of it. She clubbed him in the neck. He shrugged this off and started to get up. She heard a crashing and looked uphill. *Let it be the guards.* But it was only Alex.

18

GEORGE

He ran before Cowell could reach him. The woman had taken time, and he had still not hit her. He needed to take a moment to steady his aim.

The pond was not far away. But the woman had taken the wind out of him with her goddamned dodging, gobbling up precious seconds.

Breath cut in his raw throat. The air itself seemed to crowd in. A tunnel formed in the bright day, leading only to the gray waters.

There was a figure ahead, across the pond: Lomax. He must have followed the chillers out, without an opportunity to find George.

Footsteps from behind.

He turned. Cowell swelled like a grotesque apparition, spears of ruby radiance forking from him.

George heard something else, not a noise but a leaden silence, a huge pool of dead air in which he discovered he was drowning. Coughing. Struggling to drag thin sheets of God's oily air into heaving, pain-shot lungs.

Cowell flew at him, launched across the thick zone of stagnant air. He drove his right shoulder into George's chest, expelling the inert breath, wrapping a steel arm around his neck, throwing a hard weight against him.

The spray canister flew away.

George clawed at Cowell, found a left arm that swung lifelessly, no resistance. The arm was like a thing from the grave, a corpse limb attached to the living Cowell. George could not escape its flopping. The arm rolled over his face as he went down, thumping hard. Shiny blades of grass stabbed at his face. The devil arm was in his eyes, fingers dragging across his cheeks, and he hardly noticed the sharp slamming of Cowell's good hand into his middle.

Cowell butted him hard under the jaw, hammered a fist into his neck. George saw sparks of hellfire ignite in the venomous air above Cowell's head, wondered what they meant. He grappled at Cowell, cold fear striking into his bowels.

They rolled, face to face. In Cowell's eyes he saw depthless time, and in the pupils a flat plane of gray menace. He sucked in air and tasted sweat, an acrid bite, a stench like rotting flesh from this animated corpse.

Cowell spat out curses, tearing at his hair, smashing the one free fist into George's nose so that blood spurted hot and rich into his mouth. George yanked Cowell hard, rolling over him, getting a knee between them. Before he could thrust them apart, a sharp pain shot through his temple. He turned and saw the Hagerty woman stepping back to kick him again. Yelling something at him, eyes blazing.

Cowell punched at his chin, missed. George flailed back, hot lights darting in his eyes, and a shoe slammed into his ribs. He rolled away from the woman, tried to kick at Cowell. The grass writhed and murmured in his ear, dark earth-words he could not make out. A thick blade stuck up his nostril, jabbed sharply into his sinuses. *Arise, do battle.* He heaved up, tossing Cowell aside.

The sun boiled above. George gathered his feet to stand, and a shoe caught him in the chin, slamming him back sprawling. He recovered fast, rolling away. Purple dots swam in the clear sky. He saw a leg and snatched at it, yanked, brought down the Hagerty woman. She landed heavily. But in an instant she was on hands and knees, coming at him with raking fingers.

Bright shards of panic flared in him. An arm slipped around his neck, locking him in a choke hold. George grabbed the arm with both hands and lurched sideways, getting his shoulder into it. The arm lost its hold. Blindly he jabbed out, catching somebody. He got his legs under him and lurched up. He gasped in burning air, and the sun lanced in his eyes.

Then they were on him. Cowell hit him in the belly, and he went down. A mass slammed into him. He kicked out, heaved upward, made it to his knees. A shoe dug into his belly. Rage, fear, swarming blind confusion—all poured through him like hot oil.

Escape. Lomax would help. The thought spurted clear and quick through his turmoil. His analytical side, still there. Cool, distant.

The Hagerty woman hit him viciously in the neck. He sucked in air and punched fast, slamming his fists like hams. She was soft and went down.

He stepped back. Cowell was blinking, hair in his eyes. George shot a fist into his face and ran.

There. Dr. Lomax. Bringing to bear a shiny steel automatic pistol.

George was moving fast and he hardly registered the bang or the thump in his left shoulder. He stopped before Lomax, blinking in bewilderment. Lomax's eyes were hooded, remote. This was not the way it was to be, not the way at all.

George threw himself forward and crashed into Lomax's legs. The pistol smacked him in the head. Lomax swore and chopped at George's neck. Sparks of silvery agony showered in his skull. He heaved himself up, pushed Lomax away. Laboring to breathe, George pivoted on a fulcrum of stupefied terror.

Lomax swung a thin fist at George. He caught it in midair with his left hand and hit Lomax with an overhand punch. The man staggered. Fell.

Shouting, words spraying like shrapnel.

Heaving, eating earth beneath a cutting sun.

Hagerty, limping, Cowell trotting unsteadily.

George faced them, tried to think. Lomax was down, holding his head. If only the Reverend were here.

George bolted. Somewhere there would be shelter from this strange storm. He slowed, peering at the pond, consternation crawling in his face.

A hand landed on his shoulder and yanked him to the side. Cowell.

George tried to strike at him, but a fist smacked into his temple and the world teetered.

Arms around him, tight. He slipped free, but he had hurt his foot somehow and limped. Cowell hit him from behind. They both grappled. Water splashed on his legs. Cowell's salty sweat and roaring demon breath swarmed over his face. George swung at Cowell, got him in the ribs. He stepped back, and the chilly pond came up over his knees. He grabbed and tried to sling Cowell to the side but lost his own footing and went in, water slopping up and over his back, enveloping his chest, lapping laughing at his chin. Nameless terror leaped into his throat.

In vain he tried to twist away. Cowell shifted suddenly and got him in a bear hug from behind. He bent forward to lift Cowell, and his face went under the water, sending a stark panic into his chest. Frantically he threw himself sideways and got one of Cowell's arms loose but slipped and went into the water full, the awful chill covering his face. He rolled over and gasped. His feet thrust in all directions, seeking purchase.

He sucked in frosty vapor and was in a place of dead sound, hollow. Currents stirred in him, frenzied the air above. His arms flailed like sticks, smacked, splashed. The black lake was here at last and wintry. A gray flat plain of impassive water, and he could see only inches above it, legs struggling against nothing, no ground.

Flat, indifferent. He dipped below it. Into gray embrace.

Memory rushed out of an ebony tunnel toward him.

He was growing heavy, thick, ponderous. Down and down through grays and somber blacks, fleshy underwater growths brushing at him, schools of mottled fish, waxy reeds, plunging down through shrouded lanes of wintry water, ever colder as he grew sluggish and heavier, deeper and colder, sinking forever into an abyss more strange and awful as he felt its frigid hold wrap around him, gather, slow and creeping cold and depths beyond.

And more memories, exploding out of the black tunnel of decades lost. Slamming into him without pity.

The infinite black lake. And then the bursting forth, the blaring glare of the operating room, warped faces above him

Not a vision from the Lord. A memory.

He did not feel his feet catch the mud bottom. Massive with the weight of water and years, he struggled up the slope. Staggered into the shallows. Waded up onto the brow of the pond.

Cowell was some distance away, and people came running over the hill. Cries cut the air. He shook the heavy water from him as best he could and felt a coat of anxiety and distortion shed from his weary body.

Lomax.

George pushed aside all the other chaos and concentrated on the figure, now bent over, the gray head trembling with nausea.

Slogging uphill. George reached him before the man could look up. Others were coming, there were only seconds. George shouted, "You did that to me! You!"

Lomax's face tilted up, white with panic.

"You took me out of that lake!" George cried. "A boy, I was a boy and you did that, made me, made me—"

"I saved your goddamned life," Lomax wheezed.

"But you—but you—"

"Without my methods you would never have lived."

"I drowned—I was frozen!"

"From the water, yes, but I had to lower you further, ice you, to preserve you until I could work out methods. Until I could bring you back up to normal temperature and—"

"You made me a chiller!"

Lomax stepped back, fear darting in the leathery face. George saw the same knot he had witnessed before, crawling crablike under the stretched skin, along Lomax's jawline and into his neck, a clear sign from the Lord of the marked, the despicable. Filigrees of crimson and violet crackled all around Lomax's cowering shape. The air worked with wracking impulses.

The black lake.

The stabbing lights as he awoke, a chiller, into the hideous world without his parents.

The shiny canister lay at his feet.

"Bones of Ezekiel!" he cried, and in one step had the frail old body of Lomax in his grasp. It was featherlight as George grunted, bending down, holding his prey in one hand while he picked up the canister.

Lomax beat against him, light as moth wings.

Strident voices bursting like shells around him.

Lomax's pathetic whining, shrunken and thin.

Pop. A sticky yellow wad struck Lomax in the left eye and spattered over his nose into the gaping cavern mouth. Which had opened, George saw, to receive the bread and the wine. *This is the body and blood given to thee, in abject tribute, for I have sinned.*

Yellow foam boiled across Lomax's face. It frothed eagerly in the throat, slopped over the bands of agonized muscles in jaw and neck. Already the stink of digestion curled up in tendrils from the bubbling skin.

Gray dark time.

The lake.

Flat and cool and waiting.

EIGHT

TIME'S WINGED CHARIOT

But at my back I always hear
Time's winged chariot hurrying near
—Andrew Marvell
"To His Coy Mistress"

1

KATHRYN

The view of Niagara Falls was stunning, with frothy cascades tumbling all the way around her room, but Kathryn had to turn off the sound to concentrate. Alex sat beside her bed, holding her hand and relating a complicated story that made very little sense. It didn't help that he was already using slang like "croakers" and "wirehead," assuming they were obvious.

"Whoa—start over. Lomax started out a hero in all this?"

"Sure, he was called in when the attending physicians couldn't figure what to do with George."

"George as a boy."

"Right, he was eleven or so. Lomax had these experimental drugs developed by Vitality Incorporated. He tried freezing George down *further,* below what that cold lake had done. The kid had been in the water over an hour and a half. Then Lomax injected his drugs and slowly warmed George back up."

"For how long?"

"Took days, the old records show."

"Why did we take months, then?"

Alex looked at her with fond indulgence. "We were hundreds of degrees colder, with lots more damage. So anyway, George comes out of it, only he's frapped."

"Which means?"

"Sorry, that's some current slang. It means he's damaged goods. Synapses screwed up or something. The trauma of drowning, too. But Lomax, he figured he could work on George, repair most of the damage."

"He was sure wrong about that."

"Lomax *did* fix it—but only by using drugs that suppressed some of the memory sites in George's right brain lobe. Something made the drugs accumulate in sites of the brain. That had some side effects, mostly in aberrant behavior. George had blocked out memories of his drowning and a lot about his parents. Part of him kept trying to fill that in."

"Look, I don't care about the personal problems of that slug."

Alex sat back reflectively. His face and arms were heavily purpled with bruises from the fight with George two days before. "I know how you feel. He killed me, remember."

"I wish you'd have really drowned him this time."

"I lost him in that pond, or sure, I probably would've."

"Fernandez would have pulled him back, pretty likely."

"Right. I have the feeling it's hard to die nowadays."

"Lomax saved George in the seventies, you said. How come you never heard about it?" she asked.

"George's problems would cast a bad light on the whole method, hurt the Vitality stock, wreck his research plans. This was an ambitious guy, Lomax. He fixed as much as he could, arranged a regular series of drug therapies for George—and then got rid of him."

"Into those foster homes? Sounds pretty terrible, I have to admit."

"Lots of foster homes are fine. Lomax knew how to get George labeled 'mildly dysfunctional.' George got shuttled into some homes in Arizona, to keep him out of the media eye in California. Lomax kept his distance, checked on the kid now and then. He knew George was developing psychotic patterns, but that would reflect back on him, so he stayed low and waited."

"How does anybody know this stuff?"

"Stern went after the foster parent records. Plus some stuff the cops turned up in Lomax's own private files. I guess he was just minimizing the threat to Vitality, and to his own reputation. But then he got worried about Immortality Incorporated and saw a way to use George to do us in."

Kathryn lounged back, letting her bed massage her. She had a lot of bumps and bruises from the fight, too, and all the wonders around her didn't do much to erase the aches. Maybe a few more miracles lay down the road. Or maybe, by cosmic justice, into every life some pain must fall. "So he used Reverend Montana. Keeping his distance."

Alex nodded. "Montana says he didn't know about George's past, at first. He was happy to take on the job of harassing us, though, doing a favor for his older brother. It meant big bucks from Vitality, too, when the Rev was starting to have funding problems. I guess his line of patter wasn't working out all that well, after all. Seems Lomax had been making little donations all along, figuring he could manage the religious objections to cryonics that way. Montana says he really thought George would just pull some pranks, sabotage, stuff like that. Montana didn't realize George was psychotic until it was too late."

"I see. When that happened, Lomax told him to shut up, that Montana would take the blame if George got caught and confessed."

"So Montana says. I think he's telling the truth—he's too scared to lie very well. After all, what could Montana do? He was out on a limb before he knew it. That Karen Bocelin woman—the one Lomax used to keep tabs on George? Stern figures she did something wrong, reminded him of his drowning somehow, and he killed her. With her gone, there was no obvious connection to Lomax anymore."

"And that's how Lomax got the good Reverend to help him kill me," Kathryn said bitterly. "I'm getting some memories of it now, from seeing Montana again. Fragments."

Alex leaned over and gingerly slid his arms around her. That helped, but the blades of darting fear made her shudder. Those lost memories were in fact an accidental kindness, filling in a stark moment that she would otherwise always wonder about. She hoped no more returned to her. But something told her that her dreams would seethe with jagged images for a long time.

"So all this was because Lomax wanted to be the man who conquered death," she said.

"Lomax alone, that's the key. He hated it, I guess, when despite George, despite everything, I^2 kept on doing research using Susan's methods."

Kathryn grinned maliciously. "And got a lot of public sympathy from our deaths, from the spooky idea that the victims could return to point a finger at their murderer. Pretty gaudy stuff."

Alex smiled, obviously pleased to see her being cheerful again. He gave her a careful hug and nuzzled into her neck.

The mere sight of George would have been bad enough, she thought, even without all the violence. In some sense, revival from suspension demanded that the mind sort itself out at deep levels. The worst traumas might not be the visible ones. George himself was clear evidence of that. The human body was a marvelous machine, but it was still better understood than the vastly more complex mind that rode atop it.

Dr. Blyer was keeping them away from the media entirely, not even allowing them to see the coverage on their wall screens. Even Detective Stern had gotten only one interview after the assault. So as she glanced up from nuzzling Alex's neck, Kathryn was surprised to see Niagara Falls wither and a full-size image transmission take its place.

She gave Alex a squeeze and murmured, "We have company." It was a moment before she recognized the grinning, matronly black woman who seemed to be standing a few feet away as Sheila, from Fashion Circus. Kathryn blinked, then cried out in incoherent surprise. Sheila looked older and wiser and yet somehow the same.

"My, I'm glad to see that some things in this world don't change," Sheila said with a chuckle.

Alex looked startled and released Kathryn, but recovered nicely. "Yeah, you're still interrupting us just as the going gets good."

Then he looked sheepish. Kathryn knew just what he was feeling. This was an awesome event, being revived, and all the staff here were appropriately solemn. But to Alex and Kathryn, Sheila was the jazzy girl they had known just a few weeks ago, and that Sheila didn't have a solemn bone in her.

"Y'know, it's amazing—you two really are the same as back then," Sheila said. On Kathryn's wall she turned and walked across to a tan overstuffed couch and sat down, the camera somehow knowing to follow her. She was in a spacious, airy house. "Hard to believe. After all the times I thought of you . . ."

Her voice trailed off, and for a moment a kind of awed sadness came into the familiar yet lined face. Kathryn, determined to keep things light, said, "I see you haven't given up your passion for high heels and leather skirts."

Sheila brightened. "Heels, sure—I got all dolled up for this. I been calling you every day. They say nobody lower than the pope gets through. Then this Dr. Blyer calls *me,* says he wants to wall me right into you. But leather? *Nobody* wears that anymore—this is synth. Looks the same, wears better, and the animal neuros don't nag you."

Kathryn made a mock grimace. "My Lord—I've got to learn thirty-eight years of fashion!"

Sheila waved a hand airily. "Naw, two days in the shops, and you'll be givin' *them* tips. All anybody needs is to know the last six months—before that, it's like the pharaohs wore it, for all most people care. This is the thirties look, puff shoulders and all, dancin' round again."

"Come on, spill. What's happened with you?" Kathryn had been uninterested in the standard briefing tapes, full of recent political and economic history and slabs of facts, but catching up on friends was different.

"Lots. Let's say that if I had it to do all over again, I'd make the same mistakes—only sooner."

"You aren't starving," Alex said, gesturing at the house they could see behind the couch. It seemed to stretch to the horizon, a coordinated symphony of fabrics, glass, and rich woods.

"Wish I was. I'd have some hope of getting into a size eight again. I've got a little clothing operation, brings in the pocket change all right."

"I *knew* it! Remember, we used to talk about starting up a chain where a woman could get sharp clothes, not just knock-offs? At reasonable cost?"

"Yeah, we *did,* and after you were—well, gone, I guess is the word—I finally got my squeezers on and did the dance."

"So you own the business?" Alex said.

Sheila lounged back, letting a grin play across her broad features. "Yep—all of them. Got seventy-eight outlets for Steppin' Out."

Kathryn was thrilled. She realized that she had been hanging back from really engaging this world, out of a vague fear that it would lie beyond her abilities. Sheila made it seem possible, though. They talked for several moments about the business, and little seemed to have truly changed since the Fashion Circus days. Sheila had a wry amused attitude toward it all and shrewdly studied them both. Then she said quietly, "Kath, you've got to remember, the future is always going to be a lot like the present. People don't change as fast as their toys."

"Enough philosophy. How about the real stuff?" Kathryn asked.

Sheila winked. "Ah, I know this gal—time to dig the dirt."

"There must be plenty," Alex said.

"Only maybe a mountain range or two. One thing I learned, the two hardest things to handle in life are failure and success."

Kathryn shook her head. "I don't believe it. You always knew how to handle yourself."

"Let's say I learned that a husband's there while the marriage is on, but an *ex*-husband you've got for *life.*"

Kathryn grinned. This *was* the old Sheila all right, irreverent as a whoopie cushion. The world seemed a lot more comfortable with her in it.

"I see a surfboard stashed in the hallway behind you," Alex said. "That's not your style, so there's a man around somehow."

"That's Alex's—my son." Sheila raised her eyebrows. "Right—I named him after you. I remarried, been that way for eighteen years."

Somehow this made Kathryn's eyes mist. The incredible collapsing perspectives of life and time overpowered her emotions at times. But the dominant emotions were good—not of the still well-remembered past, now lost, but joy and wonder for this strange present, so rich in possibility.

"I snagged a big fellow, name of Albert. And that's what I call him, not Al. He'll be home soon from the office, you'll see him. I had him zap you over some contracts to look at, get the jump on the competition."

Kathryn looked confused. "Competition?"

"Why, *everybody's* going to be trying to hire you. You're famous, gal. I figure that'll wear off, though, and I been looking for a new buyer in the high-fashion end of the operation. Want it?"

Kathryn blinked. "Uh, I guess so."

"Pays two twenty-five plus expenses. I'll be working with you and—"

"That's two twenty-five *thousand*?" Alex blurted.

"Sure. Hey, you think inflation froze up while you did?" Sheila grimaced in mock alarm. "Man, I can see you two are gonna need an agent. You might as well soak the media for some walkin'-around money. Famous folks, they got to leave big tips, y'know."

"My lord." Kathryn remembered suddenly that she had borrowed money from Sheila to make the down payment on her own suspension. Well, she could pay it back. Late, but in full. She held Alex's hand tightly. All this was daunting, and she would need him. They would need each other.

Sheila gave her a wise, warm look. "Hey, it'll come natural to you, believe me. One thing I've learned for sure, it's possible to live happily ever after, all right—but only on a day-to-day basis."

2

ALEX

The vault was bright, high-tech, and oddly chilling.

Alex followed Stern among the gleaming steel canisters, marveling at the old fittings, heavy valves, thick lines—and especially, the enormous double-jacketed liquid nitrogen vessel that dominated one wall. His heels sank into thick carpeting, scented and air-conditioned mild air brushed his cheek, and except for the absence of windows there was no way to tell they were deep underground.

"Lomax built it right into the foundations?" Alex asked.

Stern gestured at thick concrete footings along the cream-colored walls. "I guess he didn't want any sign from outside that the mass of the house was carried by these. So he had it planned back when the buildings went up. The county's blueprints show this as a big wine cellar."

Alex sniffed. A musty, still quality to the place. "Well, he did store for long term."

Stern scowled. "I figured maybe you and Mr. Constantine could tell us something about this gear. It's pretty old."

Ray was still staring in disbelief at the long, low-ceilinged room. He was slightly heavier than Alex remembered from the far past, but his face held the same laconic skepticism, beneath the heavy lines and erosions of age.

"Primitive," Ray said. "Kinda clunky. And amazing."

Alex realized that this gear lay nearer in time for him than for Ray. He could even recognize some of the brand names on the piping and valves. "Well engineered for the time, though. Top of the line. Must be an automatic control system."

Ray bent over to inspect the couplings, his movements a bit fragile. "Looks like. Catch those electro-servos over there, ought to be in the Smithsonian."

"Control of what?" Stern asked.

Ray gestured. "These lines carry the liquid nitrogen from that big vessel. The system must top off the nitrogen in the canisters."

"You guys had stuff like this?"

Ray nodded. "Better done, sure."

"So the people in here, you figure they're still preserved?"

Ray shrugged. "Hard to say. I wouldn't trust any machinery for decades."

"Lomax's records say he had an attendant for this. 'Wine steward,' it says. Looks like he's skipped. We're trying to find him."

Alex said, "He probably just tended the refilling. It's a simple job."

Stern leaned against one of the polished, curved canisters. Ray wandered slowly away down the aisle. It was a big room, and there were at least a hundred whole-body cylinders here, lying horizontal in long rows. Stern looked pained. "Alex, I was thinking you might look this over before you spoke to any of the media. Maybe if you break the story, things will be a little easier."

Alex was still taking it all in, and he didn't follow Stern's diplomacy. "Easier?"

"We looked pretty bad, letting Lomax get George onto the Vitality-Immortality grounds. There's a big clamor about it. Way I figure, you meet your first press conference and show just what Lomax was doing, how slick his operation here was, it takes some of the heat off all of us."

"Off you."

"Hey, off you, too. Immortality Incorporated comes out the angel in all this. Probably you guys can sue Vitality for every buck they've got left."

"Sue?"

"Harassment, persecution, the works. Lomax used Vitality corporate research to control George. He developed that spray as a side product of a Vitality product. A nasty little combo, brewed up by corporate technicians. Not easy to trace. And Lomax was planning to shoot

George, cover his tracks. Then there's misuse of corporate functions, every bit of it. And all directed against you, against Immortality Incorporated. Plenty of lawsuits there."

"Look, I'm not interested in games like that."

"Vitality and I^2 are still separate corporate entities, y'know, even though they're close collaborators throughout the whole cryonics industry."

Alex gritted his teeth. *"No."*

"Fine, fine," Stern held up both hands, palms out. "So take it easy, just have a look around. Tell us how Lomax might've set this up."

Alex realized that he was being courted, to keep his criticisms of the police tempered. Did he care? He felt disconnected from the strains and countercurrents of this age. A prince from a distant, frozen land.

Time enough for political stuff later; right now he wanted to study this incredible place. "Let Ray and me nose around awhile."

"Sure, have at it."

Each canister was sleek, sculpted, chromed, the look of old-fashioned futurism. Maybe that had been more convincing to big-time movers and shakers, back in the waning decade of the long-gone twentieth century. Each had a curved transparent plate in the top. Alex bent over one and peered in. The bright overhead fluorescent cast a pale radiance across a seamed, still face only an inch away. Liquid nitrogen was clear, invisible, and Alex could see tiny crinkled lines in the face of Salvador Dali. The theatrically upturned moustache, the imperious jaw, were unmistakable.

Alex moved onto the next. He had never heard of anyone putting windows in a cryonics vault. The plaque beneath the next little viewplate read HOWARD ROBARD HUGHES, 1905–1979. An emaciated, worn face that conveyed a hint of granite resolve. And perhaps a gleam of madness.

The next two names and faces he did not recognize, but the third was familiar from the Pink Panther movies. PETER SELLERS, 1925–1980. There was an odd look of pain to the features.

Several more names and faces, two of them women, meant nothing to him. Many of the very wealthiest managed to keep their names and pictures out of the media, then and now.

But the next one aroused pangs of remembrance. Richard Feynman had been a great genius in theoretical physics, Nobel Prize winner, and a madcap prankster of insatiable curiosity. Alex had loved the books that recounted Feynman's exploits in his own taped conversations. The face seemed about to break into a grin, open to the world. What would a second Feynman lifetime give the world? At a minimum, a lot of deliciously crazy stories.

He heard an indrawn gasp from Ray and walked over to the next aisle. Ray was leaning against a canister that was slightly longer than the others, shaking his head. "Who'd have believed?" he mused.

Alex looked in. Surprise made him momentarily back off. For some reason the eyes had opened, and the famous face seemed to look directly at him, assertive and mellow. The chiseled features had sagged a bit from how Alex remembered them, but they still conveyed the rough and ready spirit. The plaque said MARION MICHAEL MORRISON, 1907–1979, which must have been the real name of John Wayne.

Ray said, "There are a hell of a lot here. All rich, I guess."

"I saw Getty over that way," Alex said blankly, trying to digest the implications.

"Yeah, that Onassis guy is two aisles over. Her, too."

"Really?" There was enough supply of sensationalism here to last the trash media for years.

"Why the windows?" Alex asked.

"I wondered the same," Ray said. "Looks like they're triple-paned, with interior lighting so you can see the face. They're a heat path, so it costs you some in liquid nitrogen."

"No point in regularly looking in on the patient. They don't change."

When Alex had arrived here at the Lomax estate, escorted by Stern, Ray had already been at work with other police specialists, scanning through Lomax's computer records. Everybody seemed surprised that Lomax's data-bomb protection programs had failed, until they saw that it was old software, easily outfoxed. As Lomax had aged, he had apparently not kept up with security technology. His large system had proved unable to quickly kill the files Lomax wanted scrubbed in an emergency.

Ray leaned against a vessel, his back bowed by fatigue. "From what I saw in Lomax's files, I figure it was for advertising."

"Huh? For who?"

"Big-shots being taken on the tour, into the inner sanctum." Ray smiled wryly. "Imagine you're old, plenty of bucks, you see that the big guy, John Wayne himself, has done it. Better than any lecture on the glorious march of technology."

"I see. And plaques could be fake. But if you can *see* rich and famous people who've already bought in . . ."

"How many you figure there are in here?"

Stern answered, approaching. "Two hundred and seventeen."

"Wow." Alex gazed at the aisles stretching away, still trying to take it all in. "How in the world did he keep such a big operation secret?"

"Tight security," Stern said. "Dividing up functions, so very few really knew what was going on. After all, Vitality was a registered archival tissue bank. It had permits, did cryopreservation research, then moved into biotech. Plenty of room in there to hide a little quiet freezing on the side. Especially since it was all here, under his estate."

Alex placed a hand gingerly on John Wayne's shiny cylinder, still a little unnerved by the man's unwavering stare. In a real sense, the big movie star was still there, his essential personality intact but inert. Something in Alex wanted to see the old guy tug at the bill of a Stetson and swing heavily up onto a sleek horse again, leather creaking. The world would spin a bit truer on its axis.

Stern said, "One of our technicians found the billing system. Lomax would get the corpse from whatever funeral home was doing the burial. He was supposed to do some special embalming technique. His clients had it all nice and legal, written right into their wills. Lomax would pull a switcheroo, give the funeral home back something that looked like the corpse but wasn't."

"Why all the secrecy?" Alex asked.

"These were famous people, remember," Ray said. "Folks like that, they mind to their public image, even after they're dead. Lots of them have their papers burned before they've even cooled off."

Stern nodded. "Figures. But Lomax didn't want to be known as a cryonicist, either. Look at all the persecution you guys suffered."

"Most of it at taxpayers' expense," Ray added dryly.

"I figure the big shots liked belonging to a secret, exclusive club, too," Stern said. "Lomax charged a million bucks a pop."

"My God, suspension shouldn't cost nearly that," Alex said.

"He only had a half dozen or so customers per year," Stern said. "He funneled the money into his company, used it for research." A sardonic smile. "Then too, he lived pretty well."

"Then Lomax was really a cryonicist," Alex said wonderingly. "He was one of us."

"Nope, afraid not," Ray said.

Stern asked, "You mean somebody else was behind this?"

Ray said, "No, just that Lomax never intended these people to come back out of the nitrogen."

"Come on," Alex said. "Look at this gear. First class all the way, better than anything from its time. Sure, Immortality Incorporated had better stuff later, but—"

"Lomax didn't perfuse them."

"*What?*"

"The records are plain. He just slipped them in these containers and piped in the liquid nitrogen."

"But that would cause massive cell rupture!" Alex was shocked.

"It sure must've."

"But why?" Alex looked in at John Wayne and thought of the burst membranes and ravaged chemistries that lay beneath that apparently alert face.

"I've been trying to figure it out." Ray ran his weathered hands along the canister, their backs splotched with brown spots. "Maybe we'll never know. Lomax was a ruthless egomaniac. He knew how hard the cryosuspension problem was. He was attacking it on his own, spending a lot of money on his research—money from these rich folks. But he didn't think the technology would get good enough to bring them back out while he was still alive."

Alex whispered, "So . . . why bother?"

Ray nodded. "Perfusion, all the cooling stages—that takes time. Care. Money. Personnel. Easier to keep things secret if he did it himself."

The enormity of it stunned Alex, squeezed his chest. "He just went through the motions?"

"He was running a con game. For decades," Ray said.

Stern had been subdued, frowning. "I don't get it, then," he said. "Why'd Lomax use George to go after Immortality Incorporated?"

"Competition," Ray said. "Lomax was suckering millionaires. Every time he took one down here to show him the celebs, the scheme snowballed. On the other hand, I^2 started suspending people for much less. We even took on charity cases. I^2 hurt business."

Stern said cynically, "Volkswagen hurting the Rolls-Royce guy."

"Right. He was the luxury end of the market, and we were an upstart cheapo outfit," Ray said. "Okay, so he sells himself as discreet, private, tasteful. Not a bad marketing strategy. But then Susan started doing first-class research. Lomax must've seen his empire threatened. Worse, Susan was successful with reviving dogs—which he knew about, through contacts at UCI, who gave him documents. Imagine his nightmare. We might even start bringing people back." Ray smiled without a trace of humor.

Alex grinned. "How terrible."

"Then where'd he be? Rich people have estates. Watchdog committees. Those would start wondering why grandaddy wasn't getting thawed out, like the ones over at I^2."

Stern said, "I'll bet a lot of estates *don't* want grandaddy thawed out. Think what that'd do to inheritance law."

Ray chuckled. "Already is. The lawyers are turning purple already over cryonics. Inventing 'rights' of children who got willed stuff and don't want to give it back to the old man, now that he's walking around again."

Stern slapped the John Wayne capsule, the report ringing in the cool silences of the basement. "Me, I'd be happy to be back alive. For a lot of these people, it would be more fun to rebuild your fortune, starting over."

Alex said, "But Lomax never intended that they'd come back."

Ray pursed his mouth with grim disbelief. "Hard to get your mind around that, isn't it?"

Alex felt the same, but the logic seemed inescapable. He had never truly believed that evil lurked in the world in a pure form, but Lomax—a man he had only glimpsed in the final skirmish on the lawn—embodied pure malevolence.

A strange thought struck him. That man he saw for just a few moments had shaped Alex's entire life—no, lives—from offstage.

"All for money. Just money. No concern for people at all," Alex said disbelievingly.

"Cryonics is always about money as well as life," Ray said. "Same as medicine generally. You stop to wonder why I'm an old codger, showing every year?"

Taken aback at this shift, Alex said defensively, "Hell, you don't look so old."

Ray poked at his arm. "Skin's looking like saddle leather, knees creak, eyes don't want to read—but sure, I'm doing great for an old fart. Point is, the biotech that brought you back can also fix me up. Only I can't afford it yet."

Alex had in fact wondered why anybody aged in this brave new whirl, but he hadn't brought it up. While he searched for a reply, Stern said, "Yeah, me, too. I've saved up, withdrew most of my retirement account. I'm going in for a refab soon as I can get a slot."

"Refab?" Alex asked to cover his confusion.

"Refabrication of tissues—the really important organs, anyway," Stern said. "Molecular agents that clean out the cholesterol deposits, rebuild kidneys, stand guard against cancers. Costs a fortune, but adds years, decades."

Alex had to admit that both men looked a good deal younger than their years—which numbered in the seventies. Ray had an unreadable expression. Alex wondered if Ray envied him, fresh and young and rebuilt with microscopic agents Ray could not afford. Medicine and money and the movements of time.

Embarrassed, Alex decided to step around the issue. "Lomax looked pretty good for a man his age, too. He must have spent his money on the best biotech treatments."

"I imagine we'll find out in the records," Stern said. "They go back deep into the twencen."

"Funny, y'know—back when he got started, Lomax never really believed in cryonics enough to bother treating his clients right," Ray said.

"Until Susan started getting her results at UCI," Alex said. "That's when he sent George after us."

"I wonder how he knew about her results that early?" Ray asked. "Somebody at UCI leak it to him?"

A small, tingling suspicion wriggled through Alex's memories. He would have to look up the records on that guy—what was his name? Blevin.

Ray grimaced. "That kind of thinking led him to this—suspending people without treatment. Great technical guy, but he had no faith."

Alex remembered Sheila from long ago, smiling at a party conversation and saying that cryonics was just another kind of faith. He wondered if even then she had understood how right she was. Technology without a dash of faith was stale, barren.

"Plus he was psycho," Stern said vehemently. "At least with George, we have an assignable cause. Those resuscitation drugs that Lomax used on him, they went straight to certain focal spots in the brain. Overdose, as he did, and you burn away capabilities, balances. Made George a barely controlled sociopath. A human Rottweiler. But what was Lomax's excuse?"

Evil needed no explanation, Alex thought. It just was.

Faith, evil, immortality—deep stuff, aswarm in mystery. And he had always thought of himself as a technical type, clear and precise and objective. He had used to say on radio talk shows that one way of viewing cryonics was to imagine that any medical treatment that could *ever* be developed could, in principle, be available to the patient of the present—if you saved the structure of them, suspended it, then just waited for the future to arrive.

But that was too intellectual a way to go at it. This reached into the deep swamp of the human psyche. "I hope the religious people don't try to read too much into all this," he said distantly.

Ray smiled, this time with amused warmth. "Too late. You're the modern Lazarus yourself, buddy. This is a weird world we've got here, but it still needs icons, and you're going to be one."

"Huh? Wait a minute."

"You're a founding cryonicist, one of the reborn. People will want you to help them, heal them. Tell 'em what you heard from God while you were in there. Pester you to death, I'll bet."

Alex grinned and wandered down the aisle. "Geez, and here I thought I'd woken up into utopia."

Ray said, "No such thing if it has real people in it."

Alex stopped beside a canister that was a bit different from the others. Older, less outfitted. He bent to peer inside, straightened up, and asked meditatively, "Do you think we can bring these people back after all?"

Ray frowned. "Wow, that's one hell of a job. Have to repair all the wreckage in every cell. Where structure was completely scrambled, you'd be forced to make a shrewd guess about what information was lost. It would take a whole mess of special microbugs, new techniques."

"I'd like to work on that," Alex said distantly. "There's a hell of a lot of talent down here."

He looked around, not seeing the stretching stillness of the vault at all. Here was a legacy Lomax never truly meant to leave. But it could be made real and vibrant. Something splendid could come out of malignant blackness.

"Well, a man's got to have something to do," Ray allowed.

Alex slapped the old canister. "There's a fellow here I'd sure like to shake hands with, if we can recover him. Kathryn would, too. She and I visited his grave once, a long, long time ago."

3

GEORGE

It was simple, really.

Ezekiel had said it long before in fiery words that cascaded down through millennia. About the dancing bones. Bleached white and yet dancing, holy gambols in the risen sun. The shining valley. The fertile fields where happy holy women in long dresses worked unceasingly.

It had been that way in his family. Warmth, order, certainty. Parents who loved and cherished. They had been wonderful, and he had spent his life trying to get back to them, to someone like them. Lomax had prevented that. Had blocked off a part of him with gray walls of drugged forgetfulness.

Those granite slabs had come crashing down inside him, at last—there in the pond, where the waxy plants had beckoned to him like the bloated limbs of corpses. He had remembered it all.

The maggot-covered bodies of his parents, dead in a crashed car and found by the sheriff a week later.

The yearning, the pain that the boy could not quell.

The black lake. So serene.

Then coming back to the raw world again. Into shrieking hard lights, twisted doctor-faces, a loveless antiseptic hell. He had tried to flee that Godless place, and Lomax had worked the medical madness on him, taking away the memories. Stealing from George what he was.

So that when shards of memory had come to him in unguarded moments, he thought they were the Master's Messages. Signs from the Lord. Images of what the chillers would go through.

When all along it was what he had already done.

Now Lomax had joined his parents in the valley of seared bones, as was only right, and the grand day would come when he too would rise in the valley of Ezekiel, Lomax and his parents, together.

George would be there, somehow, and he would speak to the Lord of all this, tell the story of twisted years, and the Lord would send Lomax farther into the bowels of the great earth.

Forever. Eternal fire awaited Lomax, not the chill.

The chiller people—his people, now—could not save Lomax's carcass, devoured by corrosion. So Lomax would not rise from the sinful cold to greet George some future day, and of that George was most thankful.

He fell to his knees in his little room with no windows. Kneeled and prayed and wrestled with the memories. So many.

The pain had been so great, so lancing for a boy. Both parents gone. A world hollow and aching. His feet had led him to the lake. He had marched right in, never stopping, never doubting that another, better world lay on the far side of the black lake, the side he could not see because it lay in the dark waters. He had known that he would find Mommy and Daddy there and laugh with them again in God's sunny embrace. So he had started to swim and the wise weight of water in his shoes and socks had known his intention, had drawn him downward even as he stroked for the far shore.

The healing waters had betrayed him in the end, he saw that now. The strength had drained from him, the chill had made him sluggish and fearful. In his waterlogged clothes he had not been able to swim to the deepest part of the lake, where the kindly darkness would have hidden him. The man who saw him from the distance had called others and though they were slow in coming, they had known where to look. They had dragged him away from his reward, snatched the holy promise from him, cut the last cord to his mommy and daddy. In the long moments of sinking, down through silvery schools of fish, he had felt his daddy reaching out toward him, calling, smiling the broad grin, big hands ready to help. Then gone.

Gone for all these years.

In the hospital, long after, he had wanted to take himself away from this rotted world. But Lomax and the others knew his desires and stopped him, gave him no chance at a sharp edge or a simple length of cord. Until they had adjusted his injections properly, they said.

No chance. Just as now. His cell was narrow and bare, as clean as the bleached bones of Mommy and Daddy that would dance on that distant day.

They said they could fix him. *Let me go,* he had shouted at them. *Let me die.* But they wouldn't.

Even the Reverend had nothing to say now. George had asked to see him. The man apologized and explained and finally begged for forgiveness. George had thought he would try to kill the Reverend in some way that the doctors could not fix, make him like Lomax so that there was not even any point in turning him into a chiller, too.

But the Reverend had seemed small, shrunken, pitiful. He had fallen to his knees and asked George to join him in prayer.

For a long time George had stared down at the ruined face full of doubt and finally turned his back on the man and walked to the far end of the interview room, thinking of the lake.

So they said now they would fix him. People had been fixing him all his life.

There was only one way to fix him through and through, and it would come to him sometime. He just had to wait. He could do what they said, ape their cues. Con them, just as he had conned people and computers alike, all his life.

They would declare him all repaired and then would let him out of this place without edges. He would pretend to be anything they wanted. It would bring that day closer.

Then he would find another dark lake, one without watchers. Then he would go to his mommy and daddy.

To dance. The bleached bones. It was simple, really.

4

SUSAN

She watched the wall as it rather pedantically explained itself. Susan
had found that the brutality of days before had calmed her somehow.
She was content to stay in her new room, enjoying the quiet pleasures of
reading, listening, watching the walls.

At the moment the illustrated lecture she had requested showed her
a glittering cityscape. It zoomed in on a slender building, gossamer sea-
blue steel and glowing glass. A tapered peak caught the sunrise, refracting the radiance onto the plain of trees around it.

A green splotch had wrapped itself around one edge of the steel and
glass. It was huge, the size of a football field and about the same color.
This was one of the new biofilm cleaners, the wall murmured, working
its way with excruciating care while it absorbed dirt and tarnish. Another
technofix, shaped from the traits of grass and plant digestive systems.

Susan watched the immense brown cleaning plant crawl another few
inches over the glass cliff. Safer and more thorough than putting humans up there. And the biofilm lived off the waste it ate. Tidy.

It was a small part of a vast strategy for dealing with the greenhouse
crisis, she had learned. The world was warming, the poles beginning to
melt. Oceans had already risen a meter, and dikes held it back, bulwarks
from Orange County north to Ventura.

So all the immense miracles around her were matched by fresh problems, equally huge. Maybe it had been that way down through countless
centuries. Humans were the species that went forward by putting a foot
in front, losing its balance a bit, and then catching itself.

She clicked the wall into a soft sapphire sheen. Enough homework.

She was learning to not think obsessively about how close all three of
them had come to a second death, out on the broad lawn. The terror of
it still tightened her jaw, she noticed clinically, and increased her heart
rate. No wonder, really. She still saw George's demented face, if she
closed her eyes.

It had been a near thing, a damned near thing. Only George's deep confusions had slowed him enough for Kathryn's disfigured face to shatter his resolve. That had tipped him into his personal abyss.

Susan shook herself to break her mood. *Brrrrr!* Madness drew back the curtains of civilization, revealing naked savagery.

Dr. Blyer had given her a preliminary analysis of George's multilayered psychosis. So many assaults upon the fragile cradle of a young mind! His parents, rotting in their wrecked car. His wrenching suicide. The trauma of freezing and slow revival. Then having to relearn how to live, with a brain damaged in subtle ways. The "treatment" by Lomax, a brilliant but unprincipled man who used hit-and-miss methods.

And when they yielded a boy with muddy emotional patterns but high intelligence, Lomax had consigned him to the casual brutalities of the foster home system in Arizona. No wonder George had clung to his religion, made it the fulcrum of his warped, lonely life.

Even so, she had assumed that George would go to prison. Blyer seemed startled. "With his ingenuity throughout this entire matter? He is a valuable person of superior intelligence. If we can fix him, get to the root of his disorder, we will learn something of postcryonics mental trauma. Prison is a waste! A very twencen idea. With such intelligence and resourcefulness, his talents might be of considerable use."

"Uh—twencen?"

"Oh, it means 'twentieth century.' 'Old-fashioned.' "

They seemed assured, as though murderers could obviously be patched up into model citizens. It was just another example of how far the world had come—or thought it had.

There was still the customary craziness, of course. In scrolling through the newspaper she had come upon an advertisement for help in crucifying a man, who wanted assistants to play the Roman soldiers. "Historically accurate, real swords used." Another article recounted a sighting of the Madonna by three housewives, and Susan had read nearly to the end before realizing that the apparition was not of the Virgin Mary, but of some rock singer of decades before, since perished. Not all craziness was curable.

And just to underline her own limitations, there was a big, 3-D advertisement for a new restaurant, based on "90s nostalgia." The gay nineties, the 1890s? Nope—her own seemingly bland 1990s, which she had filled with work. Apparently, she had failed to live through her own times. She made a note of the restaurant's address.

For a moment she recalled her now-distant past and the people who had not made it to this strange land. Blevin, who had apparently worked for Lomax, dead of liver cancer. Many of her colleagues at UCI General, succumbing to the usual erosions of age.

And even some cryonicists. Poor Boyd Zeeman, who gave such generous parties, drowned while swimming off Huntington Beach. No technology could protect you from the random rubs of fate.

She sighed, sat before a mirror, and tried to remember how to put on makeup. Lipstick, blush, eyeshadow. Ancient crafts.

Time to move on. There were better things to remember.

She had felt the subtle yet remorseless pressure in her, the wedges of forgetfulness like stone slabs in her mind. She had battered against their cold solidity, but nothing got through.

After the mess with George had calmed a bit, she had sat Dr. Fernandez and Dr. Blyer down and told them directly that something was wrong deep inside her. The two had glanced oddly at each other, the way they had several times before, and then decided to admit the truth.

There were memories she carried in long-term storage that they had feared would make her recovery more difficult. Stern had argued that they could easily disturb her recollection of her murder, too.

Memories deep and powerful. They knew the locations in her brain and had simply blocked them with microtechnology. She had flared into anger, shouted, thrown a cup into the wall screens. And before the coffee had run down the wall, she had been sobbing, head in her hands.

All without knowing what the memories were, or why they might be so damaging.

Susan stood at the large transparent patio door to her new room and gazed out over the long, sloping grounds. She slid the glass aside and caught the heady scent of orange blossoms from the great sweeping groves that began a short distance away. They were part of the global strategy for taking carbon dioxide out of the thick air, she knew, but that was nothing compared to the luxuriant wealth they brought to the simple act of breathing.

Again, after too long, there were grand orange groves in Orange County.

An hour before, Dr. Fernandez had come with his staff. In mere minutes they had canceled the blocks. Her mind was her own again.

The richness had come flooding into her. Heart-thumping moments of passion. Quiet, dear interludes. Laughter and spitting anger and long walks on the beach.

The most amazing thing was how they had been able to do it at all. They had erased a fact at the core of her life. And somehow the many threads that dovetailed into that nexus had not led her to it, when she recalled them. It had been like a blind spot in her vision, a dead place whose very absence went unremarked. She had felt it several times—an acute, congested discomfort—but never was able to trace it down.

She saw Kathryn and Alex in the distance and waved, hoping they were heading this way. More than anything she wanted contact, the rub of ordinary life. She had been sealed within herself for a long time, she saw. It was time for the blossom to finally crack through the crusty husk that had grown around it through the years.

Not that she wouldn't have use of some crusty nature in this strange world. She had a thing or two to say about the medical ethics of depriving patients of their memories, the very essence of themselves. Whatever the Crunch had brought, not every change was an improvement.

Already she felt an itch to get back into medical practice, to fathom the implications of all this gleaming technology. And to have a fight or two over it, she was sure.

A knock at the door.

She thumbed the release. The door slid aside. And there he was.

"Roger. You're—"

"The same?" His smile still had the funny dip in the left corner, his eyes the crinkling laugh lines. His resonant baritone struck through her. "Nope, I'm better."

Then they were in each other's arms, and there was a long time when she thought of nothing at all.

It was some hours before Roger suggested they go out for a walk.

She stretched with a catlike luxury she had forgotten in her long years of loneliness. "Ummm, I'm having more fun here."

"Part of my rehab program. Five miles a day."

"I suppose I'll be doing that soon. Come to think of that, how come you could be revived when the rest of us were? I mean, I used an earlier type of transglycerol for your suspension, not the one that Alex and Kathryn and I had."

Roger shrugged. "They say it worked well, saved the structure. There's more than one type of perfusate that'll do the job. I was just lucky."

"So am I." She kissed him deeply, sliding hands over him.

"Come on, I've got to do my exercises—vertical ones, not horizontal."

"Sure? What if I just . . ."

"I may be rebuilt and all, but I'm still just a man."

"Can't prove it by me," she said. "That last bit of horizontal exercise was divine."

He made a funny joke while they got dressed, and she had to stop herself from laughing so hard, sensing that somehow she had no right to feel this good, that this was the territory of the gods. Then she kissed him, light and airy, and slipped on her sandals.

Stern and Blyer had suppressed her constellation of memories associated with Roger, sure they were doing the right thing. Now that she felt her full memories of Roger, with all their passion-laden crispness, she knew they had been wrong. Nothing justified intrusion into her personality itself. She could see she had her work cut out for her in this brave new world.

Alex and Kathryn were on the brow of the far hill. They had been waiting the whole time, she guessed.

She waved and started toward them, keeping one arm around the man who had been her husband once and now would be again. She was different, but he was the same, and there would be problems with that, but that was what life was, simply—problems that you enjoyed.

A gangly form darted by Alex and loped across the grass. The Irish setter's coat was glossy, and it tossed its head with a certain jubilant air. Susan felt a burst of heart-stopping surprise.

Sparkle carried a tennis ball in her mouth, bounding merrily with youthful energy, bright and sure beneath a new sun, and ready to play.

Acknowledgments

This novel is based on the existing cryonics movement and especially on the Alcor Life Extension Foundation's site at 12327 Doherty Street, Riverside, CA 92503. I thank them for innumerable conversations in which I learned how cryonics works. However, my fictional Immortality Incorporated should not be taken as a depiction of Alcor or any other specific cryonics organization. All present-day cryonics technology depicted here is that used in the early 1990s.

I am grateful to Mike Darwin, Saul Kent, Mike Perry, David Pizer, Arthur McCombs, Ralph Whelan, Fred and Linda Chamberlain, the late Jerry Leaf, and Dr. Thomas Donaldson for much time spent with me. For advice on the manuscript I thank Dr. J. Jones, Dr. C. Brigham, Dr. D. Brin, Dr. M. Coleman, Charles Platt, Jennifer Hershey, Elizabeth Mitchell, Lou Aronica, and Wayne Baglin.

For advice on both technical and narrative issues, I especially thank Dr. Stephen Harris and Dr. Mark Martin. Hugh Hixon made innumerable cogent suggestions. Sheila Finch gave me the benefit of a detailed reading of the manuscript. Throughout this work I was greatly helped by my agent, Ralph Vicinanza.

None of the famous people named as having been cryonically suspended were in fact suspended, to my knowledge—though such matters are highly confidential, and all expressed interest while alive. In summer 1992 there were forty-one persons suspended by the three public cryonics organizations, and two known to be privately suspended.

The position taken on cryonics by the Society for Cryobiology, representing international medical research in this area, remains as depicted in this novel: they refuse to publish, or allow presentation at meetings, of any research relevant to the suspension of humans, but not that applied to human organs such as skin, kidneys, and the like.

Sterling Blake
September 1992